FU

S<small>HE</small> TUGGED AT THE ~~...~~ lanced the darkness and—

The Count's voice, barely human, "You should not have—not the light—I will change now—change—"

The curtain fell away and the moonlight streamed in across the glittering fields of snow.

The Count . . . his face . . . his nose had elongated into a snout. Even as she watched he was changing. Bristles sprouting on his cheeks. His teeth were lengthening, his mouth widening into the foaming jaws of an animal. The eyes . . . bright yellow now, slitty, implacable. His hands, already covered with hair, were shrinking into paws. With a snarl the Count fell down on all fours. His teeth were slick with drool. The stench intensified. Her gorge rose. She tasted vomit in the back of her throat. Then the wolf leapt.

She was thrown back. She fell down into the patch of moonlight. The beast was ripping away her dress now. It still desires me, she thought. The wolf's spit sprayed her face and ran down her neck. She tried to beat it back but it straddled her now, about to sink its teeth into her throat—

It touched the silver necklace—

And recoiled, howling! Speranza scrambled to her feet. The wolf watched her warily. Where its snout had touched the necklace, there was a burn mark . . . an impression of the silver links in the chain. The wolf whined and growled. . . . She found the door, flung it open, ran, clambered across to the next car, entered. As she slammed the door shut, she heard an anguished howling over the cacophony of steam and iron.

Tor Books by S. P. Somtow

MOON
DANCE

a novel by

S. P. SOMTOW

A TOM DOHERTY ASSOCIATES BOOK
NEW YORK

MOON DANCE

Copyright © 1989 by Somtow Sucharitkul

A Tor Book
Published by Tom Doherty Associates, Inc.
49 West 24th Street
New York, N.Y. 10010

Cover art by Joe DeVito

ISBN: 0-812-51127-1

Library of Congress Catalog Card Number: 89-39883

First edition: November 1989
First mass market printing: April 1991

Printed in the United States of America

0 9 8 7 6 5 4 3 2 1

For "Uncle Bob,"
one of my career's chief building Blochs

ACKNOWLEDGMENTS AND DISCLAIMERS

The following people either helped in my meandering researches, encouraged me, or exhibited a godlike forbearance during the longest gestation period any of my works has ever experienced:

Tim Sullivan, Bob Halliday, Brett Prang, Eleanor Wood, Beth Meacham, Gardner Dozois, Harriet McDougal, Hank Stine, Art Cover and Lydia Marano, George Scithers, Ryan Effner, David Gish, Walter Miles, Ed Bryant, John Douglas, Janet Alvarez, Col. Michael Sinclair, Sharon and Bryan Webb, Algis Budrys, Daniel Jacobson, Betsy Mitchell, Michael Meredith, Margaret Brown and Thomas Wilson Brown and their family; and countless strangers in Nebraska, the Dakotas, and Wyoming who bemusedly tried to answer the questions of someone who must have appeared to them to be, at the very least, a lunatic—

any faults herein being, of course, my own.

CONTENTS

PROLOGUE

The Laramie Ripper

1
1963: South Dakota
three-quarters moon, waxing

THIS IS NOT THE BOOK I SET OUT TO WRITE.

This is not the book I dreamed of as I crossed the snow in my battered Impala. I was young then. I chased after sensations. I wanted the frisson of coming face-to-face with a mass murderer whom the world had long forgotten. I was going to write the ultimate exposé. I saw the book—a fat hardcover, of course—gleaming on the racks of the neighborhood bookstore. I imagined the Carltons next door shunning me and retreating into their split-level ranch-style mansion, muttering darkly about how girls shouldn't go to college, look how weird they get when they come home. She'll never find a husband now. I laughed and pondered the book I was going to write. As I glided along the empty road between endless snowbanks, looking out over snow and snow and more snow, the book I dreamed of became clearer and clearer to me. I could almost heft it in my hands and read the gold-leaf lettering on the spine:

A KILLER'S LIFE
by Carrie Dupré

The snow was steady, hypnotic. I turned up the heat. I luxuriated in it. It was making me drowsy. It was four in the afternoon. I realized that I wouldn't have much daylight left this far north, in the dead of winter. Well, I had to be somewhere near my destination. It must have been an hour since Wyoming. Maybe I'd overshot. Many of the road signs were smothered in snow. Maybe I'd missed the turn somewhere. I decided to pull off the road and look at a map.

The car clunked and wheezed as I stopped. I looked up at the mirror and teased my bouffant into shape. I left the car running so that the flakes wouldn't pile up on the windshield and so I could keep the heat on. Then I opened up the map I'd bought back in Laramie and struggled to make head or tail of it. All I knew for sure was that the Black Hills were to the north; I could see them at the horizon across the expanse of white. The sky was gray. There was no sun. I was alone. Sunny suburbia was more than a week into the past. I was determined not to be afraid. It had been my decision to be a writer, my decision to pick the kind of sensationalist subject that women weren't supposed to write about . . . if I didn't go through with it now, the Carltons were going to laugh at me.

Maybe I just need to get up and walk around, I thought.

I squirmed into my shaggy coat and started to get out. It was windy and I had to push to get the car door open. When I was all the way out, the door slammed shut behind me. I hardly had time to feel the cold when I realized that I had already pushed in the lock, and that my keys were in the ignition with the motor running. I was too stunned to panic. All I kept thinking was, They're going to say, "Just like a woman," and laugh the whole misadventure off. Light snow tickled my face. I stared through the window at the warm interior of the car.

Soon it was going to be sunset.

The wind whined. I started to feel numb. I rubbed my hands up and down the inside of my coat. I looked for something, a branch or a rock, to break the window with. There was nothing. Maybe beneath the snow. I began shovelling at the snowdrift with my bare hands, wincing at the cold. I could feel the joints getting stiff. I was getting angry. Could the Carltons be right about me? The wind was roaring now. I plunged my arms into the snow all the way. My fingers met something hard. I grasped and tugged, cursing in frustration.

"Need some help?"

I screamed.

Then, feeling stupid, I looked at the man who had come up beside me. "I'm . . . I'm sorry," I said. "I didn't mean to—" He lifted a finger to his lips. He wore a black leather jacket. Dark, shoulder-length hair, frosted with snowflakes, held back by a blood-colored headband. "Where did you come from?" I said. "I didn't hear anything. . . ."

"The rushing wind hides many sounds," the stranger said.

Behind him, across the road, I could see a motorbike leaning against the embankment. I could have cried with relief. Instead, I straightened my coat and nervously tried to shield my hair from the wind. He said, "And what's a woman doing all alone on the reservation in the middle of nowhere?"

I flinched a bit at the question, although I guess I should have expected it. "I must have missed a turn somewhere, I guess . . . reservation? You mean I'm not in Fall River County anymore?"

"No ma'am. This is Shannon. You're on the Pine Ridge Reservation. We're about two miles from Wounded Knee. That was the White River you crossed back yonder."

"River?" I hadn't even noticed.

"I guess I'd best get you and your car together again first." He walked over to his motorcycle, rummaged around, pulled out a coat hanger, came back. "Always keep one of these on me case I run into one of them damsels in distress." He began methodically to unwind the hanger, then slid it down the side of the window. In a second he had popped the lock.

"You must really be handy at this stuff," I said, earnestly trying to make conversation.

"Condescending white bitch," he said.

"I'm sure I didn't mean—"

"Yeah, right, you're sure."

We didn't talk for several moments. He kept staring at me, as though expecting me to say something. In the twilight his shadow stretched all the way across the road, and his eyes gleamed. "Well, ma'am, I suppose you'll be wanting an escort to Winter Eyes."

I started. "How did you know where I was going?" I looked around me in panic. The wind was screeching, my hair was flying into my eyes. He didn't move.

"I know a lot about you, Carrie Dupré," he said.

"My name. . . ." Slowly I backed away, feeling for the car door. My fingers fumbled at the icy handle. "Get away from me! Are you some kind of psycho?"

"You got mass murderers on the brain, don't you?" He didn't smile. His eyes glittered in the dark through the mass of hair that fluttered across his face. "You got some cowboy movie ideas about Injuns too, I bet. You think I'm gonna rape you and scalp you or something. Shit, you'd probably even enjoy it. Don't you even recognize me? Shit, you even condescended to screw me once! But it was dark in the drive-in. And you were smashed out of your mind. And anyways we all look alike. You were the snottiest girl in Berkeley, Carrie, and you ain't changed one damn bit."

"Jesus," I said, "you're—"

"Preston Bluefeather Grumiaux," he said softly. "I work part-time for the tribal police force."

"Dr. Murphy's Indian Studies class," I said. "You used to sit in the back and make fun of everything. Whenever Murphy tried to get serious you'd start saying 'how' and 'ugh.' It can't be you. You rejected all this Indian heritage stuff. What are you doing back here?"

He said, "I was wrong."

We were silent for a long time. It was all so unlikely that I couldn't quite accept that it was happening. I remembered Preston Grumiaux clearly now. He hadn't looked anything like this. In those days he had a crew cut and did everything he could to look like a Xerox copy of Wally Cleaver. It was pathetic in a way.

We had gone out once. I couldn't remember having sex with him, but I could have been stoned. "Even if you are Preston," I said at last, "that still doesn't explain why you know where I'm going."

"I'm a part-time tribal policeman," he said. "My other job is at the institute. I guess I got a natural affinity for fruitcakes. Dr. La Loge sent me to look for you, stupid. You're a day late and they were getting worried. Didn't think a city girl like you could make it through the storm."

"I waited out the blizzard in Laramie," I said, self-consciously rearranging my blond hair. "I'm not that dumb."

"Reckon you ain't," he said.

"Christ," I said, "since when did you start saying 'ain't'?"

"I got fed up with your kind and your highfalutin sixty-four-dollar words, I guess. I learned something after all. I ain't one of you. I don't like hamburgers, and if I ever see another jar of mayonnaise I'll puke. I burned my fraternity blazer. They only took me on as a token anyway, the sons of bitches. Show how fucking liberal they were. I ain't one of you. *Lamakota!* You know what that means? *I am Sioux!*"

I managed to get the car door open. I couldn't look at him, couldn't deal with his raw emotion. I felt a blast of heat in my face. He held the door open. "Look," I said, "can we talk this over some other time? It's getting dark. Let's just get on the road."

"Certainly, Miss Dupré," he said. "But first, tell me why you, of all people, are coming to interview the Laramie Ripper?"

"I'm doing a book about him," I said. "A couple of publishers are interested. And . . . well, I was doing my family tree, and . . . there was a woman mentioned in the hearings, an old woman who used to take care of him, who died just before all the killings started. Her name was Hope Martin. There's a good chance this woman was my great-grandmother."

"So you're exploiting a family connection, huh?"

"It seemed like a way to break in."

"Don't you think you oughta leave the old man alone? All that stuff happened thirty, forty years ago. He's a dying, sick man. You're gonna do this big scandalous book full of gore and sordid details. I bet you have a title for it already . . . 'I Was a Crazy Sex Killer . . . as told by Carrie Dupré'! I see it all. In lights. Maybe a movie, too. Hitchcock'll do it."

"Come on."

"You're shaking," he said. "I bet you're scared shitless."

"It's just the wind. And the snow." The wind had not let up. It was dark, so dark. Snow was gusting in through the car door. "Can we start now?"

"Don't bullshit me. You're terrified."

"No."

"Terrified! But there ain't nothing out here. Only the bleakness. The desolation. Nothing's gonna jump at you and tear you apart. Not right now. You got three days yet."

"Three days?"

"Until the full moon."

"The full moon . . . don't be ridiculous."

He started to cackle like a banshee as he crossed the powdery pavement. The growl of his bike was drowned in the roar of the wind. I slammed the car door and skidded onto the road. He was right. I was shaking. But it was only because of meeting him so unexpectedly, and because I loathed him yet felt so helpless without him. That was all. Full moon indeed. I couldn't understand why Preston was trying to freak me out.

I had come to interview a psychotic, not a werewolf.

* * *

I had no impression of the town of Winter Eyes at all the first time. I was too intent on following Preston Grumiaux, a sooty whirlwind streaking through the snow. Later I would come to know the town all too well. At first I would be disappointed. I had come from the city thinking that all remote towns were invested with a romantic magic. The reality of Winter Eyes was otherwise. In the end I would find another magic here, malevolent and seductively beautiful. It would always be astonishing to me that the first time I passed through Winter Eyes I had noticed nothing at all. Of course, all that I saw was the squalid, modern town and not the ghost town hidden behind it.

We seemed to be going uphill. The town itself was behind us now. The road was narrow and wound through fields of snow. Preston didn't slow down.

We turned at a crossroads. The snow was falling thick now. All I could see was the cloud of smoke that was Preston Bluefeather Grumiaux. Now I remembered making love to him. He was right. I had done it to show how much more liberal I was than the others. I felt bitterly shamed. I drove on. Through the veil of snow I could make out the twisted outline of some rock formation. Perhaps it was a mountain. There was no perspective in this ocean of cold and gray. The light was almost gone.

Abruptly we turned again. I remember spiked wrought-iron railings in the mist. We slowed down. The snow was bloody in the sunset. We stopped. The snow ended in concrete steps, and Preston was already striding up, two steps at a time, his hair and his leather jacket flailing behind him. I got out and followed, I couldn't keep up. The cold was unendurable, and I could hardly see through the curtain of snow. The doors were of oak. Preston rapped on the brass knocker. Steadily I climbed up, treading in his bootprints to avoid the seeping slush. Above the doorway, in letters of iron, were the words:

The Szymanowski Institute

I knew, as my tongue struggled with the unfamiliar name, that this was the place I had been driving toward for the past weeks. Dread touched me once again. But when I stepped inside the door I felt a blast of heat and I stood in a well-lit hallway and was being warmly greeted by a receptionist, and I left my fear outside in the snow.

"Dr. La Loge will be with you in a—" the woman at the desk began. Before she could finish he had already stepped into the room. He was tall, blond, bearded, not at all the mad-scientist type.

"Ms. Dupré, I presume?" he said, extending a hand. "We were quite worried about you." He turned to Preston. "Thanks for going after her."

"Oh, it was nothing, Doc," he said. He looked at me with an emotion I couldn't quite understand . . . anger or longing maybe. Then he turned—as though tearing himself away—and walked over to the elevators. I let the receptionist take my coat.

I had a speech all prepared, and began: "I'm so thrilled to be in the presence of—"

"The notorious Sterling La Loge, mind-prober extraordinaire!" He started to laugh. "Come on. You must be starving to death. We'll have to eat in the commissary, I'm afraid. The town is completely shut down, because of the weather. I was hoping to lodge you at the Red Cloud Motel, twenty miles down the road—it's the only one anywhere near here—but they're snowed in and their phone lines are down." He started to steer me down the hallway, then paused. "Luggage? Give Greta the car keys. She's a local, she's used to freezing." I dug them out. The receptionist didn't seem fazed at the prospect of going out in the snow, and I was too weary to be polite.

I followed La Loge meekly as he led me down a corridor, its walls steel-gray, its wooden floor polished to gleaming. The air held a mélange of medicinal odors. Now and then I heard someone screaming in the distance, but that was only natural in an insane asylum. Certainly it wasn't the oppressive, Dickensian hell that I had half expected.

The dining room was something of a surprise. I had expected something rather like a high school cafeteria; instead we entered an expansive lounge with bay windows that looked out onto a grand snowscape at whose horizon loomed the contorted hillock I had seen on the way over. "Impressive, isn't it?" said Sterling La Loge. "It's called Weeping Wolf Rock."

"What an unusual name," I said, making small talk. I was

starting to realize how famished I was; frankly I wasn't in the least
bit interested in the colorful chunk of local history that I was sure
Dr. La Loge was going to disgorge. Luckily, he didn't. Instead, he
pointed to a table beside the window and I sat down. A few others
were eating at another table. They all wore lab coats. This was
clearly not the patients' dining room.

Going to an intercom by the door, La Loge paged Preston
Grumiaux. "Perhaps a familiar face at dinner will help you get
acclimated to this desolate place," he said, sitting down. We
waited in uncomfortable silence.

I sat staring at the landscape. Weeping Wolf Rock was all that
breached the flat monotonous white. The moon, not quite full, had
risen. Though it was warm in the room I shivered. I wondered
what gave the rock its name. It didn't look like a wolf.

"A hundred years ago it was all forest," said a voice behind me
in a Hollywood British accent. I jumped and turned to see an old
man carrying a tray . . . a waiter. I looked at him. After a while
it occurred to me that Dr. La Loge was studying me intently.

"That's James Karney," said La Loge, "an inmate here. Quite
harmless, I assure you. But alas, he has no family, and the
institution is all he has left. Pour some wine for the lady, James."

He did so with a shaking hand. In doing so, his hand brushed
mine. I felt an odd tickling sensation, and I retracted my hand
hastily. The waiter stood stiffly to attention, but I could not help
noticing that his hand was trembling still, and that the back of it
had a silvery sheen, almost as though it were covered with fur. It
must, I decided, be the moonlight.

"Ms. Dupré . . . ?" Suppressing a shudder, I turned away
from the waiter. "Or should I call you Carrie? In these parts we're
not much given to formality, I'm afraid."

"Of course you can . . . Sterling." He lifted his wineglass.
We toasted each other. I drank deeply, more deeply than I should
have. James refilled the glass and brought us each a bowl of clear
soup, bland but warm. Preston joined us. Again he looked at me
with that look of indignation and desire. And I was beginning to
remember more and more of that one night stand in Berkeley. It
had been after one of Professor Murphy's soirées. . . .

"The Laramie Ripper," Dr. La Loge said abruptly. "I suppose
you'll want to meet him soon?"

"Yes, please. As soon as possible."

"Good. But what do you expect to gain from all this? He's just a sad old man. It was all so long ago."

"Well, you might say there's something of a family connection," I said, "or at least I think there might be. But mostly it's . . . well, the romance and the sensationalism. I mean . . . small-town America during the Depression . . . a series of wild, bizarre killings in which the victims seem to have been viciously torn apart by a wild animal . . . Jonas Kay, a madman, brought to trial . . . but there's no trial . . . and then the coverup. The Laramie Ripper is spirited away across the South Dakota state line into an obscure mental institution . . . and the whole story simply dissipates."

"And this is where Carrie Dupré, girl reporter, moves in for the kill?" Preston said, sneering.

I had been expecting this. "I happen to be a liberated woman," I said, trying not to come on too strong. "I'm hardly the Lois Lane type. As far as I'm concerned, Superman can stay on Krypton."

Dr. La Loge laughed. "Considering the chip on your shoulder, Preston, I hardly think you should be making snide remarks about the one on Carrie's."

Preston dug into his soup bowl, sulking.

"Chicken or fish?" said James in sepulchral tones.

"Ignore his little act," La Loge said, his eyes twinkling. "I think it's rather therapeutic, don't you? This little playacting, I mean, this English butler shtick."

"Chicken," I said nervously.

The hand placed a steaming platter in front of me. It retreated before I could look at it more closely. Since La Loge seemed ready to talk, I pulled my notebook from my purse and opened it.

"What I want to know," I said, "is why the Szymanowski Institute—"

"You might as well learn to pronounce it," La Loge said. "Shima*noff*ski. There. No relation, by the way, to the famous Polish composer who wrote the opera *King Roger*."

I'd never heard of anyone by that name and I didn't know whether he was putting me on. I decided to ignore this piece of trivia, but I did correct my pronunciation, which had been distressingly off. "Why did the Szymanowski Institute go to such lengths to get hold of Jonas Kay? Didn't the institute cough up funds to get him some kind of fancy lawyer? Isn't that why it never came to trial?"

"Jonas Kay was a very sick man, Carrie. As you will find out. And we at the institute are particularly interested in . . . cases such as his."

"Such as his?" I said.

"Well, the Laramie Ripper wasn't . . . isn't your average psychotic killer. In fact, he doesn't suffer from any kind of psychosis at all."

"Are you trying to tell me he's perfectly sane?"

"Not exactly. He is what we call a multiple personality."

"Right," I said, "a schizo."

"Let's get one thing straight before I let you meet our friend, Carrie. He is not a schizophrenic. Multiple personality is classified as a neurosis, not a psychosis. Most of the subject's personae are perfectly charming people. Some are artistically talented. One of them is a brilliant pianist. Some are socially maladroit, but hardly the sort of thing you'd have a person committed for. One of them is a woman. Unfortunately, one of them . . . well, one of them isn't quite as . . . sane as the others."

"The one who killed all those people." I thought of the newspaper clippings in my suitcase. They were subdued, of course, except for a few "true stories" from the sleazier crime pulps. They talked of victims torn in two . . . their heads found miles away from their torsos . . . the flesh savagely ripped open with a serrated device . . . livers half eaten, shredded hearts. "Jonas Kay."

"Jonas hasn't come forward in years, Carrie. You see, we're in the process of trying to reunite our poor friend's fractured mind. And one of the personalities has emerged as a kind of core, drawing in the fragmented selves one by one . . . we call this process 'fusion,' and when it is done our friend will be Johnny Kindred and no one else."

"What's Johnny Kindred like?" I said.

"He's an eight-year-old boy. Oh, the body doesn't change. But Johnny Kindred *is* eight years old, just as James Karney is . . . however old he is. You'll love Johnny. He's charming, bright, full of joy. You'll meet him soon. This evening, maybe. Would you like that?"

"Very much," I said.

The waiter whisked our plates away and poured coffee. All three of them were staring at me: the waiter, standing stiffly, out of the corner of his eye; Dr. La Loge with a detached curiosity; and Preston Grumiaux with the kind of intensity that always seems to presage a sexual overture.

It was Preston who broke the silence first. "Come on, Sterling. A joke's a joke, but the suspense is killing me. Tell her."

"Tell me what?" I said in alarm. I spilled my coffee on the table. The waiter moved in with a napkin. "I'm sorry to be so jumpy," I said. "But the long drive and. . . ."

I saw the waiter swabbing at the tabletop with brisk, mechanical strokes. I stared at his hands. I laughed at myself for thinking they were covered with fur. He was just abnormally hirsute, that was all. Hanks of silvery hair protruded from his sleeves.

"Oh, all right," Sterling La Loge said. I waited for some dramatic revelation, but he simply said, "You can ask all the questions you like, but I must insist on one condition. . . ."

"Oh, utter confidentiality, naturally," I said, trying to sound smoothly professional.

"Oh, no, I don't mean that. I mean . . ."

I waited.

"I mean," he said sheepishly, "do you think you could get me some kind of cameo role in the movie?" He started to giggle uncontrollably. Before I could answer, he asked me, "And what about one for James, too?"

I studied the waiter, who stood to attention now. He had a craggy face; at a pinch it might have done for a geriatric Byron. He had a wild mane of white hair that pointed every which way. "He's certainly a colorful character," I said. The waiter surveyed me with his nose in the air.

"Yes . . . I see it now," La Loge said. "Hitchcock, I think, don't you? Co-starring Sterling La Loge and James Karney. What do you say, James?"

The three of them—the waiter standing behind the two seated others—gazed expectantly at me. I got the impression they were laughing at me, although their faces revealed nothing. I looked from one to the other, my puzzlement increasing. They think I'm just a dumb broad, I thought, fuming. Screw this! I was about to cry out with frustration when Preston couldn't control himself any longer and began to laugh out loud. "Don't you get it?" he cackled. "James Karney? J.K. . . . J.K. . . ."

I looked straight into the waiter's eyes and saw—

"No," I whispered. "No!" James Karney . . . Johnny Kindred . . . Jonas Kay . . . it couldn't be.

"You seem overexcited, Ms. Dupré," the waiter said, unruffled. "Perhaps I should show madam to her room?"

"What? Me alone with the . . ." I got up from the table.

"Alone with the Laramie Ripper?" said the waiter. His eyes brimmed with an exquisite sadness. "Ah no, madam . . . that was another person . . . and another time, so long ago. Such terrible crimes! To think some people think that I . . . I am just a foolish, harmless old man, Ms. Dupré." He came to me and put his hand on my shoulder. "I wouldn't hurt a soul." His hand was cold as the snow outside.

"Preston, you'd better escort her as well," La Loge said.

He came to me. I stood between them. Between Scylla and Charybdis. The two glared at each other. There was an old animosity between them. I felt like an intruder.

"Come on, Carrie," Preston said. Briefly he touched my other shoulder. His hand was as warm as James's had been icy. It made me tingle. I remembered more of our lovemaking than I cared to. He'd been angry that night. I left with him just to annoy Wilbur Hart. I remembered a drive-in. And him thrusting and thrusting like a machine. "Bitch," he'd called me, "white fucking Anglo-Saxon fucking bitch." I'd been turned on, in a way, but afterward I felt abused and I ached inside.

I twisted myself free of both of them. "I can walk myself," I said. "I'm not entirely helpless, you know."

"I forgot," Preston said softly, "you being, like, liberated and all."

"I shall lead the way, madam," James said. "If Mr. Grumiaux would care to take up the rear?"

Sterling La Loge was chuckling over his coffee as we left. I'm not going to let them make me feel this stupid again, I swore to myself as I started down the corridor, trying to keep pace with the clockwork footsteps of the Laramie Ripper.

We took an elevator to the fourth floor. We took passageway after passageway. We turned into another wing of the institute, the floor heavily carpeted, the walls intricately carved old wood. Although no madmen screamed and no chains clanked, the air seemed heavier here. Maybe it was the smell of the oily, polished wood. At least I was beginning to feel the brooding oppression I had expected. Clearly this part of the institute had been around since Victorian times. We said nothing, but I caught Preston and James glaring strangely at each other more than once.

"I'll never be able to find my way back," I said. My tone was light, but my unease was real.

"Don't worry," Preston said. "If you need help, there's an intercom in your room. . . ."

We turned a corner. James opened a door; I stepped inside.

". . . and anyhow, I'll be nearby. This week anyway. Next week it's back to my other job on the reservation."

A cozy room . . . peeling wallpaper, a design of primroses and carnations . . . a view of the snow. My luggage was waiting for me. I couldn't wait to unpack and settle in.

There was a mirror on the nightstand. As I looked into it, I saw that the old man was studying me. I only half believed that he was the Laramie Ripper. His face was a mass of wrinkles. His eyes seemed soulless.

But as I watched his face it seemed to shift. . . .

I started to scream but nothing came. I watched. The furrows in his brow smoothened. His cheeks stopped sagging. He seemed to be weeping. I turned around. His features were already freezing back into a mask of old age. But in the few seconds before the butler's persona took over, I heard the voice of a small child. It could not have come from the old man, but it had. It was a voice all innocence and longing, and it whispered, "Speranza."

I started to answer, almost as though he had called me by name. I stopped myself. The child had gone completely; James Karney was standing stiffly, with his nose in the air.

"Happens all the time," Preston said ruefully. "Looks like magic, but it's just this incredible control of the facial muscles. He *is* all those people. You should see it in slow motion. Reckon you will. Film in the archives. Just like magic."

James Karney glared at him.

"You can't talk like that!" I said. "It's not like he wasn't there. He's a human being, too, even though—"

"He's a fucking murderer. Guys like him, they shouldn't be put away, they should be shot, man."

The old man stood at the door. "Sir," he said quietly, "Jonas Kay *was* shot. He's dead. We killed him, together, Johnny and James and Jeffrey and Jonathan . . . and Dr. La Loge. Why do you go on speaking of such terrible things?" And the little boy in him said, "Speranza," and disappeared once more.

I was alone with Preston.

I didn't look at him. I went straight to the window and looked out at the snow, hoping he would go away.

"You can't stare at the snow forever," Preston said softly.

He came up to me. Stood behind me. I could feel his breath and smell him, axle grease and sweat and mud and musk and leather. "Don't touch me," I said, "don't, don't . . . not yet." I knew that it would happen, knew that I couldn't escape him. I was remembering more and more of that night. It was beginning to mean more and more to me. "I'm afraid."

"Bitch," he said. But not angrily.

I let him touch me. Very lightly. His lips brushed the nape of my neck. His lips were chill. I shuddered. He held me more tightly while I looked out at the moonlit snowscape. He crushed me against him, his stubble rasping my cheeks. Stonily I watched the snow.

Suddenly I saw—

Eyes. Red eyes, burning against the white—

I screamed. Twisted away from him. He shouted after me, "What's the matter? I ain't good enough for you anymore?" and I just pointed dumbly at the window—

"Fuckin' psychopath," he said. He turned toward the door. The door slammed shut. I heard footsteps. "Oughta chain him up tonight, he's restless. Oughta tie him down and pump him full of Thorazine."

"Was it him?" I said. He tried to touch me again, but the desire I had felt was gone, gone completely. "I'm not saying no," I said, "but—"

"You're saying no."

"Well, for now—" There was something disarming about him. "But I want to know if it was him. I mean—"

"The Laramie Ripper?" Preston laughed, a dry, comfortless laugh. "Dr. La Loge is right . . . he really is harmless now. But if you want, I'll arrange to have him locked in for the night. In case he decides to stake out the shower."

"That's not funny. Those eyes . . . they were bright red! They seemed to be on fire! They weren't . . . they weren't *human*. Am I being too melodramatic? For God's sake, I've been on the road for so long, I'm tired . . . you and the doctor have been screwing with my mind all evening."

"Carrie, this book you're wanting to write is gonna give you nightmares."

"I'm strong enough to face them," I said. I was young then.

He left me alone at last.

I ran to the door and bolted it shut. I didn't turn out the light. I didn't undress. I just lay down on the bed, afraid to close my eyes. But in the end I did. And I didn't dream of mad slashers. I dreamed of surfing.

Surfing. . . .

Red eyes, submerged, glowing like watery gemstones.

And once, behind the shatter of the waves, a child's cry penetrated my dream. It was a plaintive, despairing voice . . . the voice of a child who has witnessed something too terrible to describe, too brutal to comprehend . . . a voice that whispered, over and over, the word "Speranza."

In the dream the oceans turned to ice and my surfboard became a weather-beaten Impala careening through snow without end.

2
One Day Before Full Moon

IN THE MORNING AN ORDERLY I HAD NOT SEEN BEFORE KNOCKED ON my door. I readied my tape recorder, took a three-inch reel of tape (all that the portable would hold), and followed him. I could not recognize any of the corridors we passed down. I had an irrational feeling that my room had drifted to a different part of the building, that nothing in the Szymanowski Institute had a fixed location.

Dr. La Loge was already waiting for me. We had a quick breakfast, hardly exchanging more than a few perfunctory courtesies. It had never quite stopped snowing.

He said, at last, "I wanted you to meet our friend in this unorthodox way, Carrie, because I wanted to make sure that you didn't have any preconceptions about mad slashers."

"Unorthodox?" I said. "It sure was."

"Now you're going to meet him in a quite different situation, a clinical situation. But everything will be under control. You needn't be afraid of Jonas Kay emerging and making a dash for your throat."

"I'll be perfectly okay," I said, as I gazed out at the white and gray. I was determined to let nothing faze me. I had avoided hysterics last night, hadn't I? With a madman right beside me, staring at me with bloodshot eyes.

Bloodshot. That's all it had been. Nothing supernatural. Dr. La Loge isn't a medium, he's a psychologist! And we're not about to have some kind of séance. I was jittery, but I gulped down a second cup of coffee. Thank God, I thought, they haven't pulled this James the butler stunt on me again.

"Will Preston be there?" I asked him. I wasn't sure if I wanted him or not.

"He'll be joining us later today," Dr. La Loge said. "He went over to the reservation." He seemed to be waiting for me to say something. "Is there anything you want to ask me? Maybe a pocket lecture on multiple personality, that sort of thing?" I could tell that he thought I was some kind of idiot.

I wanted to clear the air right away. So I said, "Look, Sterling, I don't know why you agreed to let me come and do this research if you think I'm some kind of baby, that I'll just jot down your pocket lectures and regurgitate them later. Maybe I don't know that much yet, but—" I started to improvise, since I really had very little idea of what the book was going to be like. "I don't want to do a simpleminded sensationalist book. Sure, they'll package it like one, but—"

"How touching. A sensitive, loving portrayal of the man who ripped Inge Holst apart with his teeth, who ate the liver of Natalia Denisovitch . . . I can't wait to read it."

"There's got to be *some* reason why you let me come up here, Sterling," I said. "For decades this man has languished up here, isolated, seen by no one. And you let *me* come here, me who you consider a total idiot, it seems. I don't understand it."

"Nor do I. But let's get one thing clear, Carrie. Before you go in and see him. *I* didn't choose you from the dozens of names and résumés that have come in over the past thirty years. We haven't been flooded with inquiries, at least not in the past ten or fifteen years. But we have our share of them. Some of it is hate mail—you know, why don't you just lynch him, hang him, castrate him, whatever. Some of it's bleeding heart mail. Many of them are letters from people who claim they're related to him or to some other person involved in the case. So much for your being the great-granddaughter of Hope Martin, or whatever. I would just as soon not have anyone here. Although I'm sure we'll all get to know and like you, you'll be a nuisance. People like you always are. And then what?"

"Who did choose me then?" I said.

"*He* did," said Dr. La Loge. "He saw that picture of you in your résumé. He took a fancy to you."

Then he took me to see him.

The Laramie Ripper lived in a small cluttered room, sparsely furnished with a couple of chairs and a hospital bed. The window was barred. Snow was piled on the sill; the glass was frosted over, and you could hardly tell it was daytime.

At the head of the bed, taped to the wall, there were four faded photographs. I couldn't see them that well because he was sitting on his bed. He had not yet seen me. Another anomaly was a dusty Victrola and a stack of old 78s, piled up on a desk by the window. In the doorway's shadow I studied him. He was stooped, sunken; he seemed much older than last night when he had played the butler. He was busy with a piece of notepaper, creasing and uncreasing it.

"Ah, Jonathan," Dr. La Loge said softly. "Jonathan Kippax." He must have done that so I would know that it was a different J.K. this morning. "Jonathan is rather a dull character, you'll find, compared to some of the others; he's sort of a perennial hospital patient, a geriatric ward type. Rather a hypochondriac, too."

"Been waitin' on you all morning, Doc," the old man said. "I got this powerful ache." His accent was different, too, not at all British-sounding. "Where is she?"

Dr. La Loge held his hand up. I kept back. "She's on her way."

"Get her out of here, I didn't ask to talk to nobody, don't want to talk to nobody." A tired voice, a cranky old man.

"Didn't you want her to come?"

"Johnny Kindred wanted her to come. He's got this notion she looks like someone he used to know. But I don't think so. I never knowed her anyways."

"Where is Johnny now?"

"I killed him."

"Come now. You know he's there."

"He ain't comin' out. I got all the others locked up, Doc, they ain't comin' out till she's gone. It's too dangerous. I never harmed no one, I just want to be left alone."

"*Lupus!*" the doctor said.

At once the old man subsided. Dr. La Loge beckoned me into the room. All the expression seemed to drain out of his patient's face. He no longer seemed old or young. He wasn't stooping anymore, but sitting straight up.

"What did you do?" I whispered.

"Sit down." I did so, and turned on my tape recorder. "That was a post-hypnotic suggestion, Carrie. Whenever I say that word to him, he goes into a trance. Now, I don't want you to act like this hypnosis is a big deal. It's not a parlor trick. We do this every day. It helps us talk to him. All of him."

I waited, fidgeting with the controls of the tape recorder. My gaze darted across the room. Once more I tried to make out the four photos on the peeling wall; they were the only objects of interest in the room, and I would have to describe them in the book. To lend atmosphere.

Dr. La Loge said, "We're going to meet Johnny Kindred now." He sat down directly across from the old man and said softly, coaxingly, "Johnny Kindred, are you there?"

The face transformed itself . . . though none of the features had changed, he was acting with all the mannerisms of a little boy. The voice had a trace of some accent; English, maybe, or Eastern European. He looked straight at me. He got up. He came to me. He was crying. "Speranza," he said. "Speranza, I knew you'd come if I waited long enough—"

"She's not Speranza," Dr. La Loge said coldly. "Johnny, go and sit down. Behave. Or I'll have to spank you."

"Yes, Doctor. I'm sorry, Doctor." He looked at us with soulful, tearful eyes. Who was Speranza? I wondered.

"Oh, Speranza, how could you leave me for so long? Speranza, I feel myself fracturing into teeny pieces, I think I did some bad things. Oh, Speranza, protect me from the Count. Don't let the Injuns scalp me."

"What is he talking about?" I whispered to La Loge.

He was scribbling in a notebook. "This is as new to me as it is to you," he whispered back. "We'll just have to wing it."

"I'm not Speranza," I said to him. It was terrible, it felt as though I were breaking his heart. "I'm Carrie Dupré."

"Are you sure?" Johnny Kindred said. "Maybe you've fractured too. Maybe it's just a part of you you don't remember anymore. Like all the parts of me."

He reached over and gripped my hand with such desperation, such familiarity. It was cold as the snow outside. I did not pull away; I was held, transfixed, by those child's eyes in the old man's face. Somehow I belonged in his world. Or he thought I did. I was frightened, because I felt his madness tugging at me, I thought I was going to get sucked in. Firmly, brusquely, I said, "I'm Carrie Dupré, I'm Carrie Dupré."

"Look, Speranza, I made this paper airplane for you." He tossed it at me. It was the notepaper that Jonathan Kippax had been nervously creasing and uncreasing. In Johnny Kindred's hands it had become a sleek, streamlined work of art. It made a corkscrew in the still air and seemed to home in on my outstretched hand. In spite of my terror I found a kind of charm in him.

"Carrie's come to write a book on you," La Loge said. "She's going to make you famous."

"No! Speranza's going to do a book about me." Johnny Kindred pouted and looked out of the window.

With his head turned I caught a fleeting glimpse of the photographs. All four were group photos; the group seemed the same each time. In the first the clothes were definitely Victorian. There was a tall man with bushy eyebrows, in evening dress; he wore a cloak. He was flanked by several people who seemed to be retainers. In the very front was a small boy wearing a ruffled shirt. He seemed to be crying. Behind the boy was a woman. Severe-looking, wearing a prim, high-collared dress and holding a book in her hand. They were standing on a cobbled street; behind them was the façade of a town house, guarded by weathered gargoyles. There was a sign on the street; it was in old German script, and I couldn't read it.

I barely glanced at the other photos before Johnny Kindred turned back and his head obscured them. "Do you remember?" he said. "Come closer, look, look." He giggled. He was looking at me with feverish excitement, like a kid with a favorite aunt. "Look, remember me?"

I came closer. He pointed at the ruffle-shirted boy in the first picture. "This was where we went first."

"First?"

"On the train.

"Don't you remember the old house? The Count? There he is. He always looked very formal in photographs. But you liked him. You always wanted to, you know, *fuck* him." He smirked when he used that word, but he didn't really seem to know what it meant. The transformation into a child was absolute.

I said, "I don't know what you mean."

He said, "You've got to know. I've been waiting so long for you to come back . . . I'm not talking. Tell Dr. La Loge to wake me up, I've had enough."

I turned, bewildered, to the doctor. He shrugged. "This is all new," he said. But he made no move to protect me. I could see he was far more interested in these revelations about Johnny Kindred than in me.

Johnny seized my arm. He dragged me toward him. He had surprising strength. He shoved me onto the bed, forced me to look at the picture once more. "Don't you see yourself? Yourself in all of them. See, see?"

I looked. The other pictures showed the same group . . . in front of a bleak, Old West train station . . . in front of a saloon somewhere, perhaps here in South Dakota, with the tall man shaking hands with what appeared to be an Indian chief . . . and then a snowy plain, with only a few people . . . the only constant people were the boy (a little older in each one) and the Count (as I had already begun to call him in my mind) and the prim-looking woman. "Who is she?" I said.

"Why, you're playing tricks on me like we used to on the train, going all the way to Vienna that time, just you and me. But I don't want to play guessing games. That's you, Speranza Martinique."

Suddenly I knew. Speranza . . . Hope. Hope Martin. My ancestress. I stared into the face of that woman. She was dour and pinched. She didn't fit my self-image at all. "She's nothing like me," I said, resisting.

"Actually," Dr. La Loge said, "you know, allowing for the Victorian mode of dress, the resemblance is pretty remarkable. You could pass for twins. Play along with him, Carrie. We can probably get a whole lot of new information if you pretend to be who he thinks you are."

I panicked. This wasn't what I'd come for. I felt myself teetering on the edge of this madman's world. I stared at the old pictures, stared at the woman who was supposed to look like me. She seemed to stare back. I didn't like her, I didn't want any part of her. "He's crazy," I said. "I don't want this. I've changed my mind, I don't need any of this."

The old man wept . . . a pathetic parody of a young child's sobbing. "Don't be cruel, Speranza."

"I'm not Speranza!" I screamed.

There was a long silence. It seemed that a spell was broken. For Johnny Kindred's face shifted abruptly, and his posture slumped, and he was suddenly again the stooping, whining Jonathan Kippax. Only then did I notice that Preston had joined us. He had come into the room like a shadow. And I thought that the soundlessly creeping Indian brave was just one of those stereotypes.

"When you gonna give that medicine, Doc? I'm aching somethin' fierce."

Dr. La Loge said, "That's never happened before." He seemed perplexed, out of control. "He's never spontaneously snapped out of hypnosis like that before. I've always been able to lead him gently out of—*you* did this to him. Whatever you said, it awakened the memory of something very traumatic, Carrie."

"I just want out of this place." Anguished, I turned to Preston. He seemed far more attractive to me then than he'd ever been before. "Preston—"

"Come on, baby," he said. I didn't even mind his tone of intimacy.

"Please . . ."

La Loge turned to his patient and whispered the magic word

once more: "Lupus, lupus, lupus." No effect. Then La Loge leaned over the desk and put one of the old shellac records on the gramophone. It was very scratchy, but I could make out a whiny, reedy tenor voice singing in what sounded like German, and there was a tinny plinkety-plonking piano accompaniment. The song sounded vaguely familiar. It was minor key, haunting. It seemed to remind him of something. Me too, though I didn't know what. It soothed him. He settled back on the bed, shifted into the small boy, sucked his thumb in the corner.

Johnny Kindred said to Preston, "You're going to fuck her now, aren't you?"

"Yes," Preston said, blatantly, defiantly. I didn't contradict him. It was exciting to hear him say that, because it was so alien to the way I'd been brought up.

"Be careful," said Johnny Kindred, looking at us with lost, longing eyes. "I feel something bad. I think someone else is coming. Someone we haven't seen in a long time."

"I'll join you at lunch," Sterling La Loge said. "I think he's had enough excitement for now, don't you?"

Dr. La Loge was even less communicative than usual over lunch, but I was too busy brooding to notice. Preston ran off somewhere. We sat over sandwiches and coffee. It was snowing so hard that it seemed like evening. I felt as though I'd come for nothing. Just at the moment when I might have been the catalyst, the key to the unravelling of the Laramie Ripper's strange sickness, I'd chickened out. Maybe the Carltons were right about me. About women. It was an infuriating thought.

"You're very silent," La Loge said suddenly. "That jolt of the real thing was a bit much for you, I guess."

"I have to think."

His eyes narrowed skeptically. "Do you want to go home?"

"No. But I didn't realize I was supposed to get so . . . involved. I don't get the plan behind all this."

"Nor do I. You know, we're supposed to be the guardians, controlling the lives of these poor inmates who can't deal with the world. But in J.K.'s case . . . I think he may be controlling us." I shivered. "I *know* he thinks he is. But I was wrong about you. I think you *can* be helpful after all. Because of who he thinks you are."

"Now maybe you'll believe that Hope Martin really is my ancestress," I said.

"Tell me, Carrie, do you menstruate regularly?"

"Doctor, what the hell—"

"No. Just answer me. A hunch."

"Like clockwork," I said. "Around the full moon."

He nodded thoughtfully.

"Why on earth would that have anything to do with anything?" I'd heard that lunatics are affected by the full moon, but wasn't that just a myth? Besides, I wasn't one of the patients. I gulped down more coffee and tried to look intelligent. Perhaps I should try another tack. "What was that music you played to him? And the photographs?"

"All things that have always belonged to him. The music is a song cycle by Schubert, *Winterreise*. It means 'a journey in winter.' The words of the first song are: 'I came here a stranger; a stranger I depart.' When the post-hypnotic suggestion doesn't work, the song always seems to get him into the right mood. The pictures . . . he's always had them."

"He knows German?"

"Who knows?" La Loge shrugged. "I don't even know how old he really is. His body is so good at contorting itself into whatever age his dominating personality is at that particular time. Physically, he could be a hundred. Judging by the earliest of those pictures . . . could be the 1870s, 1880s. He's maybe five or six years old in it. Then he'd be eighty-eight, eighty-nine."

"*Winterreise*," I said. "It sounds so familiar. Like I just heard it somewhere."

"Of course you did," La Loge said. "It's the name of our town. Winter Eyes. Another of your coincidences, I guess."

"Winter Eyes. *Winterreise*." I repeated the words over and over to myself.

"You going to eat that sandwich?" It was Preston. He startled me. The silent-Indian stereotype again, I thought. I stared dumbly at my plate. I hadn't eaten a bite. Preston grabbed the sandwich and hunkered over us, chewing noisily. When he'd finished it, he said to me, "I have the evening off. Let's go into town, baby." Before I could protest he was dragging me from my seat.

I was going to twist away from him when I realized I didn't

want to. I wanted to be with him, anywhere, away from this labyrinth of madness.

We rode into the snow like children. I hung on to his jacket. He left the road and we slipped and slid along channels of slush. He turned into a snowbank. We threw snowballs at each other. We laughed. Anything to avoid thinking about the morning's interview.

As evening fell we went into Winter Eyes. The general store was already closed. There was a diner next to it. We were the only customers. There was nothing newer than 1959 in the jukebox. A huge poster of Jacqueline Kennedy dominated one wall. The waitress was hostile. In a small voice I asked Preston why. "You stupid white bitch!" he whispered savagely. "It's 'cause I ain't one of you, I'm a wagon burner. And I don't got the right to be out drinking with real folks . . . now, don't get that bleeding heart look. It's true."

I didn't want to stay after that. I fidgeted. I didn't drink my beer. But I didn't dare say "Let's go," because I was afraid of another outburst.

At last he said, "Come on. There's more to Winter Eyes than this sleazy strip."

It was dark outside. "Where now?" I said, brushing the snow from my hair.

"I'll show you." He was already mounted and pulling me up.

We turned a corner. Went past a few houses. The town ended abruptly with a ruined church and a cemetery. The gravestones peered over the snow; mostly headstones, here and there a cherub or a cross poking out of the mass of white. It was snowing only lightly now; through the dense fog shone the moon, almost full, ringed by a ghostly rainbow fringe. Preston turned his motorbike and we went into the graveyard through a gap in the fence.

"What are we doing here?" I said.

"You'll see." I could distinguish a few worn names among the headstones: *Thomas Simon, Capt. James Sanderson, Scott Harper, Mrs. Prudence Carmichael*. The dates: the late 1880s; there was one that read 1901. Nothing later than that.

I clung to the jacket. Its smell, leather and man's sweat, pervaded me. I saw where we were headed. Ahead . . . almost as though they were condensing out of the swirling mists . . .

there were more houses, houses with ornamental gables.
"Where?"

"Old Winter Eyes. Abandoned. Ghost town. No one lives
there."

"No one?"

Another gap in the fence. He stopped the bike and leaned it on
a tree. There was a boardwalk; there were wooden buildings, their
eaves groaning with the weight of snow. A wooden canopy still
stretched over most of the boardwalk. Wondering, I followed
Preston, wishing it were daytime so I could see every detail of the
ghost town. We were sheltered from the snow. Ahead, a light
flickered in a doorway. I edged closer to Preston, reached for his
hand. He laughed softly. It was a swinging door, just like a saloon
in an old western. I could make out a bar, a few stools, a
table . . . beyond, coming from the back room, the source of
light.

I followed him there. It was one of those kerosene lamps. Inside
was a bed. On the wall was a portrait of an Indian chief, rather
garish work done in acrylics. "My hideout," Preston said. "I
come here sometimes and I imagine . . . I imagine I'm in the
Old West, and the bar is full of them drunken gold diggers on their
way to the Black Hills. It's a private place. No one knows about
it but me. And you now, I guess." The floorboards creaked, even
though we were tiptoeing toward the bed. "I can almost hear their
voices." A howl in the distance. "Just a coyote. Or maybe a gray
wolf. But they never come this far south no more." More
howling. "Sometimes I imagine the howls are the secret signals of
Lakota warriors. They got anger in their hearts on account of the
broken treaties. They're coming to raid the town, hundreds of
warriors, and their call is the call of the gray wolf that the white
hunters have driven from the land."

"You're spooking me," I said. The one tiny window was
completely blanketed in snow.

"I know," he said. His eyes glowed in the unsteady light.
"Come on, baby."

With a kind of desperation I fell into his arms. It was freezing
in the room, but Preston's body burned. I clutched it harder, trying
to siphon his warmth into me. I kissed him, scraping my cheeks
on stubble, breathing in the smell of gas and sweat and leather. He
squeezed me hard. I tottered. I fell back onto the bed, and we

made love, urgently and with a graceless haste. I don't know why there was so much sadness and anger in him. Or so much need in me. We weren't thinking of each other, I'm sure of that.

When I drifted into sleep, I thought I saw the eyes again.

In the window, imprinted on the snow. Yellow-red slits of eyes, not human. I blinked and they were gone. "I want to go back," I said, and prodded Preston lightly where he lay snoring.

He jumped, came awake as though he'd been guarding against an ambush. He saw me. Bitterly he said, "No like-um tipi, white bitch?"

"Please, I didn't mean. . . ."

"Okay. I'll take you back."

He led me through the maze to my room. "Look, if you start freaking out or something, I'm two doors down the first hall on the left. That's my room whenever I'm staying over at the institute."

"Yeah. I'll need someone to talk to after tomorrow's interview."

"So you're going through with it."

"Guess so," I said, knowing that I couldn't back down now.

"I thought you would." He turned to leave. I didn't touch him. Somehow our lovemaking had left me more disturbed than ever. He said, "You can have the day off tomorrow, though. You won't be able to talk to him. Tomorrow's the day we lock him up in his padded cell for a couple days."

"Why?"

"Full moon," he said. "That's when he turns into a werewolf."

"Oh, cut it out," I said. "I'm nervous enough as it is."

Preston leered at me. Then he howled, a mock horror movie wolf howl. I slapped his face. He laughed. "We'll party tomorrow," he said. "Day after, I have to go back to my other job."

"Sure."

I shut the door and locked it. Then, on impulse, I bolted it too. And drew the curtains so I couldn't see the snow.

3
Full Moon

OVER BREAKFAST I ASKED LA LOGE IF IT WAS TRUE THAT THEY WERE going to lock him up for the next couple of days. "Yes, it's true, I'm afraid. But there's really no danger. It's just to protect him from himself more than anything else."

"What about the full moon? Preston said—"

"Ah, the old werewolf joke? Surely that's wearing a little thin. I'll have to have a word with him about it." He was noticeably more civil to me now that I had become indispensable to his research. But getting information out of him was still like milking a stone. "Seriously," he said, "there was some relation between Jonas Kay and the full moon; but Jonas Kay hasn't been around for some time. As Johnny Kindred told you, we disposed of Jonas in therapy many, many years ago." He offered me a cigarette; I refused. He went on: "What did you think of Johnny Kindred?"

"Disturbing. That's really his 'core' personality?"

"He only comes out during hypnosis."

"That's not true," I said. For I had seen Johnny the very first night and heard his voice cry out, "Speranza." He had manifested himself to me of his own free will, without any help from a hypnotist or a drug. It dawned on me that there might be things I knew about Johnny that even the doctors didn't know. I didn't say anything, though. I could be as tight-fisted with information as La Loge, if I wanted to be.

It wasn't as if a thunderbolt struck me and I declared, "This means war." But I thought, two can play at these deceptions, these false hints, these misdirections. Let him think he's manipulating me.

It was a mindless day. I borrowed a typewriter from Greta down at reception, and I tried to work on my book. I wanted to start with something brooding and romantic . . . the snow. That would set the scene. I sat down in my room and typed paragraph after paragraph, all opening paragraphs about the drive from Laramie, all descriptions of snow.

I pushed the little desk over by the window so that I could look out. I could see Weeping Wolf Rock poking up. It was the only thing that wasn't white. The snow was light and the air was clear.

"It's like some kind of goddamn Victorian novel."

"Preston!" I whipped around. Hastily I covered the sheet with my arm.

"Like being caught masturbating, ain't it?" Preston said. He smiled easily. I didn't know how long he had been standing behind me. He rifled through the wastepaper basket and pulled out some crumpled sheets. "What's this! 'It was a dark and stormy—' Not that one."

"I was just joking," I said. "You know, when you're blocked, you start just typing anything that comes into your head."

"Sure. 'It was the best of times, it was the . . .' 'Call me Ahab.'" He started reading the whole sheet. I was embarrassed. He tossed it back in the trash and started to pull out another one. "This one's a bit better," he said, and started to read aloud again. This was one of my serious attempts.

"Give that back," I said. But I made no move to stop him.

"Wanna fuck?"

"Preston! I'm working."

"Yeah, but you're blocked, anyone can see that. Why don't we—but you WASPs are all alike. You always seem to have a log permanently rammed up your—"

"You think you're going to turn me on by talking dirty?" I said, laughing suddenly.

"Worth a try."

"It's not even night," I said.

"Another WASP fixation. Gotta have a time and place for everything. But look, it's okay. Why don't you come down to the institute library with me? Maybe you'll find some good background material. I promised La Loge I would help them sort out their index cards for a couple of hours. Then I gotta go and walk the loonies for an hour, and tomorrow I'm off for a week, back to patrolling the reservation and picking up drunks." He tried to sound nonchalant, but I sensed bitterness in him.

I didn't want him to go, I realized. "You mean I'll—"

"Be alone? Yeah. But you can call me at the reservation. There's a phone at the general store, a half mile down the road from where I'll be. Besides, there's still tonight. And I'll be back, baby, I will."

I didn't like the way he implied that I somehow needed him. But it was true. I was disoriented here . . . the people might as well be from outer space for all I understood. I was getting dragged in far deeper than I'd thought possible. I clung to him like a child.

The library, with its mahogany panelling and nineteenth-century oil paintings, seemed forbidding. An upper gallery could be reached by spiral steel staircases at each corner. The shelves were so close together that two people could barely squeeze between them, and the dust was thick. There was a skylight, but it was piled with snow; the room was dimly lit; there were a few people in lab coats working at some kind of microfilm device. "Come on," Preston said, "I wanna show you the back room." We passed through a façade, Ionian columns imitated in wood. Behind was a small room even gloomier than the one we'd left behind. Books were piled everywhere. A row of filing cabinets, many of them dented and crooked, leaned against one wall, blocking out half of the light from the only window.

"God, how old is this institute?"

"There was a loony bin here in the 1890s," he said. "Parts of it were cannibalized into this building. That's why there don't seem to be no order to the place."

"Yeah, I see."

"You might want to rifle through this stuff." Preston pulled out a file drawer and casually emptied it onto one of the desks. Then he set to work on some other books and index cards. I was left staring at a mass of material.

There was a file folder marked *Jonas Kay*. So that was why Preston had brought me here.

I opened it. Some pictures fell to the floor. I saw that they were reproductions of the ones I had seen on the wall in J.K.'s room. I looked at them more closely. "I still don't think it looks like me."

"You have Speranza's eyes," Preston said, not looking up.

I looked at the first picture more closely. It was an odd group.

I noticed the one J.K. had called "the Count" right away; the one who was supposed to look like me, and the little boy I remembered. There were others too; one was a turbaned gentleman who seemed to be dressed in elaborate silks; another an old woman in a black dress, with cruel eyes set in a vulpine face; a third, inconspicuous, a skeletal old man with a black bag. More people were standing in the shadows. It was hard to make them out. I looked at the train station again, and then the one in front of the saloon . . . and then the one in the snowy plain.

"Isn't that Weeping Wolf Rock in the background?" I said.

"Yeah."

I looked through the records some more. There were old news clippings with details of the slasher killings. The paper was yellow and brittle. I didn't read them; I had my own copies. There were notes and reports and diagnoses. "Can I borrow these?" I said.

"I guess. They're dupes, anyways. The real records are in La Loge's office. I came across this stuff when I was clearing out the files. Thought you might want them."

"Thanks." Preston perplexed me more and more. He seemed to want to help me. But I always got the feeling that he was withholding information . . . waiting for me to ask the right questions. Playing a game with me.

I continued looking at the pictures. The last one had a strange sadness to it; the three protagonists seemed utterly lost in the landscape. "Why do they call it Weeping Wolf Rock, anyway?" I said at last.

"First reasonable question I've heard all day," Preston said.

Frustrated, I waited.

"That rock formation," said Preston, "marks the boundary of the sacred burial grounds of the Shungmanitu tribe."

"I've never heard of them," I said. "And, considering we were both in Murphy's Indian Studies class—"

"They're extinct."

"But we talked about other extinct tribes in Murphy's class . . . I mean, the Miami, the Delaware—"

"The Shungmanitu were not destroyed by the white man," Preston said. "They chose to become extinct. Even their true name is no longer known. Shungmanitu is a Lakota word for 'wolf.' We don't know what they called themselves. They lived a little to the north of here, in the forests, above the plains."

"Are you . . . is this some kind of . . . tourist thing?" I said. After all, I had gotten an A in that Indian Studies class. Preston snorted and turned back to his work. It was a take-it-or-leave-it proposition then. "But why would they decide to destroy themselves?"

"You wouldn't understand. But I'll tell you the person who knows all about it. Your friend J.K."

"Why would he—"

"But you have to get him in his right mind, if you see what I mean."

We heard a scuffling sound from the next room. "Shit," Preston said, "he's loose." He flung the door open. I followed him out.

It was J.K. But he was moving so fast he was almost a blur. His features were shifting even as I watched . . . his eyes growing bloodshot. A couple of orderlies were chasing him. He sprang up on a bookcase. Dust was flying everywhere.

"Get the hell down," one of the orderlies was shouting. He was holding a straitjacket.

J.K. was looking down at them, taunting. A strange smell permeated the room . . . the smell of a damp forest floor, of a wild animal. He growled. He was on all fours now, straddling the bookshelf, clawing at the air.

I wanted to run back into the inner room. But Preston held me. "This ain't happened in years," he whispered. "It's on account of you. You've gone and awakened something in him. Something that was lying dormant. Something the doctors thought they'd killed." I shivered, although the heat was blasting from the radiator right behind me.

J.K. glared. Who was he now . . . had he been taken by Jonas Kay, the mad killer? An orderly was climbing up to him on a stepladder. J.K. scratched at his face. The orderly screamed and clutched his eye and fell on the ground. I heard an alarm go off somewhere.

La Loge came in. He sized up the situation. He looked at Preston, who rolled his eyes and raised his palms in frustration. Then he saw me.

"*Lupus!*" he shouted.

But his patient wasn't buying. Instead he pawed the dust of the bookshelf and howled. I was chilled by his cry. There was nothing human in it at all.

Dr. La Loge noticed me for the first time. "Call to him!" he shouted. "Yes, you! You're the only one who can get through to him."

"Me?"

I tried to back away. But my voice had attracted his attention.

"Johnny," I said softly.

"Speranza?" His facial muscles twitched, twitched, transformed. "Is it time for bed?"

"Yes."

"Where am I? Will we be there soon?"

"Soon," I said, "soon. You're having a nightmare," I said, improvising. I saw La Loge encouraging me by his gestures. "But it's all right . . . come down from there now."

"How much longer till we get to Vienna?" A frightened, little-boy voice. So convincing. I was drawn to him, drawn into his make-believe. Slowly I approached him. I reached up. I felt his hand in mine. I squeezed it to give him reassurance. I could not doubt his sincerity. I was disturbed by the way he trusted me implicitly . . . but it also moved me the way nothing else had ever done.

His hand went limp. Dr. La Loge had climbed the stepladder and had shot him full of tranquilizers.

I tried to start the book again that night. I kept the curtain tight shut and the door bolted. I filled the wastepaper basket to overflowing. I found myself drifting off.

The central heating was stifling . . . I was sweating. I got up from the desk, got into my nightgown. It wasn't any cooler. I thought of opening the window but I didn't want to see the snow.

I went back to the typewriter. After a while I began to type just for the sake of typing, paragraph after paragraph of garbage . . . about the snow . . . running through the snow . . . my tongue hanging out, the moon full, my body low to the ground, feeling the snow damp and chill against my thick fur . . . my tail high in the air, with the windstream moist and icy . . . a howl of terrible passion and yearning torn from my lips . . . lips that weren't lips, that were jaws glistening with sharp teeth. . . .

I shook myself awake. A dream, a vivid dream. Almost like those visions the Plains Indians used to have in their sweat lodges. Well, it was hot enough in here. So much talk of wolves in the past few days: werewolves, the doctor's magic word *lupus,* the Shungmanitu Indians, whoever they were . . . and Preston in the ghost town, telling me about the gray wolves driven north by the white hunters.

Back to the Laramie Ripper! I told myself.

But the howling had sounded so real. . . .

It *was* real! I realized that I was still hearing it. It was coming from somewhere far away . . . maybe upstairs. I got up, put on a robe. I went to the door. Yes, I could hear it. Somewhere.

I unbolted the door. I could hear my own heartbeat.

I stood in the corridor.

The howling was distant, but it was somewhere in the building. I thought of Johnny Kindred in his straitjacket, in his padded cell. That's all it is, I thought. He thinks he's some kind of wild animal. I shouldn't be afraid.

I took a few more steps.

The howl came again, closer, bloodcurdling.

I stopped thinking and started running.

I have to find Preston! I thought. I wanted to be with him. Where had he said his room was? First left . . . two doors down . . . I ran to it, banged on the door. No answer. The howling seemed to come from just around the corner. I didn't dare look behind me. I slammed my fists into the door—

Cold. Cold. The curtains were rustling. Snow was flurrying into the room. The window was wide open . . . no, not open, shattered. Glass all over the floor.

I looked around. Disarray. An unmade bed. On the sheet, two flecks of blood.

I didn't stop to think about consequences. I ran back to my room and got my car keys. Somehow I found my way downstairs. There was a watchman at the reception desk, but he was fast asleep. As I left the building the cold blasted me. I was only wearing my nightgown and a thin robe, but I couldn't go back. I dashed down the steps, found the Impala in the parking lot, turned the heat on full, and headed out toward Winter Eyes.

It wasn't snowing anymore. The moon was full and huge in the clear night sky.

I turned onto the road. It hadn't been plowed. I skidded into Winter Eyes, telling myself over and over, I'm just panicking for no reason, I'm going to be embarrassed in the morning. But I didn't turn back. I parked the car in an alley and headed out toward the cemetery.

The wind roared. My skin felt sore and flaky. My ears hurt. I didn't stop. I stumbled through the gap in the fence, through the snow. There were deep bootprints. And other prints too, something four-toed, with claws. The air was laced with that musky animal scent I'd smelled in the library. My robe was damp and the water was freezing to my skin. As I ran I relived the dream—was it a dream?—the sensation of running wild in the snow in the forest with the cold tickling my nose and my tail held high. I ran.

I reached the ghost town. The old wood clattered as I climbed onto the boardwalk. There was a dark trail beside the outlines of boots. I couldn't tell if it was blood. In the moonlight it was dark, silver-edged. There was the old saloon.

I went in.

The doors swung; back and forth, back and forth, creaking. It was pitch-black inside. I listened for breathing. Once I thought I heard the howling, but it was the wooden floor, groaning as I leaned into it. Gingerly I felt my way toward the back room. The door was closed.

Between the door and the floor there was a crack of yellow light. The floorboards next to the door were stained with sticky blood.

I crept up to the door. "Preston," I whispered.

I tapped.

I pushed the door open.

On the bedside table, a candle was burning on a small dish. It was almost all gone. In the flickering light I saw Preston lying on the bed. He was covered with a blanket from the neck down. His eyes were open. "You had me scared," I said softly. He didn't move.

I went and sat beside him on the bed. I stroked his hair. His face was cold, utterly cold, and he didn't blink. I touched his chin. Gently I rubbed his neck. My hands slid down to touch his chest. They met something wet and slippery. I recoiled. The blanket moved and I saw that Preston's abdomen had been ripped open. His intestines, tangled, steaming, protruded from the opening. I stepped back. The blanket fell to the floor. I saw that his penis had been cut off. I realized that it was lying on the nightstand, next to the candle holder. It had been there the whole time, but it had never occurred to me that that was what it was.

I didn't scream. I couldn't. I stood there, staring, disbelieving. After a long while I heard the howling again. Far away.

I had to get back to the institute. I had to tell someone. I still felt no fear; I was too numbed. I ran back to the car and drove back. Inside the lobby, I shook the watchman awake. I was starting to get hysterical. I hollered at him, incoherent words.

"Reckon I ought to call La Loge," he said finally, and pushed some buttons. Dr. La Loge came in right away. He was completely dressed. It was almost as though he were prepared for this moment.

"It's Preston!" I was shouting. "He's been killed, horribly killed—the Laramie Ripper—"

"Calm down," La Loge said. "What are you talking about?"

I started to tell him about it.

"I think you're just getting a little overexcited . . . having bad dreams . . . would you like something? Nembutal? I can give you something stronger if you want . . . Valium? Harvey, run down to the storeroom and get some, will you? Our poor friend is still locked up in his cell, you know."

"I've just seen a dead man lying in his own guts, and you're trying to make me take sleeping pills! Call the police, for God's sake! I've had as much of this as I can stand—"

"All right. Just to prove that there's nothing the matter . . . why, you're shivering. Fetch a coat or something for Miss Dupré, Harvey."

I felt something warm being put over my shoulders. I was trembling. It was just starting to hit me that I had seen Preston dead, torn apart . . . a man I had made love with only the day before.

"I'm not crazy," I said quietly.

"No one's suggesting you are, Carrie. In fact, let's go down there now. In case it's true. We'll take one of the ambulances. Harvey, get the keys."

We didn't speak until we reached the edge of Winter Eyes. We had to walk from there. Grimly I led the way. In the saloon, La Loge realized there was no electricity and sent Harvey back for a flashlight.

I strode over to the back room and threw the door open.

There was no corpse.

There were no bloodstains on the floor. A kerosene lamp burned brightly beside the bed. The blanket was gone. Instead there was a patchwork quilt. "I don't understand it," I said. "God damn it, is this some kind of coverup or something?"

"Let's go back now," La Loge said. The watchman had returned. He had one of those industrial-strength flashlights, and the light poured into the back room. There was no sign of Preston at all. Not even the leathery, sweaty smell I had come to know so well.

"Don't worry about him," La Loge said. "You'll see him again next week."

"I won't! I won't!" He stared at me. I started to sob helplessly.

I saw Johnny Kindred the next morning in his room. He was already in hypnosis by the time I got there.

When he saw me he said, "Help me, Speranza."

"Did you—" I began.

"I've been away . . . on a long journey . . . it's like I'm lost under miles and miles of snow and there's no one to pull me out."

"You killed Preston Grumiaux!" I screamed. "Where's his body?"

La Loge tried to restrain me. But I ran at him, I started to pummel him with my fists, this sunken old man with the eyes of a child. Johnny didn't resist. I went on hitting him, while orderlies hovered over us with hypodermics.

At last they managed to pull me away.

"I didn't do anything," Johnny Kindred said softly.

"Tell me I didn't see Preston's body in the ghost town. Tell me that."

"I can't tell you that." It was another voice entirely, an oily, deep voice. La Loge looked up, startled. He seemed alarmed for the first time. "Perhaps, in time, the boy will reveal everything. If you cooperate, Miss Dupré."

"Jonas," La Loge whispered.

Jonas Kay was a man in his prime. He sat erect and spoke without fear. His eyes were slits, and he constantly clenched and unclenched his fists.

"I'm going to go back inside now," Jonas said. "The boy

doesn't know who you really are, Carrie Dupre. .
You'll get a lot more out of him if he thinks that you
nanny." He laughed. "Kid doesn't have much grasp of reality,
afraid."

"Murderer," I whispered.

"Oh, you're wrong. I didn't kill Preston Bluefeather Grumiaux.
I didn't kill those women either. The doctors haven't really figured
out the full extent of my . . . metamorphic nature. The fact is,
I had the ability to change inside me long before the childhood
trauma split my mind into many cubbies. You see, I am a
werewolf."

I looked at the doctor, who said, "Yes, Jonas. Go back inside
now. You know you're not allowed out anymore. We killed you.
Remember. You're still under hypnosis, and I want you to do as
I say."

Jonas Kay spat in the doctor's face. But before La Loge could
respond Jonas had retreated, leaving Johnny Kindred in his place.
Johnny was crying.

"Jonas," La Loge said, "suffers from certain delusions." He
gestured to an orderly, who injected Johnny Kindred with something. "Isn't that so, Johnny?"

Johnny said, "I'm scared he's come back. You told me he was
dead, Dr. La Loge. I don't trust you anymore. I'm only going to
trust her from now on."

Tentatively I went to him. He seemed so vulnerable.

Johnny said, "You probably won't remember anything, Speranza, because it's been so long. So I'm going to tell you all of it.
Everything."

"Turn on your tape recorder," La Loge whispered to me.

I started the book a few days later.

It was not the book I dreamed of as I crossed the snow. It wasn't
the sensational, instant bestseller I had thought I would write. It
was more like a novel than a piece of journalism, and I was glad
of this, because I don't think anyone will believe the truth, and
besides, it doesn't matter anymore.

The mystery of the Laramie Ripper was only a tiny part of the
complex tapestry of Johnny Kindred's story. Johnny spoke to me
in many voices; with his affliction came an uncanny knack for
mimicry. And so the book came to be written in the voices of its

many characters: the Europeans, the Americans, the Shungmanitu, who were and were not like the other Indians of the Plains. In
time I too was to become a part of the story, inextricable from it.
This was not the stuff of journalism, partial or impartial.

The story had begun more than eighty years before. The
protagonists came from many countries; they were separated by an
ocean and by a cultural gulf that was to have tragic consequences.
One thing they had in common, as they began to journey toward
their predestined meeting, was their nature, which was to be
wholly human yet always apart, always alien.

The other thing they shared was the snow. It had been a terrible
winter on both sides of the ocean.

PART ONE

Crossing the Snow

1
1880: Dakota Territory
half-moon, waxing

"SNOW. SNOW STREAMING DOWN SINCE THE ONSET OF NIGHT. SNOW heaped up against the tent flaps, whipped up by the wind, seeping through the places in the walls where the hides have worn thin. Snow piling on the treetops outside and bending the branches to breaking. Snow on the ground packed hard, stubborn snow. Snow caking on the buffalo robes, not melting. Snow hanging in the air even beside the dying embers of the fire. Snow on your clothes and your hair and even your eyebrows, my son. Are you surprised, my son, that this winter the snow has crept inside me, and turned my old woman's heart to ice?"

He did not answer her but continued to squat cross-legged on the buffalo robe. Perhaps he was listening to the wind. Was he awake, even? But his eyes were open.

"It is time for me to go into the snow, my son. There is only enough pemmican for you and your wives and their children. You will slaughter the dogs one by one to fill the hunger from moon to moon. The time has come. The wind whistles and whines, and sometimes I think I hear my name. Do not be sad. I know that is why you will not speak to me. You also hear my name on the wind, my son. Is it not so?"

He still would not look at her. She studied him. His hair was almost as gray as her own; here and there it was flecked with snow. In the shadow, away from the fire, a baby cried; she heard a young girl's soothing voice and did not know which of her son's wives it was, for her ears were failing her. She knew it was from deep reverence that he did not speak to her directly; whenever he did it was always with the politest of speech forms. She wished it were not so now. The cold had burned its way into her bones. She could feel them creaking. Her bones were like flutes through which the winter wind whistled.

"The hardest thing of all, my son. . . ." She paused. He looked up at last. He is clenching back some terrible emotion, she thought. I must not shame him. "I can no longer change. Do you understand? I have lost the gift."

"*Ina,*" her son said at last. "Mother. Will you go to join my *inachikala*, your sister?"

"Yes." Her sister had left the encampment only a few moons ago. She too had been unable to change. But it was the four-legged that she favored. She was certain that it was her sister's voice she had heard on the wind, speaking in the secret language of the Shungmanitu. But she did not say this aloud; she did not want to distress her grandchildren. Some of them at least were awake and listening to every word. She was sure of it. Her little sister must be hungry too.

She thought: But at least I will be able to stave off *mitankala*'s hunger. As my children and my children's children will butcher and feast on the meat of our dogs, so I will be meat for the mighty dog of the darkness.

The cold was numbing, so numbing; she forced herself to think clearly. She imagined lines of heat radiating outward from the smoldering fire, imagined them weaving a web around her. The image warmed her a little.

"I must array myself with what finery I have," she said. "I do not want to enter the other world dressed like a pauper." While her son watched, she rummaged in her belongings. There was a wooden chest that had come from the white men by way of the Arapaho. She opened it and pulled out a hairbrush made from a porcupine's tail, stretched taut over a buffalo bone handle. She began to straighten the tangles of her sparse, dry hair, wincing from the pain. Then she took the robe that had been hers even before she had come into her son's household, and wrapped it around herself with the fur inside; the skin side was painted with a design of mating wolves. She selected a walking staff, one she had made herself when she was only a girl. She spread a little bear fat on her face and arms. Perhaps it would protect her from the cold. For a little while at least. Until she could find her sister.

"Will you be able to make it as far as the burial ground?" It was her son, trying to speak in low, measured tones, though she knew his heart was breaking.

"Yes. I will even dance the moon dance for the last time," she said. "We will dance together, my sister and I, under the light-in-darkness. And you will be proud."

She went to the door and lifted the flap. Snow streamed into the tipi. The child cried again, and, called after her: "*Unchi, unchi.*"

"Don't fret, Mahtohokshila, Little Boy Bear," she whispered. "Come to Grandmother." The child toddled to her across the robes. She held him in her arms. "I'll tell you a story." She rocked him gently to and fro.

"When Wakantanka made all things," she said, "he made some of our brethren wingeds and some four-leggeds and some two-leggeds. And they flew and they scurried and they ran to the four corners of the universe, each one singing his own song . . . except for one: the one we call Wichasha Shungmanitu. And Wakantanka said, 'Why do you not rejoice like the others? All have chosen what they will be, winged or four-legged or two-legged, creatures of air or earth or mind. Why do you remain here?' And the Wichasha Shungmanitu said, '*Tunkashila*, Grandfather, I want the intelligence of man, and his skill at war and his understanding of the universe. But I have in me a darker longing, and it is to be wild and swift-footed and fierce like the wolves, and to be free of understanding. For understanding is both the greatest of gifts and the most terrible of curses.' And the Great Mystery said: 'You understand me too well, *michinkshi*. I have put light and darkness in all things. And because you have understood, I will divide you from the race of men, and give you the power to change; and the power will come at the time of the greatest-light-in-darkness. You will be brother yet not brother to the Lakota and the Cheyenne and the Arapaho and the Apsaroke and the Sarsi and all the peoples of the earth. You will be brother and not brother to the creatures that fly and run and scurry. It shall be so.' And that is why, *takozha*, we are here to this day."

She smiled, seeing that the boy had fallen asleep to those familiar words. Mahtohokshila's mother was there now; she was kneeling, her arms outstretched to take the child.

She thought: The time has come.

She lifted the tent flap all the way and crawled out.

When she stood up, she was knee-deep in snow. The wind keened; she could hardly hear the cry of her sister, deep in the forest beyond the clearing. As she began to trudge away from the tipi, the distant cry was drowned out by the ululation of her women relatives, and she could hear the griefstricken sobbing of her son. She was proud that he had reined in his emotion until she could depart with dignity. But now she feared for him and for his wives and children. She did not know if they would survive the winter even without a useless old woman to feed.

"Sister!" Her voice was barely audible above the mourning songs and the squall. But she knew that her sister would hear. For her sister had gone over to the dark side; and the creatures of the dark side hear much more keenly than men.

She thought she heard an answer: a growl. Somewhere ahead, beyond the snow embankment. Across the frozen creek.

I *will* dance the moon dance once more! she told herself. I *will*!

The snow came, stronger, colder. She shouldered the gust and staggered, unflinching, into the wind.

2
Victoria Station, London

"EXCUSE ME. MIGHT I RESPECTFULLY INQUIRE . . . ARE YOU . . . might you possibly be Mademoiselle Martinique?"

"Sir, this is the ladies' waiting room. I trust that you will recognize the impropriety of your presence amongst these unescorted ladies, and that you will retire a few paces beyond the entrance and state your request without the forwardness you have just exhibited?"

"I say. Awfully sorry, I'm sure."

Overhearing this conversation and her own name, Speranza Martinique looked up from her Bible. A corpulent woman, whose feathery hat ill suited her belligerent demeanor, was having an altercation with a bearded gentleman in morning dress. Perhaps this was the messenger that His Lordship's secretary had mentioned in his letter to her. She rose and tugged at the fat woman's sleeve. "Your pardon, madam, but I think the gentleman is looking for me."

The woman turned on her with a look of sheer disdain. She shuddered, and her unnatural plumage shuddered with her. "A railway station waiting room is hardly the place for a furtive encounter," she said. "I find the fact that you seek to disguise your unnatural intentions behind a *Bible* most revolting."

Mildly, Speranza said to the aggravating woman: "Look to the mote in your own eye, madam; it is the best way, I have found, of alleviating the harm that a prolonged meditation on the world's evils can afflict upon a lady's refined sensibilities."

"I never!" the fat woman said, as Speranza swept past her and accosted the bearded gentleman, who was waiting by the entrance. She could see that he was amused by their exchange; but seeing her approach, he suppressed his laughter and was all gravity.

"*Mademoiselle*," he began in atrocious French, pulling a sealed paper from his waistcoat pocket, "*j'ai l'honneur de vous présenter cette lettre écrite par—*"

"Heavens!" the fat woman remarked. "I should have known. A Frenchwoman. What an unprincipled lot, those frogs!"

"Only half French, actually," Speranza said, "and half Italian. Oh, sir, do let's continue this conversation elsewhere! Certain people are becoming most tiresome! Surely the crowds that are gathered here will render a chaperone unnecessary."

"I say, you speak English awfully well, what."

"I do," Speranza said, "and if it is not too forward of me, might I ask that we use English from now on? I think my command of that tongue might be a little . . ." She tried to say it tactfully, but could not; so she changed the subject slightly. "I was, after all, the governess of the son of Lord Slatterthwaite, the Hon. Michael Bridgewater, before he was unfortunately taken from us—"

"Consumption, I understand," said the messenger, shaking his head. "But I have neglected to introduce myself. My name is Cornelius Quaid. I represent . . . a certain party, whose name I may not at present divulge."

"Lord Slatterthwaite assured me that this party's credentials are impeccable. I will take him at his word, Mr. Quaid. And where is the boy?"

"Soft, soft, Mademoiselle Martinique. All in good time. First let me go over the plans with you. Here is the letter I spoke of; it will allow you and the lad safe passage to your destination. Attached to it is a banker's note which, you will find, will cover any emergency you may encounter; I trust you will not abuse it. The travelling papers, tickets, itineraries, and other paraphernalia are here as well. You depart in a little over an hour. Your things are at the left luggage office, I presume? I shall have my man see to them. Furthermore"—he reached into a capacious trouser pocket and pulled out a small purse—"I have been authorized to give you a small advance." Speranza was very grateful for this, for her dismissal from Lord Slatterthwaite's service, though no fault of hers, would have left her destitute, had it not been for this rather mysterious new development. "Count it at your leisure, mademoiselle. It contains one hundred guineas in gold. The rest, you may be sure, will be forthcoming upon the safe delivery of the boy to a certain Dr. Szymanowski, in Vienna."

"I will take your word on it, Mr. Quaid," Speranza said, tucking the purse into an inside pocket of her coat. Where was the child? His Lordship had told her that her new duties would involve escorting a young lad across Europe, for which, he said, she was eminently suited; for not only was she trained in the care of children, but she was acquainted with French, English, and Italian, and had a smattering of the many languages of the Austro-Hungarian Empire. There was no more information about the boy, however, and Speranza was anxious to learn all she could. She regretted having left the relative warmth of the ladies' waiting room. The station, imposing though it was, was not well heated; and she could see, clinging to the hair of beggars and urchins and to the hats and overcoats of those who could afford them, evidence of the snowstorm that was raging without. It was a veritable bedlam here: flower girls, newspaper vendors, old women hawking steak-and-kidney pies, and of course the passengers themselves. Rich and poor, they shuffled about, their expressions bearing that self-imposed bleakness which Speranza found all too common amongst the English.

"The boy?" she said at last.

"Ah yes, the boy." For the first time, a look of trepidation seemed to cross the face of Cornelius Quaid. Was the boy ill? Consumptive, perhaps, and capable of spreading the disease? But Speranza had remained at poor little Michael's bedside day and night for many weeks. Surely, if she were going to catch it, she would have done so already.

She said, "Sir, I take it that disease is at issue here, since you desire me to deliver him to this doctor. A specialist, I assume? I assure you I will take the greatest pains to—"

"Mademoiselle, the boy's affliction is not physical. It is of the soul."

"Ah, one of the newfangled dementiae?" Speranza was aware that certain research was being done into the dark recesses of the mind; but of course such subjects were not within the boundaries of decent discourse.

"No, I mean the soul, mademoiselle, not the mind."

She stiffened a little at this, for the fat lady had been unwittingly right in one thing: the Bible that Speranza Martinique carried upon her person was a purely cosmetic device. For Speranza suffered constantly from thoughts that, she felt, should correctly be suppressed; her severe dress and her Bible were intended to deflect the suspicions of strangers, who she was certain could see into her very soul did she not stand constant guard against discovery.

"The boy is possessed," Mr. Quaid said in profound earnest. "Sometimes, when the moon is full . . ."

"Tush, Mr. Quaid! This is the nineteenth century; we don't believe such superstitions anymore, do we?" she said, a little uncomfortably, shivering a little, thinking to herself: I have every right to shiver, do I not? It is the dead of winter, and these beastly English do enjoy the cold so. "Let us just say that the boy is . . . ill."

"Very well, then. I am no expert on the young. But I will tell you this. The boy's parents are dead. They were killed under most unpleasant circumstances. I wasn't made privy to the details, but there was . . ."—he lowered his voice, and Speranza had to strain to hear him—"devil worship. Heathen rites. Mutilation, I believe. Terrible, terrible!"

"If so, then the boy's distress is perfectly understandable. Possession, indeed! Grief, confusion, perhaps a misunderstanding of the nature of good and evil . . . nothing that proper, attentive care won't heal," Speranza said. She did not add—though she almost blurted it out—that she found the English notion of loving care most astonishing, consisting as it did of little more than an assiduous application of the birch to the behind. Ah, where do they get their love of flagellation from? she mused.

"Well," Mr. Quaid said, interrupting her reverie, "it is time you met your charge."

He gestured. So imperious was his gesture that the crowd seemed to part. Two men came forward; they appeared to be footmen from some well-established household. The boy was between them. The shame of it, Speranza thought, having him escorted like a prisoner! After all he has suffered!

"Come, Johnny," said Mr. Quaid. "This is Mademoiselle Martinique, who will assume the responsibility for your welfare until you are safely in the hands of Dr. Szymanowski."

Speranza looked at the boy who walked toward her with his eyes downcast. She had expected a rich, pampered-looking child; but Johnny wore clothes that, had they not recently been cleaned, might have come from a poorhouse; his coat, she noticed with her practiced eye, had been clumsily mended. He was blond and blue-eyed; his hair was clipped short; only prisoners and denizens of lunatic asylums had their hair that short, because they had sold it to wigmakers. She wondered where Johnny had been living before his nameless benefactor found him. And no more than seven years old! Or perhaps he was small for his age, improperly fed. He came closer but continued to stare steadfastly at the ground. He had clearly been mistreated. Those English! she thought bitterly, remembering that even in the final stages of his consumption the Hon. Michael Bridgewater had occasionally been subjected to the rod.

And to the fresh air, she remembered. That fresh air that they love so much here, freezing though it might be. She was sure that the fresh air had driven little Michael to his death. She was determined that no such thing would happen to this Johnny. Already she felt a fierce protectiveness toward him.

"Johnny Kindred," Cornelius Quaid said, "you are to obey your new guardian in all ways. Understood?"

"Yes, sir," the boy mumbled.

"You may shake Mademoiselle Martinique's hand. Bow smartly. There. Now say, 'How do you do, Mademoiselle Martinique?'"

Speranza grew impatient. "Mr. Quaid, I trust you will allow me to exercise my particular speciality now." She turned to the child and took his hand. It was shaking with terror. She gripped it affirmatively, reassuringly. "You may call me Speranza," she said to him. "And you needn't shake my hand. You may kiss me on the cheek, if you like."

Mr. Quaid rolled his eyes disapprovingly.

"Speranza," the boy said, looking at her for the first time.

She did not wait for Mr. Quaid to harangue her. Without further ado, still grasping the boy's hand, she steered him towards the platform. Soon they would reach the sea. Soon they would cross the English Channel and reach a land where men did not hesitate to show their feelings.

Already she had begun to love the child they had entrusted to her care. Already she was determined to heal his anguish. Affliction of the soul indeed, the poor boy! Speranza believed that love could cure most every illness. And though she was a woman possessed of many accomplishments, it was love that was her greatest talent.

3
Dakota Territory
three-quarters moon, waxing

"LIEUTENANT HARPER! ZEKE SULLIVAN! REPORT TO CAPTAIN SANDerson right away. There's some kind of trouble."

Scott Harper stared with dismay at the open door of the commissary, through which he could see the sergeant major tramping back out into the snow. "Shit! I ain't but drunk two sips of this whiskey," he said to Zeke, the scout he had befriended in the first few days of his brief sojourn at Fort Cassandra.

Zeke grunted. "You'd best straighten our yer uniform, Lieutenant," he said. "Sanderson's a prick about regulations."

They left and crossed the courtyard. It was noon, but the sky was gray. It had been snowing ever since he arrived two weeks before. Beyond the wall, tendrils of smoke rose from the tipis of the Crow scouts. The ring of a blacksmith's hammer pelted the air. Somewhere in the compound a bugler was practicing. Now and then he'd flub a note.

Scott had never expected it to be this drab here in Dakota

Territory. He hadn't seen one Indian in these two weeks except for
the Crow scouts, and they were hardly the glamorous, colorful
Sioux and Cheyenne that he'd heard so much about. Mostly you
were just sitting around shivering your butt off, or doing one of
Sanderson's pointless exercises. Zeke was the only friend he'd
made. They didn't have much in common. But Zeke, who
normally never spoke a word, took kindly to the lieutenant, who
was young enough to be his son, and always told him wild stories
about how he used to live among the Indians.

They knocked on the door marked *Capt. James Sanderson*.
When they were summoned inside, Scott saw the captain sitting at
a desk; on the chair facing him was a woman whose pinched,
worried face peered at them from within a tightly laced bonnet.

"This is Mrs. Bryant," the captain said, scratching his mustache. "Her husband's missing. I want you two to investigate."

"Yessir," Scott and Zeke said at the same time.

"Explain to the two gentlemen," Sanderson said impatiently.
He already seemed to have lost interest in the matter; he was now
perusing a thick, leather-bound book. "Exactly where did you last
see your husband?"

"He's a miner, Captain. He's been diggin' up in the hills for
nearly two year. A fortnight ago, he sets off east by himself,
headin' out Flint Rock Creek way. Said he had a map. He
wouldn't take no one with him. Said he'd be back in a couple of
days. I said, there ain't no gold veins that way, but he said, it
weren't a deposit, but a hoard that the old man Cavanaugh hid
afore he died. I tried to stop Eddie, but he were possessed. He had
that crazy look, that gold-fever demon glint in his eyes. I got
scared, I guess. That's why I come down to the fort to ask for
help. I got a copy of the map. Lord, he told me never to tell no
one, but if he didn't come home in three days, to set off after
him." She took out a piece of paper. It was a handbill, printed on
one side with an advertisement for guns, new and used. The other
side had a rough drawing of the area east of Fort Cassandra. She
spread it out on Captain Sanderson's desk and they crowded
around it.

Zeke saw the map and sucked in his breath. "Captain, that's
inside Sioux territory. Them miners ain't supposed to cross over
this here line." He scratched it on the paper with a chewed-up

fingernail. "He got what was comin' to him, I reckon. Beggin' your pardon, ma'am."

"That is a most heartless remark, Sullivan. Our job, as you know, is to protect the settlers and the miners." Sanderson peered hard at Zeke and Scott.

"Sir," Scott said diffidently, "ain't we supposed to protect the treaty, too? Between us and the Injuns, I mean. We can't cross the line without—"

"When I want your opinion I'll ask for it, mister!" said Sanderson. He glared at Scott, then asked abruptly, "Why do you only have eight buttons on your coat?"

Scott was taken by surprise. He stepped back a couple of paces. "Don't rightly know, sir. Must've been loose or something."

"Lieutenant, the regulations clearly state: 'There will be one row of nine buttons on the breast, placed at equal distances.' You are short by a button, Harper, and those that remain are decidedly not equidistant! Don't let me catch you like this again. Don't get uppity. Remember, you're only a *brevet* lieutenant."

"Sir." Obviously the captain had it in for him. He'd have to watch his mouth, if he could. It was going to be hard. People said what was on their minds, back in Missouri.

"Now, I want you two to take the map and try to locate Mrs. Bryant's husband. Be cautious, now. You will, of course, be inside the hostiles' territory. Try not to make a mess of things, will you?"

A solid day slogging through the snow now. The ford across Sulphur Creek was frozen solid. The horses slid uneasily on the ice. They had four horses, two to ride, one laden with gear, and the last to carry the body.

Alongside the creek there were oaks, denuded and piled with snow; in the distance, uphill, there were clumps of pines, patches of desultory green. The wind blew briskly, but the snowfall had thinned; here and there you could even see a break in the cloudbanks, a strand of startling deep blue. They dismounted and walked the horses for a while, chewing hunks of jerky as they trudged through snow that sometimes came up to their thighs. Zeke was silent almost all the time. Scott wondered how a body could stay quiet that long. He asked the scout about it, but he already knew what Zeke was going to say:

"Learned it from the Injuns."

"You reckon Bryant was killed by—"

"Could be. Keep alert."

Night: they camped and rode on at dawn.

Forest: they led their horses through twisting trails often blocked by fallen conifers. After several hours of this, Scott couldn't bear it anymore; he had to talk. "Why would a body risk his scalp on account of a map? There's plenty of gold that's near civilization."

"And plenty of other miners," Zeke said. "Quiet. Listen."

"Something growling? A wolf?"

"It's daylight. Wolves is nocturnal. No. Someone is follerin' us."

"Shit!" Scott whispered. "And fixin' to jump us."

"Maybe not. Just act like you ain't scared of nothing. And don't shoot until I say so."

Scott fingered the ivory stock Colt that his father had given him. He could feel the initials carved on the handle, and he remembered how his daddy had used the gun during the last war.

About a hundred yards farther was a clearing ringed with firs. Zeke strode out into the middle, took his rifle from his horse's saddle, and fired straight up into the air. Then he started shouting: "*Toki ya la hé? Echâ! Chiktepi kte lo!*"

"What in tarnation—you want us killed?"

Zeke turned and whispered urgently: "They know where we are. We might as well let 'em know we ain't a passel of cowardly squaws. That way they might let us be. Or least give us a fair fight. Sanderson may think Injuns is just savages, but they got a thousand times more honor than he does. Now stand yer ground, boy, and look fierce. Appearances counts considerable with Injuns."

Scott took a deep breath, cocked his revolver, and waited. The wind stirred up the snow and made it swirl before his eyes. It was hard to see straight. By and by Zeke began firing again and hollering out more native insults. Any minute now they were going to be surrounded by caterwauling braves. Scott stood, tense, uncomfortable in the searing cold. I should've traded in this .31-caliber antique, he thought uneasily.

Something moved.

Instinctively Scott fired. A high-pitched howl sounded above the roar of the wind . . . an utterly inhuman sound. Against the white, something shifted, something silvery gray . . . it lunged for him out of the firs. He fired again . . . it *was* a wolf, it had been a wolf all the time . . . the biggest wolf you could imagine . . . Zeke had been wrong! The scout, unnerved, stared open-mouthed for the merest second, then fired his own rifle at the animal.

The wolf didn't stop.

"Shi-it! That critter's stuffed with lead and it ain't even slowed down!" Zeke said, bewildered.

Scott fired four more shots. They ripped into the wolf's flesh. Blood sprayed into their faces. But the wolf didn't stop—

Another howl . . . somewhere in the darkness of the forest.

Slowly the wolf came to a halt, only a few feet away from where they stood. The snow was spattered with crimson. Scott thought: It's dying now. It couldn't survive all that lead. The wolf snarled. Scott saw teeth, knife-sharp, glistening from the wolf's drool. It looked up at them. And Scott saw something in the wolf's eyes, something almost hypnotic. He had been reloading his pistol, but somehow he couldn't shoot.

That distant howl again. The wolf pricked its ears.

Then it turned away. It was in pain, that was obvious. But the wounds . . . they were closing up . . . healing before their very eyes . . . and then they heard a voice. An old Indian woman was standing at the edge of the clearing. She looked at the two white men. There was pride in her face, and rage, too, and a terrible resignation. Softly she said, "*Mayakte shni ye. Winmáyan ye.*"

"What's she saying?" Scott said. The woman's eyes were like the wolf's. That was the strangest part of it. They were almost like . . . like twins. Even though one was a human and one was an animal.

"She says not to kill her, she's only a woman."

She stood in the gathering snow.

"I think she wants us to follow," Zeke said.

"Maybe it's an ambush."

"No."

He started off in the direction of the woman. The wolf was seated at her feet now, and she was stroking its fur and speaking softly to it, a singsong phrase, over and over. As she saw them approach, she gestured to them once, beckoning them forward. Then the snow gusted up and she and the animal vanished. They left the clearing. She was nowhere to be seen. They saw tracks leading deeper into the forest.

Then they came upon Bryant leaning against a tree.

He didn't smell bad yet. It was too cold for that, and he was stiff as a board. His clothes were torn to shreds. So was his body. His chest and stomach had been ripped open. His entrails hung to the ground in ribbons. They were frozen solid. Brown icicles of blood hung from his arms. His sleeves and pockets were crammed with gold nuggets.

"Come on," Zeke said. He was emptying the dead miner's pockets. "This oughta keep us in whiskey for a few days."

"Mrs. Bryant'll be powerful sore iffen she suspects her gold's been stole," Scott said.

"How's she to know any different?"

Scott decided to pretend not to notice the scout sneaking one into his trouser pocket. "Now, will you help me haul this here stiff on top of the hoss?" Zeke said.

"I can't understand it," Scott said to himself. "Why didn't that blamed wolf *die*?"

On their return, they paused only long enough for Scott to sew on his ninth button before making their report to the captain.

"Murdered by those rapacious savages," Sanderson said. "Just as I feared, I'm afraid! Well, we're going to have to retaliate." He was sitting in his office just as before, still wrapped up in his leather-bound book.

"Beggin' your pardon, sir," Scott began, "he was mauled to death by a wolf."

"How can you tell me that, with all this evidence of mutilation and atrocity?"

"Sir—" It was useless. Sanderson had made his mind up even before they had started out. They might as well not have found the body.

"Did you not find one of the savages standing right beside the body?" Sanderson said.

"Captain," Zeke said, "it were nothin' but an old squaw."

"Retaliation is absolutely essential in such cases. I have selected a suitable target . . ." The captain opened a map of the

Dakota Territory and pointed to a region just within the boundary of the Indian lands. "Intelligence reports that the men of this little encampment have left the reservation in search of game. It seems a perfect opportunity to inflict punishment," he said grimly. "They have to understand that they can't go around murdering white men. Those bloodthirsty Sioux are going to have to learn that—"

"May I speak, Captain?" Zeke said.

"Go ahead, scout."

"Sir, them Sioux ain't done nothin' you and me wouldn't do. Not this time. You can't expect them to live on maggot-ridden government-issue beef and stale crackers."

The captain tapped his fingers impatiently, while it slowly dawned on Scott that they were about to go and attack an Indian village for no obvious reason at all. He'd come seeking adventure and glory, but he couldn't see what glory was to be had in butchering infants. He remembered the old woman in the forest and the soft song she'd used to calm the wolf down . . . that blamed unkillable wolf. Nothing seemed right.

"Something on your mind, Lieutenant?"

"Sir, I—"

"Doubtless you feel a little anxiety over the coming fray, my boy. It's only natural. But when you start hearing those whoops and screams you'll lose all your fear. By the way, I do not prohibit rape, as long as it is discreetly carried out and the victims are immediately disposed of. Understood? I don't want any breeds cluttering up the landscape."

Scott must have paled, because the captain softened his customary severity. "If you have any problems, Harper, you must feel free to come to me."

Zeke said, "Sir, who's fixin' to tell the Bryant woman she's just been made a widder?"

"I'll take care of that, Sullivan," said the captain. "Don't you worry. I shall use tact; I shall refrain from lurid descriptions of the Indians' atrocities. The gold you've found will be a poor consolation, unfortunately, but should render her more attractive to prospective second husbands. . . ."

They ambled down to the supply store. A small crowd of enlisted men had gathered around them, hoping to hear all about their adventure. Scott realized that there was no way the widow wasn't going to hear all the goriest details of how her husband was set upon and murdered by Indians. The mood in the fort was dark. They were out for blood. They'd never believe the truth now.

"What we goin' to do, Zeke?"

"Get drunk," Zeke said. "That's the best advice I can give you, boy. When they tells you to go in and burn down a village and kill women and children, you'd best not do it sober."

4
Bavaria
two days before full moon

ON THE TRAIN FROM LONDON, ON THE FERRY ACROSS THE CHANNEL, the boy said nothing at all. In France he merely asked for food and drink at the appropriate times. Their benefactor had bought them second-class tickets; Speranza was glad of that, for she had had occasion to travel by third class, and she knew that it would be crowded and cold and crammed to bursting with unpleasant characters.

When they crossed the German border, the two old priests who had been sharing their compartment left. The boy's mood lightened a little. There was not much to watch but fields and fields of snow, and now and then a country station with an ornate, wrought-iron sign and a bench. Speranza decided that the best tactic would be to wait. The boy was afraid of everything; she already knew that, for whenever she tried to touch him, he flinched violently from her as though she were on fire.

A few kilometers into Germany, the boy asked her, "Have you any games, mademoiselle?"

At last, she thought, he is giving me an opening. Another part of her reflected: Yet I must not become too attached to him; he is mine for only a few more days. And in the back of her mind she

saw Michael Bridgewater's pathetically small coffin being lowered into the ground. That too had been in the snow.

"Speranza," she said to him, reminding him that they were to
be companions, not opponents. She opened a valise which
Quaid's people had provided, labeled *Entertainments;* it contained, she saw, a pack of cards, a backgammon set, and a snakes
and ladders board. "Shall we play this?" she said, pulling it out
and setting it down on the middle seat, between them. Steadily the
fields of snow unreeled. The game was not printed on cardboard,
but handpainted on a silken surface. The snakes were very
realistically depicted. There was a velvet pouch with a pair of
ivory dice and tortoiseshell die cup.

The boy nodded.

"Good, Johnny," she said. She wished she could pat his cheek,
but knew that he would flinch again. Instead she handed him the
dice.

He threw a 3 and eagerly moved his counter three squares.
There was a ladder, and he clambered up to the third row.
Speranza threw a 5, and was stuck on the bottom. They played for
a few minutes, until Speranza encountered her first snake and slid
back down almost to square one. Johnny laughed.

Then he said, "Those snakes, they're just like a man's prick,
aren't they, Speranza?"

Speranza did not quite believe she had heard him say that. She
was flustered for a moment, then said, "Why, where did you learn
a word like that, Johnny?"

"Jonas taught me."

"And who might Jonas be?" Speranza asked, intrigued. Clearly
the boy's upbringing had had almost nothing to commend it.

The boy said nothing; he had a guilty look, and Speranza felt
that to probe further would perhaps be inopportune. They went on
playing. Johnny's counter hit a snake and slid. He cackled. "Right
through to the snake's bleeding arsehole!" he said. His voice
seemed different; harsher, more grown-up.

"Johnny, I am a rather unorthodox woman, but even I find your
language a trifle indecent," she said mildly.

"Fuck you!" Johnny said. He looked her straight in the eye.
There was anger in those eyes, blazing, unconscionable anger.
"Fuck, fuck, fuck, fuck, fuck!"

"Johnny!"

He started to cry. "I'm sorry," he sobbed, "I'm sorry, sorry, sorry. Jonas told me to do it, it wasn't me, honestly it wasn't." He crumpled into her arms, dashing the snakes and ladders board to the floor. Seeing how much he needed affection made Speranza hug him tightly to her. But as he buried his face in her breast she heard him growl, she *felt* his growl reverberate against the squeezing of her corsets. It was like the purring of a cat, but far more vehement, far more menacing. She thought: I cannot be afraid of him; he is only a child, a poor hurt child, and she clasped him to her bosom, struggling not to disclose her anxiety.

They crossed the Rhine. At Karlsruhe, they waited for several hours; part of the train was detached and sent north, and they were to be joined by another segment that had come up from Basle. Thinking to give the boy some exercise, Speranza took him for a walk, up and down the platform. Although the station was canopied, there was some snow and slush on the cars and on the tracks. Many of the passengers milling around outside had snow in their hair and on their coats. The car that joined theirs bore on its sides the crest of some aristocratic family.

"Let's go and see!" Johnny said. There was nothing in him now of the obscene, deep-voiced child that had emerged earlier. He was all innocence. She was convinced now that his problem was some kind of division within his soul, some combat between the forces of light and darkness. Taking his hand, she took him up to the carriage.

Heavy drapes prevented one from seeing inside. The car seemed dilapidated, and the coat-of-arms had not been painted lately; beneath it was the legend "von Bächl-Wölfing" in the Fraktur script which Speranza found difficult to read. The arms themselves were fairly ordinary-looking. Two silver wolf's heads glared at each other across a crimson field. *Argent*, she reminded herself, and *gules*. Little Michael had always been very particular about heraldry; but then he had been the son of a peer of the realm. As she mused on her former life as the young aristocrat's governess, she saw that Johnny had stepped up very close to the track, that he was shaking his fist at the coat-of-arms . . . that the same menacing growl was issuing from his throat.

Then, to her alarm, Johnny pulled down his trousers and urinated onto the side of the train.

"Johnny, you must stop!"

"I am Jonas!" He turned; their eyes met once; she saw that his eyes were slitty golden . . . like the eyes of a wild animal! Terrified, she started to follow him, but he growled and sprinted to the front of the train, across the track, clambered up to the other side of the platform. She called, then started to run after him.

I'll have to take a shortcut, she thought. She dived into the train. An old peasant woman with two hens in a basket looked up at her. She tried to open the door on the other side, but it would not come open.

She pressed her face against the window, called his name. He was urinating again, on the track, on the steps into the train, and shouting, "This is my place I'll not run in your pack I'm me I'm me leave me alone alone alone!"

"Help me," Speranza whispered. "If you please, though I can't speak your language . . . *au secours, j'ai perdu mon enfant.* . . ."

Some of the others in the carriage were looking out too. A burly man said to her, *"Is' es ihr Kind dort aufm Gleis?"*

She nodded, not understanding. The man began shouting, and an official in uniform came and opened the door. Speranza and some of the others leapt down onto the side of the track.

"I'll not run in it I'll not I'll not!" Johnny screamed, spraying them with piss.

"Was sagt er denn?" The strange man caught the boy and held him tight as he wriggled. Johnny grew still.

"Thank you." Speranza reached out to take him from the man. He was curled up in fetal position, sucking his thumb. His clothes and his face and arms were stained and foul-smelling; it was an unfamiliar odor, as though his urine were somehow not quite human.

In the compartment, she filled a jug with water, moistened a towel, and began to swab his face. He did not stir. A whistle sounded, and the train began to ease itself away from the station. The odor was pungent, choking. But Speranza had cleaned and washed little Michael every day in the last weeks of his consumption, and her stomach was not easily turned. The boy seemed to be fast asleep. She did not want to embarrass him. She took off his coat and laid him on it. Very gently she began to undo his back

and front collar studs and to pull his shirt over his head, and to
unbutton his braces so that she could unfasten his trousers. The
shirt tore as it came away. The backs of the child's hands were
covered with fine, shiny hair. His back was unusually hairy too;
when she started to wipe it, it gleamed like sealskin. There were
welts and scars all over him; she knew from this that he had been
beaten, probably habitually, since many of the marks were white
and smooth. She wrung out the cloth, soaked it in water again, and
cleansed him as best she could. Though she tried to look away, she
could not help seeing his tiny penis, quite erect above a tuft of
silver-white hair. She did not think little Michael had had hair
down there. This boy definitely had some minor physical abnor-
malities as well as his obvious emotional ones.

The sun began to set behind distant white hills. She managed to
get him into a nightgown that had been starched stiff; clearly it had
never been used before, like all the other clothes in the trunk that
Quaid's men had loaded onto the train. The sharpness of the fabric
must have disturbed him. He opened his eyes and said, "Tell me
a story, please, Speranza. Then I'll be fast asleep and Jonas won't
come. He never comes when I'm asleep."

She was going to ask him about Jonas, but she was afraid her
questioning might bring more strange behavior; so she merely
said, easing back into the padded seat and allowing him to lie with
his head against the lace and black satin of her skirts, "What story
would you like? A story about a prince in a castle? A beautiful
princess? A dragon, perhaps? Or would that be too frightening?"

"I want Little Red Riding Hood," he said in a small voice. "But
make Little Red Riding Hood a boy."

She tried not to show how startled she was at his request. She
felt a strange indecency about what he had asked, though she
could not put into words why it would feel that way. She did not
look at him while she spoke; she watched the fields go by, the
snow slowly blooded by the setting sun. "Once upon a time there
was a girl—"

"A boy."

"—named Little Red Riding Hood who lived by the edge of the
forest." When she reached the part about the wolf dressed in the
grandmother's clothing, the boy clung to her in terror, but that
terror was also something a little bit like lust. She had always
known that children are not pure and innocent, as the English liked

to believe. But the idea that the boy was enjoying her discomfiture, actually, in some inchoate way, taking advantage of her person! And yet she knew already he loved her. So she went on: "And the wolf said, 'The better to eat you with, my darling boy.' And ate the little boy up. In one gulp. And then the hunters—"

"That's enough. They just put the hunters in so little children won't be frightened. But you and I know the truth, don't we?"

"The truth?"

"The hunters don't care. And even if the boy was still alive inside the wolf, then the hunters' rifles would just rip them both apart anyway, wouldn't they, Speranza?"

"It's only a story," she said. The sexual tension had abated; perhaps, Speranza thought, it was just in herself, she had imagined it; how could a seven-year-old boy, even a profoundly disturbed one, manipulate me in this fashion?

"It's not a story, Speranza. Believe me. And if you can't quite make yourself believe me, maybe you'll talk to Jonas one day." And he drifted into sleep, lulled by the clanging, and she covered him and sat thinking for a long time. They had missed the early session in the dining car.

There was a knock at the door.

"*Darf ich herein, bitte?*" A slimy voice; the sort of man used to toadying; not the kind of voice she expected for a railway official. Her heart beat faster.

"*Je m'excuse,*" she said in French, "*je ne comprends pas l'allemand.*" Then she added in English, "Please, sir, I have no German."

She unlatched the door of the compartment.

It was a man in evening dress, very stiff and proper, bearing a silver tray. "May it please you, Fräulein Martinique," he said, "my master would very much enjoy the pleasure of your company at dinner, now that the boy is asleep."

"How does he know—"

"He felt it, *gnädiges Fräulein*. In his heart."

"Sir, I do not think it is quite proper for a man to invite a woman to whom he has not been properly introduced—"

The steward, or butler, or whoever it was, handed her the little platter. There was a calling card on it, printed on rag paper, with a gold border. It contained only the name *Graf Hartmut von Bächl-Wölfing*.

Speranza knew that the word *graf* meant "count" or "earl" or some such title. What did this man know about her and the boy? How could he have felt the boy's waking and sleeping? And why did Johnny try to urinate all over the Count's railway carriage? She was afraid of what this might be leading to. She felt a premonition of something . . . unnatural. Perhaps even supernatural. But Speranza was not superstitious, and curiosity vanquished her fear.

The Count's servant was waiting for her reply.

"I will be glad to come," she said, "if you will send someone to watch the child while I dine; and perhaps the Count's cook could prepare some small tidbit for me to bring back to him. Poor Johnny is worn out, but he hasn't had his supper, and I think he may wake up hungry in the middle of the night."

The servant paused, perhaps translating her comments to himself; the train clattered as it negotiated a curve. "Yes, *gnädiges Fräulein,*" he said at last.

"Now, be so good as to leave me so that I can dress. If I am to meet a count, I ought perhaps to try not to look so shabby," she said, feeling suddenly frail.

When the man departed, Speranza looked through her trunk and found little to wear; she changed into a somewhat cleaner black dress, tried to tidy her hair, and threw over the drab costume a rabbit fur pelisse. She did have a few articles of jewelry; she selected a silver necklace studded with cabochon amethysts. A little ostentatious, perhaps? But it was all she had. She looked at her reflection against the glass and the snow. Perhaps, she thought, I could be more attractive. In the window I seem to be a governess, only a governess . . . but I have dark dreams for a governess, dark and daring thoughts.

Presently a serving maid, perhaps fourteen, in a uniform came, curtseyed, said, *"Für den Knaben."* Speranza assumed she had come to watch the boy, and left; the manservant was waiting to conduct her down the corridor and to let her into the domain of the Count von Bächl-Wölfing.

The first thing she felt was gloom. The curtains were tightly drawn, and the only light was from a gold candelabrum in the middle of a table of dark Italian marble. The candles were black. The servant showed her to a fauteuil, overplump, dusty, dark velvet; a second servant poured wine into a crystal goblet. Were it not for the ceaseless motion of the train, she would have thought herself in a sumptuous, if somewhat ill-kept, apartment in Mayfair.

The servant said, seeming to address the empty room, *"Euer Gnade, das französische Fräulein, das Ihr eingeladen habt."* He bowed.

"Welcome," said a voice: liquid, deep, suggestive, even, of some hidden eroticism. At first she saw only eyes; the eyes glittered. Strangely, they reminded her of Johnny's eyes, while he had undergone that eerie metamorphosis into his other, demented self: clear, yellow, like polished topazes. Now she saw the face they were set in: a lean face, a man clearly middle-aged yet somehow also youthful. His hair, balding, was dark save for a silver streak above his left temple. His upper lip sported the barest hint of a mustache.

He said, *"Ou est-que vous préférez que je vous parle en français, peut-être?"* His pronunciation was impeccable.

"It doesn't matter," Speranza said, "what we speak. But perhaps you can explain to me . . . oh, so many things . . . who are you, why do you seem to know so much about the child and me?"

"I am but a pilgrim," von Bächl-Wölfing said. "I journey to the same shrine as you, my dear Mademoiselle Martinique—or perhaps you will permit me the liberty of addressing you as Speranza. Your name means *hope*, and without hope our cause is doomed, alas."

"Your cause?"

The Count moved closer to her, and seated himself in a leather armchair. "Ah yes. We are all going to see Dr. Szymanowski, are we not?"

"I am to deliver the boy to him."

He sighed; she felt an almost unbearable sadness in him, though she could not tell why. It was as if his emotions were borne on the dust in the air of the carriage, as though she could smell his melancholy. "And after?" he said.

"I do not know, sir. Perhaps I shall return to my family in Aix-en-Provence." A maid was serving a fish course; the Count nibbled distractedly, but Speranza was more hungry than she had thought. "Something your servant said . . . that you *felt* that

Johnny had gone to sleep . . . in your heart. What did that mean?"

"We have a secret language."

"But you did not even see him."

The Count wrinkled his nose. "I most certainly smelt him, mademoiselle! Still that odor lingers in the air . . . ah, but you cannot smell it . . . some of us are more . . . deprived . . . than others."

"If you are referring to Johnny's unfortunate accident . . ."

"It was no accident!" the Count said, laughing. "But he has much to learn. A youngling cannot usurp the territory of a leader merely by baptizing his environment with piss! The boy knows only instinct at the moment; soon he will combine that instinct with intelligence. To be able to help mold his mind, so malleable, yet so filled with all that separates our kind from—"

"I have no idea, Count, what you are talking about."

"I apologize. I begin to ramble when the moon waxes. It makes up for the times when I am robbed of the power of human discourse."

Why, Speranza thought, he is as mad as the boy is! Who was this Dr. Szymanowski? Surely the purveyor of a lunatic asylum. And they were going to use Johnny. Experiments, perhaps. Speranza had read *Frankenstein*. She knew what scientists could be like. She wondered whether the young serving girl who was alone with the boy was really—

"She knows nothing," said Count von Bächl-Wölfing.

"You read minds, Count?"

"No. But I *am* observant," he said softly. "I know, for example, that—though you appear to me in the guise of a prim, severe governess—that is merely a shield behind which hides a woman of passion, a woman who can take agonizing risks; a dangerous woman, a woman fascinated by what other women shy away from; a woman capable of profound, consuming love."

Speranza's heart began to pound. "Count, I am perhaps a more modern woman than many of my occupation; but I hardly think the first few moments of a meeting, even when the difference in rank between us is so great, is a suitable time for—"

"You are quite wrong, Speranza. I do desire you, but . . . some things one can perforce live without. The boy is important, though. He is a new thing, you see, a wholly new kind of creature.

But I see you do not understand me." He sighed; again she seemed to sense that perfume of dolorousness in the air. "It is all so unfair of me . . . but believe me, I would not say these things about you without having first ordered a thorough investigation into your character."

"My character is unassailable!" Speranza said, feeling terribly vulnerable, for the Count had ripped away the mask, so painstakingly assumed, and exposed it for the flimsy self-delusion that it was. "How dare you pry into my life, how dare you have me brought here! I think that under the circumstances I should depart immediately."

"Of course. But before that there is something I ought perhaps to tell you."

"We have nothing to say to each other—"

"Except, Mademoiselle Martinique, that I happen to be your employer."

"You! Who communicated with Lord Slatterthwaite—who sent Cornelius Quaid to Victoria Station—" She was trembling now, she felt as lost and bewildered as poor mad Johnny Kindred, who did not know if he was one person or two.

The Count merely smiled, and offered her another glass of wine.

5
Dakota Territory

OUT OF THE FOREST, SOUTH, TOWARD THE PLACE OF THE MOON dance; the buttes glistening with frost; the old woman and the wolf her sister. *"Chuwitamateyela kte,"* the woman would cry out, "I will be frozen to death."

The wolf replied in the language of night, though night had not yet come; but they understood each other, for they had both crossed the boundary between the two-legged and the four-legged many times in their long lives. The woman tried not to think of the people she had left behind: her son Ishnazuyai, who for many summers had been *blotahunka,* a war chief, among the Shung-manitu; she was proud he had shown no emotion when she left him. And her son's wives, especially Tiptowin, the youngest, mother of her grandchild Mahtohokshila. These names should be nothing to me now, she thought, as I and *mitankala* no longer have names that men can utter.

Sometimes they half ran, half slid, down the slick white slopes. The wolf-sister was no longer fleet, and the woman was getting blind. Though there was nothing to see but snow, so that it made no difference, she could tell direction from the smell of the wind.

Once she asked her sister, "Why do you not devour me now? I cannot really reach the place of the moon dance. I will never be buried in the sky with the rest of the wolf-people. I only thought to give you sustenance, so I could be inside you when you reach the sacred place."

The answer came, blended with the whine of the wind: "The flesh of the *washichun* will sustain us for a while, my sister."

"But why have the white men crossed over into the land of Lakota?"

"Sister, I cannot tell."

There came the wail of flutes, carried by the wind. But these were not the *siyótanka,* the bone flutes that bore messages of love; they had a grating metal timbre; they were harsh like the speech of the *washichun.* Where was the sound coming from?

"Look," said the old woman. The wolf tensed, sensing her sister's feelings; the woman wished she could smell more keenly. But she would never regain her power to transform; old age had hardened her into a woman's shape, her face wrinkled and pitted as the Badlands. But her dim eyes saw, in the chasm between two twisted mounds of rock, plumes of fire and tendrils of smoke. The she-wolf reared up and howled; the woman knew that she could smell death in the air. It must be a war, she thought. But what of the *rat-tat-tat,* rebounding from butte to butte? She had heard rifles before, but these rattled in inhuman unison. Disturbed, her sister sniffed and pawed the air . . . the odor of death must almost be choking her . . . even the woman sensed it now, like burning rancid buffalo fat.

She felt an odd detachment from it all. Deep within her heart she knew she would never reach the burial grounds. The great cycle of the moon would end and begin without her.

"Shall we go down to the village?" she asked her sister the she-wolf. But they were already descending the hill. I am close to death, she thought, and so it is that I am drawn toward the dying.

Scott and Zeke spurred on their horses and burst through the circle of burning tipis. Coughing and screeching, women were running into the center of the encampment. A woman on fire was rolling in the snow. Through the smoke haze Scott saw three or four soldiers raping a woman while another was jabbing a bayonet into her face. The body lay limp; perhaps it was already dead. Above the screams, fife and drum were playing a jaunty air.

Scott dismounted. A woman ran up to him. She was naked. Her face was streaked with tears. She flailed aimlessly at him with a tomahawk. He stared at her, uncertain. A shot rang out. The woman crumpled onto the snow. "Are you suffering from qualms, Harper?" said a voice behind them. It was Captain Sanderson. "But here is your chance to do battle for your country!"

"Rapin' women and slaughterin' children just ain't my idea of glory, sir," Scott said defiantly.

The captain stalked toward them, pausing only to kick a whimpering baby in the face. "No mercy, Lieutenant," he said. "Give an inch and they'll take a mile." The baby, still strapped to its cradleboard, rebounded across stones piled over the snow. It did not cry out. Perhaps it was already dead. "You think me cruel?" the captain roared. "Remember the Minnesota massacre, Harper! You were only a boy then, but remember!"

Zeke whispered, and Scott heard bitterness in his voice, "You can't fight it, boy. It's a damn shame, but there ain't nothin' you can do."

"I can't believe you could be acting this callous, Zeke Sullivan. You lived with them Injuns."

"I ain't callous. Just old and tired. I seen the future, lad, and it ain't got no Injuns in it. Just miles and miles of railway track. And miners and farmers and churches and cathouses."

The captain reached them. "Are you two contemplating mutiny?" he said.

"Sir, I protest—"

"Come with me, Lieutenant! We'll make a man of you yet."

The captain began striding off. The two younger men followed him. Smoke swirled. It seemed to Scott that he was walking into a nightmare. None of this could be real. He was vaguely conscious of the captain's unrelenting gait. Zeke had become separated from them. The acrid smoke made Scott's tears spurt. Everything swam. There was no perspective. The tipis were like burning pyramids. Horses were whinnying as the soldiers slaughtered them. The wildness in the captain's eyes . . . the same gold-haunted wildness in the eyes of miners . . . Scott followed the captain. There was no one to fight. Of course not. Only old men and women and young children.

They were upwind of the smoke. Behind them it coiled up snakelike over the melting snow, over mounds of human bodies. The captain was waving his pistol. He seemed possessed. Scott could barely keep up with him. There were trees ahead. Among them were Sioux funeral scaffolds. He could see the dead resting in their finery. The skulls of men and buffalo peered out from their snowy covering. "There'll be a few hiding amongst these remains," the captain was muttering, "thinking we wouldn't be fool enough to violate their sacred burial grounds . . . what simpletons these savages are! To think their heathen beliefs can shield them from our righteous wrath. . . ."

He darted into the shadows. Scott watched, appalled and fascinated, as he pulled a woman out by the hair. He threw her face down into the snow, knelt down and pinned her fast, held his pistol to the back of her head. "Look!" Sanderson screamed.

He kicked the woman and the snow. The cries of dying people were muffled by smoke and wind. They seemed to be somewhere else completely, the mad captain and the woman about to be killed and Scott. Why didn't she at least scream? That was the trouble with the way they'd all been dying, it wasn't like how his daddy had described the last war—the panic, the shrieking, the pleading, the desperation. "Look at them all," Sanderson said, waving at the burial scaffolds. Bones and snow. "Look at this squaw. I have nothing against her. But she can't stop the march of history, can she? Kill her. That's an order."

Scott hesitated. Behind the captain, in a thicket, just beyond the last of the scaffolds . . . was it that wolf again? Just eyes. I'm seeing things again, he told himself.

"Kill the woman!"

"I'm right sorry, Captain. I can't do it." He couldn't believe he was saying those words. Scott had always been trusty. He'd joined the army because his daddy said they were all one country now, that it was time for forgetting. Scott knew the meaning of authority and the meaning of disobedience.

"Kill the woman or I'll have you court-martialled!"

"No."

The eyes again . . . burning in the snow . . . the same eyes. The wind changed and smoke was pouring into the clearing, searing his eyes and his nostrils. The wolf and the old woman were enveloped in smoke. Both were emaciated, skeletal. Where were they going? Were they following him? Their eyes held him. They shone through the choking haze. He seemed to see his own destiny in the cold smoldering of those eyes.

So mesmerized was he that he barely heard the captain's ranting or the gunshot that rang out; he hardly noticed that the snow at his feet was blotched with the young woman's blood and brains. What happened next seemed like a dream. The captain was kicking the corpse, sending up flurries of crimson snow. Now he turned his anger on the burial scaffolds, shaking them, trying to knock them down. His trousers were soaked with blood. Bones rained on them, bones and ancient feathers. All the while Scott and the wolf-woman and the woman-wolf faced each other across the smoke . . . he felt he could almost speak to them, that their language was just on the tip of his tongue.

The wolf-woman howled. Her keening pierced the distant chorus of the dying. What was she saying to him? He fancied he understood; he drew a kind of comfort from it, though the cry was heartrending. "In your anger, forget not that we do not choose what we are." That was the message he seemed to hear.

"I don't mean to . . . I mean, it ain't right for me to . . ." He wanted to say more. This is driving me crazy, he thought. I'm having visions, I'm hearing things.

The captain was rattling one of the scaffolds. A shield of buffalo hide fell. It covered the dead girl's head. Scott was glad of it, because Sanderson had shot her at point blank range. More feathers flew. A small hand dangled from the buffalo-rope canopy.

"Farewell," the wolf-women seemed to say to him, and disappeared into the mist and smoke. There was music in the air: shrill music of fife and drum to drown out the screaming.

Scott didn't answer. He had to attend to the captain's raving now. He watched him flailing. He noticed that the hand that had emerged from the scaffold wasn't limp and rotting . . . it was reaching down, grabbing at the air . . . "Watch out!" he shouted. But it was too late. The hand found Sanderson's hair and yanked it sharply upwards. Another hand shot out and started digging into the scalp with a knife.

Scott fired at the scaffold. Over and over. The captain's tirade cut off abruptly. Blood was spurting down his face. On the scaffold, feathers and bones and buffalo skins writhed . . . the bloody scalp flew from the hand to the snow. Sanderson darted after it. He seemed to shocked to feel any pain at all. A figure rolled off the scaffold. There was no thud; the soft snow muffled everything.

For a long moment Sanderson tottered, holding out the circle of skin and hair, matted with coagulating blood, dandruffed by the snow. He still did not scream, did not seem to feel pain at all. At last, hoarsely, he whispered, "You see, Harper? It's easy to kill a child, it's easy, easy." And fell, fainting, beside two Indian corpses . . . and Scott started to holler for help.

To kill a child . . . what kind of a taunt was that? As others began to filter in from the burning encampment, as they prepared to carry the captain away, Scott noticed for the first time whom it was he had killed.

He couldn't have been more than twelve years old. He was naked except for a breechcloth. Scott's Colt had inflicted only flesh wounds. The boy had already been bleeding to death, slowly and painfully, from a deep gash in his abdomen. Perhaps a cavalry sword, Scott thought. The boy's mouth gaped in an unuttered cry, more of surprise than anguish. His face was daubed in paint; even Scott could tell it had been inexpertly applied; unmatched streaks of blue, sloping down either cheek, lent an angular asymmetry to his features. His guts were seeping into the snow from the deathwound. One fist was tightly clenched around a hank of the captain's hair.

"I reckon they wouldn't let him go on the big hunt, on account of he was too young." Scott looked up and saw that Zeke had come up and was standing beside him. "So he stays with the women and children, chafin' to go into battle like his brothers and uncles. Then he gets sliced up. He knows he's gonna die. Not soon, but he seen he's just gonna go on spillin' his blood and entrails till he's nothin' but a husk. He reckoned he ain't got long for this world, so he figured on dyin' proper. A man's gotta look good in the spirit world. He managed to paint his face somehow. Hid among the dead—he was practically one of them anyways. Figured on taking one of the *washichun* with him."

"You talk like you knew him, like you was there."

"Shit, I've knowed plenty that was like him. Well, one of us palefaces done blasted him right out of his final restin' place."

"I ain't proud of it," Scott said. "Not one dad-blamed bit."

"It were you?" Zeke said. "Well, boy, you're a real soldier now, you got blood on yer hands, on yer mind."

"I'm mighty surprised to hear you talk like this. You lived among them. You married a squaw once. The way you talked about the boy's death, it was like . . . like poetry! Shit, Zeke—"

"I ain't so old I can't tell truth from poetry."

"It don't feel . . . the way I reckoned it'd feel. Besides, the captain's fixin' to have me court-martialled for —"

"Court-martialled? They's all saying you saved his life! You gonna get yourself a medal for this, boy, you gonna get yourself promoted."

"We don't choose what we are."

"What do you mean?"

Scott realized those had been the words he'd heard in his mind, the words the wolf-people said. And his next words came out without thinking: "*Shungmanitu hemakiye.*"

"Where in tarnation'd you learn to say that?" Zeke was staring at him, profoundly disturbed.

"It just slipped out of my mouth. I don't even know what it means." Then, panicking, "Zeke, what *does* it mean?"

"Never you mind," Zeke said sullenly. He turned away, not giving the corpses another thought. Scott watched him as the mist swallowed him up. The bitter cold warred with the heat from blazing tipis. I'm a hero, he told himself, but the words meant nothing, nothing at all. Later, he would remember this only as the moment Zeke stopped trusting him.

6
Bavaria
one day before full moon

SPERANZA HAD LEFT THE COUNT'S PRIVATE COACH AS SOON AS SHE could. She had found the child awake, picking at the light supper which had been brought in for him: a little pâté, a bowl of soup, a loaf of black bread, a goblet of hot spiced wine. The maid, seeing her approach so soon after she had left to join von Bächl-Wölfing, curtseyed and departed, smirking . . . or was Speranza only imagining the worst?

"You stink of him," the boy said. It was the other one. The one with a tongue of a guttersnipe. "You reek of him, he's bursting with animal spunk, he's been wanking all over your cunny, did you let him get inside?" Speranza did not attempt to respond, but waited for the fit to end. At last Johnny Kindred emerged long enough to say, "I'm glad you're back; stay with me always." And then he fell asleep in her arms.

The night passed uneasily. She blew out the lamp, eased the boy onto his back on the seat opposite hers, and stared at the passing snowscape. Dark firs, silvered by the moon, stretched as far as she could see. Cold, dappled, light streamed into the compartment. She tried not to think of the Count von Bächl-Wölfing. But her dreams were of being pursued by him through the dank forest, the stench of earth and wolf piss burning her nostrils, the wind sharp and ice-cold. . . . In the dream she remembered thinking that they had left the German forests behind, that this was some quite alien forest of leviathan trees and unfamiliar animals, a forest in some strange new world.

In the morning the same servant appeared with an invitation to breakfast. "You should bring the child," the man said. She looked at Johnny. He seemed contrite; he offered no resistance as she dressed him from the clothes they found in the trunk. For herself she again selected dark colors; again she wore the silver necklace, although she was afraid he would think poorly of her for wearing the same jewelry two days in a row.

The curtains in the Count's car were still closed. She could not help noticing the smell; she recognized it from last night's dream. The boy began to growl. "Quiet, Johnny, quiet," she said softly. Some daylight seeped in between the closed draperies; dust swam in the rays. She could see the Count's back; he was seated at a writing desk, paying them no heed. She took in details she had missed before; the car was partitioned by a curtain of heavy purple velvet bearing the wolf crest; perhaps there was a sleeping area behind. Suddenly she was afraid the boy would start pissing on all the priceless furniture. But his growling seemed more for show; soon he became withdrawn, fidgety, his eyes following a dust mote as it circled.

The Count moved, shrugged perhaps; abruptly the divider drew open, and music played from the adjoining section, soft-pedaled chords on a piano. After a few bars, a clear, sweet tenor voice joined in with a plaintive melody in the minor. Sunlight streamed in.

The boy's attention was drawn immediately to the music. At last, for the first time, he smiled.

"Schubert," Speranza said, for the song cycle *Winterreise* had not been unknown in the Slatterthwaite household, though His Lordship had sung it in his cousin's stilted English translation, with little Michael pounding unmercifully on the family Broadwood. She had not known it could be so beautiful.

The Count said: "'*Fremd bin ich eingezogen, fremd zieh ich wieder aus.*' Do you know what it mean, Speranza? It means, 'I came here a stranger; a stranger I depart.' How true. Look, the boy understands it instinctively. He is no longer annoyed with me."

He clapped his hands. The music stopped; the boy's smile faded. "Shall we have breakfast now?" He got up and beckoned them to follow; as he crossed the partition, he nodded and the music resumed almost in mid-note. She took Johnny by the hand and led him. As they passed the desk where von Bächl-Wölfing had been sitting, she saw that he had been writing a letter

in English. She had already read the salutation—"My dear
Vanderbilt"—before realizing her appalling breach of manners.
Of course she would never normally have contemplated scrutinizing another's correspondence; it only showed how powerful an
effect the Count had had on her. She resolved to be more prim,
more severe in her demeanor. She would not step one inch over
the line of propriety—not one inch!

They had a pleasant enough breakfast of pheasant pâté, egg-
and-bacon pies, and toast and marmalade. Coffee was served in
blue-and-white Delft demitasses. She admired the china. She
admired the cutlery, whose ivory handles were carved in the shape
of lean wolves, each one with tiny topaz eyes. Throughout the
meal the Count said little. He stared at the boy. The boy stared
back. They spoke without words. She became aware that she was
babbling, trying to fill an uncomfortable silence with chatter. She
stopped abruptly. The music filled the air. Schubert's song cycle
spoke of beauty and desolation. And so it was here. The windows
had been opened a crack, driving out the musky animal odor. The
train moved out of the forest, past frozen lakes and somnolent
villages. There were mountains in the distance. In a few hours
they would enter the empire of Austria-Hungary, teeming with
exotic peoples and dissonant languages. She sipped her coffee,
which was flavored with nutmeg and topped with whipped cream,
and watched the wordless communion of the deranged boy and the
worldly aristocrat.

At last the Count said, "You seem to have made quite an
impression on the boy, Speranza. He loves you very much, you
know. You have a certain magic with children . . . and even, I
may add, with the middle-aged."

He smiled disarmingly. She blushed like a schoolgirl even as
she forced herself to purse her lips and respond with unyielding
decorum. "You are pleased to flatter me, Count," she said.

"You shall call me Hartmut," he said expansively.

"I would not make such a presumption," Speranza said. Her
pulse quickened. She steadied her hand by meticulously buttering
a slice of toast and applying the pâté to it, patting it into place and
making firm, precise ridges with the pâté knife. Before she could
finish, he had reached across the table and was grasping her hand
firmly. His hand was hairy and slick with sweat. She felt as though
her head had been plunged into a furnace. Quickly she snatched it

away. The Count smiled with his lips, with the contours of his face; but his eyes betrayed an untouchable sadness.

"What are you thinking? That you should touch that sadness?" How strange, she thought, that he could read her mind so accurately. "Ah, but you have not yet learnt the impossibility of the task you set yourself. You are young, so terribly young. Can you not cage the beast within, Speranza, even though you are fully human?"

"Sir, you are forward."

"It is because you wish it."

There was danger here, though the compartment was awash with light. Speranza decided that she might as well be direct. "Why, Count von Bächl-Wölfing, have you had us brought here? Why do you keep hinting of mysteries? There is an air that you affect, a feeling almost of some supernatural being. I do think that it is merely the result of your high birth, if I do not overstep—"

"Everything you have imagined, mademoiselle, is true."

But she had not yet imagined . . . the boy was growling again. He was toying with his food. He leapt onto the table on all fours. The Count turned to him. In a second his face seemed transformed. He snarled once. The boy slid sullenly back into his seat. The Count's face returned to normal. Speranza studied him for some clue as to its metamorphosis, but saw nothing.

"What did you do to make him stop?" she asked him.

"We have a way with each other."

"To return to this subject . . . why are we playing at these guessing games, Count? I am a modern woman, and not fond of mysteries."

"I am a werewolf."

The train clattered harshly against the Schubert melodies. Her rational mind told her that the Count was once more entertaining some elaborate fantasy to which she was not privy. Once more she considered the notion that he might be as mad as little Johnny. But another part of her had already seized on the statement. She could not deny that it was intriguing. Though she hardly dared admit it to herself, she even found the idea glamorous.

"*Noch was Kaffee, gnädiges Fräulein?*" the manservant said, smoothly gliding into position on her right. She nodded absently and he poured.

"I hear no reaction, mademoiselle, to what must constitute a most singular revelation." Was he laughing at her? But no, he seemed all seriousness. "Perhaps I should go on about wolfsbane, about nocturnal metamorphoses under the full moon, about silver bullets and so on. But you will only say, 'I am a modern woman,' and dismiss with that specious argument the accumulated knowledge of millennia. Let me suggest, instead, that you ask the boy. He knew at once. He knows now. By the way, he's a werewolf too."

"Perhaps you, Count, are suffering from some dementia that convinces you that you are . . . other than human," she said. "But Johnny's troubles are far less simple."

"True," said the Count. "How quickly you have divined, mademoiselle, the dilemma that is at the very heart of my involvement with him!" He did not seem to want to expand on the subject, and turned his attention instead to a snuffbox which his manservant had brought him on a silver tray.

She was bursting with curiosity and frustration. Instead she asked him, "And Dr. Szymanowski? Who is he?"

"A visionary, my dear mademoiselle! Whereas I . . . I merely pay the bills. By the way, what is your opinion of America?"

Taken aback by his change of subject, she said, "Why, very little, Count! That is, I know that it is a wild country of savages who are ruled by renegades scarcely less savage than the *Indiens peaux-rouges* themselves."

The Count laughed. "Ah, a wild country. Perhaps you will understand why it calls to the wilderness within us. In humans, but especially in us, who are—humor me at least for the moment—not entirely human. It cries to us across the very sea." Almost as an afterthought, he added, "I have been making a number of investments there. They are, I think, shrewd ones."

Speranza had the distinct impression that he was attempting, in a roundabout manner, to answer her questions; at the same time he was testing her, daring her to reveal the darkness inside herself. There was also something in him of a small boy with a secret . . . the frog in the waistcoat pocket . . . the Latin book coded with obscene messages in invisible ink . . . he wanted to know if he could trust her with the truth, but the truth excited him so much that he could hardly restrain himself from spilling everything. Even the sadness in his eyes seemed to have lifted a little.

She had an idea. "But the cutlery . . . is it not silver? And if it is true that you are indeed what you claim to be . . . is not silver a substance that might cause you distress?"

"My dear Speranza, heft my spoons and forks in your dainty hands! Are they not of unwonted heaviness? I have no cutlery on my dining table that is not purest platinum."

"And the full moon . . ."

"Will soon be upon us. Oh, don't worry, my dear Mademoiselle Martinique. You will be quite safe, as long as you observe certain conditions which I will spell out to you before moonrise. Ah, I see that you are skeptical, are you not? You think little of these extravagant claims?"

"Only, Count, that you are possessed of a powerful imagination." She felt uncomfortable, since both man and boy were staring intently at her, so she continued, "Oh, come sir! Here we are sitting amidst brilliant sunshine, doing nothing more supernatural than eating a pheasant pâté; how can you expect your ghost stories to have their full effect?"

"Ghost stories! Is that what you think they are?"

"Is it not what they are?"

"You mistake me, Speranza. I do not believe in ghosts. Nor spirits, nor demons, nor any of the trappings of damnation. How can I allow myself to believe in such things? I would fall prey to the utmost despair, for in the Christian hegemony in which we find ourselves, creatures such as I dare hope for no salvation, no redemption from the everlasting fire: we are damned already, damned without hope, damned before we are ever judged! *Quindi, Speranza, quindi bramo la speranza!*"

He spoke to her in her mother's tongue, the tongue of gentleness and warmth; she felt as though he had violated her final, innermost hiding place. She did not yield, but continued in English, to her the coldest of languages: "And why, Count von Bächl-Wölfing, why is it that you so ardently yearn for hope?"

"But I forget myself." The Count's passion had been but fleeting; now he was all correctness. "I apologize for inflicting my religious torment on you, mademoiselle; I trust you have not been too disturbed by my words?"

"On the contrary, the fault is mine," Speranza said automatically, thinking nothing of the kind. "I should perhaps be going now?"

The sun hung low over the snow.

Johnny sat with his nose pressed against the pane.

"What do you think?" he asked her suddenly. "Shall we trust him? Shall we run with him in the cold, cold forest?"

"I don't know what you mean."

"You're going to go to him tonight, aren't you? He'll invite you. Maybe he won't, but you'll find some excuse. Because you're dying from curiosity. You want to know if it's true. And you want to fuck him."

"Johnny, I really must insist—" But she knew that all he said was true. He understood her so well, this lunatic.

"My language. I can't help it, though, I'm possessed by demons, you see. Everyone says so."

"Johnny, there aren't any demons. Even the Count says so."

"I don't want to be this way."

"You don't have to be, Johnny, because I'm going to help you, I'm going to pull you out of this sickness of yours somehow."

"Will you love me, Speranza?"

"Of course I will."

"Then you must fuck me, too, mustn't you?" The words no longer offended her; she knew it was part of his illness. Somehow these things had become terribly confused for him. How could she blame him? Even she was confused, and she was a sane woman, was she not? She tried to pry him from the window, thinking to comfort him; he resisted at first, but then threw himself into her arms with a hunger that was like anger, and it frightened her, how so much passionate anguish could come in so frail a package; and as she hugged him she heard him wailing, with a desperate concern for her and for his own future, "When you go to see him tonight, you have to wear the silver necklace, don't ever take it off whatever he says don't you ever ever ever take it off!"

7
Deadwood, Dakota Territory
full moon

HE CREPT INSIDE THE SALOON LIKE A CAT, HOLDING BACK THE DOORS so that they hardly swung at all. No one noticed him at first. They probably couldn't think that well above the raucous chatter and the pounding of an out-of-tune piano. Beside the piano, an operatic soprano was shrilling away in German—someone's misguided attempt to import a little culture into the wilderness. It was the woman whose steatopygous image had adorned a billboard that hung on the wall outside: "Amazing feats of vocal artistry— straight from the court of King Ludwig of Bavaria—Amelia Nachtigall!" No one was paying any attention to her, although she was warbling earnestly and inaccurately away. It was, he noted, a Schubert song. Over their heads.

He was uncomfortable in these clothes; somehow, by affecting some of their garments, he felt tainted by their wildness. Still in the doorway, half in the shadow cast by a flickering oil lamp, he stood, fastidiously brushing the snow from his greatcoat. Listlessly he surveyed the scene. It was much the same as those he had been witnessing for the past weeks, in a score of saloons in Lead. He wondered why he had bothered to come to this town, knowing it would be like the others; his master would be none the wiser if he sent him a somewhat doctored report. But he knew how important it was to all the . . . people . . . all the members of the Lykanthropenverein whom he, like his colleague Cornelius Quaid in England, served. Why had the Count not sent Quaid? At least Quaid would have been speaking his native tongue.

The room was pungent with human sweat, with tobacco smoke, with the smell of alcohol and old puke. Men sat around tables, drinking and playing cards. Their garb was outlandish in the extreme: he never failed to be amazed at their slouch hats, their canvas trousers—Levi's, they were called—and especially their extravagant boots. In Lead, one of them had told him he never took off his boots even in bed. It did not surprise him in the least. He was glad that he had left Natasha in the vestibule of the quaint wooden church that stood not far from the stage depot. But he would have to fetch her soon; the sun was setting, and he would have to make sure she was properly taken care of before moonrise. Or else there would be trouble.

He had just about composed himself enough to go on into the saloon when the door was pushed open behind him, hitting him in the shoulder. He felt something cold and sharp digging into the small of his back, even through the greatcoat.

A voice whispered, "Get out of my way or I'll blow you to kingdom come."

"I'm terribly sorry . . . I'm sure I did not mean to—"

"A furriner! I'll be!" Another dig in the ribs. "You ever felt the cold steel of a loaded derringer in the small of your back before, stranger? Ever know what it is to be frightened plumb out of your cotton-pickin' mind?"

"If you'd just permit me to go about my business—"

"Turn around and take it like a man! Slowly!"

I'm going to be killed, he thought, murdered in this savage, godforsaken country—and Natasha! left to her own devices, stranded in this place without anyone who would understand her—

Suddenly he realized that everyone in the saloon was staring at him. They had all stopped talking. Through the tendrilling smoke he could see their eyes . . . all of them filled with a kind of cold, malicious mirth. He turned to face his assailant. "You want money?"

Laughter broke out. It dawned on him that this was these people's idea of a joke. They lived so near to death all the time, these denizens of America's Wild West; no wonder they thought death was funny.

"Howdy," said the man, slipping his derringer smartly back into his sleeve. "Allow me to introduce myself, mister. Cord-wainer Claggart's the name. Ah, you recognize it? Even in your distant land they've heard tell of Cordwainer Claggart, the great *in*ventor, creator of Claggart's Patent Floccinaucinihilipilificator?

I'm right flattered, mister, right flattered!" He turned to the others almost as though expecting applause, a tiny man, bald, wearing a white frock coat and a silver waistcoat from which depended one of those fashionable Dickens watch chains. "And who might you be?"

"My name is Vishnevsky," he said. It was his real name, but he had been too confused to invent one this time, despite the Count's admonitions. Too late to retract, so he continued, "Valentin Nikolaievich Vishnevsky."

"That's a mighty mouthful," said Claggart. "What might you be doing in these here Black Hills? Are you lustin' after the gleaming yellow stuff? Cravin' to be rich as Cressida?"

"Croesus," Vishnevsky corrected automatically.

"That'll cost you your life, mister!" said the little man sharply. "Draw!"

"I mean no quarrel, Mr. Claggart," Vichnevsky said uncomfortably, still thinking of Natasha and wondering how long they had until moonrise. "I merely came here in search of a room."

The "world-famous" Amelia Nachtigall, who had been relentlessly singing her Schubert lieder all along, now launched into a series of slightly bawdy ballads. These were greeted with much more enthusiasm; some of the clientele were even joining in for the choruses.

"A room!" Claggart guffawed, and Vishnevsky wondered whether he still intended to shoot him.

"If you please, Mr. Claggart, permit me to make my inquiries unmolested. I am travelling in the company of my cousin, a lady, whom I have left waiting at a nearby church; I am desirous of seeing her safely bedded for the night."

"Bedded, my friend! There's a dozen lusty bucks'll be right glad to take you up on your kind offer," Claggart said, smirking. "She speak English? Well, there ain't no need for that, when it comes to panderin' to the desires o' the flesh."

"Have I not made myself clear?" Vishnevsky said, aware that he was being stared at from all sides. He took out his watch—occasioning more stares, for his timepiece was a fine one, of Swiss manufacture—and saw that he had only an hour left until sunset. And the moon was scheduled to rise . . . when? I must not panic, he thought. For Natasha's sake, I must not panic! "There was a sign that advertised rooms, was there not? I will pay well—though I must say that two dollars a night seems somewhat excessive. One would not pay that much even in a more—" He was about to say "civilized part of the world," but stopped himself just in time.

"There ain't a spare room to be had in all of Deadwood," Claggart said. "Ain't that so, Ebenezer?"

The bald bartender, who was evidently also the proprietor of the boardinghouse, nodded, and said in a gruff voice, "Since they uncovered that new vein last month, mister, them gold diggers just ain't stopped coming. The snow ain't even slowed 'em down. I got 'em packed three to a bed at six bits a head. Some calls it highway robbery, but most charges more'n me."

"Three to a bed!" That would never do. Not this night of all nights. Vishnevsky could sleep in a corner, in a barn, anywhere, but Natasha . . . had to have that special treatment. Or else . . . he shuddered. Even I am not immune, he thought. The ties of blood mean nothing to . . . to one of those creatures. He hated the Count at that moment. He had fed on the girl's infatuation . . . his wealth and his title and his frayed good looks . . . and then he had made her into one of his kind. And bullied young Valentin into entering his service, saying, "It will be so lonely for her. She will need someone from her past to be always with her, to show her she is still loved. You cannot imagine how desolate it is to be . . . as I am."

He was rudely awakened from his reverie by the voice of Claggart. "But of course, I, Cordwainer Claggart, inventor of Claggart's Patent Floccinaucinihilipilifactor, ain't come unprepared for this here contingency. As a regular and welcome customer and friend of the proprietor, I comes in for a bit o' *magn*animosity now and then. Ain't that so, my friend?" He waved his derringer grandly at the bartender.

"Sure is."

"It just so happens that I chances to have me a private room in this here establishment. Which can be yours for a night of private bedding with your"—he leered—"cousin, you said, har, har, har?"

"Name your price," Vishnevsky said, trying to mask his desperation as he looked once more at his pocket watch.

"Well, such an esteemed commodity's gonna take a moment or two of bargaining," Claggart said, steering him toward one of the tables. "And I reckon you must be thirsty from all that fright. Let's have a drink." To the bartender he shouted, "Two of the usual!"

They sat down. Vishnevsky slung his greatcoat over the chair. The bartender poured them two glasses of something whose color and odor reminded him of horse piss. To his dismay, Vishnevsky noticed that floating in the bottle was something that looked alarmingly like the head of a rattlesnake. "That'll be four bits," the man said. He looked helplessly at Claggart, realized the he had been conned into treating, and hunted in an inner pocket of his greatcoat for his purse. He pulled out a fifty-cent bill.

The bartender held it up for all to see. Derisive laughter echoed around the saloon. Even the warbling wonder gurgled in mid-note. "Where'd you get this from?" the bartender said.

"Why, the bank," said Vishnevsky, who had drawn a large sum in cash from the local Wells Fargo on a letter of credit from one of the Count's New York accounts.

"Didn't they tell you we don't take no shinplasters here?" the bartender scoffed. "This is the West, my friend! Around here folks believes in gold and silver, not pieces of paper."

Claggart said, in a mournful, sympathetic voice, "Hoodwinked again, Mister Vichyssoise or whatever you're called. Well, I'd be mighty honored to come to your assistance. Shall we say, fifty cents on the dollar?" He reached into his pocket and pulled out a handful of coins. Before Vishnevsky could lose his temper, he continued smoothly, "Ah, but you're a stranger, and I reckon you oughta get off lightly the first time. Six bits to the dollar's my last offer."

If I stop to argue, Vishnevsky thought, it will be too late. Wearily he nodded and handed Claggart a sheaf of greenbacks. Claggart counted out some coins. "But those do not even look like American dollars!" Vishnevsky said, bewildered at the appear-ance of some of the coins, which appeared to be inscribed in Spanish.

"They's dobe dollars," Claggart said.

Vishnevsky thought: I will never understand this. He slipped the coins into his purse, carefully replaced it in his greatcoat pocket, and took a sip of the yellow liquor. It was, he reflected, no worse than peasant vodka. "Did I imagine it? But did I actually see a snake's head in the vessel from which—"

Claggart laughed. "Nothing better'n a rattler's head for that extra punch. It's the venom. I've been known to add a jigger of it to the Floccinaucinihilipilificator, too, when it don't taste powerful enough. Folks never has faith in a bland medicine. And faith, mister, is what mirac'lous cures is all about." He pulled a flask from his tail pocket and branished it. Vishnevsky barely caught a glimpse of its label, which consisted of a fearsome list of diseases, from consumption to warts, from which the potion purportedly proffered surcease. "I don't often do this, stranger, but seein' as you're new to these parts . . . here, take it. It's proof against ills that would horripilify the stoutest heart."

Either Vishnevsky's command of English was barely sufficient to understand Claggart's complex metaphor, or . . . "The room," he said, trying to return to pressing matters. "How much is it you want for the room?"

"Ah, the room . . . well, how much do you think it's worth a man to give up the hard-earned comforts of life and doss down with two or three stinkards on a rope bed three foot wide?"

"I will pay what I must," Vishnevsky said.

"Well . . . let's you and me be gentlemen about this. I won't make you pay—"

"No?"

"—if you can beat me at a few rounds of blackjack."

Although Scott was a bit uncomfortable with popery and mumbo jumbo, he was too well brought up to show it at Eddie Bryant's funeral. He and Zeke had been ordered to escort Widow Bryant and the corpse to Deadwood.

It was better than staying at the fort and having to take Captain Sanderson's orders from his bedside. The captain wasn't a pretty sight, although his recovery had been, in its way, amazing. But if they had thought him petty and tyrannical before, the men found new things to fear in the new Captain Sanderson. He insisted on being carried about the fort in a makeshift litter, and seemed almost proud of his demonic tonsure, the mass of purple tissue and gangrene at the top of his head. There'd been no more talk of a court-martial once word got out that Lieutenant Harper had saved the captain's life; but his act had earned him no gratitude from the enlisted men either.

It was maybe a half hour before sunset. Whitewood Park

straddled the horizon, glistening with scarlet snow. He and Zeke were standing a ways off from the grave site, where the priest was mumbling in Latin. A boy, shivering beneath the thin cassock and surplice, was swinging a censer over the open shaft. The Widow Bryant was standing beside the grave. There were few friends and no family. A couple of miners had come down for the funeral. Their trouser legs sported the stiff creases of factory pantaloons; they'd probably bought their funeral finery only that day, and hadn't had time yet to disguise the creases. Mrs. Bryant stood weeping into a lace handkerchief. Behind the reek of incense was the faint odor of liquor from the saloon down the street.

"They don't need us here," Zeke whispered. "I reckon we oughta go get ourselves a swig of rattlesnake venom." He started to tug Scott in the direction of the church.

Scott said, "We're supposed to make sure the widder don't come to no harm. But maybe—" He turned around then and saw a woman standing in the church's shadow, staring at the hilltop where the sun was setting. "Look at her!" he said.

Zeke grunted.

The woman walked slowly toward them. She was running her hand lightly over the top of each wooden grave marker, brushing off the snow. She wore a serge travelling dress and an ermine stole, and her face, framed by startling red locks, was shadowed by a fur-trimmed bonnet. Her gait had an air of command; it reminded Scott somehow of his mother, whom he had buried more than ten years ago. Her eyes were wide and golden, surely a trick of the evening light; her face was pale, bloodless almost. Unthinking, he had already begun to move toward her, ignoring Zeke's muttered "Leave her alone." As he approached her he saw what it was about her eyes that was so familiar.

"Excuse me, sir," the woman said. "I am too forward, no? But I am stranger here."

A foreigner, Scott thought. "We ain't much for Old World civilities here in the Dakota Territory, ma'am," he said. But he doffed his hat to her and bowed, and she smiled at him. "Are you in need of some kind of assistance? I reckoned, you being without an escort and all—"

"You will talk with me a little, and stay beside me? I am to wait for my cousin. But I have not told you my name; I am Natalia

Petrovna Stravinskaya." She laughed. "It is . . . a mouthful no? Have I got that right, a mouthful?"

Scott laughed. "Why did your cousin go and leave you here alone? There's a lot of crazy folks in this town."

"He wished to spare me the . . . I cannot explain. Do you speak French?"

"Just a few words, ma'am. But I thought—from your name— you must be Russian."

"One only speaks Russian to the servants."

"I see," Scott said, though he really didn't. They stood in silence for a while, listening to the sound of the priest's voice. The breeze was flecked with snow, and the shadows of the grave markers were long and fringed with crimson. Scott knew he should be rejoining Zeke and the others, but he stood mesmerized. It was like that time in the Indian village. And this time it was also because of the eyes . . . the woman's eyes, wolf's eyes. And the feral odor of earth and piss that the woman's perfume couldn't quite disguise. Maybe I'm going plumb out of my mind, Scott thought. I'm seeing a wolf inside every woman I look at. He wondered whether it was because he hadn't had a woman since coming to the territory. "I'm sorry for staring, ma'am," he said, suddenly realizing how boorish and rude he must appear to her.

She didn't answer him directly, but said only, "These markers are so quaint. Why are they made of wood, I wonder? They are so impermanent. When they rot away, the dead will be quite forgotten, isn't it? Often I have hoped to die in this manner."

"What do you mean? You wouldn't want nobody to remember you after you're gone?" Scott said, bewildered.

She said, "It would not be worth remembering. But I'm troubling you, no? Pardon me." She extended her hand to him. "But you must tell my your name."

"Lieutenant Scott Harper, Eleventh Cavalry, ma'am," he said. And he took her hand, and, because it seemed expected of him, he kissed it. She wore no gloves, despite the cold. But her hand was hot to the touch, and his lips tingled from its warmth. It was as though she were burning within. He wondered whether she was ill.

"But you must put your hat back on, Lieutenant," she said, "for it is cold, and you are excessively polite." She paused, and said, "And you are still staring. But I don't mind."

"Ma'am—" He averted his eyes, embarrassed suddenly. "I thought—you reminded me of—"

"Many in my family have compared me to a wild animal." Had she read his mind? She went on, "You please me, Lieutenant Harper."

Flustered, Scott said, "What shall I call you, ma'am?" He had a vague notion of trying to find out whether she was married. "I reckon maybe I should call you Miss Stravinskaya, but . . . well, from the way you look . . . I had you figured for one of them aristocrats, a countess or somethin'."

"You should address me as Natalia Petrovna," she said. "That is the formal mode of address in my country. Oh, but I am flattered you should think me a countess. Alas, I am not, nor can I ever be one . . . though I am so close to it!"

"What do you mean?"

"I am rather intimately attached to a certain count. I am, in fact, his mistress." Seeing Scott's reaction, she continued, "But you are shocked? Perhaps you think me a whore? That is correct word, isn't it? But it is not the same thing at all." And she began to weep bitterly.

"Natalia Petrovna—" Scott didn't know what to say. She was part of a whole different world . . . a glittering, glamorous world of counts and kept women and fabulous wealth. He felt inadequate. "Don't cry, ma'am," he said softly. "I hate to see you cry. I mean, you're so pretty and all. And—tarnation, I'm as tongue-tied as a schoolboy, and—" Not knowing what else to do, he undid his yellow silk kerchief and handed it to her. She took it and dabbed at those distant, amber-colored eyes.

It was at that moment that Zeke Sullivan, with Widow Bryant on his arm, approached them. Natalia Petrovna dried her tears.

Scott introduced them all to each other. Zeke said, "*Préférez-vous que nous parlons en français, Natalia Petrovna?*"

"Didn't know you could speak French," Scott said, a little resentful when Natalia beamed with pleasure. "And don't tell me you learned it from the Injuns."

"To tell the truth, I did," Zeke said. "There's tribes up north that's been dealing with the French for two hundred years."

"But you knew we speak French in Russia," Natalia Petrovna said. "That is the remarkable thing."

"Not really, ma'am. See, there was this Russian feller—the

Grand Duke Alexis. A few years back, he come to the territory with Buffalo Bill to try his hand at huntin'. That was when I was scoutin' for Custer. Anyhow, one time they got me to interpretin' for this duke, or whatever he was, and we got along famously. He took such a fancy to our Smith and Wesson .44s, he ordered a couple thousand of 'em for the Russian army."

"How astonishing!" Natalia said. "I myself have never been granted an audience by the grand duke. But I believe my cousin has one of those very revolvers you speak of."

There was a lull in the conversation as people filed past, offering their condolences to Widow Bryant. At length, Zeke said, "We should leave." They were not due back at the fort until the day after tomorrow, and they had taken lodgings at the saloon and boardinghouse down the street. One of Zeke's many friends, a trainman, was going to meet them there at sundown. The widow was to stay with the family of one of her husband's friends. Zeke said to her, "Are you about ready for us to escort you to the O'Gradys?"

She said, "I feel all empty inside me. I wish I was a man and I could just walk into a saloon and order me a double shot of whiskey."

Scott was a little shocked that she would say that at her husband's funeral. But Zeke didn't seem surprised. "Today's a special day, Mrs. Bryant," he said. "You've had enough grief to last ten years. I reckon we oughta escort you right down to the saloon me and Scott is staying at. Besides"—he took a flask of liquor from his coat and took a swig—"there's a feller waitin' for us there right now. He's a right fascinatin' individual. And, well, to get to the point, you could do worse than gettin' to know Claude Grumiaux, the trainman." It seemed improper to Scott for Zeke to talk about meeting new men, with Eddie barely buried, but the widow didn't seem to mind. Maybe, now that she was rich, she reckoned that she'd be calling the shots this time around.

Suddenly Scott realized that they were going to leave Natalia behind. He turned to her and said, "And what about you, ma'am? It ain't right for a woman to loiter here alone, even in a church. One of the miners is sure to try and bother you—"

"My cousin will come to fetch me soon, I am sure."

"Where's that cousin of yours now?" Zeke said. "He ain't got no more sense than a rattler's ass, beggin' your pardon, leavin' a lady out here by herself—"

"He'd down at the . . . the Diamond Spur Saloon, I think they call it."

"Now if that ain't exactly where we're headed!" Zeke said. "Come with us, ma'am. If your cousin's as much a furriner as you, he's prob'ly down to his last three-cent shinplaster by now. It's my Christian duty to protect him from them cardsharps and them two-bit, uh, ladies of the evenin'." He turned to Scott and winked.

Scott heaved a sigh of relief. He was going to have the company of this mysterious, beautiful woman a while longer—and he had been saved the embarrassment of asking her himself.

"You are not a formal people," Natalia said. "I like that about you." And she held out her arm to be escorted.

As she touched him, Scott felt the burning once again. It was even more powerful now; only politeness kept him from snatching his arm away.

"Please, we must hurry," she said urgently, "it may already be too late."

That rank forest smell assailed his nostrils once again. He almost choked on it. He slipped in the snow. She steadied him. Her hand, which had seemed so pale and fragile, had a grip as firm as a man's. The sun was almost completely gone now, and her eyes glowed with a harsh, unnatural light. He stared at the slush as he guided Natalia around ruts and piles of horse dung to the opposite boardwalk.

"We must hurry," she said again. There was a metallic rasp to her voice, and when he looked up at her at last, he thought he saw, behind those elegantly painted lips, the glint of fangs.

As the game proceeded, it became obvious to Vishnevsky that Cordwainer Claggart was cheating. There was something about the way he peered intently at the back of the cards. There was a way he had of anticipating Vishnevsky's hand. At last he could bear being made a fool of no longer. He was too enraged to think about Natasha, and the vile rattlesnake's-head liquor was pounding inside his skull. "I suspect you are playing with marked deck," he said, his English deteriorating as he became more drunk.

"Now that's a mighty impolite thing to say in the middle of a friendly game of blackjack," Claggart said. "Don't you have no manners where you come from?"

"Insist! We use my cards!" He fished in his greatcoat pocket. He had come prepared for this, for the Count had insisted that Vishnevsky bring playing cards to this wilderness—themselves marked, of course. He thrust them on the table and glared at Claggart until the man took them sullenly and began to shuffle them. Vishnevsky found that the game of vingt-et-un became childishly simple once one knew every card the opponent had, and he was too inebriated to bet with caution.

Claggart started to lose. "You ain't as easy a mark as I thought," he said grudgingly.

Smiling, Vishnevsky ordered another round of drinks. They were served by the world-famous opera singer, who seemed to have more than one function. They had begun to attract an audience. He downed the venomous fluid in a single gulp, much to the amusement of the miners who had gathered.

"You're cheatin'!" Claggart announced at last. "Them cards is marked!"

"Just give me the room," Vishnevsky said, "and that will be end of matter."

Enraged, Claggart pounded his fists on the table. The cards flew to the floor. Claggart bent down and began to grope under the chair. Vishnevsky became aware of a tugging at the greatcoat he had hung over the chair. He looked down and saw a hand reaching for the inside pocket. "You are trying to steal my purse!" he shouted, and snatched up the coat. Paper money flurried and coins scattered.

Claggart seemed nonplussed for only a second before he pulled his derringer from his sleeve and shouted, "Watch who you're accusing, mister! Or you're liable to end up dead."

Vishnevsky had no time to react. He had a gun too, somewhere, in one of the pockets . . . one of the Russian-model Smith and Wessons. He fumbled desperately for it.

A shot rang out.

Vishnevsky dropped everything he was holding. He was surprised that he felt no pain. It took him a moment to realize that he had not been hit . . . that Claggart's gun had not even gone off. Claggart was staring at his hand in disbelief. A chunk of flesh was missing around the knuckle of his index finger, and blood was pouring out. His derringer had been knocked clear across the table and onto the floor. The bottle of Claggart's Floccinaucinihilipilificator was shattered. Noxious fumes clouded the air. The odor was disquieting . . . and then he heard a shriek, more animal than human, and he knew that she had come.

"Natasha—" No sooner had he spoken than he saw her standing in a far corner of the saloon. Could he have been so absorbed in this ridiculous card game that he had not seen her come in? Her eyes had already taken on their wolf's color. The transformation had already begun, but she was swathed in furs and smoke, and no one had noticed. Standing next to her was a cavalry officer in dress uniform and several other people. The man who had fired the shot approached, and Vishnevsky's cousin followed him, avoiding the ragged pools of lamplight. "Thank you," he said to his rescuer. "I am—"

"Yes, Valentin Nikolaievich. Your cousin has told me something of you. It is fortunate that we have met." He had a slight French accent. His beard was straggly and his hair, black, silver-tinged, hung down to his shoulder; he smelled of tobacco. "I am Claude-Achille Grumiaux. This is my friend Zeke Sullivan; he has brought with him Lieutenant Scott Harper, Mrs. Bryant, and of course, your cousin." To Claggart he said disdainfully, "Give him the key to the room. After all you've put him through, it's the least you can do, you low-down snake-oil merchant. I've a mind to make you give back all the money you cheated him of, too."

Claggart threw a key on the table and slunk away, not, Vishnevsky noted, without pausing to eye Mrs. Bryant; perhaps it was with lust, or perhaps he was appraising other prospects.

"You are one of those . . . gunfighters?" Vishnevsky said.

"Hardly," said Grumiaux, "although in so rough a society as this it would not do to let one's markmanship slip. Far from it, sir; I am a trainman by profession, and at present I am surveying for the Fremont, Elkhorn and Missouri Valley Railroad. That is why I knew immediately who you were when your cousin told me your name. You're working for that Austrian Count, aren't you? The one who has been investing heavily in the very railroad I work for."

So the Count's investments had been less inconspicious than he had hoped. Obviously he would have to interrogate this fellow further. As soon as the most pressing matter—Natasha—was taken care of. "We'll talk—" he said. His speech was still slurred from the liquor.

"Yes. But first I must—"

"Of course. Natalia Petrovna, *bonne nuit.*" He bowed deeply to Natasha as Vishnevsky made his way through the onlookers. Ebenezer the barman directed him toward a flight of stairs at the back of the saloon, and promised to dispatch a boy to the stage depot to pick up their luggage.

"Just leave it outside the door," Vishnevsky said. "On no account is anyone to enter the room."

Scott and Widow Bryant didn't speak much. The widow had already downed two drinks and was working on a third. Scott was thinking about the Russian woman. He felt drawn to her, though they had known each other less than an hour. It had something to do with the wolf-vision that had come to Scott during the massacre, in the middle of the captain's raving and the smoke and the bloodshed and the snow . . . and the mysterious words in the Sioux language that had sprung to Scott's lips, the words Zeke had refused to translate.

Scott sat staring at his drink. The other two men conversed animatedly. They were old friends, but Scott had never met the other man at all. They were reliving some ancient argument. Apparently Grumiaux had run off with Zeke's wife a long time ago. Or maybe it was the other way round. It had been an Indian woman, anyway.

The more Scott thought about the Russian woman and the wolf-women in the forest, the more confused he became. There was some raw emotion in himself, one he didn't want to face. He decided, instead, to join in the conversation. So, during the first lull, he said, "That was mighty strange, wasn't it? I mean, the Russian happening to be someone you'd heard of."

"Not really," Claude Grumiaux said. "I have been pursuing him all the way from Omaha. I fully expected to meet him here."

Scott was even more confused.

But Grumiaux explained, "This Count, you see, from Austria, he has been putting a lot of money into my company's railroad. That in itself is not strange; with the influx of miners into the territory, a narrow gauge line from Omaha all the way into the Black Hills, avoiding the perils of the Cheyenne-Deadwood stage route, is bound to be profitable, and we have been laying track as fast as we can, though the winter makes it hard . . . but our mysterious Count wants more than a share in the money. He seems to want control. He's demanding a tangential spur into the foothills going off to no one quite knows where, except that no prospector's ever found gold in that direction. Does he know something we don't ? And if he does, how can he know it all the way in Austria? That's what the company sent me to find out. I'm supposed to befriend him."

"So this Russian and his cousin are . . . spies?" Scott said. It didn't surprise him anymore that a body would go to such lengths to get gold. For he'd seen Eddie Bryant's corpse, stiff and stuffed with nuggets. "You think they're up to no good?"

"Maybe. I see no other explanation," the trainman said. "Except, perhaps, for black magic."

For some reason that made Scott shudder.

Vishnevsky bolted the door. He drew a silver chain from the lining of his greatcoat.

"I won't be chained!" Natasha said. But her voice was already losing its human quality. He came closer. She circled the bed, pawing the floorboards, her haunches up, foul-smelling.

"You must, Natasha," he said sadly.

"I beg you . . . I beg you, Valentin Nikolaievich," she said, switching to Russian.

She did not protest as strongly as she usually did. Perhaps, as he suspected, Claggart's snake oil did contain traces of wolfsbane. Or holy water. That was what had caused her to cry out so incautiously, and why she seemed enervated now. Quickly, methodically, he forced her onto the bed and chained her wrists to the posts. Welts broke out on her arms and hands as the silver touched them. She moaned, and even as she moaned the sound was transformed into a she-wolf's howl. He drew the chain tight. "Forgive me," he whispered. And kissed her on a cheek that was already bristling as the moon rose. He closed the curtains. Sometimes the metamorphosis was less severe when no moonlight was admitted. But if Natasha should break free—

"Fetch me someone!" she cried out. "I'm hungry!"

"Stay until morning," he said.

"The boy . . . did you see the young soldier boy? . . . the boy was beautiful, and so naïve . . . Bring him to me."

"Of course, of course," he said with surpassing gentleness. He hung a Greek cross on the door, and on the windowsill, behind the curtain, he placed a tiny icon of St. Basil. He did not think they would be much use against the wild and ravenous beast his cousin might become. But it was better than taking no precautions at all.

"I will be back," he said. "While you still possess some understanding, let me impress on you the importance of this mission. Don't jeopardize it by letting yourself be seen." Natasha thrashed against the metal and whimpered each time the silver grazed her skin. He steeled his heart. "I must try to make friends with the trainman," he said, "and glean more information for the Count, your lover."

"Get me the young lieutenant!" came the growl of the she-wolf, the last barely human sounds she would make until dawn.

Claggart had a tryst with the opera singer planned that night. Actually she wasn't a star of the German stage at all; Claggart happened to know that she was born and raised in Council Bluffs, Iowa. Blackmail had helped him lift her skirts and get beneath her unmentionables.

But seeing Widow Bryant made him wish he hadn't planned anything for the night. Claggart had an unerring nose for money, and there was something about this widow . . . he'd heard the rumors, of course . . . but how much gold was there? Was it worth making a play for this dumpy, weather-beaten woman?

He sat a few tables away from their group. The woman wasn't really participating in the conversation, he noticed. Good. They weren't really her friends. He smelled an opening.

He saw her pay for something with a gold coin.

He started to move toward her, but saw the Russian coming back down the stairs. "God damn all Russians," he muttered.

Then he thought: I'll just neglect to tell Amelia I'm no longer sleeping in that room! Let the Russian have her, if he can stomach her!

He caught Widow Bryant's eye and smiled at her. She looked away. He moved a little closer. He had forgotten his little scam with the cards and the shinplasters. This was bigger game.

He saw her look up again. She was lonesome, that was obvious. Probably always had been. Husband probably never even diddled her, he was so busy digging for the yellow stuff. He wagged a finger at her. His joint chafed against the bloody handkerchief he'd used to stanch the wound.

She looked away. He waited. A third time, he thought, just one more soulful gaze and she'll be dancing to my tune. I've been selling panaceas for twenty years, and I know that I've got the cure she wants, right here between my twitching legs.

8
Austria
full moon

THE INNER WORLD OF JOHNNY KINDRED WAS LIKE A FOREST: NOT THE picture-book forest of fairy tales, but a forest of gnarled trees knotted with rage, of writhing vines, of earth pungent with piss and putrescence, of clammy darkness. At the very center of the forest there was a clearing. The circle was the center of the world, and it was bathed in perpetual, pallid moonlight. When you stood in the circle of light, you could see the outside world, you could hear, touch, smell. You controlled the body. But you always had to fend off the others. Especially Jonas.

And when you were tired, they gathered, surrounding the circle, thirsting for the light. Waiting to touch the world outside.

Waiting to use the body.

Right now the circle was empty. The body slept.

"Let me through," Johnny said faintly.

The darkness seethed. Vines shifted. And always the wolves howled. There were unformed persons in the depths of the forest, their strength growing. Johnny could smell them. He could smell Jonas most of all. Jonas hanging head downward from a tree. Jonas laughing, the drool glistening on his canines. Calling his name: "Johnny, Johnny, you silly boy, you're just a fucking figment, you're just a dream."

"Let me through—" He had to step into the light before the body wakened. Because the moon would be rising soon.

"Through? You don't even exist. I'm the owner of this body, and you're just a little thing I made up once to amuse myself. Get back, get back. Into the dark, do you hear? Or I'll send for—"

"No!"

"Our father."

"Our father in hell," Johnny whispered.

"In hell." He could see Jonas more clearly now. The other boy was swinging back and forth, back and forth. He looked like one of the cards in their mother's tarot deck . . . the Hanged Man. "Fuck you! Why did you have to think of our mother, simple Johnny? Do you want to go back to the madhouse? Perhaps you have fond memories of your mudlarking days, my little mad brother?"

"I forgot. That you can read my mind." The thought of their mother could still hurt Jonas. Johnny tried to think of her again, but he saw only a great blackness. Jonas had been at work, striking out any bits of the past that displeased him, tossing them aside like the offal that lined the banks of the Thames, like the rubbish piled up against the walls of their old home. Jonas used to bully him all the time at the home. Whenever the beatings started he would push Johnny out into the clearing so that Johnny would feel all the pain. Even though it was always Jonas who had done wrong. "Get out of my mind!" Johnny screamed, despairing.

"Our mind. No. My mind. It's my mind, you're in my mind. Why can't you be more like me? I'm not a snivelling, snotty-nosed boy who's afraid of the truth. Our mother never could face the truth, could she? You're weak, like her, weak, weak, weak."

Johnny started to run. The mud clung to his toes. Brambles slithered around his ankles. Thorns sliced into his arms, opening up fresh wounds. The clearing didn't get any nearer. He leapt over rotted logs and mossy stones. He had to reach it first, he had to. Dread seeped into him. He knew that Jonas was swinging from tree to tree, his animal eyes piercing the dark. There it was! He was at the edge now, all he had to do was step inside—

He fell! Twigs and leaves flurried. He was at the bottom of a pit. He breathed uneasily. His hand collided with something hard.

Pale light leaked in from the clearing. He saw who was in the trap with him . . . a skeleton, chained to the earthen walls with silver that glinted in the light, cold, cold, cold.

"Let me out—"

Jonas stood above him. "The body is mine," he said slowly, triumphantly. Johnny could see that he had already begun to change. The snout was bursting from flaps of human skin . . . the eyes were narrowing, changing color.

Desperate, Johnny beat against the wall of his prison. And Jonas cackled. His laughter was already transforming itself into an inhuman howling.

Speranza watched the boy as he slept. The moon was rising. She had half believed the Count's insane suggestion that the boy would now transform into a wolf . . . but he lay peacefully, his eyes closed, curled up on a woolen blanket.

Speranza watched the moon. She knew she would soon go to him. Since crossing the Austro-Hungarian border she had felt dread and desire in equal measure. They were moving into a thick forest. Bare trees, their branches weighed down with icicles, obscured the moon. The train rattled and sighed and seemed almost to breathe. She steadied herself and watched the trees go by. Soon, she thought, I will be free of these madmen. What then?

The boy stirred. He moaned. Beneath closed eyelids, his eyes moved feverishly. She touched his hand. Recoiled. The hand was burning. Burning! It must be a fever, she thought. Gingerly she touched his forehead. It was drenched with sweat. She shook him. He would not waken. "Johnny," she whispered, "Johnny."

He moaned.

"Johnny!" Why am I panicking? she thought. This dread is quite unreasonable . . . I must cool his brow.

She opened the door of the compartment. The servant girl who had looked after Johnny before was sleeping in the corridor. She awoke instantly. "I am sent . . . by the Count, *gnädiges Fräulein.*"

The Count. . . .

"Has he done something to the boy?" Thoughts of cruel scientific experiments . . . potions in the food . . . mesmerism . . . "Fetch some water. Quickly."

"*Jawohl, gnädiges Fräulein.*" The maid hurried down the

narrow walkway. Wind from an open window whipped at her and
left sprinkles of snow on her black dress. She was still wearing the
necklace of silver and amethysts.

A powerful odor was wafting into the corridor . . . the reek
of animal urine. She heard a trickling sound from within the
compartment. The poor child, she thought. He is wetting himself.
She went back in.

She looked at him in the moonlight. His nightshirt was stained.
The urine was running onto the floor of the compartment. His eyes
were darting back and forth beneath squeezed lids. His whole
body was slick with sweat. The flow of urine never stopped. She
held a handkerchief over her nose, but still the stench was
suffocating. Where was the maid? Could they not understand that
the boy was sick? She went out into the corridor once more. The
cold blasted her. The dread came again, teasing at her thoughts.
The maid, she thought, the maid. . . .

"At last!" she cried, seeing the girl come back. She was
clutching something in her arms . . . a small bottle and a
book . . . a Bible, Speranza saw. "I sent you to get water!"

"Holy water," the maid whispered. The terror in her face was
unmistakable.

"What's the matter with you?" said Speranza angrily. "Come
inside and help me with the child." She went back into the
compartment and put her arm under the boy's neck to lift him into
a sitting position. The boy was limp, lifeless-seeming. Piss
spurted all over Speranza's dress.

The maid stood at the door.

"Come and help me—"

The girl made the sign of the cross and looked down at the
floor. The train rocked and clattered. The girl held out the holy
water and the Bible—

"This is nonsense, purest nonsense!" Speranza cried. "Superstition and nonsense! This Count of yours has you all under the
diabolical influence of his mad illusions . . . you must calm
yourself, girl." How much did the servant understand?

"Ich habe Angst, gnädiges Fräulein."

"Stop chattering and—" She tried to seize the bottle from the
girl. It smashed against the seat and broke. Water mingled with
piss and began to seethe. An acrid steam rose up. Speranza
coughed. The maid screamed. Still the boy slept. "You can see

quite clearly that the boy is not a werewolf," Speranza said, trying to keep calm. "Stay with him. I'm going to fetch the Count. We'll settle this matter once and for all. Stay with the boy, do you understand?"

The girl had thrown herself against the wall and was sobbing passionately. "What's the matter with you?" Speranza said. "It's not going to kill you." The maid's hysteria grated on her ears. The burning odor—doubtless some bizarre chemical reaction between the urine and the holy water—seared her nostrils. She could endure it no longer. She stalked out into the corridor and slammed the door of the compartment.

In that moment Jonas leapt into the clearing, seized control of the body, forced open the child's tired eyes, which glowed like fire in the light of the moon.

And howled.

Speranza felt the dread again. It must be the wind, she thought, the desolate relentless wind. It howled down the hallway. The walls were damp, and snow glistened on the threadbare carpet.

She had to see him. She had to unmask his terrible deception, had to allay this dread . . . she made her way to the end of the corridor, stumbling as the train lurched. She opened the door.

The wind came, whistling, abrasive. She grasped a handhold. There was no one to help her step over the coupling mechanism, which groaned and clanked between the two cars. An animal's cry sounded above the pounding of the train and the clanging of the couplers. The forest stretched in every direction. They were moving downhill. She took a deep breath and skipped across, feeling frantically for a railing. The howling came again. So close . . . it almost seemed to be coming from the train itself and not the forest.

She peered into the Count's private car. Black drapes shrouded the window. "Let me in!" she cried, banging on the glass with her fists.

Abruptly the door opened. She fell into utter darkness.

She heard the door slam. She could see nothing. The air was close and foul. Even the clerestory windows had been covered up. "Count . . ." she whispered.

"You came."

His voice was changed. There was a rasp to it. She stood near the doorway. She could see nothing, nothing at all.

"Come closer, Speranza. Do not be afraid. The utter darkness does tend to impede the transformation a little. You see, I do have your interests at heart."

She hesitated. The stench filled her nostrils. Its fetor masked a more subtle odor, an odor that was strangely exciting. She backed against the door. The train's motion made her tingle. She was sweating. Still she saw nothing. But she could hear him breathing . . . breathing . . . breathing.

"You're driving the boy mad," she whispered. "Though it is true that I am being paid, I ought perhaps to dissociate myself from—"

"You did not come here to discuss business, Speranza. Am I wrong?"

The smell was seeping into her . . . she felt a retching at the back of her throat . . . and a stirring, a dark stirring beneath her petticoats . . . "No, Count—" she said softly, at last admitting her shameful desire to herself.

Something furry had reached up her skirts. It touched her thigh. It was searing hot. She whimpered. The hand stroked her, burned her . . . moved inexorably up toward her private parts . . . it caressed them now, and she cried out in pain, but there was pleasure behind the pain, and the warmth burst through her body as it shuddered, as it vibrated with the downhill movement of the train . . . "You must not . . . you ought not to . . ." she said . . . she felt something moist teasing at the lips of her vagina, and she felt her inner moisture mingling with sweat and saliva . . . I must resist him, she thought, I would be ruined . . . yet she made no move to escape, for the fire was racing in her nerves and veins. . . .

The hands roved, brutal now. Something lacerated her thighs . . . she moaned at the sharp pain . . . were they claws or hands? My imagination is running wild, she thought. The madness is infecting me. The cloth was tearing now. She felt hot blood spurting onto the other fluids. "No," she said, gently trying to tear herself away, "no, don't hurt me." The Count did not answer her with words but with a growl that resonated against her sexual organs. She tried to inch away, but the hands gripped her thighs tighter.

She could see nothing, nothing at all, but the railway car smelled of musk and mud and rotten leaves, the air was dank and clogged with the smells of rutting and animal piss . . . at last she managed to free herself. She groped along the wall . . . the wall was clammy, like an earthy embankment . . . her feet were sliding in damp soil. . . .

I'm dreaming! she thought. It's because of the darkness, I'm starting to imagine things—

Her hand touched something soft now. Curtains. I have to let in the light, she thought. She tugged at the velvet. A sliver of moonlight lanced the darkness and—

The Count's voice, barely human, "You should not have—not the light—I will change now—change—"

The curtain fell away and the moonlight streamed in across glittering fields of snow. . . .

The Count . . . his face . . . his nose had elongated into a snout. Even as she watched he was changing. Bristles sprouting on his cheeks. His teeth were lengthening, his mouth widening into the foaming jaws of an animal. The eyes . . . bright yellow now, slitty, implacable. His hands, already covered with hair, were shrinking into paws. With a snarl the Count fell down on all fours. His teeth were slick with drool. The stench intensified. Her gorge rose. She tasted vomit in the back of her throat. Then the wolf leapt.

She was thrown back. She fell down into the patch of moonlight. The beast was ripping away her dress now. It still desires me, she thought. The wolf's spit sprayed her face and ran down her neck. She tried to beat it back but it straddled her now, about to sink its teeth into her throat—

It touched the silver necklace—

And recoiled, howling! Speranza scrambled to her feet. The wolf watched her warily. Where its snout had touched the necklace, there was a burn mark . . . an impression of the silver links in the chain. The wolf whined and growled. There was a smell of charred fur. Her heart beat fast. The trickling drool scalded her neck, her exposed breasts.

She found the door, flung it open, ran, clambered across to the next car, entered. As she slammed the door shut, she heard an anguished howling over the cacophony of steam and iron.

* * *

For a long moment she stood. The howling died away, or was drowned in the clatter of the train. She stood, her arms crossed over the front of her tattered chemise, the chill air numbing the places where the wolf's touch had seared her.

She touched the silver necklace. It was cool to her fingers. She thought: Impossible, it's all impossible.

Could it have been done with conjurer's tricks? With pails of animal dung, with suggestive disguises, preying on a mind already primed to expect a supernatural metamorphosis? Moonlight streamed into the corridor. They were emerging from the forest now. There were mountains in the distance. In the middle distance was a church, enveloped in snow, its spire catching the cold light and softly glittering.

She thought of Johnny.

Whatever the Count was, he was trying to make Johnny into one too. Perhaps it was all some inhuman scientific experiment . . . or some kind of devil worship. Had Cornelius Quaid not spoken of mutilations and atrocities? The poor child!

I must steal him away, she thought. I cannot suffer him to remain here, succored by lunatics, a lamb amongst wolves!

Perhaps they had done something to him already. . . .

She opened the door of the compartment.

Wind gusted in her face. The window had been smashed. The floor, the seats, were blanketed in snow. "Where is he?" she said.

She could see only the young maidservant. She was lying on one of the seats, covered in a blanket, staring oddly ahead.

"Where is the boy?" Speranza said.

The maid did not answer.

"Where is he? He was entrusted to your care!"

Still there was no response.

"I have had enough of these enigmas!" Speranza said. Anger and frustration deluged her. She slapped the servant's face.

The young girl's head rolled onto the floor. The train's movement sent it thudding, back and forth, back and forth, between the two seats.

Slowly the blanket slid away. Beneath it was a tangle of body parts. And amongst them, wrapped up in the bloody entrails like a newborn baby entwined in his own umbilical cord, was a small boy, naked, clutching something that looked like a human heart, disconsolately sobbing.

"Johnny!" She was too shocked to feel revulsion at first.

Slowly the boy's cries ceased. Slowly he lifted his head up from the mass of blood and human tissue. His mouth, his cheeks, were smeared with blood, black in the silver moonlight. His hair was matted with it. He said, "I tried to stop Jonas from coming. I tried, Speranza. Oh, I didn't want you to know, I threw most of her out of the window, but I didn't have enough time . . . Oh, Speranza, it's hopeless, I'm never going to be like other humans."

Speranza remembered what the Count von Bächl-Wölfing had said to her also: "Therefore, Speranza, I long for hope." She knew she could not abandon the boy now. Even though he had killed. It was a sickness, a terrible sickness. She swallowed her dread and allowed him to come to her arms. "Oh, Johnny, you must have hope!" she cried out.

"Yes, I must, mustn't I?" said the child. And he wept bitterly, as though the world were ending, the tears mingling with coagulating blood.

9
Deadwood
full moon

THE BACK OF THE SALOON OPENED UP INTO AN INNER COURTYARD. IT was there that Cordwainer Claggart retired to count his money and to contemplate the night. He smiled when he saw that the Widow Bryant was already there, heedless of the chill air. The wind was damp and bitter and the snow heaped high against the walls. It was dirty snow, reeking of liquor and vomit.

She was watching the moon that hung, bloated and deathly white, over the hills. She's only pretending not to see me, Claggart thought. Damned if she ain't already shopping for another man. She was right plain, but she had painted her face a little, and she had already taken off her veil.

He observed from the shadow of the doorway for some moments, putting off his move, imagining himself a lone wolf, sniffing out his prey, circling, toying. At length it was she who gave the signal, a slight tilt of the head. Claggart's spirits lifted. I was right—she must be desperate! he thought, and wondered about what kind of a man her dead husband used to be. Neglected her, that was obvious. Lived and breathed gold. Beat her up sometimes. Probably thought of it as warming up the body for the night. Well, there was no harm in beating your wife now and then. Claggart sidled up to her, pondering which opening to pick from his ample repertoire. His finger was still bleeding some but the cold made it numb.

Before he had a chance to speak, though, she said, "You've been eyeing me all evening, mister. I ain't got looks to speak of, so you must be after the money. With my husband barely buried! Shame on you, Mr. Claggart."

Claggart felt a momentary panic. And yet, he thought, she must have been interested enough to find out my name from someone. "You sure do have spirit, ma'am," he ventured.

"That I do," said Sally Bryant.

"I was merely hoping to . . . offer you a moment of . . . consolidation . . . in your bereavement," he said. He shivered. The snow had almost stopped completely, but the wind was bitter cold.

She smiled suddenly. "Consolidation!" she said. "Do you say them wrong words on purpose?"

Claggart frowned. "I never went to no school. Ran away from home when I was seven years old. I just couldn't take it, ma'am. Any long words I learned I heard from my paw, when he wasn't taking a hickory to my bee-hind." That part, at least, was true, though Claggart had told the tale of his sad childhood so frequently that he now thought of it as just another story. Those yarns were like a dog-eared deck of cards, and every time he shuffled them, he could deal himself a brand new past. "My paw was a . . . preacher, I guess you could call it. That's what *he* called it. There ain't nothing like preachin' for reachin' deep into folks' pockets—not cards, not snake oil, not runnin' rifles to the Injuns. I know 'cause I've tried it all. Paw was hard on us, so I ran away from home." That part was true too, although Claggart did not tell the widow that he had burned down his father's house and stolen his second-best horse, nor that he had tried for a while to eke out a living in Abilene by selling, for four bits an evening, the favors of his ten-year-old sister. Doubtless the widow had already guessed that his past was less than honorable; but he did not think she would be overly choosy. After all, the goods she had to offer were less then store-boughten. Nevertheless, he thought he'd better hint at respectability, so he went on, "Made my first fortune in gold, but my pardner took off to California with all my profits. Then I dabbled in railway shares, ma'am, but they cheated me and didn't build the railway where they told me they was going to. So I become a scientist, Widder Bryant, and turns to helping the sick with my world-shakin' discovery." He brandished a phial of the Floccinaucinihilipilificator.

"You're a scoundrel," said Widow Bryant. "I don't believe a word." But she smiled a little, and Cordwainer Claggart suspected he had already won.

In the closet of a room that the innkeeper allowed her to occupy during her stint performing at the saloon, Amelia Nachtigall divested herself of her wig, her corsets, and her German accent.

And, of course, her name, for she was really Verna Smith from Council Bluffs, and her knowledge of German was gleaned entirely from immigrants and guidebooks.

There were no windows in the room. She stared at herself in the mirror by the light of a candle. Carefully she put on a dressing gown which did little to conceal the amplitude of her bosom. It was a tattered old thing she had bought secondhand from one of the Chinamen who lived at the other end of Deadwood, and clearly designed for one of those small-framed oriental women, although the vendor had told her that its former owner had been a veritable giantess.

The kerosene lantern, flickering, sooty, seemed to soften the lines on her face. Verna Smith sighed and wondered whether she should apply more powder. Why bother? she thought. It's only the old snake-oil merchant, a skinflint if ever there was one. Perhaps I'll be able to sneak something out of his purse. If I get him excited enough.

She placed a fresh candle in a ceramic holder and lit it from the kerosene flame. Then she gave her dressing gown a perfunctory smoothing-out, turned out the lantern, and slipped out into the cold creaky corridor.

Vishnevsky had come back downstairs determined to solicit more information from the mysterious Grumiaux. He found the train-man still at the same table, deep in conversation with the lieutenant and scout. Several bottles of the vile liquors these people favored stood open on the table. The room was shadowy and full of smoke, but there was no more singing. The men talked in low voices. He stood awhile, grasping at fragments of conversations, not quite understanding them. They spoke of gold and women and cards and liquor and occasionally of Indians.

Vishnevsky was still concerned about his cousin. He had barely chained Natasha up in time! What if something had gone wrong? Had he drawn the curtains, and was the material of which they were made dark enough, opaque enough, to shield Natasha from the light of the moon? If she were to become only partially transformed, would she nevertheless become strong enough to—

"Ah, Monsieur Vishnevsky," Grumiaux said in French, noticing him at last and motioning him to join them. "You have been having rather an exciting time here in Deadwood, is it not? I do hope the remainder of your stay will be a little less . . . interesting." He gestured to the bartender. "Ebenezer, a drink for our friend."

Vishnevsky did not really want another drink; but it was cold here despite the stove and the roaring fire. He could hear the mountain wind outside, and through the window he could see that the snow, which had abated earlier, was flurrying down again. He took the proffered drink and downed it quickly.

"We were just discussing the Fremont, Elkhorn and Missouri Valley Railroad," Grumiaux said, "a matter, I think, of not inconsiderable interest to you."

"My employer, le Comte von Bächl-Wölfing," said Vishnevsky cagily, "is not averse to my gathering . . . information. He intends to pay well for it, and I carry a letter of credit from Wells Fargo—"

Grumiaux laughed. "You've seen, I think, how well paper money is regarded in this town!"

Zeke Sullivan said, "What I don't understand is why a man like your Count, or whatever he is, wants to do business in the territory."

Switching to English, Vishnevsky said, "Sometimes is difficult for me to understand Count's motives."

"But I heard a rumor," Grumiaux said, "that your Count isn't just going to be sitting in Vienna getting rich on the profits from the railroad . . . that he intends to come here personally—with hundreds of retainers—that he's planning to buy out the entire town of Deadwood—Chinatown and all."

"Where did you hear such an idea?" Vishnevsky said, startled. "It is idle rumor." But dangerously close to the truth, he thought uncomfortably. Perhaps Grumiaux was merely speculating on the chance that Vishnevsky would blurt out some of the real facts. "I can tell you, for certain my employer has no interest in Deadwood."

That much was true, and the others seemed convinced.

"But he does have an interest in the Fremont, Elkhorn and Missouri Valley Railroad," said Grumiaux. "You cannot deny that, surely, Valentin Nikolaievich. I've heard your Count wants to meddle in the actual routing of the railway. Should he not leave such things to the experts?" And he looked him in the eye, challenging him.

"I do not pry into Count's affairs," Vishnevsky said, "I only do what I'm told."

"I reckon you ought to take the man surveying with you, Claude," Zeke said. "Give him the feel of the place."

"Why not?" said Grumiaux. "We are, after all, on the same side, are we not?" He looked straight at Vishnevsky, his face a mask of ingenuousness. "Will you do me the honor of making a small trip with me tomorrow? You can watch our men at work. It will be very dull, I'm afraid—a snowplowing expedition. Some say it's an impressive sight, that huge plow barrelling through the snow, being pushed by five, six, as many as a dozen locomotives, and the snow flying on either side."

"That would indeed be an honor," Vishnevsky said, affecting the same ingenuousness, as they each downed another glass of foul whiskey to seal the bargain.

The lieutenant had been sitting distractedly, only half listening to them. But he sat up abruptly and said, "Listen! It's that blamed wolf again—"

"A wolf? In the middle of town?" Grumiaux said. "Surely not."

Vishnevsky became alert. He listened. Were there any unusual sounds coming from upstairs? He listened for the telltale growl, the keening, the unearthly howling. Nothing. Surely he would have been the first to notice. Could Natasha have—

"Scott," Zeke was saying urgently to his friend, "you have been seeing some mighty strange things, but . . . there ain't no wolves in Deadwood."

"I know I heard something!" Scott Harper said.

Vishnevsky listened. There were voices all around him: rough voices, men playing cards, swearing. Then he heard something else . . . a high-pitched howl . . . far away, almost blending with the keening of the wind. Surely it could not be Natasha . . . even if she had broken free of her chains, even if she had gone through the entire metamorphosis . . . how could she have gone outside unnoticed? Was there a balcony from which she could have reached the roof and thence leaped down? Vishnevsky's mind raced. He could not remember. He had to find out.

"Tarnation . . . I do hear wolves," Zeke said.

Someone from another table said, "They feel the warmth of the the town. They got nothing to feed on out there. I reckon them wolves is hungry."

Grumiaux said, "I suppose we should go search for it—"

"No!" Vishnevsky blurted out.

It seemed as though everyone in the saloon stopped talking and was staring at him. "I only mean . . ." he said lamely, "I only mean that it is dangerous. We should not risk—"

One of the card players said, "Sounds like it's coming from the Chinee end of town. I ain't risking my neck for no heathens."

Grumiaux got up. "I will go," he said. "Zeke, come with me."

A few others rose too. In a moment it seemed as if they were all getting ready, putting on their greatcoats, reaching for their Smith and Wessons. What if it *were* Natasha? Their guns would be useless against her. How could he tell them that? They were already trooping out, and gusts of snow were billowing into the room. He shivered.

Zeke said, "You ain't coming . . . of course not. A foreign gentleman like you. But Scott, mayhap you should stay behind and look after him . . . and the lady upstairs."

The lieutenant nodded. It seemed to Vishnevsky that the young man was not reluctant to remain behind. Though he strove to mask it, there was fear in his eyes . . . more fear than a mere wild animal should evince in a trained soldier, Vishnevsky thought. He wondered whether Harper had somehow guessed the truth . . . but no, how could he have? I am allowing these people to frighten me too much, he thought. There is nothing superhuman about these frontiersmen.

The howling came again, closer now. It was a wolf; he was sure of that. But it's cry is strangely weak, he thought. Natasha's howling is a huntress's war cry, angry and aggressive. Perhaps it is a true wolf . . . a mere dumb animal . . . motivated only by hunger and the need for warmth . . . a creature without a soul. This land is full of true wolves, Vishnevsky reflected, and felt a little better. But he was still uneasy.

Horses neighed. Boots trampled the boardwalk outside; a few shots rang out. Men shouted and the wind squalled.

He sat back down and took another slug of whiskey. There was no one left in the room but Scott and the bartender.

He and the lieutenant looked at each other. Scott Harper smiled at him, a trusting, easygoing smile. Vishnevsky looked away. "If you will excuse me for a moment," he said, "I had better see that my cousin is safely bedded. She is very much afraid of wolves," he added.

And he got up from the table and started up the stairs.

Verna Smith knocked gingerly on the door. When there was no answer, she opened it and stepped inside.

It was dark, so terribly dark. "I'm here," she said softly, holding up her candle. There was a four-poster bed at the other end of the room. The drapes of the bed were drawn tight, as were the window curtains. That Cordwainer Claggart always had a flair for the mysterious.

The first thing she noticed was the smell . . . like the stench of a woman's monthly bleeding, but much more powerful. She almost choked on it. Why, she thought, there's been another woman in this room. A woman shameless enough to let a man take his pleasure while she was . . . what kind of a harlot could sink so low?

"I know you're in that bed, Claggart," she said, "you two-timing bastard."

There was a dressing table beside the bed. She set the candle down on it. Beside it was a washbasin and a crystal carafe full of water. There was a mirror, a hairbrush, a key, and two bullets . . . bullets that glinted oddly in the candlelight. She realized they must be made of silver.

"You going to come charging out of that bed now, lusting like a wild animal?" she said, laughing.

Something moved behind those drapes. But no one spoke.

"Come on," she said. "You play too many games. One of these days . . ."

No answer.

"Maybe you want me to take off all my clothes?" she said, teasing him, allowing herself a lascivious shudder at the thought.

A man even modestly well brought up wouldn't dream of making a lady take off all her clothes. Let alone removing all his own. But Verna knew all about making love without clothes on. A Comanche had taught her. Injuns were shameless and were always rutting like animals. She had heard that niggers made love naked too. Animals! There are some disadvantages in being civilized folks, she thought, sighing.

A low moan came from the bed.

"I knew that would get you to answer me," she said.

She took the candle in one hand and yanked the curtain aside with the other. And gasped.

The smell was stronger than ever. There was a woman chained to the bedposts. She was naked. Though the room was chilly the woman was drenched in sweat. She moaned again and stared up at Verna Smith with slitty eyes. "Help . . ." she said, "please . . . the key. . . ." Were they words or were they the growls of a hungry animal? She could barely understand.

"Lord, did Claggart do this to you?"

"Please, the key. . . ." In the near total darkness the woman's eyes glittered like those of a nocturnal animal. "I haven't much time . . . I'm burning up. . . ." She spoke in a strange European accent that Verna could not quite place. Why had she been chained up? Foreigners did such incomprehensible things sometimes. And what was that around her face . . . a fur shawl? No, the fur seemed stuck to her sweaty cheeks. . . .

"Free me!" Not words but an animal barking.

"You want me to fetch some water?" Verna glanced at the washbasin.

"No . . . the key . . . free me!"

"Of course, of course." Trembling, she fumbled for the key on the dresser. Lord, the woman's wrists were scored where the chains had chafed them. Verna undid the fetters and as she did so the woman gripped her wrists so tightly that Verna cried out. The stench assaulted her nostrils . . . behind the odor of a menstruating woman there was another, even fouler smell . . . why, Verna thought, it's dog piss, she smells of dog piss. . . .

The woman moaned . . . she drew Verna to her, grasping her by the shoulders, ripping the fabric of her dressing gown. "The heat, the heat," the woman cried. "Please help me, please . . . hold me, touch me . . . the pain. . . ."

To her astonishment, Verna realized that this woman was demanding carnal knowledge of her. And despite the overpowering stench, there was something irresistibly erotic about her. She shuddered, she shivered, her arms, her breasts slick with perspiration. And always those eyes burned. Verna could not look away. Roughly the woman pulled her onto the bed. The dressing gown was in shreds and the fingernails drew blood now, and Verna cried out . . . again the woman whispered, "The heat, the heat, you must draw the curtains and open the windows . . . help me, help me, I am burning. . . ."

"Are you ill? Should I go wake up the doctor?"

"The heat. . . ."

Verna said, "Let go of me and I'll let in some fresh air." But the woman gripped her tighter, tighter, pushing her down onto the satin sheets. The chain still lay on the bed. It dug into Verna's back, and she rolled aside and the chain touched the foreign woman's breasts . . . suddenly the woman let go, screaming, and Verna saw a deep gash across her breasts, she saw the blood seething . . . the woman was writhing now, thick sputum dribbling from her lips . . . clearly she was ill, maddened by her pain.

Verna extricated herself and backed away, reaching behind her for the window drapes. She drew the curtains and unfastened the casement. Then she turned and looked down into the courtyard below. Cordwainer Claggart was there . . . paying court to that widow! Why, the impudence of that man! She was so furious that for a few seconds she did not notice the bitter cold.

Moonlight streamed into the room. The wind whistled and the cold battered her half-naked body. Snowflakes settled on her hair and her eyelashes. She turned around and spoke to the sick woman: "There, there, you must go back to bed now, you must try to get some rest."

In the distance, she heard gunshots. And the howl of an animal—perhaps a wolf.

The odor had grown even more powerful. She couldn't breathe. It was definitely dog piss mingled with the stench of woman's blood . . . from far away, on the Chinee side of town, maybe, came the howl of the wolf once more. And then came an answer to that howling—

It tore out of the throat of the madwoman. She was howling too, howling like a wild dog, and as she howled she was changing, her nose jutting out into a snout, her mouth widening into a slavering maw, her teeth glistening with drool. . . .

Verna had no time to scream as the beast leaped at her. She saw the door fling open and the tall Russian stand in the doorway and she heard him shout out something in his native tongue. She tried to warn him to stay away, but she knew it was already too late. . . .

The widow and the snake-oil merchant held hands and looked into each other's eyes. Claggart was thinking, I do feel some kind of love for her, damn it! and he bent down to kiss her. Far away, an animal howled, and another answered from somewhere inside the building.

He heard something thud into the snow behind him.

Sally Bryant's eyes opened wide. Suddenly he realized that her expression was one of terror, not desire. There was something wet dripping down his forehead . . . down his nose . . . his lips tasted blood. She backed away from him, pointing hysterically. She was trying to scream but could not.

He twisted around and saw what had fallen from the window—

And took her in his arms, letting her bury her face in his greatcoat, because what he had seen wasn't a fit thing for a lady to look at—

It was a human head.

He held the widow hard in his arms. And looked up, and saw the torso of a naked woman flailing at the window. Blood was gushing from the stump of her neck. That was what had spattered his face. He stared at the head in the snow. It was, he realized, that of the self-styled German opera singer. The face stared back at him with an expression of stark terror. From the upstairs room came the howling of a wild beast—a wolf! It was damn fortunate he had not kept his date with the luckless Miss Nachtigall—or Miss Smith, or Miss Trestail, or whatever she was calling herself that week. I avoided a monster, he thought, and found me a gold mine.

Blood seeped into the snow, a delicate spiderweb pattern around the severed neck. The singer's lips were parted. It's just as well, he thought, we ain't a-cursed with that cheap whore's yowling no more.

Claggart had seen savage mutilations before. He had seen the remnants of an Indian massacre in Minnesota. His stomach did not churn at the sight of Amelia Nachtigall's head, nor did he flinch from the torso in the window above. He turned his attention to the woman who trembled in his arms. "I love you," he said soothingly, as a man might comfort a puppy. "I surely do."

Scott heard the Russian stumbling around upstairs. I'd better try and help him, he thought.

The stairs were steep and the corridor dingy. Rips in the wallpaper revealed previous layers, garish once, but smothered in dust now. A foul stench filled the air . . . the stink of a bitch in heat . . . and the reek of urine. Scott saw the Russian standing in an open doorway. He was looking inside, saying something in his native language. The tone was such as one might use to calm a wild animal. Scott crept up beside him.

"No!" Vishnevsky said, in an anguished whisper. "You must let me deal with her, only me, alone."

Scott looked into the chamber, past the Russian's hulking frame. It was awash with moonlight. The headless body of a naked woman was propped up against the windowsill. The casement was open, and the corpse was already covered with fine, powdery snow. The back and buttocks were scored with scratches. Smears of coagulating blood gleamed in the moonlight like a tacky lacquer. The smell was even stronger here. But there was no fetor of decay. It was too cold for that to set in yet.

Scott didn't know who she was. Maybe one of the loose women who plied their trade outside on the boardwalk. Surely it was not Natalia Petrovna. A well-born lady like that'd have no business taking off her clothes.

He drew his Colt.

The Russian did not move, but went on speaking softly.

"Who are you talking to?" Scott said. "Is it your cousin? Is she hiding somewhere? Under the bed? Is she in danger?" He was about to say more when he heard the growl.

Something moved. From beneath the bedspread. Panicking, Scott shot at it. A flurry of goose feathers. Another growl. From the closet. From behind the dresser. Shadows, shadows where the moonbeams did not fall.

"Do not shoot her!" Vishnevsky stepped into the room and Scott followed, their boots making the floorboards creak. "I beg you. She is not always beast." He tiptoed to the dresser and groped about for something. When he turned around again, Scott saw what he was holding—a pair of bullets.

Something about those bullets, the way they glinted. . . .

"Silver," Scott said.

"Natasha," said the Russian, loading his gun. Scott saw that there were tears in his eyes, that his expression was one of unbearable grief, as though at the death of someone close to him. . . .

The wolf came bounding from behind the bed. He had no time to react. Vishnevsky fired once, wildly, cursing in Russian. The wolf leaped upon him as though in an embrace. The gun clattered to the floor, slid toward the doorway. Scott fired. No more bullets. He fell to his knees and groped for the Russian's pistol. Where was the wolf? He found the gun. He froze, listening. The sound of panting . . . where was it coming from?

A thud. He whipped around. No. It was only the headless corpse, shifting, hitting the floorboards. Clouds and snow obscured the moon and it became suddenly darker. The panting went on. Somewhere in the room.

Or was it the Russian sobbing quietly to himself?

"Sir," Scott said quietly, "that dead woman ain't your cousin,

I know it. She must be hiding somewhere. She ain't dead, I promise you."

"Give me back the gun . . . is better if is done by . . . one who loves her. . . ."

"You're distracted, sir, begging your pardon. It's best I handle any shooting. There being only one bullet left and all. And that blamed animal fixin' to kill us. Try to calm yourself." He spoke as much for himself as for the foreigner.

More sounds! No. Gunshots on the street outside. They'd gone looking for a wild animal . . . but it had been lurking inside the whole blamed time.

Stay completely still. Don't move. Listen.

And then . . . almost as if it had materialized out of the shadows . . . it was there, trampling the floorboards, streaking across to the door, running into the corridor. . . .

"Please . . . let me . . . " said the Russian weakly. "Only I can take the life of Natalia Petrovna."

He's a madman! Scott thought. He's hunting the woman, not the wolf.

Scott saw her face in his mind's eye for a moment, and remembered her smiling at him in the graveyard against the setting sun. He couldn't let the Russian have his gun back or he'd kill her. "Don't talk," he said. And slipped out into the corridor.

He looked around. No sign of the wolf.

A single candle burned on a bookcase on the landing. Shadows danced dimly on the walls. Scott readied the revolver and inched along, his free hand skimming the cracked, waxy wallpaper.

Movement! Silvery fur, hard yellow eyes in the circle of candlelight. Paws scraping the wallpaper . . . the candle rolling onto the floor, a frayed rug bursting into flame. . . .

"Water! Someone fetch water!" Scott shouted. Flames leapt up. Heat blasted Scott's face, his hands. He was sweating all over the gun. And behind the flames . . . the wolf.

He saw it clearly for the first time, framed by the doorway. Its fur glistened in the firelight. Its eyes glowed. He gazed into the wolf's eyes . . . and he thought, I know those eyes, they're like the eyes of a woman, a woman I've known, a woman I could love—

The Russian stood beside the wolf. His arms were upraised in a gesture of pleading. The wolf ignored him completely, its eyes fixed only on Scott's. There was smoke now, curling, twisting, muting the flickering firelight, and through the smoke the wolf's eyes shone. Scott could hardly breathe.

"Get water—in the room, beside the bed—" he choked.

Vishnevsky was still speaking to the wolf. The wolf growled and was about to spring. Scott's shouts seemed to penetrate his babbling. He snapped to and hurried inside.

The wolf turned back to Scott, and Scott fired—

A thin line of blood along the wolf's left cheek. Only grazed it! Scott thought. A howl escaped its throat, a sound curiously human . . . and then the creature dashed back into the room as Vishnevsky came back out, wielding the washbasin in his arms.

The Russian emptied the basin onto the rug and scurried back into the room. The flame smoldered and was spent. Someone was tramping up the stairs, carrying a lamp; he turned and saw that it was Ebenezer. He had a pail of water.

"Fire's out," Scott said. He took a few deep breaths. "Got a gun?"

Ebenezer set down the pail and pulled a derringer from his waistcoat pocket. "I don't know how much use this'd be, but—"

"Come on with me. There's a wolf in there with the Russian. He's gone plumb crazy, he's talking to the wolf in Russian. There's a dead woman, too. It ain't pretty."

Scott and the bald bartender went inside. Ebenezer held up the lamp. The curtains had been drawn, shutting out what was left of the moonlight. The drapes around the bed, too, had been drawn shut. Only the faintest trace of those foul odors lingered in the air.

Vishnevsky stood by the window. The headless corpse lay at his feet, supine, in a pool of blood.

"Amelia!" Ebenezer said. "Oh, no." He looked blankly at the body, not quite understanding.

Scott felt a moment of relief because it was not the body of the Russian lady . . . but guilt overcame that relief, and he stared at the floor, not wanting to meet anyone's gaze.

"Wolf is gone," said Vishnevsky. "He jumped out of window."

"Funny," said Scott. "I didn't hear no crash."

Then came another voice from behind the bed-curtains: "He is right, Lieutenant Harper. I saw it with my own eyes—a terrible sight. A huge creature, lumbering after me . . . terrible, terrible."

A white hand, slender-fingered, parted the curtains a little, and Scott saw Natalia Petrovna reclining. She wore a silk dressing gown, and she had wrapped a scarf demurely about her face, hiding her mouth and her cheeks. But the eyes were unmistakable. "Thank the Lord you're still alive, ma'am. I was afraid something terrible had happened to you, and I'd hate that more than anything in the world."

"How gallant you are, Lieutenant!" She smiled with her eyes, but the scarf remained tightly wrapped about the lower part of her face. "You hardly know me, and already you are breaking my heart."

"Where were you hiding?" he said. He wanted to move closer to her, to comfort her, put his arms around her perhaps. But he felt awkward because he knew that he desired her.

"I hid behind . . . behind some drapes. Oh, I was so frightened. I did not dare even scream. You saved me from that monstrous creature."

"But . . . I never saw you at all, ma'am. You must not have even breathed."

"Sometimes I am almost like an animal myself, blending with the darkness."

"Don't be afraid, Natalia Petrovna. Tomorrow Mr. Grumiaux has invited us on a tour of his railroad. It sure would be an honor, ma'am, if you would allow me the pleasure of escortin' you."

"*Vous êtes trop gentil, cher monsieur.*" She inclined her head to him. Then she looked across at her cousin and spoke to him in Russian, harsh words whose meaning Scott could only guess at. And her eyes burned with anger so intense that he could scarcely believe she was the same person.

Vishnevsky mumbled something back, an abject apology.

Scott was about to say something when they heard voices from below. The huntsmen had returned. He could hear Zeke's voice, shouting: "Blew the bastard to smithereens! We saved the ears and the tail. . . ."

Ebenezer said, "Well, it seems the beast won't be troubling us folks no more."

"Reckon it won't," said Scott .

But he noticed that Vishnevsky did not concur, and that, as he spoke to his beautiful cousin, there was beneath his obsequious manner a hint of resentment, even hate.

10
Vienna
full moon

SPERANZA DID NOT SLEEP AT ALL THAT NIGHT. SHE HELD THE CHILD firmly to her bosom, and allowed him to sob until he was quite spent. No one came to remove the mangled remains of the servant. Little Johnny trembled in her arms, and behind the clatter of the train and the wind whistling through the broken windowpane she could hear a faint and plaintive howling from von Bächl-Wölfing's private car. She dared not close her eyes; no, she told herself, I cannot, not until I am sure that the moon has set behind those snowy mountains.

It was cold, unconscionably cold; but a feverish heat arose from the boy's body, and now and then he seemed different, his arms dangling at a straight angle, his nose oddly distended, his cheeks covered with silvery down. Each time she thought he had somehow transformed himself she would look away, her heart pounding; but when she looked back he was always a little child again. And she thought: I am mad, I am imagining everything. But however hard she concentrated on wishing it away, the mutilated body on the opposite seat would not disappear, and after some hours it had begun to exude a dank odor of putrescence. Speranza turned her face away from the body and resolutely faced the shattered window, letting the fresh chill wind mask the faint stench of decay.

"There are no monsters," she whispered to herself over and over. "Only bad dreams."

At dawn she drifted into sleep. And dreamed.

There was a forest. She ran among thick trees. She wore no corsets, no confining garments. Her hair was long and free to fly in the hot wind. She was naked but she felt no guilt because she was clothed in darkness. The air reeked of a woman's menses. Her feet were bare. They trod the soft earth. Moist leaves clung to her soles. Twigs lacerated her arms, her thighs, but the pain was a joyous pain, like the pangs of a lascivious passion. Worms crawled along her toes and tickled them. She laughed and her laughter became an animal's howling.

A brief memory surfaced: she was helping young Michael Bridgewater with his Euripides one day, only to come across passages which she could not in all decency translate . . . at least not into English, for in that language things that could be made to sound elevated in Italian or French were rendered intolerably crude. It was this enforced crudity, she had reflected at the time, that gave the English their preoccupation with prurience. And then they had lowered young Michael into the ground and it seemed as though it had not stopped snowing, as though she'd never escape the snow, not even by fleeing across half of Europe. . . .

Here there was no snow.

No snow at all. There was moisture that dripped from the branches overhead, that oozed out of the earth, that was wrung out of the very air. The ground was slippery. She slid, glided almost, cried out with childish delight as the very earth seemed to carry her along.

Light broke over leaves streaked with black and silver. Moonlight over a stream. She sat at the edge, bathing her feet. The water warm, like fresh blood . . . the ground trembling a little, with the regularity of a heartbeat . . . and she heard the cry of a wolf, distant, mournful. The sound was both repulsive and somehow alluring. She knew it might well be a love song, if she could but understand its language. . . .

And in the dream she knew, as by a profound inspiration, that the howling came from the waters' source. The beast was waiting for her upstream. And that she was drawn to the beast as the beast was drawn to her. . . .

She heard horses' hooves on cobblestones. She opened her eyes. The boy was tugging at her hand: "Speranza, Speranza, do wake up! You've slept ever so long."

She sat up. They were in an open carriage. The sky was

overcast. It was hardly snowing at all, only a few flakes now and then. Johnny Kindred was sitting beside her; someone had dressed him. He smiled shyly at her.

"Are we in Vienna then?" she said.

"Yes, Speranza. Some of the Count's men lifted you and put you on this carriage with me. They're very strong."

She looked around. They had swathed her in several layers of blankets; clearly they had felt too embarrassed to dress her. The street was narrow, the snow piled into heaps every few yards. There were shops on either side. The signs were in German. There was a faint fragrance of coffee and nutmeg in the air, and when they turned a corner she saw a little coffeehouse with a turtle emblem hanging in the window and a sign that read *"Schildfröte."*

She looked at the boy. There was no trace of blood on his face, and his hair had been perfectly combed. He smiled again. "There was quite a to-do, last night, wasn't there?" he said. "Someone told me that one of the servants had . . . fallen frightfully ill, and there was such a fuss. No wonder you're so tired yourself, Speranza. Oh, you slept and slept and slept. I missed you. Was it awful, seeing her, I mean . . . when she . . ."

"Of course." Could he have forgotten all that had happened? Did I imagine the boy crawling out of the innards of the bloody corpse . . . the Count's bizarre metamorphosis in the midst of his romantic attentions? she thought wildly. Already her memories were becoming blurred, and the dream, with the stream and the forest and the distant wolf, seemed so much more vivid. She asked him, "And why would I be exhausted, Johnny? I was not sick myself."

"You really are very funny, Speranza. Why, you sat up with the sick maid all night long. That's what Sigmund told me."

"Sigmund?"

The young man who had been sitting beside the driver turned around and climbed over into the carriage. He was dark-haired, bearded, and had a serious demeanor. "If you will excuse my forwardness, *gnädiges Fräulein:* my name is Freud, and I am a pupil of Dr. Szymanowski's. I shall be receiving my medical degree next March. You do me great honor to allow me the privilege of escorting you to the professor."

Speranza was a little unnerved by the gentleman, who, though he gazed at her with great intensity, seemed at the same time somehow distracted.

"I understand, Fräulein Martinique, that you were very self-sacrificing indeed in your ministrations to the servant girl; indeed, your labors seem to have rendered you prostrate with exhaustion. I shall have to obtain for you a prescription for some cocaine; it is a wondrous new substance, a panacea indeed for the weary mind. Indeed, I have a phial of it in my waistcoat pocket, should you have need of urgent revival."

"One hopes it will be a little more efficacious than fresh air . . . that was the only remedy one ever encountered in England, Monsieur Freud," said Speranza.

"It is very sad that the maid . . . passed away. She has no family, alas, so the Count has gone to make all the arrangements himself; he is so solicitous of the servants; he really does seem to have the common touch." Speranza could only sit in bewilderment, trying to absorb a version of the events so utterly different from that which she remembered.

"Sigmund has been very nice to me all morning. He helped me put on my clothes. He asked me about my nightmare." Speranza had not seen Johnny so loquacious the whole trip. It pleased her that this student seemed to have drawn him out of his shell.

"Nightmare?" Speranza said.

"Oh, you remember. There were wolves in the nightmare. Prowling through the train, attacking the passengers. It was very frightening. Also there was a woman calling to me in a dark forest from the banks of a river of blood. . . ."

She was silent for a while, pulling the blankets tighter around herself. The nightmare the boy described seemed familiar, almost as though she had shared the same dream. It had to be some kind of exhaustion, gnawing away her memories and substituting insane visions.

They turned a corner. An ornate sign read "Spiegelgasse." It was little more than an alley. On their right, there was a little private park, fenced in, with a wrought-iron gate in a design of singing angels. The ground was blanketed with white, but in the center of the park, emerging from the snowy embankments, stood a well, and in front of it a statue of the Madonna. At least it seemed like a Madonna to Speranza, except that in her bosom she clasped not the Christ child but a wolf cub who sucked at her bare breast.

"That statue is—" she began.

"Fascinating, isn't it?" said Freud. "They say that her face is an uncanny likeness of the late Gräfin von Bächl-Wölfing—the Countess, that is—who was murdered years ago in a particularly bloody manner. The sculpture is one of those avant-grade things . . . done by a pupil of Arturo Marano's . . . apparently a reversal on the famous statue of Romulus and Remus, founders of Rome, being suckled by a she-wolf. Faintly blasphemous, some would call it. But we are in Vienna, and to be decadent is, shall we say, de rigueur."

On the left, twin staircases led up to a baroque façade. There was a long line of carriages along the side of the street. Some were the ordinary station carriages; others were private, and blazoned with various emblems and insignia. One was an imported American Concord, and it was this one that bore the von Bächl-Wölfing arms. People were dismounting from their carriages and being escorted up the steps by footmen. The air was cloudy with horses' breath and rank with their manure; two brawny lads in uniform were sweeping dung off the snowy pavement, chattering to each other in some Slavic dialect.

"This is the residence of Dr. Szymanowski?" Speranza asked.

"Oh, no!" Johnny piped up. "This is the town house of that Count, the one who frightens me so."

"There is nothing to be afraid of. He is a very generous man."

For a moment Speranza panicked, thinking that the boy would once more attempt to baptize the Count's dwelling with urine. But there was no invasion from the mysterious Jonas, and the boy was nothing if not angelic—almost alarmingly so, Speranza thought.

"Dr. Szymanowski comes from a little town in Poland—Oswieçim—Auschwitz, we call it in German—and the Count has graciously allowed him the use of an apartment in the town house, along with some basement space for his experiments. He's a harmless old fool, the doctor. He is an expert, you know, in the . . . ah . . . in the mating patterns of wolves. Something of a delicate subject—perhaps a lady such as yourself—"

"Oh, please, Monsieur Freud! I am so tried of gallantries, of constant references to my refined sensibilities!"

Freud smiled a little. "It is strange, is it not? I have barely made your acquaintance, yet you are already confiding in me your most repressed desires . . . I seem to bring that out in people."

They did not speak for a while. Speranza watched as the Count's guests ascended the steps. There was a turbaned gentleman now, whose silken garments, stitched with jewels, almost blinded her with their colors: turquoise, shocking pink, lemon, and pea-green. There was a ragged, stooped old woman who looked just like one of those operatic Gipsy fortune-tellers. There were elegantly dressed men, in top hats and opera cloaks, and there were those whose origins seemed less than aristocratic; but all were accorded equal deference by the Count's retainers.

"Ah, I have a small favor to ask of you, *gnädiges Fräulein*."

"Please."

"The Count is not at home—he is with the embalmers, trying to arrange for a proper disposition of the body of that poor dead maid—and the boy's arrival is supposed to be, well, something of a surprise. I hope you will not be incommoded if we were to use the tradesmen's entrance? Dr. Szymanowski is out as well—he is teaching a class in brain dissection until suppertime, I'm afraid— but the butler will be glad to take the young lad off your hands and pay you the remainder of your stipend, and arrange some accommodation for you at an inn until such time as you choose to continue your journey. . . ."

"I won't go!" the boy screamed. "Not without *her*!"

"I was afraid something like this might happen," said Freud. "Your long confinement together has produced a powerful bonding. I warned the Count, but he wanted to do it this way. It was your name, you know: *la speranza . . . Hoffnung bedeutet das*."

"Yes. My name means 'hope,' " Speranza said, but that meaning had never seemed so contrary. She knew she could not abandon the boy to these people; the contract she had made in London meant nothing. Johnny was not completely like one of them. Perhaps he was capable of undergoing the same metamorphosis as the Count; perhaps he was indeed a werewolf, preposterous as the idea seemed in the light of day. But there had to be something different about him—something to justify the expense of transporting the child across Europe. What was Dr. Szymanowski going to do to him? This talk of brain dissection . . . surely they would not. . . .

"I won't go anywhere without Speranza," Johnny said firmly.

"Well, perhaps the Count will not be entirely inflexible on the matter," Freud said. "But," and he gazed earnestly into Speranza's eyes as he said this, "you must realize that the Count's circle of friends is decidedly . . . eccentric. You must be prepared for anything."

Screaming, the boy clung tightly to the edge of Speranza's blanket, and the horses, unnerved by his outburst, reared up and neighed. There was a sudden wind, stirring up the snow; as Speranza looked away from the façade of the Count's town house, she fancied she saw tears streaming from the eyes of the obscene Madonna.

She did not feel put out that they entered through the tradesmen's door, concealed from the street by the twin ornamental balustrades of the grand façade. Lord Slatterthwaite, kind though he had been to her, had never treated her as other than a servant; Speranza expected nothing better, despite the fact that the master of this household had made little secret of his base desire for her person.

First Speranza was given an opportunity to change. She put on her finest clothes, such as they were. A vague impending dread impelled her to put on the silver necklace.

The three of them were ushered through the basement, which contained the kitchens, the scullery, storerooms, and the apartments of some of the servants, up to a little parlor which was apparently where the upstairs maids prepared coffee, tea, and chocolate, and waited to be summoned.

It was a cozy room; two plump, frayed fauteuils faced the fire, and there was an ugly sofa, whose upholstery had been patched in several places, against one wall.

Maids and footmen came and went, but hardly glanced at the three visitors. They bore trays full of delicacies, and wine buckets, and platters of crystal goblets. There was no silver. Even the wine buckets were made of gold. The servants were constantly going out through a curtained doorway from which Speranza could hear the sound of chattering, of glasses clinking, of small talk in many languages.

The three of them did not converse. Johnny stood by the doorway, eagerly trying to puzzle out what the guests within were talking about; Freud was dosing himself with a certain white powder, which he inhaled, one nostril at a time, like snuff.

Presently Speranza heard a round of desultory applause.

"Ah," said Freud, "Dr. Szymanowski has arrived."

"Do they always clap their hands when he comes?"

"He is, after all, their savior . . . the founder and sustainer of the Lykanthropenverein . . . though I daresay von Bächl-Wölfing's money has something to do with it too . . . are you sure you don't want any cocaine?"

At that moment the curtains were drawn, and a stranger stood in the doorway.

Johnny Kindred growled. He was slipping into that animal state again. "Johnny!" Speranza said sharply. The boy growled, tensed, coiled up into himself as though he were about to spring—

He was a slight, stooped, ancient man, almost bald. Wisps of white hair covered his chin. Red blood vessels crisscrossed his cheeks. He propped himself up with the help of an ivory-handled cane. His voice, when he spoke, was a phthisic wheeze.

The boy rushed at him, and he lifted a hand to ward him off, and whispered: "*Sei still!*" Though barely audible, his voice carried authority, and Johnny stepped back, cowed, reaching for Speranza's hand.

"*Der Junge versteht aber kein Deutsch,*" Freud said quickly.

"Then shall I English speak," Szymanowski said. "You are the Speranza Martinique? I have here your money ready."

"I don't want your money . . . I must insist on staying with the child until I am satisfied that you intend him no harm!"

Szymanowski thought for a while. Then he turned to Freud and said something in German.

"*Jawohl, Herr Professor,*" Freud said, and bowed smartly. He turned to Speranza. "Perhaps I will see you again before you leave. But I am wanted at the university." He turned smartly and stalked off down to the basement.

"Your insistence is very awkward situation for us," Szymanowski said, peering at Speranza as though she were a microbe in a magnifying glass. "If you stay you will see many things perhaps that will frighten you."

"I'm not afraid," said Speranza, though she did not feel terribly brave.

"The Count will return soon. He must return before the moon

rises. That is only an hour from now. Are you understanding my meaning?"

The boy whimpered and snarled again. She caught a whiff of fresh urine in the air, and she began to shake.

"Come quickly then. You will want to meet other guests. While they are still in human form."

She followed him to the doorway. She listened to the chatter, the laughter, the strains of a string quartet. Was it her imagination, or was there mixed into that laughter a sound like wild wolves' howling? She beckoned to Johnny and, gripping his hand, stepped out into a vast ballroom, lit by glittering chandeliers, filled with guests in opulent clothes, decorated with marble statues and unicorn tapestries and pastoral paintings, permeated with the faint but insistent odor of canine piss. . . .

11
The Black Hills
full moon

NIGHT. THE OLD WOMAN HUGGED THE SHE-WOLF HER SISTER AS THEY lay together in the shade of a lodgepole pine. She had gathered enough wood for a fire, but it gave little warmth. She had built a low wall of snow and packed it hard to keep away the mountain wind. The wall and the fire were meager protection from the elements, but the old woman made no complaint. The moon dance was but a day's journey away. The moon would still be full enough tomorrow for the dancing, and many of their kind from the northern mountains and the southern plains would doubtless be there. And I too, she thought, if only I live long enough. But in her heart she did not quite believe she would see the moon dance again. My heart is blind now, she thought, blinded from the bitter snow.

She lay back against her sister, but her fur was soggy; she

spread her tattered buffalo robe over them both and sang a lilting
song, a lullaby of death. And her sister howled, for the moon
shone through the branches of the popping trees. And the old
woman longed to be able to change with the moon, to shift to the
four-footed. Then she might have a warm pelt, and not this thin
skin and these aching bones. She might be able to hear the racing
blood of young animals as they scurried through the snow and to
smell their sweet flesh and hunt them out. Her sister could do
these things still, but she was too weak to run fast. They had not
eaten well, except the day of that terrible massacre, when she and
her sister had glutted themselves on the flesh of their slain Lakota
brothers and she had scrounged cold scraps out of the gutted tipis.

"It was a terrible slaughter," she said. "I do not know why the
washichun did what they did, *mitankala*. They even defiled the
burial grounds. . . ."

Her sister whimpered in response. Perhaps her spirit had slid so
far into the animal world that she no longer understood the speech
of men.

"And yet," the old woman mused, "there was that young pony
soldier who saw us . . . once, twice . . . I think he recognized us, he saw our true natures even through the snow and
smoke that can deceive men's eyes. I know he is not one of us. But
I think I spoke to him. I think he answered. Is it possible that some
of the *washichun* are not evil?"

Her sister whined, a piteous sound.

The fires had died down quickly in the snow. It had not taken
long to kill the women and the children. The old woman and her
sister had dined after a fashion. There had been a kettle in the
embers of one fire, a few hunks of boiled dog, a couple of pieces
of pemmican. And her sister had found the body of a young boy
who had been shot while hiding in the burial grounds. Even as he
was dying he had been trying to scalp one of the soldiers. He had
been so brave, and well deserved the honor of becoming one with
the Shungmanitu; and as her sister gulped down the shreds of
flesh, the old woman had sung a triumphant song, her voice
quavery in the night wind.

But they had not waited for the return of the warriors from the
hunt. They did not want to witness any more grief. For the journey
toward the moon dance should be a time of rejoicing, even their

final journey, even their death dance. So the two of them had hastened onward, skirting the city of the white men.

"Last night, when we passed by the houses of the *washichun*, did you not hear wolves howling? And the men, pursuing them on horseback through the streets, firing their thundering weapons? Those wolves were not our kind. They were the true wolves who cannot change. The brothers who are not brothers. They must be starving if they dare to venture into the very lair of their enemies."

She waited for the she-wolf to answer. But though her sister howled again and again, watching the moon through the flickering firelight, her howling hid no words. She had lost her voice, she had become quite dumb.

"It is good that you no longer think like a human being," the old woman mused. "You are closer to the heart of things, closer to the rhythm of the universe. I understand why you no longer wish to speak." She still felt her sister's love; why else had the she-wolf not killed her and eaten her? And so she went on speaking, for herself as much as for her sister, recalling old memories. "Do you remember the first time we saw a white man?" she said. "It was when we were children. We found a beaver caught in a trap. There was metal in the trap and we did not know what it was. And the man came up to it and killed it while we hid in the berry bushes. We thought he must have some disease, but Grandfather told us, 'Their sickness is not of the skin, but of the soul.' And I asked him, 'Do the white men, too, have those among them who walk the path between man and beast? Do they have their own Wichasha Shungmanitu?' And he laughed and said, 'They do not know themselves. Every one of them carries a beast inside him.'"

The fire was dying. The ice on the tree tinkled in the wind. She drew the buffalo robe even closer, tucking it under her sister's prone form, covering the she-wolf's head, all but the tiniest opening for the snout. She squeezed in closer.

And whispered: "I doubted my grandfather for the first time when I saw the pony soldier, how he seemed almost to understand me when I spoke in the language of the wolf . . . but later I knew he was not truly one of us. Perhaps he can become one. Perhaps it is a premonition. But later, when we passed the town . . . when we heard the wolves and the huntsmen . . . I thought I heard another voice too. There was someone else there . . . not running wild with the animals, but in another part

of the town altogether . . . I heard a voice akin to one of
ours . . . and yet the language of its howling was not our
language. I knew there were words and yet I understood none of
them. And I thought for the first time, there is a Wichasha
Shungmanitu among them."

She brushed the snow from her hair with her hand. Then,
tenderly, she worked her bony fingers through the she-wolf's fur,
plucking out the pests that infested her, for her sister was too weak
to groom herself. And sang to her until they both fell asleep and
the fire died. . . .

In the morning they descended into a valley. Snow was falling,
steadily but not heavily. The place of the moon dance was not far
from here.

They crossed a frozen creek. There was no food. The hills were
a wall of white behind them.

Her sister ran ahead, panting. The old woman could not follow,
but the scent of her sister hung in the air, and she knew her sister
would stop and wait for her now and then. She moved slowly,
painfully, stopping to draw breath many times.

Suddenly she heard the she-wolf yelping. What had she seen?
She made her way downhill as best she could. She could not help
crying out as she slid along the slick slope. And then she saw what
her sister had unearthed with her paws.

It glistened in the snow: something long and shiny, too straight
to be something from nature. It was metal. She came up beside her
sister and shovelled away some more snow with her hands, and
she saw that the metal rod stretched for a long way in either
direction . . . there were two rods, parallel to each other, and
wooden planks that joined them at regular intervals. How far did
this artifact extend and what was its purpose? Did the human
brothers know of its existence? The Shungmanitu were a secretive
race; they kept to themselves, high in the hills, and there was
much that their two-footed relatives had learned about the *washichun* that the Shungmanitu did not yet know.

The she-wolf howled again. "What are you telling me, *mitankala*?" cried the old woman.

But she felt it in her bones . . . the earth was shaking . . .
far in the distance, a column of dark smoke rose in the cleft of the
valley . . . and she could hear the bellowing of a monstrous

creature, and the thunder of metal feet, and she could smell the foul fumes of death on the icy wind.

The she-wolf shrieked. There were words in her cry: ragged, broken words: "Iron . . . monster . . . with no face. . . ."

"You still speak, my sister! You have not vanished completely into the four-legged world. . . ."

She howled again, but this time the old woman understood nothing. Perhaps I merely imagine that she is still with us, she thought.

"Let us sing again, my sister. One last song."

They sang, their voices blending over the clattering drumbeat of the approaching monster: together they sang a song of mourning, the woman, the wolf, and the wind.

12
Vienna
full moon

JOHNNY CLUTCHED HER HAND TIGHTLY AS THEY STOOD BESIDE THE doorway. The guests paid her no regard at all; most were deep in conversation with one another, and a few stood next to the dais beside the French windows at one end of the ballroom, where the string quartet was performing, the four musicians immaculately dressed in tails, starched wing collars, hunched over their music stands. The French windows were shuttered, admitting neither fresh air nor evening light, and although the hall was spacious, the air was dank and close. Speranza was getting used to the reek of urine now.

She stood, a little embarrassed, not quite certain what she was expected to do. Presently one of the guests—it was that richly attired Indian whom she had seen enter the town house earlier—accosted her. "Mademoiselle," he said, and continued in heavily accented German, "*Sie sind also auch beim Lykanthropenverein—*"

"I have no German," she said with a smile.

"Oh, I am jolly glad," he said. "It is good to be encountering fellow subject of Her Britannic Majesty, isn't it?" He surveyed her haughtily, twirling one end of his mustache as he spoke, and extending to her, with his other hand, an open snuffbox made of gold and inlaid with amethysts, emeralds, and mother-of-pearl. "You will perhaps be caring for snuff?" When she demurred, he clapped his hands and a little Negro boy, costumed in an embroidered silk tunic stitched in gold thread, sidled up to him and took the snuffbox from his hands. "Perhaps you will be preferring a cigarette? I know that amongst you people cigarettes are considered more becoming in a woman than the more vulgar incarnations of tobacco. But where we are going, cigarettes are very costly, so I understand."

"We are going—" She noticed that Johnny was sniffing the air and glancing shiftily from side to side, and held on to him even more tightly. "I am not quite sure what you mean."

"Ah, but let us not be speaking of the stark, pioneering future! Let us revel in our past while we may. I will jolly well be missing my homeland. You are, from your manner of dressing, an Englishwoman, isn't it? How excellent it is to be able to converse in my mother tongue, for I am of course being a most loyal subject of Her Britannic Majesty the Empress of India, Victoria, may she live a thousand years."

"I'm French, actually. But I have lived in England. And this boy, who has at the present been entrusted to my care, is English, as he will tell you himself."

"Nevertheless—for we cannot all be fortunate enough to be born beneath that destiny-laden Britannic star—I salute you, madam." He bowed deeply to her, and the peacock plumes that adorned his turban quivered. Johnny reached out and tried to touch them, and laughed when they tickled his fingers. "And, young sahib, I salute you most humbly. I am called Shri Chandraputra Dhar, and was once Lord High Astrologer to the Nawab of Bhaktibhumi, before I was sent away in disgrace and shame, for reasons which no doubt you will already have guessed."

"I'm sure I don't know what you mean," Speranza said. They all seemed to assume that she was one of them, that she knew their secrets.

The young Negro page reappeared as if by magic with a tray,

some glasses of champagne and a small dish of caviar, and Chandraputra idly ran his finger through the boy's curls. "I no longer serve the Nawab, but His Grace the Count is being kind enough to allow me a position in his household, for which I am being most humbly and abjectly grateful. But you are doubtless understanding me when I say that blood is thicker than water. Especially that blood that runs in the veins of those who walk between the two worlds. You will of course know this from your own experience, Miss . . ."

"Martinique," Speranza said. His talk of blood disturbed her. She remembered her dream of the river of blood. The air seemed thicker now, as though the ballroom somehow had been transported to the edge of a dark forest. "And the boy's name is—"

"James," the boy said distinctly. His manner of speaking was quite different from any she had heard him use before: refined, almost haughty, like that of a servant in a highborn household. "My name is James Karney, if you please, sir."

"Oh, nonsense, child!" Speranza said in exasperation. "Do excuse my charge, Mr. Chandraputra . . . we are both very tired from our journey across Europe, and young Johnny Kindred is very much given to make-believe—"

"Ah! He is the one with many names!" said Shri Chandraputra. "Now I understand everything." To Speranza's amazement, the Indian fell on his knees before the child and gazed upon him with a humility that would have seemed comical were it not so full of earnest. He rose, grasped Speranza's hand fervently, and stooped to kiss it. His nose felt curiously cold against her hand, almost like a dog's. "You, madam, you, you . . . all our company is honoring you . . . you, *you* are, in all truth, the very Madonna of the Wolves incarnate! Ah, Countess, to have given birth to the one who will be a bridge between our two races . . . permit me to be the first to worship. Boy! Boy! Champagne, mountains of caviar! Or shall I be fetching the gold, the frankincense, the myrrh?"

"Surely, sir, you are making fun of me," Speranza said, laughing out loud at last, for the fellow was making an astonishing spectacle of himself. "This is no Christ, but a poor, half-crazed young child who cries out for affection; and I am no madonna but a mere governess, a creature in the Count's employ."

"Then you are not having privilege of being the child's

mother?" said Shri Chandraputra, scratching his luxuriant beard and raising one eyebrow skeptically.

"No," she said, "I am afraid that honor is not mine," and started to turn away. "Come, Johnny, let us see whether Dr. Szymanowski can explain . . ."

"Madam," the boy said, again in that curiously adult voice, "please refrain from holding on to my hand; I have not yet had the pleasure of being introduced to you. Perhaps you would be so good as to release me, so that I may retire to the pantry and continue my duties?" Dexterously he twisted free from her grasp and proceeded out through the curtained doorway, his nose in the air, in an almost comical parody of a stage butler.

What is he playing at? Speranza wondered. He has shown three personalities now: the demure Johnny Kindred, the bestial Jonas Kay . . . and now James Karney, who apparently thinks himself one of the domestics of this house. Could the child really be entirely unaware of these distinct personae . . . is that the nature of his malady?

"Interesting, is it not?" Szymanowski said abruptly. She was suddenly aware that he had come up to her and was regarding her with a kind of curious contempt.

"Interesting! I suppose you might call it that. But it is also very sad, Professor."

"Sad! Ah, but such melodrama. Doubtless you see this whole affair as something similar to your penny-dreadful novels. You have, perhaps, formed a theory as to the young one's problem?"

"The child's soul is deeply disturbed, that much is clear, Professor. I had originally thought that there must be some war within him between the principles of light and darkness. But—"

"Soul! Light and darkness! *Liebes Fräulein*, what for antiquated notions to which you subscribe!"

She was not comfortable in his presence. But he was standing between her and the doorway into the inner parlor. Since she could not retreat, she steeled herself and dived into the throng, seizing a glass of champagne from a passing footman as she did so. She saw the Indian whispering into the ear of another guest and pointing to her. A couple who had been waltzing stopped and stared with naked curiosity. Speranza turned and saw others pointing, tittering. The music was abruptly cut off as one of the guests rushed over to tell the latest gossip to the quartet players.

Frantically she looked down at her dress, wondering whether she had accidentally exposed some part of her person.

"Why are you all staring at me?" she said.

As she spoke, all conversation ceased.

The guests stood stock-still, their jewels glittering, their eyes narrowed, like predators preparing to pounce.

The smell intensified. Sweet-sour fragrance of rotting leaves. A dank forest. The rutting of wild beasts.

Then she heard a whisper somewhere in the crowd: "*Der Mond steht in einer halben Stunde auf.*" The others nodded to each other and slowly backed away from her. And glanced warily at each other, taking each other's measure, like fellow beasts of prey. And the Indian astrologer growled at her . . . growled, like an angry hound!

"*Der Mond steht auf . . .*"

Moonrise . . . in half an hour!

She began to tremble. It could not be true, could it? The last time she had witnessed the metamorphosis, it had been dark, in a moving car. Perhaps a train was a universe in and of itself, touching the real world but not quite part of it. But she was in Vienna now, in a grand ballroom in the midst of a huge metropolis, and the chamber was well lit. Surely, if anything were to happen here, she could not call it imagination, she could not call it a nightmare . . .

"A dance!" A woman in an embroidered gown stretched out her delicate arms and languorously shrilled: "A dance, my dears, before we all turn into ravening beasts!"

Shri Chandraputra said: "Ah, but the transformation will not render us utterly bestial, for we are shutting out the moonlight, isn't it? And the effect is being mitigated by us, we are being in control of our dark natures, thanks to discoveries of the esteemed Dr. Szymanowski—"

"A dance—a dance of metamorphosis—a dance to honor the power of the moon, my dears, which is to us as the sun is to the puny race of mortals—"

Dr. Szymanowski smiled, acknowledging the flattery of the Indian astrologer.

As though at a signal from him, the string quartet, joined by a pianist, burst into a rhapsodic waltz, and all around Speranza guests formed couples and swept out to the center of the ballroom.

"Speranza, Speranza, I'm frightened!" Where was the voice coming from? She thought she saw the boy, scuttling behind a tall man who was doffing his hat to a petite old woman wrapped in a voluminous shawl. She made off in the man's direction, and he turned to her, smiling, his arm outstretched to invite her to the dance, and his teeth were white, and knife-sharp, and glistening with drool . . .

"Speranza!" It was coming from somewhere else . . . from behind her. The music welled up, and with it the mingled smells of lust and terror . . .

Where is the child? she thought. I must find the child, I must protect him from these madmen!

There he was, talking to Dr. Szymanowski . . . were her eyes deluding her, or was the professor's face becoming longer, his nose more snoutlike, his eyes more narrow and inhuman? His smile had become a canine leer, and his tufts of hair pushing up through his bald scalp—

No! She rushed to the boy's side and grasped his hand. His palm was bristly, hot. She pulled him from the professor's side. "We've got to get away from these people," she said. "Come on, Johnny. Please." I mustn't let my dread show, mustn't startle the child, mustn't provoke the monster inside him—

"I've killed Johnny forever, I'm with my own people now!" The boy's voice was deep and rasping. Dr. Szymanowski snarled at her, and she saw saliva running down his chin, which was sprouting dark hairs, and she held on to Johnny and elbowed her way through the guests as they danced frantically to the accelerating music, the jewelled gowns and the chandeliers whirled, she lashed out with her free hand and sent champagne glasses crashing onto the Persian carpet with its design of wolves chasing each other's tails in an infinite spiral—

"Speranza, I'm afraid—" Johnny's tiny voice was interrupted by the voice of the other: "Get back inside—it's not your turn anymore—back inside and let me kill the bitch!—"

"Johnny!"

Shri Chandraputra Dhar had torn off his turban now and had dropped down on all fours. He was sloughing his face. He howled. Pieces of flayed skin hung from his neck, his palms. Blood gushed from his eyes like tears. His nails were lengthening, his hand shriveling into paws. Speranza could not move, though her heart was pounding, for there was in his transformation a fierce, alien beauty.

The woman in the elegant gown screeched, "Oh, how tedious, my dears . . . it's that hot-blooded oriental nature . . . even with the moon shut out he's off and howling. Oh, someone see to him before he sets everybody else off—" Her words trailed off into inchoate screaming, and fangs jutted from her moist, painted lips, and hairs were poking through her porcelain complexion—

Speranza ran, dragging the boy behind her.

Two footmen guarded the double oak doors that led to the vestibule. They bowed and let her through. The doors slammed shut behind them. Speranza was shaking. The boy wrested himself free of her grip and looked at her.

"Why are you taking me away from them?" he said softly. "I understand their language a little, I think. And I belong to them somehow." It was the voice of Johnny Kindred once again: always afraid, always a little child.

From behind the massive doors came howling, snarling, screeching, growling, to the accompaniment of passionate music. The vestibule was dark. A single candelabrum, at the foot of a sweeping staircase, flickered forlornly. The walls were hung with purple velvet drapes, and the floor was richly carpeted, siphoning away the faint sound of their footsteps.

And Speranza was at a loss to answer him. There was fear here; there was a palpable, brooding evil; and yet she too had felt the allure of darkness. She dared not remain, and yet . . . she thought of the times when, helping the Honorable Michael Bridgewater with his Latin verbs, or pouring tea at one of Lord Slatterthwaite's interminable garden parties, she had fallen into a reverie of thoughts too dark, too sensual to allow of public expression. Even then she had dreamed of being touched, in the midst of a primal forest, by a creature barely human, and of succumbing to a shuddering delight that was laced with pain and death. And she had thought to herself: I am vile, I am utterly without shame, to let such lewd thoughts surface in myself. She knew that it would be best to take the child away forever. But the abyss at whose edge they both stood called out to them.

So she did not respond; she merely held the child close to herself. He seemed dazed. He moved, scratching her arms and drawing blood. She stared at his fingernails in the half-light. They had lengthened and crooked themselves into the shape of claws. But his face had not changed.

"We'll go away from here," Speranza said. "If you're away from these people, you'll not become one of them."

"Could it be so simple?" said the boy.

Ahead was the massive front entrance she had earlier seen from the outside; the doors, inlaid with ivory and gilt, were shadowed, and she saw only glimpses of the sylvan scene depicted on them. There were trees, curved, their gnarled trunks catching the candlelight; there were tree nymphs, sensuously entwined about the limbs of the trees, their hair streaming, highlighted with gold leaf; there was a river; there were wolves, baying at an unnaturally huge moon that was actually a stained-glass window, of roseate design, set in the archway above; on it was depicted the coat-of-arms of the von Bächl-Wölfings.

The doorknobs were the paws of wolves that faced each other in a contest of wills; in the meager light their eyes, which were cabochon topazes set into the wood, glowed with an intense ferocity. She backed away, still carrying the child in her arms.

Behind her: laughter, music, the howling of wolves.

Gingerly she touched the doorknob, turned it—

The portals swung open! Footmen stood on either side. And, framed in the doorway, tall, dark against the driving snow, his cloak billowing in the wind, stood the man she most dreaded: the man who had brought her to the brink of darkness, and who had awakened in her such unconscionable desires . . .

"Speranza," he said. "I see you have decided to remain with us."

"Your guests—they are—they are changing—becoming wild animals—"

"Tush! Could they not wait for moonrise? They will destroy all that I have worked for! I begin to regret that I called together this gathering of the Lykanthropenverein."

"Lykan—" She had heard the word spoken many times now; it was one of those Germanic portmanteau words, and she had paid it little regard. But now she looked at him questioningly, and he responded:

"The Society of Werewolves, my dear Speranza. Of which I find myself, by right of single combat, the Herr Präsident. Oh, it was stupid of me to arrange for the meeting at the Vienna residence . . . we could be seen, we could be noticed . . . far better to have the gathering at my estates in Wallachia . . ." The Count sighed. "But . . . you were on your way out, were you not, Mademoiselle Martinique?"

She summoned up her last reserves of defiance. "I cannot allow you or Dr. Szymanowski to take charge of this child, Count von Bächl-Wölfing. I apologize for my failure to perform my duties, and I shall attempt to repay your generous stipend when I have obtained some other employment—"

"What will you do? Bring up the boy yourself? Surely you must realize that a woman of your means—"

"If I have to, I will!"

"Have you consulted the child?"

"No . . . but of course he doesn't want to stay here! He's a lamb amongst wolves. He needs tenderness and warmth, not your mad professor's bestial experiments!"

"Ask him."

"I don't need to ask him . . . I can see the terror in his eyes, I can tell by the way he clings to my side."

"Ask him!"

He clapped his hands. The doors slammed shut, and the footmen, holding their kerosene lamps aloft, entered and stood on either side of the Count. She heard a voice shriek out from the ballroom within: "Only one more minute until the fatal hour— only one more minute until moonrise!"

The boy extricated himself from Speranza's arms. In the lamplight he cast a huge double shadow against the velvet drapes. He shrank away from the Count; and yet there was in his eyes a certain awe, a certain love.

"Oh, Speranza, don't ask me to choose between you. Oh, Speranza, I do love you, but I have to stay, don't you see? I know that now." As he spoke the reek of canine urine became suddenly more powerful, choking her almost. And the boy spoke again, in the deep voice of Jonas: "He is my father."

Jonas had seized control. In the forest clearing at the center of Johnny's mind, the wolf that was Jonas possessed the whole body. Johnny was at the clearing's edge. There were other persons near him, hiding in shadows, flitting from tree to tree.

"My father?" Johnny cried. "How can you say he is my father?"

Jonas shouted: "I can smell it . . . I can remember smells, even if you can't. I can do all sorts of things you can't . . . I can smell, I can hear, I can kill. This is my body, not yours. The wolf-man, the beast in human hide—he's our father, you stupid boy. That's the reason you can't escape from him."

"No!" Johnny cried out. He tried to make tears spurt from the body's eyes, but Jonas was in full control. Johnny wanted to reach out, to tell Speranza that he would not abandon her. But Jonas was more powerful than before. It was because the moon was rising.

I'll have to retreat, Johnny thought. He could see Jonas, dancing wildly in the light, racking the body with convulsions. He knew that when the spasms were over Jonas would flee into the forest, leaving Johnny to enter the clearing and feel the body's pain. Jonas loved to give pain, but when it came to taking it he always left that task to Johnny or one of the others.

"You see?" said von Bächl-Wölfing. "The child knows instinctively. Instinctively! He is my son, conceived of an English harlot in Whitechapel, raised in a madhouse, but my blood runs true—he has the eyes of the wolf, the senses, the memory; he knows me for what I am. And, since he has learnt to call me father, I acknowledge him, I embrace him as mine."

"You can't mean—" Speranza began, trying to shield Johnny from him with her arms. But the boy himself pushed her brusquely aside. His eyes glowed now.

The Count spread his arms wide to receive his child. With halting steps the boy came forward. Through the stained-glass moon above the door, Speranza could see the rising of the real moon, pale and haloed by the icy air.

The boy stood close to the Count now, dwarfed. The Count enfolded him in his cloak. Speranza cried out the boy's name, but her voice was lost in the wind's howling and the cacophony from the ballroom . . .

The Count looked longingly into her eyes. His gaze mesmerized her. There was in it a kind of love. The Count advanced toward her, and already his lips were being wrenched apart as the wolf's jaw began extruding itself from within. As she stood transfixed, he began to court her in Italian: "*Come sei bella, fanciulla; come sei bella, o mia Speranza.*" The voice was harsh, guttural, a travesty of her native tongue . . . yet the wolf was wooing her, trying to make love to her. Her blood raced. Her skin tingled. A hand reached out to her from under the cloak: a twisted, furry hand. A claw grazed her cheek. She closed her eyes, shuddering, desiring yet loathing him. Her cheek burned where his paw had touched it. She did not retreat from him, for he held the child captive still, and she told herself that to effect the child's rescue from this brutish destiny must be a sacred task for which she must sacrifice what small chastity she could lay claim to. She met his gaze with defiance.

"I'll save him yet . . . somehow . . ."

"Will you, my Madonna of the Wolves? I have a fancy to make you one of us this very moment. A bite from me should suffice. Or else I could force you to drink the dew that has formed in one of my footprints; we keep phials of such precious fluids in this house for just such an occasion. Or perhaps you would care to wear the sacred pelt of my ancestors, which being worn can be cast off only by death?"

"I could never become one of you," she said. But she was tempted.

His paw continued to stroke her cheek, drawing blood now. She shook her head, loosening the silver necklace from beneath her collar. The Count recoiled. His voice was barely human: "Consider yourself fortunate, mademoiselle, that you are wearing the necklace!"

His forehead was flattening now, his brow creasing and uncreasing as bristles began to shoot out from folds of skin. He howled, and a uniformed servant emerged from an antechamber, lantern in hand.

"If the *gnädiges Fräulein* would care to follow me," he said, bowing deeply, "I can show her to a safe room, where she may wait out the night's festivities without fear for her person. May I escort you upstairs?" The servant spoke French in the Viennese fashion, interspersed with German words whose meaning she had to puzzle out.

She hesitated. She was about to protest when the Count cast aside his cloak and she saw the wolf cub leap from his arms, and she knew that Johnny was beyond help, that night at least. In the morning she would see what could be done with him. Perhaps that young student Freud would have some idea. She could not abandon the boy now, never, never.

The wolf cub was running in circles, whining, and the Count himself was falling to the floor, and she could hear the guest's paws pounding and scraping against the doors of the ballroom, and she could smell their rage . . . she turned and followed the servant up the staircase, with its gold and onyx balustrade, past marble statues and dusty portraits.

From the mezzanine, the sounds of chaos seemed far away, for the heavy drapes muffled them. "If you do not mind, *gnädiges Fräulein*, I will give you a suite in the servants' quarters; things will be far safer there, I assure you."

"Why do they not harm you?" Speranza asked him. "They are ungovernable."

"We are all branded with a certain mark."

As he held up the lamp, she saw on the back of his hand something she had taken for a blemish or birthmark; looking at it more closely, she saw now that it was a kind of brand, burned into the flesh, and that it was the image of a flower.

The servant explained, "If you decide to remain in the Count's service, you will doubtless come to know this insignium well. That poor serving maid, alas . . . the young boy, apparently, did not know the meaning of the brand . . . the Count was devastated. He has done everything he can to appease her family and compensate them in their bereavement . . ."

"Compensate?" Speranza said, remembering that she had seen little Johnny crawl forth from the entrails of that girl . . . no, it had been no nightmare, she knew that now. "He caused her to be killed—brutally, horribly!—and he is devastated?"

"The Count is not without compassion," said the servant, "or else his retainers would not have remained with him for generations, as I have, humbly and loyally."

"It is so strange, though," Speranza said, "that so bloodthirsty a household should have as its mark of servitude so beautiful an image as a flower . . ."

"Not so strange, mademoiselle. It is a flower worshipped and feared by those who walk on both sides of the forest path . . . they call it wolfsbane."

13
Deadwood
the same night

"No! NO MORE HAVOC, COUSIN!" VISHNEVSKY PULLED THE SILVER fetters tighter. The only light in the room came from the candle he was about to blow out. Soon the moon would be setting, but he would take no more chances. "I don't even want to look at you." He was wary of eavesdroppers and spoke Russian to her; he knew that she would think it vulgar and peasantlike of him, but the situation did not warrant the preservation of such niceties as might preoccupy the minds of folk at home.

Natalia snarled. Her eyes glittered. "You didn't send me the young lieutenant."

"We are supposed to blend in with these tiresome people somehow, not arouse suspicion."

"He is a beautiful young lieutenant, is he not? I'm half in love, half ravenous." She continued, petulantly, "Why did you give him the silver bullet? I'll not be able to show my face. It grazed my cheek."

"If only the Count had sent Quaid! It is so difficult to keep all these people straight . . . they do not think like civilized people, and I am constantly afraid I may reveal one of the Count's secrets. And then there's you . . . a burden, a constant embarrassment. What if they find your secret?"

"My foolish cousin," Natasha said. There was the barest hint of a growl in her voice. "You know why Hartmut sent me. It is I who will ultimately determine the location of his little colony. It is I who will bear the litter. Only I can decide where we will den."

"You believe, then, that you are your leader's chosen consort?" Vishnevsky knew that since the death of the Gräfin, the Count had gone through a dozen mistresses, yet not one of them had been awarded the von Bächl-Wölfing name. He had not seen fit to choose a consort, yet the Lykanthropenverein needed a female leader, for in a wolf pack only the leader's consort might whelp, and only she could dictate the birthing place. That was the law among these creatures. "I cannot believe, cousin, that you remain so certain of your position. Especially in view of your unfortunate . . . disfigurement."

Natasha tried to sit up, her wrists straining against the chains. He winched as he saw the burn marks form on her pale flesh.

She said, spitting the words out, "You arranged for this to happen! You hope for me to fall into disfavor. Then you can abandon me and go home. Don't think, my dear cousin, that they'll take you back into the village . . . you're tainted . . . doomed to spend the rest of your days in subjugation to us . . . you have the flower of servitude branded on the back of your hand, like every other servant!"

"I bow to Your Lycanthropic Ladyship," Vishnevsky said, unable to stop himself from sneering a little. But when he caught sight of his own right hand, curled around the candle holder, he felt the bleak hopelessness that all slaves experience from time to time.

"I know you hate me, cousin. I know that you tried to kill me."

"Natasha . . . you know that I have always loved you." He searched for sincerity in his words but found them curiously empty.

"How easily love is transformed into hate—just as I can change from woman to monster and back again!" The moon was setting now; Vishnevsky could feel its influence fading.

He regarded her face in the candlelight. Yes indeed . . . the silver bullet had sheared off an irregular patch of flesh from her cheek. But what remained was more than a scar, more than an ugly blemish on her otherwise perfect complexion. For silver was silver, and the bullet had worked a powerful magic upon her skin. Where the bullet had scarred her, she had not transformed. There was a streak of wolf's pelt, sleek reddish hairs with just a tinge of silver, grafted onto her face, and at its edges the human skin was peeling, like the skin of a leper.

"I am sorry," he said at last. "You know that I had to do it. The Count himself . . . gave orders that . . . the secret must at all costs be concealed."

"Then your love for me is not entirely dead, Valentin," she said in Russian, suddenly vulnerable.

"No, Natasha."

He turned away. It would not do for her to see him weep. Who knows, he thought, what use she will put my weaknesses to, next time she transforms?

Natalia Petrovna, of course, did not weep; for hers was a species denied the solace of tears.

Claude Grumiaux and Zeke led Scott away from the saloon, downhill. They followed him as he turned off the street into an alley. No boardwalk here, Scott thought, as they trudged through the slush and he felt the cold and damp seep into his boots.

The alley intersected with a slightly wider street. There were tumbledown rowhouses. A paper lantern hung in a window. There were signs in Chinese. The wind, whistling in their faces, carried a faint whiff of opium.

Zeke suddenly started to laugh. "Are you living in the Chinee district, Grumiaux? I'll wager you got yerself one of them yeller women, too."

"Why not, Zeke?" Grumiaux said. "I had an Indian wife once. As you well know."

"Bastard! Still rubbin' my nose in it after all these years."

"I always know where the real excitement is in any town," said Grumiaux mildly. "Here, Lieutenant Harper. I will treat you to a few amusements you perhaps did not know existed so near to Fort Cassandra. And I think that my lodging, meager as it is, will be preferable to you than paying eight bits for a room. Not that you could even find one."

To reach the Frenchman's dwelling, they entered a laundry, descended through a basement doorway in the back, and negotiated a network of narrow passageways with dirt floors. There were rooms with bead curtains. Scott heard the speech of Chinamen from behind those curtains, singsong, alien. The corridors were lit with paper lanterns. At length, Grumiaux paused in front of one of the bead curtains, and said something. He directed his companions to go inside. Scott had to stoop to pass through.

There was a vestibule in which a wizened Chinaman lay in a hammock, puffing away at an opium pipe. The smell filled the chamber. There was a cramped, hemmed-in feeling that made

Scott's hair stand on end. He took in opium with every breath, and it gave him a strange sensation of floating. Somehow it made him think of the Russian lady, and when he thought of her—

They passed into another room, much wider than the first. A tiny, slender woman with oriental features greeted them. She wasn't wearing all those fussy clothes, those bustles and frills, like white women, but a simple tunic. She had a delicate kind of beauty; clearly Grumiaux was a man with a taste for the exotic in women.

"*Ma femme*," said Grumiaux, "Mei Ting."

The woman said a few words in French, but seeing that Scott could not follow her, switched to English. "Let me prepare you some food! I heard that you have been hunting the wolf, no?"

Before he could answer, she retreated into another room, and unfamiliar scents—spices he did not recognize—began wafting into the chamber. Grumiaux bade his friends sit down. The table was covered with black lacquer and inlaid with mother-of-pearl. A map hung on the wall, and Scott saw that it depicted the Nebraska, Dakota, and Wyoming territories, with railway lines linking the various towns.

"This is where my railroad will go when it is completed, a few years hence," Grumiaux said, and he drew a line with his finger from Omaha, a shallow northwest curve that crossed into Dakota Territory about due south of Deadwood and climbed northward through the Black Hills. "And this is where your Austrian Count is demanding his spur." He drew a westward fork from the foothills, just above the Nebraska border, stretching into nowhere. "I know of no gold being mined there. Do you?"

Zeke shook his head.

At that moment, Grumiaux's wife came in and set down a tray of astounding delicacies, plates full of rice and chopped-up meats and vegetables. The mouth-watering smell blended with the fragrance of opium. Scott realized that he hadn't eaten since midday. He didn't know what this food was, but it sure looked a lot tastier than the son-of-a-bitch stew he'd been expecting.

The bizarre surroundings, the constant inhalation of opium, made Scott feel as if he were dreaming. He was chasing morsels around the bowl with chopsticks, much to the others' amusement. Zeke told of the wolf hunt, and pulled out the wolf's tail he had been carrying in his vest. "Tomorrow I'll turn this in. There's bound to be a bounty on wolf's tails in this town."

"One dollar," Grumiaux said.

"A dollar! That much? I'll be a rattler's ass. I'll buy dinner for the three of us . . . and them Roosians too, if you like."

At last the subject of the two Russians had come up. For some reason, Scott found himself blushing. Zeke said, "I seen the way you look at that woman, Scott. You sure do set your sights mighty high."

"She's mighty pretty," he said, "but there's something about her makes my hair stand on end. The way she seemed to appear out of nowhere. Right after I shot that wolf. And the way that cousin of hers acted. Calling the wolf by her name. The way he was fixin' to kill the wolf, saying he was the only one as had the right to kill her. And putting those silver bullets into his pistol . . . and I didn't hear nothing crash through that window, no matter what she said."

"Perhaps," Grumiaux said, smiling, "she is a *loup garou*."

"He means a werewolf," said Zeke. "There's legends of them creatures all over the world. The Injuns believes in 'em too."

Scott didn't say anything, because he was thinking about how the wolf had looked at him, and about all those other times he had encountered wolves and had seemed almost to understand their speech.

"Among the *Indiens peaux-rouges*," said Grumiaux, "these werewolves are not considered creatures of Satan, but have their own part to play in the great cycle of being. Some of the Sioux believe there is an entire tribe of werewolves to the north of us, and that they prey on slain warriors and old people who have outlived their usefulness, absorbing their essence unto themselves."

"I ain't saying your Russian friend's a werewolf," Zeke said. "But here in the territory, we ain't really part of the civilized world. A lot of things is possible here that just ain't so back East."

"Or in the old country," Grumiaux said. "In Europe they are so damned scientific these days, they sometimes cannot see what is happening under their very noses."

14
Vienna
the same night

FROM HER LITTLE ROOM—A GARRET, MORE OR LESS—IN THE ATTIC of the von Bächl-Wölfing town house, Speranza was able to see the street below and the private park with its Madonna, for the snow had abated a little and the moon was full. She sat at a little dressing table, brushing her hair and organizing her possessions. She turned up the lamp as far as it would go, for she did not feel like sitting in the dark. The room was a little spartan, with frayed, faded rugs that did not entirely cover the unstained wooden floor, and the fourth wall was papered differently from the other three; but there was a modest fireplace, and a small bucket of coal beside it. They had left a bedwarmer in her bed, and the pillows, stuffed with goose down, seemed to have been borrowed from the master's side of the house.

She had opened her trunk, and was pulling out the objects one by one. All those that contained a little silver she placed on the table; the others she threw back.

There was not much to work with: the hairbrush had a silver handle, and she had a letter knife that also seemed to be silver, and a small mirror whose handle was of the same design as the hairbrush. And a few small items of jewelry apart from the necklace that had already saved, if not her honor, at least her life.

She studied the articles for a while. What has happened to me? she thought. I have turned from a rational, modern woman into someone positively mediaeval . . . yet this thing exists. Perhaps it is some disease, some dementia so extreme that it manifests itself in the outward form as well as the mind . . . perhaps it is some taint in the blood which little Johnny has unwittingly inherited. But it cannot be incurable. I have seen the boy resisting it, and I too must resist. For his sake.

But, she told herself, there is so much here that seems to do with old wives' tales, with nightmarish superstitions. I cannot sort out the truth. So I must do things with silver. Just to be sure.

She got up, bundled up the objects under her arm, and studied the ways of entering her room. She moved a chair next to the door, and propped up the mirror on it. She took four trinkets and placed them on the floor at the corners of her bed. There was only one window—the one beside the dressing table—but she placed the hairbrush carefully on the sill. The letter knife, she decided, she would carry on her person, in her bosom, when next she was called into the Count's presence.

She sat down once more. It was beginning to snow again; the stone Madonna was almost buried. From below there came howling: not the cacophony she had witnessed in the ballroom, but something far more purposeful. First came a single note, drawn out, with an almost metallic resonance. Then another joined in, on another pitch, stridently dissonant with the first; then came a third and a fourth, each adding a note to the disharmony. The window rattled. Her very bones seemed to feel the vibration. How could the servants live in such surroundings? Did the mark of the flower really protect them? It had not protected the maid on the train . . . but then little Johnny could not have known . . . not little Johnny, the unwitting beast.

The howling crescendoed. The floor trembled against her feet. The chair she sat in was shaking. And suddenly it was over. She heard a slamming sound, and she saw the wolves pouring out into the street. They streamed past the row of parked carriages. She was glad none of the horses had been left outside.

When they howled they had seemed hundreds, but now she saw there were only perhaps twenty. They stood, still as statues, for a few moments, in the middle of the alley, their breath steaming up the air. Snow flecked their pelts. Their leader's fur was black and streaked with silver just as the Count's hair was . . . and beside him stood a young pup, the very one she had seen leaping out of the Count's opera cloak . . . and behind them other wolves. Even from this far up she could see how their eyes glowed. The moon was low, and the wolves cast giant shadows across the wrought-iron angel gates of the park. The leader shook the snow from his fur and looked from side to side. Then they moved. Sinuously, with an alien grace, almost as one. A sharp bark from their leader and they began to trot down the Spiegelgasse. Quite silently, for the deep snow muffled the patter of their paws. At the corner, the wolves turned and vanished behind a stone wall.

She watched a while longer. But at length she was overcome by an intense weariness, and went to her bed. Her sleep was fitful, for she dreamt of the forest, and the river, and the lupine lover waiting for her at its source.

The wolfling sniffed the chill air and shook the snow out of his pelt. At last he had quelled the rebellion in his soul . . . at last he was as he was meant to be: proud, ferocious, one with the darkness. He was unsteady on his feet at first. But he imitated his father's gait and soon fell into its liquid rhythm.

The wolves moved silently. Now and then the wolfling's father paused to mark his scent, arrogantly lifting his leg to urinate on some memorable spot: a stone, a brick wall, the wheel of a cart. They spoke a language of the dark: now and then with a whine or a bark, more often with a quick motion of the head or a quiver of a nostril or a glance.

"My son," said the leader with his eyes, as the pack slipped into the shadow of another alley. "My son. How much I rejoice that I have found you . . . and that you are truly one of us, able to change . . ."

"Why did you not seek me out before?" the wolfling cried out with a shrug and a circular motion of his paws.

"Because," said his father, lashing the snow with his tail, "I was afraid. Your mother was not one of us."

"My mother . . ."

There was another voice within the wolfling's mind, a voice that seemed to cry out: No, I am not one of these . . . I am a child, a human.

Whose was this inner voice? The young wolf followed his father, faster now, darting from shadow to shadow. The voice distressed him. It did not belong here. It was good to be this way. Good to paw the ground and sniff the air. The air was vivid: he could smell the blood of distant prey, racing, already sensing death. The inner voice spoke again, saying, This vision is bleak, gray, colorless . . . but the wolfling did not understand what the voice meant, for his eyes could not see color, only infinite gradations of light and shadow. And the possessor of the inner voice could not seem to grasp the richness of sound and scent he was experiencing, but continually bemoaned the absence of this thing he called color.

He pushed the voice further back into his mind. It was a useless thing, a vestige of some existence. He followed his father. The pack had split up now. There were the two of them, hunting as father and son.

Hunting! For the pit of his stomach burned with an all-consuming hunger. Not only for fresh, warm meat, but for the act of killing. . . .

Abruptly his father stopped, cocked his head. The wind had dropped. The snow fell straight down. Footsteps, human footsteps. He smelled blood: sluggish blood, tainted with the sour smell of wine. "Come, my son," his father said with an imperious bark. "We will celebrate together, you and I, the mystery of life and death. The quarry is nigh."

He saw nothing. They did not move. The smell came closer. There was a shape to the smell, a two-legged shape. He stood beside his father, tense, waiting. A second shape, much smaller, beside the first. What were they doing in the cold, in the dark? His father growled . . . a faint, ominous sound, like a distant earth tremor.

The snow thinned and the young wolf saw more. The quarry was on the steps of a church. There was a woman and a child, perhaps four or five years old. A half-empty bottle lay next to them. There was a small puddle of wine on the snow. They were shivering, huddled together under a man's greatcoat.

The woman was muttering to herself in some Slavic tongue, and rocking the child back and forth. She wore a woolen shawl; beneath it he could see wisps of gray hair. She had a drawn, pinched face. The child was sullen, distracted. He could not smell what sex the child was; it was too young.

"They are street people," said the wolfling's father. "They have strayed from the herd. They have sought the desolation of the cold and dark. They belong to us."

And loped up the steps, his jaws wide open, while his son followed closely behind.

At first the woman did not even seem to notice. The wolf circled her several times. Then he pounced.

She let go of the child. The child began to whine. Its scrawny shoulders showed through the torn nightshirt. It began to clamber up the steps toward her. The wine bottle rolled away, chiming as it hit each step. The wolfling watched his father and the woman. For a few seconds they gazed at each other, neither of them moving, oblivious to the bawling of the child. In those moments it seemed almost as though they were exchanging vows, each choosing the other as partner in the ritual of death.

Then his father leapt. He tore out her throat with his jaws. The wolfling caught a momentary glimpse of the woman's trachea, still pulsing. There was an eerie whistling as the wind left her. She crumpled as the wolfling's father ripped her chest cavity open. The child, crying, was pummelling at the wolf's side with its fists, but the wolf ignored it. Blood gushed down the steps now, mingling with the spilled wine. The woman's shawl, pinned between her torso and the steps, fluttered in the wind.

The wolfling smelled the child's fear. It maddened him. He rushed at the child. The child's eyes widened. It backed away, up the steps. Then it turned and began to run. The wolfling followed. The child's blood smelled warmer than the woman's.

There was a door at the top of the steps. The child pounded at it with tiny fists. It did not budge. The wolfling jumped up, clawing at the nightshirt, gouging out great gashes in the child's chest and arms. Suddenly the door gave way. A rusty bolt, perhaps. The child ran inside. Through the rips in the nightshirt the wolfling saw its tiny vulva, and knew its gender for the first time.

He smelled incense. And dust. And sweet fragrance of over-varnished, rotting wood. In the distance there was an altar. A painted stone Pietà stood guard in the antechapel. There were candles everywhere.

The girl ran. He followed the sound of her footsteps, shoeless on the stone floor. She was hiding somewhere among the pews. She was panting. He could smell her exhaustion, her desperation. It was only a matter of time. He felt his heart pounding. He heard her heartbeat too, and paused to pinpoint it.

There! He scurried down the aisle. She was under the altar. He ripped the altar cloth with his jaws and found her huddled, clasping a leg of the altar, sobbing. Roughly he threw her down, hulking over her, teasing her face with his tongue and the edges of his teeth, urinating on her to show his possession. And gazed at her, as he had seen his father gaze into the eyes of the woman.

He saw her fear. And behind her fear he saw something else too . . . a kind of invitation . . . the dark side of desire. He sensed that what they were doing together, hunter and quarry, was a sacred thing, a dance of life and death. The girl trembled. Pain racked her body. He spoke to her in the language of the forest, asking her forgiveness; and she answered in the same language, the language that men believe they have forgotten until such moments as these, giving him permission to take her life.

He was about to tear her apart when a long shadow fell across them both. He looked up and saw his father. Blood dripped from his jaws. There was a trail of blood from the antechapel all the way up the nave. His eyes glowed. His breath clouded the musty air.

"Now," said his father. "Kill. Feel the joy. Feel the spurting blood. Bathe in its warmth."

"I feel no joy," the wolfling said, "only a strange solemnity. I feel a kind of kinship with her."

"Good! You understand the law of the forest well, my son! Men see us as unreasoning, ravening beasts, but that is not all we are. We are not simply Satan's children. There are some of us to whom the killing is nothing more than the exercise of lust. Perhaps most of our little society are like that. But with you it is something more. Good. You are truly my son. To lead the Lykanthropen-verein you must be more than a crazed creature of death . . . you must also feel a certain love for your victims . . . now, kill quickly. Shock her nervous system so that she will no longer feel pain."

The wolfling bent over the girl, ready to dispatch her. Then he heard the inner voice: "Get away! Go back into the darkness! I want the body!" There were several other voices too. Voices of humans. There was a mutiny going on inside his mind! The other personalities were seizing control! He struggled. But he was losing his grip. The girl was fighting him. And there was something going wrong with the vibrant layers of scents and fragrances around him . . . he was losing his sense of smell . . . the shapes were shifting too, darkening, becoming fringed with garish colors. . . .

Johnny Kindred snapped into consciousness beneath an altar

inside a huge church, with a little girl in his arms. Her eyes
widened. She began jabbering away in a foreign language. She
pointed. There was a black wolf in the church. Staring at the two
of them. Its fur was matted with bright red blood. Blood and drool
dribbled from its teeth, which glistened golden in the candlelight.

"Jonas won't harm you," Johnny said to the girl. "I've sent him
away."

The wolf growled. Johnny felt that it could almost understand
what he was saying. If Jonas were nearby he could translate, but
Jonas was being held down by the others. He was not to go
anywhere near the clearing.

"The big bad wolf won't harm you," Johnny said, stroking the
girl's curly hair. "He's . . . my father."

There was a knock on Speranza's door.

She reached for her dressing gown, sat up in her bed, and called
out, "Come in."

The little boy who opened the door was subtly different from
Johnny Kindred. He wore morning dress: a tailcoat, a starched
linen shirt, an old-fashioned stick-up collar, and a white tie.

"Good morning, ma'am," he said solemnly.

"Oh, Johnny," she said. She had better not quiz him about the
night before, at least not until she had had a chance to regain her
composure. "I see you're very well dressed this morning."

"Johnny has gone away for a little while, ma'am. I am James
Karney, in service to this household; and I have been sent by the
Count to extend to you his profound respects, and to invite you to
join him and his guests in partaking of a little breakfast."

Ah yes. She remembered this character now; he had emerged
briefly during the chaos of the previous evening. He stood stiffly,
awaiting her response. She nodded and told him she would be
down shortly.

She recognized the music at once: it was, again, the Schubert
Winterreise, being sung by a young tenor to the accompaniment of
a Blüthner grand piano.

A long table had been set with some two dozen places—about
the number of wolves she had seen leaving the house last night.
There was one empty seat . . . one directly opposite the Count,
who was absorbed in some letters. Johnny—she was sure it was

Johnny this time, for he was slouched in his chair, not sitting up straight as she was sure James Karney would be—was at the Count's right. He was playing with some lead figures of American Indians.

The men stood up when she entered. She saw among them Dr. Szymanowski, Chandraputra, and Sigmund Freud, who was occupying the seat to her own right. The women included several she had seen at the ball, including the bored, screeching one in the elegant dress. Today she wore an amazing assemblage of plumes, and was puffing languidly at a cigarette in a golden holder.

"I thought it best to have one of your fellow humans sitting next to you," the Count said, not looking up from his notes, "as you must be feeling rather outnumbered, my dear Speranza. Some caviar, perhaps? Or would you prepare something more English? I believe we have kippers."

As she sat down, Freud said to her, "They've gone quite mad! It's rather thrilling, actually."

"Mad?"

"Ah, yes! hallucinations en masse . . . delusions of lycanthropy . . . really, it's very exciting. You haven't seen this morning's paper, have you?" He thrust it at her. "Oh, but it is in German. *Je m'excuse,* Fräulein. Attacks by wolves . . . a petition to the bishop . . . the Kaiser disturbed in the middle of the night, for heaven's sake!"

"I did see something," Speranza said cagily.

"I'm afraid that we're indirectly responsible for the whole thing," Freud said. "You see, some of Dr. Szymanowski's wolves—the ones whose, ah, mating habits he is studying—escaped their cages last night. Might I offer you some cocaine?"

"Perhaps . . . yes, I think I will," Speranza said, her mind spinning. He offered it to her in a snuffbox; she took a pinch and inhaled it much as one might take snuff. "You say the wolves escaped? They are normally kept here?"

"In the sub-basement," Szymanowski said. "They are now all fully recaptured."

Freud whispered to her: "But they're all playing this game now . . . and we have to participate. Since the Count is frightfully rich, and the neurology department of the University of Vienna is, alas, very poor, we have all learnt to humor our dear Count. It's not all that bad . . . you should have seen the games we had to play when King Ludwig of Bavaria paid us an official visit! You can't imagine how boring it can be to talk about Wagner all the time! At least, with the Count, one can play bizarre party games that toy with the darkest recesses of the mind."

"Do you believe that the Count is insane?" Speranza said.

"Tush, Mademoiselle Martinique! The wealthy do not suffer from insanity . . . merely from eccentricity," Freud said, and partook of some more cocaine.

The Count cleared his throat. Silence fell.

"The pieces of the plan," he said, "are falling into place one by one. But you must understand that, until we are ready, we cannot have any more spectacular diversions such as last night's. There has never been so complete a gathering of the Lykanthropen-verein, and we must control ourselves thoroughly if we are to avert suspicion. This may be the nineteenth century, but remember that most of our peasants are still living in the Middle Ages! The effects *can* be mitigated if the moonlight is shut out. Self-control *can* be exercised to some extent—though not if you are going to stand out in the open basking in the moonlight!"

"Enough of these words of caution!" said one of the women.

"Yes. I think we are wanting to hear about America," said Shri Chandraputra, picking his teeth.

"America . . ." Speranza said.

"Bang! Bang!" said little Johnny, making his lead Indians chase each other across his toast.

"Very well. America it is." The Count spread out his letters in front of him. "I have some preliminary reports from my man Vishnevsky. The land we have picked—it is called Dakota Territory—is desolate. I am taking steps to gain control of the one railroad they are thinking of building there. There are some garrisons of soldiers, a few miners and missionaries, and several tribes of natives."

"Natives! Oh, jolly good," said Chandraputra. "Helpless, unsuspecting natives. No more will we be shot at with silver bullets or buried at crossroads. No more this persecution."

"Have you considered," said Freud, "what these aborigines might feel about it?"

"Ah, but they are only natives," Szymanowski said.

"Herds and herds of food animals," said the Count. "A new land. Unspoiled by civilization. Freedom at last. We shall roam where we will. Our women will den; our pack will become many packs, perhaps. And natives to feed on, natives unacquainted with the folklore and superstition that cause the peasants of Europe to hide behind their silver and their wolfsbane. And endless territory we can mark as we please. Dr. Szymanowski is a true visionary; I, alas, am merely a writer of cheques. But the professor's dream is now within our grasp."

There was a burst of applause from the guests. Freud turned and whispered in Speranza's ear: "He really is very good at extemporizing these comic speeches, isn't he? Sometimes I think he really does suffer these delusions."

"And now," said the Count, "I must address a question to Mademoiselle Martinique, who has arrived at the banks of her personal Rubicon. Last night you told me that you felt that this boy could be saved . . . that you were determined to effect that salvation somehow. Perhaps you think that there is a kind of tug-of-war between us for the soul of this boy—and you see yourself on the side of the angels, and me, of course, on the other side. Will you continue the struggle, having seen all that you have seen? Of course, since you will be in my service, we will give you a mark, so that you will not be molested by any of us. . . ."

She could not leave Johnny's side now. Perhaps her confidence was bolstered by Freud's cocaine, for she felt unusually belligerent that morning. All her life she had been commanded by others. All her life she had been little better than a domestic servant. It had not occurred to her to go to America, but it was true that she had nowhere to go except back to a dreary existence in Aix-en-Provence; and she yearned for a distant country where she could become a wilder person, something more than a mere governess. "I'll go," she said. "But not as your slave. On my own terms. You will not brand me. I'll survive by my own wits. Or perhaps with this."

She plucked the silver letter knife from her bosom and brandished it. I look ludicrous, she told herself. But the others recoiled, and the plumed woman actually screamed in terror.

"Bravo!" said Freud to her. "You are really getting into the spirit of this."

"I think I'd like a little more cocaine," she said, and took another pinch.

The Count glowered. "I do not make bargains. Come with us on my terms or not at all."

She pointed the knife at him. He looked at it curiously, but she thought he seemed a little shaken.

Johnny looked up from his toys and said, "Please, Father, I should like to have her with us."

She waited.

"Very well," the Count said. "My son has spoken."

She looked around. It was a moment of discomfiture for all of them. At last it was Freud who rose to his feet and spoke: "A toast to your lycanthropic utopia, then, Count! Have you named it yet!"

The Count clapped his hands; servants poured champagne for all the guests. "In memory of this pilgrimage we have all taken across the snows of Europe . . . to this city, the capital of the world . . . to hear and realize the vision of the great Dr. Szymanowski . . . I shall build a city for our people in the New World. I shall call it *Winterreise*, after the Schubert song cycle . . . in memory of our winter journey."

"America!" the plumed woman cried, downing her champagne.

"America!" the others shouted, Speranza among them.

She drained her glass with the others. They smashed their goblets on the floor, and servants brought in fresh ones. Johnny left his seat and ran to her side, beaming, and she kissed him on both cheeks. Somehow, she thought, my life really is beginning again, after all.

The champagne was an unusual vintage, being very light and sweet, with a bitter aftertaste.

15
The Dakota-Nebraska Border
one day after full moon

THEY HAD BEEN TRAVELLING SINCE BEFORE DAWN. THE DOWNHILL road was not easy; Scott marvelled at how Natalia Petrovna, riding sidesaddle, the scarf masking her face, kept pace. She did not flinch at the icy wind, but stared steadily ahead as they rode. Several times he pulled alongside and tried to talk to her. But she never answered him. Grumiaux, who knew the way, rode on ahead.

No snow fell. It was a day of dazzling brightness. It burned your eyes, the sight of so much snow. The snow still hung heavy on the fir branches. It would be weeks before it started to thaw. He longed for summer. He craved the woman, too, though he didn't quite know how he could ever tell her. He was still confused from last night's opium. He had dreamed about she-wolves that stood erect and wore serge travelling coats and had red, luxuriant hair. She was driving him plumb out of his mind.

It's just that it's winter, he told himself, it's been winter too long. Anything new and I'm right obsessed.

They stopped for a quick meal at Sheridan, a town of tents with a general store and a seven-room boardinghouse; Zeke spent his one-dollar bounty for turning in the wolf's tail on bread and stew for all of them, and had four bits left over. Then they left the main road. The pathway was steep, but the two Russians rode relentlessly. Of course, Scott thought, they're used to this cold where they come from.

Towards evening they reached a ledge. The hillside sheared sharply down where they stood, but there was a gentler grade not far off and a twisting path into the valley.

He saw Grumiaux dismount, and the Russians follow suit. He

did the same. The five of them stood at the edge. The snow was firm and crunchy beneath their boots. Zeke pulled a flask of whiskey from his saddlebag and passed it around. And Grumiaux pointed.

First Scott saw the smoke. Around it was a cluster of tents. He could make out people, Chinamen, he thought, sitting around the fire. There was a pile of logs.

"The railway," Grumiaux said. "But, of course, to you Europeans, our great new marvel must seem a little primitive."

Scott could see nothing at first. Then Natalia Petrovna said, "Yes, I see it now—" and he looked where she was pointing and saw a slender gleaming sliver of metal in the snow . . . here and there a railway tie poked out of the white, but mostly the track was buried.

"Come down," Grumiaux said. "The snowplow should be arriving in, perhaps, an hour."

They led their horses down into the valley. The Chinamen greeted Grumiaux dourly, and he answered them in their native speech. He turned to his guests and said, "We have only laid twenty more miles to the northwest, although I have surveyed several possible alternatives for the rest of the route. The work goes slowly; I doubt we will reach Deadwood in the next year. Especially since your Count is so anxious to buy up control. Chicago and Northwestern is showing an interest too. By the time the various companies have ceased wrangling, it will be 1886!"

The valley sloped downhill to the southeast. The track rounded a corner and disappeared behind a steep hill some three furlongs away. The Russians had gone off a little way and were conversing in their own language.

Zeke took a gulp of his whiskey and handed the flask to Scott, who refused. His head was still full of queer thoughts from the opium. Sometimes he wasn't quite sure if he was awake.

To the south and west, the snow stretched, level, monotonous, as far as the eye could see. Except for a twisted hillock that jutted up, almost at the limit of their vision, a contorted black shape, almost like an animal writhing in an agony of death. Or birth. Was it the opium, or was the hill moving? A mirage? He squinted, trying to make it out, until tears came to his eyes.

"I see you are looking at Weeping Wolf Rock," Grumiaux said to him. "It is a sacred place to the natives, you know. Some say

it is also sacred to the Wichasha Shungmanitu . . . you will
recall, last night, Scott, that we were discussing the legend of the
loup garou."

"More talk of werewolves!" Zeke scoffed.

Vishnevsky looked up. Natalia Petrovna started. Like a frightened animal. The scarf slipped on her face, and she rewound it
with such haste that she lost, for a moment, her grace of
movement.

"What's wrong, ma'am?" Scott said, going to her . . . instinctively putting out his hand to steady her.

She sighed. He had touched her bosom, and he felt it heave a
little under the thick serge. "I do beg your pardon, ma'am . . . I
was afraid you were fixin' to swoon." He tried to extricate his
hand, but she placed a gloved hand on his, and, as in the
graveyard the evening before, he felt the almost feverish heat of
her body. He flushed. The heat seemed to reach right down into
his loins. He snatched away his hand, embarrassed at his own
arousal.

She looked straight into his eyes and said, "Lieutenant, your
attentions do not . . . displease me. Alas, the Count . . . I do
adore him, of course, but . . . he is far away, and I am
afraid . . . perhaps I am sent here because he is . . . bored
with me?"

"Listen," said Zeke suddenly, relieving Scott of the necessity of
replying.

The ground rumbled a little. In the distance, to the east, a
metallic wheezing . . . a rhythmic clanking . . . a column of
smoke wafting in from behind the hill. A whistle blew. Wheels
clattered.

"There it comes," Grumiaux said. Workmen were scurrying up
to the tracks. There was a lot of smoke now. Scott coughed.
Natalia Petrovna arched an eyebrow; her cousin took a notebook
from his greatcoat and began scrawling something with a lead
pencil.

The snowplow rounded the curve—a railway car whose front
was a huge angled scoop—resembling a gigantic steam iron on
wheels. Snow was flying furiously in front of it and to either side.
Pushing the plow uphill was a bright blue engine with two pairs of
little wheels and two pairs of big ones, puffing noisily. A man was
shovelling wood from the tender. Scott was about to remark on the

sight when he saw a second engine pushing behind the first—and a third was emerging from behind the hill—and then another, and another—like segments of a garish centipede.

"Impressive, no?" said Claude-Achille Grumiaux.

The Russian woman cringed. Bolder now, Scott put his arm around her shoulder and said, "It's nothin' to be scared of."

But she rebuffed him and went to her cousin, screaming hysterically at him in French, pummelling his chest with her fists.

"What's wrong with her?" Scott said.

"I can't hardly foller what she's saying," Zeke said, "but it's something about how this territory is marked already."

"Marked?"

"I'm tellin' you, that woman's got one of them mental diseases that only rich folks gets."

"Wait!" Grumiaux cried. "What's that?"

The snowplow came closer. It moved painfully, jerkily, as the locomotives rammed and pushed. Scott saw what the matter was. Something was wedged in at the tip of the scoop. Something gray and furry.

"There's some kind of animal stuck in it!" Grumiaux said.

The snowplow came to a shuddering stop. Several workmen ran forward. They shouted out to Grumiaux.

"Something about a wolf . . . and a woman," Grumiaux said. The five of them went to look.

The Chinamen were at work with shovels. Grumiaux pushed his way through. Then he turned back and said, "Madame, it might perhaps be best if you did not see this."

"*Je n'ai pas peur*. I have seen a great deal, Monsieur Grumiaux, more than you might imagine. Please, I must see."

The Chinamen stepped aside and Scott, standing beside the Russian woman, saw what it was the snowplow had turned up.

Grumiaux was saying, "Strange, how it seems to have made no effort to devour the human. . . ."

There was an old Indian woman and a wolf. Lying in a tight embrace, like lovers, wrapped in the same buffalo robe. They were frozen. In death the old woman smiled and the wolf's snout nuzzled against her neck. They were at peace, the woman and the beast.

"Shit!" Zeke said, pulling out a knife and kneeling down beside the animal. "I think I'll cut off its tail and earn me another dollar."

"No!" Scott shouted, making Natalia Petrovna turn and look at him curiously.

Zeke paused. Flustered, Scott said, "I mean, you didn't exactly make the kill. You ain't exactly entitled to the bounty. Maybe you ought to give it to one of the Chinamen."

He did not want to remind Zeke—perhaps Zeke knew, but did not want to be reminded—that they had seen these two, she-wolf and old woman, before.

Twice.

Grumiaux averred that they might want to ride in the cab of one of the engines for a few miles. Vishnevsky readily consented, for he wanted to remove his cousin from that ghastly sight. They crowded into the front engine and, as soon as the corpses had been removed by the workmen, continued working their way uphill.

"It's useless," Natasha said. She did not mind speaking Russian now. The need for security was too great. "It's quite useless, the land is taken. I smelled them even before I saw them. This land—this perfect land—made for us, don't you understand? Nothing but the Lykanthropenverein . . . and a few frontiersmen . . . and a few savages. But *they* are here, too!"

He knew she could not be wrong about something like that. "I will have to write to the Count. I only hope it will not be too late. Perhaps we can find another location . . . in the southern desert, or in the far north. . . ."

"No!" she said fiercely. "I have seen the denning place. It is near the hill that man called Weeping Wolf Rock. I feel it in my heart. That's the place, the only place."

"But if it is already marked—"

"I don't care! You know very well that the pack will den where I say it will den. We are just going to have to dispose of the others. We will have to mark the territory ourselves."

"But it changes everything."

"We will den here," she said, pulling the scarf tighter around her face. "I have spoken, and I won't be moved."

At least it was warm in the cab. That was the best that could be said for it. But as the grade grew steeper, they were being continually thrown about. Only Grumiaux and the engineer seemed completely at ease. Zeke, Scott saw, was on the verge of puking. The Russians were huddled together in a corner, conferring in Russian. He concentrated on watching the scenery go by. Snow was spewing out on either side of the plow. Ahead, the sun was setting, dyeing the snow in vivid hues of vermilion, carmine, scarlet. To the north, the snow-clad firs were stained with the colors of twilight . . . the sky was streaked with russet and deep purple.

Gradually he became aware that Natalia Petrovna was no longer in the cab.

The others all seemed engrossed. She's probably just gone out back, he thought, to look at the tender. Impulsively he decided to follow.

He stepped out. The wind was bracing. The train heaved, shuddered like a metal beast. In the tender, cords of wood were neatly stacked, leaving a passage down the middle that a man could squeeze through. He saw the scarf flapping from somewhere beyond the piles of wood. Evidently there was a bench or platform at the other end of the tender where a person could sit.

He slid into the space between the piles. He thought he saw her scarf . . . or a fold of her serge coat . . . somewhere along the top of the woodpile. He moved slowly, not wanting to startle her. Peering from a stack of wood, he saw her. She was sitting on the edge, precariously balanced. His head was level with her buttocks.

I don't dare say a word, he thought. If she knows I'm here she's liable to scream and maybe even fall off.

He held his breath.

She was loosening her coat. She shivered out of it. It fell right beside Scott's face. Now she was lifting her skirt . . . carefully peeling it up over her thigh . . . he could see the whalebone of her bustle as she rolled up her petticoats.

What could she be doing? Nothing could surprise him now. Perhaps she was going to metamorphose into a werewolf, as Grumiaux had jokingly suggested. He was ready to believe anything of her. There was a musky odor to her private parts, more powerful than he remembered from playing in the stables with his cousin Prudence.

She turned in his direction. Her face was still muffled by the scarf. He shrank back. But her eyes were closed, and she seemed to be clenching back an unconscionable rage. Could she smell him? he wondered. But he was downwind of her. Maybe that was why the smell of her unmentionables was so overwhelming.

She sighed. Then, very intently, she began to urinate into the snow.

What a blamed thing, Scott thought. So ladylike when they're in your company, so different when they think they're alone. To think I believed she was up to some mischief . . . the Frenchman even had me suspecting she might start howling like a wolf! When all she was doing was answering the call of nature.

PART TWO

Winter Eyes

1
1963: Omaha, Nebraska
new moon

From the notes of Carrie Dupré

I had seen winter before the winter of '63. My parents always used to take me skiing in St. Moritz when I was little, and when I was at Berkeley, I would go to Colorado on weekends with friends. Snow was pretty, snow was exciting and romantic. But before that winter at the Szymanowski Institute, I had not known how you can be steeped in winter, how winter can numb you, seep into you, steal your soul away.

I hardly left the institute all winter. Mornings I spent with Johnny Kindred and the tape recorder. Afternoons I read in the library; twice La Loge had Harvey drive me all the way to Rapid City so that I could check out more books and delve through microfilm archives of nineteeth-century newspapers.

Evenings I worked on my book. Once or twice I even tried to revive "A Killer's Life." Johnny's story was so obsessive, and so full of detail, that—at least while he spoke—I was fascinated by every word. And as I read more of the historical records, as I drove past the desolate bleak places of his story, it became harder and harder to sustain the notion that it was all some madman's fabrication. He drew me into his world so completely. I wanted to be Speranza. I had reconstructed her thoughts, and especially her dreams, from the way Johnny talked about her and mimicked her voice, her mannerisms. After I wrote about her dreams, I started having them myself. I am not sure where her dreams ended and mine began.

Preston hasn't come back. But there was no funeral, nothing about foul play in the paper. Sometimes I'd ask La Loge about him and he'd just say something like: "Indians are like that, you know. They just vanish sometimes. Maybe he's on a vision quest or something. They're always doing things like that."

I think about Preston sometimes. They are all so certain that I dreamed up the whole event . . . that I suffered from premature cabin fever or something. Johnny knows something. But since the time I confronted him and accused him of murdering Preston, he hasn't said a word about him again.

Did I dream it?

I read a lot of academic papers about multiple personality. I discovered that it's really nothing like *The Three Faces of Eve*. For one thing they never have only three personalities. They usually have a dozen or more—even in the famous Eve case, Joanne Woodward notwithstanding, the author had simplified the actual case history. Maybe he just didn't think anyone would believe the truth.

Johnny's case—like the other known cases—is thought to have been precipitated by severe, intolerable child abuse. You're a kid and all these terrible things happen to you and you just shatter into a dozen pieces. They still have no idea of the sequence of events that let to his first dissociation, but it probably occurred very early in his life, long before he first met Speranza Martinique and the Count von Bächl-Wölfing. I plan to try to get to the bottom of that next.

As to the werewolf aspects of the story. . . .

I just don't know yet. *I've* never seen him turn into a werewolf or anything like that. Not yet. But when he talks, you can see it. You can feel it. Shit, you can *smell* it.

Jonas Kay has stayed away from the interviews. Except once. When he broke through and told me about the transformation in Vienna . . . and the little girl in the church. He crawled around the room, howling, whining . . . he even pissed himself. That was probably the most nerve-racking session I went through all winter.

A few days ago, Johnny started telling me about the journey to America. He made La Loge leave the room.

Then he pulled a cigar box from under his bed, rummaged around in it, and took out something.

"Close your eyes," he said. He was still under hypnosis. His voice was a little boy's.

I closed them. I felt his hands around my neck . . . and

something cold. I opened my eyes and saw myself reflected in the window by his bed. He had given me a necklace—a silver necklace with cabochon amethysts, five of them, not quite symmetrical, tear-shaped. I knew the necklace from his story.

"For your protection," he whispered. He was so close to me. I was frightened, but I fought it. Then he kissed me.

It was such an unnerving feeling. His lips are old and chapped, and yet when he is Johnny Kindred he speaks like a little boy, and he's skittish and temperamental like one, and yet his lips, his lips . . . are withered. And he said to me, still in that piping voice, "I'm so glad you've come back to me. When you were gone, I had to let Jonas out. I think Jonas did a lot of bad things. But now you're back. You haven't changed at all. We can start all over again."

I'm still frightened. Because, for a fraction of a split second, I was beginning to kiss him back. Even though I knew that he was the Laramie Ripper.

I have to get away. Spring is getting here at last. I think I'm going to climb into the Impala and just drive off for a few days. I'll take the back roads down through the foothills and into Nebraska. I hear Omaha's a pretty funky town, or what passes for funky around here. They have heard of the Beatles there.

Maybe I'll try to find the old Fremont, Elkhorn and Missouri Valley railway. Yeah, it really existed, all right. It was completed in 1886. It only lasted a few years. A pretty obscure fact for a supposed basket case like Johnny to know about. And he was right—it was bought up by the Chicago and Northwestern line. But I couldn't find any evidence of a takeover attempt by an Austrian count. Once again it's a case of being able to dig up virtually every bit of background and find that Johnny hasn't made a single error, and it's all so convincing . . . and then, when you get to that part of his story that involves the miraculous, the supernatural, the psychiatrically deviant . . . when you get to the crucial part, the key event his whole argument hangs on . . . suddenly the evidence evaporates and you're left with—

Dreams.

But you want to believe so badly, because, because . . .

In every sane and superficially responsible person there's a kid who *wants* the wolf to swallow Little Red Riding Hood whole.

Because Little Red Riding Hood is such a loser, such an unliberated prude, that it serves her right.

A couple of days to get to Omaha. I was taking it easy. For luck, I wore the silver necklace. Route 20, with snow still capping the twisty hills, with tall grass that's so green you think it must be artificial, with yucca-studded fields and stony shapes, humanoid almost, looming up . . . it was a lonely road. There would be no cars at all for thirty minutes, an hour. Long after sunset I pulled off the side of the road to sleep and no one bothered me. I didn't care. I didn't even brush my hair anymore . . . my bouffant had gone to seed and I'd gone to a pageboy style because I was too obsessed with the story to care.

Route 275 went along the Elkhorn Valley. I hadn't realized that the Elkhorn was a river until I crossed it at dawn, with the sunrise in my eyes.

Omaha, gateway to the West, twin city of Council Bluffs, Iowa (gateway to Omaha): I checked into a motel. It was late afternoon. I had a feeling that this was going to be one of those towns that die at seven in the evening. I thought I had better do the tourist thing, so I walked downtown. It was chilly, but there was no snow at all. I wandered up and down the purportedly funky main street with its curio shops, antique stores, and eclectic bookstores, but, to be charitable, it wasn't Berkeley.

Union Pacific headquarters had a museum, but it was already closed. There was also a Union station about ten blocks away, and, as the sun was setting, I decided to check it out.

It was an Art Deco kind of place—white and pointy and perverse. A big portion of it had been converted into a museum. I went inside and there was a huge, almost cathedral-like lobby. The place was quite empty except for a woman in a ticket booth who didn't even look up at me. I went on in. No one tried to take my money, so I walked back and forth for a while, peering at various historical exhibits.

There were some battered stagecoaches, a Conestoga wagon with some wax pioneers standing around with those wax museum expressions. There were artifacts in glass cases. I never knew that they had sewing machines back then, but there was one. There were diagrams, maps, and enlargements of contemporary prints. There was a big board explaining how passengers used to have to get off the train at Council Bluffs, carry all their baggage across the river, and get on the Union Pacific on the Nebraska side; rival railroads didn't do much cooperating with each other in those days.

Then, on the lower level, in a yard, were a bunch of historic trains. Some had been restored; others were rotting away. There was no one down here either, so I just walked up and down the railway platforms.

It was getting much darker. The silence was beginning to get to me. It's like a graveyard, I thought. Twilight glinted on rusty-flecked wheels, on dusty cowcatchers and passenger cars with peeling paint and faded gilt lettering.

The date 1881 caught my eye. It was on a sign that was telling me that the train I was standing in front of had an engine called a mogul, with one pair of little wheels and three pairs of big ones, and that this particular locomotive had been put into service that year.

It was a beautiful engine: its body was painted bright red (they had refurbished it so that it seemed almost new) and highlighted in blue. There were several passenger cars, each one about thirty or forty feet long, a couple of freight cars, a caboose. One of the cars was dimly lit up from within and I could see the usual wax figures sitting inside. I decided to go on in. There was no one to stop me.

I leaned on the railing for a few moments, trying to imagine the thing puffing and clattering along the Nebraska landscape at twenty-five miles an hour. Then I went inside. There were velvet drapes in the windows, and some plump armchairs. Two of them, facing each other, had wax figures, one of them a gentleman in gray, with a high hat and a cane, and a royal straight flush in his right hand; the other was a woman with a sort of disapproving glare, one of those horribly pinched waists, and a satin dress with layers and layers of frills. They didn't have any pockets, those Victorian women, I thought to myself. And those corseted waists—that's why they were always able to put things into their bosom—clench them between their breasts—without any danger of the articles slipping into their underwear. Those clothes! No wonder they were so repressed.

Bolder, I ventured farther into the car. There was a wood-burning stove, a piano, a little bar with a couple of stools and a bottle of whiskey—or brown Lucite. There were a few posters on the walls advertising lush western farmland and opportunities for all.

"We meet again," said a voice.

I jumped.

The piano began to play.

I turned. Someone in the shadows, close to the drapes. It was dark outside.

Long, black hair. A headband. Red, glowing eyes—

"No!" It couldn't be him. He was dead. Wasn't he? Or gone off somewhere. . . .

He sauntered out of the shadow, whistling. Stubble on his face. I stepped back.

"You think I'm dead, don't you?"

"I—"

"I bet your wondering where my dick is, ain't you? You're thinking, didn't that Injun Joe's pecker get chawed off by a werewolf?"

"Preston, I—"

He came close. I was backed against the wall. He cuffed my cheek, not gently, with a callused hand. I caught a whiff of him for the first time. A faint smell of animal urine clung to my lips.

"You're bringing the dead to life, Carrie. All of them. In your words, I mean. Speranza. The Count. Claude-Achille Grumiaux. You must've guessed by now that I'm descended from him and his Injun bride. Yeah, I'm part white. Kind of embarrassing, but there it is."

"But I saw you . . . lying there . . ."

"I didn't exactly die. Let's just say I got into a squabble over the right to rut with the pack bitch . . . sorry, Carrie, but things ain't quite as refined in the animal kingdom as they are in your whitebread suburbs. No, I ain't dead. I . . . well . . . I crossed over into another plane of existence. I transcended humanity. You can psychobabble all you want, but we're all playing into his hands."

"Whose?"

"Your friend, the lunatic, that fucking mass murderer—he's like the werewolf messiah, did you know that? The Shungmanitu Indians were completely extinct before you came. Now they've come back. There's at least one of them around. Me! Yeah, I'm one of them! I've turned into a fucking werewolf! Scared?"

I was terrified, but I didn't want him to see. I tried to make a run for the exit but he blocked my way. And grinned. He had knife-sharp teeth, and they glistened. "Hey, easy, babe," he said. "I ain't gonna do nothing to you! I've missed you."

"I've got the silver necklace!" I said, holding it out like a crucifix to a vampire. I felt frightened and absurd at the same time.

"Careful with that thing! You could hurt someone." His eyes shifted from side to side.

"Leave me alone!"

"You think I'm gonna rape you? I'm gonna stuff my primal penis into your oh-so-sophisticated pussy?" He pulled something out of his jeans and waved it in my face. "Don't worry, *washichun* bitch. I don't do that anymore."

I couldn't look at it.

"You never seen a dried redskin dick before?"

"Preston—"

"My—ah, rival for your affections wanted to make sure I'd never stand in his way again. Don't worry about it! I'm used to it by now. Penises, shmenises. The cavalry used to take 'em all the time. They used to make tobacco pouches out of our balls."

"I—"

"You want it? Here, catch."

"Leave me alone!"

"C'mon, babe. I still feel down there, you know? You ever heard of phantom pain, like when people have their arm amputated and they feel like it's still there? Well, I get phantom pain in my dick. I get phantom erections. Ever been fucked by a phantom dick? I could come phantom come. It's the latest form of birth control."

I tried to push him aside again. But he just laughed. He gripped my arm. He was strong, stronger than I thought possible. I gasped. "This isn't happening," I said. "This isn't real, somehow—"

"Been having dreams, Carrie? Been falling into the dreams, not knowing where the dreams end and the world begins? Welcome to the narrow path . . . between two worlds . . . welcome."

"Yeah, I've been having dreams, bad dreams."

"You think when you've done the book you can throw it all away, you can hide inside it, you can say there it is, it's just a

fiction, a study in criminal psychopathology. It's a house of cards!
I'll huff and I'll puff and I'll blow it down."

"So now it's the Three Little Pigs?"

He smiled. A sinister smile. "You know, I do like you, Carrie.
I want you. I still want you. Kiss me, Carrie." He pulled me hard
and I felt his lips crushing mine, chapped, sandpapery. There was
a hint of tongue. I shuddered. He looked at me, his eyes clear and
emotionless. Then he let go. Slowly. I twisted my arm free. He
just went on smiling. I don't know what happened next. I think he
kind of faded out. Like the Cheshire cat. Only his smile remained.

Then the smile faded too, and there was just the starry glint of
a single canine tooth, and then that too was gone.

Was I going insane?

I had to sit down. I found a seat next to the wax Victorian lady.
I was trembling. It felt as though the seat was vibrating . . . the
train was vibrating . . . moving . . . huffing and puffing its
way across the prairie.

2
1881: Council Bluffs, Iowa
crescent moon

JOHNNY HEARD HIS GOVERNESS'S VOICE CALLING HIM FROM ACROSS
the lobby of the Transfer Hotel. But he didn't want to be with
Speranza right then. Latin grammar was fine when you were
cooped up in a closet-sized cabin aboard a transatlantic ship, or
stuck in a train compartment for days on end. But they were not
due to leave until tomorrow, and until then he wasn't going to stay
in one place long enough to conjugate a verb.

Not when there was so much to see, so many people to talk to,
so many sounds and smells to experience.

He saw Speranza beckoning to him from the stairway. The
lobby was full of travellers. A game of poker was in progress on

the carpet, several men sitting around on wooden chests, with a ragged boy peering at them, trying to see their hands. He noticed Johnny and Johnny smiled shyly back.

Speranza threw up her hands in exasperation. Johnny decided he had a good half an hour before she would set out to look for him. He was about to go outside when he heard the ragged boy mumble something to one of the card players, who got up, threw his cards down on the floor, and cuffed the boy on the ear.

The boy kicked him in the shin and ran for the door.

The card player shook his sleeve. A miniature gun popped into his hand. He twirled his mustache with his left hand and aimed with his right; then thought better of it, wiggled his fingers, and made the derringer disappear back into his sleeve.

"Hey, boy!" A voice just behind him. "Come on."

He whirled around to see the ragged boy. "Let's get out of here. I'm bored," the boy said, tugging at Johnny's sleeve. He grabbed his neck and shoved him outside, smudging the fresh paper collar that Speranza had put on him only that morning. "Damn that cardsharp!" the boy went on. "Every time I think I'm fixin' to figure out his technique he kicks me out of the way."

They stood in front of the hotel, a stone's throw from the banks of the Missouri. A bridge spanned the river, and there was a continuous stream of people crossing, on foot and by buggy, in both directions, and endless carts of luggage. The depot was next to the hotel, and Johnny could see another depot on the Omaha side of the river.

"Who was that man, anyway?" said Johnny

"His name's Claggart." Johnny's new friend was about eleven. He had dirty, tousled black hair, wide brown eyes, a dark complexion, and a brown jacket that had seen better days. He was always smirking. "He works the Union Pacific route, up and down, from Cheyenne to Omaha and back again."

"Works it?"

"You know. Blackjack. Poker."

"Oh. Gambling." Johnny noticed for the first time that his new companion was barefoot, and his trousers had a couple of yawning holes through which he could see scrawny, hairless thighs.

"You an immigrant, boy? You got them high-society airs. I reckoned your ma's a widder; I seed she was wearing black. I thought maybe she was comin' West to find a man. Then I got to wonderin' why there wasn't no men for her back East. Maybe she couldn't find one that was man enough for her. On account of them eastern gentlemen is so busy sticking their fool noses in the air they can't never seem to do the same thing with their pricks."

"Oh, no. The woman you saw is my governess, Mademoiselle Martinique. I'm with the Austrian Count's party. My name is . . ." Suddenly Johnny hesitated. The others inside. They were clamoring at the outskirts of the circle, all of them wanting to get acquainted with this new person. Except Jonas. Jonas was sulking somewhere in the depths of the forest.

"Hey! You got a tongue?"

"Sorry. I'm Johnny Kindred. Yes, I am an immigrant. We're going to a new town in Dakota Territory. It's called Winterreise."

"I'm Theodore Grumiaux. Teddy. I'm a news butch. That means I goes running up and down the train selling newspapers and tobacco and anything else them passengers want. Funny, though—I been workin' the Omaha-Cheyenne run since I was nine year old, and I ain't never heard of no town called Winter Eyes. But why does folks like you want to mine for gold anyhow? You look like you's wearing fifty dollars' worth of clothes right here—and it ain't even Sunday."

"Actually, the Count gave them to me. He's been very good to me."

"Good to you! What are you, his bumboy?"

"I'm afraid I don't quite know what you mean, Teddy." But he felt Jonas stirring a little for the first time in weeks, and he wanted to change the subject. "Is it exciting, working on a train?"

"Sometimes. C'mon! I'll show you around. We can cross over to the Omaha depot if you want. There's a new mogul. And they just brung in some private cars. I think they's for your friend the Count."

"I don't know." Time was running out. Speranza would be looking for him soon, and when he was too long without her he always felt afraid that one of the others would escape and take over the body. "I'm wanted back. I'm supposed to be learning my Latin conjugations."

"Race yer!"

And Teddy was already off, kicking up dust with his bare feet. Johnny started to follow, but a corpulent woman, lugging her trunk toward the depot, bumped into him and knocked off his hat.

The breeze picked up the hat and sent it whirling toward the river. Johnny sprinted after it, picked it up, and caught up with Teddy. The river had a sharp, clean smell. Their footsteps thudded on the planks. They wove in and out of the lines of passengers. A padre wagged his finger at them. They laughed. He ducked a swipe from the parasol of an irate, schoolmarmish woman. The news butch squealed with laughter.

"Look! The mogul's comin' in now!"

Johnny heard the whistle in the distance. They reached the platform, almost out of breath, and Johnny saw the engine almost head-on, a monstrous, breathing, clanking machine, its brilliant red and blue paint peering from layers of dust and soot. It was braking. Behind it he could see dozens of tracks, mating, dividing, curving; beyond them, the town.

"Let's run down to the yard," Teddy said, tugging at his arm again. They ran toward the tail end of the slowing train.

Beyond the edge of the platform, an official shouted at them: "Get out! Oh, it's you, breed. Well, be careful."

"What does 'breed' mean?" Johnny said.

The boy stopped running abruptly and stared at him. "You really don't know? I'm half Injun. My daddy is a trainman, but my ma is a full-blooded Sioux. But he left us for a Chinawoman, and I run away from the reservation to look for him. But anyone can see what I am. You hadn't noticed?"

"No." The train was screeching against the tracks as it slowed. A man was sprinting along the top of the freight cars, pausing to turn the brake on the roof of each one. "Does it matter?"

"It means that decent civilized folks treats you like a buffer turd, boy. It means you spends your whole life not knowin' who you really is."

"I understand," Johnny said softly.

"Hell, no! Rich feller like you?"

"I'm one too," Johnny said. "I understand you perfectly." And he put his hand on Teddy's sweaty wrist and patted it a couple of times.

"Hey! Friends?"

"Brothers."

"You stay with me and I'll take good care of you. Look for me when I come sellin' newspapers."

The two boys smiled at each other. A man in uniform was

running alongside the slowing train, darting in between each car. "What's he doing?" Johnny said.

"Oh, he's just uncoupling the cars. In these here primitive parts, they still does it by hand. They runs in and grabs this bolt and pulls it and tries to get away before—"

A crash—steel on steel. The man screamed. Teddy gazed curiously, but Johnny couldn't look. The official who had shouted at them earlier was running to the scene and calling for help. The man had fallen and lay, twitching, on the track. The train had finally ground to a complete halt.

"You all right?" Teddy said.

"It's—well, it's the blood—" From where they were standing Johnny couldn't see any blood, but inside him there was someone else, someone who could smell it as it gushed from the trainman's hand, someone who was quickly becoming aroused by the smell and who wanted to burst out into the clearing—

"Hey, pardner, you better develop a stronger stomach!" Teddy said gruffly. But he let Johnny hide his face in his jacket, which stank of sweat and other things. "It's a rare trainman that can keep all his fingers."

Johnny didn't answer. In his mind, he was too busy fending off Jonas. He could hear Jonas laughing. He didn't want Jonas to make friends with Teddy. Teddy was *his* friend, not Jonas's. But he could hear Jonas whispering, and the others tittering along with him. The alliance he had forged after Speranza agreed to stay with them was beginning to tear apart at the seams.

They were carrying the trainman away on a stretcher. "I have to get back now," Johnny said. "My governess—"

The card game was still going on when they reached the Transfer Hotel. Teddy gave his new friend a quick punch in the ribs and ran off, mumbling something about having to pick up supplies for tomorrow's trip.

Johnny stood for a moment, feeling desperately alone amid the crowd. They jabbered, they strolled back and forth, they drank, they played cards; two of them sat playing a clunky, out-of-tune duet at the lobby piano.

In his mind, in the forest, he saw Jonas's eyes, watching him.

"Speranza! Speranza!" he screamed, and ran toward the staircase with all his might.

3
Fremont, Nebraska
crescent moon, waxing

IN HIS PRIVATE CUBICLE IN ONE OF THE FIRST-CLASS COACHES, Cordwainer Claggart dressed himself very carefully, as befit his newfound status as a man of substance. Two hours had passed since dawn, when the *Pacific Express* had started to pull out of the Omaha depot; they were probably a good fifty miles from Omaha, and due to pull in at Fremont soon. It would soon be time for the second session of breakfast in the dining car, and Claggart knew from experience that the richer passengers would hardly be expected to breakfast at the first session.

What a prime prospect Sally Bryant had proved to be! She had willingly handed over all her gold, just for the privilege of being pumped full of juice every couple of weeks. A little house in Deadwood, the acquaintance of some of the soldiers at Fort Cassandra, who were only too eager to part with their hard-earned silver . . . and enough cash to set himself up as a cardsharp, working the *Pacific Express* and clearing, after expenses, close to five hundred dollars a month.

Of course, there was the small price he had to pay . . . negotiating the unappetizing flesh of the insatiable widow. But until she actually consented to marry him, he was compelled to perform, at intervals, that distasteful act. Why sure, he had been in love with her that winter night in Deadwood; but love could wear thin after a while, and for him a while wasn't that long. He was a man who craved variety. But there were other women in the world, and even without women there were alternatives, for he wasn't one to turn down a bit of spice.

He used the window as a looking glass, mindless of the plains that reeled endlessly past. The land was green; the last of the snow had melted. The train rattled on. He drank from a flask of whiskey on the seat of his velvet easy chair.

He opened his valise. Among the bottles of Claggart's Patent Floccinaucinihilipilificator was the device to which he owed his success in gambling. He took it out. Part of it he strapped to his bare thigh before pulling up his trousers. A thin cord ran up to his belt, where it was hooked in place; a wire ran up his back and down his sleeve to a metal band buckled to his forearm. From this there extended a steel claw—a sneak—in which he proceeded to place several cards: an ace of spades, two kings, and a queen of hearts. Fortune had smiled on him since he had ordered this holdout from a Montgomery Ward catalog and adapted its rather primitive mechanism to his own purposes.

Claggart put on his shirt, fastened the starched linen front, took a fresh collar from his valise, and attached it with an ivory stud in the back and a gold one in front. He ran his cravat through the collar, knotted it, and tucked it smartly into the sides of the collar.

Keeping his face impassive, he practiced the slight squeeze of the knees which pushed the claw out toward his shirt cuff, which had an extra pocket sewn into it. There was a luxuriant lace ruff around each cuff, which served conveniently to conceal any eccentric movements that the holdout might make. Having made sure that everything worked correctly (and after putting a few drops of grease on the joints, for they were a mite stiff) he buttoned up his vest, which was made of pea-green Chinese silk, embroidered with butterflies in gold thread, and put on his coat over it. Then he loaded his derringer and stuck it in his vest pocket. He'd had a gold chain put on it so people would think it was a watch.

He topped his bald head with a fine bowler hat, slicked down his mustache with a bit of the same grease he'd used on his holdout, and sallied forth to inspect the victims of the day. He sniffed the air. It smelled of money, he was sure of it. Why, he'd heard there were counts and dukes and European dandies on board.

"By the time we pull in at Grand Island," he said, pulling the curtain of his cubicle tight, "I'm going to win me a sack of gold."

"Oh, do let me go now, please!" Johnny said to Speranza. "I promised Teddy I'd go up and down the train with him and help

him sell his newspapers. And I do so want to look at the second-
and third-class passengers. Teddy says that in third class they're
crammed in like maggots."

Speranza sighed. The boy had become more skittish, more
willful, since they had arrived in America. "Well, you'll have
some breakfast first. A piece of bread at the very least." She
handed him a slice, buttered and covered with jam, and he ran
down the aisle of the dining car, munching furiously at the same
time. He bumped into a little man in a bowler hat—rather gaudily
overdressed, Speranza thought—who was just entering from the
rear of the car.

"I do apologize for the boy—" Speranza began.

"Oh, never you mind, ma'am! Ah, the foibles, the ferocities of
youth! Might I join you, now that your boy has vacated his seat?"
He tipped his hat and revealed his baldness.

"This table is reserved, I'm afraid," Speranza said, for the man
was being most forward. Pointedly, she placed her Bible on the
table. Claggart immediately apologized and backed away.

Shri Chandraputra, who was seated alone at the table opposite
hers, said, "By all means, sir, you are being welcome to share my
repast." He inclined his head. His crimson turban contrasted
violently with the bright green of the plains as they rushed by.

"I'll be damned! Beggin' your pardon, ma'am, but I mean, an
honest-to-goodness Oriental Pumpkintate! Cordwainer Claggart,
sir, at your service. I am the *in*ventor of Claggart's world-famous
panacea, the Floccinaucinihilipilificator. Perhaps you know of
it?"

"It is not something I have run across."

"I don't suppose you play poker?"

"The game is not altogether unfamiliar to me. But perhaps you
would prefer vingt-et-un?"

"Done! After breakfast, in the parlor car," Claggart said,
sounding terribly pleased with himself. He turned to Speranza and
said, "You know anything about that millionaire Count folks is
talking about?"

"My ears burn. You are speaking, perhaps, of me?"

He had arrived. Speranza had not heard him approach. She
should have grown used, by now, to the noiselessness of his
movements; but he never failed to startle her. He looked at
Claggart, a little bemused by his flamboyant attire; he himself

wore black. "I am Count Hartmut von Bächl-Wölfing." The Count sat down at her table and ordered breakfast.

"Pleased to make your acquaintance, Your Highness—is it Your Highness?"

"I'm afraid not. 'Count' will suffice, although that, and the Barony of Kodaly, were the least of my family's titles before the Austro-Hungarian union. Of course, my ancestors did once lay claim to a hereditary dukedom in the Kingdom of Wallachia; that is why my servants still persist in calling me 'Your Grace'; but Wallachia is, alas, no longer independent, so I do think that is a little hubristic, don't you?"

Speranza had to suppress a laugh at Claggart's confounded expression.

Claggart watched them with undisguised interest, and the Count immediately switched to French.

"This infernal American coffee! It tastes like river water. Not even a pinch of nutmeg or a dash of whipped cream!" He sipped fastidiously and paid the waiter fifty cents for the vastly over-priced steak, ham, eggs, biscuits, butter, and marmalade he had been serving during von Bächl-Wölfing's brief explication of his family history. "Tell me, Speranza . . . you are pleased with the boy's progress?" Before she could answer, he went on: "I must say I am not."

"Oh?"

"You are hiding his true nature from him. The moon has waxed and waned three times since your coming to us, and not once has he transformed."

"Most assuredly not! If you desired that he be instructed in the ways of an insensate beast, would you not have released me from your service by now?"

"Come, Speranza! The boy would never forgive me for letting you go. And yet—"

"Perhaps it's true that you are his father. But he must have had a mother too. And his mother was not one of you. That much is clear. But are you the father of all his disparate personalities? Or only the father of Jonas Kay, the twisted shadow, the one I am endeavoring to make him forget?"

"Why are you so sure that Johnny Kindred is his true self? Did he not tell you, Speranza, that, when I visited his mother in Whitechapel, I identified myself to her by the name John Kay?

The boy wants to take after his father. That is why he has chosen this name for himself. . . ."

"We are fighting over his soul, Count."

He thought for a moment, and at last said, "Yes. I suppose we are."

"And you are no longer desirous of my person, Count? You have ceased belaboring me with your attentions. . . ."

"On the contrary, mademoiselle. I have been exercising the most exemplary self-control. One should never love one's enemies, should one?"

"Am I your enemy?"

"You have just told me so."

Speranza sipped her coffee. Soon the others would arise and gather for breakfast: Dr. Szymanowski himself; the screeching Baroness von Dittersdorf, who had made herself so raucously noticeable at the soirée, that first night in Vienna; Azucena, the Gipsy woman; Father Alexandros, the Orthodox priest who was also of the lycanthropic persuasion; and the others, a pack of some two dozen. They had all, of course, brought servants; the priest had even brought his own confessor. They were so many, and she was but one; how could she hope to win? And the Count: though the experience on the last train journey had never been repeated, the dark attraction she had felt for him had been by no means mitigated by the passage of time.

But she knew now that he had a mistress waiting for him in the Dakota Territory: as was the custom amongst his kind, the queen wolf had gone first, to claim a denning place.

In only a few days she would be meeting Natalia Stravinskaya. What kind of a woman could be the Count's mistress? To her own horror, she had begun imagining herself in that position. The prospect had not filled her with the darkest opprobrium she felt she ought to feel.

I cannot mate with an animal! she thought. Surely I can draw the line there!

But the Count continued to transfix her with his penetrating gaze . . . mesmerizing her . . . making her tremble.

4
Columbus, Nebraska

"GARFIELD INAUGURATED PRESIDENT! JAMES G. BLAINE APPOINTED secretary of state! Congress in an uproar!"

Teddy barked out the news as he and Johnny made their way through the first-class carriages. He wore a leather apron stuffed with broadsheets, tobacco, medicines, and sweetmeats. They passed through cars shrouded in smoke, where men sat poker-faced at card tables; a parlor car, where the passengers strutted about, the women displaying their plumage, the men all dandi-fied, to the accompaniment of a piano. Johnny had been with people like this all winter; he was much more interested in the second-class section. There were stern-faced men with guns strapped to their belts; soldiers; miners; women who did not hesitate to use profanity; Catholic priests; dirty-faced children. They stared at Johnny, in his costly clothes, with naked curiosity and envy.

"Headache? Cramps? I got Gessler's Magic Headache Wafers," Teddy said to an old woman who was clutching her head. "That'll be five cents." Turning to Johnny, he said, "Come on, boy! You want to see shit-ass misery? I'll take you down to third."

They reached the next car. Teddy was right. They were jammed in together on straw, men, women, and children in tattered clothes, some looking vacantly ahead, others babbling in foreign languages: Johnny recognized Polish, Low German, Italian, and Croatian among them. "Immigrants," Teddy said. "Californy bound. I should say they coughed up their last pennies for the eighty-dollar fare to Sacramento." The air was pungent with the stench of unwashed bodies. The straw, the dust made Johnny cough. He felt uncomfortable; the scene reminded him a little too much of the last place he had lived in. The madhouse.

"They won't be wanting nothin'," Teddy said, and dragged Johnny away.

Back in the second-class section, Johnny saw his first Indian.

He was seated all by himself; an old man, his braided hair almost white. His face was deeply pocked; his brows were knitted. He was dozing by an open window. In his sleep he scratched his wide, flat nose. He wore a single feather in his hair, which twisted in the wind.

Johnny felt Jonas stir. "Keep back!" he whispered in his mind. "You've no business coming out now." Aloud he said, "Who is he?"

Teddy said, "Oh, he just rides back and forth between Cheyenne and Omaha, same as me. When they made the treaty for the land to build the railroad, they done give some of them chiefs the right to ride the train free of charge in perpetuity. I don't think this feller was one of them, but as far as U.P.'s concerned, all them Injuns looks alike."

The Indian woke. Johnny stepped back. They looked at each other. Suddenly the Indian smiled. And began to sing in a wheezing falsetto: "*Kola anpa zi kin wana hinape lo! Hehanl wani ye lo!*"

"What's he saying?"

Teddy said, "I ain't sure; I don't remember too much Injun talk no more. I think it's a called a *shungmanitu olowan*, a wolf song."

"I think he wants me to be his friend."

"Take care, Johnny." Teddy started to drag him away, but Johnny could not take his eyes off the old Indian.

Later, in the little railinged balcony between two cars, Johnny watched the scenery. Green, green, a monotony of green. A freshness in the air, like the smell of summer lightning.

Teddy said, "What did you mean when you said you understood me? About bein' a breed, I mean. You ain't got no mixed blood. Have a chaw."

Johnny took the tobacco and put it in his mouth. He tried to imitate his friend as he chewed glibly. "But I am of mixed blood. I'm a foundling. I spent my life searching for my father, like you. And now I think I've found him, and he tells me I'm only half human."

"You ain't making much sense, pardner."

"No, it's true. That Indian knew about me. I'm not quite sure how, but he knew. What was that wolf song anyway?" For Johnny was sure that his friend knew more than he was letting on.

"When I lived with my ma, I heard a song like that once. Some bucks come back from a war party, and one of them who was friendly to me on account of he was a kind of uncle, he says to me: 'As we was comin' over the hill toward the enemy camp, we heard a pack of wolves singing this song.' And he sung it to me. It means, 'It's dawn, my friend. So I'm still alive.'"

"How could he understand what the wolves were singing?"

"Beats me."

Claggart was immensely pleased when he arrived in the parlor car that served as a makeshift gambling house. Chandraputra, a heathen prince if ever he saw one, was already there, puffing opium from a brass hookah on a cushion by his feet, which were even now being massaged by a little Negro boy. "Ah! You are ready for playing vingt-et-un now, Mr. Claggart!" he said.

"Sure am."

He sat down and pulled out a pack of cards.

"Surely you are not thinking I am such a fool as to trust your cards, Mr. Claggart! Let us be using mine." The Indian waved his own deck, and Claggart saw that it did not match his, either in size or design. He did not allow his dismay to show.

"Then I would be the fool, mister." He looked around and saw the news butch breeze through with his new friend, that solemn little blond boy who seemed to belong to the Austrian Count. "Sell me a pack of cards, boy," he said.

Teddy Grumiaux paused and handed him a fresh pack, wrapped and sealed. It was precisely what he wanted, for he had made sure beforehand that the cards the boy sold were identical to his own—he had supplied them himself!

Presently they were joined by Baroness von Dittersdorf and Father Alexandros, a black-robed priest of some Eastern Orthodox faith with a straggly black beard that trailed all the way to his waist. Claggart had little difficulty divesting them of about four hundred dollars in about an hour of intense play. Blackjack soon palled, however, and they switched to poker.

He was annoyed to find the news butch peeking over his shoulder. That boy was getting to be quite a pest, even though once or twice he had been useful to him. Why, the day before, he had damn near made him forget what he was doing, with his peering and staring.

"One o' these days," he said under his breath, "I am going to take a hickory to your bee-hind."

"Oh!" exclaimed the Baroness. "I should very much like to watch!"

Chandraputra laughed. "I am afraid my aristocratic friend is being a little too fond of inflicting pain," he said. "It is very Teutonic of her. I will see you."

"And I will fold," said the priest.

The boy didn't move. "Don't you have papers to sell, boy?" Claggart said, for he noticed that the boy's gaze was drawn precisely to his sleeve. He was about to squeeze his knee, operate the holdout, and have a fresh ace pop into his hand, but the boy's presence was preventing the operation.

"No sir," said Teddy. "They is all gone."

Claggart sighed, pulled a silver dollar out of his pocket, and thrust it at the youth. The boy beamed with delight. The instant he looked away, Claggart deftly substituted the card. "I have," he said, "four aces," revealing them with a smirk, and preparing to sweep up the pot.

The Indian astrologer had been bluffing.

The Baroness burst out laughing. "Ha! You have been cheating, for I have here a full house, aces and kings, and I do not believe that even in America there can be six aces in a single deck!"

"Now, look you here, ma'am," Claggart said in an injured tone, "that's a hell of an accusation to bring against an honest, hard-workin' cardsharp like my humble self. Mayhap *you've* been cheatin'. I never heard that Europeans was exempt from the noble art of switchin' cards! But, you being a highborn aristicritical lady and all, I am just too chivalrous to go making accusations of you, so I will just let you have your own way. Take the pot, ma'am. Be my guest. I ain't a covetous man." He tipped his bowler hat and waved the money away.

The Baroness ironically acknowledged his gallant gesture and began gathering the coins into her kerchief. As she did so, Claggart put his hand under the table and sharply wiggled his knee so that a fresh ace was hurled from his sleeve into the Baroness's shoe.

"Did I hear something fall?" he said. He turned to the news

butch, who was gossiping in the corner with his young friend. "Boy! The Baroness has dropped something; you are small, so crawl under the table and retrieve it for her."

He did so, and emerged brandishing a card.

"Beggin' your pardon, ma'am," the boy said, "it must have dropped from under your petticoats. . . ."

"I see!" Claggart said indignantly. "You have one of them holdouts concealed in your corsets, ma'am! The ladies of today—so brazen—I ain't never going to understand them . . . you accuse me of hiding aces . . . when you yourself have an ace in your petticoat!"

"Oh, this ain't no ace, Mister Claggart," the boy said. "This is the queen of spades."

But Claggart was sure it had been an ace that he . . . suddenly he realized that the Baroness had indeed been cheating the whole time . . . he began to laugh heartily, and the Baroness joined in, cackling like a witch.

"What was all that about?" Johnny asked Teddy as the two of them sat, chewing tobacco, between two cars, their legs dangling between the railings.

"Look." Teddy took a handful of coins out of his pocket. "Mister Claggart been payin' me for helpin' him, distractin' the other players, you know. But I don't play favorites, and that Baroness's money is just as good as Mister Claggart's."

Johnny said, "You mean you've been taking money from both of them to help them cheat against each other?"

"I know. I'm liable to git myself kilt . . . but I needs the money. I don't want my paw to think I'm a pauper. When I finds him. I want him to be proud of me."

He said this with deep feeling; Johnny felt there was a lot he was leaving unsaid. "What's next?" he asked.

"Grand Island . . . some buffler hunters will come on board, and if we encounters a herd, they will give a grand old demonstration of their prowess. The U.P. pays them to put on a show."

"When will we get to Cheyenne?"

"Depends. Did you know there's 230 stops betwixt Omaha and Sacramento?"

Johnny slipped away and found the second-class car where he had seen the old Indian.

He was still there. Johnny sat down beside him. The sun was setting. Johnny unfastened his cravat and gave it to the Indian. The Indian plucked the feather from his hair and gave it to Johnny.

The Indian said: "We will meet again in the high country. You see me now, but I am here in spirit, in a dream. I have come to greet you, my brother, and to welcome you to the new land."

Wondering, Johnny said, "But you speak English so beautifully!" Not until several long moments had passed did he realize that the old man had not opened his mouth. He had spoken to Johnny in another language . . . a language of movement, touch, smell.

"He spoke to me, not you!" cried a voice inside his head. "It's the beast language, you silly boy. You don't even understand it. You only know what he's saying because I happen to be listening."

"Get away, Jonas!" Johnny whispered fiercely.

Jonas laughed.

Claggart surprised the news butch as he was trying to pry open the lock of his valise. Angrily he shoved the boy out of the way. "Trying to steal from me! I ought to see you hanged."

"I wasn't trying to steal nothing, sir—" The boy looked properly abject, Claggart decided. "I was hopin' mayhap you could learn me . . . well, some of your secrets."

Damn! Slapping the boy had torn his sleeve, and revealed the steel claw of his holdout! And the boy had just noticed it. He was staring at it wide-eyed . . . admiring.

"Fixin' to become a cardsharp?"

"I'll pay back all the money you been bribin' me with, just so you'll learn me some tricks."

"I don't need no money, boy. And remember, I could report you for stealing." Claggart peered at the boy, who was trembling something fierce. "But it's always good to have a 'prentice. I could use a little diversion, boy, on these long train journeys, away from my woman. Do you catch my drift?" He arched his eyebrows.

"Oh, please, sir! I don't hold with no cornholing."

"Don't lie to me, boy. I know you lived among the Sioux, and them Injun bucks is always cornholing their enemies. Show their contempt for them. A breed like you, by the time he's your age, has probably fucked everything under the sun, including his own ma. But that ain't what I want. I want a little bit of spying done."

"Sir?"

"That little friend of yours . . . he has something to do with the Count, don't he?"

"He's an orphan, sir. But the Count gives him everything. I done asked him if he was the Count's . . . you know . . . but he acted like he didn't understand."

"Find out everything you can about the furriners. Pump the Count's little catamite for information."

"I'll do my best, Mister Claggart."

"Good. I'll learn you something right now, if you like." He took out his cards, shuffled them, threw them in the air, made them dance between his hands, threw them up again, plucked the aces out of the air. . . .

The boy gasped.

"But before I gives you your first lesson, I want you to help me relax." He began to unbutton his trousers.

"Please, sir. . . ."

"Remember that I caught you a-stealing from me, boy! Well, if you ain't no thief, I ain't no filthy sodomite, neither."

"You don't have to worry, my dear Speranza, that there will be any incidents on this trip; we have a full fortnight before our next . . . ah . . . festivities," the Count said, finding the governess moping in a corner of one of the parlors, apparently studying her Bible.

They were alone together, for almost everyone in first class had gone to the gambling car to gossip, gawk, or try his luck.

"But there are other mysteries we could perhaps celebrate," the Count said. And cupped her chin in his hand, forcing her to look into his eyes.

"I should remind you, Count, that you have a mistress waiting for you in the Dakota Territory; and that I am not your abject slave, branded with a yellow flower; I do not have to submit to your—"

"I have a terrible failing, Speranza, which has led me into trouble before . . . I have loved many women. Once or twice, I have loved a woman so passionately that I have made her one of us . . . but somehow it is no longer the same after that . . . so it has been with Natasha. The flame . . . has spent itself. I find myself . . . attracted to another."

She received his kiss without response at first. His second kiss was more urgent, more demanding. She yielded to him a little, closed her eyes, tried to block from her mind the memory of that horrifying night on the train to Vienna. He smelled of autumn leaves, of damp earth. She did not know whether what she felt for him was love or a desire for what was bestial in him. Without warning tears came; she wept passionately, uncontrollably.

"Is it from joy that you weep? Or sorrow?"

"I have no shame!" Speranza cried, understanding at last that she had always known that she would eventually succumb to his advances . . . had known from the moment she first laid eyes on him.

"There is that in us which is beyond shame . . . beyond the repressive trappings of our civilized society. Men imprison their bestial selves . . . as a woman cages her body within a whalebone corset. But we of the werewolves are free of those constraints . . . we are more truly alive than they . . . for we dance the dance of life and death!"

He kissed her a third time. All the passion she had buried within herself came bursting to the surface. She drew him into her embrace. What did it matter that she was a fallen woman? They were in another country now—a country of wildernesses, far from the civilized world.

Perhaps I will change him, she thought, remembering the story of Beauty and the Beast. Perhaps I shall redeem him.

As he kissed her he murmured, as though in agreement, "My Madonna of the Wolves. . . ."

5
Deadwood

THE SNOW STILL CLUNG TO THE HIGH GROUND. THE WIND WAS STILL bitter cold at times. But the sun shone every day now, and there was a subtle new fragrance in the air . . . the promise of spring.

Scott Harper had returned from Deadwood to find himself promoted; his superior, the Indian-hating Sanderson, had been elevated too, for his role in that terrible massacre. He was a major now, and confirmed, rather than acting, commander of Fort Cassandra; but Scott knew that the munificent salary of $187 per month and the allotment of two servants instead of one had done little to dull Sanderson's fury.

His scalp, carefully tanned and set in a glass case on his desk next to a marble bust of the late General George Armstrong Custer, was ample evidence that Major Sanderson had no desire to forget that bloody day.

As they rode along the Deadwood road, Scott remembered the shock he had felt the first time he had walked into Sanderson's office and seen that scalp so carefully preserved and so prominently displayed. He rode side by side with Zeke. There was to be a grand ball in Deadwood, and Sanderson had been given the honor of opening the festivities; he and Scott and half a dozen others had set out at dawn to escort the major. It was to celebrate the inauguration of President Garfield; Silas Snodgrass, fervent Republican turned gold miner, had rented the St. Ambrose church hall for the occasion.

It was a wet morning; the new leaves glistened, and the canyon walls were slick with rain. It was hard slogging uphill, with frequent stops to haul the mule cart, which held their dress uniforms, out of the mud. But Scott looked forward to the evening. Life at the fort had been dull as before. He'd had a taste of what Sanderson called combat—that massacre—and he sure didn't want another. But there had been nothing more the rest of the winter, and the Sioux had stayed subdued and gone on eating their maggot-ridden rations. But Sanderson was crazier than ever. Bizarre exercises at all hours of the day and night—and sometimes they'd find him walking up and down the walls, quoting Xenophon and Wellington. Scott reckoned it was what they had taught him at West Point.

"Captain Harper!" Sanderson called sharply to him. The major had taken off his hat, and there was nothing to cover the circle of purplish scar tissue that adorned his head like an obscene tonsure. "You are daydreaming again, mister!"

He stopped. He had left the rest of the detail far behind. They were busy unsticking the cart again. The drizzle made him blink. He turned around and rode back. "Sorry, sir."

Sanderson peered at him, no doubt trying to find some imperfection for which he could dress him down. When he could not, he allowed him to carry on.

Scott was indeed daydreaming. He was wondering if the Russian lady was going to be present at the ball. Rumor had it she'd gone off and started a new settlement south of Deadwood . . . somewhere near the place where they'd found the Indian woman and the she-wolf buried in the snow.

He'd been dreaming a lot about her. There were no women at the camp except for some of the Crow squaws that were kept around for general use. When they were on leave, the men would frequent the Green Door in Deadwood, but Scott didn't hold with whoring; his daddy had brought him up well, even if they had not been well off since the end of the war between the states.

But the Russian woman was different. . . .

The band was starting up—violins, guitars, and the grating, nasal voice of some local singer. "We should never have come," Vishnevsky said to Natasha. "You always attract too much attention. Already too many people know about your little project. . . ."

"Come, cousin. If we had turned down Snodgrass's invitation, it would have been equally suspicious. We cannot yet snub the influential people of Deadwood, not until we are quite sure which of them we can manipulate, and which of them we will have to . . . destroy."

It was true that Natasha could not fail to attract attention. She was wearing a ruffled dress of scarlet satin stitched with pearls. Over it she wore a camisole of the same material, and a sacque highlighted in mink. She wore a crimson veil, for nothing could disguise the streak of wolf's fur that now marred her cheek, even though her sacque had a high turned-up collar whose fur matched hers almost exactly in hue. Her appearance was so striking that, although they had not yet set foot inside the dance hall, those in the antechamber where they were standing were all pausing to gape.

A Catholic priest stood at the entrance, checking over the guests and now and then consulting a list he carried. The doorway was adorned with streamers—red, white, and blue—and the unvarnished floorboards were strewn with petals.

As they approached, they heard the priest say: "Please leave your weapons with the deputy here."

There was a table, decorated with flowers, beside the entrance to the hall, and an excessively corpulent man was divesting himself of gun after gun there. A lanky sheriff's deputy sat beside the table.

When the fat man had finally laid down all his weapons—all his visible ones, at least—it was the turn of Vishnevsky and his cousin. Vishnevsky had had the foresight to bring only a pair of derringers, one concealed inside each shirt cuff. The deputy waved them both through.

"We'll stay for as a brief a time as courtesy will permit," Vishnevsky said. The scheduled arrival of the Count von Bächl-Wölfing was but a few days away, and Vishnevsky did not entirely share his cousin's confidence. He had been profoundly shaken by her discovery that there were others of their kind already in this territory. "Even though the construction of the new town is proceeding apace," he told her, "something could go wrong. We've made Winterreise as inaccessible as possible by keeping it clear of the Cheyenne-Deadwood road and almost on the border of the Sioux territory. But rumors of gold deposits are leaking out and there's not much we can do to discourage them . . . especially considering how ostentatiously you dress, my dear cousin."

"We have to be here. I have to see that famous Indian fighter, the major with no scalp, Sanderson, for myself."

"It *is* important that we take his measure. Your master and mine will need a description."

"Look! It's that trainman, that Monsieur Grumiaux!" Natasha said. She pointed to the street entrance.

Grumiaux was wearing a somewhat tattered tailcoat. There was a slender Chinese woman on his arm. Her pink lace and calico dress, though in good condition, was at least fifteen years old, for it had a hoop skirt, not a bustle.

"Ah, Valentin Nikolaievich," he said in French. "And Natalia Petrovna. I had not expected you. Rumor has it that you are off building towns."

"I told you!" Vishnevsky whispered to Natasha in Russian. "These people suspect something . . . even if the truth is too unthinkable, they suspect *something*!"

Ignoring him, Natasha said, "*Est-ce que c'est votre femme, Monsieur Grumiaux? Elle est vraiment charmante.*"

Grumiaux bowed and his wife curtseyed. The two men shook hands solemnly, and Grumiaux turned to hand his weapons over to the deputy.

"Beg pardon, sir, but . . . we can't allow her in here." The deputy looked uncomfortable, but glared at the Chinese woman. "This is a respectable church hall, and . . . well, she's, I mean . . . a heathen."

"Ah," said Grumiaux, "but I received an invitation for Mr. and Mrs." He pulled it from his waistcoat pocket, a card beautifully engraved in copperplate and bordered with gold. "Nowhere was there any mention of my wife's religious beliefs. This is a Catholic establishment, isn't it? Yet I see"—he peered past the deputy into the hall proper—"Presbyterians, Mormons, even, heaven forfend, a Jewess!"

"You know what I mean, Frenchman. If we start allowing niggers and Chinamen to socialize freely with white folks . . ." He turned and appealed to the priest.

"Well . . ." the priest said, "it's on the list all right, but—"

"Let the woman pass, skunk!" said a man who had come up behind them. Vishnevsky saw a decidedly plain-looking fellow with a pistol in each hand. He was not in evening dress, but wore a buckskin coat and leather trousers. For all his bluster, he had a peculiarly high-pitched voice. "An honest Chinawoman's better than any dozen of them Green Door whores that's in there already!" The deputy reached for one of the guns on the table. "I wouldn't do that if I was you," said the man. "Less you figure on losing that trigger finger permanent."

"Don't shoot, Jane," said the priest. "You know Silas Snodgrass doesn't want a scene."

It was only then that Vishnevsky noticed the curve of female breasts beneath the gunman's shirt. "That must be the notorious Calamity Jane," he said to Natasha, "a skilled gunslinger who always wears men's clothes—a sort of rustic American version of Joan of Arc."

Rolling his eyes, the deputy let Grumiaux and his wife pass; Vishnevsky and his cousin followed them into the grand hall, where the band was playing what passed for a waltz among these people. There were some soldiers in their glittering dress uniforms, some wealthy miners, stiff and awkward in their evening finery, ladies of both good and ill repute.

"Let's look for Sanderson," Vishnevsky said, "give him a quick appraisal, and leave. . . ."

"That female gunman . . . she is rather intriguing, isn't she? She smells terrible, of course," said Natasha, "but I do find her . . . exotic."

Vishnevsky struggled to control his panic. The moon was not, of course, full . . . but Natasha had been scarred by the silver bullet. Part of her had never changed back to human form. As the body, so the mind, Vishnevsky thought. How much of her mind was still wolf?

He turned to smile at Grumiaux and his wife. Calamity Jane had stalked off to talk to some miners. He fingered the vial of Claggart's panacea in his inside coat pocket. What a strange coincidence, that one of its ingredients that mountebank had mixed into his worthless brew turned out to be wolfsbane!

He hoped he would not have to use it tonight.

Little Elk Woman had walked six days through the melting snow. It was Istawichayazan Wi, the moon of the sore eyes blind from snow. It was a dangerous thing that she did, and she had told no one. She did not think that she would be sorely missed. Her Lakota husband had been killed in the massacre and she had performed *wikhpéyapi*, giving away all her belongings, moving into the tipi of her husband's brother, who had never cared for her, a woman who had once loved two white men.

She had tried to make herself beautiful for him, even though she knew he no longer loved her. She had painted her lips with the white man's garish cosmetics, and powdered her face, and wore, beneath a buffalo robe, a calico dress she had preserved for this occasion. The slush leaked into her moccasins. The journey was mostly uphill, and she was always afraid that soldiers or perhaps the Crow, who were friendly with the soldiers, would violate her. She walked near the road but never on it. The *washichun* clothes were difficult to walk in, and it would have been impossible to ride. The whites were not a practical people, and impracticality was a trait they actually admired, especially in their women; they valued a woman who knew nothing, who never worked for fear of sullying her clothes or herself, and who expected to be deferred to and waited on hand and foot, even without the benefit of great age or a powerful vision. They were crazy, these folk! In a way, she was glad her white husband had left her.

The moon was a thin crescent. The nights were dark. She lit tiny fires, chewed pemmican, and worried about what she was going to tell him, how he would react. She wondered how his new wife was, and how she would react to having a senior wife appear. Most women were glad of another woman in the tipi to share the labor, but white women were insanely jealous; some said they even castrated unfaithful husbands in their sleep. But her husband had not taken a white wife; he had married one of those yellow women from across the sea. She wondered whether this woman would think the white women strange too.

Night was falling as she reached the edge of the town. She knew where the house was, though she had never set foot in it.

She overcame her trepidation and knocked.

The door swung open. An old Chinaman paused only briefly from his opium to inform her, in halting French, that Claude-Achille Grumiaux was not there; he had gone to the ball.

"Then I will find him there," she said. She could not afford to waste the trip. Too much was at stake. She asked for directions and began walking, down the muddy alley, to the boardwalk on Main Street.

"Why, look at him!" Natasha whispered. The famous major was at the other end of the room. His hat was under his arm, and he made no attempt to hide his disfigured scalp. Beside him was the young lieutenant who had been so taken with her before; and deep in conversation with the scout, Zeke Sullivan, was the woman in men's clothing, her hands in her coat pockets. "He's very distinguished, isn't he? And the man-woman . . . quite, quite captivating . . . and the young soldier . . . he's no longer a lieutenant, is he, but a captain? . . . he's still as charming as ever. Oh, he's seen me."

"For God's sake, Natasha! Don't do anything rash!"

She was already moving in their direction. Vishnevsky could not see, through her veil, whether she was smiling that smile, at once cruel and seductive, that so many found irresistible.

"She's here! The Russian woman!" Scott tried to attract Zeke's attention, but he and Calamity Jane were outbragging each other as they helped themselves to liquor.

The music had started up again. Scott watched, open-mouthed, as Natalia Petrovna made single-mindedly for Major Sanderson. He bowed smartly to her and led her to the floor. The Russian woman was veiled, but Scott could tell who she was by the way she moved across the floor . . . like a beast of prey in the forest. The captain, so crude and ruthless in combat, danced with a surprising litheness.

"Who is that woman?" he heard Calamity ask Zeke.

"Oh, she's the mistress of some fancy furrin count," Zeke said.

Zeke laughed drunkenly. Scott stared at Natasha and Sanderson. They whirled their way through the other dancers. Why was the Russian woman veiled? Sanderson's scarred head bobbed up and down in the sea of clashing colors. He saw the ostentatiously wealthy Silas Snodgrass, their host, oiling his way about the floor with an overpainted girl on each arm.

The floor was unvarnished and the walls unpainted, but the womenfolk were ornament enough, Scott thought. Though the surroundings were shabby, it made Scott think of his childhood . . . when his parents would sometimes take him up the river, to a grand old ball at the plantation of his cousin Harold. Only the Widow Bryant, drinking with Ebenezer the barman in the far corner, wore black. From the platform where the band was fiddling and plucking away, a woman started to sing in a raucous contralto, and Scott thought of the opera singer whose head had been flung from Natalia Petrovna's window.

I ought to warn her about him, he thought, about his cruelty. He moved toward her, pondering whether the major would be offended if he tried to cut in.

After a brief uphill walk, she came to a building beside a church. Lights, music, the strange, harsh tones of *washichun* speech. Screwing up her courage, she stepped inside. If he is there, she thought, I must not shame him. I am his wife.

There was a vestibule where one of the black-robed *washichun* shamans stood. He was reading from a piece of paper. There was a table piled high with guns of every description. Beside it sat a man with a silver star pinned to his jacket. Perhaps he would be able to help her.

"*Excusez-moi,*" she began. "*Je cherche Monsieur Claude-Achille Grumiaux. Où se trouve-t-il?*"

The deputy said, "I'll be damned! Savages puttin' on airs—speaking French, or I'm a rattler's ass! We don't allow no Injuns here . . . this is a church hall."

"*Je suis la femme de Monsieur Grumiaux,*" she said.

The priest looked at her, then at his sheet of paper. "She says she's the Frenchman's wife . . . the trainman, Grumiaux," he said.

"But he's married to a Chinawoman, not a damned squaw!"

She could not make out all they were saying. Although she had learned flawless French from her husband, she had never understood English very well. But she drew herself up as tall as she could and spoke in the pidgin that was the lingua franca among traders, Indians, and Chinamen: "Me wife of Claude Grumiaux. Bring message. Heap important message!"

The deputy laughed. "His wife's already inside."

"But this is scandalous!" said the priest. "I never knew that trainman was a bigamist!"

"Heap important message!"

"Look here," said the deputy. "I ain't got nothin' against Injuns . . . in their place. But I already let in a Chinawoman. If I let this inside, who knows what's gonna breeze in through that door next . . . a couple of niggers, maybe!"

Little Elk Woman did not enjoy men's work, but she was quick.

She sprang onto the table and had a bowie knife to the deputy's throat before he had time to reach for any weapon.

"You redskin bitch," the deputy gasped.

The priest laughed. "Let the woman in," he said. "I'll not have violence in God's house . . . you know their customs are different from ours . . . savage as she is, she may sincerely believe that she is the wife of the trainman; and my guest list makes no mention of the number of his wives."

She relaxed her grip.

"Find him," the priest said. "Deliver your message."

Vishnevsky tried to keep an eye on his cousin as she and the major danced. But he was also trying to attract the attention of some others with whom he had business that evening . . . business he did not yet want to tell Natasha about. He knew how she could be with secrets sometimes. There they were, the men he sought . . . gathered around the buffet, which was laden with the simple foods these people loved: steaks, turkeys, pork loins, hams, and platters of overcooked vegetables. Criminals! The lowliest of men! How he hated to deal with people of their ilk! But he needed their help, and the Count's money would buy their silence.

He made his way toward them, elbowing his way through the dancers. Then he stopped suddenly. That young soldier . . . the one who had inadvertently caused Natasha's present condition . . . was hovering behind her, waiting for an opportunity to interrupt her dance. He did not want him near her. He did not want him to know what jeopardy he had placed his life in that night at the inn. He did not want him to be sucked into their lives. Could he not see the trap he was walking into?

Harper stepped forward, about to cut in—

She noticed him. She nodded at him. Of course he could not see her smile through the veil, not clearly at least. But he started like a surprised rabbit. It was good to toy with these young men. They were so pliable, so pathetically worshipful.

She was wondering whether to allow him to break in. No. Let him stand there, she thought, sweating, clenching his legs together to hide the bulge of his manhood! Little does he know that the smell of his arousal has already reached me.

"You have killed many Indians, Major?"

"Innumerable, ma'am. You see, on my lacerated head, the evidence of their savage brutality. But, outnumbered though we were, we routed them roundly. We shall soon be rid of them all. We of the Eleventh Cavalry shall protect all settlers and miners from the depredations of the red man . . . and, I may add, his bestial, uncontrollable lusts."

"Ah, such a courageous man. . . ."

"My duty." They danced awhile in silence. Then the major said: "What brings you to this desolate territory, Natalia? There have been rumors at the fort . . . of a new town being built with mysterious money from Europe . . . a town in the middle of nowhere, off the road, far from any projected railways. The rumors seem to connect . . . *you* with this town."

"A completely inaccessible town! Why, Major, why would anyone want to build such a thing?"

She looked for her cousin, but he was walking toward the buffet. Who was baiting whom? Had the major sought her out merely to extract information from her?

"If it's gold, ma'am, I can keep a secret as well as the next man."

"No gold is involved, Major."

"If it's something other than gold . . . be assured that I will help all I can."

"We will remember," Natasha said. But she looked away from him. The beautiful young captain was approaching. He stared at her with a certain longing . . . the kind of emotion, Natasha reflected, nurtured by penny-dreadful novels and preposterous romantic poetry. If only he could know the true longing . . . the thirst for darkness. She wanted him.

He extended his hand to her and bowed—

Another man pushed him roughly aside. But no, it was not a man at all . . . it was that female gunman who had so gallantly defended the Chinawoman's honor earlier. She bowed stiffly, like a man, and looked at her with an ironic smirk. Natasha laughed. "Major Sanderson," she said, extricating herself from his grasp, "it may dismay you if another man cuts in, especially officer of lesser rank; but surely you cannot complain when offender is but a woman!"

Sanderson did not seem pleased; but he was forced to laugh or be thought a fool. Several people around them stopped to stare and point as the feminine gunslinger led her back to the waltz. She noticed that Valentin Nikolaievich was looking up too, and that he wore an expression of profound annoyance. What a stroke of luck! she thought. I've found another way of annoying my fool cousin. Hartmut sent him as my guardian, my protector . . . and he thinks he can be my jailkeeper. Let people stare at me! Let me attract attention! When one cannot disguise oneself by appearing inconspicuous, the best disguise is no disguise at all.

"Tarnation!" Zeke said. "You've been beat by superior gunpower . . . and female gunpower at that!"

Scott tried to put a good face on it, but Zeke just kept right on chuckling to himself. He was about to change the subject when Zeke seemed to freeze up in mid-chuckle. He went white.

"Don't move. Look at the door. Look. You see?"

Scott couldn't make anything out at first, because so many people were drifting past. Then he saw a slender woman in a yellow calico dress. She had long black braided hair. "An Indian," Scott said. "But—"

"That woman," Zeke said, "would have been my wife, if that low-down son of a bitch Grumiaux hadn't gotten to her first!"

"What's she doing here?"

"We'd better go and see."

"Grumiaux's noticed her too. He seems mighty confused, and his Chinawoman looks like she's fixin' to give him a tongue-lashing!"

They hurried through the mob. Grumiaux and his wife were heading for the entrance, and others were pushing through the crowd too—Major Sanderson, he noticed, was in a fine passion, and shouting about godless savages.

They circled her completely. Scott saw that the woman was afraid, but was making a show of bravery. When she saw Major Sanderson, she stiffened. Was this one of the women who had survived the massacre?

"*Toi!*" Little Elk Woman's husband was distraught as he approached her. "Why have you come? Is something the matter with the boy?"

She spoke quietly, a steady stream of Lakota.

"What's she saying?" he whispered to Zeke.

"She says the kid run off three years ago to look for his paw.

Life on the reservation didn't agree with him none. But she ain't come about the kid. It's the massacre."

Grumiaux spoke again, and she responded, her words more ominous than before. Zeke said, so only Scott could hear, "After he left her, she come to live with an old Injun name of Seven Horses. In the same encampment that we—"

"Oh."

"She wanted to warn us. Her husband is dead, his brother don't care for her on account of she used to belong to a white man, so she decided to come and try her luck with her first husband. When the braves come home and found half their women and kids cut to pieces, they was considerable angry and was all for going on the warpath right away. But their allies, the neighboring bands, is all too discouraged. They decided to wait for spring. Some of them gone up to Canada to try to talk Sitting Bull's renegades into joining them for another assault. But I been hearing another rumor that Sitting Bull's planning to give himself up at Fort Buford soon . . . the Great Grandma, Victoria, ain't been as generous to him as he hoped she'd be."

"I cannot abide any more of this heathen jabbering! Get that insolent barbarian out of here!" Sanderson was shouting. He unsheathed his ceremonial sword, which, being ceremonial, he had not yielded up at the door. "Or I'll run her through myself."

"That is most ungentlemanly of you, Major!" Grumiaux said, blocking his way. "Why don't we all enjoy the ball? I would hate to mar the celebrations in honor of President Garfield with bloodshed . . . even if it is merely, as you would say, the blood of savages."

"Damn civilians . . ." said Major Sanderson, but he sheathed his sword and stepped back into the crowd.

"My friends . . ." Grumiaux gestured to Zeke and Scott. "We are going to have to talk. I know that at least one of you has understood everything this woman has said. I think it best that I escort her back to my house . . . will you come?"

Zeke turned to Scott. "You don't want to hear what she has to say . . . if you hear, and you don't report . . . it'll be treason."

"But—" said Scott. He was trapped. He knew that Zeke was right; he knew what Zeke was risking too, if he listened to anything else the woman had to say. A discharge at the very least, if not a hanging.

Zeke spoke to the woman with a tenderness Scott rarely saw in him: "*Hekhakalawin.*"

The Indian woman seemed to see Zeke for the first time. "Zeke," she said.

Grumiaux was about to say something, but his Chinese wife gripped his arm tightly.

Zeke said: "I know you didn't mean to come back to me, Little Elk Woman. But I reckon that's just what you done."

The two woman looked at each other. Despite their shabby, antiquated finery, they both managed to look dignified and indignant at the same time. Suddenly, they both burst out in a fit of giggles, and started to chattering at one another, each in her own language. What a cacophony! Zeke and Grumiaux and the Indian woman and the Chinawoman left Scott standing alone by the door. They made no move to invite him. And though Scott understood why Zeke had excluded him, it hurt him a little. Once more there were things that had come between them, things he wasn't allowed to understand. The music started up again, a polka this time.

He saw the major stalking up and down, cursing; Vishnevsky deep in conversation with some seedy-looking dudes by the buffet; and Natalia Petrovna still dancing with the infamous Calamity. He felt thoroughly confused and miserable. Might as well go get myself a drink, he told himself.

6
North Platte, Nebraska

SUNDAY ON THE U.P. WAS CELEBRATED IN EXEMPLARY FASHION, with all the priests and preachers on board taking turns to hold forth in one of the saloon cars. The second- and third-class cars had their own services too, for there were plenty of clergy in every class, and some of the more enterprising first-class men of the cloth took it upon themselves to journey down the entire length of the train, preaching to whomever they could find of the appropriate persuasion.

Johnny explored the train by himself. Behind the third-class section there was a horse car; he could smell them and hear them neighing. They were agitated. The smell made Jonas stir a little, and Johnny did not want to stay, so he came wandering back to where Speranza awaited him with his morning's breakfast and Latin.

The clergy were many, but, alas, the faithful were few; for an hour after dawn, just as the North Platte depot was disappearing to the east, a herd of buffalo was sighted. Johnny watched the passengers crowd around the windows and squeeze into observation platforms. Breakfast was done. He slipped away from Speranza once again and went to find the news butch.

He could not see much. People crammed into the parlor car, where there was no one preaching. There were legs everywhere; legs in creased, machine-made jeans; legs in old pants that stank of sweat and alcohol and old piss; legs in elegant trousers trimmed with gold . . . and women's skirts, their bustles swaying, satin and calico jamming the aisles. There wasn't much for a young boy to see, wedged in between so many legs.

"Teddy!" He saw the boy, with his penny broadsheets stuffed into his apron, elbowing his way easily through. He wore a slouch hat much too big for him; it covered his forehead. That was why Johnny had not noticed him before. "Here I am!"

"Come on!" Teddy said, yanking his hand. "You ain't gonna see nothing down here. But I know a place."

He pulled Johnny outside. The space between the two Pullmans was full. Gunshots in the distance. Startled, Johnny gripped his friend's hand harder. "This way!" said Teddy.

"If you please, young man!" an old woman said, smacking him on the buttocks with a parasol. He leered at her, then pushed his way to the railing. There was a ladder to the roof. "Hurry!" he said.

Johnny clambered after him. There was a strong wind that blew their hair into their eyes. Teddy helped him onto the roof. He stood up. Teddy's slouch hat blew off and he ran after it, his arms spread wide to keep his balance.

"Shit! I done lost my hat!" Johnny watched Teddy flailing at the air. He saw the wind catch the hat and send it spinning up high, like a big deformed bird. He laughed as Teddy cussed out the wind. "You fuckin' whoreson thievin' varmint!"

"It's just the wind . . . there's nothing you can do about it," Johnny shouted.

Teddy shrugged. "I reckon I can steal me a new one just as quick."

The train shook all over and smoke blew in their faces. It was a fine feeling . . . the wind whipping at them, the plains stretching endlessly on either side, the thin metal ribbon of track splitting the green world in two. It seemed that they rode the wind on the back of a dragon of fire and iron. To their right, north, was what seemed to be a vast, swirling lake of brown . . . moving toward them . . . writhing, twisting, churning. Johnny couldn't make out any individual creature, but he knew what they must be.

"It's . . . it's grand!" Johnny said. "There must be hundreds of them. Thousands!"

"You ain't seen nothing. Before the buffler hunters come, there was millions in one herd, millions. You couldn't see no grass at all, not from one end of the whole world to the other."

They were rushing straight toward the herd now, and Johnny heard more rifle shots. Behind the clanging of the couplers, behind the puffing of the engine and the scream of the wind, he could hear hoofbeats too . . . and the falsetto whoops of hunters. "Look!" Teddy said. "That's Buffalo Bill!"

"Who's that?" said Johnny.

Galloping toward the herd, a hunter with a mane of yellow hair led a group of others, all struggling to keep up. The leader's white horse was actually outrunning the train.

"He's the most famous buffler hunter in the world, and the U.P. has hired him to entertain you passengers along this route."

The herd must have been upwind of them. The buffalo made no attempt to flee as the hunters charged them. Dozens were falling. Johnny stared, appalled, and inside Johnny someone else stirred, someone who could smell the fear, could hear the racing blood. The wind shifted and all at once the herd stampeded in a pounding, rhythmless thunder. And the person inside Johnny smiled. He began to whisper in Johnny's ear.

"Go away!" Johnny shouted. "Leave me alone, don't talk all the time, I can't hear myself think!"

"What's the matter with you? Skeered of the stampede?"

"No," Johnny said, struggling to silence Jonas, knowing that Jonas was busy trying to enlist the support of the others in the forest, to lead an insurrection to oust him from the clearing . . .

Teddy stared at him strangely. Johnny thought: It's showing in my face. No one must know! Jonas, Jonas, go away, I don't want to play today!

The two boys lay down on the roof. Teddy shouted above the roar of the stampede: "Want a chaw?" and pulled a hunk of tobacco from his apron. "It's Pride of Durham . . . the best, and it don't come cheap!" They chewed. Johnny didn't like the taste, but he knew that some of the others did, and he let one of them take over for a moment, to take away the taste. That was a mistake. He could feel Jonas lurking just out of sight, ready to make his move.

With their eyes level with the clerestory window, they could peer into the car. It still swarmed with people oohing and aahing over the sight of the buffalo. They couldn't see the hunters anymore; they'd retreated and were performing one of their celebrated stunts, pushing their steeds into a flying leap onto the horsecar in the rear.

Presently Johnny saw Buffalo Bill himself striding into the car . . . he even saw Speranza smile at him and proffer a little notebook for him to autograph. He felt a stab of jealousy. Or was it Jonas's jealousy? It was Jonas who wanted to be near Speranza, who wanted to smell her, touch her, nuzzle against her breasts . . . Johnny trembled even to think of it.

"Ain't it a fine feeling!" Teddy declared. "Like we was on top of the whole world. We can do anything we's a mind to, ain't nobody can catch us, ain't nobody can see us." He rolled over and lay close to Johnny . . . casually he put his arm over the younger boy's shoulder. "You ever get . . . I mean, *hot?* . . . down below? Inside your trousers." His hand probed lower. Lower.

Jonas growled. "Fuck you!"

Johnny retreated from Jonas's intensity. He tried to hold Jonas back, but he was already striding into the clearing, pawing at the ground.

"Hey, I didn't mean no harm." He said nothing for a few moments, then went on: "You want to see my Li'l Charlie?"

Jonas leered.

"I knowed you was more worldly than you was lettin' on." Teddy unbuttoned his trousers and Jonas glanced at his half-erect penis. "Want to give me a few whacks?"

Jonas laughed. "You haven't even got any hair," he said derisively. "You're just a baby."

Teddy giggled, a little nervous, seeming much younger suddenly. Jonas glared at him through slitty eyes. He loved the wind. He loved the scent of the grass, spiced with the odor of fear and fresh animal blood. The train plowed on, straight west, straight as an arrow.

Jonas said: "The time is not right for me fully to be myself. But I shall show you . . . I shall show you, you foolish little boy!"

Teddy suddenly laughed out loud. "Hey, you been looking at too many penny melodramas. You ought to get a job in one of them Wild West shows!"

Jonas let out a wild howl. Then he began tearing off his clothes, flinging them aside. The wind picked up his jacket. It snagged on the ladder. Teddy scrambled after the clothes, crying, "You's plumb out of your mind!" Jonas cackled as Teddy gathered the clothes under his arms. "These is good clothes, rich folks' clothes. You ought to be ashamed of yourself. I have to buy machine-made jeans and wear them till they is in tatters."

Jonas stood naked in the wind. He crouched down. Chill wind sheared hard against his body. I wish the moon was full! he thought. Only then am I complete. He growled. He imagined himself holding his tail high, snout to the ground, lifting his hind leg, pissing in the wind. "*You* want *me* to give you a few whacks!" he said, his voice raspy . . . he was all Jonas now, and that other one, the one the others listened to more often, had taken refuge in the dank and dismal darkness. "I'm bigger than you, I'm hairier, I can impale you, slice you up, cut you to ribbons with my big bad wolf's prick . . . you're nothing. I can play more rough than you ever dreamed. Stick your nose up my arse and smell my shit."

He moved toward Teddy. Teddy couldn't move. Jonas saw fear in his face, but also fascination. He narrowed his eyes and sniffed the air. In his mind's eye he was all wolf, all beast, hackles raised, fangs bared, ready to spring, to subdue.

Teddy grinned a little. "Well, I don't hold with no cornholing. I mean, it's . . . I mean, well, little kids play around with it, but . . ."

Jonas leaped up. Teddy slipped and fell. Jonas exulted. He sprayed the roof with piss. The discarded clothes were flapping around them as Jonas pinned Teddy down and clenched his face between his thighs and wedged his nose between the cheeks of his buttocks. The boy struggled, but Jonas pulled his wolf strength from deep inside himself. He howled his exultation to the wind. "I am king! Smell my shit! I am king!"

Suddenly he heard footsteps.

He looked down at Teddy. He felt himself shifting, being sucked into the forest . . . just as he was beginning to have so much fun! he thought. When the moon comes, I'm going to get revenge on the pack of you!

Teddy shrieked: "Help!"

James Karney woke up and found himself naked and grappling with a strange boy. They always do this to me, he thought, letting me emerge at the most awkward moments, when none of them are capable of wriggling out of the situation. "I'm so sorry, sir," he said, and stood up, letting the scruffy-looking boy sit up and wipe something off his face. Excrement and urine. Ah, yes. It was usually Jonas who sent him out. Jonas liked to have his fun, but hated to deal with any consequences.

The strange boy said, "You fuckin' . . . you fuckin' . . . you ought to be hanged for what you done."

The footsteps came closer. Teddy's eyes widened. He shouted, "He's plumb out of his mind, Mister Claggart! He attacked me!"

James said, "I apologize for any inconvenience, sir. If you like, I would be delighted to serve you luncheon." A calm, authoritative voice: that was what usually sufficed to—

He turned to look at the newcomer.

A little bald man, somewhat overdressed, the tails of his morning dress flapping behind him. He stopped quite still and peered at the two of them. "I clomb up here to get a good view of the last of the *pro*ceedings, and see what I found! If it ain't that furrin Count's little painted catamite! Getting a little practice on the side, if I ain't mistaken! And you, Teddy Grumiaux, a foul participator in the lusts o' the flesh! And on the Lord's day!"

Teddy spat. "You ain't the one to judge."

The little man came closer . . . and James Karney suddenly found himself whisked out of the clearing . . . Jonathan Kippax woke up for a moment, blinked his eyes in the strong wind, took in the situation and retreated instantly . . . Johnny Kindred found himself being pushed, protesting, into the light. . . .

It's freezing cold! he thought. Where are my clothes?

Claggart was almost upon the two of them. Teddy cowered, but still seemed defiant. Johnny had awoken as though from a dream, for when Jonas burst loose he did not often like to watch what Jonas did. He was terribly afraid. Claggart scowled at them, and when Teddy made a fist at him, dropped a derringer into his palm from his sleeve.

"Ain't you a hairy one, boy!" Claggart said. Johnny flinched as the man ran the old end of the gun up and down his chest, making his hair stand on end. "Your eyebrows knit together . . . look, even the backs of your hands is covered with that golden down . . . like a wild animal . . . like a wolf-boy." He whistled. "I reckon that's what your master likes about you, ain't it? The feel of that silken fur, rubbin' up and down him, when he buggers you? Hey, Wolf Boy, I'd gladly donate you a dollar for the minstrelations of your puckerin' arsehole . . . heh, heh, heh."

"Don't touch him!" Teddy said, protective suddenly. "When you says lewd things to him, he goes all weirdlike, changes into a different person, a monster."

He felt Jonas stir again. "Stay away!" he shouted. "Stay far away . . . in the dark . . . where you belong."

"Wolf Boy!" Claggart hissed. "Wolf Boy!"

"Get your clothes on," Teddy whispered to Johnny, in a tone half timorous, half pitying.

Speranza sat beside Count von Bächl-Wölfing in the parlor car. They did not look at each other. She was dressed in her most severe apparel. She clasped her Bible to her bosom. But her other hand reached out to brush the hand of the Count. She dared not face him, yet the mere touch of Hartmut's fingers on her palm sent a deep thrill through her. She let her eyes stray, and saw his face, stern, absorbed in some private meditation. He did not meet her gaze. Last night, she thought, he told me that he loved me.

The car was crowded. They had come to listen to a preacher

who inveighed against the sins of the flesh. The sermon had been interrupted by Buffalo Bill's demonstration, but now the U.P.'s star entertainer had retired to a private saloon car with a group of well-heeled hunters, the carcasses had been left, rotting, miles behind; and the preacher resumed where he had left off.

"Them as fornicates, sodomizes, or practices the solitary vice," the voice boomed over the rattling of the train, "all goes to the everlastin' fire. The Lord sees everything you do, and ain't no way you can 'scape the wrath of the Almighty. I bring not peace but a sword. If you covet another man's wife, sure as the night follers the day, your flesh will be rended from you with red-hot pincers by devils with forked tails and forked tongues . . . your heads will be stricken off and stuck back on again, fifty, sixty times a day . . . you will be burned alive on heaps of human ordure . . . terrible, terrible are the torments of hell! And if the Lord sees you touchin' yourself in a impure way, your manhood will be riven from your body and thrown to wild animals . . . not once, but time and time again, until you screams for mercy, but it will be too late, unless you repent . . . repent . . . but woe betide them as lies with mankind as with womankind! Your nether orifice will be continually buggered with red-hot pokers . . ."

The Count started to chuckle to himself. Several passengers turned disapprovingly in his direction.

"Ha!" the preacher screamed. "You mocks me now, but you'll be right sorry when you burns in hell—"

Abruptly the Count stood up. There was silence for a few moments. Speranza saw in his expression a terrible anguish, which he could not quite mask. Softly he said, "You know nothing about hell, Reverend. You have not done it justice; I may say so with some authority, since I speak from the experience thereof."

He turned and left the car.

7
Deadwood
half-moon, waxing

A GRAY MORNING IN DEADWOOD: IN FRONT OF THE CHURCH HALL, streamers lay, trampled in the mud. Miners trudged uphill, their breath steaming, their scarves flying. Wind howled along the boardwalk. Wanted posters flapped against the wooden walls. Old women walked, scrunched into their bonnets, hunched against the wind. Wind toying with young boys' hats and with Chinamen's queues.

Major Sanderson's contingent had arisen at dawn to load the cart; Scott Harper was in charge. The major had disappeared that night . . . gone somewhere with the Russian woman. Zeke and Grumiaux and the two women had vanished too, and Scott had not dared follow them. He had spent the night at the same inn where he had taken Natalia Petrovna that winter night, the night of the wolves. This time he had shared a bed with a sergeant and two miners who stank of alcohol and didn't take off their boots to go to sleep. He had not had an easy night of it.

He had expected to find Zeke here, but an hour past dawn he had still not turned up. He hardly paid any mind to loading up the cart with the fresh supplies. Sanderson's going to be here any moment, he thought, and Zeke won't be here, and the major's going to ask questions.

Sanderson appeared at just that moment, striding up Main Street. Where was Natalia? What had they been discussing, and where had they gone off together? Scott felt a twinge of jealousy, but suppressed it quickly as the major bore down on him. "I trust we will soon be ready to depart, Harper?" he said.

"Yessir."

Sanderson looked around him and his countenance darkened.

"We appear to be missing a man, mister! Your friend the scout, Sullivan, I believe."

"I ain't seen him since last night, Major."

He looked around, and the other men mumbled about not having seen him either. "You don't suppose that the man has deserted? These Indian squaws can bewitch a civilized man sometimes. I sincerely hope nothing of the kind has happened to your friend, Harper."

"I don't know, sir." He was glad now that Zeke had not chosen to tell him anything.

"I do believe you are telling the truth, Captain," said Sanderson. "Nonetheless, I want you to find him. Doubtless you know where his favorite haunts are; if he is merely lying, drunk, in some gutter, then perhaps you are likelier than most to know which gutter he is to be found in! Go and find him, Harper, and arrest him; then catch up with us. We'll see about appropriate punishment as soon as you reach the fort."

Scott turned away. He knew that Zeke had come to some fateful decision. It had happened when Zeke set eyes on the Indian woman. If Zeke had indeed deserted, and if Scott found him and brought him back, there was only one possible outcome: a hanging. What was it that could be worth that much?

Sanderson was busying himself with directing the other men, barking orders, making them scamper about. "I expect he's at the trainman's house," he said, "in Chinatown. I won't be but a few minutes looking for him." The major merely grunted, and Scott turned, mounted his palomino, and turned downhill in the direction of Chinatown.

They had left Deadwood in the dead of night. At least they did not have to walk; Grumiaux had given them a horse. It would not have been wise for Zeke to try to get his own horse out of the livery stable.

"I can't believe I'm doing this," Zeke said to Little Elk Woman. She smiled secretly to herself as she grasped his coat with both hands. The road was dark; only now and then did the half-moon peek out from the dense forest that lined the downhill trail.

His Lakota is rusty, she thought, but perhaps I was wrong about him; his heart is with our people, not with the *washichun*. "What an irony," she told him. "I came to warn one husband . . . and now I'm returning to my people with a different man, one I never thought I would see again!"

"I never forgot you," Zeke said. "And I was right angry you chose him over me. And then, when he left, you didn't even look for me—but ran straight into the arms of that Seven Horses feller—"

"I did not want it said that I disdained my own people," Little Elk Woman said. "Besides, he offered four horses for me. The Appaloosa is particularly beautiful, and when you build your tipi to shelter us I will give him to you."

Just before dawn they left the trail and went into the forest. Little Elk Woman gathered some firewood, then made a soft bed of brush and twigs, on which she laid her buffalo robe. Before they made love, she whispered: "I am glad you have come back. When Seven Horses' brother and the others make war on the white men, I wouldn't want them to come home with your scalp. It would be terrible if, when I joined the other women in dancing the scalps of the slain, I was forced to hang your hair from a stick and leap for joy."

These were morbid thoughts. It was time to give him pleasure and to be pleasured by him. Time enough in the future to think of death. . . .

Grumiaux told Scott nothing. But when the trainman avoided his gaze, Scott knew that his suspicions were true. He noticed that Grumiaux's horse wasn't tied up in front of the laundry. Fresh hoofprints led away from Chinatown, east. Not too many people would ride out of town after midnight. It wasn't too hard to pick up Zeke's trail; and Scott knew only too well where Little Elk Woman's village was. Nothing would ever eradicate that memory from his mind.

About twenty miles east of the town the tracks veered off into the forest. Scott tethered his horse to a pine tree and followed carefully. He knew he was making too much noise, stepping on twigs, sliding in the mud. He decided to follow Zeke's advice and simply announce his presence by shouting: "Zeke! Zeke!"

The forest swallowed up his words.

The tracks were hard to follow now, except where the snow had not yet thawed. He walked deeper into the forest. He stood still for a moment. Footsteps? A twig cracking beneath an animal's paws?

He looked up. Too late! Someone jumped him from an overhead branch. Arms locked around his neck. He stumbled. He tried to grab whatever was on his back. There was a knife. His assailant was light, unusually light—a boy perhaps. He managed to shake him off. He reached for his Colt, turned, and saw who it was. She lay on the ground, trembling with rage. The knife glinted in the dew.

"Little Elk Woman?"

She said, "You no touch him. I kill. I kill!"

"I—"

She rushed at him again. Pummelled him with her bare fists. He seized her arms. She wriggled, screeched, tried to bite. "I won't hurt you," he said softly. "I won't."

Then he heard Zeke's voice: "*Wichakte shni yo.*"

She subsided, sobbing.

"I told her not to kill you. She would have, you know, eventually, long as there was a breath left in her." Zeke came walking out from behind a tree. He had a Winchester pointed at Scott, but Scott didn't drop his Colt.

"Gimme that gun, boy. Not that I don't trust you, but we ain't fightin' side by side no more."

Scott said: "Major Sanderson ordered me to—"

"I ain't goin' back. I remembered the first time I set eyes on this here Injun woman. Damn near killed that bastard Grumiaux on account of her. The Injuns got something us civilized folks don't got, and I aims to find it again."

"But I got orders, Zeke!" He pointed his gun but he couldn't bring himself to shoot.

"Then, son, you will just have to kill me. You can say I was resistin' arrest. No one will think the worse of you."

The old scout walked up close. The woman stood beside him. Scott looked at his old friend. His face was weather-beaten, but his eyes seemed young. "I can't kill you, Zeke!" he said. "But—"

"I ain't got the stomach for the army, Scott. That last massacre done burned me up. When I seen Little Elk Woman and heared that her people was gettin' ready for another war, I knowed what side my heart was on. This land had a soul once. But iron horses don't got no souls, rifles don't got it, army don't fight with it. If you can kill me, it just goes to show how a good-hearted boy like you can get sucked into that great big soulless machine . . . and throw aside friendship."

"What do you want me to do?" Scott cried out. "You want me to become a deserter like you?" His daddy had never deserted even when they knew there was no hope for the Confederacy. He'd stood his ground. But here there wasn't any easy path to honor. Such things as duty, honor, and self-respect seemed much more clear-cut back in the sixties. . . .

"Go back. Tell them you lost me. Or that I set upon you and you couldn't catch me."

"That won't stop them looking for you, Zeke."

"If you ever sees me again, Scott Harper, kill me."

"All right."

The woman said something in Lakota. "She wants me to kill you and take your scalp back to the village. Thinks it'll gain me back some of the respect I lost when I left them all them years ago."

"Maybe you should," Scott said.

"Reckon so," said Zeke. "You see, my friend, I am torn too. You best leave afore one of us does something he'll regret for the rest of his life."

Scott turned away.

"I want the hoss," Zeke said. "The old nag Grumiaux gave us ain't going to carry us both clear through to the Sioux lands . . . and it ain't more than four, five hours' walk back to Deadwood. You can get you a fresh hoss there. Tell the major the horse was stole when you was jumped. If they want to hang me for desertion, a little hoss thieving ain't going to make it no worse, nohow."

Scott started walking toward the trail.

8
Ogllala, Nebraska
half-moon, waxing

NIGHT. SPERANZA STIRRED FROM A FITFUL SLEEP. IT WAS THE SAME dream as always: the forest, the creek, the howling . . . the water crimson and warm as living blood. And the lover who waited for her at the source of the stream. . . .

She sat bolt upright. She was wide awake now. The Count's private car was dark, save for the flame of a single candle beside the bed. The Count lay sleeping beside her. He was quite naked. The indecency no longer shocked her; how could it? I am a fallen woman, she told herself, and I feel no shame at all. A fine, silvery down covered his chest, his arms. His forehead was furrowed, as though he were brooding in his sleep. His eyebrows met in the middle. She touched his arm gingerly. He did not move. He did not snore; he hardly seemed to breathe. His smell clung to her fingertips. The smell of wet earth and animal sweat.

She slipped from the bed and put on a silk dressing gown over her night shift. She lit a candle from the one by the bed, put it in its holder, and stole away. A Chinese screen separated the bedroom from the parlor where the Count sat for his coffee. There was a wood-burning stove, the one incongruous item amid the plush appointments. Its embers cast a reddish glow over the onyx table with its Union Pacific map, the vase of oriental lacquerware with its wilted, week-old roses, the ebony limbs of the furniture. There was a chaise longue, upholstered in purple velvet, where Johnny often slept. It was empty. She wondered where he had gone. Out exploring with that newspaper vendor boy, no doubt! There were plenty of people still up and about; even though it was past midnight, a poker game continued in one of the saloon cars.

She sat down in the chair. She closed her eyes, but the dream tormented her. She rose to part the curtain a little way. The half-moon cast a ghostly light over the great emptiness that stretched to the limits of her vision. Tall grass swayed, like strands of tarnished silver. She wondered what the Count's mistress was like . . . the woman he had sent in advance to seek out the denning place . . . and whether he had already fallen out of love with this Natalia Petrovna Stravinskaya. Was that what he meant when he told her of his weakness, his inability to love those women whom he had transformed into his own kind?

And am I next? she thought.

She leaned against the windowpane. Prairie after prairie. She tried to keep her eyes open. But even as she stood there, lulled by the rhythmic rocking of the train, she began to fall once more into her dream.

In the dream she had already begun wading through the river to the source of the howling.

Johnny Kindred was not with Teddy at the time. The game of poker did not really hold his interest, but Teddy was so engrossed that he did not say a word to the younger boy at all. Something had come between them, though Johnny could only remember coming to, without his clothes, on the roof of the observation car. He knew that Jonas had done something, but Jonas wasn't talking, and the others would only make dark hints about it.

Johnny left the saloon car and started walking to the back, toward the second-class cars. Men and women lay snoring there, scrunched against walls, stretched out in the aisle, their heads and limbs tucked into strange positions.

The Indian was sitting, quite still, his eyes open, staring out at the fields. Even though the rest of the car was crammed, the seat beside his was empty; it was as though the others abhorred him, or perhaps they feared him. The air was foul with the stench of sweat and farting, but in the air around the old Indian there hung a certain fragrance . . . the smell of flowers that only bloom in moonlight.

Johnny spoke to him, very softly: "I've put away the feather you gave me, sir. It's in a little cigar box that I got from the Count. I think you're a very kind old gentleman. Even though I heard the Baroness von Dittersdorf say that all Indians are savages." The

Indian did not answer; he seemed not to have heard Johnny speak at all. "Are you really a savage, sir?"

Jonas whispered in his mind: "I told you! He speaks only to me, you stupid child. I am the master of the beast language. Smell my shit! I am the king!"

The Indian said nothing for a long time, then spoke suddenly. "You are the shattered fragments of one being. You have been broken apart, tossed out of the great circle. But the wolf essence is in all of you, and the man essence is in all of you." He had not moved his lips. The words were in small twitches of the face, in odors, in little movements of the hands.

In his mind, Jonas said, angrily: "He lies! I am the one true person in this body—I am the one who is both man and wolf. Don't try to tell me anything different, little boy Johnny."

And Johnny answered: "I understand him without your help, Jonas. I *can* understand him the way you understand him."

"So change! Transform! You can't do it. I rage, I burn, I roar, and when you come rushing out you're just a little boy again, mewling and whimpering."

Johnny looked hard at the Indian, hoping he would speak again. But only a guttural humming escaped his lips. The man was singing to himself. It was that song again, the *shungmanitu olowan*.

Johnny tried to twist the odd cadences to his own lips. But he couldn't imitate the wobbling tones the Indian made in his throat. Abruptly, the Indian turned, looked at him, and laughed. Johnny crept away, half ashamed and half exhilarated.

She felt hairy hands shaking her by the shoulders. "We must get ready!" said the Count. "Something very exciting is about to happen. We must make sure that the boy is safe with us."

She rubbed her eyes.

"I smell it in the wind," he said.

She saw his eyes sparkling, red in the glow from the wood burner.

Teddy crouched in the shadows where Claggart couldn't see him. He had been initiated into the mystery of the hidden holdout. Now he was trying to see it in action. Baroness von Dittersdorf and Chandraputra were among the players he recognized; the Baroness smoked one of those machine-rolled cigarettes that came all the way from Europe. A little Negro boy was buffing the fingernails of the Indian's left hand. A fourth player, Teddy saw, was the Greek priest who seemed to be attached to the Count's party.

"Very interesting spectacle indeed, this buffalo hunt of yours," Chandraputra was saying. "This Buffalo Bill is most accomplished at horseback riding. In India, he should no doubt be playing polo regularly at the British country club, isn't it? I will raise you fifty dollars, if you are not minding."

More gold on the table. Teddy's eyes widened.

"Tush!" said the Baroness, quaffing champagne, "I shall see you, and raise you, shall I say, another fifty?" A bit of champagne dribbled from her lips and smudged a beauty spot that had not been there the previous day.

"Ain't it an honor, ma'am, to do business with one of such intrepiditude and courageousity!" said Claggart, whistling. He looked at his pocket watch.

"We shall be playing until dawn," Chandraputra said, "unless one of us is deciding to . . . how do you say it? chicken out."

Father Alexandros put down some money, but said nothing.

"What a powerful-looking man, that Buffalo Bill of yours," the Baroness said. "What a pity he left us at Ogllala. Do you suppose we shall ever see him again? He does have a certain crude fascination . . . an animal magnetism. We should have recruited him for . . . our cause."

"Baroness! You are growing indiscreet in your inebriation!" said the astrologer, horrified for some reason Teddy could not figure out.

The Baroness let out one of her witchlike cackles.

Teddy leaned forward a little more. He read the little imperfections in the patterns on the cards, just as Claggart had taught him to. He couldn't help smiling to himself. There were thousands of dollars riding on this hand, yet every single player appeared to be bluffing. That took guts, especially since each of them knew that one or more of the others was cheating. Teddy couldn't help admire the way they just sat there, conversing idly, as though all this money mattered not a bit.

"Well," Claggart was saying, "you furriners have sure proven yourselves apt and sportsmanlike poker players, I'll give you that.

But I can't bring myself to fold, so I'm just going to have to raise you another hundred dollars."

Another five gold double eagles dropped on the table. What was happening? Claggart had thrown caution aside. It was as if he no longer cared about the outcome. There was something in the air, something serious. He could almost smell it. That was the oddest thing about it. It smelled a little bit like dog piss.

Suddenly both Chandraputra and the Baroness seemed to freeze. They kind of sniffled, the way a dog does when he's on to a fresh scent. Teddy crept forward.

"We must end the game," the Baroness said languidly. "I am afraid something has come up."

"You're folding?" Claggart said.

"It is of no consequence," the Baroness said, and rose from the table, throwing down her cards.

The Indian astrologer did the same. They whispered among one another in some foreign language, German, Teddy thought. The Negro page went scampering down to the next car, babbling incoherently. Presently the others followed suit, and only Claggart, Teddy, and the Orthodox padre remained.

From somewhere in third class, maybe, came the sound of a woman screaming.

And gunshots.

Teddy stood up. Claggart looked bewildered and then shrugged. "Reckon I've won, then," he said, and began scrambling, rather ungracefully, to gather up all the gold.

At last Father Alexandros spoke up: "You should have waited for me to say my piece. I will see you, Mr. Claggart."

Startled, Claggart threw down his cards. He only had a pair of eights. His panic did something to his holdout, though, and three aces shot out of his sleeve.

"I trust we can ignore those?" said Father Alexandros, toying with his beard. "I, as it happens, have a pair of nines." Nonchalantly he began sweeping up the coins and stuffing them into his robes.

Claggart said, "Wait. Don't think you can hide your cheatin' behind your religious vestments, padre! I seen you palm them nines—"

"It hardly seems to matter now," said Father Alexandros, "considering that we are under attack."

A window shattered, and a bullet ricocheted around the saloon car.

"God damn it, duck!" Claggart screamed, diving for the underside of the gambling table.

"Not the sort of bullets that can kill me," the priest said calmly. Then he turned and left.

Teddy crawled over to the nearest window. In the light of the half-moon he could see horse riders—a dozen or more—bearing down on them from the north. They were wearing masks. One of them was neck and neck with the saloon car. He had the barrel of a rifle pointed at them through the window. "Shit!" he said. "Train robbers!"

"Come and help me pick up the rest of them coins!" Claggart shouted at him. "Maybe we can jump off before they board us. I ain't losing my hard-earned money to a passel of marauding thieves."

Another shot. Teddy saw Claggart grip his arm, screaming. Blood gushed out onto the gold. "What a damned uncertain profession!" he gasped, and fell to the floor. His head slammed against the leg of an armchair. Teddy crawled over to him and tried to shake him awake. The rider was still abreast of them, beside the broken window. His eyes peered over the mask that flapped in the wind. He looked like he was about to spring through the window—

"Shit! I ain't stickin' around no more," Teddy said to himself, and ran for the exit.

In the next car passengers were screaming, crawling around like turtles. A child bawled. Teddy elbowed his way between two fat women, who were jabbering and wringing their hands. Suddenly he saw Johnny Kindred standing at the other end of the car.

He wasn't panicking at all. He just looked over to Teddy and gestured to him. Teddy had to fight his way across. Johnny said, "The Count wants us to gather in his car. I don't think I'm supposed to bring outside people, but you're my friend. I don't want to be . . . alone . . . among them." Teddy had to strain to hear him.

They went outside. Banged on the door to the next car. They could see frightened people huddled, pressed against the glass.

"God damn it, let us in!" Teddy shouted. The other boy stood still, as if nothing was going on. "Help me force this thing open."

They stepped across. The coupler groaned. Sparks flew at their feet. Teddy hammered on the glass with his fists. It gave way. He didn't feel the pain of the splinters but he could see the blood. Three or four more cars to go.

"Hurry up, Teddy," Johnny said, smiling.

He looked up to see someone leaping across from roof to roof. His ears rang from the gunfire. They pushed their way into the car and shoved their way through the crowd, not looking back.

9
The Sandhills of Nebraska the same night

"THE BOY, SPERANZA!" THE COUNT WHISPERED URGENTLY, SHAKING her. "You must find him!"

The private Pullman was already filling up with the members of von Bächl-Wölfing's party. Confusion flooded her. Gunshots . . . anguished cries from the other cars . . . talk of an attack . . . by whom? for what? The new arrivals brought in kerosene lamps, and the car was filled with flickering, sooty light. They crammed onto the floor; three or four of them squeezed onto the bed where only hours before she had known the bleak passion of Hartmut's lovemaking. "Johnny," she cried out. There was no answer. Where could the boy have gone? Now of all times! "I'm going to look for him," she said.

"Yes. You must." Suddenly she saw in the Count's face no concern at all for her . . . only for the boy, the all-important boy he had put such hope in . . . she felt a twinge of almost unbearable jealousy and quickly suppressed it. And left the car in search of her charge.

Third class: the seats were on fire. A child screamed. It's mother's eyes had been shot out. She heard footsteps directly above, on the roof. Women with abject eyes huddled under straw. Speranza went on.

A saloon car. She recognized Cordwainer Claggart. He was wounded, groping for a handful of bloody gold coins. Broken glass on the floor. A man with a shotgun climbing through the window. She moved like an automaton, pushing her fear deep into herself. She went on.

A second-class car. Two dead miners had been piled against a window; men with Winchesters knelt behind them, using the corpses as shields, shooting into the plains. Hoofbeats. "Johnny! Johnny!"

In the aisle an old Indian danced. He sang a wheezing, high-pitched song to himself, and he capered wildly, waving his arms. "Have you seen a boy?" she shouted at him. "A young boy?"

He danced. "Have you gone quite mad?" It seemed that the whole world had. The Indian began to howl like a wolf. It was so lifelike that she thought of Vienna—the night of the Count's grand ball—and she felt terror for the first time. She squeezed past him. Stepped over the body of a woman whose bustle had been blown to bits. She stepped on shards of whalebone and thighbone. Wind whined wildly. The dead woman's wig flew up into Speranza's face. She pushed it away and walked on. Her heartbeat quickened. She had to find him.

The old Indian howled.

A dining car. The tables had been set for breakfast, but now the floor was littered with shattered china.

A car packed with passengers. Men with guns and rifles piled against the windows on the right side. On the left, women and children cowering on the floor between seats. She saw Johnny and the other boy. They were on their knees, crawling toward her, weaving in and out of the heaps of living and dead. There was blood on Johnny's face. She cried out to him. She struggled to reach him.

She heard someone say: "I hear they shot the engineer."

"I hear the brakeman's overhead, trying to stop the train."

"He don't have time. He'll be dead afore he gets to all them brakes."

He dashed into her arms. Over their heads, the continual thumping of boots on old wood. "Why did you come looking for me?" he gasped. "I was . . . on my way back . . . to my father's place."

"Are you Johnny? Or one of . . . the others?"

"I don't know. Please, let's go."

They pushed their way to the back door. Leapt across to the dining car, ran through the smashed dishes . . . and reached the carriage where the Indian danced. An eerie, wavering singsong that often changed into wolflike howling. She smelled a familiar odor . . . the pungent canine piss that presaged a time of heightened emotion for the werewolves, a war over territory, a battle over a bitch, a lust for human blood. But it was not the full moon!

She stared wildly at her charge. It was too dark to see if his trousers were stained. She saw only that he seemed transfixed by the Indian's frenzied dance. Their gazes were locked as in a mystical communion. Wind roared through broken windowpanes. But that was not why she felt so cold, cold to the very bone.

"Ma'am," said the news butch suddenly, "I think we'd best be gettin' on."

"You feel it too, don't you?"

"I seen some mighty strange things with your boy, ma'am. He ain't . . . he is considerable touched, ain't he? I mean in the head. Look at him and that Injun!"

Johnny's arms and legs moved spasmically, out of control. Suddenly he gave a terrible, deep-voiced cry: "Take the damned body, arsehole, the only thing you're good for is feeling the pain, the humiliation!"

"Johnny!" Speranza said.

She seized his hand. She led him onward. More fighting. Men's faces, pale in the half-moon, and the gunfire brilliant against the night. Onward. The cardsharp lay still, his hand still clenching gold. Teddy cried out: "Is he dead?" but did not stay to find out. They reached the entrance to the Count's private car.

The door opened. "Quickly. You and the boy."

Von Bächl-Wölfing stood outside. That odor emanated from him and from the others within. The train rocked sharply. She tottered, held out her hand . . . he took it. A burst of warmth shot through her. "You and the boy. This other creature"—he regarded the news butch with a look of distaste—"well, I'm afraid he doesn't belong with us." His cloak flapped. His eyes had taken on a little of that lupine luminosity. He seemed unmoved by the shouts and the rifle reports.

Teddy looked him right in the eye, defiant. "I ain't afraid of you, mister. I come here because my friend wanted me. I'm used to not belongin'."

"Go away, boy. You cannot understand what is happening."

"Get fucked, mister high and mighty."

Speranza looked from one to the other. She stepped across to the other car. Johnny would not move.

"My son," said the Count, "you must come to me now."

"Teddy's coming too."

"I have humored you too much already! First with this governess, who already knows too much—and now—"

So that's how you regard me! Speranza thought. Even though you touched me in my most profane places, even though you wrung from me a kind of frenzied, twisted love. I'm a supernumerary—a woman who knows too much—untrustworthy.

She looked at Teddy. There was a bond between them. Not just Johnny's need, but the fact that they were human—not this other thing that the Count was.

A clamor from above. A man's voice: "Pay dirt! Hostages!" Someone was climbing down the ladder. The Count jerked her roughly into the car. Johnny followed. He gripped Teddy firmly by the hand. The door slammed shut. Speranza turned to see a masked figure through the glass. She screamed.

Teddy had been through the narrow corridor that allowed access to the next car, but he had never set foot inside the private compartment itself. The furniture was all velvet and plush. There were paintings in gold frames. A screen separated the boudoir from the retiring chamber, where he could see a four-poster bed, draped, with an ancestral crest.

He hardly had time to notice all this because the chamber was crowded with the most eccentric collection of people he'd ever seen in one place. He knew some of them from the poker game: the turbaned astrologer, the Baroness, the padre; but there were others too. A bald old man with an ivory cane peered at him. All of them were dressed to the teeth. They had money, that was for sure. But mayhap they were all like Johnny Kindred, plumb out of their minds. Could be, he could try some of old man Claggart's tricks on them. If any of them survived the night. He stuck close to Johnny for the moment. This was Johnny's turf.

As for the governess. . . .

The way she'd looked at him, outside there . . . almost as though they were somehow kin. He'd have to study her more.

They murmured to each other in foreign languages. They looked at him strangely. Almost as if they were . . . stalking him. He was uneasy. He stayed close to Johnny, whose terror seemed to have lessened in these people's presence.

They heard a tremendous crunching sound. "Behind us!" someone shouted. They all crowded toward the bedroom area. Teddy knew that clanking, groaning sound well. Someone had uncoupled them from the cars behind. He watched through the tiny window. The gap was widening. There were horsemen galloping on the track, speeding toward them. Masked men springing from horseback onto their car. Climbing the ladder. Running overhead: thump, thump, thump. The governess put her hands over Johnny's eyes, but he pushed them away. Then came the thunk of uncoupling again. The wheels screamed at the loss of power. The Baroness shrieked like a maddened witch. Through it all the Count stood, unshakable. Father Alexandros was muttering in Greek. Teddy slipped. Collided with Speranza and Johnny. The three of them slammed against a plump velvet armchair. They were slowing, slowing . . . as the rest of the train sped hastily away.

Damn rich folks! Why did they have to travel in private Pullmans full of fancy furnishings? No wonder the robbers had singled out this one car. He could hear the squealing of iron on iron as the brake was being turned.

They came to a stop.

A head poked into the compartment. "Out! With your hands up! All of you! One at a time!" A harsh voice.

He followed the others out.

There were about a dozen armed men on foot, and several more on horseback. They wore black. Their horses were dark. Their masks were black, their dark hats pulled down hard over their eyebrows. They looked fearsome. But Teddy knew he had to do something to try to talk his way out of this. These damn foreigners weren't about to talk their way out of anything—they just stood around like sheep. Mayhap they didn't even understand what was going on. Hell, they didn't even look scared.

Teddy shouted, "There's more gold back there"—he pointed

with his thumb to the train that was disappearing into the west—"some poker players dropped a couple of thousand in gold in the saloon car. It's just laying on the floor. Why don't you leave us alone and go after it?"

"Shut up!" He felt the butt of a rifle slam into his face. He recoiled. Blood in his eyes. He looked at the others, who were staring at him, half incredulous, half mocking.

That's the thanks I get, he thought bitterly. They'll probably kill me now and I ain't even found my paw yet.

"Now walk. Single file."

They turned north, away from the track.

And started walking. Making no noise at all. The horses whinnied, their captors occasionally barked orders, but the foreigners moved quite silently, like nocturnal animals.

A huge explosion behind them. Liquid fire in the sky. He did not look back; none of the others did.

The fields were black and gold in the firelight. There was a light, hot breeze, smelling of burnt grass. And thousands upon thousands of stars. They walked on, past hearing the sizzling of wood and the tumbling of shattered metal.

They walked on for about an hour, two hours, three. They never seemed to tire. Except for the governess. She was walking in front of him. She was the only one whose footsteps he could hear, a steady crackle of shoes on grass.

Presently he could see the outline of low hills far in the distance. They were the Sandhills. Chalky boulders glistened in the moonlight. There were some trees hard by, the first he had seen since they left the track. Next to them were wagons, campfires, and tents.

Other horsemen were approaching them.

Teddy had to talk, even though his head still ached from the last blow. He said to the governess, "They ain't gonna hold *me* for ransom, ma'am. I ain't worth two bits even as a 'prentice."

Speranza said, "Something very strange is going on."

"Them friends of yours is acting mighty peculiar," Teddy said. "Like they ain't human, almost."

"They're not," she said. "They're werewolves."

She was aware of how preposterous it sounded even as she said it. But the boy did not seem taken aback. It was as if she were confirming some inner conviction that he had had all along.

She had been suspicious even as they had been attacked. For the members of the Lykanthropenverein had not panicked; they had simply been waiting. She was not surprised that they were indifferent to the carnage on the train. But if these had been ordinary robbers, she did not doubt that the wolves could more than hold their own in a fight, and would not have allowed themselves so meekly to be captured.

"Stay close to me, Teddy," she said. She owed him that much. He was another human whom Johnny had drawn into his world. Johnny needed humans near him. To keep him from being imprisoned forever by the mind of Jonas Kay.

They came to a stop. Their captors dismounted and they all took off their masks. They stood to attention, waiting for a signal. The Count smiled. The horsemen who were coming toward them bore torches; others with lanterns walked behind.

Dr. Szymanowski turned to them all. It was the first time he had spoken more than a curt word or two since their journey had begun. "It has been a most excellent idea, Excellency. The robbery—the diversion—the burning of the Pullman. It will be presumed that we were lost, perhaps killed, by the brigands."

"And the land journey?" said Chandraputra. "How long will that be taking? It is only a few days to our . . . transformation, and we must feed, that much is certain."

One of the captors addressed them. "Do not worry, honored masters," he said. "There is ample provender to the north, on your way to the denning site . . . an entire village of Indians awaits your pleasure."

"What are they talking about?" Teddy whispered.

"Later," Speranza said. He could not be told all at once. And some provision must be found for protecting him from them—before the night of the full moon.

Among those who approached there was someone riding sidesaddle. A woman in red. A veil covered her face. Her skirts trailed almost to the ground, and she lifted her arms in a flamboyant gesture of welcome.

Suddenly all the members of the Lykanthropenverein, all except for the Count, fell to their knees. And gazed at her with adoration . . . and a certain lust, Speranza thought. And Speranza knew who this woman must be. She had dreaded this moment since she had known of this woman's existence. Is this the true Madonna of the Wolves, and I a mere stopgap to assuage the Count's uncontrollable urges? If I could but see her eyes—

But she never raised her veil.

Even so, Speranza had seen her countenance in photographs. She knew it must be the queen wolf, the woman Natalia Petrovna Stravinskaya, the Count's mistress—the woman whom she had displaced in the bed of the Count von Bächl-Wölfing.

10
The Lakota Lands
three-quarters moon, waxing

"AN OLD MAN HAS COME. AN OLD MAN OF THE SHUNGMANITU HAS come, dancing."

Little Elk Woman heard the voices as she and her sisters were dressing hides beside the creek, a little way off from the cluster of tipis that was their village. Her sisters were gossiping about men, and their talk was becoming tiresome; she decided to go back to the village and see this wonder for herself.

And there he was next to the fire at the center of the village, a man whose weather-beaten face and white hairs spoke of many long years, and whose eyes held that not-quite-human quality that men said distinguished those of the Shungmanitu. The young children were already seated at his feet, waiting, no doubt, for fierce tales of prowess in battle and the hunt. She stood apart from the others, just drinking in the stranger's wondrous appearance. He danced in the light of dawn, his bare feet stamping the ground with a power that belied his years, and from his lips came a wolf song.

Soon they would invite him into the tent of one of the warriors, and the women and children would be shut out from the ceremony of the pipe. She wanted to hear all she could.

He danced and she moved closer. She could catch his words

now, between the wordless *eya-eya* of the refrain: "A wolf is born. I rejoice."

But why had he come to their village? The children watched him, intent, unmoving. She did not question them, for they seemed transported into another world entirely.

Dancing, punctuating his words with long silences and outbursts of howling, the old man said: "Among the *washichun* I have seen a young wolf. A young wolf, the youngest of the pack, one of them yet not one of them. Listen and hear me! I have seen white wolves among the white men, Wichasha Shungmanitu among the dead-eyed people who ride the iron road across the plains. I smelled their urine even in the swift wind of their journeying. I smelled the fetor of their breath. No man believed it could be true, but I have seen it, I, an old man of the Shungmanitu, I, whose mother and aunt perished in the Moon of the Popping Trees as they sought out the place of the winter moon dance."

Zeke sat in the tent and listened to the words, but he couldn't make head or tail of them. Yet his Indian friends sat quite still and paid as much mind to this old man as if he were a preacher.

They done put on their Sunday best, thought Zeke. Old Wambliwashté had even come bedecked in a war shirt that must have been fifty years old, the hanks of enemy hair frayed, half the buffalo bone ornaments missing. There he was now, passing the pipe with the ritual words *na* and *ku*. There was smoke everywhere in the lodge, smoke that stank so badly it made you want to retch, except that retching was unpardonable bad manners in a council as important as this one.

The stranger went on. His dance became wilder and his voice more wavery. "For many moons I have ridden the iron horse, availing myself of a free passage granted me by the white men who built it in exchange for my pledge that my tribe would not intervene in the building of it. I have ridden it back and forth and seen many strange things. But none was stranger than the boy who is both *washichun* and Shungmanitu. I met his gaze and he knew me for what I was. And then came many men, attacking the iron horse, and slaying the travellers, who captured the boy-wolf and took him along themselves."

There'd been some kind of train robbery then, Zeke thought.

Just when folks were beginning to think the territories would get civilization.

He sat back and breathed in the smoke. The smoke curled up around him and seeped into him and filled up his lungs. An acrid smoke that held a hidden sweetness. This was the smoke of visions, of seeing things far away. Though he had smelled it many times, he had never had a vision himself. Old Wambliwashté now, he was sitting there with his eyes closed, rocking a little. Maybe he was talking to some spirit animal. To an Indian, visions were just as natural as breathing, and a dream was as real as though it had happened in broad daylight.

The dancing old man sang, "This child was born in a distant land and he has been sent to us to be our savior, to lead us out of this dark time."

And Zeke sat bolt upright at those words. "You're wrong," he said, forgetting in his astonishment to speak Lakota. "You been listenin' to them missionaries too long, old man. There ain't no such thing as a wolf cub messiah that's comin' to save the Injuns. Times is dark, but they ain't gettin' no brighter."

He stopped himself short. No one had understood him. They watched him, dead silent, waiting for him to continue perhaps. The old man had paused in mid-syllable, waiting out the interruption.

Zeke looked into the old man's eyes. Mayhap it was a trick of the firelight and the smoke, but his eyes seemed almost yellow, slitted, like the eyes of a wild animal. He had seen those eyes before.

He had a sudden recollection: that day of Sanderson's massacre. The death-smoke sweeping up from the snow flurries even as now it welled up from the circle of life. The smoke choking him, making his eyes smart. The boy bleeding to death in the snow. The old she-wolf among the dead ones buried in the sky. The words that had sprung to Scott's lips: *"Shungmanitu hemakiye."*

"A wolf told me this!" That was what young Harper had said—ritual words to be spoken when a Lakota Indian returned from seeking a vision—ritual words that identified the spirit animal who had been his guide!

Yes. He had seen eyes like those before.

Tonight he would have to ask Little Elk Woman how long it was until the full moon.

* * *

That night they feasted the old man's coming. Little Elk Woman sat beside her husband, a little way off from the celebrations. There was no buffalo meat, but she had grown used to the tough salt beef that the soldiers provided them, and they were boiling a sweet young dog. The dancers sang, the women shrilling, the young men raucous against the pounding of the drum. By rights she should have felt joyful. Had not great news come to the village? But her husband had not spoken a word at all since he had emerged from the chief's lodge. It was almost as though a spell had been cast over him.

"I know," she said, touching him lightly by the arm, "that once you were *washichun*. Though now you have shed their ways and become human, it's not always possible to forget entirely the ways of white men. I'm scared for you." Was it possible that he longed to be with them again?

"The *wichasha wakan* says that the *washichun* have no souls at all, that they are dead inside. Today we were all happy because the old man came. You're the only one who is sad."

Perhaps there were some advantages in not having a soul; she knew that it gave the *washichun* a tremendous, uncaring ruthlessness in battle. It was hard for her to imagine why a man would choose the white man's way of life deliberately, but even among the Lakota there were some whose souls, it seemed, had been stolen from them; how much easier for a man who had been born among whites to be sucked back into their world. She was afraid for him and could not stop speaking, though he seemed not to hear her.

The young boys were running in circles around them, shouting war cries and poking each other with blades of dried grass. Kneeling by the fire, old Wambliwashté was telling war stories. Little Elk Woman retrieved a piece of the dog from the kettle and gave it to her husband, who munched it silently.

At last he asked her, "How long is it till the full moon?"

"That's a strange question to ask," she said. "Four days at the most. But the old stranger will know best of all. He is of the Shungmanitu, and he'll probably change into a wolf then."

"You really believe that, don't you?"

"Is there a reason not to?" But she knew there was; the white men did not have visions, and saw only the surfaces of things. That was the way they themselves were.

But he only muttered to himself, in English: "World's goin' crazy. Wolf messiahs. Old men changin' into wild animals."

She could not understand what he said. She clasped his arm to her, trying to give comfort, but he would not answer her; and that evening, as they retired beneath the thick buffalo robe, she lay on top of him, trying to stir him, urging him on with soft cries and little movements. But though she roused him to the semblance of a mighty passion, it seemed to her that his mind was in a place she could not reach.

11
Dakota Territory
full moon

SINCE THEY HAD FIRST SET EYES ON ONE ANOTHER, NATALIA Petrovna had not deigned to speak to Speranza. By day the convoy headed north, with carts and pack animals, over hills speckled with yucca. Rain slowed them and made the grassy seas smell fragrant. She shared a cart with Johnny and with the news butch.

Nights, the Count's vassals erected tents: a huge pavilion for the count and his madonna, smaller apartments for the lesser wolves in order of rank, and mean, tipilike structures for the humans. The wolves gathered around the campfire and took turns boasting of their prowess or telling tales of being persecuted in the old country. Or played poker. They were suffused with joy at their freedom, and they laughed easily. It was hard to believe that the carnage she had witnessed on the Omaha-Cheyenne train had been part of their plans.

As befit his station, the Count's son stayed at his father's pavilion during the night. Speranza could not guess with what evils they were indoctrinating him there, but during the day she tried to undo them as best she could, with wholesome games and with the discipline of Latin conjugations and by treating him with a steadfast affection in the face of all his strange metamorphoses of personality. It was harder and harder to do. Johnny Kindred was being pushed more and more into the background, and Jonas Kay was coming into his own. She suspected that Johnny came out only for her, and that when the boy was with his father, Johnny was suppressed entirely.

She shared a tent with Teddy Grumiaux. At night the Count slipped in and out like a shadow. He was so silent that Speranza did not think that Teddy was ever awakened by him; although once or twice, startled and shamed by the pleasure she knew with the Count, she had not been able to stifle a cry; whereat she would imagine the boy staring, wide-eyed, from the far corner of the tent where he was wont to lie with his blanket wound round and round him like a shroud, and the thought would vex her and keep her sleepless long after the Count had vanished into the night.

As the first day of the full moon dawned, she knew that she would have to tell Teddy what these creatures were. The three of them were riding in the wagon together, hunched up against bundles of canvas. The wagon groaned and jerked, pots and pans clanged as they made their way uphill with the sunrise behind them to their right. She had been reading her Bible; when she looked up, she saw that she and Teddy were alone together, for Johnny had gone prowling among the canvas-heaps.

She put down the Bible. The last words she had read had been: "and the wolf shall lie down with the lamb," and it had brought back so vivid a remembrance of the preceding night that her face flushed with shame. She quickly looked down again for fear it would be seen, but she was too late: the young half-breed said, "Are you sick, ma'am? You looks feverish."

"Oh, Teddy, there is something I simply must tell you! But you'll think me mad."

"About werewolves."

"You couldn't have seen any . . . transformations yet."

"I've known it from the time we started travellin' north. I got eyes in the back of my head and ears in my britches, ma'am. I may be unschooled, but I ain't stupid. And I seen how Johnny behaves. He ain't one of us and he ain't one of them."

"That's why I'm still here."

"Reckoned you wanted to keep him human somehow," Teddy said. He fished some tobacco out of his pockets and offered her a chaw; she declined. "Do they really change shape?"

"I've seen it."

Teddy sucked in his breath and said nothing for a while. The wagon rocked to and fro, and now and then she could hear Johnny cursing at some imagined foe.

Teddy said, "And when they change shape—what do they eat?"

"Oh, Teddy," Speranza said, "I have seen things I wish I could not remember."

"So it's people then."

She nodded. "That's why they've come here—to live in the wilderness and use the poor savages to sate their brutal hunger. And I came because somehow I thought that Johnny—that I could prevent—that I could—"

"The poor savages!" Teddy said, imitating her tone of voice. But behind his easy mockery is a certain sadness, Speranza thought. "Did you know, Miss Speranza, that we're headin' right in the direction of the Indian lands? I reckon we'll reach the village by moonrise."

"The village—"

"The village I run away from. My mother's village. I went to search for my paw, but I guess I'll never find him now."

"Your mother is in danger!" Speranza said. It was the first time she had ever thought of the Indians as something other than an abstraction. Oh, the Indians along the trip had been picturesque enough, but she had always had the feeling that they existed merely to lend their journey a festive note. Of course the boy was half Indian—how foolish of her not to perceive before that he must have ties with their world no less strong than those he felt for the community of the white man. "She must be warned somehow," Speranza said. "You must go . . . you, a poor child, alone into the wilderness!"

He laughed. A bump in the road jolted them, and they touched each other by accident. She could feel his derision in the way he snatched away his hand. "A poor child," he said, taunting her tone once more. Then he whispered, "If you help me I could get a horse. We could be at the village in time to warn them. . . ."

"Help you! I can ride passably sidesaddle. I know nothing of the wilderness."

"I ain't askin' you to come with me, ma'am. I just need someone to distract the Count. So he won't see me steal one of them horses up front there."

"But I must tend to Johnny—"

At that moment she heard the young boy howl and saw him scramble past her, his arms low to the ground, and she thought: I am too late. They have him. He has slipped away from me; the wilderness has made him a wild thing; I cannot save him. I cannot even save myself; the beast has made a plaything of me.

Speranza wept. It seemed to her that she had lost all the qualities she had possessed on the day she stood in Victoria Station waiting for Cornelius Quaid: her self-assurance, her belief in men's innate goodness, her strength. And as she wept, she saw Johnny standing beside her, laughing at her as he emptied his bladder over the side of the wagon.

Teddy made no move to console her, but stared out at the landscape, chewing his tobacco. At last she touched him lightly on the shoulder and said softly: "Tell me what to do."

He leapt from the wagon and ran alongside it. The mud squished in between his toes. Jonas exulted. Each time I change, he thought, I become more and more myself. He sniffed the air and knew the scents of all the members of the pack. There was odor of fear, too, mingled with the familiar smells: he knew that there were prey animals among them, and that they had already begun to dread the coming night.

The procession was coming to a stop. It was time for a mid-morning break: champagne, cards, tobacco, conversation. He saw the Baroness playing poker with Father Alexandros; the Indian astrologer was measuring the position of the sun with a miniature astrolabe. His father was already seated on a chaise longue that the servants had unloaded from one of the wagons. In a fauteuil beside him sat Natalia Petrovna, his father's abandoned mistress. She had not been formally put aside, and she sat proudly, her face half smothered in an ermine stole.

Two horses were tethered to the tree that sheltered them on the grassy embankment overlooking a shallow northward slope.

Beyond them were foothills; and farther still, dark outlines, perhaps mountains.

With his attenuated senses he could hear the servants whispering as he approached his father: "There he comes, the wolf pup!" . . . "They say he is the most dangerous of all." . . . "How harmless he seems, and yet. . . ."

Yes! He could smell their terror on the wind, sour, with a sweet aftertaste, a little—he grinned as the thought sprang to his mind—a little like an orange soufflé. A delicious thing, this fear.

He knew that his father smelled it too, for the Count von Bächl-Wölfing smiled a little and said, "*Mein Söhnchen.*" And rose, his arms outstretched, his blood-red silk dressing gown flapping in the breeze against the mid-morning sun. Jonas cried out, "Father, Father," and ran to embrace him. Under the silk he felt the hardness of animal muscle, the prickle of wolf's hair. Though nightfall was far off, the moon was already exerting its power a little.

"Father," Jonas growled, "I'm strong now. I don't need that governess anymore."

The count put a finger to the boy's lips. "Perhaps not. But now . . . alas, my child, it is I who have need of her." He smiled mildly and seemed indifferent to the boy's transformation. Could he not see that Johnny was gone, banished to the forest depths?

"Weakling! You should be leading your people! You shouldn't be fucking humans!" Jonas bared his teeth. Why did he have no fangs? He could feel them, phantom fangs, ready to burst from his gums. Where was the moon? Feverishly he struck out with weak fists that were not claws.

His father slapped his face. Then, not raising his voice above a whisper, he said, "Youngling, you still have much to learn. I, not you, am the leader here. Perhaps, one day, you will have the temerity to challenge me, and you may even fight me to the death; it is a possibility I entertained when I conceived you. But you will not defy me yet."

"Nevertheless," Natasha said, "I think he is right, Hartmut. We should put her away, or better yet, devour her."

"Nonsense, Natasha," said the Count. And to the boy: "You loved her so much."

Jonas's face burned. He looked steadfastly into Natalia's eyes. Perhaps there was an ally there.

She said: "Dearest Hartmut, if I am to be dethroned, let it be swift. I cannot bear it when you show indecision. There she comes."

Jonas turned and saw her climbing up the knoll. She was an unwelcome presence, incongruous among the gaily clad celebrants. Walking behind her was that dirty boy Johnny had befriended. Come nightfall he would be the first to be disposed of. As she came closer Jonas felt another presence too, stirring within himself, at the edge of the forest clearing. Johnny was trying to repossess the body. How irritating! The others could be controlled, but Johnny, for all his whining childishness, had strength. There it came again, that puerile snivelling: "Let me out! I want to speak to her! I have to speak to her!"

"No!" Jonas struggled to maintain an impassive expression. But the muscles of his face were twitching, forcing his lips into an infantile pout, flushing the fluid from his tear ducts, and suddenly it was Johnny in the clearing and Jonas felt himself melting into the darkness beyond it. . . .

All was not lost. At first the child had growled and snarled at her, but, with startling suddenness, there were tears in his eyes and he looked forlornly at her and seemed almost as out of place as she herself did.

"My son has just informed me," said the Count, "that he doesn't need a governess anymore."

She reminded herself that she must try to create a diversion so that Teddy could steal a horse. She could think of nothing to do that did not seem like a scene from one of those torrid penny-dreadful novels, so, bracing herself, she flung herself at the Count's feet, almost doubled up, her corsets chafing against her abdomen.

"Speranza!"

"A fine moment to tell me this!" she cried. "After uprooting me from all I held dear, after dishonoring and defiling me in the worst possible manner—"

She stopped. The Count's guests were actually laughing at her! And the Count himself smiled indulgently and reached out his hand to stroke her hair, confident that he possessed her utterly. "I did not say," the Count said, "that I agreed with my son's contention."

"Enough!" It was Natalia Petrovna who spoke. "I want to get a close look at this woman who means to oust me."

"I intend nothing of the kind!" Speranza said.

"Shall we fight it out now?" Natalia turned to the others. "Now, while you still have sporting chance? If we wait until moonrise, I shall simply tear you limb from limb."

She pounced. Pinned Speranza to the ground. Her knee dug into her waist, cracking the whalebone, making her gasp in pain. Natalia's lips foamed. Drool streamed over Speranza's eyes, her mouth . . . stinging, reeking drool. Her fingernails dug into Speranza's wrists almost as though claws had already begun to sprout from them. She was choking on the stench of her, even though she knew the smell well from the Count's lovemaking.

"Let her go!" Johnny cried out. And began tugging at Natalia's skirts, her stole . . . he ripped it from her neck, and Speranza saw the patch of fur and scar tissue that it concealed . . . Natalia screamed as the boy pummelled her with his tiny fists, but as Speranza watched, the boy's eyes turned slitty, yellow, and he seemed to draw some of Natalia's identity into himself, and he was on all fours suddenly and slavering over Speranza, and she thought she saw a hint of fangs, glistening, fetid . . . and from around her came the cries of other beasts . . . and she saw the Count himself rise from his chaise longue and lumber toward them with emberlike eyes. . . .

And Teddy, dashing toward the horses.

She closed her eyes, squeezed them tight, but in her mind's eye they were already wolves, their canines stained with blood, their howls lancing the chill night air. . . .

When she opened them again, they all had their backs to her. They were standing at the edge of the knoll, and as she raised herself up, she could see, in the distance, a horse and rider speeding northward. He was a blur now, lost in the windy grassy sea.

She saw the Greek priest heft a rifle to his shoulders and aim it carefully.

A shrill laugh from the Baroness, his poker-playing partner. "I see you have been picking up a few hints from that Buffalo Bill person," she said.

"Let him be," the Count was saying quietly. "Let us not forget, my friends, that until night we still have a veneer of civilization about us."

"What of the governess?" someone said. It sounded like the Indian astrologer. She closed her eyes, expecting them to turn on her again.

Then she heard the Count's voice: "I will not have her harmed. I intend she will become one of us. But it will have to be of her own free will."

And Natalia's mocking voice: "That is what you said to me, Hartmut, and not too many years past. *Merde!* I have since learnt hypocrisy of this 'free will' of yours."

She opened her eyes. Natalia was looking at her with naked hatred. The Russian spat on the grass at Speranza's feet, then turned her attention to the Count.

As she started to walk back toward the wagons, Speranza heard a child's voice: "Speranza, Speranza." And felt the small hand in hers, and gripped it hard, and knew that she was Johnny's last hope. "Hold my hand," she said. "I will lead you out of the forest, Johnny."

"If there is a way out," the boy said sadly.

12
The Lakota Lands
that evening

THERE WAS A FULL MOON. A SHAFT OF MOONLIGHT FELL ON LITTLE Elk Woman and her man through the opening in the tipi where the poles met. And from the distance came a new kind of howling—cold, anguished, almost like the screech of the iron horse as it clattered across the dead buffalo plains.

Little Elk Woman thought: When wolves howl, you can sense the joy of their oneness with the night. You can hear the urgency of their hunger even as you lie huddled in your buffalo robe, afraid. But these are not wolves who howl from hunger. Their howling is more akin to lust—not the lust of lovers but the mocking lust of a warrior who humiliates a fallen enemy by entering his anus. These cannot be the wolves that have always lived in these lands. They have somehow partaken of the white man's qualities—they are cut off from nature, they do not know themselves.

The fire in the tipi had died down. She sat up, thinking to wake her husband. But he was not there.

"Zeke?" she whispered. There was no answer save the distant howling. She rose from the buffalo robe and covered herself in a blanket, for she could feel the night wind tugging at the tipi flaps.

"Zeke!" she said. Perhaps he was just outside, listening to the howling. Was it possible that he felt a kinship with it? There was no answer. But then she heard the flute.

She was sure she had imagined it at first. But it came again, soft-toned, erotic—the sound of *siyótanka*, the low-voiced instrument of courtship. "You are teasing me," she said quietly. "Yes. I am not a virgin anymore, and you have not come with horses and scalps to give to my father to buy my love. I am old and have borne children and known too many men." And she laughed. The music came louder now, drowning out the cries of the wolves, dispelling her fear.

She crept outside the tipi. The moon hung in a cloudless sky. Where was the sound coming from? Beyond the clearing. She thought she saw someone move, but when she turned to look at him he had blended into a tipi's long shadow.

She followed the sound. Left the clearing. Walked into the forest. Too quickly—as though she had not been walking, but transported through the magic of dreaming—she arrived at the edge of the creek where the women did their washing and bathing. The whine of the flute came stronger now, piercing the still air. In the shadows of the trees . . . was there an old man playing? She could not see, because where he stood the leafy canopy was so thick that no moonlight fell on him at all.

And then she heard her husband's voice. He was railing at the old man. She saw him now, standing half in, half out of the moonlight.

"You ain't got no business comin' here," Zeke was saying—

Little Elk Woman could not understand why he was speaking a tongue of the *washichun*. "Givin' them false hopes. There ain't goin' to be no wolf pup redeemer, old man, and you ain't John the Baptist neither. Go back where you come from."

The music stopped. Once more she could hear the howling, and she was afraid.

Blood! The scent of it filled the air, maddening him, goading him on as he writhed on the hillside, racked with the agony of shifting. All around him they were transforming! There was the Count's cloak, tossed aside as the claws tore loose from the fingernails. Chandraputra's turban unwinding across the silvery grass. The Baroness's fur bristling as she dropped on all fours. And he, Jonas Kay, screaming as his wolf shape ripped from his human skin and his forepaws shredded through his silk shirt, his flannel trousers. And always the servants standing stiffly in their starched uniforms, their faces impassive, as their masters howled with the pangs of metamorphosis.

Next to the tethered horses stood Natalia Petrovna. She was still in human shape. She had thrown off the scarf that hid her silver-scarred cheek, and her face was contorted in agony. Howling she raged, but the toxic silver within her flesh retarded the transformation and made it a torture. How strange to watch her, her body fighting itself, the poison working against her true nature. . . .

No anguish in Jonas's transforming. None! How high the wind keened to his lupine ears, how pungent the air smelled, how intoxicating the stench of fear and the rush of blood! He rejoiced as he ran full tilt toward the others even as the hair began to rise along his spine, prickly, tickled by the wind. "Father, Father!" he cried, but the cry was already turning into a snarl, a guttural growling.

They changed. They raced toward the northern woods whence wafted the faint scent of human prey. In the last moments before his human nature left him, Jonas Kay saw Speranza standing in the moonlight in her black dress. The Count his father was circling her, nuzzling her, caressing her with his paws. She clutched a Bible in her arms and wept. Moonlight enfolded her; her face shone; her tears glistened; he could hear the racing of her blood and the pulsing of her heart, intense and rapid as the patter of rabbits' feet.

And Speranza saw him too now.

I hate you! *I hate you!* She still holds that other creature captive—that part of me that would draw me out of the forest—that mewling human child. He's drawn to her, he wants to make love to her. She even holds my father captive—my father, king of the beasts, lord of the dark places! Even now as he clawed at her, growling, howling, whining as the wind whinnied, he would not draw blood, would not devour her . . . even now, when the whole pack craved the taste of manflesh, he was drawing about the place where she stood in a circle of protection, lovingly cutting her off from harm with a barrier of piss, shit, semen.

His last thoughts were of hate, before his animal nature swooped down on him and swept from him his capacity for thinking.

Teddy Grumiaux stopped at the creek to sniff the mist. There was an odor of boiled dogmeat. The encampment must be nearby, not quite where it had been when he had run off to look for his father. From somewhere on the other side of the creek came the breathy whisper of a wood flute. Someone out courting, he thought. Good time for it. With the full moon setting the leaves to shining with their pale fire. If only they knowed what I know.

The sound came louder. Pierced the still night. Teddy shivered and looked back at the horse he had tethered to a lodgepole pine. The horse stood unnaturally quiet. There was fear here. If there was anything Teddy had learned from the Injuns, it was what fear smelled like. But the smell of boiled dog was stronger, and Teddy was hungry. No wolf cries yet. The pack was still far off. The fear came from the horse, because the horse knew what his masters were and knew they were on their way.

Suddenly he saw the flute player. Just for a moment. When the mists seemed to part. A ghost? He was startled. He stepped back. The music died down and he heard the crunch of dead twigs. Behind the mist, the outline of tipis.

"You ain't no ghost," Teddy said softly. An old man standing by the bank. An old man dancing. Half naked and dancing in the bitter cold.

And Teddy had seen him before. It was the mad chief who

always rode the train, back and forth, Cheyenne to Omaha to Cheyenne. He had always been there, rocking back and forth and singing to himself, and Teddy hadn't ever paid him no mind, excepting he and the wolf-boy seemed to speak to each other in a private language.

And then he heard another man talking to the old Injun, so he surely knew it hadn't been any spirit.

He couldn't catch all the words, but it was English. Here in Sioux country the words sounded alien. "No messiah . . . you go on feedin' your people them lies, and givin' them false hopes, and they'll foller you all the way to perdition . . . I heard another Injun like you tell about the ghost dance from the south . . . that there's one messiah for the white folks and one messiah for the red . . . and they can wish the buffalo back into the plains with their own selfs and dream the white man back into the sea if they believes and dances the ghost dance with all their hearts. And you're just one more of them crazed old men the Injuns loves to pay heed to. I don't want my woman believing you."

The old man bent down to pick up his flute and in the same fluid motion put it back to his lips and picked up his melody in mid-phrase, and never stopped dancing.

"You can dance all you want, old man, but you ain't never going to make the clock turn counterclockwise."

What did that mean? He was about to step out of the shadows and show himself to the old man. Hadn't he sung the *shungmanitu olowan* on the train when he caught sight of that Johnny Kindred for the first time? Teddy knew that these Sioux had a sixth sense about danger. Didn't he realize what was going to happen? No . . . his dancing was full of joy.

Teddy saw that the white man was walking away now. He hadn't been able to convince the old man of whatever it was he was talking about. He looked angry. I'll wait until he's out of sight, Teddy thought. Then I'll tell the old man and he'll know what to do to warn the rest of the village.

For the first time since he had reached the creek, Teddy heard distant howling. The white man stopped, listened. Teddy shrank back, trying to find a patch of shadow somewhere. Then he saw the woman.

She had been standing in the mist behind the two men. Now the clouds must have shifted. Her face was mottled by twigs and moonlight. Teddy hadn't seen her in a long time, but he knew his mother at once, and he couldn't help calling out to her: *"Ina, Ina!"* like a little boy craving a teat.

It was too late to retreat. The white man saw the woman and she looked demurely at the forest floor.

"I was lookin' to protect you, Little Elk Woman."

"Yes, Zeke."

Teddy knew who this man was. Once or twice his mother had spoken of another white man, a friend and sometime rival of his father's. So he called out to his mother again and waded to her across the stream.

The old man stopped playing.

"Mother—" Teddy said. There were so many other thoughts whirling through his mind—the long absence, the regrets, the old quarrel. But he didn't have time for that. He spoke to her in Lakota: "Something terrible is happening. White people are becoming Shungmanitu. They want to swallow up your village. *Hechitu welo!*" He shivered, drenched from the creek. She moved toward him, covered him with a part of her blanket. There were familiar lost smells in the fabric . . . like the dried sweat of a woman who has spent all day dressing hides.

I don't know why I run off like that, he thought. I was a fool. She loves me. No one ever loved me when I worked that train. Even when they done things to my body five minutes after they come from listening to their favorite preacher.

"If it ain't old bastard Grumiaux's kid!" Zeke Sullivan said. And came closer.

He's her man now, Teddy thought. I hope he don't try to call hisself my daddy. But he's like me, trying to walk the path between two worlds. Likely as not he'll understand me better than her old Injun husband did.

Teddy looked at his mother and the stranger. Instinctively he shrank into the gritty folds of the old blanket and his mother's arms. And put up his hands as if to ward off a blow.

But Zeke only said, "I'm glad you come home, kid. Your ma's been worryin' herself sick about you."

And his mother said: "My son, you must be hungry," as though he had never gone away.

The old man did not resume his piping, but stared strangely at the three of them. He sniffed the air three times. He said: "I smell fear. I smell anger. I smell the hunters." He dropped down on all fours, haunching his withered buttocks at the moon. He pawed the ground, he buried his nose in the soil. He turned his head sharply as though listening to distant voices.

Came the faraway howling once again. Teddy felt his mother's trembling. "There is a wrongness in this howling," said Little Elk Woman, "and that is why I came out to find you. They are not real wolves."

"Damn right they ain't!" Teddy said. "Werewolves—all of them werewolves—all of them fancy furriners on the train."

"So that was what Harper meant—" Zeke said. Teddy didn't know who he was talking about, but he seemed scared. In Lakota Zeke added, "I had a friend once and my friend, though a white man and a soldier, he saw a true vision. And after that we were never as good friends again."

The old man looked up at them from the forest floor. His face was covered with wet leaves. He picked up the flute in his mouth and tossed his head back so that the flute flew up in an arc and then he scampered after it and caught it in an outstretched hand, and his fingernails seemed like claws. The three of them watched. The howling came again. The old man answered it. His eyes narrowed. They glowed. Reflected moonlight, Teddy thought. But he wasn't convinced.

The old man darted through the dead leaves, stirred them up, scattered them. The forest smelled like . . . Teddy remembered how a lady taking the train out from Boston had paid him four bits to slide his tongue into her unmentionables and wiggle it back and forth, slowly, while she leaned back against the shuddering seat and the train rolled on past Grand Island. That was how the moist earth smelled. Of a woman's private parts. There had been blood, Teddy remembered. Clotted over the frilly lace. Gooey on his tongue.

And the old man . . . again and again he howled as he scurried, more lithe than a man could scurry, mixing up the dirt and the dead twigs. Why, the old man was one of them too! Teddy cried out, "I came to warn you, but there's one of them here already, and fixin' to change into a monster afore our very eyes!"

"Noooooooo!" the old man shrieked. "I am dancing to protect you . . . I smell the peril that stalks the boy!" And reared up, and loped around them in a circle, stopping at the four compass points to make water, gasping. "I am too old to change completely . . . *yahéhéhé* . . . but I can still piss on the ground to make it holy . . . *yaháháhá* . . . and draw a circle of protection against your enemies . . ."

The mists were rolling away. The moon shone down on them. Teddy was still wet and cold, and the blanket pricked his cheeks, the backs of his hands. He could see the village clearly now. Here and there a tipi glowed from an unspent fire. The sound of wolves came closer, closer, closer. . . .

Teddy screamed out: "The *washichun* Shungmanitu are coming! Wake up, wake up!"

"There is nothing you can do now, boy!" The old man stopped what he was doing and spoke with a sudden lucidity. "The wolves will eat their way through the village. The village means nothing now. I am here to draw the circle . . . the circle that will draw in the one who is to save us all . . . though you have no place in the drama, you shall remain within the circle and be protected also. . . ."

Then came more howling, huge, cacophonous, terrifying.

Wildly Teddy looked at him. His mother mouthed a silent song: was it a death song? He could not read her lips. Behind them, people were stirring from the tipis, peering from the flaps, staring wild-eyed at one another.

Then, from across the creek—

Hoofbeats. Whinnying. Snarling. The crackle of paws on brushwood. And Teddy saw a man on horseback marking his way toward the stream. The wolves were at his heels. He wore a cavalry uniform. He had been riding a long time. The wolves were leaping onto the horse's flanks, rending flesh from bone now. And Zeke shrieked out: "Harper!" as the palomino staggered and swayed and the wolves swarmed over it—

Around the four of them was the circle the old man had drawn . . . it was a circle indeed, Teddy saw now, a circle drawn in pale blue fire that shed a ghostly flickering light over his mother and the others . . . that made the eyes of the wolves seem crystal-cold.

And Zeke screamed, "I'm coming to get you!" and began to run toward the creek's edge, but the old man stilled him with a gesture, and he himself strode out of the circle. He raised his arms. The wolves hesitated. Their jaws were bloody.

The old man played a brief melody on the flute, and the wolves howled in response and parted so that the young cavalry officer could crawl to the water's edge, his face bleeding, his uniform ripped. Zeke and Teddy went to the circle's edge. They leaned over as hard as they could to drag the man across the boundary.

A single wolf stood apart from the pack. Teddy knew who the wolf was from the streak of silver fur on his forehead. He said: "That's their leader." The wolf leapt the stream and came to the circle's edge. As his paw touched the blue flame he drew it back sharply with a bark of pain. The old man played and the flame grew brighter.

The wolf gazed long and hard at the old man. Teddy knew it was the stare a wolf gives its prey when it means to tell his victim that the stalking is done and it's time to die.

But the old man, he went right on playing, and he stared back at the wolf, as though they were equals, leaders both of them. And there was a calm in the old man's eyes.

The wolf that was also the Count von Bächl-Wölfing lifted his tail high and roared his rage and tried to put out the blue fire with his own piss. But the old man went on playing.

And the other wolves waited.

Scott Harper lay in the circle. He was gasping for breath. Lord knew how long he'd been riding. He said: "Sanderson done sent me to bring you in, Zeke Sullivan. He's fixin' to hang you for desertion."

"He sent you?" Zeke said. "He knowed you was my friend."

"He knew. He wanted to make an example. Zeke——" Scott's voice cracked and Teddy moved to throw the blanket over him. "Zeke, I don't want no part in this army no more. I have nightmares. I see the way Sanderson kicked that baby in his cradleboard down the hillside. I see the dead baby rolling in the snow. And the blame wolves. They're trying to tell me something, I know it."

The Count, the wolf king, turned his back on the circle of flame. He set off toward the village, his tail high, and one by one the other wolves came splashing across the creek.

Teddy started to follow, but the old Injun gripped his arm and would not let him go. "Many will die," he said.

The old man answered: *"Chéyewakinicha,"*

"What's he saying?" Scott said feverishly.

"He says he can't hardly keep himself from weepin'," Teddy said. "But we can't none of us leave the circle. Or the werewolves will get us."

The wolves had reached the village. Teddy could hear the screaming. He forced himself not to look.

They huddled together, four of them now, while the old man went on dancing. And then Teddy saw another person come toward the stream from where the wolves had come. She stood behind the carcass of the palomino. Teddy's horse was done for too; it lay limp against the pine where he had tethered it. When the cavalryman saw the woman he seemed to plumb lose his mind.

"Natasha!" He could barely speak; the words tore from his throat like a dying man's. He started to stumble out of the circle.

"Don't leave the circle!" Zeke whispered harshly, and tried to grab ahold of Scott. "Teddy, hold on to him!"

Teddy gripped a fold of Scott's shirt, but it ripped away in his hand. It was soaked in blood. Scott staggered toward where the woman was standing. Teddy recognized her. "Don't you go to her," he said. "She's the queen wolf, the Count's bitch, and you're just a man—"

Natalia Petrovna smiled at him. Her face was half fur, but she still stood erect. Why hadn't she changed with the moonlight? "Don't you go to her!" Teddy shouted, but Scott had already reached the stream and was wading to her through the blood-blackened water.

"Do not stop him," said the old man. Behind, from the village, Teddy fancied he heard the scream of a child being ripped limb from limb. "He is already dead."

Scott said, "Ma'am, you can't be here alone amongst these wolves and Injuns. . . ."

Natalia Petrovna opened her arms wide to greet the cavalryman. Her gown, black and red, rustled in the wind. Like the grass, like the treetops. In the moonlight, her smile had a phosphorescent glow, and her teeth glinted like tiny daggers.

In another circle, south of the forest, on a promontory that overlooked a desolate plain, Speranza stood, her Bible under her arm. Around her the servants bustled, making ready for their master's return. Fauteuils and sofas were being loaded back onto the wagons. By torchlight, a butler played cards with two parlor maids.

From inside of the wagons, Vishnevsky watched her. She could not bear his gaze. She knew that his fortunes were linked with those of Natalia Petrovna. How tortured he must feel, to see his cousin's destiny fading thus! she thought. And yet he is human, like me, even if he bears the wolfsbane brand on his palm. He must long to be freed from his servitude.

A footman attracted her attention; he bore a tray with a glass of spiced wine and a little soup and bread. He bowed to her and said, "*Gnädiges Fräulein*, it will be quite safe to leave the protective circle. In perhaps three hours the moon will set; and it is most unlikely that any of the masters will return with their appetites unsated. And you, it is agreed by all, are protected not only by the circle, but by the Count's express commands."

Speranza stepped out of the circle. Quickly the footman put a chair for her in the shadow of a covered wagon. A fire crackled. She heard the butler and the parlor maids laughing. She sat down and took a few sips of the soup. It was a hearty brew of diced venison and chopped carrots, and the wine was French. She wanted to talk to someone, but the servants left her alone. They fear me, she realized. Because I may soon become their mistress . . . because I too may fall prey to the temptations of lycanthropy. . . .

It was then that she noticed a figure struggling up the hill, waving to her. It was not one of the servants; nor could it be one of the wolves, for they had all departed; even Natalia Petrovna, who had experienced some difficulty in transforming, had followed the pack on horseback.

As the man approached, she could tell who it was by his high hat, his overcolorful silk vest, and his swagger. His clothes were torn, and he was unshaven; but that could doubtless be attributed to the difficulties he must have undergone to arrive at this place. "Why," she said, "Mr. Claggart! Fancy your tracking us down."

"Made-*moyzel* Martinique!" said Claggart. "I never thought to find a lady of quality in this here den of iniquity. Won't you spare a square meal for a dyin' man, ma'am? And mayhap a beaker or two of rotgut?"

"How did you find us?" she said, clapping her hands and

summoning another stool, and bidding the footman pour another glass, for though the man was a charlatan and a trickster she could hardly refuse him hospitality. "I had thought that your segment of the train managed to continue on after the unfortunate . . . robbery."

"Why, sure enough, ma'am, we reached the next station safely enough. But there was a marshal lyin' in wait for me at Big Springs. Seems that the last time I departed that town, I left some folks with some unpleasant memories—mayhap it's best I don't dwell on those, ma'am. But as you might guess I was in a position of profound vulnerablance, and it was easier to rustle me a horse and flee the county. I thought I would get me to Deadwood—my wife ain't seen me for some months, but wives, bless 'em, can be a refuge in times of adversity. Then I picks up this wagon trail in the Sandhills and I get to wonderin' who would travel north by such an outmoded route when you have the Cheyenne-Deadwood stage route as well as the trains. And I fall to thinking, folks that craves to travel this way must surely have something to hide. Am I wrong, ma'am?" he said, and downed the entire glass of red wine.

"I cannot say," Speranza said.

Cordwainer Claggart leered. "There was a boy you was looking after—a right pretty boy, an aristocrat."

"Little Johnny is my charge," Speranza said, "but he is with his father at the moment."

"The day before the robbery," Claggart said, staring her strangely in the eyes, "I seen something very strange about him. I would be most curious of knowin' him better."

Speranza was disturbed by the cardsharp's arrival, and even more by the way he harped on the subject of young Johnny. She tried to change the subject. "If you have journeyed all this way to find someone on whom you can practice your card tricks, mister, you will find fools aplenty amongst the servants."

"Alas, Mademoyzel, I think that my days of cardsharpin' are over. By now they've done spread the word all over Nebraska Territory, and Dakota can't be far behind. A career ain't worth more than three or four year before you does something that merits a hangin'. I blame near got myself hanged in Cheyenne once over my Patent Floccinaucinihilipilificator, and that's why I switched

over to gamblin'—they told me to go get me an honest profession.
I reckon it's time for another change now."

Speranza could not help smiling. After the supernatural horrors
she had seen that evening, a display of honest, human roguery had
its charms. She said, "Perhaps the Count will employ you. He has
need, occasionally, of someone who knows the territory; and I am
sure that no one can know it better than one whose occupation
skirts the law." Perhaps the man can be an ally, she thought.
"Perhaps you will travel north with us? The servants can prepare
a pallet for you beside the fire . . . though for your own safety
I will suggest that they make your bed within that circle."

She pointed to where she had been standing earlier. Where the
Count had marked it, the grass had an eerie blue glow, as though
it had been painted with phosphor. Cordwainer Claggart looked at
it; then he shook his head. "I'm no man's servant, ma'am; I'd
rather be a criminal, and wanted in four territories, than take
orders from a furrin nobleman. I have plans, ma'am, extravaga-
tious plans. It was the young wolf-boy made me think of them.
But I'll thank you kindly for a loaf of bread and a bottle or two of
holy water, as the Injuns call it." He drained his glass a second
time. "I can get meat by myself," he added, flicking his wrist and
making a derringer appear by magic in the palm of his hand.

"As you wish," Speranza said, and ordered the servants to
bring him fresh supplies.

"And if you could see your way to selling me a fresh
horse . . . misfortunately, the horse I stole from Big Springs
was set upon by a pack of wolves not a hour ago—the fiercest,
vilest-lookin' critters you ever did see. They never touched me,
though."

Speranza noticed for the first time that Claggart wore a silver
watch chain that dangled from his waistcoat pocket—and silver
cuff links. And a heavy silver chain around his neck from which
depended some gaudy amulet or talisman, encrusted with turquoise. Did he but know how narrowly he had escaped with his
life! she thought. "The horse?" he asked her again.

"Alas, I do not give the orders here."

"I can't pay you now in money, but I can give your Count a gift
he sorely craves . . . my silence, Mademoyzel Martinique."

He looked her straight in the eye. She did not know how serious
his threats were, or how much credence the authorities would give

him; she was under the impression that the Count's gold had already purchased the silence of those who wielded power in the Dakota Territory. And yet . . . Hartmut would want to be absolutely certain.

Speranza nodded. She motioned to the footman. "Give him what he wants," she said, "and see that he is escorted far from here . . . all the way to Deadwood, if need be." The footman bowed and hastened to obey. They already see me as the Madonna of the Wolves! she thought. But what of Natasha? Perhaps we shall have to fight for the honor. To the death, like two ancient Roman gladiatrixes.

She watched him ride down the hill. If she had been discomfited by his presence, she felt little joy at his departure. Vishnevsky was still observing her from his wagon.

Why had Cordwainer Claggart been so interested in the boy? What had he discovered, and what was the great plan he had conceived, somehow inspired by her young charge? She could not guess. Resolutely she looked to the north, watching for the wolves' return, determined not to fall asleep, for if her waking life was terrifying, her dreams were even more so. . . .

Scott could not help himself. The Russian woman was calling to him. Perhaps she was hurt . . . perhaps the wolves had wounded her. He fought off Zeke and that young half-breed who reminded him oddly of someone else. He didn't stop to think about how unlikely it was that Natasha would happen to be standing at the outskirts of the very same Indian encampment to which Sanderson had sent him. When she looked at him, he couldn't think straight at all. He forgot about Major Sanderson and about whether or not he should be arresting Zeke. All he could think about was the woman with her golden eyes and her half-laugh in her lips.

"Why, it's Captain Harper!" she said softly. "You are far from Fort Cassandra." And she held out a gloved hand to him. "You must help me across river. I am such a weak woman."

"You shouldn't be here, ma'am." He stared at the patch of fur that seemed to disfigure her face.

Zeke and the boy shouted to him from the circle. The old medicine man—if that was what he was—was dancing up a storm, and the crazed wolves had reached the village and were tearing down tipis. But Scott only saw the woman.

He held out his hand to steady her. She said, "I must go where the wolves are, you see."

He did not question her. He was mesmerized by her. He lifted her in his arms and carried her across the stream. There was an animal reek about her that her perfume barely masked, and the smell was driving him crazy, stiffening his desire. She held on tight. Her fingers dug into his shoulders, sharp as claws. Zeke and the boy were gesturing frantically to him. Her tongue snaked along his moist lips. "I have always wanted you," she said. "I wanted you in graveyard. I wanted you at dance. But you eluded me, no?"

"I didn't know." He was confused by her nearness, by her unseemly passion.

"Kiss me."

He held her hard. But before his lips touched hers she gripped his hand so tightly that he cried out in pain, and then she slipped from his grasp so suddenly that he tripped on the wet earth and fell, and he tasted dew water mixed with mud and offal from the forest floor. . . .

When he looked up, she was changing. And speaking to him as she changed, her voice becoming more and more guttural, more and more like the growl of a dog. "You have drunk water from my pawprints, my little blond soldier!" And the streak of fur on her face was throbbing, pulsating, widening across her features.

"Water—" he gasped.

"Soon you will be as I am. If Count wishes to cast me aside for a spineless governess, then at least I shall have what I want. Oh, Captain Harper, you are beautiful, but soon you shall be more than beautiful . . . you will be animal, animal . . ." and as she said those words her mouth distorted into a slavering jaw and her eyes narrowed and glittered and she threw herself down beside him and her smell came even stronger now, charging him with insensate lust, and she fell upon him, drooling on his face, rending his uniform with her canine teeth, straddling him, almost suffocating him with the tatters of her shredded cloak . . . he could feel her paws thrusting between his fly buttons, could feel the fur and claws teasing at the shaft of his prick, and he thought, This ain't natural this ain't right I can't be having these feelings, and he tried to will away his erection but her odor came stronger now as she pinned him to the ground and stuck her bitch's cunt in his face and she was all wolf now, spiky-furred, muscular, her laughter a harsh, high canine yelping . . . he fought to free his face. He screamed, "Zeke, Zeke . . . help me . . ." and tried to ease his Colt out of his belt but it was stuck. . . .

"Too late!" the Natasha-wolf growled, her voice a parody of a woman's. "You—have—drunk—water—from—pawprints—"

He heard the woman shouting: "*Hiyá, Zeke, hiyá!*" and the boy's anguished shriek, "Zeke, stay inside the circle!" and the wheezing, falsetto singing of the old Indian.

The next thing he knew, Zeke had flung himself on the Natasha-wolf. As Scott rolled clear, his hand touched the edge of the protective circle. And encountered a dull, throbbing pain. As if it didn't want him to get inside. As if it were protecting the child and the woman from *him*. He sat upright and saw his friend and the she-wolf. The Indian woman uttered a shrill cry. Scott knew it was the cry of a woman bereaved of her husband. And then he saw what the wolf was doing to Zeke. He sat there dully, too shocked to act. His eyes were brimming with tears and cold sweat. The creature was tearing Zeke apart . . . there was blood everywhere, blood dyed metal-black by the moonlight . . . he heard the snap of a human spine, saw the she-wolf unreel the small intestine from the ripped abdomen . . . too late, Scott found his ivory Colt and fired every bullet in it at the she-wolf, but he knew it was too late, he knew his friend was gone . . . that his murderer was the creature he had lusted after.

"You have to come inside," said the boy. And tugged at his wrist. He felt the woman pulling at his other arm. The flaming circle seared him, but he gritted his teeth and stood the pain and knew that he wasn't yet one of the Natasha-creatures, no matter what she told him. He sat and stared at the wolf as it continued methodically to rip the body apart. She looked up at him with a severed hand in her jaw. And when their eyes met he could still feel the lust, and his penis stirred again, and he screamed, "No, no, no," and squeezed his eyes tight shut until the tears streamed down his face. . . .

"You fool!" the boy hissed. "Don't look back at her, don't even think of her."

"Zeke—he's my friend, you don't understand—"

"He's done for," said the boy.

"His woman—"

"She'll live. She's Injun through and through. She knows the meaning of life and death, mister. And I'll stay with her. I ain't running away no more. I'll never find my paw nohow. I'll stay here and hunt for her and make sure she don't get thrown out into the cold come winter, sure as my name's Theodore Grumiaux."

Amid the welter of conflicting emotions came a fresh realization—that this boy was the son of Claude-Achille Grumiaux the trainman. Softly he said, "I know where your daddy is, Teddy. I can carry you to him iffen it's what you crave."

The she-wolf was already changing again, even as she was rending the body of his friend. The snout was retracting, the luxuriant red hair sprouting from the mass of fur, the breasts bursting through the pelt. And she was speaking again, though the words were barely distinguishable: "Now I know what will counteract the silver's poison . . . a man's arousal . . . we need each other now . . . we are bound together . . . by your lust and by my affliction. . . ."

In the moonlight Natasha's face was pale, unearthly pale. Her hair fell down to her breasts. Coyly she shielded her private parts from his gaze with a bloodstained hand which, even as he felt the stirring of fresh passion, was tightening into a claw. He turned away. "Don't let me look," he whispered to the boy. "Cover my eyes."

He felt clammy fingers over his face. When they were removed, the apparition was gone. But the remains of Zeke still lay there, and the woman's shrieks of lamentation never ceased, nor the old man's frenzied dancing. Lord, he thought. There's his head, half buried in the brushwood.

"You're all a-tremble," said the boy. "And I can't make no sense out of my ma or the old Injun."

"He was my friend," Scott said. "I never thought he'd die. Not him. He knew the forest as well as any red man." And he remembered the corpse of Eddie Bryant, spread-eagled against the tree, and all the gold pouring from his pockets into the snow.

"You drank from her pawprint," Teddy said. "I reckon that means you're going to change, too. That's what the Russian woman meant." And he told Scott what he had heard from the werewolves, that the Count had cast her aside for a French governess who was always clad in black. "She wants a new mate," he said, "and I heared tell that when a body drinks dew water from the pawprint of a werewolf, he can't help but hear the call of the moon hisself."

"I ain't fixin' to be a werewolf," Scott said, "that I ain't."

There came screams from the encampment, and Scott could feel the heat of burning tipis and smell burning flesh. But he did not look. He did not want to see Natasha again. He could feel the moonbeams pricking at him, tugging beneath his skin like needle and thread. "Throw a blanket over me," he said, "and shut out the moonlight."

The boy took the blanket from his mother and threw it over Scott. The thick cloth muffled the sounds of death, but he could still feel the moonlight.

"I ain't never changing," he said. "In the morning I'll ride back to the fort. I'll never let the moonlight touch me."

But he knew what awaited him at Fort Cassandra. He knew he would fail to bring in Zeke for punishment. He knew that he would have to face the wrath of Major Sanderson. He couldn't go back. Sanderson had never forgiven him for the day he turned his back on the massacre and then went on to save his commander's life.

But when he thought of not going back, the future seemed even more dark, and he despaired. His daddy had been so proud of him when he had given him that ivory stock Colt and sent his son to join the very cavalry he had fought against in the last war. Scott didn't think there was anything to be proud of now. His friend had been killed by a hell-creature, and he could feel the contagion in himself too, even though he hid from the moonlight under a squaw's blanket.

"It won't happen overnight," Teddy Grumiaux said. "The change comes slow, they tells me. But one day you wake up and you think like them and you start lookin' forward to the next full moon. . . ."

Why was that blamed old medicine man still dancing away?

As though in answer, Zeke's woman said something in Lakota, and Teddy said: "That old man was on the train with us. He came to tell the people what he seen, same as me. But what he says he seen ain't nothing like what I think I seen. He thinks something good will come of this. Now ma says he's dancin' to summon up a spirit—"

"Like calling up the devil?" said Scott.

"No. He's calling up a spirit child which is going to bring the Shungmanitu together. I don't rightly know what she's talkin' about, mister." When Scott peered from the blanket, he saw the boy staring steadfastly at the stream, trying to shut out the sights, sounds, smells of the Sioux village. After the first outburst of lamentation, Zeke's woman showed no signs of grief at all. How could she just sit there while her man lay in pieces on the grass?

Perhaps she saw his unspoken rebuke. Little Elk Woman said, "We no more important. Only spirit child important now."

Spirit children . . . supernatural wolves . . . circles of pale blue fire . . . nothing made any sense at all. But Zeke's mutilated corpse lay just beyond the circle, and no amount of chanting or dancing or philosophizing could make it go away. He wanted to weep, to discharge his grief, but all he could feel was a dread that just kept on mounting up and wouldn't go away.

13
the same night

THE WOLFLING FOLLOWED HIS FATHER ACROSS THE STREAM. THERE were a few humans outside the village who had found protection inside an alien wolf's territory. He could smell the alien's urine—it was disquietingly sweet. It seemed familiar. Perhaps one of the other persons within him had encountered this wolf somewhere else. But none of those persons were there now—he had exiled them all, he occupied the body alone, exulting, triumphant. He cried out to his father in the speech of wolves: "Who is it who dares to cast a piss-spell against you, the most powerful of all the wolves?"

His father did not speak but scurried swiftly, churning up clods, snorting. His head and tail were erect. The king wolf's sinews rippled through the fur and his eyes burned, coal-red. He stopped to let the wolfling catch up as they reached the encampment. The others ran beside them. They had ceased their howling and they bounded in step, in silence, save for the crunch of hard paws on dry wood.

Somewhere beyond, the wolfling could hear the whinnying of panicked horses, for they had already smelled the wind of the hunters' coming. Fiercely the young wolf ran. The ground was firmer now, baked hard by the constant campfires.

An Indian woman peered from a tipi entrance. The wolves gathered. She shouted at them, made warding-off gestures with her hands, screamed for help. Behind the king wolf were the others of the pack—the Gipsy Azucena a magnificent black; the Indian astrologer wolf of silver fur and fierce countenance; Dr. Szymanowski mangy, losing his fur; Father Alexandros with his sleek sable pelt; the Baroness von Dittersdorf with a ring of white about her neck like the minks she so affected. They waited for a signal. The horses and the forest animals they had attacked on their way to the village were forgotten now. The young wolf knew that this prey was different. To kill a human meant to extinguish consciousness. The smell of terror laced the air, subtle as perfume, and as erotic. Why don't you charge her now? he thought. He stifled his impatience, knowing that he could not alter the measured rhythm of this violence. He waited. They all waited for their leader to spring.

The young wolf's father opened his mouth. His teeth glistened pearl-like in the moonlight. Yes! thought the young wolf. Here it comes . . . the stare of possession . . . as the woman's eyes widened and the scream caught in her throat, the Count leapt, jaws wide, embraced the woman in his paws, lacerated her cheeks, tore open her throat to expose the still trembling trachea. There was no scream, but a melancholy whistling as the crushed windpipe surrendered her last breath. She fell and the wolves fell to and feasted.

Yapping, the young wolf darted between the legs of the other wolves. And tasted sweet blood. Breathed it in, soaking his nostrils, matting the fur of his cheeks. Sweet, sweet and warm. Joyfully he barked as the blood that was the woman's life-fire gushed out, bathed, renewed.

Only for a moment did he feel the other voices in his mind,

clamoring to be let out. But he was stronger now. He was with his family, he was strong, and the woman who always sided with the others . . . she was far away. This was as it was meant to be.

And then his father put back his head and howled with blood-madness, and soon they were all howling, and they rammed into the side of the tipi, sending the lodgepoles crashing, setting the hides on fire, fire that ran along the dry grass of the camping ground and spread to other tipis.

A man in flames sprinted from one lodge, and the pack harried his heels as he ran crazed toward the creek. The wolves ran swifter than the stream. As the man fell and the water steamed up they crowded him, yelping, pulling at him, biting off chunks of cheek and hanks of hair, and he saw Father Alexandros gouge out an eyeball with his teeth and gulp it down, and the Baroness gleefully crunching the feathers that had once adorned the man's hair. . . .

Another howl from his father . . . and the wolves were hastening back toward the burning tipis . . . the wolfling was about to follow when he heard another sound, high-pitched, almost like the whisper of the creek . . . he stopped, pricked up his ears, listened for it . . . it stirred dim memories. He did not know he could remember that far back.

The sounds came from a ridiculous old man, stooped, playing a flute. He was standing next to that circle where the three puny humans were huddled. Though he was human in appearance he gave off an odor that the wolfling recognized at once. He was angry. This was the creature who had dared to piss-challenge the Count himself! A creature not even capable of transformation!

Let him stare! I will transfix, mesmerize, turn to stone, thought the wolfling. I will stare him into a puddle of blood and torn body parts. I will, I will. I shit on him, I piss into the wind of his flute playing, I piss piss piss.

He slid his paws from the moist soil, tensed, turned to spring. The old man watched him and did not cease playing. The young wolf hunched down, raised his haunches to fart out his disdain. Their eyes met. Let my gaze be cold! the young wolf thought. Let him see the final darkness in my eyes . . . let him see hell. The old man did not look away, but played another sequence of notes, lower in pitch, mellifluous. And the wolfling heard voices inside himself: "Free me, free me."

No! Not those voices! Anger exploded in him all at once, and he sprang up, sprang for the stooped throat, sprang to stop the source of the music, but—

He landed on rock-encrusted mush. And the old man's playing sounded from far off. The light had tricked him. I must close my eyes, he said, abjure the human senses, trust to the smell and the sound of him. He shut his eyes and stalked the scent and the song of the flute, stalked it along the bank of the stream.

He could feel fire now. He could hear his father cry out in the language of night. "Come away, my son . . . come to where the blood calls. Do not follow the stranger . . ."

But the song of the flute was stronger than the song of the blood. He almost choked on the smoke of burning leather and charring flesh. Hot ashes swirled about him. He still did not open his eyes. He could see well enough with his nose and ears, could see the baby on whom the Indian astrologer was feasting as it still mewled for its mother, could sense the arrows whistling in vain as Indians strove to stave off the invaders. He yelped as an arrow lodged in his side, but still he ran on. The wound closed up and spit out the arrowhead. He felt no pain from the arrow. The music was far more painful. He followed the music. The old man's bitter scent softened, became more sweet, reminded him of the time before he knew his true father . . . the time before Speranza . . . before the madhouse in London, before . . . before his soul had splintered into a dozen quarrelsome persons . . . had there not been a time when he had been whole? The music stirred this remembrance in him. And when his father cried out to him, "He is feeding you delusions, false hopes . . . you are the way you are, as I am, as we all are . . . rejoice in your damnation, exult, be glad, be what the darkness has made of you," he did not heed the words as they came, howling in the acrid wind, for the music was more sweet. It lured him on. His feet felt fleeter. He danced on the very moonbeams.

And the old man said, in the language of the wolves, "Listen. You are hearing an echo of the music of the moon dance. You can hear the music because you are one of us. You are Shungmanitu. Come to your people. The moon is the source of the river of light. We dance with the moon. We are one yet not one with the people of the plains and the forests and the hills. We are one yet not one with the four-legged and the winged and the finned and the scaled. Hear the music."

And his father howled, a howl of such desolate grandeur that the spell was almost broken. The wolfling opened his eyes. He was in the middle of the village. A group of children, not quite awake, were huddled around the corpse of their mother. An old man, his neck snapped, lay with his spine jutting from his torn back, two wolves circling him, growling, each unwilling to yield his title. In the center of it all was his father. There were dead bodies stacked in a heap on the ashes of a fire, and his father stood on top of the pile, howling, howling, clawing the air, howling his rage.

And all the wolves howled together, and the meaning of their howling was: "Death, death, death, death, death."

And then came his father's voice: "Do not listen. Darkness we are and unto darkness we shall return. Abandon hope, my son. Rejoice that we are the instruments of chaos. We are the beast in man. Rejoice that we have no hope."

And they howled again, and their howling meant: "Chaos, chaos, chaos, chaos, chaos." And they prostrated themselves before the king wolf, and he anointed them with his urine and marked them with his scent, and they howled his name again and again.

The young wolf watched. His father shook the last drops of piss from his leg and bent down to gnaw at the genitals of a dead Indian brave.

The fluting came again. His father stopped, cocked his head, bared his fangs, growled softly. The old man was dancing down the dirt path, playing his flute, fearlessly moving straight toward the pack. The young wolf's ears pricked up; he faced the old man; it seemed that he was floating toward him, floating in a sea of moonlight. . . .

All at once a wild and angry barking broke out. The other wolves surrounded them. The wolfling's father leapt down from the pile of dead bodies and flung himself at the old man, but an invisible force rebuffed him and he fell howling to the ground.

The young wolf screamed: "Father, Father—"

But his father seemed far away. He followed the old man now, past the gathering of wolves, past the burning tipis, to the edge of the stream, to the circle of blue fire—

And the other wolves ran after him and tried to enter the circle but fell back as though on fire, but he and the old man passed

unharmed over the barrier, and the voices inside him were all
clamoring for attention, battering down the barrier he had put up,
peering through his eyes, feeling the burning wind through his
pelt, and now he felt the presence of that pathetic Johnny-child,
inside his skin, struggling to burst forth—

The wolves would not get inside the circle. But their howling still
chilled him, and Teddy couldn't stand to look into their eyes. The
cavalry captain was all wrapped up in his blanket like a corpse,
and his ma was just holding on to him and rocking to and fro. She
was having one of her Injun visions, he reckoned. She was singing
to herself, and Teddy was scared it might be a death song. It
wasn't unknown for one of the Lakota to just up and sing hisself
into the grave.

Then Teddy saw the old man with the wolf cub at his heels. The
young wolf's pelt was pulsating; patches of human skin showed
through. The eyes were widening, the snout shriveling up and
spewing out pus and blood. He knew who the wolf pup must be.
"Johnny . . . are you in there, Johnny?" he said softly. The
moon hadn't set yet, but he knew that Johnny was no werewolf . . . only the other boy, the one who had emerged the day
they were playing on the roof of the train. He knew that Johnny
wouldn't harm him . . . if it was Johnny and not one of the other
people who lived inside the same body.

The boy's face was almost all Johnny now; only the ears were
still pointed and some of the hair was still bristling as it was
sucked back into the cheeks. Weeping, the boy called for
Speranza, Speranza.

The wolf that was the Count von Bächl-Wölfing continued to
run in circles around them. Now and then he tried again to burst
through, then snatched back his forepaw, screeching in agony. The
old man paid him no mind, but just went on dancing. He had
been dancing since the moon rose, Teddy reckoned, but he wasn't
even sweating. The music he played didn't make any sense.
Sometimes it was full of sobbing high notes; other times it was
way down low, the kind of sound a woman could make if you
touched her in just the right places.

The old wolf roared. The old man laid down the flute and spoke
a kind of gibberish, human words mixed up with the whimpering
and barking of a dog. Teddy couldn't tell what he said, but it made

the wolf angrier and angrier, and finally he turned around and his tail dropped and thudded on the ground and he slunk away.

And all the wolves ran with him, splashing over the stream, their paws pounding on the packed earth, a cloud of fur and dust streaking across darkness.

And Teddy said to the boy, who stood naked, covered, like a newborn, with splotches of gelatinous blood: "Speranza ain't here; she's back at the camp, waiting. I come to warn the villagers, reckon I came too late."

Johnny said, "She'll be waiting a long time. I have to go with *him* now." He pointed at the old Injun.

The old man said, "Ishnazuyai." It appeared to be his name.

The boy seemed untouched by all that had happened. It was as though he'd just been dreaming. The bloodstains on him were going away all by themselves, too, and his ears were folding up into human shape. The boy stood there and his downy body hair had a silvery sheen because of the moonlight.

Ishnazuyai put his flute down on the ground. As soon as it touched the soil the magic circle vanished. Softly, almost imperceptibly, it started to rain.

The old man squatted down and Johnny jumped onto his back. The rain slicked downy hair. The old man got up. Johnny smiled.

"Piggyback ride?" he said.

Without another word, the old man started walking with the boy clinging onto his shoulders. He was going north, toward the sacred hills. Johnny never looked back.

"How far are you goin'?" Teddy screamed after him.

Johnny never answered him. But Little Elk Woman said softly, "The land of the Shungmanitu are hidden high in the Black Hills, where no white man has dared go even in search of the yellow metal."

The raindrops were coming down thick and fast now. Teddy could see that some tipis were down and smoldering. "Be dawn soon," he said, and tried to nudge Scott out of his cocoon. But he was sound asleep. Teddy didn't want to wake him. He reckoned he had been through plenty, seeing his friend torn up by the she-wolf, and maybe about to change into a wolf himself come next full moon.

Finally his mother seemed to wake up from her trance. She

looked at her son. "I'm home, Mother," Teddy said. The language of his childhood came easily to his lips.

"I'll make food," Little Elk Woman said. "I think our tipi is still standing." From the village he could hear the wailing of bereaved women, but there were also the more normal sounds of daybreak: dogs barking, children laughing, women chattering.

He pulled the brim of his slouch hat over his ears to ward off the rain. "Yes," he said, "I think I am a little hungry."

"We killed a dog for the kettle yesterday; I think there may be a few scraps left. And we have to see to our guest, too; he should be put to sleep on a real buffalo robe, not this uncomfortable blanket." How brave she was, holding in her sorrow like that. A white woman—why, you'd have never heard an end to her caterwauling. He was right proud of her.

The anguished search for his father, the months of hardships on the railroad, the torments he had suffered at the hands of strangers . . . suddenly they seemed only to have been bad dreams. But when he saw, in the light of dawn, the destruction that the wolves had wrought upon the village, and the corpse of the man his mother had loved, he knew that he had only exchanged one nightmare for another.

14
the next morning

SHE HAD BEEN LYING IN THE COUNT'S PAVILION, UNABLE TO SLEEP; moonlight flooded the sleeping area, silvered the oily wood of the divan, forced her eyes open when she tried to close them.

The moon was setting, but it was not quite dawn when she heard the tumult of their return. The servants were bustling about outside the tent, and an odor of Viennese coffee was wafting into the pavilion. She sat up on the bed, expecting Johnny and the Count to come bursting in.

But there was only the Count. Even as he entered he was

sloughing off his lupine body. There was a liquid grace to his transformation; one could not tell when the wolf ceased to be and the man began. But he was standing there, naked, in a pool of twilight, and even as she started to murmur a greeting he was striding toward her. He was enraged about something. Where was the boy? His eyes still glowed. He seized her by the shoulders and threw her onto the rug. She put out her arms to steady herself, and he was already ripping her nightgown with fingers whose sharp nails were still retracting, and he began thrusting at her, inconsiderate of her unreadiness, thrusting and thrusting as she bit her lip so as not to scream. He bared his teeth. There were still fangs, though they were slithering back into the gums. She turned her head this way and that. The costly Persian carpet was woven in a dizzying moiré. The patterns swirled. She cried out in confusion.

Why was there this savagery? Was he still in the throes of some bestial passion? She gasped, screamed . . . and then, abruptly, he was done. And he rose up, spun around, seized a cloak from the hat rack and threw it over himself. She tried to sit up but could not; pain stabbed at her lacerated thighs. "The boy—" she whispered. "What have you done with him?"

"He's been taken from us!" the Count cried. Never had he seemed to her to have so lost his composure. "My child, my son—and I could not fight the power that robbed me of him!" He sank down on the divan, and it seemed to her that he wept, though she could not be sure of it in the half-dark. "My son."

She raised herself up, and for modesty's sake tried to pull the tatters of her nightgown about her. She said, "I thought there was nothing that could stand in your way."

The Count said, "We are not the first lycanthropes to settle this land. Natasha hinted at it, but I thought she must be mistaken. The dream that Szymanowski presented to us was so perfect that I could not admit of the possibility of a flaw."

And there it was. At last, Speranza thought, after all these months, he seems vulnerable. "They stole Johnny from us?"

"More than stole. They prevented me from taking him back with a powerful dark magic. My child, my child . . . in the hands of savages! They mesmerized him with music."

"With music. . . ."

Speranza put on one of the Count's silk dressing gowns—heavy with his animal scent—and went outside. She could see the others coming up the hill. Servants were rushing down with coats and robes. The werewolves were shedding the last vestiges of their animal selves. The sun had almost risen. There was blood in the air. The werewolves ran uphill as their servants covered them with cloaks, for their old clothes had long since been shredded by their transformations. Lagging behind, riding a roan, was Natasha. Even now the Count's butler was throwing a blanket up to her, and she was pulling it over her shoulders, looking sadly back at forests to the far north.

The Indians had wanted to bury Zeke like one of their kind, exposed to the elements on a platform. At first Scott Harper was appalled at the paganness of it; but Teddy Grumiaux took him aside and, as they sat in the shadow of Little Elk Woman's tipi, still intact after the previous night's raid, told him about growing up in two cultures. "I know he was your friend," he said, "but I reckon they is doing him a mighty honor by letting him be buried amongst their own braves."

"They ain't Christians," Scott said, but even as he said so he knew he was starting to sound like Major Sanderson.

"But if you says a private prayer over him . . ."

Scott agreed. They stood up and started walking toward the burial place. It was still drizzling. The rain was fragrant with the spores of spring. They could hear drumbeats in the distance, and the wheezing voices of chanting mourners. As they walked away, they saw that Little Elk Woman was stripping the buffalo hides from the tipi. A crowd of women stood around, watching her but not speaking.

"What's she doing?" Scott asked the boy.

"I think it's . . . it's a *wikhpéyapi*," said Teddy. Beyond the village clearing, they were performing whatever funeral rites for the dead were customary among the savages, but what was happening here had an even more tragic air about it. Little Elk Woman emerged from the tipi bearing a small wooden chest, and she began distributing its contents among the other women.

Each woman muttered something but would not look Little Elk Woman in the eye as the widow handed out good trader knives, hairbrushes, an old mirror with an ivory handle that might have come all the way from France. When the chest was empty, she handed it to a little girl who carried it off. It was almost bigger than she was. Then Little Elk Woman went back inside and came back out with an armload of blankets, all neatly folded, and she began to give them away.

"What's she doing that for?" Scott asked the boy. "She'll need those blankets come winter."

"She ain't expectin' winter no more."

"What's that supposed to mean?"

Teddy wouldn't answer him. Little Elk Woman was giving away clothes now—there was a calico dress that must have been a gift from Claude-Achille, and beautiful shirts, painstakingly embroidered with beads and sewn with scalps. Scott was getting an inkling of what the woman purposed.

At last Teddy's mother seemed to notice Scott and the boy. She walked up to them. She stood very proudly, not weeping, like the wife of the grandest general in the cavalry, and she said something to her son. Teddy turned to Scott and said, "She's asking you to take me to see my paw."

"What about her? Your paw is living with a Chinawoman in Deadwood now."

"She don't intend to stand in anybody's way," Teddy said, almost choking.

And Little Elk Woman observed Scott without apparent emotion, waiting for his answer.

"You shouldn't let her," Scott said, realizing what Teddy meant at last. Among these Indians, he had heard tell, a woman with no man would just up and leave so that she would no longer be a burden to her people. "She's a woman—she can't just up and leave the village—she'll—"

"Die."

"You're just going to let her?"

"Ain't nothing I can do," Teddy said, and if his heart was breaking he hid it well. "Your friend Zeke would have understood. Death don't mean the same thing to them as it does to your kind, Captain Harper. My ma has no man to hunt for her now. She knows she'd only be a hindrance to her people, and they lost so many last night, they can't feed a useless woman no more."

Scott wanted to reach out to Little Elk Woman, to clasp her by the hands and console her, but when he tried to do so he saw for the first time that she had lost three fingers of her left hand. The wounds were still fresh, the bone showed through. It had been cleanly done, as if by a surgeon. Horrified, he backed off.

"She done it herself," Teddy said softly, "and she didn't make a sound." And now she was going to walk away from the village and go into the forest, she might survive the summer, but winter would surely kill her.

Scott thought of all he had been taught about the sanctity of human life, of womanhood. His faith in those values had already been sorely taxed when Sanderson had ordered him to take part in the massacre of these people. He knew that suicide was a sin, and yet when he saw how this woman was willing to part with all her possessions and lay down her life for her people, he could see that there was something ennobling in it too. And that was another nail in the coffin of his beliefs.

And then there was Natasha's assertion that he was going to become a werewolf, a creature of Satan, irrevocably damned—yet he did not feel damned. "I ain't no hellspawn," he murmured to himself, "and iffen they tell me that my soul be already doomed to perdition, I know in my heart that it ain't the truth." To the boy he said, "Come, let's go up to see Zeke's restin' place."

The werewolves sat in council. Breakfast was served, although none appeared hungry. Now and then there was a light drizzle, and the servants hastened to stand behind their masters' chairs with umbrellas held high. The breakfast was an Italian collazione of prosciutto, cheeses, and breads, which were fast becoming soggy. But no one was eating. There was a heady exhilaration in their faces, tempered by worry over the disappearance of young Johnny.

Speranza sat on a footstool beside the Count's fauteuil; for she feared Natasha's wrath, and felt that the proximity of von Bächl-Wölfing might provide some small protection. They were all there, even the frail Dr. Szymanowski, who reclined on a divan and supped at a posset of red wine and herbs. All talk was of the child, the child.

"I warned you," Natalia Petrovna said, "in my letter." Her cousin Vishnevsky added, with some bitterness, "We have done you much service, Count. Perhaps you might have trusted us a little better. . . ." And he looked straight at Speranza, and she knew that he hated her, because she had usurped Natalia's place, and Natalia's welfare was the only thing he had left to live for.

"While they're holding my son," said the Count, "we'll have to be more cautious. Perhaps they plan to use him as a hostage . . . perhaps they won't yield him up until we turn tail and point our noses back to the old country."

"They are simple savages!" said the Baroness von Dittersdorf. "They will not be able to stand up to us, we should weed them out like vermin."

"They are not only savages," said the Count. "They are not just fodder for our appetites. Didn't you see the old man's territorial circle? I, the leader, even *I* could not trespass onto the ground where he held my child captive. And they have been observing us, waiting for us. I am sure now that I remember seeing that old man on the train, though I did not smell his spoor; somehow he managed to mask his scent, though I believe that he communicated with my son."

Then Dr. Szymanowski spoke. "Perhaps," he said, "they will merit some study, some experimentation; we should not too hasty be in their extermination."

And Chandraputra, who was the only one eating, said, "I fail to see why we are so concerned, he was only half one of us anyway, isn't it? I have never been approving of crossbreeding."

Speranza thought: I am alone now. I only came from Europe because of Johnny's need. There is no one here to whom I can confide. The servants are loyal to the wolves; even that little half-Indian boy has gone.

Never had she felt so isolated. She knew now that she did feel for the Count a kind of love. She looked around her at the members of the Lykanthropenverein, and she knew that they were a family of sorts, and that she was an outsider, an observer; she saw that they shared a secret language of looks and gestures at whose meanings she was only beginning to guess. She did not belong here. She thought of trying to escape, to go back to Europe. But she had no money; and what was there in Aix-en-Provence?

It was with no small horror that she realized that there were some aspects of her new life that she actually relished. The train robbery and its sudden reversal had excited her a little. That the man who nightly made love to her was part beast was repugnant to her, but there was also something ineluctably arousing about him. No, she could not go back. What if Johnny were found, and she had abandoned the Lykanthropenverein, and he was left alone, unfriended, to descend all the way into madness? No. All that she cared about was here: all that she loved, all that she loathed.

It was a mention of Johnny that awoke her from her reverie. Von Bächl-Wölfing was saying, "It is clear that this colony of savages must know where the boy has been taken. They were not lycanthropes themselves, or they would have transformed; the old man was alone, a rogue perhaps, and too advanced in years to change into a wolf himself. But there must be a settlement of wolves somewhere in the territory; we must send out scouts. Obviously there is only enough prey for one tribe of lycanthropes. They will have marked the land. We must not rest until we've recovered him."

"Though it would be interesting," Szymanowski said drily, "if they decided to try to rear him as one of themselves . . . for we cannot yet know whether these are creatures exactly like ourselves, or subject to other laws we do not know about . . . whether they are affected by silver, for example. It would be of some scientific interest to have the child brought up by these imperfect savage versions of ourselves—"

"Not my child!" said the Count.

And Speranza thought: He is not all evil. He loves his son. As a man must love his child.

She clung to this shred of humanness in him; she knew she must cherish it.

For she needed to give the gift of love. If she stayed with him, if she continually reminded him of human emotions, he would not turn completely to darkness.

Scott Harper watched the medicine man muttering incantations and shaking a bundle of sacred objects over Zeke's mangled body. Then two braves hoisted it up onto a platform. A buffalo skull, painted in three colors, was placed at his feet. They had found all the parts of him they could and put him back together like a jigsaw puzzle.

Teddy said, "Them wolves ought to be kilt for what they done." He had relieved one of the women of the bottle of whiskey his mother had given away. He had drunk more than his fair share. But Scott didn't feel like telling the boy not to.

Scott didn't know his Bible too well, so he just murmured the Lord's Prayer and then all he could remember of the Twenty-third Psalm. Teddy didn't know all the words, so instead he spoke in Lakota. He told Scott he was praying to Wakantanka. "I reckon God don't care what name you calls him by," he said.

The Indians' ritual was solemn and dignified; nothing could be further from the bacchanalian screechings and cavortings that were, according to such as Major Sanderson, the only religion of which the Sioux were capable. The elder sang in his wobbly voice, punctuated by the measured beat of the drum; there was, Scott thought, almost a touch of popishness in their ceremony.

But through the whole thing Teddy was cursing under his breath: "Them wolves—blame fucksters—ought to be kilt, ought to be burnt up alive, shot full of lead, sliced up with knives— blame fucksters."

He couldn't watch anymore, so he and Teddy started walking back downhill, toward the encampment. When they got there, Little Elk Woman's tipi had already been stripped, and she was nowhere to be seen. The rain streamed down the bare lodgepoles. The women—more like vultures, Scott thought—had already gone off with their new possessions.

"Dadblamed fucksters," Teddy said.

"You shouldn't say that," said Scott. "You think I'm going to become one of those creatures. Lessen you want to kill me, too."

The thought seemed to sober Teddy up a bit. He backed away from Scott, and the fear in his eyes was real enough. So Scott said, "I'll prove to you whose side I'm on. We'll get revenge. You and me and the people of this village—if they want it—we'll track down those sons of bitches and kill ourselves a few."

"Got any silver?" said the boy. "I got two dollars we can melt down for bullets."

The caravan wound its way northward. Their destination was only days away, and the atmosphere of expectancy, of excitement, was becoming more and more heightened. The wolves had fed off the land, as Szymanowski had planned; soon they would be reaching the homeland they had all dreamed of for so long. But Speranza was alone.

She sat in the covered wagon, not looking outside, for all that the countryside would have ravished a Wordsworth or moved a Keats to tears. At long last, she thought of something she had been endeavoring to forget: a small package that had been waiting for her in Chicago and which she had carelessly placed in a chest with some useless bric-à-brac she had brought over from Europe. It was a letter from Freud; she had not wanted to read it for fear she might remember too much of the horrors of the Viennese winter.

She realized that she had in fact been hoarding the letter for just such a moment of desolation.

The caravan smelled of musk and animal urine, and of an expensive red wine that had been carelessly spilled during the morning's festivities. She turned up the flame of the kerosene lamp with care, for the road was bumpy and she did not want the caravan to catch fire. Then she broke the seal—it bore a legend in Latin over the arms of the University of Vienna—and read the accompanying letter.

> *Chère Mademoiselle Martinique,*
> It is with no small concern that I turned my attention to your most recent epistle. I know that the members of the Count's fraternity are eccentric, but I hardly expected them to infect you with their peculiar brand of *dementia*, for you seem to be an eminently sensible woman, and well able to distinguish reality from illusion; it is precisely for that reason that I felt it best for young Johnny to have someone like you there to succor him.
> Mademoiselle, I am enclosing herewith a small supply of the coca powder which you so enjoyed when you were staying in Vienna; perhaps it will induce within your spirit a state of transcendental peace that will still the madness that threatens you on every side.
> *Mit vorzüglicher Hochachtung,*
> Your most ardently admiring
> Sigmund Freud.

There was a small sachet of cocaine in the packet, carefully wrapped in a pouch of Prussian-blue velvet. She put a little of it in the palm of her hand, and wondered for a moment whether she should indulge herself. It had been one way she had found the

Viennese winter tolerable, and yet she feared becoming addicted to the powder, much as others favored tobacco or hemp.

After all, she thought, where would I be able to obtain this substance in the wilderness, if I were to grow dependent on it? And yet—it is from the Americas that coca comes, and here I am nearer to the source, not farther from it.

The wagon lurched as they encountered some obstacle, and the white powder slipped from her palm onto the rough wood. I cannot let it go to waste! she thought, thinking suddenly of her thrift-loving family in Aix-en-Provence, and quickly got on her hands and knees to recover it. And before she knew it, she had already inhaled a little pinch of it; it was already working its magic on her, a magic far more puissant and seductive than snuff or laudanum.

15
Deadwood
two nights after full moon

CORDWAINER CLAGGART WAITED TILL LONG AFTER NIGHTFALL BE-fore he slipped into town. He doubted whether any would care that he was a wanted man in Big Springs, but you never could tell.

The Count's servants had brought him all the way to the outskirts of town. They took his horse to ensure he would not follow them back. He did not mind. It was time he made his peace with his woman, one way or another, for he had need of her money now.

Stealthily he made his way to the house. When he reached the front porch, he couldn't help thinking what a stroke of luck it had been, that he'd been able to inveigle himself into the control of the Widow Bryant's wealth. Though no priest had consecrated their marriage, Claggart didn't hold with any such ceremonies anyway; for a preacher was no better than a snake-oil merchant—and, having been both, he knew there was no difference betwixt them.

What a door, he thought: polished mahogany, with a stained-glass window in it and all. He could see the design on it because there was a kerosene lamp on inside the hall.

He let himself in, hung his slouch hat on the rack, and, because he wanted to give Sally Bryant a surprise, even took off his boots and put them by the door. At which so foul an aroma arose from his feet that he almost forgot what he had come back to Deadwood for.

Sally had become an encumbrance once he had managed to acquire her wealth, and she might well object to his latest plans. He would, he realized, have to kill her—or at least to engineer some kind of accident.

He heard a faint sound coming from upstairs. A rhythmic creak-creak-creak, as though the bed were—

The bed! Was the old hussy so desirous of carnal satisfaction that she was occupying herself with a tallow candle? A rope end? Or perhaps even a broken-off chair leg? he thought, almost laughing out loud at the ludicrous image.

Perhaps I should give her a few whacks of the old cock-a-doodle-doo, he thought, before I do away with her. For old times' sake.

He took the lamp in his hand and tiptoed up the stairs.

As he turned the knob on the door to his bedroom, he felt the barrel of a shotgun poking him in the ribs. "Take it easy, darlin'!" he said. "It ain't but tired old Cordwainer, come home at last to kiss his woman and say he's sorry he didn't come home sooner."

"So the perfidious Claggart has decided to come home!" came a voice out of the darkness. It was decidedly male.

He held up the lamp and he was staring right into the face of Major Sanderson—who was sitting, bear-naked but for his boots, on the edge of the bed. Even in the half-dark there was no mistaking that mass of purple scar tissue where the major's scalp used to be. Sally sat up on the bed and covered her unappetizing flesh with a sheet. She looked at Claggart with utter scorn, but Claggart was inwardly amused.

"Kindly git off my wife, sir!" said Claggart, and reached for the topmost dresser drawer, where he had always kept a loaded Smith and Wesson.

He found it easily enough by feel and pointed it at the major.

Another stroke of luck! he thought to himself. Now I can be rid of her—just as I was planning—and have the law on my side. "As you know, Major," he continued, "having discovered you and my wife in the flagrant dereliction, as the lawyers would put it, I am perfectly within my rights to blow the two of you to kingdom come; ain't that so?"

"Good God, man!" said the major. "You won't even do me the gentlemanly courtesy of challenging me to a duel?" He was reaching for his uniform, which hung on a wicker-backed chair next to the bed, trying, Claggart observed, to negotiate for his life with a modicum of dignity.

"Why should I? You know as well as I do I'd lose. I ain't getting myself dry-gulched over a woman, especially when I has catched another man in the act of fingering her factotum. Nope, I think I'm just going to kill the both of you good and dead, right here, right now."

A curious feeling of excitement took hold of him. He fired and hit his wife right in the chest. It was a good clean hit. She shuddered, thudded on the headboard and slumped over, and there was a good deal of blood. He looked at her for a moment before suddenly realizing that, with the moment of her death, he had abruptly experienced an untold rapture that was even now oozing down his thighs and onto his trousers.

Why, he thought, if it ain't better than a day in church for relievin' all them pent-up cares.

He wondered whether such a thrill could ever be replicated . . .

Major Sanderson stood up, shielding his privates with a ragged undershirt. "Now I know that you're no gentleman, Mr. Claggart, and that I was quite right to come at the request of this deprived woman, to lend her what small comfort I could in the perpetual absence of her gambling, good-for-nothing husband. And now, murdering her in cold blood . . . disgraceful! Even though you are, of course, quite correct in claiming the legal right to kill a spouse caught *in flagrante delicto*."

"It's right generous of you to say so, Major Sanderson, ain't that the truth," said Cordwainer Claggart. He continued pointing the gun at the major as, trembling, the latter donned his uniform. "And I am obliged to be generous in return. I feels no partickler rancor at you, Major, and my thirst for vengeance has been aptly slaked by the killin' of that there whore. I can surely 'preciate how you might be driven into the embraces of such a strumpet as the late Mrs. Claggart, after a hard day's work killin' innocent unarmed Injun women and children."

"You're quite right, Mr. Claggart," said the major, and Claggart saw that he was feeling a mite relieved that he wasn't imminently about to bite the dust. "Savages every one of them." He rubbed that skinless pate of his. "I regret having caused you the inconvenience of having to do away with your wife, but I would be happy to pay the undertaker's costs as a small compensation for putting you through this bother. I am glad to find you so reasonable and such a gentleman besides, Mr. Claggart."

"If you would be so kind as to come down to the sheriff's office with me, mayhap we can discharge all this unpleasantness in a civilized manner."

"Of course. We should straighten out the paperwork right away," said the major, sighing.

"You are one hell of a slimy varmint, Major Sanderson," Claggart said, without putting away his weapon, "and you may take that as a compliment, for it takes one to know one."

He cast no more than a momentary glance at his dead wife. He had never shot a woman before, he realized, let alone killed one; the thrill of it was not something he would ever have imagined possible. And he was infinitely grateful to the major, for his adulterous act, of course, made the killing eminently reasonable; not that he felt any guilt, for he had been meaning to dispose of her anyway, but this way he need not even feel guilty about his lack of guilt; he had merely done what any righteous man would have done, and the murder had the backing of both law and scripture.

"But I'm neglectin' my duties as a host, Major," he said. "Come on downstairs, and let me pour you a glass of bug juice."

As they toasted each other in the living room, Claggart impressed upon the major the need to contain the scandal, and elicited from him a promise of help, for he would need to sell all his newly inherited belongings in order to set himself up in his new career.

"Shall we go to the sheriff's office now?" said the major. "I must be going soon; I received a dispatch from back East whose contents will be of interest to the trainman, Grumiaux; and then I have business in Winter Eyes."

"Winter Eyes? Where's that?"

The major looked away. "South," he said, and changed the subject. But Claggart seemed to recall the name of the town; was it not something to do with that foreign Count? He could not quite place the name, but thinking of the Count reminded him once more of that wolf-boy.

As for the wolf-boy. . . .

He did not really need the wolf-boy, he realized, to set his plans in motion. But it was the sight of the child that had first inspired him to imagine this grand design, and he did not think it would be complete without the child.

He was uncertain at this stage how he would go about obtaining the child. But there was a price for everything. When the time came, when all was ready, the major would help, he was sure.

I is damned obsessed, Claggart realized with a start, as he prepared to cheat the major at a few hands of blackjack.

It was a ways past midnight when Teddy Grumiaux and Captain Harper sneaked into Deadwood. They tiptoed behind saloons and whorehouses. The town stank of stale liquor and old tobacco and horseshit. It smelled a lot worse than Omaha. Teddy kept close to the captain, who was wrapped in a buffalo robe but would hardly pass for a blanket Injun; he walked too much like a white man. Teddy kept to the shadows and tried to keep Scott from tramping too hard on the boardwalk.

After a bit he could smell opium. The streets were narrower, murkier. "Where there's opium there's Chinamen," Teddy said. "I thought you said we was going to find my paw."

Scott didn't say a word. He hadn't said much at all since they'd left the Sioux country. He was grieving for his dead friend, but he wasn't showing much emotion. Teddy reckoned he had to keep his wits together. If the army got him, being a deserter now, he'd be about ripe for a necktie party. And Teddy didn't want him to get hanged.

This captain is a good man, he reckoned. Treats me like a human being. Not like a witless breed that's only good for kicking around.

Footsteps. Jaunty, confident. A familiar snigger. It couldn't be! "Duck!" he whispered. "Just do it!" They slipped into an alley.

"What the—" said Scott. Then, as a second voice joined the first, he suddenly froze. Teddy peered from the shadows.

Two men were crossing the street. One was a man in military uniform. Where his hair should have been there was a mass of purple scar tissue. He'd been scalped and lived. The man he was with was Cordwainer Claggart. Teddy stiffened. He thought he'd seen the last of the cardsharp.

"Shit," he whispered, "that varmint must have nine lives. Last time I seen him, he was bleedin' to death on the *Pacific Express*."

"The other man's Major Sanderson," said Scott.

The two men were right by them now, walking in the direction of Main Street. "You certainly vanquished me at blackjack, Claggart!" the major was saying. "Five hundred dollars! If I hadn't dealt those seven consecutive blackjacks with my own hands, I would have fancied you a common cheat."

"A fine thing to say, Major, to a man which has lost all his goods to a passel of train-robbing desperadoes, and which comes home to find he has lost his wife to a philanthropizin' lecher."

They walked out of earshot, and Scott finally said: "I can't understand it—what they were doing there."

"In Chinatown? They was probably just buyin' theirselfs some opium."

"No, Teddy, not just that . . . it looked to me like they were just quittin' your paw's place."

Later, at long last, Theodore Grumiaux came face-to-face with his father. It was a difficult moment for him. The Chinee woman he was hitched to didn't make things any easier. There were some points of similarity with his mother—his paw liked them small-boned, that was for sure—and she moved the same way, kind of like a rabbit almost. And the room smelled strange: not just because of the opium wafting down the corridor. The food they were cooking smelled odd and so did the woman who was cooking it. She gave him a bowl of the stuff, though, and although she called it something else, damned if it didn't taste exactly like son of a bitch stew—veal kidneys and sweetbreads mushed together and sweetened with brains—as normal a white folks' supper as you could ever find.

His paw didn't say a word to Teddy, not a word. And Teddy didn't say a thing back either. Things were sure different here. Leastways there was a stool to sit on and four solid walls around you, not like in the tipi. But the air was dank and close, and the wind didn't blow all around you, and you couldn't smell the fresh scent of grama grass—just that opium, almost choking you, the way it just seeped inside your pores.

Teddy contented himself with sitting in a corner and listening to the men talking. They spoke about a lot of things he didn't understand, but one thing was clear—his paw knew everything about the foreign Count—had actually worked for him, in a manner of speaking.

"That explains the information that Major Sanderson just came to give me," he was telling Scott. "Apparently there has been a dramatic movement in the stock of the Fremont, Elkhorn and Missouri Valley Railroad. This Count of yours has been playing some strange games with the shareholders, and . . . well, it looks like all construction will be coming to a standstill for a while. Perhaps until 1886. The Count did everything he could to acquire the railroad and then—when he seemed to have gained control of it—he appears to have engineered its collapse, at least temporarily. You might say that I am out of a job."

Scott said, "Shit, he never wanted that railway built. He was fixin' to stop it in its tracks the whole blamed while."

"*Vraiment,*" said Grumiaux. "I think that you are right."

Then Scott told Grumiaux how Zeke had been killed. Teddy's paw was shaken; you could see that they had been friends. Grumiaux didn't scoff at the description of the werewolves; he was familiar with what they were, and did not disbelieve in them.

But Teddy couldn't help being hurt some, because his paw didn't seem to show much emotion when he saw his son, but when he heard about Zeke, he was almost crying.

I wonder if my paw ever thought I was dead, he thought. I wonder if he cried any tears for me. I don't hardly know this man which I been looking for all these years past.

He stared at his father, trying to figure him out.

"We have to get ourselves going now," Scott said, "before they catch us. I calculate I'll be a wanted man soon."

"Where will you go?" said Grumiaux.

"Into the hills. Mayhap I can help the Sioux fight this new enemy. Get even with them. For Zeke's sake."

"For Zeke." After a moment Grumiaux said, "Since I will no longer be working for the railroad company, perhaps a little hunting would do me good, no? In Canada I once dabbled in wolfing for the bounty on pelts. But with these *loups garoux* it will not be possible to collect money—their bodies revert to human shape when they are killed, so I am told."

Teddy didn't exactly understand why he felt so strange inside. Perhaps it was because his mother had gone walking off into the forest . . . perhaps it was envy, because his paw seemed to burn with revenge for the death of a man Teddy hadn't known for but a few minutes. And hadn't so much as spoken a word to his own son except for a grunt or two.

Then his father said, as though walking from a dream, "But Harper, I cannot go with you—it is only a fantasy. You see, it is that I have the boy now. He has been through so much to find me, and I must at least try to find a less adventuresome life for him for a time."

Teddy looked his paw straight in the eye for the first time and he knew that deep down he loved him; so he said, "Hardship ain't no bother to me, Paw." Then he added, fervently, "I want to get even with them sons of bitches, Paw."

"*C'est mon fils*—my son!" said Grumiaux, beaming with recognition and sudden delight, and kissed the lad on the cheek.

"I guess we're at war," Scott said.

16
The Black Hills
three-quarters moon, waning

THE OLD MAN ISHNAZUYAI CONTINUED TO STRIDE TIRELESSLY NORTH-ward with the young boy on his back. Every few hours he would kneel down by a stream and lap up some water, and the boy would do so too; now and then he would mark the way he had come with a dab of concentrated urine. They did not speak to one another for many days. And then, slowly, they began to say a few things to each other.

"Water," said the boy, his head swaying from side to side.

Leaves rustled. Both of them tensed as they smelled a prowling bear no more than a furlong away. The boy smiled when a male lazuli bunting fluttered by, a flash of feathery blue amid the forest's earth colors.

The boy knew no human speech—oh, he could speak many tongues of the white men, but he could not yet form the shapes of Lakota words—and their only communication was through the language of the four-legged, which the boy knew but imperfectly: he lisped, he floundered for the right groans and howls, he stuttered. The Shungmanitu from across the Great Water had lived far from the center of the world, Ishnazuyai reasoned; only from a tremendous distance had the Great Spirit touched them.

The boy said, "Why have you taken me from my people?"

And Ishnazuyai replied, "When I was a young boy—before my first changing—I had a vision once, and in this vision I saw wolves coming to our land across a river of iron. Wherever they went the land was laid waste; and the mark of Wakantanka was undone, for though the Great Mystery fashioned these wolves at the beginning of time, they had lost their way and no longer knew where the center of the universe was. And they rooted up the forests and they flattened the mountains, and they scattered the two-legged and the winged and the four-legged creatures across the face of the plains, and replaced them with creatures that had no life, only the appearance of it."

As he spoke he went on walking, he sang rather than spoke the things he had seen in his vision, and kept time with the rhythm of his own footfalls; and he could feel the child entranced by the vision, seeing it with his own eyes; for the child had the gift of seeing with the eyes of many persons.

He went on: "All possibilities led to the annihilation of the Shungmanitu, all except one. For in my dream I also saw that there would come one who was one of them yet one of us; one whose heart was fractured into many souls; one who was wholly human yet wholly Shungmanitu. Time passed. My mother grew old and left our village to dance her final moon dance. And so I came to ride the railways, back and forth, back and forth, waiting for the one who might yet save us from the end. And when I met you I knew who you were, and when I sang the song of recognition I knew you had understood it. And then when I saw you being led by the other wolves, and how you balked at their wanton killing, I saw that you have compassion, little wolf, and I could not bear to see you among them. I meant only to speak to you, not to take you from them, but when I saw you in the village I felt a great love for you, and I knew that to leave you among those others, so far from the center of things, would be like leaving you to die."

The hill was getting steeper now. They trudged beside a stream. He could smell the fish leaping through the water. Here and there, through the canopy of pines, there shone a patch of brilliant sky. Even the birds seemed silent; they know, Ishnazuyai thought, they are witnessing the passage of an important person.

"How much longer?" the boy said in his lilting half-speech.

"A few more days yet." Even now the snow had not left the peaks. The boy played with the feathers in the old warrior's hair, and wonderingly stroked his smooth cheeks; doubtless he was used to the pocked and hairy complexion of the *washichun* wolves.

"Will you let me down so I can walk beside you?"

But Ishnazuyai was reluctant to do so. Not that he feared that the boy would run away. But the child was so precious, so vital to the survival of all wolves, that he was afraid to let go of him. Yet when he did, he hardly noticed the burden gone from his shoulders; he was a slight boy, almost weightless. What he did notice was the breeze, the sudden chill; for the boy generated a powerful heat, like the heat of transformation, even though he was not changing shape. He was more than a Wichasha Shungmanitu; even in human form he was constantly transforming from one aspect of his fractured self to another.

Before he can save us, he himself must be healed, Ishnazuyai thought.

Jonas Kay had been in hiding since the old Indian had somehow hypnotized that impressionable little weasel into leaving his father behind. He had stormed about in the forest, but whenever he tried to burst into the clearing of the body's consciousness he had encountered stronger resistance than usual. That bastard had managed to forge some kind of alliance against him! And what he had begun to suspect during the train journey was true—Johnny *did* understand the speech of the wolves—there was a part of

Johnny as animal as Jonas. And this infuriated Jonas, for Jonas wanted the beast all to himself.

Sulking, he hung upside down from a tree, swinging back and forth, jeering now and then. "I don't know what you're after," he said. "You were perfectly content before. You had that ingenuous Frenchwoman, and I . . . I had the night—the wolves. If you had half a brain . . . I wish I had left you behind in bedlam!"

He swung once more, over the branch, and landed on all fours on the soft ground. He tried to get a glimpse of the world outside through the body's eyes, but they were all peering, crowding him out. When he managed to peek, he saw that it was no different from the world inside the mind. Another forest. The air close and rank and damp. And they were climbing, climbing. Another forest but also the same forest. A strange sensation, as if the body were being turned inside out.

Johnny had climbed back up onto the Indian's shoulders. The silly child was giggling, playing with the Indian's greasy hair— the lice looked fat and delectable. If Johnny would lose his concentration for just—

There! He was turning to make cooing noises at a badger that was scampering across the forest floor. What a sentimental little thing he is, Jonas thought, despising him utterly. But it gave him the opening he needed. Jonas reached out and bit into one of those luscious lice and then rapidly retreated into the darkness.

"Enjoy, Johnny-boy!" he said, cackling as Johnny was propelled back into the clearing.

Johnny spat it out at once. He grimaced. Jonas was down there somewhere. "Back," he whispered, "back, back, back."

Ishnazuyai paused. Perhaps he interpreted it as meaning that the boy wanted to be let down; he let Johnny climb down from his back and run on ahead, though he never let him out of his sight.

The boy was quick. He scrambled uphill. It was easier on all fours, because the hill was steep. He was naked—he had lost his clothes in the transformation—and the loose stones stung his hands and elbows. He could hear Ishnazuyai far behind him, and knew the old Indian was watching, but he could smell another human being too—he could smell sorrow in the air—and the odor of a woman who has been trudging for many days.

Crouching, he peered through the bushes.

And recognized the woman he saw squatting beneath a pine tree, singing quietly to herself, though the passage of only a few days had emaciated her features and coarsened her scent. There was death in her song and death in the drooped way she sat, sunken, hollow-eyed. It was Teddy's mother.

He called to her softly: "Little Elk Woman."

Startled, she looked up. Doubtless she saw his eyes and little else through the thick foliage. He parted the leaves with his face and said in English, for he did not know her tongue, "Why aren't you with Teddy?" and then again, "I am sorry your husband was killed. It wasn't me who did it . . . I would never have done a thing like that, believe me." Though he heard the mocking laughter of Jonas deep inside himself.

She looked at him fearfully. He knew he must seem strange to her, a naked white child in the wilderness. From behind him came another sound . . . Ishnazuyai had started with his flute again. The music calmed the woman, and she said, in an accent somehow both Indian and French, "You are medicine child Ishnazuyai tell of."

"You've left the village . . . to die, haven't you?" said Johnny. "Because there's no one for you now. But what about Teddy?"

"I tell him go find father." And she turned away from him and went on singing her death song. And Johnny smelled death on her, and a passive acceptance of death . . . the smell of a quarry who knows that the hunter is nigh. He knew then what form she expected her death to take.

If the wolves of urban Vienna mesmerized their prey with their eyes, the old man was doing it with the song of the flute.

He felt that the old man was closer now, standing directly behind him. The breath of the flute was cold on the nape of his neck. He turned and said harshly, contorting his facial muscles to the language of night: "I don't want you to stalk her, hunt her down, kill her. Only days ago you were her protector."

"Other wolves will come. I am too old to change."

"I want you to protect her still."

"But that is contrary to nature. She has sought death out, child, and we cannot unsing what she has sung."

But Johnny cried out to the woman, feeling her pain. "You mustn't die now . . . because I've found you." Feeling the old man's unease, he went on, "What was sung *can* be unsung! If I am all the old man says I am, then I am the one who will unsing what has happened—the coming of the white Shungmanitu—and what will happen—the catastrophic war between the wolves." He didn't know what part of himself he plucked those words from. They seemed to ring true, though. Even the woman smiled a little. And then he said to her, as though he could guess the fate that had caused her to leave her village, "I still need a human mother."

There came to him a painful memory of Speranza in the camp of his father the Count; and he thought: She is lost to me now. She loves him too much.

Grief flooded his senses. But he pushed the grief away. In his mind, he heard Jonas laughing from just outside the clearing: "Forget her! She's gone, you simpering little puke. And soon you'll be gone too, because it's me they want, me, the werewolf, not you, the crybaby." But he knew that for now, the other selves sided with him; as long as the alliance held, Jonas could be beaten back. Aloud, he told the woman, "Come with us. I'll need someone who is all human if I'm to live among werewolves."

Softly, Ishnazuyai said to Little Elk Woman, "I was right. Truly our hopes rest in this child, for he alone among us is compassionate."

Somewhere ahead of them, a stream whispered; leaves rustled in the mountain wind. Johnny Kindred shivered from the cold and the thin air. He hoped his journey would end soon. But it was to be several more days' travel before he and the old man and Little Elk Woman reached the most sacred place of the Shungmanitu, the wolf encampment whose whereabouts no human had ever dared ask.

17
Winter Eyes
half-moon, waning

THE TOWN LAY IN THE FOOTHILLS, NOT FAR FROM WHERE A MASSY rocky outcropping loomed, bald and long-shadowed, over the deep green grama grass plain. The Count von Bächl-Wölfing rode in front of the procession, with Natalia Petrovna by his side, for Speranza had been banished to the supply wagon. Until Natalia was officially stripped of her position as queen wolf, it was unseemly for Speranza to take official precedence, although it was now to her that the servants deferred. A duel of sorts between the two women was inevitable. But Speranza wished to stave it off for as long as she could. Meanwhile Natalia's cousin Vishnevsky, who seemed to have lost considerable rank in the hierarchy of the Count's retainers, continued to treat Speranza with utter opprobrium; and she sympathized with that, for she knew that as Natalia's fortunes fell so too did his.

Cottonwoods ringed the town and concealed it from view. A mile or so before they could even glimpse the town itself, they met the railway tracks which had followed the curve of the foothills. They followed the tracks until they ended abruptly, swallowed up in a sea of knee-high grass. It was here that you could see the town. The bulbous domes of an Orthodox church peered from the treetops. Behind, hints of the façades of buildings.

A few hundred yards from where the tracks stopped, there was a wide stretch of road that wound its way into the wall of cottonwoods. A gleaming Concord stagecoach was making its way toward them. A driver in livery wielded the whip whilst another servant rode shotgun, and the coach was drawn, as in a grotesque parody of the Cinderella story, by six white horses.

The Count fell back, leaving Natasha to lead the procession, until he was riding abreast of the wagon where Speranza sat.

"Our carriage," the Count said to Speranza, not without a certain dry irony. "Somewhat like a fairy tale, is it not? Although I now doubt we shall be living happily ever after."

"You seem sad, Hartmut," Speranza said.

"Can you be surprised? The New World, alas, is not entirely what I dreamt of. But look, Szymanowski is pleased." He pointed out the bald old man, whose horse had cantered up to Natalia's; the two were engaged in animated conversation and looking at the sights with interest. "Ah, Speranza, could you but know the paradise of which I dreamt! The perfect world where I, my queen, and my son could dwell, far from the madness of our nineteenth-century life. Now my son has been taken from me, and as for my queen, my queen. . . ." He reached his hand toward her. It was cold, almost the hand of a dead man.

They held hands as he rode side by side with her, Speranza leaning from the side of the wagon. She was wearing black, as always, but now she permitted herself a scarlet sash and a dab of rouge in her cheeks and a touch of crimson on her lips. She knew that he found her beautiful; and this in itself was strange to her, who had but a few months before pronounced herself forever plain as suited a governess.

Then came a sign: *Welcome to Winter Eyes*. A painted plank nailed to a tree trunk.

And the Count laughed softly, almost to himself, and said: "Thus it is that dreams change. I thought we had named our city *Winterreise*, after our journey across the snow; instead, some wag of a sign painter has made it into a pun. Another blow to Szymanowski's grand vision, I'm afraid."

He rode on ahead, joined his mistress, entered the carriage drawn by white horses. The servants cheered. Their enthusiasm seemed genuine enough; at least, Speranza thought, they will not be travelling again for a long time.

Thus it was that the werewolves entered the town of Winter Eyes. There were a few there to greet them; one, in particular, stood in the town square, a military man. He removed his hat to salute the Count, and many of the servants gasped, for instead of hair he had a mass of scar tissue. Evidently he had survived a scalping. It was almost noon, and the spring sun shone on them from a clear sky. It was not warm; a breeze gusted through streets that smelled too clean, through mudless boardwalks, fresh-painted signs that

clattered against fresh-painted doors, hitching posts without
horses.

Speranza climbed down from the cart and came closer. At one
end of the square was the church, and the unholy Father
Alexandros was already preparing to enter. The military man was
helping Natalia down from the coach. The square was flanked
with a hotel and saloon, a general store, a barbershop—but all
these buildings seemed somehow unreal, for there was no activity
within, and they gleamed with fresh paint. She had the feeling that
they were empty shells, that Winter Eyes was only a simulacrum
of a human town. From within the saloon came the tinkle of a
piano, but no sounds of conversation. Perhaps it was one of those
popular new mechanical pianos that needed no player.

Next to the saloon was a building whose façade bore the legend
Szymanowski-Institut. Perhaps it was where the old man planned
to continue his experiments.

"Madam," said the officer, bowing deeply to the Count and his
mistress. And Speranza knew at once, from his fawning, that he
had already become one of the slaves of the werewolves—that he
had already been branded with the wolfsbane insigne of servitude.

Natasha said to the Count, pointedly looking straight through
Speranza. "This is Major Sanderson, Hartmut. He is the commander of Fort Cassandra, and he has proved most useful to us. I
managed to exert my . . . fascination . . . on him. He's going
to help deflect curious people away from Winter Eyes, and he'll
keep us informed as to the whereabouts of the Indians."

"Anything that keeps the savage Sioux in his place, Your
Excellency, is a good thing," said Major Sanderson. "They should
be exterminated like vermin, but my hands are tied by the new
treaties."

"I am so glad," said the Count, "that we are able to help each
other in this manner."

More pleasantries were exchanged. Speranza found her attention wandering. The piano continued to play, its rhythm so strict,
its volume so unvarying that she was convinced now that it was
playing automatically. She mounted the boardwalk and peered
inside the saloon. No one was there.

She walked on, not caring to watch the servants unloading the
wagons and carrying the supplies to the various houses. Past the
church, a little way uphill, she could see the houses that had been
built for the members of the Lykanthropenverein, all identical

save for one, larger than the others, higher on the hill, with Grecian columns along the front porch, stained glass in the windows of the upper story. She found herself walking into the churchyard itself. The smell of incense drifted from its open door; Father Alexandros was already at work. As she entered the vestibule, she saw that there was a graveyard next to the church, but she did not think there were any bodies there; the markers were there to lend an air of authenticity, like Adam's navel.

"You are surprised we have church here?" She turned to see Natalia Petrovna advancing toward her, the cloak of black velvet and scarlet satin billowing behind her, an ermine stole muffling her cheek. "Ah, but you should not be. You think, perhaps, we come from Satan, cannot touch holy relics, cannot take communion. Oh, but we cling to past, to familiar things." She laughed. "Oh, but we were all human once. Until something—someone— released the beast within."

Speranza said, "Have you come to fight me?"

"Here? Now? Are you so eager to be queen of all this?"

Speranza thought of Johnny Kindred, kidnapped by savages, lost, perhaps, forever. "What else do I have to live for?" Her voice echoed. There were no pews in this church; those of the Eastern persuasion, Speranza recalled, stood through entire services of three hours or more. But there was an altar, and Father Alexandros was at that very moment kneeling before it, his lips pressed to the altar cloth, whilst a boy waved a censer and filled the nave with cloudy fumes. The fragrance masked almost completely the stench of urine. . . .

"A church—sham though it may be—is hardly the place for a battle," Speranza said. "I didn't ask to be the queen wolf. I'll yield to you, if you like, and if you will ask the Count to provide money for my passage back to Europe; for without the child to care for, I'm just a supernumerary here."

Natasha laughed.

"I am not yet one of you," Speranza said. "I am not needed here—" But the Russian woman was not listening.

"You need not tell me that. There's a human smell to you. I suppose you've held on to human nature because you know what he's like. When you've changed, he'll cast you away. Only miscegenation excites him, is it not?"

"I—"

Natalia leapt at her, clawed at her face. "Your little boy is not here to help you now!" Speranza held her hands up to ward her off. She took several steps backward, felt herself backing into Father Alexandros, who continued to murmur his prayers. The Russian woman was trying to throttle her! Speranza was choking as she tried to steady herself, clutching the altar cloth . . . she kneed Natalia and she barked in pain. Her grip loosened and Speranza twisted free. Then Natalia was on her again, thrusting her against the altar. She felt her corsets crack, a shard of whalebone rip through the black satin of her bodice. The woman was thrusting hard against her, tearing at her clothing with an anger that resembled lust . . . *was* lust, Speranza realized suddenly as their eyes met.

She turned to see Father Alexandros standing silently behind the altar, a bemused half-smile on his lips, idly stroking the nape of the incense boy's neck. "Help me," she managed to whisper, but the priest did not move. Natalia seemed wrapped up in some private universe of her own, squeezing Speranza's body tightly to her, mechanically manipulating her private parts with ice-cold fingers. Speranza felt the woman's body shuddering, quaking, gripped by a passion larger than herself. Again and again she tried to dislodge Natasha, but she was wedged hard against the sharp stone of the altar, and suffocating from the incense fumes.

"Is this what drives Hartmut insane with desire?" Natalia whispered. "I fail to understand. You are like stone, like wood, unfeeling."

Suddenly her outburst of lust ended. She backed away from the altar and Speranza slumped against it. Natalia's attack had come and gone so quickly that she had not had time to react. It was only now that she felt violated, shamed. She was about to speak when they heard gunshots. And the pounding of boots on rooftops. . . .

"Hartmut!" Natalia screamed, and ran outside.

Speranza followed. The sight that greeted her eyes was as comical as it was appalling. Several of the servants lay in the dust, bleeding to death. Dr. Szymanowski was staggering about the square, an arrow in his neck; footmen and maids were scuttling about, and the werewolves were making no move to help.

The Count had taken cover behind the swinging doors of the saloon. Natalia was shrieking wildly. No one ran to help Szymanowski, who was lurching like a circus clown, a ludicrous stick figure. Blood spurted from his neck. "Why doesn't someone help him?" Speranza shouted, forgetting the danger and running across the open square to where the Count was. More gunshots. And now Major Sanderson, rifle in hand, was shooting back. Their attackers were perched on the roof of the church itself. She could make them out . . . one of them was a dark-skinned boy with dirty brown hair . . . the news butch from the train. Beside him were two white men she did not recognize, and next to them an Indian who was nocking his bow. Another Indian was behind him. Perhaps there were more attackers. But the sun was in her eyes and she could not see.

"Teddy!" she screamed.

"Get out of the line of fire, Miss Martinique!" came the boy's piping voice. "You're liable to get yourself kilt!"

"Teddy—" For a moment the attackers seemed uncertain of themselves. "Teddy," she screamed, "don't try to fight them . . . run away, or they'll devour you. . . . "

Then Natalia, seeming to recognize one of the attackers, cried out, "Harper, Harper," and there was almost a kind of triumph in her voice. "You are fighting on the wrong side, you beautiful young soldier . . . you are one of us now, not one of those filthy human beings." The younger of the two white men, seeing her, became confused, and held his rifle unsteadily.

"Harper!" cried Major Sanderson. "You dare show your face to me? I'll have the entire Eleventh Cavalry combing the territory for you—I'll have you hanged, drawn, quartered, sliced, served to the wolves for breakfast." He drew and began firing at the roof as Harper hesitated.

The two Indians looked at each other. Then they began to loose arrow after arrow into the square. Another arrow struck Szymanowski, and a squawk escaped his lips. Sanderson retreated behind the Concord.

Speranza ran toward von Bächl-Wölfing. "Do something to help Dr. Szymanowski!" she cried. "Surely you cannot simply stand there, protecting yourself, when a man is shambling about with an arrow in his throat—"

"I can do nothing!" said von Bächl-Wölfing. She saw an inconsolable sadness in his eyes. It was the same world-weariness she had first seen in him that evening, so long ago, on the train to

Vienna; since then she had never seen him appear quite so helpless.

An arrow whistled past. It lodged itself in the boardwalk at her feet. It was then that she saw the glint of the arrowhead half buried in the wood . . . silver.

"They know," she whispered.

"Our ancient enemies . . . the humans . . . have found us again. How shortlived was my hope for a utopia! Oh, Speranza, I despair," the Count said.

Szymanowski lay in the dust, twitching as though in the throes of epilepsy. More arrows pierced him. He wriggled like a porcupine in a trap. Queer whining noises escaped his ripped throat.

The servants were finally organizing themselves, and were returning fire, using the wagons and the Concord stagecoach for cover. The Indians stood on a ledge and taunted them with a whooping war cry. They fired but the Indians were nowhere to be seen. Suddenly she saw Teddy and the two white men leaping from rooftop to rooftop, and an Indian following them. The servants turned and fired again. Speranza did not know whom to side with. But she knew that Teddy had been Johnny's friend, and that he had been in the Indian village the night of the werewolves' assault. She did not want the boy to die.

Gunfire again. Smoke in the air, making her eyes water. She was too confused to feel fear. She stood in the cross fire, screaming at Teddy to flee. And Natasha stood beside her, shrieking imprecations at the man she called Harper.

Suddenly a man fell from the roof and slammed against the hitching post. Blood was pouring from a wound in his chest.

She heard the young boy's shriek: "Paw!" and understood that this must be Teddy's father . . . the man he had run away to seek.

Pattering footsteps on the rooftops. The attackers were escaping. The shuffling sounded farther, farther, farther . . . then she heard the whinnying of horses.

People rushed about aimlessly. Speranza ran to look at Teddy's father, who had slumped onto the boardwalk. No one went to help him. They were crowding around Dr. Szymanowski and the dead servants. She knelt beside the man, tried to stanch his wounds with a shred of the dress that Natasha had ripped.

"*Non, non!*" he cried out as she bent over him. She saw fear in his eyes. He began to mutter something to himself in French about the *loup garou*. He thought she was one of them!

Softly, Speranza said, "*Pas moi*." And squeezed his hand, very gently, feeling the life drain from it.

"My son," he said.

"They've escaped."

"I never thought he would . . . be so brave." She thought she saw him smile before he died. There was blood everywhere—matting her hair, slippery on her fingers. Two servants roughly heaved the body up onto their shoulders and began to walk away.

"No!" she cried, making them stop.

She felt the Count's hand on her shoulder. "They must dispose of him," he said. "Wolves like to feast on rotting meat sometimes, did you know that? It would not do to leave him lying here; you would not like to look on him with great chunks gnawed out of his face."

"Then bury him in the churchyard—like a human being," Speranza said.

"You ask much. They have declared war on us. Did you see Szymanowski?" She shook her head, but as she looked across the square she could see him lying on a blanket. It looked as though a wolf had been trying to burst loose from within him; fragments of skin hung loose on him, and a pair of stiff forepaws erupted out of his abdomen, which was slick with dark blood. The jaws of a wolf protruded from torn cheeks. The dust around his head was flecked with brain tissue from his shattered skull. The sight exerted a morbid fascination over her.

Natasha was weeping disconsolately over the corpse, flinging her arms about and screaming extravagant expressions of grief. Vishnevsky stood above her, his face impassive.

"He was like a father to us all," said Hartmut. "I did not expect him to die. . . ." As he watched the servants bear away the body of Grumiaux, he said, and his grip tightened on Speranza's shoulder, making her wince with pain, "And you want to give *that* a decent Christian burial, I suppose! When he's one of the enemy, he's declared war on us! Never can we coexist with them, Speranza—you must understand that if you are to become one with us!—we are the hunters, they are the prey!"

"And I too am the prey, I suppose?" Speranza said bitterly.

"You must choose sides, Speranza. Especially since you are going to bear my child."

He paused. Speranza cried out: "Your child! No, Hartmut, I can't bear it . . . I have told Natalia Petrovna that I want no part of this rivalry, that I will ask to be allowed to travel back to Aix-en-Provence . . ."

"I must have a queen, Speranza."

"I will not become as you."

"I could compel obedience," said the Count, and Speranza could tell that he was toying with the idea of forcing her to drink the dew of his footprint right then and there. "But I would prefer to have you . . . grow to love me. I do not think you find me entirely repugnant." Speranza could not gainsay that. "My child, reared in bedlam, has been taken from me by werewolves who live amongst the savages. I had thought that such a child, half man and half beast, might be the salvation of us all; but it is not to be. Do not say you will not bear another child. There you have no choice; the seed is sown."

He let go of her shoulder and walked into the saloon, whence came, uninterrupted, that inhuman piano music.

From a hilltop they looked down on the town. The sun was setting. The two Indians who had come with them were roasting a haunch of deer over a fire.

Teddy Grumiaux sat, half swallowed up in the tall grass, and did what Scott had never seen him do before—he was bawling his eyes out. It was time for him to weep, Scott thought. The kid had done enough of acting like a man. Like that Indian boy who had managed to scalp Sanderson even though he was fatally wounded. Scott left the boy alone until the sun was almost over the edge of the westerly hills; then he went over to him with cold coffee in a tin cup and a piece of charred meat wrapped in his neckerchief.

"We should be going back soon," said Scott.

"I ain't going back without seeing to my paw."

"What? Are you fixin' to slip into the town and steal the body? You must be—"

"No. I reckon they'll carry it out and leave it in the forest somewheres. So they can dig it up come next full moon. Wolves loves to feed on carrion." He spoke emotionlessly; his tears had long dried up. "There, look." He pointed. Squinting hard, Scott could make out two tiny figures carrying something wrapped in a blanket, striding out of town. "Them servants is wearing the Count's livery. We can go down there in a little while and take care of my paw's body. Say a prayer over it or somethin'. You say the prayer, Scott; I don't know no Christian prayers."

They were setting up a statue in the town square. The werewolves had all gone to Szymanowski's funeral, leaving Speranza alone; she stood outside the saloon, watching the workmen. She could hear them chanting in the churchyard. At times it sounded like plainsong, at other times it was a cacophonous wailing, like distraught wolves.

She walked over to watch the workmen more closely. The statue was covered with canvas. Doubtless there would be an unveiling ceremony. But Speranza thought she recognized the stone madonna from the park outside the Viennese town house, the one with the wolf cub in her arms.

The sun was setting. The workmen had gone off, and Speranza felt a strange urge to peer beneath the statue's veil. She touched it gingerly. Lifted a fold of the fabric. The madonna's face stared back at her. It was different from the face she remembered. It seemed to be her own, although she did not think she looked that beautiful; an artist had taken her face and idealized it somehow. Her eyes were demure, downcast; in the light of the setting sun the marble cheeks had the blush of youth about them, and the lips held the merest hint of voluptuousness.

She closed her eyes. The dream that had been haunting her surfaced in her consciousness. Once more she was wading upstream toward something that howled in anguish or ecstasy, like a lover, like a lost child. But now for the first time she could see the source of the stream. On a hilltop, a child-wolf was being crucified. Blood gushed from his torn hands and became the great river that ran through the dark forest.

"Johnny!" she cried. And thought: I've betrayed him, I've let him die, and now there's another child growing inside me and the Count is going to make him into what he could not make Johnny Kindred. . . .

And opened her eyes and saw her face in the stone, serene as the wolf pup suckled at her breast. . . .

A long shadow crossed the Madonna's face.

She turned. It was the Count. Softly he said, "I had it made in Vienna before we left."

She said, "You knew that I would . . . you had the arrogance to think you had me so much in your control that you . . ."

"Do you deny it, my madonna?"

And he stepped closer. And closer.

How could she have been so much a pawn of this man? I came to be with Johnny, she thought, not to become part of this unholy family. . . .

And he stepped closer. His musky scent pervaded her nostrils. She did not step back.

They found Grumiaux in the mud, beneath the cottonwoods, and they buried him with two silver-tipped arrows cruciform across his chest so that the wolves would not molest his grave.

Sanderson's their ally, Scott thought. He wants the wolves to make war on each other . . . anything that'll wipe out the Indians faster. He's more than their ally . . . somehow they *own* him now.

And they own me, too, he thought, remembering the bitter taste of the water from Natasha's pawprints. But I'm going to fight them to the death. I ain't fixin' to become turn into no werewolf!

But he knew that when Natasha recognized him standing on the rooftop, when she called his name, tauntingly, he had almost relented. . . .

"Johnny," Speranza murmured, "I must find him, succor him, give my love to him . . ." But when she closed her eyes she saw only the image of the wolf-boy crucified, and she thought: He's dead, he's as good as dead, he's just another failed experiment of Hartmut's, and I am to be the next experiment. . . .

"I love you," said the Count von Bächl-Wölfing. And he stepped closer . . .

"Goodbye, Paw," Teddy whispered. And turned his back on the town of Winter Eyes, his mind whirling with thoughts of war . . .

. . . and closer.

PART THREE

The War of the Wolves

1
1963: South Dakota
gibbous moon

IN THE DAKOTAS, WINTER SEEMS TO LAST FOREVER; SPRING PASSES like a dream; summer comes brief and sudden. As Dr. La Loge would tell me, time and time again, "There are only two seasons here—winter and August."

All that spring I looked for the madonna that was such an important symbol in Johnny's tale. There were attics and basements in the Szymanowski Institute. There was the ghost town to be explored. But there was nothing resembling a statue of the madonna to be found there. For a while I was sure that that would be the thing that would corroborate Johnny's story once and for all; but it was not.

Then, one day, at the height of summer, when Preston Bluefeather Grumiaux came back to work at the Szymanowski Institute. . . .

It was as though nothing had happened. There had been no bloody death scene, no castration, and especially no ghostly encounter in the Omaha Union Station. He just breezed into the dining room one morning, when J.K., in his James Karney persona, was serving me my ham and eggs.

James Karney bristled. He spilled coffee on the tablecloth. I was startled to see Preston standing behind me. And J.K. growling, baring his teeth—and angrily wetting his pants.

"Hi, Carrie," said Preston sweetly.

"Preston—you're—you're—"

"Dead? A ghost maybe?" he said. "But those things don't happen to white people." He seemed genuinely puzzled. "I've been gone awhile, haven't I? By the way you people reckon. But I've been seeking a vision. It's summer. It's about time I pledged a sun dance."

J.K. was circling the table now, hunched low, growling softly.

I didn't want to upset him, so I rang for one of La Loge's orderlies to take him back to his room.

"Johnny," I said, "if you're there, if you can hear me—I'll come to you later. I promise. And you'll go on with your story." And then they led him away and Preston pulled up a chair and sat across from me.

He watched me eat, intensely, unnervingly.

"A sun dance?" I said at last.

"A fancy way of getting my nipples pierced," he said. "No anaesthetic. You want to come?"

I looked up. There was something vulnerable in the way he looked at me. It was something he really wanted to share with me. I said, "Sure."

I didn't see him again for several more weeks. And Johnny Kindred was becoming more withdrawn, not talking to me for days at a time. Dr. La Loge was always busy. Apparently the next part of the story would have to be dragged out of J.K. We were reaching a crucial moment in the story of the young mad werewolf; and by the way that the staff avoided me, I began to suspect that I was less welcome than I had been at first—and it all had something to do with the reappearance of Preston Bluefeather Grumiaux.

I was greeted almost every morning with a memo from La Loge's office, telling me that Johnny was indisposed, or that the doctor himself was unable to see me. And one morning, opening the door of my bedroom, I slipped and fell in a puddle of urine. Was I supposed to be the bone of contention between Johnny-wolf and Preston-wolf? I didn't want to contemplate it.

I decided it was time to get away again. I'd been to Deadwood several times, trying to gather information that might corroborate Johnny's story. I had never turned up anything, except to note that the names of the streets seemed more or less right—there were no differences that an old man's failing shifty memory could not account for. For example, the Mount Moriah Cemetery in Deadwood didn't seem to be as close to a church as Johnny described it—but perhaps there were other burial places, or perhaps his memory misplaced the locations—certainly such details did not challenge the vivid realism of his storytelling.

And yet—as I have said before—there was never any concrete proof either. I realized I wanted to believe too much, that I was in danger of buying the whole thing lock, stock, and barrel. But just as I was about to give in to the wild-imagination-of-a-madman hypothesis, there did come a clue. It was tantalizing, and it confirmed the existence of only the most minor of the characters in Johnny's story, but it kept me going a little longer. It happened because I went back to Deadwood.

Deadwood in summer is touristy—the main street is lined with shops that sell statuettes of Wild Bill Hickok made in Hong Kong, Indian rugs manufactured in Taiwan, and the usual mugs, tee-shirts, bumper stickers. They have wax museums, a fake Lakota Indian village, and the oddest thing of all—a reenactment of the trial of Wild Bill's murderer, Jack McCall—done in a quaint high-school-drama style, its portentousness made bearable only by the earnestness of its amateur actors. I sat through the whole thing on three or four consecutive nights, and, after having money wired to me by my long-suffering parents, camped out in a splendid Victorian hotel. By day, I made a nuisance of myself at the town hall, snooping in old newspapers.

There were a lot of history buffs doing research—they all seemed to be of the pipe-smoking, tweed-jacketed variety, though. They never paid any attention to me except, I think, to wonder why I wasn't serving them coffee. I scoured old records, hoping to come up with the name of the Count von Bächl-Wölfing. I'd already written to a genealogy professor in Austria to ask about him, but he had never written back. Probably thought I was one of those dippy American publish-or-perish types trying to horn in on his territory.

One day, though, in the library, leafing idly through the dusty, leather-bound collections of *Graham's Magazine*—a sort of nineteenth-century *Collier's*—I came across, in an article about how quaint and silly the folks of the western frontier were compared to the sophisticates of the East, this engaging little snippet:

We must not, of course, omit the curious case of the Chinese woman who was hanged in Lead for the somewhat anachronistic offense of having unnatural congress with wolves—this woman, who was, apparently, the common-law wife of a trainman of those parts, having committed no crime more notorious than simply being the survivor of an

incident in which a pack of marauding wolves attacked,
mutilated, and killed a party of innocents. . . .

It was the word *wolf* that caught my eye, and the rest of the
article was quite irrelevant—it was all about cowboy jargon and
the lewd, immodest behavior of the women of the West—but I
could feel my pulse quickening. Grumiaux's woman—the Chinese one—surely this had to be the woman in Johnny's story. Was
there more evidence—the woman's name, perhaps, or court
records?

I drove to Lead to find out.

Lead! One of the first things you learn is that they call it Leeed,
not Ledd. It distinguishes the real people from the tourists—the
one thing I didn't want to be mistaken for. Tourists, tourists, in
their polyester suits and loud summer dresses, with their sweaty
children in cowboy hats and Hong Kong–made war bonnets
playing cowboys and Indians in the alleys.

Tourists, tourists—standing in line to get into an authentic gold
mine. An Indian boy, dressed up in a fanciful getup which, by
now, I knew had nothing to do with how Indians really used to
dress, was standing by the sidewalk and charging twenty-five
cents to pose for pictures. I took one, feeling very much like the
Great White Mother. I arrived too late to get into the library or the
town hall. The sun was setting. It gets chilly at sundown even in
the summer because it's so high up and you always feel the wind.
I found a cemetery much like the one J.K. had described to me as
being in Deadwood. I wondered whether he had gotten the two
confused. There was a drafty church—unlocked, empty—nearby.
I went in, went back out quickly—spooked, suddenly. Maybe it
was because the town had magically emptied of tourists—maybe
they were all on bus tours or something—and there was suddenly
no one there at all. I wandered around among the graves for a
while—don't really know what I was looking for—but what I
found was:

—RUMIAUX'S CHINAW—
1883

The marker was wood, and almost rotted through. But there
were fresh wildflowers. Couldn't have been more that a few hours
old. I was shaking. If this was what I thought it was—

A shadow. I turned around and—

"Fuckin' Jesus—I go looking for a vision and I find *you*!"

It was Preston. He gripped both my hands tightly, intensely. And said, "Carrie, you're following my family around like a she-wolf on a hot trail."

"What the—how did you—"

He smiled. The wind whipped at his long hair, blew it across his tight lips, his hard eyes. His cheeks were hollow and he had lost a lot of weight. Maybe he had been fasting. I knew that was one of the things they did when they went looking for visions.

"Preston," I said, "I'm not trying to—"

He wouldn't let go. "They hanged her. Accused her of fucking a wolf! Of course, you wouldn't know about things like that." He pulled me toward him. His breath was fetid and there was a reek of animal urine about him and I knew what he was turning into. "You know why I gotta do this sun dance, don't you? I want to know how human I still am. I'm still on my vision quest at the moment."

"But I thought you had to go out into the wilderness for that."

"This is the wilderness—the *washichuns*' wilderness—don't you know it?" And waved at the gravestones. And the town beyond.

"She was no kin to you," I said. "Why the flowers?"

"My grandfather watched her die. Yellow, red, black, brown, you people oppressed the lot of us."

"You forget," I said angrily, "that if J.K.'s story is true, then you're part white too."

"Don't remind me!" he screamed. And started to stalk away. Then, stopping at the gateway into the graveyard, he said, "I'll see you on the reservation next week. For my nipple piercing."

I watched him walk downhill, out of sight. I shivered. The breeze played with the flowers beside the grave marker. They started to blow away. I watched them in the wind gust. I was nervous about going back to the Szymanowski Institute, afraid of this book that was just growing and growing into something of monstrous proportions. But I knew that I would have to finish the story—that, in a way, I was part of it, even. J.K. had been waiting for something—somebody—and he seemed to have fastened on me as the vehicle for his redemption. I was scared of it and proud, too, and I also loved him a little, though at times I thought it was only because I was somehow becoming possessed by the persona of Speranza Martinique.

In the end, I returned to the institute. I started anew with the interviews with J.K. He was moodier than ever; some days he would just sit silently, and I could see him shifting from personality to personality . . . without words . . . I would blink and there'd be a different face staring at me. I knew those faces well now. Johnny Kindred's innocence always held the memory of pain; Jonas Kay's was an angry face; James Karney's had a kind of weary resignation about it; and there were the others, too, the ones that emerged only rarely and fleetingly: Johannes Klagendorfer with his sneer, Jozef Kandinsky, who spoke perfect Russian; once or twice I had spoken with Jozefina, the "twin sister," who lisped and flaunted her hips in an outlandish parody of Marlene Dietrich.

And always La Loge sat in the background, taking notes, ready with a hypodermic should his patient get out of hand. More and more, the personalities seemed to drift off into a state where they just stared into space, and I couldn't tell them apart anymore.

A week after this impasse, I remember asking him, for the hundredth time, "You were abducted by the old Indian man. What happened after that? What became of you?"

I felt sure I had been speaking to Johnny Kindred. The eyes were wide open, there was the childlike smile, and the one or two words he had said to me were in that little-boy voice.

In that same voice, J.K. said to me, "I don't know why you keep asking him. You should know that he doesn't speak English."

"Who doesn't—" La Loge looked up from his notetaking. He seemed surprised for the first time in days.

"The Indian one. You know, Shungmanitu Hokshila, the wolf-boy." His face shifted again; I was met with that blank stare, and I understood for the first time that it was a language barrier, nothing more.

"It breaks the pattern!" La Loge said excitedly. "No J.K."

Another voice: Jonas Kay's. "Stupid old man! There aren't any j's and k's in Indian talk. They didn't have no writing!"

"Eminently logical," La Loge said, not without admiration.

Then came another voice. It spoke the Lakota language, its cadences measured and deliberate, its music as hypnotic as a ceremonial drum. It was a boy's voice, but one that cracked sometimes—the voice of a boy who was almost a man. I only understood a word here and there, snippets I had picked up—the word *shungmanitu*, which means wolf; the word *olowan*, which means a song. After a few minutes, the voice burst into song. A childish treble with a hint of an old man's wheezing. I did not know the words.

"You can't expect me to understand—" I began.

Then came another voice, also a boy's voice, also a new character in the drama. "Howdy, Miss Speranza. I been sent to translate for you by my Injun brother. My name's Jake Killingsworth."

"Hello, Jake," I said softly. Dr. La Loge had started a new notepad. He was agitated. It must be another breakthrough, I supposed. "Did you know me before? When I was travelling with you?" I was still trying to fit in with his strange notion that I was somehow Speranza reborn.

"I never spoke a word to you afore this, ma'am," said Jake Killingsworth, "till today. But I seen you through the eyes of the other kids. When they was all clamorin' and carryin' on, I was deep inside the forest, waiting to come out. I was with the Wolf Boy on the day he was born, when the old Injun was a-carryin' him on his back toward the north."

"The Wolf Boy?"

"Shugmanitu Hokshila," said Jake, "and I'm the only one that can understand his talking and speak the English words for him. He's the youngest of us'ns. He don't speak no white man's talk a-tall. So I took care of him and when he had to speak English, I done spoke for him."

"Did you . . . speak for him . . . often?"

"No ma'am. It was only after he was captured by the snake-oil man. . . ."

So it went for the next few days. The new personalities told me their story in a circuitous way; more than anything this showed me how narrow and linear my way of thinking was. The Wolf Boy saw the world as a series of concentric circles, not as a progression from past through present to an unknown future. The future and the past were to him equally knowable and unknowable, equally full of mystery. My narrator was nothing like Johnny Kindred; he was not afraid, he was not uncertain. And yet he told me, through his translator, that he had not spoken in almost eighty years; that I was the first to call him out of the forest that was J.K.'s mind.

"Why?" I asked him. He was by far the most serene, the most collected of the personalities. If only he had been allowed to mature, I felt that he might have been able to absorb the qualities of the others into himself, become the center of healing. He was wise. Why did he vanish?

It was Jake Killingsworth who answered for him: "It was the snake-oil man, ma'am. Wanted to crush the Wolf Boy. Damn near stole away his soul for good."

"The snake-oil man?" But I suspected who that must be.

"He didn't come for more than three year. And we was beginning to come together. But there was one thing we lacked—"

"What?" I saw La Loge look up.

"You, Speranza," Jake said softly. "And when we seen you again, we was already in the hands of the snake-oil man."

Tomorrow Preston is going to come for me. We are going to drive down to the reservation and I'm going to see the sun dance.

I know I'm going to be disappointed. I've read all those anthropology texts that talk about the vow to the sun. I know they pierce the flesh of their chests and attach themselves to a sacred tree with long rawhide thongs, and they dance staring at the sun and blowing little flutes and waving little bunches of sage flowers—dance till the cords tear free from their flesh. Description after description is in those texts—eyewitness accounts—travellers' tales, the Indians' own words sometimes. But I've also heard it's different nowadays. They don't gouge the flesh as much—how can they, when the man has a nine-to-five he has to get to in the morning? The thongs rip free just like that and—poof—vow completed. That's what Dr. La Loge told me one morning over breakfast. The Indian Bureau banned the whole thing for a long time, but now it's coming back. But maybe it's not the same.

So I'm afraid it's not going to be what I've read about. But I know he wants me to be there.

I need to talk to him anyway. I want to see if he'll tell me any more about the Chinese woman—his grandmother-in-law?—or great-grandmother-in-law? I keep seeing this woman—I see her as delicate, high-cheekboned—swinging from a gallows, with the

crowd jeering, thinking filthy thoughts about her and a wolf
making love—sick, sick, sick. . . .

And yet . . . I've caught myself thinking those thoughts
lately.

And I've woken up in the middle of the night, and the scent that
still clings to my nostrils, from a dream perhaps, is a dark
musk-odor . . . and I'm so excited I can't get back to sleep
again and . . . I admit it . . . I start to touch, caress the moist
folds, think of sharp, mud-matted fur against my smooth skin, I
can't deny it . . . I am aroused.

2
1883: Lead, Dakota Territory
full moon

THEY WERE HANGING THE CHINAWOMAN AT NOON, BUT YOU COULD
hear them all night long, pounding away at the scaffold. By dawn
came the watchers, shuffling down the boardwalks, whispering to
each other, and music was tinkling from the saloons.

Speranza had not wanted to witness the hanging; she had
another errand entirely in Lead, one she did not wish to conduct
in the midst of so public an occasion; but it was difficult for her to
leave Winter Eyes, and she had to make do with the time she had.
The time of the full moon, when the wolves were in an uproar,
was the best time for her to come into town on the pretext of
shopping for clothes; and she had been able to come with only an
old servant as escort. The servant was even now at the general
store, collecting some supplies—for Winter Eyes had not yet
attained Dr. Szymanowski's idealized goal of self-sufficiency—
and she had been able to leave the Imperial Hotel in stealth. The
hanging, she realized now, would make a perfect excuse; for even
the Count would think nothing of a woman piqued by curiosity to
see another woman hanged.

The window of the doctor's upstairs waiting room overlooked the gallows. She could not help looking out, even while she attempted to distract herself by leafing through a Montgomery Ward catalog. She had been waiting for some hours, and Dr. Josiah Swanson had not emerged; he was performing a sensitive operation within, extracting a bullet from a gunfighter's buttocks.

At last he consented to see her; and she was much relieved, for the window of the doctor's office did not overlook the hanging square. But she was not heartened when he stood, not speaking, twirling the ends of his mustache. The gunfighter was still groaning and cursing; he lay on a table behind a discreet Chinese folding screen.

"Could we not have a little privacy?" she asked. "As you know, Dr. Swanson, this is a matter of some delicacy. . . ."

"Oh, he won't be hearing you one bit, Miss Martin," he said, calling her by the name she had adopted in the New World these past few years. "I've given him so much whiskey, I'd be surprised if he even remembered where he got that scar on his bee-hind."

"But I've come for the—"

A sound from the street—a choral murmur—hungry, hungry as a pack of wolves—how well she knew that sound—how well she knew, too, that the Chinawoman was quite innocent, whereas it was she, Speranza, who had had carnal knowledge of a wild beast—who revelled in the pleasure of it even as she reviled herself with its shamefulness.

"Let's not go talking about what I'm about to do, Miss Martin," the doctor said. "It's bad enough, a pretty woman like you, wanting to flush out the unborn child from her womb. If it weren't for the—"

Speranza drew some coins from her bosom and put them down one by one on the doctor's desk. Every one of them an eagle— one, two, three, a dozen. It was twice as much as last time. Discretion had its price.

"I mean, ma'am, it ain't as though you were some kind of a wh—" Swanson stopped himself just in time. "I mean, three times—"

"Sir, my reasons are my own. Suffice it that I can pay you for this operation, and that I am still able to afford your silence. I cannot, will not, bear this child or any other. Speculate how you will, Dr. Swanson; it shall not alter the truth." She spoke more bravely than she felt. She knew that if she had left it any later she would come to feel a kind of love for the creature within her, and that she must never allow herself. Or she would become in fact what the Count wanted her to be—the wolves' madonna—never to regain her freedom, never to fulfill her faint hope of finding Johnny Kindred.

There was a crash. The gunfighter had rolled off the table. "Son of a bitch!" said Dr. Swanson. "I'd best see to your little problem in the waitin' room, Miss Martin," he said. "I'll lock the door and make sure no one comes up until it's done."

"Is there a package for me?" Speranza asked, for Dr. Swanson had agreed, for a fee, to act as mail drop for this enigmatic Hope Martin, and she had been carrying on a correspondence with Herr Freud in this fashion.

"There is indeed," he said. "And since it seems to have come open, I aim to use some of his quality coca powder to ease the pain of my little operation. . . ."

He came to Lead with two dollars in his pocket. A dollar in small change for food and drink, and a big round silver dollar for a whore. At least, that's what Teddy Grumiaux planned to spend it on. After all, he was a man now—almost fifteen years old—and living in hiding in the mountains with a renegade soldier didn't give a man much chance to exercise his prick.

Especially a renegade soldier who now and then would start turning into a wolf.

The last two years had been hard. The Sioux village wanted them to stay there, but Scott was afraid word would reach Fort Cassandra somehow—or they'd be seen by one of the Crow scouts. They'd found some caves high up in the Black Hills, in the Sioux's most sacred country. Scott couldn't go into town, of course; so Teddy was the one who slipped in and out, stealing here and there, bringing the news of Claude-Achille's death to the Chinawoman. He never would forget how she stood, not crying, in her calico dress, her head bowed a little, then went back to cooking Teddy's supper for him without so much as a word. She was almost like an Injun, the way she could carry grief all bottled up inside her. And because he knew he could trust her, he told her how he and Scott could be reached; and over the years she had sometimes travelled out into the hills to find them, oftentimes with a hamper of ham and bread gone stale in the week it took her to reach them. And she would bring silver for bullets.

The wolf troubles started soon after the Count and his friends came to the town of Winter Eyes. And they weren't so easy to attack now; they were constantly on guard. When the moon was full, the pack would hunt. Indians and white folks alike they'd kill. Horses and cattle too, though they didn't like them as much.

And every time the full moon came, Teddy had Scott to worry about. He wasn't all the way one of them yet, but they both knew it was coming. That was why whenever the moon grew big, he and Scott would go to the far back of the cave and he'd cover up the entrance with as much dry brush as he could find. Nights they sat in the darkness and all Teddy could hear was his friend breathing. And there'd be a foul stench, filling the close air, making him choke almost, so he'd want to run outside and breathe the fresh air, but he'd sit still and let himself stifle, because he didn't want to let in the moonlight. And he could imagine Scott changing little by little. He sat in a circle of silver coins. It was like a sacred circle that the Injuns liked to make. Protection. He knew that one day Scott was going to change all the way. Particularly if he ever laid eyes on that Russian woman again.

Even when the moon wasn't full, Scott could tell who was a wolf and who wasn't. Teddy knew that he had a wolf sense about him even when he looked like a man. Sometimes he would sniff the air or look from side to side in a way that reminded Teddy of an animal.

They shot only three werewolves in those two years: the Gipsy woman, Father Alexandros, and someone who had not been on the train ride from Omaha, which meant that the wolves were recruiting more wolves into their ranks.

They also shot true wolves by the dozens. There was a bounty on wolves, and a body could sometimes get himself double as much gold by taking the ears to one county and the tails to another. Shooting true wolves didn't need silver, but it was good practice. They were vermin, nothing more or less than vermin.

It was the day the werewolves killed all the members of a mining party that the Chinawoman had been visiting with him and Scott. They heard it going on—the screams, the howling, the rending of flesh over the whispering of the stream downhill from their cave. The three of them sat in the darkness just listening and listening. Scott was all murmuring to himself; Teddy couldn't figure out if he had fallen into the wolf way of talking yet, that quiet growling sound that made your flesh crawl. The China-woman never said a word; Teddy watched her face in the embers of a dying fire. She had been cooking a rabbit for them, frying it up with chopped vegetables in the Chinee fashion.

Teddy didn't want to leave Scott behind in case he started to change. He didn't want to face all those ravening wolves alone either, and they didn't have much silver ammunition left. They just sat and listened as the sounds went on through the night.

The next evening came the hunters. You could hear them from a mile off, trampling the brush, bragging as they swilled their morning liquor, shooting off rounds at random.

"Hide, Scott, hide!" Teddy cried out. The three of them were sitting just like they'd been the previous night. But no werewolves howled outside; they didn't like to feed in the same place twice.

Scott cried out. No words. In the firelight Teddy saw he had begun to change. Teddy threw some dead branches over his friend. The hunters were near now; something must have attracted them; maybe the faint glow of the dying fire.

Voices outside: "Goldarn it if there ain't someone up here. In that cave maybe."

"Don't go in. Just your luck to find the whole pack inside, biding their time, waitin' to rip us to pieces like they done old Jebediah Snipe."

"I ain't afraid of no wolves."

Footsteps. Closer now. Tension hung heavy.

Teddy slid into the shadows. A soft rumbling in the air: that was the wolf's breathing. Teddy knew that Scott was going to change in spite of the darkness, in spite of himself. It was the fear made him change, the scent of terror that rode the high wind of the hillside.

Men were inside the cave. He couldn't tell how many.

"I tell you, I ain't afraid of 'em. They's just vermin."

Flickering light: a lantern. "Somebody been a-camping in this here cave." Sooty light over the circle of silver. "Lookit that!"

"Must be a hundred dollars lying about—Morgan dollars and dobe dollars—no gold. Here, help yerself."

And they broke the silver circle. He could smell the change in Scott even though he couldn't see him.

And Scott had leapt out at them. Scott, a half-formed wolf, snarling. They fired again and again. Little good it would do.

Until the Chinawoman stepped out, clasped the wolf, tried to hold him back. They'd wounded her, dragged her away, talking loudly to each other about the unspeakable sin she must have been committing. . . .

They were going to hang her today. For having "unnatural congress" with an animal. They'd made themselves believe it. Because they feared for their lives and their children's lives and they had to hang somebody for it.

Teddy found himself in the square, drawn to the sound of it in spite of himself. It was an hour before noon, but it was already crowded. He stood on the boardwalk outside Doc Swanson's. He didn't really want to watch the hanging, but there were so many people that he didn't want to seem like a coward in front of them. It was a sunny day, bright and summery and making you sweat inside your boots, and the horseshit rank in the streets. Teddy stood, fidgeting, for a while, thinking about the Chinawoman. Maybe there was some way he could save her—ride in with guns shooting, snatching her off the gallows. He'd heard a lot of stories about things like that, but always from a town far away, like Virginia City or Abilene.

The hotter it got, the farther back he stepped into the shadow of Doc Swanson's place. At last, with the sweat running down his face, he backed right into the doctor's. A woman was coming downstairs. He had never thought to see her again.

He doffed his hat to her. She started back, as if some awful secret had been discovered. Then she smiled wanly and said, "Teddy Grumiaux."

"Beggin' your pardon, ma'am. Did you come to see the hangin'?"

Speranza put her hand to her forehead. She's fixin' to swoon, thought Teddy. He rushed to her and reached out his arm to steady her. His callused hands touched silk, fine silk, and left dirt prints on the lace trimming of her sleeve, but she did not seem to mind. She said, "Oh, Teddy, Teddy, it's good to see someone who understands, who knows. . . ."

Outside, the crowd murmured, impatient.

"You'd best sit down, ma'am," said Teddy, "before you faints away." He helped her to a sofa in the foyer, at the bottom of the stairs. Some of Doc Swanson's patients looked curiously at them; mostly the people going upstairs were not patients, but townspeople trying for a better view of the hanging.

The jailhouse was a quarter of a mile down the street from the hanging square. Cordwainer Claggart had arranged to visit the prisoner. They were just taking her out of the cell when Major Sanderson appeared.

He and Claggart were a strange pair: the major ramrod-straight, without a button or a stitch out of place, his notorious wound concealed by his hat, the very picture of distinction; Claggart bright and brash, with a peacock-colored silk waistcoat, a twenty-dollar Stetson, puffing on a long nine.

"Sheriff?" said the major to the lanky fellow with the star. Claggart decided to remain in the background for now, though his attire would hardly permit it. The major did not introduce Claggart, and the sheriff did not seem at all curious about him. "I don't wish to delay your execution, but there are a few questions that Fort Cassandra could use answers to."

"Sure, Major, but they're getting mighty impatient out there. They're liable to storm the jail and hang her themselves."

It was then that Claggart noticed her for the first time. So this was Grumiaux's woman! A slight little thing in a calico dress worn almost to ribbons, with downcast eyes. She was handcuffed. There wasn't any fight in her. Claggart wondered whether her captors had raped her, and whether there was anything to be enjoyed in this bony creature. He liked a bit of bulk on a woman himself. And spirit. They had to fight back. Or there was no joy in the hurting.

"Perhaps, Sheriff, you could leave us for a few moments," said the major. "Military secrets, you know. No offense intended."

The sheriff seemed bewildered, but obediently went outside. Claggart could hear him trying to still the tumult beyond the jailhouse door. There was no one in the office but for the three of them.

"I have no interest in a Chinawoman, you understand," he said to Claggart, as though a little embarrassed to be involved, "but I have a mission to perform."

The major pulled out a silver dollar and held it up to the Chinawoman. She didn't wince or cry out.

"You are not one of the Count's creatures," said Sanderson. "There's no reaction to the silver, you see. That takes the matter out of my hands. I don't know why these good people are accusing you of mating with animals. But a scapegoat is a scapegoat, and it's a good thing you're drawing attention away from the truth."

"What would you have done, Major, if she *had* been one of them werewolves?"

"I have an obligation, Claggart, to the Count. I would have had to try to save her, distasteful though such a course of action would appear." Though Claggart did not answer, he thought: What a fool, what a slave he is, for all his fine airs. That foreign Count has the major wrapped round his little finger. How did he manage it? Claggart didn't doubt that that Russian woman had something to do with it.

The major said, "Is the accusation true?"

She did not answer him.

"She's all yours, Claggart," said the major sullenly.

Claggart went up to her, very close, so the major wouldn't hear him. She smelled something fierce, and she was all over scratches; but he didn't think they'd come from any wolf. No. The sheriff's men had had her, all right. He gripped her by the shoulders and looked her in the eye and said, softly, "I want to ask about the wolf-boy."

She shook her head.

"I want that boy, see. That boy's going to make me a rich man. Some say the Injuns got him. Some say he run off into the hills somewhere. Some say it weren't a wolf you was caught with, but some kind of wolf-man. Most folks don't believe in wolf-men, but I seen things. I know about them. You can tell me everything. Don't make no difference anyway; you'll hang." And he smiled a cruel smile.

"I don't know boy. Don't know nothing." A listless voice, the voice of someone already dead.

Angrily, Claggart slapped her face. The fool of a woman didn't even flinch.

"No private pleasures, Mr. Claggart," said the major, laughing dourly. "You'll take the edge off the crowd's enjoyment." Damn him to hell, thought Claggart. He'd done got what he came for—proof that the Chinawoman wasn't worth the Count's saving, wasn't one of them Winter Eyes people. But for Claggart it had been a waste of time.

He imagined the Chinawoman dying . . . oh, to be the rope that would send her to hell.

"Johnny!" she said, involuntarily, and she smelled blood in the forest, in the dank air. . . .

"Come on, Miss Speranza," Teddy said. "You needs air. Hold on to me. I'll push our way out of here."

Speranza opened her eyes. She must have fainted for a moment. The sound she had thought was the rustling leaves in the depths of the forest . . . was the murmur of the mob beyond the doorway.

She held on to the boy's shoulder. He had grown a great deal in the intervening years, but the sight of him had instantly brought back memories of the train ride, the staged robbery, the flight through the wilderness of Nebraska Territory. He looked at her, furtively looked away; but she knew what that brief glance said: We have to be allies, you and I. She sensed that the boy must have an inkling of why she had come to see Dr. Swanson.

An emptiness inside her.

She felt sick to her stomach again. She thought: If I could only swoon and get it over with; that would be the ladylike thing to do; then I would wake up somewhere else, with the smell of sal ammoniac in my nose, and perhaps I will feel less empty than before. . . .

"Ma'am . . . you'd best come outside."

"The hanging—"

"I won't let you look, Miss Speranza, I promise."

"Who are they hanging?"

"Only a crazy Chinawoman, Miss Speranza, that they say has done crazy things . . . carnal knowledge of animals . . . wolves. I can't rightly tell who's crazier, the woman or the judge." He was choosing his words carefully, Speranza saw; he knew more than he let on. She let him steady her, for she knew that in helping her he was also easing his own pain.

The boy opened the door for her. The crowd: they were all lurching forward, pushing against the hitching posts, jamming the good spots. Seven kids, alike as peas, lined up on the roof in front of Doc Swanson's sign. The stench of stale whiskey breath and

horse piss clogged the air. There were Chinamen there too, in their
outlandish costumes, their hair plaited.

"I shouldn't have brung you outside," said the boy, "it's just as
hard to breathe here as back in there." She held on to his arm; he
was taller than she was now, but lean, like a wild animal, and he
had the fragrance of moist earth—the fragrance of her nightmare.

She closed her eyes and saw . . . "Johnny!" she whispered.
For the time she had spent in the doctor's office, having the new
child purged from her, delirious from the potion she had been
given to numb her, she had also spent in the dark forest of her
dream, and she had come face-to-face with Johnny crucified once
more, and the blood flowing from his side into the river that rived
the forest. . . .

The crowd was suddenly quiet. I don't need to look, Speranza
told herself. I have already seen death.

But then she couldn't help herself, and she looked past the
jostling faces, all of them hungering, and she thought: They too
are werewolves, changed to beasts by the anticipation of violent
death. She saw the woman, expressionless, as they put the rope
around her neck. A cracking sound, and the crowd cried out. And
she began to weep softly to herself, so much so that the tears
blurred the face of the Chinawoman in the noose, and all she could
see was a dark figure kicking in the flurrying dust.

"Don't cry, ma'am," said the boy softly. "She ain't but a
Chinawoman."

"You know better than that," Speranza said. "You of all people
must know that it is I who should be hanged—I who have
had—congress—with wolves—"

"Don't say that so loud!" said Teddy Grumiaux. But she was
fortunate; the laughter of the crowd drowned her out.

"There are times when I think of nothing but Johnny. I think of
having betrayed him—of allowing myself to be drawn down the
path of least resistance."

"Reckon he's dead," said Teddy.

But she knew it was not true, and she knew that he felt her
certainty. It was good that the crowd was hollering and laughing
and carrying on all around them. For the emotion that passed
between the two of them was too powerful to be borne except
within a crowd, anonymously.

He led her away, down a side street, past a gaudy façade that

Speranza knew had to belong to a house of ill repute. The boy kept looking about as though afraid to be seen, and Speranza realized that he must have secrets of his own, worries he had selflessly set aside on seeing her.

"I'm staying at the Imperial Hotel," she told him, "and I'll be going back in the morning; please don't trouble yourself."

But he insisted on escorting her all the way there. She was pleased that the servant had not yet returned; perhaps he, too, had been drawn to the hanging. In the foyer, she started to thank the boy; but he was already leaving.

"I hope that we may meet again," she said. But he was gone.

3
Shungmanitu Village
full moon

THE MOON WAS RISING ON THE MIST-HIGH MOUNTAIN. THE WIND WAS stilled; the fire was dying; dogs lay, tense, in the circlet of warmth. In the tipis, the change was coming, the time when the children of the Wichasha Shungmanitu became as the four-legged.

In the forest within the forest within the mind of the boy, the moon shone too, shone blood-red over the clearing. Johnny Kindred, banished, watched from his hiding place, a treehouse he and James and Jake had built together to hide him from Jonas Kay. A shaft of ruddy light fell on Jonas, who circled, howled, pawed the dirt, marked every bush, rock, fallen branch with his piss—Jonas, changing in the moonlight.

"Can't stay in here forever," said Jake Killingsworth. "I won't always be here, won't always speak for you."

Johnny huddled in a corner of the treehouse. The moon made latticework of the cracks and seams. Jake's face was striped with the red light. Johnny had never known about Jake until he appeared one day, took him by the hand, showed him the treehouse he had started building.

He heard the voice of Ishnazuyai, speaking softly to him. He could not see outside, for Jonas, raging in the clearing, blocked his view of the world completely. He couldn't understand much of the Indian talk anyway. He had tried out the Indian talk on the first day that he had been captured; but after they arrived in the camp of the wolves, he had remained silent . . . for two years. And deliberately refused to understand the speech of the wolf-men.

But someone else was in the treehouse listening. He couldn't see him very well yet. Sometimes he caught a glimpse, a feather flashing, a dab of war paint, and wide, brown eyes. Johnny knew that there was someone within him who was speaking to the Indians, because he knew that the body was communicating with them, had done so for all these months of captivity. But that person hadn't revealed himself yet.

Johnny waited. Outside, Jonas Kay howled as the moonlight changed him.

Ishnazuyai sat with the boy as he had done each time the moon was full. Already the others of the village had run out into the night. But he had drawn the tent flaps tight closed, and he sat on the most shadowed corner of the buffalo robes, where the light from the ceiling opening could not touch him. He did not want the boy to change until he had spoken to him.

"Listen to me," he told the boy. "It's time for the changing again, and again I will tell you the story of how the Great Mystery came to create the wolf-people. . . ." And he spoke, as his mother had so often, of the Wichasha Shungmanitu and Wakan-tanka and the bargain they had made when the world was young.

How much did the boy comprehend? Sometimes, when the moon was full, he did not change at all, but sat by the fire sucking his thumb, seeming to stare into an emptiness that no child so young should have to confront. He knew the boy could understand the language of human beings; did he not fetch wood, tend the fire, eat his supper, when told to do these things? But when he spoke, it was always in the insensate jabbering of the *washichun*, a language that sounded, not like the wind and the creek, but like machines of iron that roared through the land where once the *pté* roamed wild, thousands upon thousands. Those few lilting words he had uttered the first day, when Ishnazuyai was carrying him on his back, never came back.

Little Elk Woman, whose life the boy had saved, lay sleeping beside him under a buffalo hide blanket she had labored over for many moons; it was covered with an intricate design of blue and white *washichun* beads that had come from a place called Praha. Ishnazuyai had taken her to wife, as was only proper, for she had no man to hunt for her, and the boy had chosen her as a kind of mother. But the woman, like the boy, hardly spoke. Sometimes the silence in the tent was almost insufferable, and he preferred to spend time in the tipi of his cross-cousin, whose wives kept up a constant stream of gossip.

He feared the times that the boy changed even more than the times he did not change. There was an obscene rage in his eyes. He was like a warrior who has pledged to be tied to a stake in battle, so that he must fight until he dies, a shamed man whose honor can be redeemed only in death.

"I must go soon with the others," he said. "We will swoop down on the forest below us. We will dance the dance of the hunter and the prey. And sometimes, if one among the Lakota has become a burden to his kinsmen, or has lost the desire to live, and has called out to the wolf-spirit to take him to the land of many tipis, one of us will come for him. And that is the most sacred thing a member of our tribe can do." Did the boy understand this? Ishnazuyai knew he was not like the other wolf-people from the white men's lands, who took on the shape of animals, but still had the hearts of white men, and who killed only for the pleasure of killing.

There was another kind of spirit in this boy; that was why Ishnazuyai had brought him to live among his people. He had seen this boy in a vision, seen him as one who would bring man and beast and *washichun* and red man together. But the vision had faded long since, and the child had not even spoken except in the white man's tongue—noise and empty air. Perhaps, Ishnazuyai thought, I was wrong.

From outside the tipi, distant howling.

From the shadows came the sound of Indian talk. Johnny couldn't understand the words, but Jake interpreted them for him. "He says he's the real wolf-boy. He says Jonas Kay is just a shadow. He says he's going to go out into the clearing."

"Who is he? Why can't he speak English?"

"He ain't English, that's why. Never set foot outside these here hills."

"What's he doing inside me?"

"He's new," said Jake, "like me."

Johnny heard the new boy's movements; they were like the rustling of dead leaves in the forest. And his voice never rose above a whisper, and never a word of English.

"He wants us to foller," said Jake.

At the entrance to the treehouse Johnny saw the Indian boy leap to the ground, a dark blur against the foliage that glowed faintly crimson in the moonlight. Just a glimpse, but Johnny could see he didn't look like any of the other people in the forest. Now he was moving through the tress, standing still, darting, emerging, vanishing. "C'mon," said Jake, "let's hightail it to the clearing."

"I'm afraid," Johnny said.

"Come *on!* Don't you know what this means, you brainless varmint? We gots us a chance to get ourselfs *cured.*"

"Cured?"

Moonlight breaking through the forest roof, dappling, the dead leaves. The mist was shifting. You could almost see the clearing. And you could hear Jonas howling. "I'm afraid, Jake," he said to his new friend. But Jake only took him by the hand and pulled him down, and he panicked because he thought the earth was going to swallow him, but he landed softly with moist dirt clinging to him. He brushed off the soil from his trousers. He looked up. The clearing was ahead. "Where'd the Indian boy go?" he said.

"Can't you see his footprints?" said Jake, pointing.

Nothing. The moonlight illuminated the path Jake indicated: here a broken twig, there a leaf a little out of place. "Those aren't footprints," said Johnny.

"When a Injun walks," said Jake, "the forest bends his way." Johnny wondered how long Jake and the Indian boy had been in the forest together, with only each other for companionship, waiting to make themselves known to the other persons who shared the body. He followed Jake . . . through twists and turns he'd never known about . . . until, suddenly, the clearing was upon them . . .

And he saw two wolves, glaring, sizing each other up, sniffing the air: the wolf that was Jonas Kay, slitty-eyed, rank, silver-furred, and another wolf, sleek and dark as the forest.

"What're they doing?" he said.

"Only one wolf can rule," said Jake.

And the boy opened his eyes and spoke to Ishnazuyai in the tongue of humans, and his first words were: "*Até, até.*"

"He's chasing the Jonas-wolf!" said Johnny. The two wolves were bounding around the clearing, snarling, trying to mark each other. Jonas roared, he growled, he clawed up clods of dirt, he slapped his tail on the earth; but the other wolf, smaller and more lithe, danced around him like the very night.

The boy twitched and foamed at the mouth, and when Ishnazuyai touched him, seemed rigid as a corpse. Perhaps it is the madness, the fear of water, thought Ishnazuyai, but when he touched his lips with a buffalo bone ladle full of fresh spring water, the boy did not flich. Ishnazuyai embraced him—for had he not called him "Father, Father"?—and tried to warm him, for he was shivering, and his sweat was cold as winter ice.

Tail down, Jonas Kay fled into the depths. The new wolf changed as the moon set, and Johnny dared set foot inside the clearing. The Indian boy was standing there now. Though he was naked from the transformation, he seemed to wear the fading moonlight and the mist.

"Zho-ni," he said softly, and he smiled. And touched Johnny lightly on the shoulder. And Johnny knew that they were brothers, and that they shared each other's nature. The wolf-boy looked into Johnny's eyes and Johnny felt strangely safe.

And spoke to him in the Lakota language, its measured cadence and uncompromising music; and Johnny knew that the Indian boy would keep them all safe from Jonas for a while. And for the first time, he foresaw a time when all of them would share the clearing together, and all of them would see out of the same eyes and speak with the same lips, and become whole.

And Ishnazuyai said, "We are glad you have come home, Shungmanitu Hokshila."

Wolf Boy smiled, and pleaded with his father to play the flute for him. The moon was setting. Ishnazuyai led the boy by the hand

to a place called Little Wolf Creek, and together they waited for
the others of the family to come back from hunting. And while
they waited, Ishnazuyai told him the story of how the wolves
became men, and for the first time the boy heard him with
understanding and gladness.

4
Lead, Dakota Territory
the same night

GETTING ON TOWARD EVENING, THE WIND FELL. THE STENCH OF THE
dead Chinawoman pervaded the air. She hung there motionless as
now and then the new wood groaned.

It was later than Teddy thought. No point in trying to make it
back now. Scott was tied up inside the cave and surrounded with
silver. He'd camouflaged the mouth of the cave with brush. He
was worried, as he always was when he left Scott alone overnight
in the full moon, but his needs got the better of him, and he
walked back to the whorehouse.

Teddy didn't waste any time picking out the girl he wanted. His
choice was made. Her name was Nita. She was a green slip of a
wench, no more than thirteen, he thought, with maybe a touch of
squaw in her; that was why he always came to her . . . breeds
fucking breeds was how the madam saw it, but his money was as
good as any dude's.

There was a new girl there tonight who looked even younger
than Nita; when he looked at her, she hid behind the ruffs that
concealed the piano's limbs from view. She was Gina Hopwood,
an orphan, an "unplucked flower," the madam called her, seizing
her tiny hand in hers and sweeping her up and away from the
drawing room.

In the room, Teddy paid Nita the whole dollar because she had
taken her petticoats all the way off.

This girl had a strange habit of acting like she enjoyed it, too, which was something only Injun girls usually did; Teddy had never encountered a white girl that would admit to liking it, but many that would carry on and weep and talk of sinning and hellfire, just to win an extra two bits.

He picked up his ivory stock Colt—Scott always let him use it with the moon full—and was about leaving; but tonight, she took a fancy to talking, and when it was over, she kept him in the room under the pretext of wanting to wash his cock with soap and water. "Soap? No way, miss," he'd told her, "that stuff'll plumb scrape the hide off a mule." But when she'd backed him into a window, and she started on his fly buttons, he realized he wasn't about to turn down any free extras.

"It's expensive soap from France," she said, smiling sweetly. "I could wash you all over if you wanted—but you'd have to take off them boots."

"I ain't taken 'em off in six months," he said, laughing, as she gazed ruefully at the mud stains they had left on the satin sheets of the bed. She started washing him off, and that perfume sure smelled something fierce. He unlatched the window to let in some fresh air, but instead of that there came the putrid odor of the rotting Chinawoman.

The girl chattered on about this and that—Teddy wasn't much interested in what she had to say, but she had a right pretty-sounding voice. But Teddy found his mind wandering. He was used to small talk, but Nita had become so carried away by her talk of petty rivalries and friendships that she wasn't even paying much mind to washing him.

That was why he found himself staring at the curtain behind the headboard, and why he noticed a strange sound coming from the adjoining room—like a dog being whipped—and a kind of whimpering—a cry of pain to be sure, but also something a little bit like playacting.

"What's goin' on back there?" he said, interrupting her.

"Oh, that's the room for the really sick customers, the ones that like a little pain with their pleasure."

"But what're they doing?"

"Probably a bit of the strap, or the paddle. Miss Hayvenhurst—she teached me everything I know—she's got a taste for some of them things they like to do. Like as not it's her in there now, with that Claggart."

At that name, Teddy felt his cock go limp.

"He's a strange one, that Claggart. I's sure glad they never made me take him. But he always pays good, and always in gold . . . you want to watch him?"

"I—"

Nita leaned over and parted that curtain a mite, and Teddy saw peepholes in the headboard set at different heights, so two or three could watch. That was why they had heard the sounds from the next room so clearly. Teddy shuddered. He couldn't think about Claggart without remembering that train journey.

"It's a slow night, on account of the hanging," said the young prostitute, "and because the smell done tainted the air. You can stay as long as you like. But you can't do it again, you know, without you pay another seventy-five cents."

"I know," said Teddy abstractedly, and he crouched on the bed and put his eye to the peephole.

It was a lot darker in the other room. There were only a couple of candles lit. There was Cordwainer Claggart all right. He hunched over the bed, his ugly buttocks up in the air, like a dog. "Why, he's bare-ass nekkid!" he whispered, scandalized. Then he saw the girl he was with, bound and gagged. She lay in a shaft of moonlight from the window, where the curtains had not been closed all the way.

"And that ain't Miss Hayvenhurst—that's that new girl," said Nita. "What a crying shame she couldn't of had her virginity took by a gentleman."

"He's hurtin' her!" said Teddy, for Claggart was engaged in lashing the young girl's buttocks with a riding quirt. "It ain't right. I gotta stop him." He could see bloodstains on the sheets. The girl was whimpering.

"You can't stop him," said Nita, "for he's paid good gold for what he's doing . . . and . . . and I'll get in trouble."

"Fuckin'—" Cordwainer Claggart had a little pocket knife out, and was about to carve something into the girl's buttocks; with his free hand he was playing with himself, murmuring.

"I'm going to get Miss Hayvenhurst," said Nita, appalled, "for she won't hold with scarring up no merchandise!" and she ran from the room, leaving Teddy by himself to watch the horror.

He lay there, unable to move or turn his gaze. Through the gag, the whimpering went on; the girl's eyes were wide and streaming with tears. She was wetting the bed as Claggart quirted her again and again, and Teddy thought, These things could have happened to me on that train . . . who'd have minded? I was just a news butch and a breed at that . . . and an orphan like her.

The more he thought about it, the more he just wanted to kill Claggart. He tried to reach for his Colt, on the dresser drawer, but it was just out of reach, and he could not tear his eyes away from the knife sliding down the girl's bare flesh and the thin line of blood, silver-black in the moon and the flickering candlelight. He managed to grab the handle but it slid to the floor and clattered and Cordwainer Claggart looked up and saw the boy's eye in the peephole, and he said, "I know them eyes from somewhere—" and began stalking angrily toward the door, and before he knew it Claggart had kicked open the thin door that joined the two rooms and was advancing on him, and the Colt still on the floor betwixt them—

Teddy couldn't reach the Colt. He tried to tell himself, I'm a man now, I can take him on, I can kill him . . . but he didn't feel like a man anymore . . . he felt like the child Cordwainer Claggart had bullied on the train to Cheyenne.

Claggart pushed him down onto the bed. He had his quirt. He lashed him in the face. Teddy could taste blood and knew his cheek was cut. "Mayhap you can tell me about the wolf-boy," Claggart said softly. "Mayhap you know something. . . ."

Teddy found himself blurting before he could think, "The old Injun's got him, the crazy old Injun that used to ride—"

"Up and down, up and down—" His eyes were terrifying. His face was full of a wild kind of joy that reminded Teddy of someone who was winning at craps. "Omaha to Cheyenne and back again—just like I done in my cardsharping days."

"I swear, the Injun took him—" He didn't want to remember the night in the sacred circle of the old man, but it all came back, and he thought, I shouldn't have betrayed him but I got to save my own hide first—

"You'd best not be trying to conceal the truth from me, little boy," said Cordwainer Claggart. "Or I'll come after you and pull out your little cocker by the roots, and dry it up good and sell it for a sausage."

Teddy spat in Claggart's eye. Claggart recoiled in surprise, and
Teddy managed to twist free of him and roll off the bed. He lunged
for the Colt again. He was cocking it when Claggart kicked it
away and it went off. There was smoke and the sound of a mirror
smashing. Teddy flew after the gun, grabbed it, burning himself a
little on the hot barrel.

Then he sprinted out through the door to the next room. The girl
was still tied to the bed. Teddy couldn't tell if she was dead or not.
She didn't seem to be moving. There was a lot of blood. He heard
footsteps. There was a window. It was open. The smell of the
hanging woman wafted in. The window looked out over the
façade of the whorehouse. Quickly he climbed out. He heard a
shot. Muffled. Somewhere inside the room. Was it the girl? Was
she dead? Would Claggart have dared. . . .

A woman screaming inside. And Teddy ran across the rooftops,
around the perimeter of the square where the Chinawoman still
hung, swinging gently now, for a breeze had come to drive away
the smell of her. There was moonlight on her tiny face, and her
eyes were all white.

Where can I go? Teddy thought. From the distant window came
the sound of more screaming. A street away, he could see the
façade of the Imperial Hotel, and he thought of Speranza.

Below, a black Concord, drawn by black horses, sped by. Black
curtains prevented him from seeing inside. Teddy thought he
knew the driver . . . one of that Count's servants . . . it was
heading toward the hotel! Teddy crouched down low, pulled
himself along the wooden ledges, hid behind swinging signs.
Perhaps Speranza was in danger. He clutched the Colt against his
heart. He was across the street from the Imperial now, on the edge
of a rooftop that extended almost all the way across. If only he
could jump, he could reach that awning. . . .

The clerk who sat behind the reception desk had been reading by
the light of a paraffin lamp. It was a somewhat out-of-date
newspaper article about the opening of the Brooklyn Bridge. He
was trying to fan away the stench of the rotting Chinawoman.

Outside, horses whinnied. The front door of the hotel was flung
open. The clerk looked up to see the two men carrying a sort of
sedan chair, completely boxed in with sheets of black canvas.
There was a feral odor—dog piss?—that masked the Chinawom-

an's putrefaction. Another man, in livery, walked behind. He came up to the clerk and said, "Miss Hope Martin." And put a gold three-dollar piece on the counter.

The clerk said, "Sir, I hope you ain't thinking of this inn as a trystin' place; the Imperial's a respectable house."

More gold fell on the counter: quarter-eagles, little gold dollars, finally a twenty-dollar piece. "My master does not frequent disreputable places."

The man had a commanding gaze, and the clerk found himself handing over the key to the room.

There was a tap on the window.

She looked up and saw nothing. She had not yet indulged in her coca powder for the evening, and she knew that when she was under its influence, she often saw dangers lurking everywhere: under beds, in closets, plots to destroy her. Surely, she thought, it is only the wind. But the knock came once again, and in the distance she heard the whinnying of horses.

She had been reading her Bible. She was startled to see the face of Teddy Grumiaux peering at her from the ledge; he wore an expression of such desperation that she got up and let him in immediately. His collar was unbuttoned, his britches were half undone, and he stared about as though he had seen something too dreadful to contemplate. She was immediately sorry she had opened the window, because the odor was intolerable. Quickly she closed it again, and, suspecting the need for secrecy, drew the curtains tightly closed. "I seen Claggart!" Teddy whispered. "He killed someone—I think."

Speranza remembered the unpleasant gambler well. "Really, Teddy," she said, "you must calm yourself. You are safe here."

"But you're not safe, Miss Speranza! That Count of yours is riding after you—"

"He cannot ride out, Teddy. It is—"

"The full moon. I know."

He was sitting on the edge of the bed now, completely in shadow. He had seemed distraught before, but now, suddenly, he seemed to break down completely, and Speranza heard him sobbing like a child; and her heart went out to him, and she reflected that, though he had burst into her bedchamber carrying a gun, he was still a child. Why, his voice is barely changing, she thought.

Though she was dressed in a loose-fitting dressing gown, beneath which she was wearing but the flimsiest of night dresses, she flung aside all propriety and went to him, and allowed him to cry in her arms. She owed him that; had he not succored her at the doctors, not even knowing the ill she suffered from?

Finally he was able to say, "Claggart's after Johnny too."

"Johnny?—" said Speranza, who so many times had entertained visions of Johnny's death, who had suffered so many nightmares in which she had seen him crucified by the river of blood in the forest of darkness. "Johnny is gone from us, the poor sad creature! Alas, I fear he is no more." She said these words without believing them.

"I know he's still alive, ma'am," said Teddy, "and I reckon Claggart means to do him harm. He's powerful obsessed with catchin' him."

She had always known he was alive, she realized. How was it that the wolf-people knew things? *In their hearts.* Well, she could feel Johnny in her heart, too . . . but through their common humanness.

"I think he needs us," Teddy said.

Footsteps outside. A knock on the door. *"Gräfin—"* She flinched at the title *Countess,* for she had never earned it.

"Told you the Count was here," Teddy said.

"It's his steward. Quick—hide—" She looked around for a place, but the boy had already slipped under the bed.

The door was unceremoniously opened, and the room was flooded with the animal odor that had filled her American nights. The two footmen set down their sedan chair—more casket than chair, for it was completely covered over—and went to secure the windows and block out the light. They had bolts of heavy black cloth with them. They threw them over the curtain rods.

Darkness.

The air quivered a little. She heard the Count's animal breathing. "How could you have come here?" she cried out. "The risk of discovery, of ruining all you have worked to achieve—"

"You are killing my children!" A little light now, as the steward lit a kerosene lamp and placed it on the bedside table. Yellow flickering light against the curtains of the four-poster bed.

"Your children—" She was at a loss to answer him. Shame tormented her.

"My children . . . and yours . . . the future seed of the wolf-people . . . oh, Speranza, do you not know how you have hurt me?"

Rough hands on her arms. "Countess," said the steward, softly, "we have come to take you back. And to guard you from now on—day and night. For nine months or more if need be."

"Release me! I will have her! Now!" A little more human now, this growling. He was controlling the change as much as he could.

More light now, candles, the light dancing, bouncing off velvet draperies, playing over the lustrous sheen of the satin bed sheets, the mottled oily texture of oak-panelled walls.

She felt herself being dragged toward the Count. The black cloth trembled a little. How far had the transformation proceeded? "My . . . madonna . . . of . . . the . . ."

She moved closer to him. She was sweating; the metamorphosis gave off a searing heat, and though she abhorred the bestial part of him there was also within her the memory of his ardent and considerate caresses, and despite her betrayal she still loved him. But she whispered: "I should be out there on the gibbet. It's I who have loved a beast."

"Perhaps . . . she died for you."

She was close to him now. A hand reached out from behind the layers of black cloth . . . a hand half retracted into a claw, the flesh not firmly under control, pulsating still. The hand grasped hers. Slid into her sweat-greased palm, the fur prickling her as it bristled and thrust out from raw wolfhide.

"Too many people have died for me," she said. "I can't endure it any longer, Hartmut . . . you must send me away . . ."

"And the children . . . whom did they . . . die for?"

She could not answer him. She too had murdered. She had fallen too far ever to lift herself up again. She did not resist as the claw began to draw her inexorably toward—

Suddenly the Count let go. "I smell another—the flesh of a boy, a human child—" He barked out orders to the servants. "*Schnell! Wir nehmen die Gräfin mit!*"

"You ain't going nowhere, Mr. Count."

It was Teddy. He had crawled out from under the bed. He had his gun cocked, pointed.

The Graf Hartmut von Bächl-Wölfing laughed. And stood up, shedding the layers of cloth that had shielded him from the moonlight. His evening dress still hung in tatters on his body, and much of him was still human.

The Count laughed. "Threatened by a little boy!" His voice had become much more human; she could see he was reining in the changes by a supreme effort of the will. "Madam, when I had you followed here, I suspected infidelity, but I had no idea your tastes extended to small boys!"

He gestured to the others. They let go of Speranza and moved threateningly toward the boy.

"Not so fast," he said. "This gun has silver bullets."

The boy fired. The recoil pushed him into Speranza's arms; the Count laughed, a little nervously, and said, "It will take more than a garbled myth to kill me, child." The bullet had only taken a piece of fabric from his coat.

"Miss Speranza, you'd best be coming with me," said the boy, and Speranza suddenly saw hope. A slender hope, but in the degradation of her condition, she had not dared entertain so much before. The boy pointed to the window. Speranza thought of her clothes, of the jewels that the Count had lavished on her, things she had never dreamed of possessing before . . . then she cursed herself for thinking of such things when now there was a way to atone for the shame she had allowed to befall her person. "Help me get the winder open," Teddy said, feeling behind him as he backed up against the wall, still pointing the pistol at the Count.

He ripped down the curtain. She could see the Chinawoman on the gallows, silhouetted against the moon.

The Count began to change. Reality blurring into nightmare. She felt revulsion and lust in equal measure. She was trembling, but she knew she could also feel the moist heat in her private parts. . . .

She backed away.

"You killed my paw," said Teddy. "You made him die. And the Chinawoman. And them miners and them Injuns. What did my paw ever do to you? So help me God, I'm going to blow you to kingdom come, I'm going to dance on your grave."

In Teddy's face she saw implacable hate. He shot again and again. Sobbing now, she knew he could not possibly see where he was aiming. But she could see flesh tearing now and blood spattering the satin on the bed, and above it she heard Hartmut's laughing. "Wounds, wounds, what are mere wounds, do you think I have not endured silver before?"

And Speranza said, "We must go now. I don't think he's going to die. He's stronger than the others. He's their king."

The boy whispered, "I got me a horse. I kept him tied up outside town a piece. Come with me, Miss Speranza. Come away."

The boy yanked the window open and began to climb out onto the ledge. A hot wind blew into the room. Speranza's heart beat fast. The odor of the dead woman melded with the reek of animal passion. The servants had run to his aid, one stanching the blood with a kerchief, another filling a basin from the pitcher on the nightstand.

She backed away, unable to look away from Hartmut's eyes. Even as the snout pushed away the strips of human flesh, even as the teeth lengthened and the tongue lolled, even as the Count fell on all fours, his evening dress in tatters, even then, his eyes were still human, and she could see within them vestiges of his feeling for her . . . his eyes said, "Pity me," and she knew that he loved her.

But Teddy Grumiaux was helping her out onto the ledge, and in time she was forced to turn away from Hartmut's face and to look instead at the corpse of the woman who had died for Speranza's unspeakable crime.

Hartmut's howling rent the air, but it was swallowed up in the tinkling of saloon pianos, in the whine of the summer wind.

It was well for them that the law had been summoned to Miss Hayvenhurst's establishment to look into the curious case of Cordwainer Claggart, for they were able to slip out of Lead unnoticed. It was well for Claggart that Major Sanderson was still in town, and vouched for his good name.

It was well for Claggart that the young boy who had been with Nita had escaped, and was therefore unable to defend himself against Claggart's charge that he had gone on a wild and drunken rampage; it was well for Claggart that Nita was a whore, and a breed at that, and her word could not be taken seriously.

It was especially well for Claggart that Gina Hopwood lay tied to the bed with her brains seeping out from a death wound. It was well that, as Miss Hayvenhurst diligently scrubbed the drying gray matter from the sheets and floor, she was already thinking of ways to hush up any scandal that might befall her house of already ill repute.

As for the dead orphan girl, her flower remained unplucked; for, as Cordwainer Claggart had learnt to travel the darker alleyways of desire, he had also learnt to disdain the more conventional means of possessing a woman.

Indeed, he reflected as he left the establishment, deep in conversation with Major Sanderson, my sensibilities is just too damned refined now for anything so vulgar as fornication.

He had already forgotten the incident, so tantalizing was this new scrap of evidence: the crazy old Indian had something to do with the wolf-boy! Already he was scheming.

He did not listen to the major's dull military exposition of the late General Custer's strengths and weaknesses, so caught up was he in his grand plan. He did not smell the putrefying Chinawoman as they walked past the gallows. He did not even notice the black Concord drawn by black horses, hurtling down Main Street toward the road to Deadwood.

5
Shungmanitu Village
half-moon, waning

THE NIGHTS WERE CLEAR; THE DAYS WERE BLAZING; FROM THE mountaintops you could see the world stretch on and on, and, with the eyes of the spirit within, the eyes of the soaring eagle, you could see past the edge of the world and into the future and the past. The wolf-boy grew stronger under Little Elk Woman's care, and it seemed that in a matter of days he had grown taller, though perhaps it was only that his stature was beginning to catch up with his true age.

It was a time of rejoicing in the lands of the Shungmanitu. Although the coming of the *washichun* had made them seek refuge in the remotest parts of sacred hills, and there was little food, Ishnazuyai's people were not sad. Had not the chieftain's vision come to pass? The white boy, saved from some disaster understood only by other white men, spoke only the true speech; it seemed that his past had been buried forever.

It was only a matter of time before the rest of the prophecy would come true . . . that the boy would lead the wolf-peoples, red and white, toward some common destiny no one could yet understand.

That first night, the boy spoke as an infant might, gleefully pointing at objects and speaking their names.

The next morning, he was speaking as a young boy, always asking questions, full of himself, strutting in front of the other boys. One of his cousins made him a little bow, and he took to riding as though he had always been one of them. Ishnazuyai gave him a horse blanket for a saddle, and a beaded medicine bag that contained a bone from a kind of lizard-beast that no longer walked the earth. The treaty said that the Black Hills were no longer Indian land; but the Shungmanitu were good at being invisible. Days they rode down to the greasy grass places, not caring whether the white man had named these lands Dakota or Wyoming. The boy learned to shoot shafts of grass; but in a day or two he was already adept at the weapons of a man.

By the time the Moon of Wild Strawberries had waned to a half-moon, he was speaking as an adult, in measured cadences, using the correct terms of respect and kinship to all the members of the band. And he began to speak of visions.

As the days went by, the boy played with the other children in the village. There were not many other children; even in the old times the Shungmanitu had not been a populous nation, and now there were only a few bands. The games they played were ancient ones: a game of war, with grass blades for lances; a game of love, with a crudely hollowed twig as the love flute that copied the call of the woodpecker. The boy played well, and it was whispered that he would soon grow tall enough to court the *winchinchalas* and break their hearts. For though the boy was of a strange appearance, he was comely, and he was maturing so fast that the summer when he might challenge the war chief for dominance might not be as far off as it seemed.

One night, he told, with the male kinfolk and friends gathered in the tipi of Ishnazuyai, a story about how he had come to be. As he spoke, his eyes were half closed in remembrance, and he used many strange phrases to describe things difficult to imagine. But the men listened gravely, and the boys wide-eyed, as though it were an ancient myth like the tale of how they themselves had come to be. And outside, the girls and women whispered among themselves. One girl, who already loved him a little, crouched beside the closed tent flap and relayed what words she could.

This is the story that Shungmanitu Hokshila told:

I am a single body with many souls. There are evil men and good men within me, young and old, male and female and even *winkte*, man-woman. But I, the Wolf Boy, was here from the beginning, though I did not know my own name, nor the language of human beings. I watched as the others warred for mastery. One of them was a wolf-boy like myself; the others were all human, turning their back completely on the beast-nature in them. The *washichun* wolf-boy in me knew what he was, but he favored the beast, he favored the shadow, he did not know about me, for I was a watcher until now, and never spoke. He believed that only he was the true soul of this body, that only he was the man-beast. But the other souls had stolen from him compassion, and feeling, and love; and all that remained to him was hate, and the love of killing.

We were not always fractured. Once we were a single soul. But I am the only one who knows this. And I do not know why it happened. I think it was when the body was very young, imprisoned in a place where madmen go—for among the *washichun* those who see visions are deemed mad; the *washichun* do not believe in the reality of dreams, for they want all things in nature to be cold, concrete, soulless.

I did not know my name at first. I did not understand their language. Only when the moon was full, if the man-beast was in control of the body, could I understand some things. And then it was only in the language of night. I understood the keen scent of fear. I understood hunger. And sometimes lust. When the man-beast attacked his victims, I saw through his eyes sometimes.

Once or twice I tried to emerge. On a train, in Europe, which is the farthest country of the *washichun*, the man-beast was ripping a servant girl to pieces. I tried to ask the girl's pardon, for even then I knew that one should not kill for the sake of killing, but for sustenance. The prey comes willingly when he hears the call of the predator, if the prey is ready to be called. This girl was not ready. She did not heed me when I asked forgiveness. Later, the woman who was like a mother to me held me as I wept. She did not know it was I who wept, for I did not have her language and could not reveal myself. Another time, in a great city of the white men, the man-beast attacked a child who had sought refuge in a place sacred to Wakantanka. The man-beast was pitiless; it was I who felt his pity. I could not stop him except by dragging him away from consciousness; and it was a human child who gained control, and I wept my tears through him.

Can you understand these things I am saying? I am a broken circle, a shattered shield. Through you I will be whole.

For a long time I journeyed. I crossed the Great Sea. I traveled in an iron horse across the prairie. It was there that I heard the song of Ishnazuyai. It was there that I heard words whose meanings I half grasped, that seemed to surface from some dim remembrance. I heard the song of his flute in my dreams. It called to me like *siyótanka*, the flute of love. I embraced the empty air like a lover. *Hechitu welo!*

The wolf-*washichun* have come to take this land from you. They have come to piss on your ground and make it foul. They have come to eat the flesh of the Lakota and Cheyenne and Arapaho and Apsaroke, not because their flesh is ready to be eaten, but because they hunger to give pain. This is what I learned from them on the journey across the prairie. Though you cannot imagine why creatures would lust after the land itself, I tell you it is so. *Shiché lo!*

And in the song of Ishnazuyai's flute, this song that was the voice of love, I heard terrible things also. I heard the death songs of many Shungmanitu. I saw our people fractured and despairing, and old women dying in the snow. I saw winter lengthening with every year until there is only winter, eternal, desolate.

But also in the song I heard healing. The song drew me from the place I had hidden all these years. I heard words I never thought I would hear, and in time I fought the other wolf-boy and sent him away. One by one I will lead the other souls into the clearing. One by one I will make them part of myself, and we shall be whole. And my healing will be the healing of the whole nation of Shungmanitu. For even the evil wolf-boy, the one who lusts only for blood, even he will I draw into myself. There must be a common destiny for all Shungmanitu. The man-wolves from across the sea are also part of Wakantanka. They are also capable of compassion. I have seen it. I will lead all of you to a common place, and all of us will dance the moon dance together, the white and the red, the dark and the light.

And the circle will no longer be broken.

When Jake Killingsworth translated these words to Johnny, Johnny was afraid. "He wants to rub me out!" he said. He was cowering in the treehouse again.

Jake said, "He'll ask the old man to go on a vision quest. He's young for it, but the old man won't turn him down. He's a sacred thing to them Injuns, see, because he's the old man's vision come to life. The word made flesh, that's what the old preacher would of said."

"But he said he wanted to draw us into himself. I don't want to be a wild Indian, I want to go home to Speranza."

"He's goin' to heal us."

"I don't want to join up with Jonas Kay! I'll be thinking nothing but terrible things, and I'll always be angry."

Jake translated: "He says we's all goin' to be reborn. All of us—and all the Injuns—and the Count's people too."

"But if we're going to be reborn . . . doesn't this mean we have to die?"

Jake had no answer. But the Indian boy, drawing aside the veils of consciousness, allowed them to see the faces of the listeners. The Indian boy had ceased speaking, and now the men were discussing his words, each speaking in turn, measuring his words. Johnny wanted to flee. He was afraid of death. It was true that he wanted to be healed. But there was something he had to go through first, something he had to remember—something in the past—perhaps from the lunatic asylum—something about his mother.

"You have no mother!" It was a harsh whisper, and Johnny realized that Jonas had never gone away at all. Whatever it was, the Indian boy was going to lead them straight to it. And they were all going to face it together.

And die.

The tipi was crowded and murky, but in the eyes of the Indian werewolves there was hope.

6
The Black Hills
three-quarter moon, waning

THEY FLED FROM LEAD EASILY; THE LAW PAID NO HEED TO THEM. Speranza's clothes were now in shreds, but she did not mind shedding the last vestiges of her dignity, riding behind the boy through the darkness. For as they left the city, the odor of decay lifted; the forest was fragrant with the faint scent of pine, and distant water murmured from its depths.

It was hard, uphill riding. At dawn, Teddy tethered the horse next to a creek, and they continued on foot. It was steep, and the air bracing, even when the sun came out. The lodgepole pines grew thick here. After a while, her shoes felt stiff and confining, and she walked barefoot. The ground was springy, moist, spangled with aster, dwarf bramble, marigold, violets. Light dappled the forest floor through the treetops that swayed in the wind, and she stepped from warm to cool, cool to warm, from pools of shadow and fire.

This was not the forest of Speranza's dream. There had never been this fragrance. No, Speranza thought, there is awe here but not terror.

Teddy helped pull her up the last few ledges. She was a little afraid of him. There was always about him a certain melancholy, even when he smiled. He told her more about himself than she had known before, more, she imagined, than he had ever told anyone. When she heard of the death of Claude-Achille Grumiaux, she felt a sliver of icy fear, for she knew that the man had somehow figured in the machinations of the Count; the dispatches that Natalia Petrovna had sent to Vienna had mentioned his name.

They reached the cave. It was noon. As she entered, a young man rose to greet her. She started, for he exuded the wolf-scent she had learnt to recognize.

"Beggin' your pardon, ma'am," he said, "for I can't doff my hat to you; I lost it a long time ago." He was sandy-haired, a little gangly, but possessed of a certain breeding. She allowed him to kiss her hand. His lips were warm, like Hartmut's.

Teddy said, "We're going to find Johnny."

In her mind, Speranza saw the crucified child. She began to tremble.

"The Injuns who took him," said Teddy, "I know about them. When I lived with my ma in the Sioux village, they sometimes talked about another tribe high in the sacred hills. Called them *Shungmanitu Tanka*—the wolves. And I know the old Injun is one of them werewolves, like the folks in Winter Eyes, but there's something different about his people. They ain't crazy killers. I reckon they took Johnny because they didn't want him to turn out like his paw."

Scott said, "It'll be dangerous. I don't understand why you want to be subjecting this lady to danger."

"I'm not a lady anymore," Speranza said softly. "I was the Count's . . . whore." It was the first time she had ever thought of herself in those terms. She shuddered.

"No, ma'am," said the soldier. "You weren't never any man's . . . but I'm neglectin' my manners, not offering you food and drink." He led her to a makeshift couch of dried grass and wild bramble, and gave her coffee from a tin cup, and a piece of smoked rabbit to chew on. The floor of the cave was strewn with silver: shiny dimes and dollars, bracelets, a few shapeless lumps . . . and bullets. As she drank, he went on: "Believe me, ma'am, I know how they can pull a body into their world. They look into your eyes, ma'am, and you are gone, sucked in, damned afore you know it."

She knew him now. He was one of the ones who had attacked the town of Winter Eyes on their first day there. The one Natasha had recognized. "But . . . haven't you crossed over? To their side. I would have thought you would have become . . . one of them," she said.

"The boy's been helping me. But I don't know as how I'd hold out too long, if the Russian woman were to come a-looking for me."

"And you've been . . . killing wolves."

"Now and then."

"And . . . turning into one."

"As I said, the boy helps me." She looked at the silver strewn about and realized its twofold purpose. It could be made into bullets . . . and it could serve to inhibit Scott Harper's transformation. How long had he been fighting his true nature? As though divining her thoughts, Scott went on, "It's been this way ever since your little boy got himself stole, Miss Speranza. Almost two years. I'm fighting it, but I know I'm fixin' to lose this war mighty soon. The next time I set eyes on Natalia Petrovna . . ."

"I do not know if there is a cure," said Speranza, reaching for the envelope of coca powder she had secreted in her bosom, for she desired oblivion above all things, and a quick surcease from the continual pain within.

After a day and a night of seeing her, he couldn't help noticing her more and more. He hadn't seen a woman in such a long time. He hadn't dared slip into town like the boy; it was hanging if he got caught, and he didn't have the boy's knack for becoming invisible.

One time, late in the night, Teddy had hinted of things he could do to help ease Scott's want of a woman's companionship. But Scott had never been one for those kinds of games, and Teddy had never mentioned it again. And now that Speranza had come to them, Scott had something to think about beside the wolf-woman with the flaming hair. Speranza was not striking like Natasha, but Scott saw that she was capable of a deep, unwavering love. Though she had fled him, she still loved the Count; and she loved the boy Johnny more, he fancied, than most mothers love their own flesh and blood. She wanted to set off in search of him immediately. But first Teddy would have to go down to the Lakota village and see if someone knew how to find the place of the Shungmanitu. And they could not go in the days of the full moon. Sometimes, even when the moon wasn't quite full, he would feel the animal come on him, and he'd hunger for blood.

They were all three of them obsessed. Teddy's obsession, of course, was revenge: for his father's death, for the Chinawoman, for Zeke, even for his mother, though he had no proof of her death. Scott's was the Russian woman and the fear that she would push him over the edge of the abyss. That was why he helped Teddy's revenge all he could; by killing werewolves, perhaps he would be killing the werewolf part of himself too.

Speranza needed desperately to find that child; mayhap she felt it would relieve the pangs of conscience. Though she never told Scott the reason for her visit to Dr. Swanson, it was not difficult to guess. She'd killed part of herself too, he reckoned. They were strangely alike, this foreign governess and him, a plain soldier from Missouri.

He did not try to touch her; but in the night, lying half asleep, he was comforted by the sound of her breathing.

One morning, he told her, "I reckon Teddy's about due to come back from the Indian village."

"How can you tell?"

"Got my animal instincts, I guess," he said. His sense of smell was getting keen.

"Shall we go watch for him?" Speranza said.

They left the cave—he wanted to hold her hand but didn't dare—and Scott led her downhill a ways, to a rock ledge that overlooked a valley. He stopped to pluck a rabbit from a trap for their midday meal, resisted the impulse to crunch it down raw. They looked down. Then Scott saw the damnedest thing down in the valley—a line of wagons snaking around the side of the hill—horses, carts, mules, soldiers, too. Just oozing gently by, as though they were stopping to admire the scenery every few minutes. It reminded him of a caravan in an Arabian Nights story.

For a wild moment he thought he had been discovered. But no, this was nothing to do with him. They had to be visitors . . . dignitaries of some kind.

The whole convoy came to a halt. Tiny figures sprang out of the last of the wagons. They were setting up all sorts of equipment. Artists, perhaps even photographers, he thought. Newspapers. Tourists. Easterners.

"Who are they?" Speranza said. "I didn't think anyone traveled by covered wagon anymore."

"Don't rightly know," said Scott, "but I reckon it must be someone blamed important."

Teddy was hiding behind some bushes, waiting for them to pass. His horse was grazing by a wide stream. Curiously he watched the convoy go by.

He didn't know who they might be, but there were soldiers among them, and he didn't want to take any risks, so he stayed hidden. Why didn't they just move on? And so many people! There must have been a hundred, two hundred cavalry, and not dressed for fighting, either—their uniforms were clean, their buttons polished, their boots spotless. He crouched down as low as he could. By now Miss Speranza and Scott would probably be worried. He had to get to them with the information he had learned about the Shungmanitu. Before something happened to Johnny.

If only they would move!

A shouted order in the distance, and they all stopped. He crept up closer. There were photographers rushing about, and tables were being set up for an outdoor feast. He could smell a pig roasting, and his stomach growled.

He came a little closer. A cook, wearing a white apron and a high cook's hat, was directing other cooks. There was a roaring fire, and the pig was on a spit, and they were butchering up some other meat too. His mouth was watering. There was a table, almost in arm's reach, piled high with meat pies. Lord, the smell was sending him to heaven.

No one was looking. He dashed from the bush to the table. A fold of the tablecloth hid him. It was real lace. Was anyone looking? He couldn't wait anymore. He reached a hand out, felt along the lace until he reached the edge of the platter—fine porcelain, he thought, wondering at the smooth texture of it against his fingertips—when—

The next thing he knew, he was being dragged out. A fat cavalryman had picked him up, was holding him by the scruff, looking him beadily in the eye. "We hang thieves hereabouts, boy—you know that?"

"I ain't but a poor hungry breed, sir—"

Wild-eyed, he looked about. There were several soldiers now, and they were laughing at him. He struggled. The fat soldier laughed. Then he saw someone he recognized, leaning against the next wagon, munching on one of the meat pies—

"Hey—Buffler Bill!—it's me, Teddy Grumiaux—the news butch on the Cheyenne-Omaha—you knows me, Bill!"

Buffalo Bill looked up from his pie. A tall, dour-faced Indian who was standing beside him shrugged.

"You know this sumbitch, Bill?" said the fat soldier.

Bill nodded and the fat soldier sighed, dropped Teddy on his behind, and went off. Teddy ran up to Bill and thanked him.

"You're lucky I never forget a face," said Buffalo Bill. "Now, go over to that table and help yourself to some food—and look like you belong here, by God, or you'll be spending the night suspended from the nearest tree." Teddy was about to dash back to the pies when Bill added, "And fetch one for Sitting Bull, too."

When he came back, the old Indian said, "*Pilamaya,*" and began to eat methodically. He was wearing a full-scale war bonnet, Teddy saw, though there seemed to be no occasion for it, and the feathers were dyed in gaudy colors, so that they looked more like plumes from a duchess's hat than something a brave would wear. The Indian must have noticed Teddy's grimace, because he said, in Lakota, "Yes, *chinkshi*, things have changed since the days of Little Big Horn. I have been forced to—ah, how do the *washichun* say it—'sell out'—become a creature in a circus, an entertainment. To live is a burden, yet I seem to lack the honor to die well. *Hechitu welo!*"

Startled, Teddy said in Lakota, "You are the Tatanka Yotanka whose great vision destroyed General Custer—"

The Indian set his face into a mask. But Buffalo Bill nodded. "What brings you here, son? Last I knew, you'd been blown to kindgom come in that train robbery."

"Well, I reckon I lived through it."

"Livin' off the land, eh, boy? Marchin' on your stomach like old Napoleon used to?"

Teddy smiled. "Could I take a couple more of them pies?"

"They wouldn't be for some companions you got concealed in them hills, would they?"

Teddy nodded, and, seeing that no one seemed to object, began gathering up more pies and stuffing them in his shirt. He knotted it to keep them from spilling out the front, for he had but two buttons left on the old thing, though it was made of good linen.

"But before you go, my lad, I sure think you ought to meet your host," Bill said.

And before he could protest, Buffalo Bill and Sitting Bull marched Teddy over to where the photographers were. Their subject, who was drinking a glass of wine as he reclined in a leather armchair, was a portly middle-aged fellow with a white mustache and sideburns. Beside him sat generals and other high-ranking cavalry officers, and they were being served wine and tea by menservants all dressed in white. There was a man in a uniform who kept setting off flares for the photographers.

"Ah, Cody," said the portly man to Buffalo Bill. "I'm so sorry you have to leave us so soon . . . but I suppose that Wild West Circus of yours can't take care of itself; still, it's been a pleasure to have you visit with us." He noticed Teddy for the first time and peered at him; the boy was so unnerved that he dropped his meat pie. He immediately dropped down on all fours and started looking for it—and another pie started to push out through his trouser fly. "And who might this young man be?" said the portly gentleman. "I must say he is very eager to eat."

Remembering himself, Teddy said, "I'm Theodore Grumiaux, sir; it's a pleasure to make your acquaintance." He bowed.

"Good name, that," said his host. He beamed. Everyone looked very pleased with himself.

Boldened, Teddy said, "And who might you be, sir?"

"Why, my boy, my name's Arthur, Chester Arthur. I'm the President of these United States."

Teddy laughed. "Well, ain't that somethin'!" he said, for he knew that no president would ever come this far west.

That set the old man laughing, and presently the whole company was laughing too, and it started to dawn on Teddy that this man might really be the President, for all he knew; and he started to get red in the face, for he couldn't see how he could talk his way out of his mistake.

At length, there was a silence, and the President said, "Now mark my words, friends; this is the stuff Americans should be made of. This boy doesn't know me from Adam—he demands proof positive. He wants facts, not illusions. Why, this sort of no-nonsense is the very backbone of our country!" Applause all around, though Teddy himself became very confused. The President went on (quaffing his wine the while), "I will tell you, then,

my boy, that I am journeying toward an historic rendezvous—a
meeting with the chief of the Shoshone tribe in Yellowstone, in the
Montana Territory. It will be the first time ever that the First
Citizen of this Great Land of Ours"—you could hear the capital
letters when he talked—"has ever made a State Visit to the Leader
of one of the Native Tribes. Mark my words, it will go down in
history! And you, my lad, were there!"

But Teddy was more worried about getting back to Speranza
and Scott, and about finding Johnny before it was too late. He
began to look about for a way to escape. Nevertheless, the
President continued in that vein for some time, finally remarking
that several entrepreneurs, knowing that Buffalo Bill was in the
area, had come to hear from the horse's mouth the secrets of
running a Wild West Show. "The country will be swarming with
them come 1890," said the President, "but by then our friends
here will doubtless be entertaining in the courts of Europe." He
looked up. "Ah, here come some of the entrepreneurs I was
speaking of. . . ."

Two or three gentlemen, all dressed to the teeth, were striding
toward the group from behind the nearest wagon.

Teddy froze in sudden terror. He recognized the man in front.

Cordwainer Claggart! Laughing and smiling and carrying on
like a proper gentleman! After what he'd done! Did no one know
what he did to helpless, naked girls? He felt such a torrent of
loathing, he feared he might attack Claggart in the midst of this
company. But Claggart had not seen him, could not possibly
expect to see him. . . .

They had all gone on to talking of other things now. He was
invisible again. He had to leave! Suddenly he realized that
Claggart was looking at him strangely. Not quite believing, his
eyes, perhaps.

Then Claggart was striding toward him, trying to get a closer
look.

He seized as many pies as he could and bolted to where his
horse was, and he rode uphill, never looking back.

7
Winter Eyes
crescent moon, waning

COUNT FRANZ MARIA HARTMUT SEVERIAN ENESCU VON BÄCHL-Wölfing lay, twisting and turning, on the bed. Servants ran hither and thither, fetching cold compresses, leeches, and possets. In the confusion, Natalia Petrovna was able to enter his suite unannounced. She ordered the servants away. "I shall tend to him myself," she said. They obeyed her instantly. How she despised the servants.

She came to him bearing a tray on which there were jars of leeches, an ointment made of essence of wolfsbane, diluted and fixed with gum arabic, a tincture of iodine, a pot of freshly brewed tea in which she had poured a liberal soupçon of vodka. She sat beside him, looking at his anguished face. How she despised him, too; she tried not to feel it, but she knew he could smell it in her, for he growled faintly.

"You act as though I'm already dead," he said. "I can hear the clockwork ticking in your mind. You're thinking of my successor—"

"Hartmut, Hartmut, how could you be so cruel to me?" She touched his brow, the human furrows crisscrossed with spiky fur. But of course, she knew that he understood her perfectly.

The Count stirred as she stroked his forehead. It was so hot with fever that she almost recoiled, but she knew that she must do it. She smiled at him, trying to recall the time she first ensnared his affections. With her other hand, she began to untie the strings of his silken nightshirt. "Do you not still love me?" she whispered to him. And touched the chest, mottled by patches of wolf's hide. "We are alike now, wounded, disfigured, creatures of the in-between." Her hand descended to explore his body, racked with fever. There were tufts of wolf hair everywhere. "So low have you fallen . . . so different you are from the Hartmut who turned my head and made me give up being human!" And she kissed him, gently, three times, above the eyebrows, knowing that her kisses were painful to him, for the flesh was scarring.

"You think I'm going to die, don't you?" he said.

She smiled again, and climbed on top of him, and rocked herself gently back and forth. "I will lock you inside myself," she said, "and you won't be able to pull free, and I will bear your child."

"It's three months past the time of denning," said Hartmut. For wolves only conceive in April.

"Are we slaves to nature, or its masters?" said Natasha, loosening the strands that held together her whalebone corset, thrusting to the floor the veil that hid the patch of wolf fur on her cheek. Teasingly, she began to push up his nightshirt. She could feel the throb of his penis through the layers of silk and calico, and she knew that in his weakened state he could not resist his own nature. She could smell his desire, penetrating the rank odor of sickness and medicine that hung in the air of the bedchamber.

"Speranza," said the Count, almost inaudibly.

She slapped his face. And tore at the nightshirt, pounding, howling, sniffing the humid crevice of his buttocks. "Don't speak that name! It is I who am the queen bitch, I, Natalia Petrovna Stravinskaya." She thought: I must take no pleasure in this! I am doing this for power alone, for nothing but power. If I carry the leader's whelp in my womb, no one will dare question that I am the queen wolf, and if Hartmut dies it will be I who choose whom I will look on with favor—and who will rule until my son comes of age.

She tried to make herself feel no passion, no joy. But the smell of lust was in her nostrils. He was bringing out the heat in her, even though the season was wrong for it. I must not show him love! she thought. I will conceive this child in anger and loathing! But, as she felt him rive her, as she rode above him, twirling herself like a stunt rider . . . she found herself squeezing him, wringing him, laughing wildly, mockingly, as he lay in the grip of instinct, incapable of reason. . . .

There came a knock at the door.

"*Euer Gnaden . . . Ihr habt Besuch . . . sehr dringend. . . .*"

Those damnable servants! Could they not understand? The Count and she were locked in her bitch's grip, they could not see anybody now. . . .

"You peasant! You indiscreet wretch!" she screamed.

The manservant had entered the chamber. But he only bowed to the Count, not bothering to acknowledge the presence of Natasha at all. Indeed, he hardly looked at the two of them; he had been in the Count's employ long enough to have learned utter discretion. But he slipped over to a closet and selected a quilt—one of those primitive but warm American things—and arranged it discreetly over them, so that Natasha appeared not to be there at all; and he lifted the Count's head and placed three goose-down pillows behind it so as to lend him some semblance of dignity.

"I am sorry, Your Grace," he said. "I told him you could not be disturbed, but he does not have much time."

From somewhere outside, Natalia Petrovna could smell tobacco; and behind that odor, the smell of a male wolf . . . but not one she could recognize. Not an inhabitant of Winter Eyes. She thought: Perhaps it is a long-lost member of the Lykanthropenverein, who has only now managed to take ship from Europe and arrive in Winter Eyes. But why then the urgency?

She huddled beneath the blanket, waiting for her vagina to loosen. The Count had not yet ejaculated; she would have to wait until this visitor departed before she could try again.

There! It had loosened enough for her to pry herself away! Carefully she wriggled around so that she was able to peer up, unnoticed, from a corner of the blanket. She knew that the visitor, if a wolf, would be able to sense her presence. But the norms of propriety must be observed at all costs, especially in front of those of their kind. She knew the Count would brook no embarrassment.

The smell of tobacco grew stronger. Then she saw that it came from an Indian pipe, a long stone thing decorated with feathers, that was being carried into the room on a platter. The servant set down the pipe. Behind him was an Indian.

The man was tall, old, perhaps, though it was difficult to tell his age. Long white hair came down in braids from beneath an elaborate war bonnet of intricate beadwork. He was dressed in all the finery of his people; his leggings and his buckskin shirt were hung with scalps and ornamented with glass beads from Prague and Vienna and Dresden. The servant fetched him a chair, and as he sat down, Natasha wondered whether he had already seen her. But he said nothing.

And now, as she stared at him, as she sniffed the air to separate out his private scent from the myriad other odors in the chamber, she realized that she knew who he was. And so did the Count. This was the old man who had come to the Sioux encampment in the midst of the raid . . . who had stolen the Count's child . . . who had fought off the werewolves with a bizarre urinary magic. Why had he come? He was outnumbered here, and without the power of the moon he was surely weakened and vulnerable.

She felt Hartmut sit up. She could sense the tension in the air. It was intolerable. She knew that the old man must know of her presence; how could he not? But still he ignored her; she did not know whether it was from courtesy or irony.

He spoke through an interpreter, one of the servants who had taught himself the language, and who translated into stilted German: "You have brought fear to this land. You have brought bloodshed. We do not seek these things. Why have you done this to us, our brothers? Lo, I have come to seek you, at great danger to myself, for the *washichun* are everywhere. I come to seek a truce. I have your child, and I know that he is a great seer, and that he means to forge a new path for both our peoples."

This, then, was the lair of the enemy. There was a womansmell in the air, though Ishnazuyai saw no female. Of course, it would not do have one present at a ceremonial smoking of the pipe. At least the enemy had the courtesy to hide its women rather than commit so blatant a transgression against the rules of polite conduct.

He had come expecting a powerful presence. They had met once before, after all, when the *washichun* wolves had come sweeping down on that village. It had taken a supreme effort for him to fight their leader then, but now, he saw, he lay wounded, in pain, and was perhaps dying. He had been hurt by the gleaming metal the *washichun* called silver—the moon-metal. The Shungmanitu did not possess this metal, but they had heard that men in the southern deserts knew of it, and that there were coyote-men in those lands who likewise could be injured by the moon-metal; but nothing had prepared the wise man for the way silver could ravage a body. The man was in constant pain, though he strove not to show it; the two shapes warred with one another, and patches of bloody fur seemed to erupt out of the human skin. His eyes were dulled, his complexion gray as a man who is laid out to die and who waits for the wind and the rain to take his spirit to the land of many tipis. Yet he was not laid on a scaffold open to the forces of nature; he was confined to this bed, in this unnatural tipi with its hard walls, the wood polished and scraped until the life was bled from it, the air stale and dank.

Yet, when Ishnazuyai spoke of the boy, his eyes took on a sudden shine, and Ishnazuyai knew how much this man loved the child, and was moved to wonderment by that, for he had thought them creatures wholly without pity.

The Count mumbled something and the servant translated, "You have the boy . . . that is good."

"I have brought tobacco, and a pipe," said Ishnazuyai. "Let there be peace between us until the boy has had his vision." He waited for the translation. "Then perhaps he will show us the way. There is enough territory for all of us."

To the consternation of the servants, he squatted on the floor. The rug was disturbing in its unwonted softness, but he tried to accommodate himself to the strange surroundings without complaint. He lit the pipe and smoked, facing in turn the four corners of the universe. Then he lifted it up to the bed, saying, "May the smoke, mingled with our breath, be fragrant to Wakantanka as it rises to the ends of the world."

And he held out the pipe, waiting.

And the Count raised his hand weakly to take the pipe, seeming to draw comfort from Ishnazuyai's words.

She could bear it no longer. She threw aside the quilt and turned to Hartmut. "How can you listen to him?" she cried. "He's come to pollute the destiny that you and Szymanowski saw for our family—to taint our nobility with savagery!" The translator began faithfully to repeat her words in the Lakota tongue, but she told him to hold his peace. "This is between me and His Grace," she said sulkily.

"Hush, Natasha," said Hartmut weakly. "How we must look to him! Is this the nobility you speak of?"

"He's using the child of that Whitechapel whore of yours—to turn you from your purpose! This is our country now, Hartmut! That lunatic whelp is no messiah—he's a mad, helpless boy, no

more—neither one of us nor one of *them*. And that Franco-Italian
creature you pinned your hopes on—*si, la speranza che delude
sempre!*—she has betrayed you—she has killed her own children.
Don't think I don't know that!"

She looked around her. Her outburst had confused the servants,
but Hartmut was wrong to think she lacked dignity. Her very fury
lent her a certain magnificence. She threw her hair back, pulled
the blanket up over her bosom that threatened to overwhelm her
half-laced corsets. She was beautiful. She knew that even the
ridge of wolf flesh on her cheek did not detract from her
appearance; even the old savage was not unmoved by the aroma of
eroticism she gave out—she sniffed his arousal amid the smell of
fear from the servants.

But the Count only smiled—the barest ghost of a smile—and
took the peace pipe, and took a quick puff from it, and handed it
back to the old man.

And said, very faintly, "There will be peace between us—"
Natasha stiffened.
"So long as my son is safe."

When the Indian was gone, she cried out: "No! Forget your son!
I, I will squeeze a new son from your loins—even if I cause your
death!"

Weary, the Count said, "I am vulnerable to him. He has what
is precious to me. Be patient, Natasha! They are savages, true, but
they have been here for a thousand years, and we have not!"

"Is this the Hartmut without pity, Hartmut the heartless hunter,
Hartmut stealer of souls? I loved that Hartmut—loved him enough
to cast aside my humanness—I am all wolf!—and you, Hartmut,
who should be more wolf than any other wolf—you are becoming
as weak-willed as a human being."

He tried to send her away, but she began to kiss him on the
forehead, the cheeks, the eyelids, at last the mouth, loving the
carnivorous fetor of his breath. She crouched above him, scratching at his chest, lapping at his wounds. The blood was warming,
tingling. She pounced upon him, pinning him down, playfully
biting at him, sniffing the pungent creases of his drawers. "I will
love you the way you love to be loved," she said, in a low voice
edged with silvery death, "I will love you the way no human bitch
can love you . . . see, see, I taste your genitals, I lick the pus

from your torn flesh . . . I scratch you with my claws, I wrap your nose in my pussy . . . you cannot flee this love, my love. . . ."

The Count turned his face away, demurring. But she knew that within that aristocratic aesthete's mind was another mind, darker and more bestial, and that intellect must perforce give way to instinct.

8
The Black Hills
one day before full moon

DAWN. HE HAD BEEN IN THE WILDERNESS FOR MANY DAYS NOW. HE had not eaten in all that time; now and then, thirsting, he crouched on all fours and lapped up chill water from the creek. He no longer knew where he was going. But the air had become thin in the past few days, and he knew he would soon reach the summit of the world. Gray crags towered over the canopy of pine. Sunlight streamed down on him; sometimes the wind burned like the breath of the white men's iron horse; sometimes it was cold.

The wind blew constantly, but the wolf-boy, though he wore nothing but a breechclout, revelled in the bitterness of it. I am part of the wind, he thought, I am sprung from tree and rock.

Uphill he ran. His feet were the wings of the eagle. Over a distant peak, a gray storm raged; but he could barely hear the thunder. Uphill he ran. And in his mind, inside the forest he had made for himself, he ran too. In the world outside, he climbed steep rocks that bordered on a creek that tumbled down toward the land of men with a sound of men laughing and women ululating over the victories and deaths of their kinsmen. In the world within, the stream was sluggish, and he could smell blood in it. But he knew he must find its source. The source of both streams. For both streams came forth out of the Great Mystery.

The source of the stream in the world outside would be at the roof of the world, the place where the fragrance of many pipes mingled and were pleasing to the Great Mystery. The source of the stream in the forest within was something dark, something to be feared. But he must overcome that fear. The others cowered in the forest, each one alone with his fear; they would never be united as long as they were afraid.

I have come, the wolf-boy told the others. Never be afraid again. Not even you, the dark wolf whom I vanquished. Even you are part of this soul; we are each other, mirror images in the stream.

The wolf-boy wandered, seeking the dream. He knew they would all have to dream before he could return to the village. They would all have to dream the same dream. Even the dark one would have to dream it. And even the dark one, whose fear was greater by far than that of all the others, though he never showed fear, even he would have to step into the circle of light.

Claggart had been tracking the crazy Indian for two days, since he spied him coming north from the direction of Winter Eyes. Bumping into the President's party, with its dozens of pack mules, its scores of curious cavalrymen, its photographers and journalists, had been a damned shame. But he had hung around, just enough to appear respectable; he had had the opportunity to practice some old tricks he hadn't used since his train-travelling days; and he had picked up a good many tips on how to run a travelling show from Cody, all the while siphoning his hard-earned eagles into his own pocket. By God, he told himself, I can outcharlatan any mountebank on the market, even the world's most famous.

But he had to find the Indian again. It was easy enough to find the trail. This fellow had the mysterious habit of relieving himself every fifty or sixty paces, and his piss had got to be the rankest in all of Custer County. Even after two days it stunk up the dwarf brambles so bad he near choked on it once or twice.

There was another clue, too—the old man had him this habit of playing an old flute of a night, and the sound carried for miles; if you listened carefully, you could hear it among the cries of the night birds and the songs of insects and the chittering of little furry creatures, weaving in and out, harmonizing with the murmuring forest. It was Injun love music, but the chief wasn't after no squaw. Probably just thinking of the past, Claggart thought, chuckling as he cradled his own engine of pleasure through the lining of his Levi's pockets.

Deeper and deeper into the hills he followed him. Into land he didn't know. Toward sundown, and he was stopping in a clearing to skin and spit a big rabbit he'd just shot, and to water his horse. Soon it would be night. The air was getting chilly, unpleasant, as he squatted down in the clearing on a bed of twigs and damp leaves. The horse seemed jumpy; maybe it was from the weight of the saddlebags, with their weapons and their silver chains. Claggart wasn't sure how much of the old wives' tales to believe, but he wasn't taking any chances. He had wolfsbane, too—purchased from a pharmacist every bit as quackish as he'd been himself in his snake oil dealing days—and garlic and crosses and everything known to be proof against any supernatural creature that prowled the night. Just insurance, he told himself.

In case the boy turned out to be everything he hoped.

Silver fetters to chain a gold mine!

Somewhere a wolf howled. At first he thought it might be one of those Indian signals, and he reached for his Smith and Wesson.

But he wasn't afraid. This wasn't Indian country anymore—it belonged to the miners, and besides, he had enough guns and ammunition in his saddlebags to kill an army of crazy old drunken Indians. And there were no more Indians in the hills, not since they had given up their sacred land and moved to the bleak reservation to make room for human beings.

No hordes of hostiles! No, just a rogue Indian with a kidnapped boy. Probably his bumboy, Claggart thought, as he stoked his fire and roasted his rabbit. And a damn sight better than pronging an Appaloosa mare, as I can figger from experience.

As he gnawed on a rabbit leg, he wondered why this Indian had gone rogue like that. There were any number of reasons it could have happened. Mayhap he had shamed his tribe by cowardice or tupped the big chief's daughter or stolen the wrong horse—Indians got themselves worked up over the peculiarest things. And what had possessed him to go steal a little white boy?

Claggart listened. Stopped chewing for a moment.

Damned if it wasn't that flute again, and nearer too. Just beyond the edge of the clearing.

He looked up and the old man was there. Of course—the rabbit—he'd come thinking to win himself a haunch of the rabbit, looking for hospitality, Indian style!

"*Hau,*" said the old man in greeting. There wasn't a hint of enmity in his face. But his eyes glowed a weird kind of a yellow color, and Claggart couldn't put his trust in anyone that acted so friendly. A rich Injun, Claggart thought, appraising the beadwork on the shirt; must've been a heap big chief in his younger days. But now he's just a derelict drunkard, come a-beggin' for a bite of my rabbit.

I shouldn't have followed him so secret-like, Claggart thought. Why, he don't know what I aims to do. Thinks I'm just a lone trapper.

In the firelight, through the smoke veil, the eyes glittered.

"Come on," Claggart said, holding out a piece of rabbit. "Come on, boy, here, boy . . . eat." Injuns is just like dogs, he thought, and tossed him the bone, half expecting the old man to pounce on it like an animal—

The blur of smoke . . . a quick movement . . . the old man was chewing meat and spitting out the bone.

"Why, I don't believe my eyes!" Claggart said. "You is limber as a young he-wolf." And he motioned the man to sit down by the fire. And poured him a shot of whiskey in a tin cup. "Here, old man . . . nothing like a bellyful of minee-wackun to dull your wits and make you talk. . . ."

"*Washté,*" said the Indian courteously. Trusting, so trusting! Pulled out something from his shirt—one of them peace pipes! thought Claggart—with eagle feathers all a-dangle—and proffered it. Claggart accepted, knowing that the Injun would never dream he'd double-cross him after smoking with him.

He waited until the Indian had drunk. And poured him another and another. "Can't believe the way you're holdin' down that licker," he said. "Never did see an Injun as could infibulate more'n a jigger of whiskey without stompin' and whoopin' and carryin' on." He was swaying a little . . . or was it because the moon, almost full, had oozed out from behind a bank of clouds? "Hey, chief—wantum more?" he said, cackling at his own parody of the trader pidgin lingo. "Wantum heap more? You takeum!"

As the Indian drank, his eyes grew mistier, less sinister. At last Claggart decided to ask him about the boy. "You're probably wondering why I'm a-wanderin' all alone in these here hills," he said. "Well, it ain't to enjoy the fresh air. I'm a-looking for a kid . . . a lost kid . . . my son," he said. His eyes narrowed as he searched for a convincing story. "Lost him in a train wreck. Yes . . . *that* train wreck . . . for to be sure, I recognize you, and . . ."

To be on the safe side, he pointed his revolver at the Indian. To his astonishment, the Indian showed no alarm at all, but merely waved his flute and smiled. Damn fool! Was he spoiling for a gunfight, a Schofield-Smith and Wesson against a cedarwood stick? Claggart had a mind to weigh him down with lead right then and there. It would be a quick release for the surging in his loins that always came now when he could taste death in the wind. But an old man's death would not be a sweet release . . . not like the slow death of a pretty young girl.

Claggart smiled, remembering the girl in Lead who had died right in the arms of that wrinkled madam. And blaming the death on the kid . . . delicious knavery! Laughing, he took a deep swig of his whiskey and jabbed his gun in the old man's ribs. "Start talking," he said. "I sure do miss that son of mine, and I will surely give you a fine *re*-ward for information that might lead to his recovery; and I will just as surely, if you don't talk, blow your fool Injun head off of your fool Injun shoulders."

"Him not your son," said the man . . . Just like one of them stage Injuns! Claggart thought . . . could it be he's just a-playin' at being a dumb drunk Injun, and he reckons he'll scalp me soon as I turns my back? "No, him not your son . . . him son of sky-spirit . . . son of earth . . . no man's son."

"Jesus-a-mighty!" Claggart laughed. "You sound like one of them travellin' preachers on the train who used to break wind from their mouths of a Sunday."

"Shiniché lo!" the Indian said angrily. *"Nichinkshi shni!"*

"We'll see about that," said Claggart, and reached out, casually, to put his arm in a stranglehold around his neck. The love flute bounced into the fire. It began to char. "I'll snap you in two like a twig," he said, "if you don't tell me more!" But to his astonishment, the Indian seemed remarkably resistant, especially considering he didn't look any more powerful than a mangy old mutt. His neck was rigid as steel, and now he'd closed his eyes and was muttering one of those heathen incantations. In a burst of anger he tried to push the Indian over but they ended up rolling in the dirt, like squabbling boys.

"Boy sacred," said the old Indian. And twisted free and shook himself like a dog after pissing. He went back to the fire and, incredibly, started to gnaw on another piece of rabbit meat. "You cannot touch him. Big destiny."

"I'll tell you what his destiny is, you old fool," he said. A wild thought struck him. Perhaps this man himself was . . . Claggart took a length of silver chain out of his saddlebag and lashed the Indian across the face. . . .

The Indian screamed! Dropped down on all fours, and started to howl. Claggart thrashed him again . . . there were welts now, oozing a reddish-black liquid . . . and a familiar smell. "Why, old man, you've gone and pissed yourself," Claggart said, chuckling as he bound the Indian with the chain.

The old man snarled. "Use moon-metal . . ." he gasped. Of course, thought Claggart, there ain't much silver in this here territory; mayhap this wolf-man don't know about its power over him. . . .

A bristle or two popped out of the Indian's cheek, and his skin was peeling. There was raw flesh around one eyeball. Claggart watched, fascinated, at the network of cracks that fanned out, spiderweblike, from the places where the silver had cut. "Moon-metal . . . good name for it, old man," he said. "Now, tell me where the boy is, or you'll get another taste of it."

"*Hanblécheya,*" the old man said. There was a deep growling in his voice.

"Don't give me no Injun talk."

"Him . . . go . . . seek . . . vision."

So the boy had gone on a vision quest! Turned into a savage himself! So much the better.

"Well, old man, I'm a-tellin' you, I've had a vision too. A vision of me and that boy . . . a vision of a mountain of gold stretchin' up high into the sky. I've been a charlatan and a mountebank, and I've lately discovered me a yen for killin' helpless women; I've gained and lost many a fortune, but I ain't ashamed to say that I wants something bigger and gaudier and better than I done possessed previous to now. I got me a dream too, old man." Eyes stared dully at him, eyes once yellow, clouding to the hue of curdled milk. "Bill Cody thought of it first, but ain't I the one for stealin' an idea and makin' it ten times grander! He gots his leapin' wild Injuns, his rodeo riders, his gunslingers o' the feminine persuasion, his dancin' grizzlies. But I'm a-gettin' me somethin' better . . . somethin' out of the dark side . . . somethin' plucked out o' the very arms of Satan hisself . . . I'm a-gettin' me a wolf-boy! Oh, I seen the signs o' the lycanthropic condition all over that there boy. And I believes in witchcraft and vampires and all them things, just as much as I disbelieves in the teachin's of preachers and missionaries, 'cause I knows they is all as full of deception as me, a cardsharp and a snake-oil merchant. I knows that when you strips away the skin of a man, be it white or red or black, beneath it lies the same color and it is dark, my friend, darker than the darkness o' hell, it is twisted and consumed with sin . . . we's all of us children of darkness . . . but I knows my own darkness, and I believes in my own darkness, and I believes that the darkness is one day goin' to overwhelm the light."

With the tip of a knife, he gingerly pried loose a segment of the Indian's cheek. It sizzled a little in his hand, and a fine mess of bristles covered it, like a hogskin. The skin pulsated; it was still endowed with life. Cordwainer Claggart breathed in deeply the fragrance of burning cedarwood. The Indians worshipped pain; that must be why this old man had not even cried out.

"The boy, the boy!" Cordwainer said, remembering the train journey of two years before as though it had been but a moment ago. "I seen the fine silvery hair as covers him. I heared his voice change from a boy's voice to the bark of an animal. I done some studyin' on his strange behavior on that train journey . . . and, by God, your reaction to my silver fetters proves that you and him is the same species of creature . . . spawned from the loins of the evil one . . . belched out of the butthole of the yawnin' darkness! Oh, I knows you and all your kind, I knows it well! I've been a-studyin' and a-learnin', and a-spyin' on that town of Winter Eyes . . . and damned if I don't discover that there's Injun werewolves as well as the white-skinned variety! Well listen up good, my friend, because I plans to kill you real soon, and to enjoy every minute of it . . . I ain't never killed no supernatural thing before, and I intends to study your death with the utmost diligency."

Again he made a few perfunctory cuts on the old man's face. It was like engraving the name of a loved one on the bark of a tree that had stood unmolested for a century in a dark forest. The Indian moaned a little, but seemed past caring. He seemed to be singing a little song to himself; maybe a death song, Claggart thought. The words came wheezing from his throat, and with his limited knowledge of the lingo, Claggart understood little of it. Maybe it was a warning, though; maybe the boy was nearby. He couldn't take any chance. With a certain regret, Claggart forced the old man's mouth open, pulled out the tongue—it was slippery as a wet snake—and sliced it off. There was a lot of blood, and a kind of gurgling sound, as if some of the blood was pouring down his lungs. Claggart tossed the tongue into the fire, which flared up. It smelled good.

"I means to have that boy for my very own, old man. Mayhap you thinks he's your son. Mayhap that rich Count thinks he's the father of the wolf-boy. But neither of you knows what I knows: neither of you knows he is truly born of the darkness. Because I truly know it, I alone can claim him kin, and I alone can be his father on earth, in place of his father in hell."

But the fool kid had gone off on one of those vision quests! It would be easy enough to find him. He would use the old man as a kind of bait. That's why he couldn't kill him just this minute . . . or the stink would filter through the forest and provide a warning signal. "Nasty wound on your tongue, that," he said. "Ought to be cauterized." He wondered whether the fire was hot enough to melt a little silver, and whether he could pour it down the old man's throat without killing him all at once. . . .

"Thank you for escort, Major Sanderson," said Natalia Petrovna Stravinskaya as the major helped her from her horse. "I will not soon forget your kindness." What a contemptible man this Sanderson was! And yet he has his uses, Natasha thought, as she gathered her cloak about her shoulders against the encroaching night. There was mist in the mountain, and they had ridden hard in the hot sun, and now the chill came suddenly with twilight.

Sanderson bowed and smiled—a twisted smile, a graceless parody of those debonair military officers she had so frequently encountered in the Imperial guards in Austria. "It's my duty," he said—again, that forced gallantry—"to be at the service of our settlers—especially one of such rarefied beauty as yourself."

She gave him her hand to kiss. The moon was almost full; already her features were being bent toward savagery, and her wide eyes were wild. "You understand, Major, why our mission must be of utmost secrecy. . . ."

"I must confess, madam, that I am somewhat in ignorance of your wishes; the urgency of your message, and the delicacy with which you phrased certain . . . ah . . . issues, was what persuaded me to escort you into the hills. As to what liberties you will allow with your person. . . ." Why, he was positively quivering with anticipation, the animal!

"Later, Major Sanderson. Now . . . I must confess to you . . . terrible secrets."

He moved closer to her. He smelled of dead flesh, of suppurating sores . . . she knew that beneath the Stetson that he now affected lay the gangrenous memento of a previous encounter with the savages. Oh, he was not beautiful, not like that officer who had fled the army to become the avowed enemy of the werewolves, who was going to become a wolf himself, who could not come to terms with his own nature.

She did not want to see him; instead, she gazed at the mountains stained with the myriad hues of sunset, crisscrossed by pine trees' shadows. She tried to find the scent of the boy on the wind; there was a trace of it, to be sure, but it was so muted that even her attenuated sense of smell could barely distinguish it among the million odors of the forest. He had masked his scent somehow—she knew it! Perhaps he had even refrained from marking territory . . . though she did not know how he could have gone so much against instinct.

"The terrible secrets . . ." said the major, persistent as only a human could be.

"The Count is dying."

"So I'd heard, Natasha. Will someone else take his place?"

"He and Indian wolves have declared a truce."

The major cogitated for a moment, scowling. She continued: "It's because of the boy."

"Boy?"

"A bastard son of the Count's. In a way, he was the reason Count agreed to Szymanowski's plan to emigrate to America. A new kind of child, a new land—you see?"

"Not quite. . . ."

"Not quite! He is not quite one of us!"

He thought about it. "A sort of breed, then, ma'am, I take it. I dislike breeds, as you know, and would willingly exterminate them all from the face of the earth."

"The Count has lived long time for the sake of a fantasy . . . it is that the child will be redeemer, a bridge between man and beast . . . not long ago, it was learned that the child did not die when captured by savages two years ago, but has lived among them, and now is regarded by *les sauvages* also as a kind of messiah . . . earlier this month, one of the *Indiens peaux-rouges* themselves came into Winter Eyes to seek an audience with the Count . . . what temerity!" The major tsk-tsked sympathetically.

"We have learnt that the Indians, too, see the child as a special creature. Do you not see? It has awakened in the Count his old love for the child, and his old visions, his old dreams. . . ."

Major Sanderson looked at the forest floor. Leaves swirled about his feet. "Madam, I have dedicated my life to subjugating the red man," he said, flushing with pride at this explication of his most cherished ideals, "and it is distressing to see that one whom I thought might be my ally might rather join with the forces of barbarism. . . ."

She said: "There is only one thing we can do . . . and . . ." Carefully she allowed a feeling of vulnerability to leak into her demeanor. "Oh, James, I am afraid we must kill the child! And we must do it in secret . . . or else . . . when the Count dies . . . I will no longer have my unborn son as trump . . . the pack will split down the middle . . . and . . . I will be unable to give *you* . . ." She paused, intimating much, much more than she was prepared to bestow him.

"You're planning to seize control of the pack, aren't you? I did not realize that women—"

"Indeed! But why not?" She turned on him a look of blazing scorn, so that he would know who was in control here. "Of all our people I am the strongest . . . and I will have his child. Why should a woman not rule?" And then she touched him lightly on the cheek, and smiled at him, and said, "But I could rule through a man, if it were right man."

"I'm not one of you!"

"Not yet—I need human to destroy the boy, because the moon

will soon be full, and I will be unable to see clearly reason. But after boy is gone . . ."

"You'll make me one of you—"

"And you will be by my side—"

"When the Count is dead."

The major smiled. Oh, humans were so gullible, so consumed by their petty little lusts. They are nothing more than cattle, Natasha thought, cattle to be feasted on, led by the nose, killed.

She had no intention of letting the major have his way with her. No; in her own way she had a kind of honor. The major would die as soon as he killed the child; that way, she would not have stained her hands with the boy's blood, and no one would seek vengeance, because she would have taken that vengeance upon herself.

"I have the silver bullets, as you ordered, Natasha," said the major.

"Then come. Deeper into forest. I think already I begin to smell him."

The dream . . . the forest . . . the crucified child . . .

Speranza stirred. A fire smoldered. Dry leaves crackled as she sat up, trying to shake herself free of the dream. A little way off, the soldier and the boy sat back-to-back against a tree trunk. Faint firelight danced in their faces.

She had taken a dose of coca powder, thinking it might calm the conflicts within her; yet they had never seemed more turbulent. She had become aware of a certain feeling for the young soldier . . . a feeling she feared to acknowledge. She closed her eyes again. In the distance came howling. Perhaps it was out of the dream.

The dream. . . .

Mist. Through the treetrops, gauzed by haze, the moon shone, bloody, almost full. I'm still inside my dream! she thought. For the forest was no longer fragrant, inviting. No. A faint odor of putrefaction in the air. From afar, howling. Surely I should have grown used to howling by now! she told herself. And she stood up, shaking the twigs from her torn clothes.

They had been travelling several days since Teddy's return, always going uphill. It had taken longer than they had hoped. Tomorrow night would be the full moon, and Scott would have to be guarded and kept from the moonlight. She looked at the two of them. She did not hear them breathe.

They did not move. She thought, panicking: The wolves have come already, they've killed them in their sleep . . . but no. The boy moaned something in his sleep that sounded like the French, "Papa, Papa. . . ." and his voice was tiny as an infant's.

Then came the whispering. Was not the forest calling her softly, *Speranza, Speranza, Speranza*? No. It was the creek, babbling as it tumbled down to the valley.

She stood still for a long time, hardly daring to breathe.

Then came the whispering again: *Speranza, Speranza*.

I will not be afraid, she told herself. I have come here because I love the boy . . . and because I must atone for the sordid life I have led with Hartmut and the other wolves. She ached to hold the boy in her arms as she had done on the train when he had crawled out, bloody, from the belly of a slain servant girl. How he had wept then.

Speranza, Speranza, Speranza. . . .

It was his voice! It had to be! When she looked behind her she realized she had strayed from their encampment. The trees were all alike . . . tendrils of mist enveloped them . . . the forest was alive with an eerie music of night birds and the chittering of nocturnal mammals. The night wind gusted.

Speranza. . . .

"Johnny!" she cried out.

Another voice now, the harsh, bestial laughter that belonged to Jonas Kay. And then a third voice, tranquil, lilting, in the language of the Lakota.

She walked toward the sound. The child was there somewhere. She must succor him, shield him. "Johnny," she cried out, "you're in danger, you must not—"

There was a path that led from the lit clearing into the heart of the dark. She must follow it. Her stomach knotted, almost as though she still suffered from morning sickness. The voice came again, and she began to walk down the path. The fog came streaming in, rolling about her ankles. The trees grew thicker now. Thicker. Darker. Leaves the color of tarnished silver. She could barely see the path ahead and had completely lost the path behind. The fog enveloped her, its dampness redolent with the smell of canine urine. The wind whipped up flurries of wet leaves. Trees swayed; blackness swooped down on her like a hungry owl.

Then, abruptly, the mist parted. The wind fell still. In the night sky, sweeping across the face of the moon, fleeting, the silhouette of an owl. A rock ledge jutting out over a chasm, and on the ledge a circle of blue flame, and inside the circle a child. . . .

And she was running toward him, running, heedless of the brambles that scuffed her feet and the stinging nettles, running toward him with his name upon her lips as he turned toward her, his solemn, wide-eyed countenance framed by long blond hair, his eyes set within circles of blue-black paint. . . .

And the boy said to her, without moving his lips: I have waited for you. You are the last thing I need for this vision to be made whole. Come to me, Speranza.

And ran and ran . . .

Into an embrace of darkness . . . the boy started, looked up with a cry, the vision smashed, splintered, dissipated, and then she saw. . . .

Tipis. Smoke. She was standing by the edge of a creek. On the other side, an Indian woman stood, staring curiously.

I've failed him! she thought hysterically. Hot tears ran down her cheeks. She began to feel faint. She was collapsing now, even as she tried to cling to pieces of her vision. She fell back—

Into the arms of Scott Harper. Teddy was not far behind.

"We heard you cry out," said Scott.

"You were having a nightmare," said Teddy. "Weeping and carrying on in—" Suddenly he stopped. He had seen the woman.

"Look," Scott said, pointing at the woman across the water. Speranza saw her, a small-boned woman in a robe of deerskin that was ornamented, here and there, with scraps of calico. She was holding out an earthenware pot, preparing to fetch water from the stream; instead, she looked at them in astonishment. The water was trickling from the pot back to earth.

"I thought she was dead," Teddy said softly.

And Speranza knew that this must be Little Elk Woman, the woman who had walked away from the Indian village to die. She wondered what accident had caused her to remain alive, and brought her to this place.

"I'll be," said Teddy. And suddenly he seemed afraid, as though the woman might be a ghost. "Ma. . . ."

And ran to embrace her. Splashing feet, cool water flecking her face, her arms. Speranza thought: He is still only a boy, in spite of all he's lived through.

"I've found her, Miss Speranza . . . I thought she was dead and I've found her—"

"But she ain't alone," said Scott urgently. "Look."

For behind the Indian woman, almost lost among the shadows, Speranza could see the outlines of many tipis.

The wolf-boy had not eaten for many days. The hunger had gone away now. He had made himself into an empty vessel to receive the dream.

He was standing on a ledge against the full moon. The wind tore at his thin limbs. It whipped his hair into his far-seeing eyes, which, blue as the sea unseen by any of his tribe, stared not at the world but into darkness; for he had turned his gaze inward and set forth upon a spirit journey.

The wolf-boy drew a circle of blue flame, visible only to those attuned to it. It was a sacred circle of the water from his body over which he had sung a magical song, so that the life remained in the water even though it had departed his body. Within the circle, the wind grew still, and there was warmth. The body would remain here, unmoving, until his soul returned to it.

But what of the other souls, imprisoned in the forest within?

They too must dream, said Wolf Boy to himself.

And cast his spirit into the wind.

Instantly he was high above the world. He could see his own body, standing quite still within the circle, gazing out over the void. Above, the clouds rolled about the moon. An eagle soared beside him. The great bird plummeted, and he too fell, sucked into the wind of its flight. And he cried out in the language of the winged: "Let me see through your eyes, Wambliwashté. Father, *até*, show me the world."

Instantly the earth seemed to lurch up and drift and shake and stretch from side to side and all around. He reeled. The mountains veered up. Black and silver, the moonbeams bending, iridescing. The eagle circled and the world seemed to circle. The mountains raced. The trees quivered. And he was rising, rising, into regions where he could feel the air thin. There was the camp of his people, the Shungmanitu Tanka.

He could see people there . . . tiny people trudging toward the campfire's warmth . . . toward the tipi of Ishnazuyai, his earthly father . . . strangers yet not strangers . . . people he had known in other lives. There was a woman who had once meant much to him . . . what was her name? One of the others would know. And the boy . . . he had once called him *mitákola*, my friend.

Why had they come? Shungmanitu Hokshila could not tell. Higher the eagle flew. Beneath, the mountains stretched like an old buffalo robe. "Father, Father, where do you take me?" he cried out. But the eagle did not answer. He only flapped his wings, laboring against the airstream. Wisps of cloud swirled about them. The wind roared. "I can't breathe anymore!" The wind was blasting his lungs, cold, searing.

And the clouds parted and the wolf-boy saw the whole world illumined by soft moonlight. It was not the world he knew, but the world before the coming of the white men. Though the wind raged as it swooped down from the mountain, shaking the million pines, though the air rang with the cries of the four-legged and the winged and with the thunder of falling water, this was a world in harmony with itself. It was not paradise—the boy remembered, from a time before he had become himself, what the white man's paradise was: a fool's utopia, a place without pain. There was pain here. There was the pain of the hunted, the pain of death. He heard death everywhere in the wind, thousands of pinprick death cries, yet in these deaths there was a profound concord, for life was never taken unless it was freely given. The prey that was ready to receive the arrow came willingly to seek it, and the hunter begged forgiveness of its spirit. There was war in this land too, but it was war that honed the spirit and brought honor, not the mindless war of the *washichun*.

At last, the eagle spoke. He said: "There is the place of the moon dance." They turned toward the far horizon, south, to the lowlands in the Black Hills' shadow. There it was, almost at the limits of vision: a towering rock formation shaped, perhaps, like a wolf, tensed, ready to leap. The eagle went on, his voice resonant with ancient wisdom: "They must all dance there, at the time of the great cycle of changes, all the wolves. You must teach them a new dance, and they must dance until the old world withers away and the new world comes in its place. Only then will the white wolves and the red wolves be at peace."

Already the vision was fading, spiralling away into the churning wind . . . he could see the houses of the *washichun* springing up, the iron horses hurtling across the prairies, the town of Winter Eyes clustering around the Wolf Rock and hiding it from view with the smoke from its chimneys . . . the world swam, blurred, shimmered, shifted, and now came other iron horses, swifter, threading the dark earth like flaming rawhide, and iron birds that burned across the sky, and men, swarming, more numberless than the buffalo that had once roamed free upon the plains. . . .

Despairing, the wolf-boy cried out: "Is it the future? How can I stop it, I alone?"

"It is only one of a thousand futures. Lead the wolves to the rock, and there let them dance . . . perhaps we can turn the world back to the old time."

"Perhaps?"

"I speak only as an eagle speaks. I am not Wakantanka, the Great Mystery. Though I fly above the earth, I am not all-seeing."

"Perhaps I'll be killed—"

"No, Wolf Boy. The one who can kill you is the one who loves you truly, and you are not one who will be easily loved. You are darker than the darkness."

And the wolf-boy remembered, from his life in the world of the *washichun*, a terrible fear of darkness, which the white men called Satan; and the fear touched him in his dream—

"Do not be afraid!" screeched the eagle. "Fear will make you lose your way in the dream—"

Too late! He was no longer insubstantial. He could feel the dead flesh invade his ethereal double as he plummeted. He gasped for air. The wind threw him down against hard rock. He was racked with pain. He was standing inside the circle now, next to his unconscious body.

He made ready to enter the body through the mouth and nostrils, to animate them with the wind of life. He hovered about his own face, waiting; he was afraid to take control too suddenly, for a body too abruptly possessed by his own soul can be shocked into death.

The body was kneeling. Its eyes were closed. The skin was

parched; he could smell the caked sweat, the rancid-sweet odor of starvation. There were shadows about his eyes, and already his forehead had become lined. There was no wind inside the circle, no sound. Time itself was still, for this little world was not part of the universe at all.

Wolf Boy was ready to enter when—

The eyes opened! And glared at him, glowing like embers! The mouth widened in a leer, the teeth glistening . . . the tongue contorting into the harsh sounds of the *washichun* speech.

Came the voice of another, more soft-spoken: "It's Jonas, Shungmanitu Hokshila! He says you should never have left the body . . . he says it's his now, and he's never going to let you back inside. . . ."

The body snarled. Hands clenched into animal claws. They could not change yet, not until tomorrow's moon. Wolf Boy could see the jaw muscles working, spit frothing up, the eyes rolling. The body was thrashing about now as the rebellious others tried to restrain the dark wolf within. Quickly Wolf Boy took advantage of the confusion to slip into the body and confront the other.

He found himself in the forest within. Beyond the clearing, the treehouse was burning, and he could see Jonas Kay now, his jaws slavering as he wielded a burning torch.

"No, Jonas! Don't you know that we'll all die if you—"

The dark wolf was past reasoning. He roared, he howled, he raged through the forest kindling piles of leaves, setting dead trunks on fire. The path was littered with smoldering planks from the treehouse.

Who was minding the body? No one! Wolf Boy seized control and peered from the body's eyes, clearing away the red filter of anger to gaze on the face of the moon—

There was the eagle, crossing the sky, calling his name!

"Father—" cried Wolf Boy.

Behind him, a hoarse animal cry, and the voice of Jake: "He says we have no father but darkness . . . he says we must give up all hope."

The eagle wheeled. Wolf Boy could not understand his cries. Had he lost the power to dream?

I must put out the fire, Wolf Boy told himself. And dream again. And dream again. And dream again.

9
Winter Eyes
full moon

OUTSIDE, THE SUN BLAZED, THOUGH IT WAS BARELY MIDMORNING. Inside the room where the Count von Bächl-Wölfing lay, though black curtains were drawn across every window, the light still shone fiercely, dyeing the room deep amber. The Count's fever was breaking. He lay drenched in sweat, the fur patches pungent from being steeped in beast-stench and foul poultices.

He called out. For a long time, no one came; the servants had all gone off somewhere, and only Vishnevsky was downstairs, sitting behind a great mahogany desk with piles of railway shares, receipts, and bank statements, trying to arrange the Count's affairs, for everyone knew that the end was near.

Vishnevsky drew the drapes of the immense bay window that faced the street. Already tumult, and moonrise ten hours away! There was the Baroness von Dittersdorf, regaling some of the latest immigrants of Winter Eyes: Edgecomb, a Negro cowhand who had wandered a bit too far from his herd; Josh Levy, a pawnbroker from Pierre; Victor Castellanos, an ex-Comanchero who had fled the law into the territory and had found himself suddenly a werewolf. The three had clearly been "collected" by the Baroness herself—for her taste in victims, like her gambling technique, tended toward hyperbole.

Behind them, footmen were readying the dark Concord stage-coaches that were the wolves' means of transport when they wished to delay their transformation until they reached a place rich in prey. The Count's chief manservant was checking the thick black velvet draperies to make sure there were no tears; the narrowest beam of moonlight could negate four weeks of careful planning.

Fools, Vishnevsky thought, and turned his mind to accounting. He had barely sat down, and filled his pipe with the local Orcico brand tobacco, when he heard another groan from above: "Valentin Nikolaievich!"

He put down the pipe and went upstairs to the Count, pausing at the landing to pick up a tray the servants had left, with a flagon of red wine and several bottles of useless medicines: Foley's for biliousness and constipation, Wisconsin dyspepsia tablets, Harford's balsam and myrrh . . . a small, never-opened vial of Cordwainer Claggart's Floccinaucinihilipilificator—strange how that hideous man had reappeared in their lives, as an unlikely comrade of that stiff, refractory Major Sanderson . . . ah, there *was* something useful there . . . a small bottle of laudanum, and an old platinum spoon with the von Bächl-Wölfing crest. Sighing, Vishnevsky opened the door, which squeaked, for the hinges had not been oiled.

And saw the master. The room was laced with the stench of decay. The Count looked up from a heap of quilts, blankets, sheets stained with urine.

"My lord," he said softly.

"*Dumnezeu, dumnezeu,*" said the Count, almost inaudibly. With a shock, Vishnevsky realized he was calling on God . . . and in his native Wallachian, a language Vishnevsky had rarely heard his master use except to the peasants on his country estate. "*Doamne ajută!*" the Count whispered feverishly. "*Ce-am făcut? . . . l-au crezut pe băjatul ăla . . .*" His glance shot rapidly from side to side, like a stalking wolf's. Suddenly he saw that Vishnevsky was standing in the doorway. Abruptly he stiffened, returned to the High German his rank demanded. "I see you have come yourself, Valentin Nikolaievich," he said, and twisted his lips into a wan imitation of that once-gracious smile. "Please don't try to force more laudanum down my throat; no more cold compresses, no more mustard plasters . . . I want to be taken to the graveyard . . . oh, don't look so alarmed, Vishnevsky! . . . where is your cousin?"

"She had gone hunting, my lord, with Major Sanderson."

"An . . . unlikely couple . . . the one so refined, the other . . ." Vishnevsky fidgeted. The Count looked sharply at him, and he stared at the floor; even weakened, von Bächl-Wölfing commanded utterly. Vishnevsky went to the window and yelled down a command to one of the footmen; he himself knelt beside the bed and wiped the pus and coagulated vomit from the Count's night clothes. But he was thinking of the succession, not of his master; at all costs, Natasha's interests had to be served.

It was noon by the time the footmen had prepared a makeshift litter and carried their master toward the church. Natasha's church, Vishnevsky thought, built for Father Alexandros, so that they might have the benefits of Orthodoxy even in the wilderness. Outside, in the square, the Madonna was a portrait of that other woman . . . but the church was all Natasha's.

Vishnevsky genuflected as they entered. Incense . . . candles . . . icons on dark wood, varnished and revarnished until their colors were all but indistinguishable . . . here the heat was stifling, the air suffocating. There had been no services here since Father Alexandros was killed, and Natasha was the only person in the town who came regularly to stand, stock-still, several hours at a time, and to relight the candles.

"Perhaps," said the Count—his voice was appreciably hoarser since they had left the house—"you can find some other use for it . . . a library perhaps, or even"—a wan smile, as though recalling some half-forgotten joke—"a madhouse."

"You wanted the graveyard," Vishnevsky said, for the atmosphere here was so oppressive that he longed for open air, even a cemetery's; unlike the wolves, he could not smell the putrefaction of buried people, and the graveyard was to him a fragrant place. Natasha had planted roses, wanting a reminder of the estate in Wallachia, where she and the Count had sometimes, in the full moon, disported themselves in a walled garden where roses grew wild and thorny. Sunlight streamed down on them as the footmen set the Count's litter down next to the burial place of Dr. Szymanowski.

The Count said, "I know you are thinking about the succession." Vishnevsky started. "About Natasha."

Vishnevsky waited.

"There is a will . . ."

As Vishnevsky watched, the Count's ravaged face began to transform still more. Tufts of silver-white bristles tore through his brows. Blood streamed down his face, soaking into the collar of his nightshirt. One cheek fibrillated as new muscles consumed old. In the sunlight, the metamorphosis seemed out of place, faintly ludicrous. The bestial odor mingled nauseatingly with the fragrance of roses. Vishnevsky swallowed his gorge; it would not do to be sick now, not when his master was about to divulge—

"I must appear ridiculous to you . . . changing in broad daylight . . . you must know from this that I am deathly ill . . ."

"No, my lord—"

"Dying."

He gripped Vishnevsky's arm and would not let go. Blood stained the sleeve of the frock coat.

"The financial affairs of the city . . ." The eyes wept pus. At last Vishnevsky could not look; he tore away his gaze and fixed it upon the wooden marker that read *Thomasz Szymanowski*, in shallow incuse characters that were already damaged by two Dakota winters. If only they were in Vienna again! he thought. A box at the Staatsoper—he had always enjoyed the harsh sonorities of modern operas such as Wagner's—the town houses glinting by gaslight in the mist—"You do not like it . . . here . . ." said the Count softly. Could he hide nothing from his master?

"No," said Valentin Nikolaievich Vishnevsky.

"I did not think I would die here without issue . . . without . . . planting the seed . . . you understand? Do not think I am ignorant of your cousin's plans. I am the leader, but it is well known that the female, too, leads, in her own way . . . for it is she who must seek out the denning place, and bear the litter. And we have had no litter."

"No, Count."

"There is a will . . . in Szymanowski's coffin . . . in the breast pocket of his dinner jacket . . . you alone are to know this . . . until I am gone."

The beginning of a snout was trying to push through the Count's cheek. Bone protruded where a flap of human skin had ripped loose from his shoulder. One eye was already clouded. The hand that gripped Vishnevsky's arm showed a dark discoloration; it was the silver within him, tarnishing, corrupting as it poisoned.

"You are in pain, Count," said Vishnevsky. "Let me fetch wine—a warm wine, steeped with herbs—or a posset laced with morphia."

"Yes. Pain." And yet he smiled. "No wine, though; I do not want to die with my senses dulled. Instead, I would have you send a footman out to the forest, to fetch me a glass of cold, clear water from the creek."

10
The Black Hills
the same day

THAT NIGHT SPERANZA SLEPT INSIDE THE TIPI OF ISHNAZUYAI, BUT Teddy and Scott stayed outside, by the dying fire. "I gotta make a circle around him," Teddy told her as she lifted the flap and peered out at the night, "with these," and he began to empty out the bag of Morgan dollars and worn pieces of eight. "Tomorrow night's the night. I keeps track."

"But aren't *all* the people in the village—" Speranza said, wondering why she felt no fear.

"They won't touch us. The Shungmanitu Tanka don't prey on humans less they *asks* to die . . ."

The night passed in surprising comfort. That night, for the first time for as long as she could remember since first making her acquaintance with the Lykanthropenverein, she had no nightmares; indeed, she did not dream at all. The smells of the tipi had been unpleasant at first—the dank odor of buffalo hides, the reek of rancid deer fat—but the buffalo robe she slept in was soft and warm and the food they had given her filling.

She learned that it was boiled dog, but she felt no more than a passing distaste; in the years since she left the service of Lord Slatterthwaite she had lost considerable squeamishness.

At dawn, the women went down to the stream to bathe and fetch water. Little Elk Woman made it clear that Speranza was to go with her. They splashed about in the creek, shielded by fir trees from the sight of the men. Though they were naked, Speranza could see that these barbarian women possessed an innate modesty that many an overdressed, overperfumed woman of means might envy. After, Little Elk Woman showed her the place where the women were dressing hides, tanning the buffalo pelts with the beast's brains, scraping endlessly with utensils of flint and bone; and again, Speranza saw that these were hardworking, industrious folk—much like the American Protestants—and hardly the hedonistic savages she had been led to expect. They were a graceful people, too; how ungainly she felt as, back in the privacy of the tipi, she laced her whalebone corsets and breathed in deeply so as to squeeze herself into her delicate lace chemise, already half ripped up from the rigors of their odyssey!

When she emerged from the tipi, it was midmorning; some of the villagers were gathered around a ceremonial shield of buffalo hide, on which an old man was painting with a bone tool and a palette of ground pigments. Scott Harper and Teddy Grumiaux were there already, and Little Elk Woman was bringing them water from the creek in a white man's iron canister, and a bowl of something not unlike porridge. When she sat down beside the soldier and the boy, she saw the resemblance between Teddy and his mother at once. The boy had abandoned his white men's clothing entirely; he wore leggings, a loincloth, a choker of beads made from deer vertebrae, a pair of elaborately beaded moccasins a little big for him. His hair, unkempt before, was now smoothed with a little animal fat, and decorated with an eagle feather. He seemed at home with this manner of dress, and Speranza realized that, with his slight, lithe body, he looked very striking, nay beautiful; he transformed himself from grubby boy to noble savage.

"What is that painting?" she asked them, indicating the old man who was daubing the stretched hide.

"It's a winter count," said the boy, "and each of them symbols shows the most important thing that happened in the year; it's how the Injuns reckons the passing of time." He pointed at the hide, and she saw now that there was a series of small pictures, almost like ideographs, arranged in a spiral; that the painter was working adding something to the very end of the pattern. "See that thing there, the blue coat and the yeller hair? That was '76, the year of the battle by the River of Greasy Grass. The yeller hair is for General Custer, for that was the name the Injuns gave him."

"And this year?" Speranza said, trying to peer at the old man's handiwork through the crowd of the curious, children mostly. At length the painter sat back, cross-legged, and began to sing to himself, the way the Indians often did; and she saw that he had been painting a representation of a baby suckling at the breasts of a mother wolf . . . it reminded her, strangely enough, of the famous statue in Italy of Romulus and Remus, the founders of Rome, who had been ferel children, abandoned and raised by wolves.

Teddy asked his mother a question in Lakota, and Little Elk Woman, addressing Speranza directly, said, "This year is the coming of Shungmanitu Hokshila, *l'enfant loup;* he will set us free."

At last the subject of Johnny had been raised. So Speranza could ask her hostess, "Is the boy not with you?"

"Oh," said Teddy, "I already found out all that. He's gone on a vision quest; they figger on him coming back around tonight or tomorrow, though, because of the full moon. But they tells us we can't reach him now, that his spirit's gone on a long journey."

"What about the man who abducted him?"

"The crazy old Injun—he's a *wichasha wakan,* kind of a medicine man among these folk—he's ridin' back from Winter Eyes. He's expected soon, they tells me. He aims to make peace with your old Count . . . because of the vision quest." He added, "Miss Speranza, he's in danger! If that Claggart gets to him afore we does—"

Scott said, "We'll just have to kill Claggart, I suppose."

His voice betrayed a certain resignation, and Speranza realized that this was not a man who enjoyed killing; she wondered what had made him join the cavalry. She pitied him, knowing how wrenching the transformation could be for the unwilling, and how he had resisted transforming utterly for so long. How desolate it is, she thought, to know one is not entirely man, yet to repudiate the beast within. And she said, "You are a very brave man, Mr. Harper. I cannot help but admire you."

"I sure appreciate that, ma'am," he said.

And she touched him, lightly, on the shoulder, and said, "I believe you will fight your affliction to the very end."

"Oh, I'll fight all right. But I never had to spend the night of the full moon in a village full of shape-changers before. I'm mighty glad you and Teddy are here to anchor me down."

Major Sanderson trembled with ill-suppressed fury; Natasha could do nothing but wait for his temper to subside. "The effrontery of it!" he was saying. "A whole village of the beggars hidden in these hills—in flagrant violation of the treaty in which the Indians relinquished their rights to the Black Hills!"

There, indeed, was the village; the tipis in a clearing around a fire over which meat was being smoked. Natasha could smell the inhabitants of the village, and she knew them for what they were. "Control yourself, Major," she whispered urgently, for the major seemed ready to burst, saber in hand, from the copse in which they had concealed themselves. "These aren't your treaty-signing Indians—they are completely different tribe—they are were-wolves such as we."

"As soon as I return to Fort Cassandra, I will be sending a detachment to root these savages out," said Sanderson. "I don't care whether they're treaty-signing Indians or Indians from Calcutta—one Indian is very much like another, and the only good one's a dead one, as I'm sure you'll agree."

"Yes, yes. But remember. We are here for the boy. Not for war. Not yet."

As evening approached, Teddy loaded his pistol with silver bullets. Just in case, he told himself.

Inside the fractured mind within the body of the boy who was once called Johnny Kindred, the treehouse flamed. Johnny watched helplessly. A charred plank fell. The smoke was acrid in his nostrils. Outside he heard raucous laughter and he knew that Jonas Kay was somewhere out there.

Another plank. Smoke weaving in and out of the gaps in the timber, smoke swirling, dancing in front of his eyes . . . Johnny backing against the wall next to the windowsill, watching the flames creep closer until they were lapping at his very toes . . .

A voice from below. "Jump, Johnny, jump—it's yer only chance!"

Johnny whipped around, stared out through the window. It was Jake, waving frantically. Johnny cried out, "Can't you see? We're all going to die—except for the Indian boy—and then he'll rule the body all alone—"

"Don't you know anything? He can't survive without you, you fool—he's part of you and you're part of him—*all* of us is part of you! Now jump!"

"No!" Johnny was shrieking. This was madness! He wasn't part of anyone else! It was a trick, they were all going to overwhelm and drive him into the outer darkness forever . . . tears blurred his eyes. The smoke seared his nostrils, dried his lips, made him choke. But, squeezing his eyes tight shut against the pain, Johnny suddenly saw a vision of Speranza. . . .

And yelled out her name, leaping—

And, sitting alone, staring at the winter count, Speranza thought she heard his voice . . . but perhaps it was the cry of a wild animal from deep in the forest.

And Claggart laughed as he pounded away at the lumps of silver bullion, shaping them into new instruments of torture, he laughed into the roaring wind—

Inside the magic circle, Wolf Boy waited for nightfall.

Little Elk Woman led her son to the edge of the encampment. The sun was setting. The hills were even darker against the gray sky streaked with scarlet and crimson and vermilion, the trees taller and more forbidding, the shadows longer.

"I thought you were dead," Teddy said. "Why'd you leave me, Ma?" And added, in Lakota halting from disuse, "My father is dead. And all your husbands have died. But there was still me. I thought you had gone away to die. There was honor in that. I could accept it. But you went to another man . . . another son."

She had no ready answer for him. Instead, she said, "You know that tonight they will change, don't you?" And saw anger in her son's face. She was afraid, knowing that the white men's wolves had caused Claude-Achille's death, and that Teddy wanted revenge so badly that he'd turned his back on the white men as much as the red.

"I hate them," Teddy said softly.

"They are not like the ones you knew."

"I know. But I still hate all of them wolf-people. They took my friends from me. They took Paw and Zeke and they're taking Scott and Johnny . . . and they've taken you." Though he did not accuse her, his eyes said much.

The sun had set. They heard the first howls, faint, like distant love flutes. Her son's face tightened. Anger was what he fed on now; she was afraid of him.

In English, he said, "I'd best go see to Scott. If the smell of all them wolves get in his nose, he won't be able to hold himself in his human skin—and I don't know what he'll do. I think he . . . fancies Miss Speranza."

"I will help you." Little Elk Woman saw what the friend meant to the boy. Teddy needed something to believe in, needed to save his friend from the darkness each time the moon was full. For each time he saved his friend he also won a small victory over the darkness in himself.

—out of the burning forest—

Smoke coiling, snakelike . . . trees on fire, snapping, crashing . . . the ground roaring as Johnny ran, stones sizzling his bare feet. . . .

And hand. Out of the smoke. Gripping him. "C'mon, Johnny! We got to get us to the clearing—"

"Jake! What's happening!"

"The world is burnin' up, I reckon."

Johnny looked back. And saw the last of the treehouse. It groaned, gave way, tumbled, the planks going crack-crack-crack against the tree trunks. "No!" he screamed. He had been safe there . . . the only place in the forest where Jonas couldn't touch him . . . smoke seared his eyes. And always Jake was pulling him forward, bounding over fallen limbs, leaping over jagged chasms that breathed brimstone . . .

"Careful, kid! Burn the soles off your feet."

"I want to see the treehouse—I want to see the last of it—"

"No lookin' back!"

And dragged him across stony ground now, the sharp rocks raking at his shins. And Johnny whispered Speranza's name over and over to himself like a prayer. Because there wasn't anybody else to pray to.

"We're almost there—" Jake said.

It wasn't the way they usually went to the clearing. But there were a thousand paths in the forest, and Jake knew his way better than any of the others he had ever talked to.

"We're going away from the clearing—" Johnny protested.

"It's gotta get worse afore it gets better," said Jake, pulling Johnny away from the path.

"But the path—" Johnny said, trying to free himself from Jake's grip.

"Duck!" Jake shoved Johnny flat against a twisted trunk. Johnny caught the merest glimpse of a fireball that caromed down the forest pathway. The roar hurt his ears. When he turned around, the path was ash, and here and there a blackened leaf twirled in the wind. "I'm a-tellin' you, we can't stick to that path no more . . . now will you move that scrawny ass of yours!"

A distant rumbling . . . another ball of flame . . . Johnny didn't stop now, he ran alongside Jake, his feet squishing into mud . . . the fire hadn't reached this part of the forest yet, but the air was clogged with smoke . . . he'd never been here before. There was dread here. He didn't know what it was. It made him run fleeter than before. The smoke seemed to follow him, to wrap itself around him—

Faces in the smoke! Faces from a time before he—

"Don't stop, Johnny, don't look at them faces—"

Gray eyelids. Gray lips. Whispering. Blood. A crossroads.

"I'm remembering something—"

He stopped suddenly.

The face glared at him. The smoke was coalescing now. The gray eyelids were opening . . . beneath them, delicate blue eyes, the eyes of a beautiful woman whose lips were parted as though to kiss him . . . he was mesmerized by the image . . . was it Speranza? Why was it he had loved Speranza so much? Was it not because she had something of this other woman about her? Suddenly a feeling of irretrievable loss came over him. "She's dead," he whispered.

"Of course she's dead," Jake said. He seemed to know something about Johnny that Johnny himself couldn't remember. "Of course she's dead . . . you killed her!"

And Johnny screamed: "No! No! It wasn't me! None of it ever happened to me! It happened to Jonas! *Jonas!*"

"You'll know soon enough," said Jake. "Come on now. All of

us is going to face this thing together . . . when the wolf-boy takes us acrosst the dark river."

They were inside the tipi of Little Elk Woman. Those of the village who felt the change come on them had long since gone into the forest. The change was a sacred thing and each had his own ritual of changing, given to him in a vision by an animal sacred to him. In the tent were Speranza and Scott and Teddy Grumiaux, and Little Elk Woman herself, tending a kettle, and one or two of the village children who had not yet had the dream of changing, and could not change shape.

Speranza and one of the children huddled together on one of the buffalo robes in a corner, watching as Teddy scattered pieces of silver in a circle around his friend. Something that emanated from the silver seemed to frighten the children; they pulled the buffalo robe over themselves and peeked out, their wide eyes watering from the effects of the moon-metal.

Teddy said, "Soon be moonrise, Ma," and Little Elk Woman rose, doused the fire, and pulled the cord that shut the vent flap. She could see that Scott was prostrate in the circle of silver, crouching on all fours, sniffing the air, his eyes narrowing, darting from side to side.

"You ain't goin' to change, Scott. We're watchin' you. Ain't one moonbeam goin' to touch your skin, Scott Harper." He said it over and over in a singsong voice. She saw it was an established ritual between them.

Little Elk Woman whispered something to one of the children; timorously the girl scampered toward the doorway and drew the flap shut. It was dark. Little Elk Woman opened up a chest and, to Speranza's surprise, produced a coal-oil lamp such as one might order from a Montgomery Ward catalog, and lit it from a tinderbox. The pieces of silver scattered among the dark buffalo hides glinted as the lamplight flickered.

There came howling. The children looked up. They did not cry out. The howling came closer.

Scott's face was drenched with sweat, and Teddy watched him worriedly. He was loading a Remington derringer with silver bullets, and when he was through tucked it into a fold of his leggings. He had three or four more guns, Speranza noticed, on the buffalo robe in front of him. A lot of silver in them.

"Johnny'll most likely come home tonight, after the moon sets," said Teddy. "And so will Ishnazuyai, they reckon. It'll all be over then." His voice carried little conviction. He played with the guns, arranging and rearranging them in different sequences, not looking her in the eye. "Oh, don't worry, Miss Speranza," he added, divining her fear, "I ain't goin' to shoot any of these Injuns. They are our hosts, and they done took in my ma and your Johnny and us. These here guns is just . . . just in case . . ." He looked at Scott. "Mayhap you should have one handy yourself," he said, fishing the Remington out of his leggings and shying it over to her. She looked at it but did not pick it up. The children, next to her, dived for cover under the buffalo robe.

"I trust we have waited enough, madam?" said Major Sanderson, who was itching to burst from their place of concealment. "The moon is rising, and—"

Natasha shuddered, and drew her black velvet cloak over her face, shutting out the transforming light that even now touched her from beyond the horizon . . . because of the silver poison in her flesh, she was doomed to be a sort of demi-werewolf, always on the verge of shifting. But the moonlight could still touch at her, tease at her, drive out the shattered beast from within.

The moon was not quite out yet. But the sky was luminous, the clouds fringed with mother-of-pearl, hinting of lingering twilight. They had spent the day scouting, and Natasha could smell something strange and new in the air; once or twice the major had attempted, in his fumbling way, to exact the payment implicit in their agreement; always she had led him on with a wry smile, a sensuous shiver of her hourglass figure.

"The Indians are leaving the village," Sanderson said. "And it's my experience that whenever savages muster, or set off purposefully in any direction, there must be villainy afoot."

"Do you see boy?" said Natasha. "We do not come for these others. In time we will—"

"No boy," said the major. He parted the leafy wall of their hiding place to look more closely across the river. She winced—what fools these humans were—did they know nothing about blending with the sounds of the forest? Surely the wolves would. . . .

"Wait—could that be a white boy?" said the major suddenly.

Natasha looked. A tall white adolescent peered from a tent flap. Like an Indian, he went stripped to the waist. His limbs were smooth; the sweet odor of boyish sweat emanated from him. His hair was dark and long, and his eyes brooding, not unattractive; Natasha's heart beat a little faster. To her senses, keened by the impending moon, he stood out sharply; she could almost taste the patches of warmth under his arms and between his legs.

He smelt familiar, but he was not the boy. "No," she said.

"How can you be sure?" the major said. "I know these savages, madam; a child captured by them is a native within a year, eating dog, covered with deer fat, reeking of the offal these savages dwell in. In two years you would not know him, I am sure."

"Believe me, Major . . . my senses are more attentuated that yours—"

"But, dulled, perhaps, by the taint of silver!"

"Come, Major; he is not even blond."

"Camouflage! These Indians will do anything to hide a white captive from his rightful people. . . ."

"Quiet . . . moon has come."

She drew the cloak tighter. She covered even her eyes. The world for her was mapped in scent; though cloaked in darkness, she found the night brilliant with brash odors; the fresh water, the urine trails of a score of wolves, the acidulous fragrance of dying pinecones, and the air heavy with the musk of bitches in heat. She heard the major go to his horse, heard the clink of cartridges in his pockets, the click of a Sharps rifle being loaded.

She said, "We cross the creek a little farther along . . . upwind. Or they will know we are here." She sniffed the air, trying to isolate one of the scents of the Count's child.

"Madam, I trust you will allow that I am as versed in the military arts as my training permits. We came here to kill a white boy, and it is surely inconceivable that this remote village would boast of more than one such. . . ."

He began to wade across the creek.

"You fool!" She gripped his sleeve. "Upwind . . . upwind!"

In the half-dark of the tipi, Speranza watched the shadows dance. "Is that music?" she said. From somewhere outside, between the howling that reverberated from all directions, came a plangent keening, perhaps one of those Indian love flutes.

"There's nothing, ma'am," said Teddy, never looking away from his friend. "Only the wind."

The sound again. The sooty flicker of the coal-oil lamp . . . she thought: I am dreaming, I am slipping out of the real world into. . . .

She reached into her bosom for her coca powder. Her supply was almost exhausted! How could she not have brought enough? Desperately, she breathed up the few grains that remained. There was a void in her that sucked up all the powder could give her and yet demanded more and more. She shook, the tipi seemed to tremble, and above it all came the high-pitched whistle of the flute . . . and her name . . . her name, in the voice of a little lost child . . . *Speranza* . . . *Speranza* . . .

She did not know at what moment the dream began. She knew only that all the others seemed to be frozen in time, that a dusty wind, pungent with the smell of summer grass, was blowing through the tipi, that she alone felt it; that her hair was billowing, her shredded chemise flapping against the whalebone of her corset, her skirts whipping her thighs and teasing at those parts beneath her petticoats.

Wondering, she gazed at the unmoving others. Still the flames danced . . . they danced . . . fed by the wind, they danced . . . smoke danced . . . as she stood there the wind uprooted the tipi, the lodgepoles went flying into the moon, the buffalo robes fluttered about her head, and now she could see the pine trees swaying as the wind swooped down upon them and could hear the treetops rustle like the voices of children . . . and she could taste the wind-burnt grass . . . and the dank musk of aroused wolves . . . and now the forest spinning about her, a blur of sable, russet, silver, the wind was in the trees and the wind was the trees and the trees were the rushing whirlwind, and behind their roar was the cry of the love flute and the child's voice calling for her.

Then, abruptly, fire. Tree trunks, charred, crashing across her path. A slender shadow, boy-shaped, slithering through the bushes—

"Johnny!" she cried out.

"Speranza. . . ." Suddenly he was there. A tiny boy, smaller even than when she first saw him in Victoria Station, dressed in torn orphanage rags, the hair clipped to the scalp, wide deep blue sunken eyes staring listlessly. . . .

"Johnny, you must not be afraid," she said. "I have come to rescue you . . . to set you free . . . you must come to me."

"I—" He ran to embrace her. She tried to hold him tight but he was insubstantial as the whirlwind. And fire was sweeping through the forest. Dry conifers sizzled, sparked, blew apart.

Was the boy a ghost? I am still dreaming, she reminded herself. I am in the tipi of Little Elk Woman.

"Come . . . please, come quickly . . ." said the boy, and began to run. She followed. A ball of flame pursued her. She ran.

"Johnny, why can't I touch you?"

"You're inside me. The Wolf Boy did it. His dreaming is real, Speranza."

Another boy was running beside them. An older boy, but his features unmistakably Johnny's. Long hair beneath a slouch hat, jeans, spurred boots, a tattered silk vest that seemed to have been scavenged from a train wreck. "Jake Killingsworth, ma'am," he said, panting. "At your service."

The forest grew darker now. Even the flames were dark. Jake had a shiny big bowie knife and was sawing away at undergrowth.

Johnny said, "Jake says we have to go this way to the clearing . . . but it's the long way. . . ."

"The way through hell!" Another figure beside them. The face pinched, sallow, animal eyes, golden, slitted, the voice growling, guttural. Jonas. She would have known his voice anywhere.

"I should explain, Miss Speranza," Jake said as he labored to clear the path, "we're all inside him . . . and we're all going to be one person now—"

"Over my dead body!" Jonas Kay leered. His breath was fetid. Blood dripped from his fangs. But his face was undeniably the face of Johnny Kindred.

The earth was trembling. Stones flew. Rodents scurried. The forest was denser, denser, denser . . . dark, humid, lubricious, like a woman's pubis. Jonas growled, snarled, howled, began to change as moonbeams pierced the foliage here and there with spears of crimson light. She could hardly breathe. Now and then she saw the dance of the lamplight and knew it was still a dream, and yet . . . and yet . . .

Other persons were gathering around them. Over there, dignified in his black morning dress, a tray in his hand . . . could that be James Karney? She thought she recognized Jonathan Kippax, Joachim Karnstein playing his twisted fiddle, many others whom she had known of only fleetingly; the crowd was pushing away from the moonlight, toward the darker than dark that lay ahead. . . .

"Why is it so dark?" said Speranza. They moved all together now, and she could hear the wind roar, but she could see nothing save the faintly luminescent shapes that were the souls of Johnny Kindred.

"Something is hidden," said Johnny. He was trying to grasp her hand, but he oozed through her fingers, leaving only a tingling sensation.

Jake said, "He means that we has to go through the dark place . . . to find the Injun boy. The Injun boy's calling us with his dream power. He's drawn him a great big circle at the top of the mountain, and when we step inside it we is goin' to be one soul, one self, one mind, and we will have all our memories. Trouble is, Miss Speranza, the way to the circle of light is through the dark heart . . . leastways, that what he tells me."

"But why am I here?"

"Because you and him is linked—because you loves him."

And Speranza knew that it was true.

"Is that why I came here?"

"Yes. I reckon *he* done called you out of your werewolf city . . . called you over across the mountains . . . called you to meet the Grumiaux boy. . . ."

"Because I love him," Speranza said softly.

"Metaphysical nonsense," said Jonas Kay. His voice was barely comprehensible, for he was on all fours now, and almost all wolf, thrusting through the undergrowth, pausing to mark his territory as they caught up with him. "Nonsense . . . metaphysics . . . nonsense . . . I am the real thing the real self the dark person the wolf within . . . I am all . . . all . . . *all*!"

And turned on them, fangs bared, howling. . . .

But above his howling was the song of the love flute. . . .

"But what's in the dark heart?" Speranza said. "Why does the path go through it?"

But it was Jonas who answered, his voice a rasp over the forest floor's rumbling. "The thing you fear most."

* * *

Little Elk Woman and the children waited for Speranza to reenter her body; they had felt her spirit leaving, seen her eyes dart back and forth as do dreamers' eyes beneath closed lids. Teddy accepted his mother's explanation that her soul had flown off for a time; when the Indians talked in this way, there was no telling if it was one of those metaphors, or if it was just plumb real to them.

No one spoke.

Something's going to go wrong, Teddy thought. Scott was doing fine, resisting the power of the moon better than he'd seen him do in months. He'd lain himself down in the silver circle and started to snore. It was too good to be true.

They were all sleeping. All except him. His mother breathing softly, Speranza hardly breathing at all.

Teddy heard something. He held his breath.

Footsteps in the encampment. Nothing to worry about, except . . . they didn't sound like Injun footsteps. An Injun, when he walks, the earth makes way for him; his feet just seem to fit the crannies in the soil; like as not there's no sound at all. These were awkward steps; breaking twigs, kicking over a stone.

The footsteps stopped.

Teddy breathed.

A shadow on the wall, moving—

Quickly he reached over to snatch the Remington that Speranza didn't pick up. He pointed at the wall, realized abruptly it had been his own shadow, tall and wavery in the light of the coal-oil lamp.

Nervous, he laughed aloud.

Then he heard Scott growling. Softly, very softly. He had thought it was a snore at first.

The growling grew louder, then—

A bowie knife ripping through the tent hides where the old *wichasha wakan* had painted an intricate design of mating werewolves, and—

Sweat pouring down Scott's face as the moonlight struck him, and the wolfhide began to push through his skin—

"No—no, Scott!"

Hearing his voice, his friend started to shift back a mite.

Troubled human eyes stared at him out of cheeks striped with fur. They wept blood.

"No, Natasha—" Scott said weakly.

Then Teddy saw who was behind the rent in the wall. It was the commander of Fort Cassandra, the one who'd joined forces with the wolves of Winter Eyes. And behind him was the Russian woman.

"Fuck you," said Teddy, "I got me a gun and I've learned me how to kill."

"I told you it was not he!" said the Russian woman. "We waste our time . . ."

"No breed with a derringer is going to stop me from venting the righteous vengeance of the American people upon these ruthless savages," said Major Sanderson.

He shot Little Elk Woman point-bank in the head.

"Ma!" Teddy screamed. And rushed to her, dropping the gun, caught her in his arms, a frail thing, bloody brains smearing her delicate cheekbones—

Teddy turned to the major, shouting, "I'll kill you I'll kill you I'll kill you—" but the major only laughed and fired two more rounds, one through the left eye of a five-year-old child, the other piercing a young girl's neck so that her death cry came as a windless squawk—

Teddy butted him in the stomach, pushing him against the side of the tipi, knocking his gun out of his hand . . . and now the lodgepoles were swaying to and fro and the coal-oil lamp was on its side and the fire was slithering down the buffalo robe, and the burning hair fumes were making him cough as the major laughed, "I'll save you for last, you damned breed . . . I hate breeds . . ."

Then Teddy realized that Scott and the Russian woman were staring into each other's eyes, like subjects of a conjurer's mesmerism act. And the Russian was changing . . . slowly, painfully slowly. . . .

"My beautiful soldier," said Natasha. "I see we can never escape each other. . . ."

Scott howled! Clawed at the silver barricade, yelped as the moon-metal stung him! "Stop, she ain't your friend she means to take you eat you up suck away your soul—" but it was like he couldn't even hear him. Just had eyes for the Russian woman.

Smoke in Teddy's eyes. Ma's dead, he thought. Just like I thought she was all them years. I grieved for her once and now I can't feel nothing, nothing a-tall.

She lay in the smoke, the two kids across her lap, their blood matting the buffalo robe. Why can't I feel nothing? he thought. Then he turned to see the major bearing down on him, fixing to throttle him with his bare hands.

"Dare—dare—dare—to cross river of silver that surrounds you—" said Natalia Petrovna. "I am here for you on other side, I am your dark desire."

And Scott burst howling from the circle, and the two, not quite wolf and not quite human, circled each other as the first of the lodgepoles caught fire.

"Help me, Scott!" Teddy shrieked. Scott seemed bewildered for a moment; he turned toward Teddy. Sniffing the ground, he lumbered toward the boy while Natasha readied herself to spring on him.

At that moment, Speranza stood up.

She stood in a tempest that stormed around her alone. Her hair flew free in a wind he could not feel. And she began walking. As she reached the wall of the tipi, the fire consumed the skin and made a man-shaped doorway for her to pass.

The major was distracted for a moment. Teddy wriggled free and ran after Speranza. Scott was with him. He was a little more human now. Natasha was at his heels.

Teddy said, "She's still in her dream . . . but it's one of them *true* dreams . . . I think she's being called . . . by *him* . . . we got to reach him 'fore he gets hisself kilt—"

Speranza was moving swiftly, purposefully. Away from the camp. Following the creek upstream. Were they, too, dreaming? Behind them, the tipi burned. They could hear children coughing and old men rousing themselves to douse the flames. Speranza walked on. Swiftly, and the forest parting for her, and the mist roiling about her. Swiftly, swiftly. He could barely keep up. He couldn't see whether her feet were touching the ground, but he knew she was floating on the wind of dreaming. Whatever force had been unleashed, it was powerful enough to carry the four of them with it . . . the Russian, the major, the renegade, the breed, all of them caught like a house in a tornado. . . .

* * *

Wolf Boy could feel the others coming near. He could not see them yet. They were not within the magic circle. Before they reached him, before they could be healed, each would have to battle a private darkness known only to himself. . . .

But . . . there were others, too . . . the woman he knew, it was the woman who loved the boy . . . but who were the others? He did not know them yet.

What should he do now? Suddenly he saw the flute in front of him. It did not surprise him that it had appeared out of nowhere; the spirit-animal knew how to supply everything needed for the vision to be most truthful. He hefted the flute; it was not cedarwood but bone; he had fashioned it himself from the thighbone of a grandmother, Ishnazuyai's mother perhaps, who had died in the snow on her way to the moon dance, died in the snow beside the tracks of the iron horse.

He began to play.

It was like the melody of the love flute, but there was also in it something of a death song. It was a slow, recursive melody that never rose or fell more than a few tones. There was a slow lilt to it, like the turning of the tides, like the faces of the moon. A new music for a new moon dance. Softly he played, and the stars began to shine, and the moon shone rainbow-fringed over silver-clad branches with their leaves shivering in the wind that dispelled the mist.

Johnny mumbled and twitched and shrank away from unseen faces. Jonas snarled and circled the others and would not let them cross the river. The other persons in Johnny Kindred's mind chattered among themselves, but none dared defy Jonas. Jonas raged, he roared, he snapped at their heels.

In the end it was Speranza who reached the river first. I know this river, she said. I have seen this river in nightmare after nightmare. And I know what is on the other side. . . .

The river raced, the river was blood, the river was rank with the menses of beasts, the river flamed, the river roared and whinnied like a ravished woman.

Beyond the river was the crossroads . . . the place where all would meet . . . the circle . . . the fire-girt rock.

Across the river, cast by the burning moon, the distended shadow of a cross.

"I won't go!" Johnny cried out. His tears spattered on the sod, made the weeds sizzle and char.

"You must, Johnny . . . you must," she said.

He buried his face in her bosom . . . she tried to hold him . . . now, sometimes, he was almost solid. He was laboring to become real. "I know this forest is just a dream," he said. "But in the dream forest I had a treehouse I could hide in. There won't be any treehouses in the real forest, will there? It's like . . . when the hunters came for the big bad wolf . . . sewed stones inside his stomach where Little Red Riding Hood had been . . . threw him into the creek. I think that's what waking up must be like . . . I am a wolf, Speranza . . . I am a wolf . . . but if I am asleep I can dream I am a boy."

"You *are* a boy," Speranza said, "a fine boy." She hugged him hard to her breast as the flute wailed from across the water. Blood streamed from his eyes as they embraced . . . not the chaste embrace of the infant and the Madonna, for as always there was something like lust in it too . . . and the wolf that was Jonas Kay clawed at her ankles and barked.

"Come," she said. And carrying him in her arms, began to wade. Blood up to her waist, soaking her unmentionables, seeping into her pores, but she did not falter. The boy looked timorously about. There were ghosts in the waters, faces that stared, voices that mocked. The others followed her. Fear stalked them all. The blood was brackish and full of bones. "Don't be afraid," she said, rocking him, "what you're seeing is all past now . . . all past."

In the shadow of the cross stood the Indian boy. He played a flute of bone. The music dispelled her terror, and she urged the others forward. But as she reached the other bank, and stood at the edge of the magic circle, she looked up and saw—

On the cross, a wolf, its paws nailed down, weeping . . . the blood pouring from its hands and feet and from the wound in its side . . . a wolf with the eyes of a young child, crying to her in a child's voice . . . "Mother, mother. . . ."

And Cordwainer Claggart laughed as he looked at his handiwork, and said, "If this don't summon the wolf-boy to me out of his vision seekin', my name ain't Cordwainer Willoughby Claggart the Third!"

Mists whirled around him. Far below, a tipi was on fire; even here there was the stink of burning buffalo hides. Claggart was sitting in the fork of a tree, biting off a chaw, rocking himself back and forth, back and forth, for he knew that the rocking would give his victim more discomfort.

"I sows destruction wheresoever I goes," Claggart said. "I'm right proud of that." His victim watched him, impassive; he was beyond pain, but he would still serve as the perfect bait.

Uphill they scrambled. Always, ahead, the ghostlike shape of Speranza, flitting between the pines, negotiating the boulders easily. They saw by the moon and the light of the burning tipi below them.

They ran, the major pursuing the woman relentlessly, Natasha pursuing the beautiful young soldier . . . that insolent half-breed boy behind them struggling to keep up, constantly calling Scott's name.

He would not heed him. Not the beautiful soldier . . . the soldier who was even now transforming as Natasha transformed. Natasha ran beside him, thrusting her nose into his flanks, driven wild by the fruity stench of his thighs. She shrieked to him in the language of night: "You were made for me, beautiful creature, made to love me."

"No—" he barked. "No—I do not love—"

She snarled at him, she teased at the fur around his testicles with her tongue, he scurried uphill, digging up moist earth and dead leaves . . . she knew he would be hers. Exultant, she bayed at the moon. It was good to run free, to cast aside the prison of human flesh and human decency . . . to forget the taint of silver that prevented her from transforming each month, for it was lust that liberated her.

Close to the ground. Good to feel the earth cling to her paws, good to smell the dirt. She paused to mark a clump of ferns. She ran on. The air was thinning.

She heard the voice of Major Sanderson: "I think this time we have found the real quarry—"

A break in the trees. A ledge overlooking a sheer drop; below them, the mountains blanketed with black treetops. The wind in her nostrils, the smell of burning . . . and the pungent sexuality of the beautiful young soldier . . . he was all wolf now, his fur golden-white like his human hair, his tail erect, his eyes smoldering . . . "Yes, my darling," she cried to him in the wolf-speech, "yes! Rejoice in the beast! Rejoice!" Her paws pounded the packed earth, she coiled, sprang, leaped, danced the dance of the hunter. Oh, he was beautiful, his muscles fluid beneath the thick pelt, his snout held arrogantly high as he sniffed in the myriad odors he could only now perceive. Oh, what a love she felt for him, newborn creature of darkness.

Meanwhile, she saw the two humans advancing toward the ledge. The creek that flowed past the Shungmanitu village had its source here, a tiny stream cascading over jagged black crags. Across the stream was the boy she had come seeking, and—

Another was with him . . . the bitch Speranza! The human who had stolen the Count from her!

Screaming, she charged toward the creek—

It is almost complete, the Wolf Boy said to himself. The music of the flute had brought them all in . . . they stood at the edge of the circle now . . . and the woman from his old life, the woman whose name was even now on the tip of his tongue, was helping them to face the dark things they must all face before they could enter the circle and be healed. . . .

And when they do, I will have all their memories and they will have mine, and I will be able to understand their language, and I will even know her name.

She looked at him from the other side of the circle. The others clustered around her. What was in her dream? Her face was lined with grief.

What did she see? The Wolf Boy knew that there was much about their lives that was still hidden from him. Was there something within the circle that he himself could not see, some terrible thing?

Suddenly the Wolf Boy heard a cry for help . . . it was the song of one who wants to die, who awaits the coming of the shape-changing wolf. The song was always the same song:

Tukte tuke esha munkin kta waun we
Hepin nan blihichiya waun we

"Soon," said the words of the song, "soon I will lie down and die. Now I stand. I go to stand upon a hill. I stand upon a hill with courage."

But he was so close to fusing the different personalities into one, so close to the magical act that would bring together the destinies of all the wolf-peoples. How could he answer such a cry now? Yet he must. He could not show selfishness now. The way of the Shungmanitu was always the way of compassion.

"Wait," he said softly as he set down his flute for the moment. "I go to send a brave man to the land of many tipis."

The others from inside him hovered at the circle's edge, waiting.

The cry for help came from the very source of the creek—

With a final shriek of triumph, Cordwainer saw his prize approach, and he readied his trap—

—and the Wolf Boy left the circle, and immediately the moonlight fell upon him and he changed, swiftly, smoothly, melting into the shape of the four-legged as he tensed and bounded up the massive rocks toward the one who had cried for help—

—and as Speranza reached up to touch the crucified wolf, the dream splintered and she saw, not a crucified wolf, but a man—

"So much for your vision quest, Wolf Boy," said Cordwainer Claggart to himself. "You're mine now, boy, you're all mine."

—the old Indian man was suspended from a tree by two rawhide cords. The cords were attached above his nipples. The old man was jogging back and forth, trying to free himself.

As Speranza stared, she heard a rhythmic banging from a branch of the tree . . . she saw Cordwainer Claggart, pounding on a saddlebag with the butt of a Sharps rifle. He wore a crazed expression. He beat the saddlebag in a steady four-four rhythm, like an Indian drum. And shouted down to her: "Good evening, ma'am! I do recollect meetin' you before somewhere . . . on a train, weren't it?"

He pounded. The Indian danced. His face was contorted in

anguish. Blood ran from his breasts and mingled with the water from the stream.

"Injuns gots their sun dance," said Claggart. "I figure, why not a moon dance too? A moon dance for the werewolves . . . fettered to a tree o' death with rivets of silver!"

She saw what he meant now. The pins that pierced the old man's breasts were silver. They gleamed in the moonlight. The old man did not scream, but sang softly to himself. It was not exactly singing . . . more an obscene gurgling . . . she realized that his tongue had been cut out, and that from his mouth there came a steady dribble of blood.

Where the silver cut the man, Speranza saw wolf bristles through the gaping flesh, and folds of wolfhide pushing through gashes in the arms and side. Crucifixion, worse than crucifixion!

"Mr. Claggart," Speranza said, "I cannot imagine what you hope to accomplish by this unspeakable cruelty!"

"You cannot imagine . . . ha, ha! What a fine way you has of talking, ma'am! Why, I can only manage to perpetrate a pale intimation of that there genteel manner o' discourse. 'Unspeakable cruelty!' I sure do like that, ma'am. But there's a rhyme and a reason for what I'm doing. You see, the way I figure it, them Shungmanitoose is pretty damn predictable. They fancies themselfs to be a kind of angel of death, sent from their almighty god, Wakantanka, to take away the souls of them as has no more use for livin'. When they hears an old man cry out in pain, and beggin' for to be released, they cannot help but run to his aid, neglectin' everything else . . . even their vision quests!"

"Johnny would never abandon his dream . . . not when he's on the verge of becoming healed of his affliction . . . not even to put this poor soul out of his misery—"

"But that," Claggart said, his legs swinging back and forth above her head, "is where you're just plumb wrong, ma'am. Look yonder." And motioned with a gesture of his head.

A young wolf was bounding over the rocks toward them. He circled them for a few moments. Then he transfixed the old man with an intense look; and the old man stared back.

"Old wolf ritual, that," Claggart said. "Never did see the use of it myself. Wolves and their prey exchanges them long, loving glances so the victim can tell the hunter that he truly wants to die;

and the hunter can ask his prey to forgive him . . . that's what the Injuns believes, anyhow."

It was a beautiful thing, the slow circling, the glance of love and death. But Speranza thought only of Johnny's chance for healing . . . of the fact that he had stood on the brink of the circle in which he would find himself whole. . . .

"Stay back, Johnny!"

Too late. The wolf sprang up, silver-gray streaking over the shadows, and the old man jerked the rawhide taut. He did not scream; only a strangled whistle issued from his throat. The silver hooks ripped loose from his chest and swung back and forth from the tree, the flesh still quivering. Blood spattered Speranza's face, soaked her skirts, so she could not tell whether they were drenched from the river of the dream or from this dying man's blood.

"Johnny—" The wolf leaped up to tear flesh now. Fangs ripping into sinews, flaying the neck tissue, biting open the chest cavity so the ribs popped loose one by one . . . and always the strips of bloody flesh swinging on the twin silver pendulums . . .

"Lord, ain't it a sight!" Cordwainer said. "But by his lights, he is doing an errand of mercy . . . puttin' that poor dumb Injun out of his misery . . . poor Injun! He pretended the boy was some kind of kin to him . . . but he has only one father now . . . a father that's goin' to show him just how evil a place the world can be."

"You are a wicked man," Speranza cried, as the boy-wolf ripped a withered arm from its socket. "I wish to God there were no place in the world for such as you. I thought the Count the prince of darkness himself, but he had compassion, and even a kind of nobility. . . ."

"Why, it's only natural you'd speak good of that Count. Ain't you his prize whore and brood-bitch? Dr. Swanson was mighty eloquacious about your murderous activities—"

"He told you! *You!*" Speranza was gripped by an intolerable rage and grief.

"Two hundred and fifty dollars in gold," Claggart said. "And I relieved him of every last gold dollar the next mornin' at a game of stud . . . damned if he didn't drink himself into a stupor and talk about everything under the sun! You, Miss Hope Martin, as you calls yourself, you may wear fancy clothes, but underneath 'em you ain't no better'n a coca-sniffin' whore—"

"I'm not addicted to the coca powder—" she protested, but she knew it was true, it was all true . . . she had used up her supply, she felt pain, waves of pain in her head, pounding at her skull, throbbing, throbbing—

The boy-wolf urinated on the corpse now, howling. He danced on the body. He tore out the heart and worried at it, chewed on it, spat out the gristly aorta. He rolled in the chest cavity and emerged soaked with blood.

And yet . . . she saw that the Indian's face was smiling, strangely at peace, though it now hung at right angles to the torso to which it had once been attached.

"Johnny, you must come to me—"

The wolf looked up. His form wavered for a moment, and she thought she could see the tormented eyes of her former charge.

"Oh, Johnny—" She held out her arms to him. He hesitated. There was recognition in his eyes—she knew it!

At that moment, Claggart threw a net down on him from a tree. A net of silver threads. And laughed again.

The wolf-boy thrashed, foamed at the mouth, squirmed. Claggart jumped off his perch and began methodically to stuff the boy, net and all, into a flour sack. Johnny struggled. Speranza ran toward him. She tripped. Went sprawling over the Indian's carcass. A half-chewed liver slithered down her bosom. I have no time for revulsion, she thought, getting up across the old man's corpse, slippery with coagulating blood. She began to pummel Claggart with her fists, but he merely pushed her against the tree trunk. A boy's face looked up from the neck of the sack, the eyes pathetic, sunken, stricken with profoundest despair.

"Monster!" Speranza screamed at Claggart.

"He was my father," Johnny said, peering at the dead man, "in his own fashion, just as the Count was."

"Well," said Claggart, "I am your father now, make no mistake."

Then Johnny said, in so low a whisper that only she could catch it, "It was always useless, you see. I'm not meant to lead the wolves to any destiny. I'm just a freak . . . nothing more or less." And another voice, the one she recognized as Jonas Kay: "A fucking freak!"

Speranza said, "He will never be cured! You must understand . . . he needs to be made whole. . . ."

"Oh, he'll be whole, all right," said Claggart. "I aims to teach him the true meanin' of what he is. I aims to give him what none of you could give him . . . a purpose . . . a *real* purpose . . . none of this goddamned talk of destiny and fate . . . he weren't made for destiny and fate, no, ma'am; he were made for killin'."

Then, faintly, she heard Johnny speak: "Speranza."

And another voice: "Johnny's dead . . . the Indian boy's dead! Yes, yes, you prim little governess with your secret little profane fantasies . . . they're all dead . . . all, all, all . . . the healing is complete . . . we are one now . . . we, Jonas Kay, always the werewolf." As Claggart stuffed the boy down the sack, she could hear wolfish whining.

He tied the sack up and slung it over his shoulder. It hung limp. The boy no longer struggled. Had he truly given up? But how could he not give up? It was hopeless. How could I have imagined that I, alone, could redeem him? There is so much pain in him . . . and he has borne the pain of so many others . . . or had their pain thrust upon him.

Claggart began to walk down the hill, whistling a jaunty tune; it was, Speranza realized, Gilbert and Sullivan.

She was about to run after him when—

A wolf-woman rushed at her, her red hair streaming in the moonlight! "Bitch!" she howled. "Bitch—" and she was on her. Butted her in the stomach so that she slipped once more on the dead man. And fell facedown, her face colliding with his face, her eye level with an eye that dangled from its socket by a single tendon . . . she turned around to see the woman-wolf ripping at the last tatters of her clothing, the fangs seeking flesh, the sharp claws rending her breasts—

It was Natasha! "I meant you no harm," she whimpered. "I did not choose to—"

But the wolf was beyond speech now, hate had hastened her metamorphosis. Speranza tried to throw her off, turning her face to avoid the slavering jaws. Fangs gleamed in reflected moonlight. Again and again the wolf dashed her against the stones, the earth, the ribs that protruded from the corpse's chest. Blood was in her eyes, her mouth. She tried to scream, but felt sharp claws clamp down on her mouth and slice into her tongue—

As he reached the ledge Scott saw that Natasha was attacking Speranza . . . so startled was he that his transformation jarred, began to reverse itself . . . "Miss Speranza!" he cried out, dimly hearing that he had only managed to produce a maddened snarl. Then, in the language of the wolves, he said, "Do not attack her!"

"So!" said Natasha, her words reeking of anger. "You desire her, then . . . that's what it is . . . you'd choose a human over your own kind . . ."

"I'm not your kind! Not yet—" But even as he said it he knew that he would never be fully human again. He felt fury and futility. He pounded his tail on the ground. He howled his anger. Instinctively his hackles rose and his hindquarters retracted . . . he leaped—

"Mr. Harper?" Speranza said hoarsely.

She had recognized him! He turned on Natasha. "You lied to me," he said in the speech of the wolves. "She knows me by my human qualities—"

"Delusion!" Natasha screamed, and dug into Speranza's cheek, carving deep gashes with her claws.

Scott could not endure it. He bit down hard on Natasha's left thigh. He tasted hair, skin, a little blood. "Do you not know who you are, my beautiful young soldier?" Natasha said, yelping in surprise and pain.

He bit down again and again. Natasha rolled away. Fur was torn to reveal the purple flesh . . . and here and there a patch of human skin . . . as her sexual appetite waned, she was transforming again. The snout was retracting, the features melting, the long red hair thrusting up through the furry scalp. . . .

"Thank you," Speranza said softly. She reached out to touch Scott's fur. She tried to smile at him, tried to reach the human part of him within.

Natasha ran howling in circles about them. Downhill a little, she saw that Claggart was exchanging gunfire with Major Sanderson. Now Teddy was climbing toward them, clutching the Remington. She breathed heavily as she tried to lift herself into a sitting position. There were shots in the background. But close to her was the Scott-wolf. She stroked him; he trembled. A vague stirring in her nether parts . . . perhaps it was a remembrance of Hartmut's touch . . . for she well knew how it was to love a beast.

* * *

Scott turned to Speranza. He wanted to say, "I'm right sorry, Miss Speranza, let me escort you away from these terrible things. . . ." but she was so near, and with his keen senses he could smell a hint of arousal beneath her terror. Trembling, she sat up, leaning against the tree trunk. The body of the dead Indian lay beside her. There was blood everywhere. Blood whose scintillant odor invaded his nostrils, filled him with lust. He had wanted her since he had first seen her, always known there was a part of him that thought of violating her . . . but his conscious mind had never dreamed of the violence, the rage in that obsession. . . .

"Miss Speranza," he tried to say, but it was another voice that spoke, a harsh deep growl that made her eyes widen and caused her to back away hard against the trunk. She was beautiful to him, her neck pale and slender, her lips half parted as though about to protest, her chemise torn, moonbeams on the pearl-silk sheen of an exposed breast . . . and eyes full of terror.

Terror! It was the terror that filled him with the most longing. In vain he struggled against that longing. Her heartbeat pounded, her body seemed drenched with the perfume of desire. He was in the grip of the beast. No, he told himself, no . . . but the lust was greater than his will . . . he pounced on her. She reeked of sweat and blood and Natasha's saliva. He was in a frenzy. She was beautiful. He touched her cheeks, felt the porcelain smoothness against his callused paws. "I love you," he tried to tell her, but only a growl came from his throat. "I love you, I love you," he said, and the more she resisted, the more his penis stiffened in its furry sheath and his tail thumped against the dead man—

Speranza could not resist. Her corset was cracked in a dozen places; now it shattered like the exoskeleton of an insect. She covered her breasts with her hands, but the wolf's tongue probed lower until it encountered her vulva. She felt the teeth teasing her clitoris. "Not you . . . not you, Mr. Harper!" she said, and looked down into the wolf's eyes. She saw no hint of the self-possessed young man she had known before . . . the eyes glittered, implacable. The wolf's tongue tunnelled deep into her vagina, abrading the delicate tissues. She screamed. "Stop . . . please stop, Mr. Harper," she said. "Please . . . sir, I am defenseless."

With a bloodcurdling howl, the wolf shoved her with his paws until she fell facedown onto the Indian's corpse, whose neck stump oozed blackish rheum into her eyes, her nostrils. Sickened, she felt the wolf mount her from behind, felt the snout push down on the nape of her neck, felt the bristly penis ram her nether regions . . . she screamed at the pain, screamed until she tasted bile and vomit in her throat and tears streamed from her eyes and ran into her nose and mouth and mingled with the taste of canine drool . . .

She became aware of Teddy Grumiaux standing beside them. Teddy was pleading with his friend . . . "You can break out of it, Scott . . . shit, Scott, you can't do this, not after all we's been through, it just ain't—"

Teddy shoved his Remington against the wolf's shoulder. The wolf continued to thrust, slamming her against the tree trunk. Faster and faster. Her head throbbed. She saw the moon through a veil of blood, bloated, like the eye of a skull. From the vibrating tree, leaves rained steadily on her, plastering the matted blood on her neck and breasts. "Save me . . . save me . . ." she whispered, but she knew what would have to be done to save her, and she saw Teddy standing there, the tears running down his cheeks, not looking at the two of them. . . .

"Oh, Lord . . . I can't do it . . . fuckin' Jesus. . . ."

With a final thrust the wolf spent his semen in her . . . she could feel the hot fluid spurting, the shaft of his penis sandpapering her canal, the seed bursting up her like a ball of fire.

"Forgive me," Teddy said. "You're my best friend. I loves you like my own brother, like my own—"

Teddy fired.

At once the transformation began to reverse itself. Sharp fur became sandy hair, topaz eyes shifted to a deep blue. The wolf howled, but by mid-howl the sound was tinged with a human anguish and by the time he collapsed into her arms it was the cry of a man mortally wounded.

He was naked. He was youthful, smooth, nothing like the Count who had possessed Speranza before. The moon, mottled by overhanging leaves, played lightly over the blue-veined tracery of his forearms. His hair, soggy with sweat, fell over one eye; the other stared into her own; the penis, still engorged, stood up from blood-matted curls of flaxen pubic hair.

She endeavored to feel the disgust appropriate to such an occasion. But when she saw the man in her arms bleeding profusely from his shoulder wound, saw the look of self-loathing in his eyes, she could not hate him utterly.

"Reckon I'm fixin' to die," he said, very quietly.

"But it's only a flesh wound," she said. "Just a little bullet in the shoulder . . . I'll bribe old Doc Swanson for you, if you like, and he'll treat it, and no one need ever know . . ." she added, but there was no conviction in her voice.

"I weren't shootin' to kill—just to get you off Miss Speranza," Teddy said, but she could tell that he knew what he had done. He was drying his eyes on a dirty sleeve.

"Did we save the boy?" said Scott.

Where were the others? She turned to Teddy. He whispered, "Gone . . . chasing each other down the hill . . . if Claggart don't got him, the Russian woman and the major done caught him by now."

Scott looked questioningly at her. "Yes," she said, weeping, "we saved him."

"That's good. Iffen he's been rescued, I guess I ain't died for nothin'."

"Yes." She could hardly see him through her tears.

"I'm right sorry about the other thing I done to you, ma'am. I didn't mean to harm you . . . it's just . . . I reckon I just didn't know how much I . . . cared for you."

For the first time since the violence had begun, she felt the icy wind of midnight. The treetops swayed; the wind sighed; and Scott Harper, his humanity fully restored to him, died.

Speranza cradled him gently for a few moments. He was light; in death he seemed even more boyish, his arms and legs slender, his chest taut and delicately muscled. She laid him down beside the ravaged corpse of the Indian.

"Johnny," she said. "They've got Johnny. . . ."

But Teddy could not be moved. He seemed past caring. He looked at his dead friend with eyes that seemed quite void of feeling. Her heart went out to him, but she knew he was too proud to accept pity from her. He had wept in her arms that evening in Lead, but he did not look like someone who would ever weep again.

"God damn it," Teddy said softly, fervently. "I'm goin' after

Cordwainer Claggart. I'm goin' to send him to hell if it's the last thing I ever do."

He stood up resolutely, feverishly reloading his derringer. And began stalking away.

"No," said Speranza. "You'll be throwing your life away—"

"I ain't goin' to get myself kilt, Miss Speranza. I can take care of myself real proper."

But he seemed so terribly young to her. She reached out to stay his hand . . . but was overcome at last. Though her corset was smashed, and there was no constriction about her waist to obstruct her breathing, the air was thin and the welter of emotions impossible to bear; knowing no other recourse, she swooned, clutching his hand tightly.

"Blast that Claggart!" said Major Sanderson. "He seems to have eluded us." He fired a few more desultory shots down the hill in the direction Cordwainer Claggart had taken.

Natasha felt the wind rise. She was in human form once more, for the stimulus of erotic arousal was no longer present. She smiled as she touched the major's arm and stayed him from his pursuit. "Let him go," she said.

"Nonsense, madam; we came in search of the boy; it would be a simple matter to dispatch him now."

"Let me show you something." She led him to the very edge of the ledge, where they could see the creek as it trickled down from the source toward the Indian village. The fire had spread across the clearing. Lodgepole piles were flaming now, columns of smoke clouding the face of the full moon. The wind was cold, but here and there was flecked with the warmth of the distant conflagration.

"You have what you want," she said. "You have killed Indians; that is greatest desire of your life, is it not?" The grin, half suppressed, on the major's face proved it amply. "As for boy, his death is immaterial. The important thing is that Indians have not kept him safe . . . and the truce, Major Sanderson, depends on the boy's safety! You have vested interest in the war's continuance, *n'est-ce pas*? And so have I. As long as there is war, we are both creatures of power."

At last, there was the shadow of a smile on Sanderson's lips. No need to kill him yet; there was dirty work ahead, and for now she could still hold out the promise of sensual gratification.

"Let us return to Winter Eyes now . . . secure in knowledge that *la guerre continue*."

"The war goes on," said Sanderson, "until the last barbarian dies. Custer will not have died in vain. I always admired that man; he was a man who knew the white man's place in the scheme of things; ruthless, to be sure, but it was a clean, Spartan ruthless that a military man such as I can well appreciate and emulate. Why, Natalia, I admire him as much as I do Alexander the Great and Julius Caesar, the greatest generals of antiquity. . . ."

He droned on for some time, extolling the virtues of this Custer; Natasha remembered that, when she and her cousin had been alone in Dakota Territory spying out the land for the Count, she had heard a rumor that Sanderson had fought under Custer in that infamous massacre; it was said that he had survived by hiding inside the carcass of an Indian pinto, and that he had not fired a single shot. That he had managed, by falsifying the paperwork, to claim that he was sick that day, being treated for a bout of pox; that he was consumed with fear that his cowardice might one day be discovered . . . that this, indeed, was the reason he was so obsessed with destroying the Indians, with out-Custering Custer.

At last she could endure no more of his inane platitudes. "Come, Major Sanderson!" she said. "Let us go down to Indian village and take measure of what you have accomplished there."

"Yes. The moon will soon be setting; we shall have to continue in haste."

"Wolves will be returning from their kills. The night is dangerous," said Natasha, turning coyly away from his gaze to mark the path with her scent. "Back to horses . . . back to Winter Eyes."

"I am now glad that we tethered the horses inside a ring of silver, as you suggested, Countess."

She smiled. At least he knew who was mistress in their relationship. She smiled at him, aware that in the moonlight, with her clothes tattered from shape-shifting, with her luxuriant hair billowing against her breasts in the gathering wind, she must be inflaming him beyond all reason. Indeed, he moved closer to her. He smelled of some scouring soap, despite the exertions of the evening; he was, she realized, the kind of man who cleanses himself over and over, not realizing that what taints him is in the soul, not the flesh.

"Natalia Petrovna . . ." he said. She knew what it was he wanted; and so, tempting and taunting at the same time, she gave him a moist little kiss just under his left ear . . . with just a hint of a bite to it. She could hear his heart pounding.

"The war!" she said urgently. "Think of war!"

"The war of extermination," he said.

"War of the wolves," said Natasha. But she was thinking of the beautiful young soldier. Dead, perhaps, by now, for there had been a faint mist of silver particles in the air . . . not a poisonous amount, but enough to irritate the lining of her nostrils. Whoever was pursuing them was not ignorant of the power of silver.

She wondered whether Hartmut was still alive.

Teddy Grumiaux helped Speranza to her feet. The wind howled. It was a good cold, for it made him numb all over; he didn't want to have any more feelings, not until the end of time.

He was too tired to pursue Claggart now. And there was all this grief inside him that he didn't know what to do with. No use crying about it. Only one answer now, a man's answer: vengeance. I am going to kill him, he whispered fiercely to himself. Ain't nobody goin' to stop me. I don't care how long it takes.

Speranza said, "I've failed."

He did not feel like sympathizing with her. "Reckon you have," he said, not looking at her.

"I can't go back to Winter Eyes . . . I've cut off my ties with Europe . . . in Deadwood, everyone already knows me for a whore and a child-killer, since I was foolish enough to trust Dr. Swanson. . . ." Teddy couldn't go back to Deadwood anymore either. Perhaps they thought he'd killed young Gina Hopwood; it wouldn't have surprised him if Cordwainer Claggart had managed to pin that on him. He didn't want to go back to the Indians anymore. All his ties with them were gone. I'm alone, he thought.

His fifteenth birthday was coming up soon.

"Miss Speranza," said Teddy, "I spent the last three years huntin' down them wolves because I figured I was doin' what my paw would of wanted me to do. I'm still goin' to kill wolves. All wolves, the four-legged and the two-legged. Reckon I found me a new vocation. And I has to practice it alone."

She nodded.

"I'll ride with you down to Cheyenne, and then you can take the train to wherever strikes your fancy. East or west, it don't matter nohow."

She said, "You must hate me . . . because of the way Mr. Harper died."

"No, ma'am," he said. But he still wouldn't look her in the eye.

"It's all right," Speranza said. "I hate myself, too. I've failed him. And you. And all of them."

Teddy said, trying to keep the bitterness out of his voice, "No, Miss Speranza. But I reckon you ain't a frontier woman. You feels things different. Guess you'd be happier somewheres civilized. You ain't hard and unbendin' like the badlands. You ain't got that savage wind blowin' through your heart."

She smiled a wan smile. "Maybe you don't know me all that well, Theodore Grumiaux," she said.

"I know that you been hurt on other folks' account and I don't want you to be hurtin' no more."

He spent the rest of the night building a platform out of dry wood, lashing it together with the rawhide Claggart had used for his mockery of the sun dance. By the time the moon was about setting, he had the platform up on the branch where Claggart had been sitting. Speranza watched him curiously. He hoisted up the Indian's body first. Then Scott's. He closed his friend's eyes with two large silver dollars. "Silver won't bother you no more," he whispered. He covered them both with a blanket of dried brush. Wordlessly, Speranza helped him gather dead leaves and wildflowers. She watched as he heaped the flowers over the bodies, drowning out their putrescence with the fragrances of summer. The wind gusted now and then and petals drizzled down over her. She was trying to lace the remnants of her corset together. Shows, thought Teddy, just how civilized she is.

Almost dawn . . . the moon was a shadowy thing, a cloudy disk behind a veil of twilight. Claggart had been riding hard, spurring the horse down ravines with the wolf-boy in the flour sack slung across the front of his saddle, chugging his bug juice on the fly. The terrain was flattening a little, and he could see Wyoming

Territory in the distance, beyond the hills . . . an expanse of buffalo grass, and, at the horizon, twisted rocky structures that reached up clamoring, like half-finished sculptures, to the reddening sky.

He eased up on the bit a mite. Listened. In the wind, the trees murmured, a noisome sound he wished he could be shut of. From the sack he heard little whimpering noises, and he knew that the wolf-boy was coming to. "Easy," he said, "easy, my little gold mine, my sack o' precious stones." He stroked the creature inside the sack. The sackcloth was hot, rough strands seared his hands. He could feel the creature move. "Easy," he said. "I been huntin' you long enough; I ain't your enemy. I been huntin' you down because we belongs together, you and me. I don't aim to kill you . . . I'll keep you alive and feed you well . . . on the appetisingest human flesh that I can find. But I has to make sure you knows who's master here."

He stopped his horse, dismounted, untied the sack so that its contents tumbled onto stony ground. There was the wolf-boy, enmeshed in silver, half changed. Slender arms ended in paws. The back was a patchwork of boy and beast. The face was all human though. And bloody: blood clotting on cheeks, lips, earlobes, forehead. The eyes sunken, deep blue peering out of circles of darkness; blond hair grown long from life amongst the Injuns, caked with the life fluids of the dead. Apathetic, the wolf-boy looked up at his captor.

"Moon'll be gone soon," Claggart said, "and you and me got some unfinished business. Mayhap you remembers the train ride from Omaha. . . ."

He knelt down beside the wolf-boy. Grasped him by the hair, forced him to look into his eyes. Hunter and hunted—the glance of love and death—not just an Injun saying after all, thought Claggart, because in my way I loves him as much as anybody else does.

The wolf-boy growled softly. A flash of yellow in those eyes. "You is mine now, Wolf Boy," said Cordwainer Claggart. "Say it. Say it."

"I—"

Holding the wolf-boy by the withers, he dragged him over by the stump of an oak tree. He gathered up a handful of grass, unhitched his britches, and defecated onto the stump; then, wiping off some of it with the grass, he smeared it on the wolf-boy's mouth and nose, ramming roughly up the nostrils, forcing the lips apart . . . he said, never raising his voice, "You being of the canine persuasion, son, I reckon there's but one way to make you know who your true pappy is . . ."

The boy wriggled, but he held him down, forced him against the lacerating bark. He smiled. Then he stood up and pissed on his face, his body. Where the piss touched the welts made by the silver, the flesh gave off a sour stench, like old wine, and the wolf-boy yelped. "Quiet now, you hear? Or I'll take a silver-tipped hickory to you." The wolf-boy was quivering all over like a suet pudding. The hairs on his back glistened; his body burned all over as with a deathly fever. Claggart's hands moved roughly along the mottled skin, feeling the heat seep into his hands, his veins; he remembered the day he had first caught sight of this shifting flesh, with the roof of the train rumbling under his feet, with the wind of the high plains blasting his face as they raced across Nebraska.

"Well," he said, "seeing as my britches is already off, mayhap it's time to teach you the second lesson of your new life." And, turning the wolf-boy so that he lay on his stomach on the stump, he moistened his manhood with a little spit and began to pry apart the devil creature's legs.

And in his mind, the forest was charred and the tree trunks bleeding from a thousand thousand gashes. The magic circle was gone. They could not find the clearing. Mile after mile they wandered over a land of burnt-out fires. Hot stones smoked, and the creeks were parched as a dead man's gullet. There was no sun, only a never-ending twilight.

Johnny Kindred did not know how long he and the others had been trudging. In the distance the trees still stood, twisted into fantastical shapes, some denuded, some buried upside down with their roots flailing in the acrid, acidulous wind.

"C'mon," Jake Killingsworth was saying, "we got to reach the clearing afore nightfall."

"Why?" said Johnny. "There's not going to be any nightfall. There is no more clearing."

"Sir," said James Karney, "I am convinced that the clearing still exists; that it has now become the domain of Jonas Kay. . . ."

"That's why we got to find it!" Jake said. "Mayhap Jonas thinks we is all dead. But we only been hurled down into a deeper part of the mind. We has found ourselfs in a kind of purgatory."

"But we're as good as dead. There's no one to lead us back. Where is the Indian boy? I can't feel him anywhere. I think he's gone, truly gone. I can't heal myself anymore. And where is Speranza? No, no, there's just the old snake-oil merchant, and he and Jonas have . . . a kind of understanding."

"I don't know where the Injun boy is. But we *can* rescue him."

"What's the use?" Johnny thought, Maybe I can blow myself out, like a candle. I think that all of us would die if I did that.

But Jake overheard his thought. And said, "Remember what the Injun boy saw in his vision . . . you can't die, Johnny, lessen you is kilt by the one which truly loves you."

"Why can't I die? Oh, God, I want to die . . . that's all I want . . . just let me die. God, let me die."

"God?" It was Joachim, who almost never spoke, but only played his violin in counterpoint to the others' conversations. "Perhaps it's time you abandoned the notion of God. That is a peculiarly human concept. I do not think there is a God for werewolves."

Jake was about to answer him. But suddenly Johnny felt himself lifted into the air, saw the whole universe spiralling away, and there was only blackness blackness everywhere and pain bursting through his whole body pain that started from his anus being ripped open pain like a club battering his shoulders a whip whistling across his buttocks pain invading him burning through his colon up his intestine through his guts all the way through to his pounding heart pain pain—

"How do you like it, Johnny Kindred?"

"No—no—send me back—"

"You don't want to come back to the clearing, Johnny-boy. It's all mine now. You don't want to come back. I can manage the outside world all by myself, you snivelling little pussy. From now on I'm only going to call you out to take the pain. Taking pain's about all you're good for anyway!"

—pain—

"Stay down there in purgatory, Johnny-boy . . . you're not man enough for hell."
 —pain—
 —pain—

And Cordwainer Claggart, his lust slaked, rode downhill toward Wyoming, whistling to himself as he adjusted his cravat and straightened his vest, for he would need to cultivate a most presentable appearance by the time he reached the next outpost of civilization.

11
Winter Eyes
one day after full moon

THEY RODE BACK INTO WINTER EYES IN TIME FOR THE FUNERAL.

The heat was stifling; Natasha could smell the dead Count even from the forest's edge. On her arrival, she changed dutifully into black, and the major donned a dress uniform (a complete set of clothing was always kept in readiness for him at the von Bächl-Wölfing house); the funeral was a lengthy one, with much weeping, but there was also a sense of inevitability to it. Few hopes were dashed by the Count's death; more hopes were aroused, for already the factions had formed.

Late in the afternoon, the major took his leave. Natasha retired to the house to confer with her cousin Vishnevsky.

That evening, as they supped, just the two of them, at the long mahogany table in the von Bächl-Wölfing dining hall, he handed her a yellowing document that stank of bodily decay. He told her that he had recovered it from the coffin of Dr. Szymanowski. They spoke Russian so that the Wallachian serving maids would not understand them. She had asked for the best wine; to her amazement, it turned out to be a case of red wine that had been bottled in 1791 on the Count's own estate in Wallachia. Almost a hundred years old, she thought, downing it by the gobletful.

"Do not drink so much!" he said. "And . . . read the paper."

It was a will, written in Hartmut's hand. In vain she tried to convince herself that the handwriting was counterfeit; she knew herself that it was not so, and every turn of phrase, every comma, was in a style whose origins she could not deny.

She said, "No one must know about this."

Vishnevsky said, "Of course . . . Countess."

She smiled a thin-lipped smile. "We are at war. As long as there is war, there is unity. And above all it is our unity that concerns me."

"Yes, Countess," said Valentin Nikolaievich, though she knew he was not fooled in the slightest.

"Oh, Valentin," she said, kittenish suddenly, "why are you not even chiding me for my presumption? And this new 'Countess . . . Countess' . . . surely you need not be so formal, *mon cousin*? Since when have you ceased to call me 'tyi'?"

"I know my place," said Vishnevsky. And bowed solemnly to her. "And even more, I know that my fate is tied to yours, and I cannot survive your downfall."

She swallowed another half a glass of red wine. But it was power, not wine, that she was drunk on.

12
San Francisco
new moon

ONCE MORE SHE SAT IN A RAILWAY STATION WAITING ROOM. IT WAS not segregated by sex—that was a European refinement most unsuited to the Far West—but there was an opulence she had become unaccustomed to in her Dakota years, from the wallpaper with its maroon velvet-chased design of Cupids to the ornamental brass lamp-brackets, the flames supported by angels with flowing hair.

Once more—as at the very outset of her adventures—she wore a plain black dress, and sought refuge from her surroundings in a Bible, though this time it was a cloth-bound edition she had bought used from a Mormon priest on the train, and contained— were she but to glance more than casually through its pages— many unfamiliar passages.

It was useless. The nightmares had not ceased. From Cheyenne she had ridden the rails through Utah and a change of road name, through Nevada, down the perilous Sierras with the train bucking and heaving and plunging by turns, across startling sunsets and twilights. She had ridden first-class—though her supply of gold was dwindling fast, she still had enough for that—and her occasional forays from the compartment to the dining car or library had been much noted by the other passengers, if she had cared to listen. For on lengthy journeys, tongues are loosened; a taciturn traveller will inevitably be the occasion of speculation and gossip. And so it was that Miss Hope Martin, as she was known to all aboard the *Pacific Express*, arrived in San Francisco with a past, or rather many pasts, each more fanciful than the last, and none comparable to the reality. She had spoken to no one in all that time, except in her dreams.

This was the substance of her nightmares:

Once upon a time there was a girl named Little Red Riding Hood who lived at the edge of the forest and she was called Little Red Riding Hood because her cunt was always bloody and it attracted the wolves and when she was afraid it would bleed all by itself and they would huff and puff and blow down her house of thin tissue paper like the pages of a Bible and—

Once upon a time there was a girl named Little Red Riding Hood who wept at the feet of the divine cross and cradled a suckling wolf in her arms and—

Dark inside the wolf's gut. Waiting for the hunters. Dull reports of distant rifles. Dark. The walls sweating blood. Menstrual blood. The walls sweating. Huffing and puffing and huffing and puffing and—

Standing at the feet of the cross—

Once upon a time there was a little boy named Little Red Riding Hood and he crawled into his mother's bed and whined what a

*good boy am I and his mother was a wolf and the last thing he saw
was her teeth the teeth around the edge of the blood-dripping cunt
and—*

*A little girl named Little Red Riding Hood who lived by the edge
of the forest that smelled of—*

"Miss Martin?"

—smelled of—

She looked up. There was a man of middle years, of sober
attire, his mustache twirling a little, the eyes twinkling. "Miss
Martin?" he repeated. "I could not help but notice you on the train
from Carson City, and I was wondering whether perhaps you
might be in need of some assistance. . . ."

She started to protest, but the man continued, in a tone so kindly
that it was difficult to interpret it as that of someone trying to take
advantage of her position. "Perhaps . . . your company at
dinner?"

"I am not in the habit of—" Speranza began. But no. The time
when she would have fretted about having a chaperone, or
questioned the credentials of a stranger who had the effrontery to
invite her to dinner, was long since past. I am a fallen woman, she
told herself. If this Bible—and my nightmares—are any indica-
tion, I must now be capable of any depravity.

The man backed away a little. "I apologize, Miss Martin, if
I've offended. But . . . although the other passengers were
always remarking on your haughtiness and unsociability, I thought
that perhaps it was simply that . . . you needed to be alone. I
have been alone a long time, I am a widower. I understand such
needs."

Speranza began to weep with a passion she did not know she
could still feel. With this outbreak of emotion came nausea too,
and she began to retch, and to look about in embarrassment.

"You are with child," said the stranger. But he did not speak
accusingly; for that she was grateful.

*Once upon a time there was a girl named Little Red Riding
Hood who was hiding inside her mother who was really a wolf,
waiting for the hunters to huff and puff and—*

She knew she would accept the stranger's invitation. Perhaps he
would be able to help her find some mindless occupation so that
she could forget all that had happened.

He extended a hand to her; she noticed that the ruff of his shirt was silk, and that a gold watch chain adorned his waistcoat. "I am a banker, a person of some consequence in this city; I hope you will not find my company offensive. My name is William Dupré."

The womb is the treehouse is blood.

PART FOUR

Moon Dance

1
1963: South Dakota
gibbous moon

From the notes of Carrie Dupré

William Dupré.

My great-grandfather.

I guess that's when I finally realized that this wasn't just the story of the Laramie Ripper . . . the most unusual multiple personality case in history . . . a family saga of lycanthropy . . . or even a spectacular, if offbeat, panorama of the opening of the American West. The story had all those things, but it was also my story.

And the nightmares were my nightmares.

They were the nightmares that visited me nightly . . . more intensely if I'd had an all-day session with J.K. The more deeply we delved into the world inside J.K.'s head, the more vivid they came. Fragments of fairy tales mixed with grand guignol and sexual imagery, horrific and erotic at the same time. Images of childbirth, abortion, deformed fetuses, babies with canine faces, fangs that dripped blood and saliva, drooling eyes. I didn't need Dr. La Loge to tell me about the Freudian overtones of this whole lycanthropy business—the overtones were made explicit for me every night. I was scared to go to sleep. Scared to face J.K. with my tape recorder and notepad. Scared to be alone. Scared all the time, scared shitless.

I'd promised myself never to smoke again after I graduated from Berkeley—not even marijuana. But about the time Johnny Kindred was captured by the Indians, about the time Speranza was becoming hooked on cocaine . . . I started on the Winston 100s. A pack a day . . . nothing spectacular. Then, sometimes, two.

I had to get out of Winter Eyes for a day or two. Summer was oppressive as hell, with air-conditioning on the blink and the very walls in the old wing sweating, the orderlies hustling about in their shirtsleeves, the inmates restive, the doctors listless. I read that there was going to be a big sun dance at the Pine Ridge Reservation, and I realized that Preston would be there. I took out the car, which I hadn't driven in a couple of weeks, not since coming back from Lead. Winter hadn't been kind to the old Impala and now it coughed and sputtered and always had to be coaxed— that was one reason why I dreaded going anywhere—and I went down to the site, notebooks and all.

Of course, I knew a lot about what was going to happen from Dr. Murphy's Indian Studies class back at Berkeley. But I was expecting something a bit like a *National Geographic* special, and it wasn't like that at all.

There was the circle of women, dancing back and forth in slow motion to the hypnotic pounding. There was the sacred tree, the men in their knee-length kilts with sagebrushes in their hands and whistles between their lips and thongs piercing their breasts, dancing to the solemn music. I hadn't been expecting the heat, or the matter-of-factness with which my presence was regarded, or . . . how can I put it . . . the corpulence of the celebrants.

I had formed quite a different picture of it all, with muscular, sweating young men leaping up and down and whooping wildly—in fact, in school, I had somehow managed to superimpose some kind of bondage trip onto this deal. It was something of an adjustment to see the real thing. I could see the intensity of the dancers and I knew that their pain must be real. But to me the sunlight was suffocating. And Preston was not there.

I was finally forced to admit to myself that it was Preston's absence that soured the spectacle for me. I'd wanted to see him suffer. Not for the sake of his people. But for me. It was hard to confess it to myself, but there it was. Beneath the eye of the Great Mystery, I couldn't lie, not even to myself.

And that was what I found most unbearable about this sun dance. The truth of it. There's no ancient hero getting crucified to take away the sins of the world. There's man, here and now, crucifying himself, suffering and giving life. And not some mighty-thewed Conan look-alike. The truth is a paunchy middle-aged man, someone without a job, perhaps an alcoholic, perhaps someone who beats his children. An ordinary, flawed human being.

"Truth hurts" is not a metaphor to the Lakota.

I am afraid of truth.

That's why I ended up fleeing the scene before even one of the pledgers had succeeded in ripping himself down from the sacred tree, why I ran all the way to the car with the pounding drum and the falsetto voices still ringing in my ears, why I jacked up the radio and peeled down the road to the familiar music of the Drifters.

I decided to drive to Wall, a peculiar town which has a drugstore the size of Rhode Island—if not Delaware—and which was always swarming with tourists. The road wound through the Badlands; I thought—with the self-aggrandizing romanticism of youth—that I might be able to commune with those twisted peaks, those strata of violent color, that splendid bleakness—that somehow it would enable me to come to terms with what I had partially witnessed.

Instead, my car broke down, and I found myself in the sweltering heat, mopping my brow with a fold of my summer dress, my bouffant looking more or less like a startled porcupine. Fumes were rising from the hood, and I was so thirsty I thought my throat would vaporize. I cursed myself. Somehow I had assumed that there would be a Coke machine or something at the sun dance—at a religious ceremony, for God's sake! How could I have been so stupid, and so damned . . . so damned . . . suburban and white about the whole thing? Then and there, in the middle of nowhere, with a heat stroke imminent, I lost my temper. I got out of the car and began pummelling the hood with my fists and telling the Impala to go fuck itself.

"Should have checked the water before you left the loony bin, sister."

I whirled around and he was there.

Lean and wiry and no, not paunchy in the least. "You didn't do it!" I screamed. "You didn't even go through with it, you hypocrite . . . all you ever do is posture . . . "

He stood there, smiling a little bit, in torn jeans and a faded JFK-LBJ tee-shirt. His hair had grown longer; in the still hot air, it clung to his cheeks and neck. He was thin; he had a sickly-sweet smell, like someone suffering from malnutrition. He let me shout at him for several minutes. Then he seized my wrists, gripped them with a calm I did not know he could possess. There was something different about him.

"I didn't not go through with it, Carrie," he said. "I've discovered . . . something else. Vision quest is a funny thing. You start off expecting a lot . . . pain, of course, but at the end of the pain you think you know what you're going to see. A lumbering spirit-bear maybe, who'll hand you a bow and arrow and say, 'Be a warrior.' Or 'Be a medicine man.' Or even 'Be a faggot!' Or whatever. And lead you to the sweat lodge and the sacred circle . . . and the sun dance and everything that follows. But sometimes a vision tells you what you don't want to hear." His eyes seemed terribly far away.

"How did you find me, Preston?"

"I could smell you. The air is still and moist now, and a scent can go lingerin' for hours, days. And I ain't afraid to be able to smell you. You know now, don't you?"

"Know?"

"Babe, you got the blood of the wolf in you. Maybe you're not a hundred percent true-blue honest-to-Jesus werewolf, but you got something of it in your bones, you can feel it. I know you can."

I stood there. Struck dumb. The nightmare came back. Speranza's nightmares. Flooding my senses. Here, in broad daylight, in the dazzling sunshine. I remembered—

Being very small, huddled in my bed with the comforter with big red roses . . . my mom reading *Little Red Riding Hood* to me. And wrapping myself inside the comforter after the lights out like a cocoon and seeing—

Dark. Moist walls. Inside the belly of the wolf. Waiting for the hunters. Waiting to be born. Me, twisted, misshapen, half-woman.

"Guess I'd better fix that old clunker of yours before it blows up," Preston said, lifting the hood. "Figures . . . no radiator water . . . you dumb broad." But he said it without bitterness, and I knew he meant nothing by it. He began to tinker with the insides of my car . . . I felt as though my own insides were being tinkered with.

William Dupré wasn't my great-grandfather.

Not the faded daguerreotype that hung in the family room next to the patio doors. . . .

My great-grandfather was Scott Harper from Missouri, cavalry officer, hero of the Indian Wars, renegade, deserter . . . were-wolf.

And that's why I understood the nightmares . . . and that's why Johnny Kindred's plight was so real to me . . . I had never believed in predestination, but I was beginning to see that my moves had been planned for me with the intricacy of a chess game. I was afraid. I let Preston pull me into his arms. I felt his lips, his tongue on mine . . . burning, dry . . . and always that smell, like overripe oranges dying in abandoned orchards.

"Jesus, what a weird ménage we make," he said hoarsely. "You and me and the Laramie Ripper."

I pulled away. "What was in your vision?" I said to him. I stopped to light a cigarette.

"Do you have to pollute the sacred—" he began, with all the old rancor in him. Then, "Sorry."

"I'm sorry, too." I carefully stubbed it out and tossed it into the Impala's ashtray. The mountains mocked me. Mountains groping for the sky, yellow mountains, pink mountains; here and there clefts of grass in the naked rock, freckled with purple wildflowers.

"My vision. . . ."

His eyes: the brown was flecked with yellow. Even in daylight there was a little wolf in him. The beast never goes away.

I waited

"November. Full moon. The great cycle comes around again. There will be a moon dance."

"A moon dance?"

"Yes. The wolf-boy will lead the way. Doors will be opened. The world can yet be redeemed. We can live with the beast within. Yes!" His eyes glittered. "Or else there'll be war, destruction, death, apocalypse. It's up to us."

"Isn't that a bit metaphysical?" I said. I started to laugh until I realized he was quite serious. So I stood there, fidgeting with the edge of my summer dress—since I didn't have a cigarette anymore—and waiting for him to tell me more.

"You were in the vision too, Carrie."

"What do you mean?"

"You, me, and the Laramie Ripper."

Returned to the Szymanowski Institute that night. Visited the graveyard: this time, the grave markers were those of old friends.

Scott Harper. Had they brought his body back to Winter Eyes even though he had been their sworn enemy? Another mystery I have to solve. Perhaps the fact that he was a white man and a werewolf overrode all that . . . perhaps, too, Natasha needed, for some reason, to distract the populace from her palace coup.

There is no grave marker for the Count von Bächl-Wölfing, and I have still not found the statue that is supposed to be Speranza Martinique, the Madonna of the Wolves.

Preston didn't come back with me. He is still out there somewhere, living in the wilderness; he needs, I suppose, to become more attuned to the beast. Perhaps he doesn't want to see civilization again until the consummation of his vision.

I sleep alone. The nightmares do not stop.

In the morning I met Sterling La Loge over breakfast before the day's scheduled interview with J.K. I had already smoked two cigarettes when he showed up. He merely smiled and said, "You're going to kill yourself, Carrie."

I ate.

"Look, I hate to sound like the classic Freudian that I am, but this new addiction suggests a strong desire to return to the oral stage of development. A kind of infantilism, actually. Do you long for the womb, my dear?"

I laughed, but when I closed my eyes I thought of—

Inside. Waiting for the hunters.

"Why no, Dr. La Loge."

"That's good." He poured me another cup of coffee. I gulped it down—I could imagine him thinking, "How oral, how oral," but I didn't care. "We've reached a kind of watershed . . . I hope you realize, Carrie, that we couldn't have done it without you . . . but we have the hardest part to overcome now."

I knew what he meant. I had learned that a multiple personality is usually triggered by a traumatic event in the patient's childhood . . . most often some kind of sadomasochistic incest. The event is so intolerable that the victim denies its existence, denies that it ever happened to him . . . and creates another personality to have such horrific things happen to. Once one splinters off, it's a kind of chain reaction, and soon there'll be a dozen or more characters, each with his own accent, age, voice, name, even brain waves. But it's not a psychosis . . . just a "personality disorder."

We had yet to face the primal trauma.

Oh, I'd learned of enough hideous experiences in J.K.'s life to traumatize a dozen people. But none of them was the original experience . . . the dark heart . . . J.K. himself had never faced it, although he came close during the Indian boy's vision quest.

La Loge said, "I'm going to have to ask you to be even more cooperative than before. I know it's been hard on you; but J.K. believes that this Speranza woman has to be somehow present for him to be able to break through the final barrier. Would it be too much to ask for you to . . . as it were . . . *impersonate* her? Think of it as blending in with J.K.'s fantasy life, or whatever, but. . . ."

Impersonate?

How could I tell La Loge how I felt? That Speranza Martinique had so far invaded my life that I was dreaming her dreams, thinking her thoughts? That, far from being unable to play along with his therapeutic fantasy games, I was in danger of becoming subsumed into Speranza, into losing Carrie completely?

I looked past Dr. La Loge, out through the picture window to the Weeping Wolf Rock, no longer rearing up out of the snow as when I first set eyes on it, but towering above a blanket of brilliant green. "I'll do what I can. Of course." I was already on my third cigarette. Better nicotine, I thought, than Speranza's cocaine.

2
1885: Rock Springs, Wyoming Territory day before full moon

THE AUTUMN WIND WAS ROARING THROUGH ROCK SPRINGS AS THE cowboys swept into town on their way to join the Goodnight-Loving trail south. The wind rattled the battened shutters, shook sheaves of dead leaves into the streets of steaming dung, slammed mud against doorways, knocked signs against walls. In front of Webb's General Store, a fluttering handbill, pasted on the post under the canopy of the boardwalk, told of the next day's wonders:

One Day Only in Rock Springs:
tomorrow at Bitter Creek
CLAGGART'S AMAZING
CIRCUS OF TRANSFORMATIONS!
For the outlay of a mere SHORT BIT (10¢)
YOU SHALL SEE
A *Gipsy Woman* foretell all;
A *Jackalope* that can do astounding
ARITHMETICAL CALCULATIONS;
a *Magician* who can charm the
BULLET out of a GUNSHOT WOUND
fired by the FASTEST GUNFIGHTER IN THE WEST
and:
(on FULL MOON DAYS ONLY)
a BOY *TRANSFORM HIMSELF* INTO A *WOLF!*

Beneath these words someone had scrawled: "And watch a Chinaman turn Christian!" in human blood.

The wind roared so loud that you could barely hear what else was going on in Rock Springs that day. But as Victor Castellanos tethered his horse in front of the general store, and watched his two companions, Negroes who as children had been slaves down Mississippi way, wander off to the saloon across the street he could smell blood in the air. The town reeked of death. With the full moon so close, Victor Castellanos could just about taste it. Even though he hadn't run with the Winter Eyes pack in almost two years, since the old Count died, he recognized the scent at once. Panic. Terror. And blood. He wondered whether the Winter Eyes people had come raiding this far west.

There was another scent too. There was a young wolf somewhere nearby. The posts of the boardwalk were well marked. Whoever it was knew how to piss straight, wind or no wind.

The roaring of the wind crescendoed. And then, when Victor turned, he realized there was more to the roaring than the wind. A small lynch mob was turning a corner, bearing down on the general store. They were dragging a Chinaman by his queue. Another, trussed up like a hog for the spit, was being prodded forward with rifle butts. The crowd was yelling. Castellanos couldn't make out the words. It was looking damn ugly.

He decided that perhaps it would be better to duck into the saloon. He crossed the street. He started to push open the saloon door. There came the sound of a piano and a fiddle from within. He stepped inside. The two Negroes were huddled in the back, with their shop glasses; the barkeep looked up and nodded cursorily; a dead Chinaman swung from the rafters like a pendulum. They'd hanged him with his own queue. His tongue lolled and his eyes bulged from their sockets, and blood dripped down onto Victor's boots.

"Better come in from under there," said the barkeep. "That Chinee blood'll tarnish them spurs just like that."

Victor Castellanos was shocked. Even among the Comancheros they had not treated violent death so casually. Even the were-wolves did not adorn their saloons with fresh kills. . . .

"What is happening?" he said.

"Just ridding the town of some man-sized vermin, is all," said the barkeep. "This town belongs to decent folks, white folks."

The Negroes looked decidedly uncomfortable.

"I am not entirely white," said Castellanos as he approached the bar.

"Leastways you ain't no heathen. Shit, even them niggers ain't heathens!"

"Lord, that we ain't," said the taller of the two black men, Ned Johnson, who was decidedly "decent folks," thought Victor, and an excellent cowhand besides, good with a lariat. His companion Samson was less savory; he'd be rustling if he didn't have an honest job.

Apart from the three out-of-towners and the bartender, and two women in daring scarlet dresses playing the musical instruments, the saloon was empty. The noise outside was getting more raucous now.

"Hey," said the barkeep at last, "I want to be out there enjoying the bloodshed. You mind if I just close up?"

Without waiting for a response, he abandoned the bar and went outside. The fiddle player stopped playing and, hand on hips, marched over to the counter. "Men!" she said. "All they ever care about is killing. More drinks?" She brandished a bottle of the house rotgut, and refilled their glasses without waiting for a response. "Oh, don't worry about the four bits, they ain't even gonna notice, not with the wild carousin' that's goin' on outside."

The piano player segued into a sentimental waltz, which she fairly swooned over, with willowy arm movements and intense facial expressions.

"And what *is* going on outside?" said Victor. He had smelled wolf in the air behind the terror and the bloodshed. Yet he was sure the werewolves were not behind this.

"They're doing what oughter have been done years ago—massacrin' the heathens that's been taking over our town."

Screams outside now. Castellanos stood up, leaned against the saloon doors. Trampling on the boardwalks. Men and women with ugly, angry faces. In the middle of the street, a dozen or so Chinese, cowering . . . a man clutching a baby under each arm . . . a woman with her dress half ripped off, fending off two men with a jade idol, screeching . . . gunfire . . . Castellanos watched the mob ooze toward the saloon, watched a man trampled, his guts catching on the boot spurs of the tramplers . . . and autumn leaves rained down from the lowering sky.

"Let's string this one up right here." Four or five young men—none of them looked old enough to lace his own boots—were kicking an old man along the boardwalk. Blood spurted from his nose, his lips. His smock was stained with blood and mud. The boys propelled him forward by their boots.

"We can put him right over the saloon door," said one.

"Good thinkin'." Another was fashioning a noose.

They dragged the Chinaman to his feet, tightened the noose around his neck, and threw the rope up to the crossbeam. One by one they spat in the Chinaman's face. He seemed resigned to death.

"We gonna run these fuckin' heathen right out of town. Barbarian coolies! Idolaters!"

"Kill 'em. Fuckin' kill 'em. God damned kill them sons of bitches."

"Watch your language, boys." It was the fiddle player, who had propped the door open with a chair. "It's one thing to rid the earth of vermin, I reckon, but it's another to take the name of the Lord in vain." She watched them tugging on the rope, a chaw of tobacco in one cheek. Then she ambled out and helped them yank the rope up. "Give you a hand."

Leering, one of the boys said, "I hear you give more'n a hand sometimes, Jenny Lee."

"Will ya stop thinkin' about women? We got more important work here. We is solving a national crisis . . . the Chinee question . . . damn straight."

Jenny Lee laughed and tugged. Turned to Victor. "Hey, give us a hand, pardner." For some reason, the Chinaman, faced with his ultimate destiny, had become rather agitated, and was trying to run off the boardwalk. The leering boy socked him in the mouth. A tooth skittered across the dirty planks.

Victor wasn't sure what to do. These people made him sick, but he knew that he could do nothing. After all, they might as easily turn on him, or on the two black cowherders.

Then he thought: I am not even a human being . . . I don't see why it should matter. And he put a hand on the rope.

At that moment, he heard the whistle of a bullet. The leering boy was collapsing onto the boards. There was a hole in his head the size of a half-dime.

"I'll be—tarnation—" his friend—a ringleader, it seemed—

said. "A stray bullet . . . " He turned to the mob in the streets. "Hey, careful where you're shootin'! You're liable to hit a white—"

He didn't finish his sentence. A second shot. Castellanos saw the kid's stomach rip open, the boy grimace in surprise and pain, and then . . . slowly . . . falling on top of his dead friend.

About ten yards down the boardwalk, a man was holstering a double-action Merwin and Hulburt.

"Let him go," he said. It was a whisper, but it carried above the uproar. A flurry of leaves: leaves piled up against the corner posts; the fragrance of vegetative decay filled Victor's nostrils. Though the man had a pale face, there was an Indian cast to his features, and he wore his hair long under a shapeless old slouch hat from which depended a single eagle feather, notched in the Sioux way, to show that the wearer had counted coup. He was young; though his face was weather-beaten and his eyes were lined, he was slender, not all filled out like a grown man; probably no more than eighteen or nineteen years old, the age Castellanos had been when he first started riding with Comancheros . . . long before Baroness von Dittersdorf had turned him into something not quite human.

Castellanos couldn't help himself; he said, "Thank you for stopping them."

The man stepped toward them. The rest of the boys disappeared into the mob; there was only Castellanos, Jenny Lee, and the two corpses.

Jenny Lee said, "Hey, there wasn't no call to kill them boys . . . they was just having a bit of fun."

"Fun?"

"Riots been going on a couple of days now. Today, tomorrer at the latest they say, troops be comin' to take control. Bring all them heathens right back into Rock Springs . . . protectin' them like they was people. Governor Warren, he done complained to President Cleveland, and—"

"And in the meantime, your boys is having fun." The gunman started to enter the saloon; Jenny Lee, nonplussed, stepped aside. For the first time, Castellanos noticed a sign, in ornate characters, on the wall next to the hat rack: "No Dogs, Indians or Chinamen."

The gunman gave the sign a cursory look and said, "Look's like you forgot niggers." He waved a pistol butt at Castellanos's two accomplices, who were staring at the floor. The pianist, perhaps in an effort to inject a little culture into the proceedings, had launched into a rousing medley of tunes from Italian operas.

"Oh . . . well . . ." said Jenny Lee. "We always meant to keep them out, but with so many of the cowhands being darkies, we just couldn't afford to turn down the business . . . but if you want, I could ask them to move to the back of the—"

"It's right good of you not to notice, ma'am, that I myself am of a somewhat impure blood."

Jenny Lee bit her lip. The strains of "*La donna è mobile,*" wrong notes cascading all over the keyboard, filled the saloon. At last she said, "Drink?" and sidled over to the counter.

"Drinks all around," said the gunman. He pulled out a handful of change and tossed it to the two blacks, then threw a silver dollar at Victor. "Catch!"

Victor recoiled. Too late! The silver glanced across his knuckles, scorching . . . he let out a canine yelp. Then, as his eyes met those of the gunman, he knew that this man knew what he was.

Softly, for Victor alone, the stranger said, "Should of been more careful, friend. I got to kill you now. It's something I swore on my paw's grave."

"I do not know why you would seek to kill me. If I by accident have killed someone who is kin to you, I assure you that I had no control over myself at the time . . . as you well understand, since you have guessed my nature." The knuckles of his left hand were raw; the silver had seared off the skin and exposed raw bone.

"Everybody I ever cared about in this world," said the stranger, "was kilt because of your kind."

"But if you swear an oath to kill every one of us just because of what we are . . . is that not the same as . . . what the people of this town are doing to the Chinamen? . . ."

"I made a vow," said the stranger, though Castellanos could see doubt in his eyes, and a great despair. They were alike, the two of them. The thing that had driven him away from Winter Eyes, that had forced him to try to flee what he had become . . . was the same impulse that drove this gunfighter. And so, when he said, "Shall we say sunrise tomorrow, then?" Castellanos found himself agreeing to the duel.

"That will give me a chance to settle my affairs," he said. He

did not remind the stranger that there would be a full moon
tonight; he was sure he already knew. "But, if I am perhaps to die
tomorrow, I would like to know my killer's name."

"The name's Theodore Grumiaux," said the gunman.

They shook hands. Grumiaux's was not sweating. The fiddle
player served them whiskey. The barkeep came lumbering back
inside, giving the Chinaman's corpse a push to start it swinging
back and forth once more. The sounds of the riot outside
continued. As the doors swung open, leaves fluttered into the
saloon, ocher, gold, vermilion.

"Goldarned army," the barkeep muttered. "They're less than a
hour's ride away now."

"Law 'n' order," Jenny Lee said derisively. She took a swig of
whiskey out of the bottle she'd been pouring from.

"Couple o' white boys clutterin' up the doorstep," said the
barkeep. The others all shrugged with studied nonchalance.
"Stray bullets, I reckon."

"Guess your fun's about over," said Jenny Lee.

"Not quite," the bartender said. "There's some kind of circus in
town tonight; that's where me and my friends'll be. Gipsies,
magicians, even a werewolf pup, I understand."

Grumiaux stiffened.

So that was the young wolf Castellanos had smelled earlier.

Little time left. He was pretty sure this Grumiaux could pump
him full of holes faster than he could draw. Castellanos had
survived many duels, but he had a feeling that this gunman had
silver bullets. But he could not honorably retreat from this
confrontation now that they had shaken on it.

Perhaps, he thought, I have just been fleeing the inevitable. I
never wanted to be a monster; perhaps my prayers are being
answered, perhaps this is how my curse will be lifted. He bore the
man no ill will. "Listen," he said, "I know it will not cause you
to change your mind about killing me, but why don't I buy you
some supper? There is an excellent bit-house down at the corner,
and—"

"Not anymore," said Grumiaux grimly. "The cook there was a
Chinaman."

"The inn then. Next to Webb's General Store."

3
Rock Springs
full moon

THE BOY OPENED HIS EYES. IT WAS ALWAYS DARK NOW, EXCEPT WHEN his master willed it. The dark came from a double thickness of black velvet that was draped over his cage, swathing the silver-chased bars; but he could feel the power of the moon, even through the velvet and the silver. His blood moved a little less sluggishly. It was stifling hot in the cage, and the smell of his own urine overpowered the cheap perfume in which the cage had been doused.

"What you got in that cage, mister?"

A woman's voice, raspy from too much smoking; he could smell the tobacco in the air. There was a faint odor of dried semen too, semen of many humans. Even in the dark he knew what kind of place he had been brought to. He growled, but the silver tempered his growling into a low purr; he could sense the velvet vibrating a little. The air was thick, so thick . . . he picked at a sore on his arm, licked the pus from the wound, hunched up, waited for what he knew was to come.

"The cage, mister! You said you was going to tell me what's inside it."

"I'll show you afterwards. Go ahead and take off that silk chemise and . . ."

He heard tearing cloth. An excited little giggle.

"Now, you know they always charge extra for torn clothing . . . the lace trim has to be replaced, you know . . . Pareeesian chantilly, and . . . ooh! you touched me with something c-cold!"

"Gold never fails to tame a woman. Here. Let me touch you with it. Let me run this double eagle down the nape o' your

slender little neck . . . down to where them twin tits o' yours
rises and falls softly, softly. Tits like . . . like . . . rosebuds,
that's it, rosebuds in the morning dew . . . tinted by the twilight. I'm a-telling you, them mamminaries is fair, considerable
fair."

"Poetry! I've never been had with poetry before."

"You're goin' to get had with more than just poetry, little angel!
I got magic . . . dark, dark magic."

"Oooh!"

"The gold. Glintin' against your belly . . . glintin' like a
knife . . ." More tearing of cloth. And heavy breathing. The boy
pricked up his ears, sat up . . . sniffed the odor of a woman's
arousal. Then an urgent, whimpering sound . . . like a doe
feeling the first bite of the hunter in her haunches . . . the sound
of thighs against bed sheets, flesh sliding against sweaty
flesh . . . the wolf-boy tensed. A cockroach crawled across the
velvet. Tense. Tense. The rhythmic squeak of bedsprings, in time
to the pumping of heartbeats . . . heartbeats . . . he could
hear them keenly, pounding at him in the close dank dark . . .
tense. Tense. He listened. He could hear the racing blood. He
could smell the fluids that swelled the sex glands to bursting.
Pounding. Pounding. The velvet soaked with sweat, here and
there stiffened by dried blood . . . the cage a womb. Sweltering.

"You want to see what's in the cage? . . ."

"Yes . . . oh, yes . . . yes . . ."

"But you can see it later this evening . . . at the show."

"No private shows?"

A raucous, unpleasant laugh.

The woman's voice. "Everyone's going to come. All the men in
town are heated up from killing Chinamen all day . . . they
need something where they can sit and get drunk and laugh the
night away. And I hear that many of the soldiers from Camp Pilot
Butte that were sent in to keep the peace, they're aiming to come.
But I can't, you see . . . I'm working. All night."

"Working! How many studs do you plan to service, young
thing?"

"I shouldn't be talking about that in front of a custo—I
mean—"

"You afraid of wolves, little girl?"

"I hear you got a wolf-boy in the show."

"I hear wolves been creeping up on decent folks in the middle of the night . . . on ranches . . . even in the towns . . . big wolves with glitterin' eyes . . . wolves that'll tear you in shreds. You afraid of wolves?"

"Y-yes . . . but they're dying out fast, got a bounty on them."

"There's a kind of wolf that can't be killed . . . the wolf that's inside every man. The big, bad w—"

"You're frightening me."

Tense. Tense. A hand moving across the velvet outside, feeling for the latch.

"I never go nowhere without what's in that cage. My most precious possession. My secret heart's what's in that cage, my secret heart's desire."

Pounding. The velvet rippling a little. A tiny stream of moonlight piercing the darkness, lancing him, and he let out a sharp whine of terror . . . he was changing where the moonlight burned him. The arm. The rippling flesh. He hunched down. The bars shook.

"Yes, ma'am . . . yes, you filthy little harlot . . . mayhap you wonder what kind of darkness lurks in the heart of Cordwainer Claggart. You lies there bone nekkid with the moonlight a-shinin' on your pretty little body . . . you ain't got no more secrets to hide because I done stripped you to the skin and under the skin there's nothing, just blood and bone and meat and corruption . . . there's nothing you can hide from me, little sister. I stands above you and sees and sits in judgment and—"

—ripping the velvet, jerking open the cage door, and—

Jonas exulted! The moon touched him all over. He tingled, the blood surged, the warmth exploded outward from his innards as the fur pushed up and the snout ballooned from his face and hot piss fountained from his penis and sprayed the sheets and the moon was in his eyes, he howled at shattered images of—

The woman's eyes, rimmed with makeup that was beginning to run, the peeling wallpaper with faded hunting scenes, the open window that let in the chill air, and—

"Do your stuff, my son," said Cordwainer Claggart gently, coaxingly.

—her skin death-pale in the moon, the lips unnaturally red,

mouth opened to scream, the vocal cords tightening so that the only sound was a high-pitched piping, like the wuthering of the wind, and—

"Told you it was magic," said Cordwainer Claggart.

—autumn leaves drifting one by one over the sill, fluttering one by one onto the oriental rug with the polished oak floor gleaming through bald patches and—

Jonas howled! The woman recoiled, palms down against the mattress, back to the headboard engraved with a design of interlocking roses, the smell of death stronger now, intoxicating him as it drenched his lungs, and even she could smell it now, and as the transformation completed itself the smells became more vivid and the smallest whimper screamed in his ears and the colors faded, softened into a photographic sepia—

"Devour, my son!" said Cordwainer Claggart.

—and the wolfling pounced—

"Devour!"

—the claws digging into her breasts, muzzle against her tinted lips, hind legs gouging the pubic mound and—

Claggart laughed. "My secret self," he said, "my darkness, my anger, my vengeance."

—ripping the rib cage, drawing the intestine out like a ribbon, blood spattering the wallpaper, seeping into the spackle where the paper had peeled, blood siphoning into the sheets, sluicing down the bedposts, pattering on the floorboards like a spring drizzle—

Claggart leaning back against the bed, clutching himself with both hands, his trousers at his ankles, whispering to himself words the wolf-boy could not make out . . . the secret language of his heart.

—a trickle of blood from the edge of the lips along the throat down to the lace-trimmed collar's edge—

He began to feed now. Rage propelled him. Hunks of steaming flesh, the juices squirting down his throat. He was drunk on the taste of blood. He squirmed and rubbed himself up and down against the body. He shook the blood from his fur. Fine spray fell onto the sheets in concentric patterns. He tore out the clitoris and gulped it down. It tasted of arousal. It maddened him. He thrust against the corpse like a lover. . . .

And Claggart watched. His eyes seemed distant, unfocused, but now and then he let out a peal of savage laughter. At last, almost reluctantly, he threw himself upon them both, lashing the wolfling's haunches with a silver-tipped flail. The wolf-boy whined. And Claggart, embracing the dead woman with the beast between them, after a few perfunctory thrusts, ejaculated. Semen met blood and coagulated on the wolfling's fur.

"Reckon it's about time you went back in," Claggart said.

The wolfling howled, protesting.

"Inside!" said Claggart, and brought the quirt down hard and stinging on the wolfling's withers.

And pushed him into the cage and slammed it shut and latched it and threw down the velvet covering. . . .

And Jonas felt himself shifting again. He looked down and saw human hands emerging from furry shoulders. He saw the claws retracting. The light was rapidly diminishing as the drape was pulled over everything. Soon he would see nothing again. He heard scurrying, scraping noises; Claggart was rearranging the room to look as though someone had attacked them. Later he would draw a knife down the back of his left arm, so that it would seem he too had been injured in a struggle with a masked stranger.

He would be believed. There was magic in the way Claggart talked to people . . . there was a kind of music in it. Not the silly flute music of his former existence . . . but a vital, vivid melody of blood and lust . . . and death.

Deep in his mind, voices stirred. He did not listen. The others did not matter anymore. It's my time now, not theirs, he thought. And I have a father now.

A father who loves me, he thought, his flesh still smarting from the whip.

And Claggart's voice said, "I guess I done turned the tables on you. You're the wolf and I'm the pig, but it's you which is trapped in the house, and it's me that's a-huffin' and a-puffin' to blow the house down clear into the next world."

4
Evanston, Wyoming Territory
full moon

TOWN AFTER DREARY TOWN, EACH ONE HUGGING THE SOUTHERN
Pacific railway line as it threaded through mountain and
desert. . . .

"Mrs. Dupré?"

Speranza had been sitting in the dining car, watching the
landscape reel past. The moon had risen behind distant hills. She
sat, hugging herself to keep out the chill. The rattling, the whine
of the whistle, the hum of the windowpane when her satin puff
sleeve brushed against it . . . all these were so familiar to her
now that she barely noticed them. But she had never travelled in
the autumn. When they came down from the mountains, and
evergreens gave way to deciduous forests, she had tried to count
the colors, a preoccupation that provided her some relief from the
contemplation of the horrors she knew lay in the future.

"Mrs. Dupré? Shall I take your soup?"

She had not touched the shrimp consommé. But she smiled
wanly and allowed the waiter to dispose of it.

As his forwardness in introducing himself to her in San
Francisco suggested, William Dupré had proved a most uncon-
ventional husband. Although they were married within a fortnight
of her arrival, she was given to understand that this marriage was
to be one in name alone, for Mr. Dupré was not a man much
attracted to the opposite sex. They were to do each other a mutual
favor: he would give the child a name, and, indeed, a fortune; she
would give him a veneer of respectability behind which he could
continue to practice certain vices.

The nature of her husband's proclivities was not a matter that
ever came up on the rare occasions in which they conversed. She

gathered, from eavesdropping on the servants' chatter one day, that it had something to do with his frequenting San Francisco's notorious "peg houses," institutions named for the oriental custom of having their merchandise seated upon greased pegs, so that the capacity of each one's rear entrance might be evident to the client. This was about as much as Speranza wanted to hear.

At any rate, Mr. Dupré was kind to Speranza and to her son, whom he named William, Jr., in a fit of wistful pride. She loved her son, devoted all her time to him, and rarely thought of that other child, the one forever in the clutches of darkness. Rarely, that is, in the daytime; at night, especially nights of the full moon, the nightmares did not cease to torment her.

Nonetheless, her duties to her child and husband were paramount. She endeavored to forget the past, to put aside all thoughts of Hartmut and of the boy who had his eyes. She did not succeed in forgetting, but she had come at least to some kind of accommodation with her inner horrors.

She threw herself into her husband's social circle, memorizing names, positions, finances of San Francisco's élite. She took piano lessons, went to concerts where she tried to drown out the nightmares in the frenzied cacophonies of such avant-garde composers as Wagner. She read voraciously; she took to reading such magazines as *Harper's, Graham's,* and *Century* from cover to cover.

One afternoon, with the boy napping and her husband at a board meeting of the bank, she had been sipping tea in the drawing room after a strenuous attempt to sight-read a Liszt étude. She had demolished the newly published *Huckleberry Finn* in a matter of hours, and was now idly turning the pages of one of her husband's investment journals. An article about the Chinese question did not hold her interest, so she flipped to something entitled "Wild West Shows: are these a remunerative investment opportunity? Or merely an enterprise for buffoons without foresight?" There was an engraved caricature depicting Buffalo Bill, Sitting Bull, Annie Oakley, and various other figures, all waving bags of money whilst a bloated Queen Victoria looked forlornly on, with representations of other European crowned heads in the background. But it was the name *Claggart* that caught her eye.

Others, such as the road show perpetrated by the notorious Claggart, boast a *few* Wild West appurtenances, but purport

to exhibit in the main magical, supernatural beasts, such as
vampires and werewolves, and pander to the most credulous
elements among our hillbilly confrères. This traveling
sideshow—despite its pretensions, it is no more than
that—can be seen in towns along the Southern Pacific route,
and its owner claims more than a thousand dollars a week in
clear profit. . . .

She was rereading the article even now as the train hurtled
toward the town of Evanston, Wyoming, at a lightninglike
twenty-five miles per hour.

Some discreet inquiries among her husband's acquaintances in
the impresarial trade revealed the existence of Claggart's Amazing
Circus of Transformations. Definitely a low-budget operation, it
was nothing like Buffalo Bill's spectacle, which had been a
triumph at the courts of Europe. But it was clearly inspired by it,
at least in its outward trappings—equestrian displays, gunfight-
ing, even a tame blanket Indian. Among the advertised attractions
was the transformation of "an innocent boy into a wild beast, done
without lights, mirrors, hocus-pocus, or miraculous powders, but
by the sheer influence of moonlight."

Mr. Dupré had raised no objection when she asked his permission to travel to Dakota Territory for a few months. He had made
sure she had an ample supply of gold, and letters of credit besides.
He did not question her; after all, she had done him the courtesy
of never questioning him.

Now she was staring at a second document, a piece of paper on
which were scrawled the words:

September: Rock Springs, Bitter Creek
November: Abilene

"Mrs. Dupré . . . are you all right, ma'am? You haven't
touched the fish course . . . and we're about due to serve the
roast."

"How long until we arrive in Rock Springs?" she said.

"Oh . . . won't be for an hour or two yet . . ."

"Why, damn it!" she said. The waiter seemed a little taken
aback at her profanity, particularly since she had her Bible laid
open on the dining table, propped against the flower vase. She

shrugged as the waiter took away her fish and replaced it with a dish of roast beef, dumplings, green beans, and buttered corn bread, the beef topped with a sauce of mustard and peppercorns. She stared dully out the window at the sunset.

She did not know how long she had been staring at her own reflection. She did not like her appearance anymore; though time had not ravaged it much, she believed that every kiss, every caress of the werewolf could be seen in her face. She studied the lines about her eyes . . . few noticed them, but she counted them each night before she went to bed.

They were moving past a forest. There was a high wind, sweeping down on the oaks, making the pine trees sway. The forest was canopied in a thousand reds against the bloody sky. She was drifting into a dream state, but she dared not sleep for fear of the nightmares. The forest blurred. From its depths she thought she heard a voice: *Speranza . . . Speranza . . .*

Was that a wolf, standing by the edge of the tracks, looking up at the passing train? She fixed her gaze on it. Was it there for her, waiting, watching?

"Johnny!" was on her lips. But suddenly she heard the thud of a rifle, and the wolf keeled over and tumbled down the embankment and was lost to view.

From somewhere far behind her, in the third-class section, came the faint sound of applause. Someone shouted out: "Stop the damn train! We want our bounty!"

She had read, in *Harper's,* that ten thousand wolves had been killed that year in Wyoming alone. . . .

The train was grinding to a halt. She picked at the beef, but could barely get down one mouthful. She looked out the window and saw the station sign: Granger. The stop was only for a moment; there was a frantic rush as people hastened to get on. Then they pulled away again. She was about to try a second forkful of the meat when she was aware of a shadow standing over her. It was the conductor.

"Ma'am," he said, "I'm afraid to tell you we're going to have to bypass Rock Springs . . . orders from the military. They just handed me a telegram."

"No!" She panicked. "It is imperative that I arrive there tonight!"

"You wouldn't want to be there nohow, ma'am, not tonight. There's riots going on . . . twenty-eight Chinamen massacred . . . the army is there restoring order."

"But you don't understand!" Speranza said. "If I don't reach him soon, he'll—"

She stopped. How could she explain to him that she had come to save a supernatural creature? That her own salvation depended on succeeding where she had failed before? That she had turned away from the comforts of San Francisco not to flee her nightmares, but to confront them? She looked at the paper that listed the times and venues for the Circus of Transformations.

"Bitter Creek?" she said.

"We should be arriving there late tomorrow, Mrs. Dupré. If you like—seeing as you're a first-class passenger—we could arrange for you to travel to Rock Springs by private coach. If you're sure that's where you want to go, ma'am. By all accounts, it's no place for a refined lady like you, not with the miners stampeding all over the town and Chinamen hanging on every corner. Women too, I hear, though with them long braids it's blame hard to tell them apart."

"Bitter Creek will be quite all right . . . the . . . business I have to transact can be done as easily there."

Let me not be too late! she prayed, as the train sped away from the setting sun.

5
Outside Rock Springs
full moon

SHORTLY BEFORE MOONRISE, TEDDY SHOOK HANDS WITH VICTOR Castellanos outside the inn.

"You know where I am going," said Castellanos. "Perhaps I will find a stray calf."

"Good hunting," said Teddy softly, and watched his newfound

friend walk away. Some soldiers were trying to clear the corpses from the street, but the afternoon mob had dwindled to a handful, mostly curious children, poking at the dead bodies with sticks. Soon even they were gone. They were all making their way out of town, toward Cordwainer Claggart's show.

A trail of torches led from the road outside the town to the Circus of Transformations. About thirty, forty horses were tethered outside the compound at a couple of long hitching posts. A lot of military saddles. A dwarf sauntered past, lugging a pile of documents. He scowled at Teddy. As the moon emerged from behind a cloud, horses whinnied. The moon was pale, with a spectral bluish cast to it; a kind of halo shimmered around it, a trick of the light on the cloud layer. A night to make children hide under the bed and old women gossip, Teddy thought.

He gave a boy a penny to watch his horse and went in past a ticket booth, where an old Mexican crone in a Gipsy costume took his quarter and gave him a short bit in change.

There was dust in the air, and he could hear hooves pounding dirt and a small crowd mumbling. The crickets were carrying on so loud you could hardly hear anything else.

Makeshift bleachers leaned against battered old wagons, relics from the pioneer days. A canvas awning shielded the audience from the wind. The arena was open to the moonlight. Past midnight, and the air was so clear, and the moon so bright, you hardly needed the torches that flamed in a circle. Moonlight played on the mountainous horizon.

There was a display of horsemanship going on: tame Injuns, mostly, got up in outlandish bright paint, riding Roman style, standing up, one Injun to two horses . . . the crowd seemed bored as Teddy came in, but soon, when they started somersaulting from horse to horse, and swinging under the horses' bellies and shooting their arrows at moving targets held up by ladies riding sidesaddle up and down the ring, they quieted down some; even Teddy had to admit it was a pretty fine display.

He tried to find a seat. Presently a couple of miners skootched up to give him room, and he sat with his butt half hanging out over the aisle.

"Get rid of the ladies and let's have some Chinamen!" someone shouted.

A booming voice. Teddy stiffened; the voice was intimately,

chillingly familiar. "And now . . . ladies and gentlemen . . . a stunt which ain't never been seen in all Wyoming Territory . . ." A melodramatic drumroll. Then—

Fire! Pathways of fire crisscrossing the arena. A giant hoop of fire carried aloft by women, dressed as Greek goddesses, standing on the backs of two white horses. And Cordwainer Claggart, outrageously attired as Jupiter, wearing a laurel wreath and riding a chariot around the circus ring, regaling the crowd through an incongruous speaking trumpet which someone had attempted to disguise as a classical cornucopia. The chariot driver was an Indian with a war bonnet—a ludicrous piece of headgear, with the feathers dyed in pinks and greens such as had never been seen in the land before the white men had come.

"Yes, ladies and gentlemen . . ." The drumroll crescendoed. "Yes! This here Chief Thousand Buffalo, ferociousest and fearlessest leader of the Minneconjou Sioux, who once single-handedly scalped one hundred and six men, women, and children in a single afternoon during the great Minnesota Sioux Uprising . . . who has now accepted the ways o' the white man and learned hisself civilization and taken almighty Jesus into his heart . . . will now perform the deadly, fiery, Leap of Faith!"

Teddy saw the ferocious leader—a man perhaps eighty years old, withered as a prune, and covered all over in garish paint—come cantering forward on an Appaloosa that was all over painted with lightning bolts and suns and moons. The crowd began to laugh . . . white teeth in the moonlight . . . they put him in mind of beasts of prey. He reached down to stroke his Merwin and Hulburt.

Someone let out a whoop. The whole crowd seemed to catch the mood. They were all screeching now. Just the thing to come watch, Teddy thought, after a hard day's riotin'.

He looked around. Two miners were handing a bottle back and forth, guzzling so the liquor ran down over their beards. A woman in widow's weeds was covering a small boy's eyes with her hand; he was trying to pry them away, whining, "Aw, Ma, aw, Ma!" A harlot with her face painted maybe an inch thick sat in the lap of a cavalry officer whose face was a patchwork of red where she'd kissed him. Torchlight danced over leering faces.

"Burn, Injun, burn!" they were shouting. "Burn, burn, burn!" The drumroll was deafening now. The Injun chief, who'd seemed uncomfortable before, with all that fake war paint, took a deep breath and Teddy saw him muttering. He knew it was some kind of courage-making song. Then, spurring his horse, the old man leapt—

"Burn! Burn!"

—a shot went off, spooking the horses, and—

"Burn! Burn! Burn!"

One of the Greek goddesses stumbled, the burning hoop slipped, by some miracle the horse and rider thrust their way through it before the hoop came crashing onto the dirt and rolled toward the bleachers. The widow had to take her hand off her son's face so she could pray . . . as she fell on her knees, her child squealed with glee, but his expression changed to terror as the hoop smashed into a nearby stand and you could smell singed hair in the wind. . . .

The chief cried out, a wheezing falsetto, and then came Injun drums pounding and rattles shaking and whistles shrilling, and you could hear the crowd sighing like one man, but you couldn't tell if what they felt was relief or terror.

The arena burned. The horses, the women, the Injun chief had been spirited away. Cordwainer Claggart dismissed the chariot, which clattered off behind the turned-over wagons, and strode into the center of the ring. A dark figure, his long shadow dancing in the torchlight, the moonlight in his eyes. He had a whip in his hand . . . a silver-tipped whip.

Teddy knew that this was what he had come to see.

A cage was being wheeled into the arena. A cage completely draped in black velvet. A system of pulleys and ropes was attached to the velvet covering, so that it could be dramatically whisked away or slowly lifted, at the showman's whim.

Something rattled inside the cage . . . something scurried, something whimpered. The fires were doused. Smoke billowed. People were coughing, retching, for the smoke was pungent, sulphurous, a brimstone sort of smoke.

Still attired as Jupiter, his toga flapping in the wind, a coronet of oak leaves for a hat, Cordwainer Claggart addressed himself to the mob, grandly waving his speaking trumpet.

"You all smells the burning brimstone . . . and that's as it should be, 'cause you are all about to witness a creature out of the mouth of hell itself! Your hearts is all a-quakin' and a-shakin' and your hair is a-standin' on end . . . and that's as it should be, 'cause horripilification is a natural consequence of the apparition of evil! Ladies and gentlemen, if there is any amongst you present here this midnight who is troubled by nightmares, who shivers at a fairy tale, who scuttles under the bed at the creak of a floorplank . . . I will personally refund your ten cents if you chooses to depart now . . . and I takes no responsibility for any heart attacks, seizures, grippe, or malcholer suffered by any individual which chooses to stay for the remainder of the spectacle!"

He had their attention now. There was no sound from the crowd. You could hear the leaves, swishing one against t'other as they fluttered down to the ground. Teddy could feel their dread. This was what they had been waiting for . . . not the equestrian displays, not the fortune-teller, not the miraculous arithmetic-calculating jackalope.

They waited.

The cage: moonlight rippled on the velvet. The crowd was silent, so silent.

Another exhibit was wheeled in; a platform on which rested the hanged body of a Chinaman. The noose was still around his neck. He was naked; someone had castrated him and hung his testicles around his neck. His queue had been hacked off and stuffed into his mouth. His abdomen had been sliced open, and his entrails draped about his loins. An opium pipe protruded from his anus.

Scattered laughter broke out. It quickly fell silent again. The tension grew.

On the far side of the arena, one of the painted harlots fainted; her companion began unlacing her corset right there in the open. Moonlight did that to people. Drove them mad.

Teddy forced himself to go on looking. He wanted to study Claggart's face. It hadn't changed much over the years. Perhaps a few more wrinkles at the corners of the weasly eyes. But the grin was still wide and predatory.

The Chinaman had begun to smell. People began coughing.

"Usually I uses a wild animal," Claggart said, "for this next and grandest spectacle. But when the most wildest animal of all the world is so readily available, I reckon I couldn't help but avail myself of it!"

Laughter; the tension, quickly defused, gathered itself again. Leaves and dust stirred about the impresario's feet.

"And now—behold!"

Cordwainer Claggart lifted his arms up as though in invocation to some ancient deity. Music sounded: an out-of-tune trumpet brayed over a vamping piano and a drumroll.

The velvet lifted. Slowly. Agonizingly. But before the drumroll had ended there was already the beginning of a howl . . . a howl like the cry of a hungry child. . . .

And Teddy saw Johnny Kindred in the cage. Hardly changed at all . . . had he somehow refused to grow? The boy was on all fours, the huge howl bursting from his frail body.

Now the transformation was starting. The audience leaned forward. They murmured. The boy paced. His eyes flashed.

"Ladies and gentlemen—the moon!" cried Claggart, and with a flourish signalled for the drape to be yanked away. There was the boy. Naked. Frightened. Angry. Hurling himself against the bars. Silver bars, Teddy thought to himself. That's what's holding him back.

"Ain't no werewolf!" a voice from the audience hollered. "He's jest a hairy kid."

The front of the cage clanged as Claggart undid the bolts. He touched the boy on the shoulders with his quirt. The boy whimpered, retreated.

"Out, my son , . . out into the light of the moon . . . the moon with its pale light that burns you up and changes you into the beast!"

Wild-eyed now, Claggart lashed at the bars of the cage. The boy ran about on all fours. The crowd began laughing. Teddy could see the anger in the boy's eyes. They were glittering, reddening . . . like Scott's eyes used to.

"Feedin' time!" said Claggart, and, hauling the boy out by the scruff, hurled him onto the dirt of the arena. . . .

Dirt slammed in his face. Dirt up his nostrils. Dirt in his mouth, hard wormy dirt. The wolfling was waking. Eyes. He saw eyes. Taunting eyes. There was the master with the silver whip. He raised himself, hind paws first, then front paws, clawing up dirt, hurling a clod in the master's face.

Claggart coughed. The audience laughed.

Eyes. He cowered from the whip. He wondered whether he
should summon up one of the others to take the pain. But no.
There was blood in the air. Blood mingled with the sour-sweet
scent of terror. The moonlight lanced his flesh and he could feel
the hunger and the racing blood. He circled. A dead man lay on
a platform. Still warm. Warm. He was changing now. Moonlight
tearing at his loins, ripping the fur out from under the human
camouflage, wrenching the muzzle from the human jaws . . .
there was pain in the moon's caresses, pain and joy . . . he
circled. The body lay still. Guts quivering. He could hear the
crowd and the wind sigh.

He leaped—

A collective shudder from the crowd. And then a scream. The
wolf-boy was rending the body now. A hand flew through the air
and Claggart caught it, and danced about the arena doing a grisly
handshake as the audience squealed in delight. The wolfling bit
down hard . . . the crack of the sternum could be heard . . .
then the crunch of bone and the gurgling of intestines. Applause.

One or two people were getting up to leave. The swooning
harlot, now revived, was vomiting into the aisle.

Teddy didn't want Claggart to recognize him. Not yet. But he
had to get closer. Closer to that beast. The crowd was roaring,
laughing, as Claggart caught a second bloody hand and began to
juggle the two hands. The wolfling had pulled the intestine all the
way out like a string of sausages now. Dragging the body around
the circus. Getting close to the bleachers. Teddy came down,
crouched in the aisle in the front row as the creature ran past.
Teddy looked the wolf in the eyes and said, softly, "You knows
me. We was friends once. You and me. You knows me, Johnny
Kindred."

The wolf howled. Was it pain? He stopped. Hackles high, tail
up, snarling, drooling. Someone in the crowd poked at him with
the silver-tipped end of a walking stick. The flesh charred. The
assailant, taken aback, withdrew the cane. The wolfling yelped as
a circle of hair sizzled on his haunches. He was all entangled in the
intestines like a cat with a ball of yarn.

Teddy knelt down beside him and whispered, "I'll come for
you. I swear. Before God, I'll come for you."

At last the wolf seemed to notice him. He turned on him.

Transfixed him with a look that might have been hatred, might have been something else. Teddy didn't stay any longer. He backed away, feeling behind him for the exit gate.

There was another cage, a cage that remained locked. It was in the heart of the dark forest. They were all in there together. Johnny and the Indian boy and Jake and Jonathan and James. A silver cage that hung from a limb of a naked tree. They were all in there but Jonas. Jonas had the body all to himself. The cage had sprung up around the charred remains of the treehouse. Inside, they were standing on each other's shoulders, clambering over each other, trying to get a peek through the body's eyes. Sometimes, when Jonas was in a frenzy, control slipped a little and they could sense things.

It was Johnny who saw the face from the past.

He tried to force the jaws open, to make them say, "Teddy, Teddy," but instead he tasted human blood. And the jaws could only howl. He tried to work the vocal cords and almost choked on a length of intestine that dangled near the opening of the esophagus.

At last he forced out a sound. A whine like the wind in a cave, not at all human.

Teddy led his horse to a nearby thicket. Dead leaves stuck in his spurs. Above the laughter, he thought he heard a human child cry out. But he wasn't sure. The wind was dying down now. Leaves pelted his face. The moon was bloated. A mist was seeping down the mountain slopes, crawling along the banks of a creek. As he sat down against a stump, he could see the mist swell up, swirl, ooze its way along the tree trunks. He could smell the moisture, heavy with the putrescence of dead foliage.

He tethered his horse and waited for the show to end.

The moon was lower in the sky, its light subdued, and the rising mist dulled the night to a uniform gray.

The cage was closed, the velvet pulled down; the audience had gone home. The ground was filthy with blood, broken liquor bottles, papers, horse dung. The torches had all been doused. In the morning they would come to strike down the show and head on out to Bitter Creek. Claggart had already sent everyone away, all except the fortune-teller, who was by way of being his partner, since she owned the jackalope.

They sat, counting their money, at a low table in the shadow of the upturned wagon, by the light of a coal-oil lamp.

"Pathetic take," said the Gipsy woman, wiping the artificial beauty spot from her cheek with her sleeve. "Less than two hundred people come; $20 in ticket sales, $112 in fortunes I tell, $102.50 for refreshments." She began to divide the piles of money. "One for you, one for—"

"Not so fast, Juanita," Claggart said. He jabbed the handle of the quirt in the Gipsy's chest. "I know you done better'n that."

"Well. . . ."

Claggart smiled as she began to pull, from the bosom of her frilly dress, an assortment of necklaces, bracelets, and gold coins. "Still a lousy take," she said, shrugging. A gold double eagle fell out of her sleeve onto the grass.

Laughing, Claggart bent down and felt for it in the grass. He scooped it up, along with a cricket, whose wings he carefully pulled off before throwing it back down. "You ain't gonna be a-singin' no more," he said softly. Then he turned his attention back to the Mexican Gipsy woman. He jabbed her again, this time between the breasts. "Now you'd best not be lying to me. I don't want to be findin' no cache of gold where your bosoms should be." He looked over the jewelry piled up on the table. For a town in the middle of nowhere, it was not a bad selection. "Beads," he said as he tossed a bracelet over his shoulder.

"Wait . . . that one got a gold clasp on it." Juanita scrambled after the bracelet.

Claggart laughed. "I commends your greed," he said. He grabbed the bracelet from her hand. "My portion."

"No!"

"You give me what I want, or ain't no telling who's goin' to know all about you come dawn." With the end of the quirt he began to unfasten her chemise. A tear ran down her cheek, gouging a canyon from her rouge and powder. Ugly, ugly. He undid another inch, feeling the muslin rip a little. . . .

"Why you torment me? You already know my shameful secret. You need not to bring it always into question—"

Claggart kicked back, opened his mouth in a soundless guffaw, as the chemise tore to reveal balled-up wads of cloth where the breasts should be . . . Juanita was sobbing now. "You're a travesty of a human bein'," said Claggart. "You ain't a man, and you ain't a woman. Just another monstrosity at Cordwainer Claggart's Circus of Transformations. Oh, don't you cry, Juanita. Put a little red back into them dainty cheeks." He lashed her across the face with the silver-tipped whip, and chuckled at the sight of blood. "Now, get on with countin' up that money."

He rooted through the treasures once again. There were some watch fobs that might be worth a decent price once they got to Cheyenne. There were some gold vest buttons. Another worthless necklace . . . in disgust, Claggart tossed it over his shoulder.

He didn't hear it land.

"Right cruel of you to taunt her." A soft voice.

"Who in hell—" He whipped around. Couldn't see anyone. The mist was coming in thick.

"Among the Injuns, they'd call someone like her a *winkte*, and she'd be a sacred man-woman, and no one'd be threatenin' to reveal no dark secrets."

Damned mist! He reached for the nearest weapon, the derringer in his sleeve. He was about pointing it when a shot blew it clear out of his hand and skinned his knuckles. He yelled in pain. The gunshot whistled, echoed.

"Pick it up, Cordwainer Claggart," said the voice . . . so soft, it seemed to be coming from right by his shoulder . . . "I aims to kill you like a man, not like the goddamned beast of prey you really is."

Claggart said, "I can't rightly place it, but there's something familiar about your voice." From beside the wolf-boy's cage, the shadow of a man on horseback stretched out across the dirt of the arena. Horse's breath hung over the mist.

Claggart didn't bend down to pick up the gun. Be safer that way. Seems this was the type of man who'd not yield on a point of honor. The fool. Claggart wasn't a bit nervous, not him. The voice *was* familiar. It was coming back to him now. "Yes. I reckon I do know you. You ain't nothin' but a dirty breed boy that I once taught how to cheat at poker. Name of . . . Groomy-Oh, some kind of fancy French name, mighty blame impressionatin' for a half-Injun news butch."

"I got somethin' comin' to me, Cordwainer Claggart."

"And what might that be, boy?"

"Your heart."

"Say, you done growed into a poet. I'll be." Ain't no boy going to outsmart Cordwainer Claggart, he thought. "My heart! If that ain't poetic justice. And what does you aim to do with my partickler vital organ, if it ain't too forward of me to be asking you?"

"I'm fixin' to rip it out by the roots."

"Ha, ha—"

"If I can find it."

"Very good! If you can find it."

Grumiaux fired.

The man-woman screamed and dived under the table. Claggart kicked her out of the way, pushed the table over to make a shield, grabbed his weapon. Crouched down. Fired. Heard the bullet strike the silver cage bars, heard the wolf-boy yelp. A pinhole in the velvet . . . mayhap the moonlight would leak into it and set the boy off.

Fired again. And again. No more bullets. He tossed the gun aside and pulled a second from his waistcoat pocket. Juanita had found shelter behind a wagon wheel, and was distractedly combing her hair.

"Careful where you're shootin'," said Grumiaux. "Less you wants to kill the wolf-boy here."

"Bullets won't hurt him none."

Inside the cage, he could hear the beast rattling and carrying on.

A shot whistled. It tore into Claggart's shoulder. He did not cry out. The boy meant business.

"Is it gold you want? I'll show you where the gold is. As much gold as you can carry. And plenty more where it come from! Marks aplenty in this here great land of ours. Simple folks . . . with simple minds." He felt blood soaking into his jacket. Won't come out, he thought, not even if I scrub it with lye. He was starting to sweat now, even in the frigid night air. The wolf-boy was howling like he was beginning to change shape again. Usually he wouldn't howl like that unless he smelled fear in the air. Maybe the fear came from Juanita, but . . .

I must be afraid, he realized.

"It ain't money I'm after. It's you."

Grumiaux fired again. And blasted a hole in the table. The

horse whinnied. Claggart heard the breed dismount. And saw him step out from the shadow of the wolf-boy's cage.

"You sure have growed some," Claggart said.

"Sure have."

He was tall. Dressed in black. His hair was a black mane that caught a bluish sheen from the moonlight. He was blowing smoke from his gun. He just stood there, a bad dream that wouldn't go away. "You always was a good boy," Claggart said, forcing a chuckle into his voice. "Always knowed you would amount to somethin'. Lord, look at you! You're mighty fast with that Merwin and Hulburt."

"Reckon so."

"I could use a good gunman on the show. Keep away the . . . pickpockets and the drunkards."

"I see you ain't had much luck keeping away them pickpockets lately." He waved his gun at the jewelry, which was all over the grass now.

"He made me steal!" Juanita wailed. Claggart saw that the cricket whose wings he'd pulled was clambering up a watch fob, dying maybe. "I not want no part of it . . . just tell fortunes . . . but Claggart, he force me to pick pockets, he say he will tell everyone about my secret. . . ."

"Your secret dies with Claggart."

It occurred to Claggart for the first time that he might not survive this night. He was going straight to hell, that was certain; that was how he had lived his life, and that was what he had chosen. He didn't think hell would be so bad. But he had to keep talking; no point giving up hope of a reprieve, however slight.

"Told you I wanted to hire you, didn't I! I likes you, boy, and I always did like you."

"When you likes a person, Claggart, all it means is you likes to see them hurtin'. Claggart, I been comin' after you these past three years, shadowin' you. Don't think I didn't know where you was, every minute of them three years. New York, Virginia, Texas, Carson City, down Mexico way . . . when I weren't follerin' you I was readin' and askin' questions. If it weren't for you a lot of good people would still be alive. And a lot more people wouldn't be hurtin'. I know about the women you done kilt, Claggart. You left a trail of slashed-up whores in every town your circus stopped in. I seen you kill a girl once. And you stole the wolf-boy from his people."

Claggart thought of hell. I'm already smelling the brimstone, he thought. He said, "*I'm* his people. I done more for that wolf-boy than anybody else ever done. I've been a father to him, more than a father. I told him the truth. Ain't nobody else ever dared tell him what he is. When you sends me down to the everlastin' fire, and I stands in front of that all-consumin' big old darkness in the world's heart, all hell is goin' to know that I'm a-standin' there as *his* emissary. All of us is the children of darkness, see? The wolf-boy is the emptiness that's inside everybody which walks the green earth; he's the darkness you all tries to flee and forget; and I, Cordwainer Claggart, am his mouthpiece . . . I am the ambassador of Satan . . . like John the Baptist was for the sweet little Jesus child . . . I am the voice which is a-cryin' in this here wilderness, baptizing the faithless with piss and blood."

"Should of been a preacher, Cordwainer Claggart."

And Teddy Grumiaux fired straight at his heart. The last thing Claggart saw was the gunman's eyes. The last thing he felt, before the split second of unconscionable pain that presaged the endless nothingness, was surprise: surprise because the bullet struck home with such precision; surprise because there was no hate in the gunman's eyes; surprise that the gunman was weeping as he holstered his gun.

It only took a few seconds for Cordwainer Claggart to die.

But in those seconds Teddy Grumiaux relived all of it. The train journey in spring . . . Claggart laughing as he pulled up his sleeve to reveal the holdout with the hidden ace of spades . . . whistling to himself as he gripped the boy's shoulders and wrung out a sordid payment for the cheating lessons . . . the bloody confrontation in summer . . . dead bodies. His paw. His mother. Scott Harper. Rage seized him at last. He fired again and again into the twitching body, striding closer and closer to it, heedless of the spattering blood. He reloaded and fired again. And reloaded. And fired. The sky grew darker. The moon was about setting.

At last he stopped. He knew there was a lot of truth in what Claggart said. When he squeezed the trigger, when he felt that anger blazing inside him, stampeding through his arteries, he could feel the void within, the emptiness that was the beast. Could be, all men really were nothing inside but this dark thing.

He put away his gun.

Snivelling behind the wagon wheel was the woman who was, perhaps, really a man. She was trying to pull together her absurd Gipsy costume. "Are you going to kill me?" she said. Her cheeks were streaked with face paint.

"Got no quarrel with you," Teddy said.

"You know what I am . . . perhaps you hate me."

"Just a *winkte* is all. I seen plenty of 'em amongst the Injuns." Her presence discomfited him a mite, but he tried not to let it show. He felt the dark thing inside, and he was afraid.

"Got nowhere to go now." She came crawling to his feet, a gold necklace in her outstretched hand. "You take."

"Don't want nothing," Teddy said.

She knelt beside the corpse of Cordwainer Claggart. In a moment she was racked with sobs and carrying on in her native language, beating her breast and tearing her hair, which was a wig, for it was on askew over the bald pate of a pitiable old man.

He turned his back on her. The moon was gone. He could hear the woman gathering up the money and the jewelry and heaping them up. He walked toward the cage. The sky was black save for a rim of pallid gray in the east. The morning star shone down over a mountain crest. He shivered. When he reached the cage, he whispered, "Johnny, I come for you. I'm right sorry I couldn't of come before."

He tugged at the covering. It fluttered to the dirt. There was Johnny Kindred. Curled up in the middle of the cage, as far as possible from the silver plated bars. Behind the cage stood Victor Castellanos. The two seemed to be talking to each other in a wordless language. The boy's head jerked from side to side, his hands moved in circles, he bared his teeth, he whimpered. Then Castellanos answered with a raised eyebrow, a twitch of an ear. They were human to look at, but that was about all.

Castellanos said, "I had to come here. In the middle of the night, prowling the high crags to find me a mountain goat, I smelled him on the wind. This is the one we were looking for, the one the Russian woman told us had been killed or captured."

"Yes," said Teddy.

"He says to me: 'Take me back to my people. Take me to the

wolf-men of the Black Hills. I will lead them to Weeping Wolf Rock. There we will dance away the white men.'"

"Johnny?" said Teddy. And reached his hand inside the cage. The boy leaped for it, nuzzled against the hand, sniffed, began licking. "Johnny, you knows me . . . me, Teddy Grumiaux. I come back for you like I always aimed to."

"Will you shoot me now?" said Castellanos.

"I already kilt the evilest beast of all," Teddy said, pointing behind his shoulder with his thumb. "I don't need to kill no more wolves."

"Teddy," said Johnny in a very small voice.

Teddy opened the door of the cage. The boy stepped out. Trembling something fierce. He was thin. There was blood on his lips. Bloodstains on his arms, his rib cage, his pubis. Teddy took off his jacket and threw it over the boy's shoulders to ward off the cold.

"I've been asleep a long time," said Johnny, "a very long time. Where's Speranza?"

"Far from here."

"I dreamt I was in a cage . . . a cage in the middle of a dark forest . . . I dreamt I was inside a woman . . . waiting to be born."

"You was dreamin' three whole years, Johnny-boy."

"I dreamt a lot about knives and claws and fangs. And dead women, draped across bloodstained beds. Was any of it true? Oh, Teddy, I'm frightened. I want to be with Speranza. Please don't take me back to Claggart."

"There ain't no more Claggart."

The boy saw the corpse. He shut his eyes tight.

Castellanos went to the hitching post to get his horse. Johnny came close to Teddy—he barely stood shoulder-high to him—and touched his face, his hands, as if he weren't sure Teddy was real.

"What now?" Castellanos said when he came back.

"We take him to the Shungmanitu Tanka," Teddy said. "Didn't you tell me that's what he wanted?"

"We take him? You and me together?"

"Less you reckons the Goodnight-Loving trail's more important than the business of wolves."

"No. This is a matter that must be settled once and for all."

Teddy lifted Johnny in his arms—though they were close in age, Johnny was lighter than a tail feather—and put him up on the horse. A glimmer of sunlight to the east. Red fire on far peaks, sliding down the slopes like cherry syrup, like fresh blood.

As they rode away, Teddy noticed the old man-woman watching them, standing over the corpse of her erstwhile partner, wide-eyed, tearless.

6
Bitter Creek, Wyoming
one day after full moon

THE BILL WAS POSTED ON THE WALL OF THE DEPOT, BETWEEN A notice about cheap land in Utah and a wanted poster of a cattle rustler. Speranza gave it only a cursory glance, enough to see that the Circus of Transformations was slated to play that night in a field left of the town churchyard. But there was an enormous *Cancelled* scrawled across the sign in thick red pencil.

A porter carried her valise to the boardwalk. She stood uncertainly, looking out of place in her fox-trimmed pink sacque under the serge travelling coat, her hat with its gaily colored silk flowers, her silk mitts, her hair done in ringlets—decidedly San Francisco. A ragamuffin ran past, kicking a ball that had seen better days. The street was filthy, plastered with dead leaves.

Across the street was a general store with a huge "Orcico Tobacco" sign. There were posters tacked to the walls, advertising the circus, and they too had *Cancelled* across them.

At a loss, she left her valise in care of the stationmaster and went to see what she could find. Her mode of dress occasioned curious stares, but she was not molested. Perhaps it was the Bible tucked under her arm. After a five-minute stroll, she could see the edge of town. On the walls were more of the circus posters which had not yet been scrawled on. She walked more slowly, thinking that someone might soon come, perhaps, to mark up the posters, and that such a person might be able to reveal Claggart's whereabouts.

The marshal's office was the last building. Her attention was drawn to a pile of wolf pelts, and to a dour-looking man with a black mustache and a silver star, who appeared to be haggling with a tall Indian—what they called a blanket Indian, off some nearby reservation most likely.

"No more wolf bounties," the marshal was saying over the Indian's protest. "I know your people been supporting your families with wolf pelt bounties, but to tell the truth, the government don't want to subsidize people that doesn't take to farming their own land like hardworkin' Christian folks."

Speranza moved closer, trying to appear inconspicuous by scrutinizing the wanted posters haphazardly tacked across the walls. One, in particular, caught her eye:

THEODORE GRUMIAUX—GUNMAN
wanted for killing three men in
Duchesne County, Utah
Reward: $1000 in GOLD

Could it really be the boy who escorted her safely to Cheyenne three years ago, the boy who had tended to Scott Harper, who cared so deeply about Johnny Kindred? There was an engraving of the putative killer's face, and she saw little likeness to the young man she remembered.

"You pay me," the Indian was saying.

"I just told you," said the marshal, "we just don't have the funds anymore. The Great White Father wants you to—" He did a pantomime of plowing, sowing, reaping, which the Indian stared at with a raised eyebrow.

"You want me to do women's work?" said the Indian at last. He spat, kicked at the pile of wolf pelts, strode away with his shoulders sunken, prideless.

"Damn Injuns just don't know that times has changed," said the marshal. Speranza being the only person present, he addressed his remarks distractedly to her, though she could easily have been a post or a blank wall. Seeing Teddy's name on a wanted poster had done little to bolster her confidence. She had hoped—fondly imagined, she knew—that she might find him somewhere in the territories, and that he might help her find Johnny; but she knew in her sober moments that finding one man in this vast land was well nigh inconceivable.

"Look!" the marshal said. He was brandishing one of those glass dishes in which biologists grew mold and cultures of microscopic creatures; she had seen plenty of them in Dr. Szymanowski's office in Vienna. "Damn Injun thinks he can kill a couple wolves, bring 'em in, go away with enough to buy hisself a bottle of bug juice. That ain't the way of the future, no, ma'am! This is it. Sarcoptic mange, they calls it."

The words sounded familiar. "Is that not a disease that affects . . . wild animals?" Speranza asked him.

"One of these here dishes, ma'am, is enough to kill a hundred wolves . . . and they die horribly, in pain. Vermin!"

"Speaking of wolves, sir, I have travelled to your town in pursuit of a circus which, I understand, boasts a man who can transform himself into a wolf; have you heard of such a thing?"

The marshal chuckled. "That'd be Claggart's show. Never seen it myself, though it came through town one time last summer. Never did go to it; the wife did, though. When the boy got to changing shape, she swooned, so to this day she can't tell me what kind of trickery was used."

Speranza was about to make some polite response when she spied an old woman making her way toward them. She was stopping at each of the circus bills and writing on them with a pencil. She had a strange, mincing gait, and when she came closer Speranza noticed that she had a pronounced Adam's apple, and that her face was caked with white powder, her lips and eyes painted so garishly as to present a mocking parody of sensuality. She wore the clothes of a Gipsy, shawls and kerchiefs and bangles. The marshal had gone back into the office and slammed the door shut, and it was encumbent upon Speranza to introduce herself to this odd creature.

"Pardon my boldness, miss . . . but you are in the employ of a certain Mr. Claggart?"

The woman jumped. Her pencil flew out of her hand into the mud. Her hand flew to her mouth as though stifling a scream.

"Do not be afraid, miss," said Speranza. "I assure you that I am after information, nothing else."

"Claggart is dead!" she said, her voice a blend of fear and triumph.

"Dead? Of some disease, perhaps? Or was it foul play?"

"Nothing was foul to Claggart," said the old woman.

"He had a child with him . . . a young boy . . ."

"Gone! To the mountains! Captured by two young men who claim communion with him . . . they will trade him to the Indians!" She gripped Speranza by the shoulders and fixed her with a stare. "But you are a fine woman . . . you should not tarry among evil men . . . I see a better future for you . . . money, a good husband . . . do not throw it away for the sake of the beast within!"

Speranza tried to extricate herself from the madwoman's grasp. The fingers dug into her forearms. The old woman raved a while longer. The poor creature, Speranza thought, perhaps her mind has been shattered by a prolonged exposure to Cordwainer Claggart's dementia. "I really must depart if I am to catch the next train east," she said breathlessly.

"Ha, ha! Next train doesn't come for three days . . . you are at my mercy." Speranza shuddered. "My mercy!" A high-pitched cackle. "I'll deal your cards and read your palm and cast your horoscope. . . ."

Speranza managed to free herself. She began to walk strenuously toward the depot, hoping that the stationmaster would tell her there was a way to leave town that very day. The old woman had told her Claggart was dead, gunned down, and the boy captured . . . it sounded dire. Unless it meant that the boy had been freed by someone sympathetic to him, and was even now being taken to the Wolf Indians of the Black Hills. . . .

She felt a prickle in the nape of the neck, an empty ache in her bowels . . . the nightmare is coming on me again! she thought. And it's not even night. She opened her purse, feverishly hunted for the envelope from Vienna with the coca powder. Something to alleviate the heartache. Quick! The very street seemed to cave in on her, to transform itself into the cage, the womb, the place where she waited for the hunters. . . .

There was no coca powder. She turned on her heel in time to see the old woman walking briskly away. There was a brooch missing, too, she realized in dismay, a silver brooch set with topazes—her husband had pressed it into her hands the day she left for the train station.

7

Red Bird, Wyoming Territory
half-moon, waning

TEDDY GOT OFF HIS HORSE TO TAKE A PISS IN A CLUMP OF cottonwoods that leaned against the side of the hill.

"Since you are dismounting anyway," Victor shouted after him, "I will set up camp. Sunset is about due." He jumped off his horse and went gathering dry wood with the boy.

A creek ran slantwise past an outcropping shaped like a crouching animal. Teddy leaned against a tree trunk and began to unbutton his fly. He waited until the other two were out of sight. Castellanos, of course, had been pausing constantly to mark a stone or a landmark with his scent; he did this casually, without even dismounting, and letting out a whoop when his aim was true.

In a few days, Teddy thought, it'll be over. The debts paid off. Time for me to start living, maybe. Almost like being born all over again—no ma and paw, no ties to the past.

It was a strange thought, one he wasn't quite comfortable with.

A shadow from the corner of his eye.

"What?" He turned. Just in time to see the boy. Squatting on his haunches like a dog, sniffing the chill fall wind. Johnny raised himself up on his fingertips, cocked his head, crawled closer. "What do you want?"

The boy circled. Not like a beast of prey, but like a pet begging for a favor. Teddy's second-best shirt, which he had thrown over the boy to hide his nakedness, was streaked with mud, for the boy had been prowling with his belly against the ground.

"Aren't you going to piss all over me, Teddy?" the boy said, and whimpered.

"Course I ain't . . . why would I do that?"

"I have no master now . . . I have no father . . . I need to belong to someone . . . don't you see? I don't exist except to be someone's shadow, someone's inner darkness." He watched Teddy, eyes wide with hope and yearning.

Teddy didn't answer him.

"I can't run alone, Teddy Grumiaux. I've got to have a pack. I'm not me, I'm no one, I've got to be someone's . . . I'm not a whole."

"We're goin' to take you home, boy. Then you'll belong."

The boy clasped his knees, panting, moving his head from side to side, kicking up dirt with his legs. "Please, Teddy Grumiaux, I'm alone now, you don't know how alone. I'll fetch and carry for you, I'll lick your dick for you, I'll roll over and play dead for you, I'll die for you. But you have to mark me . . . mark me!"

"I can't do that, Johnny."

"I'm not Johnny."

His face was subtly different. Especially his eyes. Tinged with yellow. He shook the dead leaves from his hair and reared up and threw his arms around Teddy's waist. The hair was sweat-damp; he was hot, burning up almost. Teddy said, "You ain't catched yourself a fever, I hope. Living in that cage all them years, without any clothes."

"You're not listening, are you? Johnny's gone away forever."

"I heard Johnny's voice, asking for Speranza. When I saw you at the circus."

"They're all dead, all but me. There was this Indian fellow tried to suck all of us into himself. But Claggart came. And now I'm going to suck them into me, see? Johnny and all the others. They're all going to be inside me . . . but I'm going to be the king. I'm going to shit all over them and mark them with my piss."

Another voice suddenly, and Johnny's face grew rigid, his brows knitted, as though he were speaking in a trance . . . the words all in the language of the Lakota: "Do not listen to him. We have all been waiting deep in the forest. Inside the circle of moon-metal, waiting for a man who will come and smash the circle so we can be born."

"A third voice: "I'm frightened, Teddy—"

"Johnny!" said Teddy.

The Lakota speaker: "The dark wolf is almost right. He did swallow up the others for a time. But in absorbing the others, he became less dark; he took on some of Johnny's pain and fear, some of Jake's wisdom, some of James's servility. He did not like these things, for these things were starting to draw him out of the darkness, and he does not love the light. He wants a world in perpetual shadow. He tried to swallow the sun, but he was burned by it and so spat it out again in anger and pain."

"Don't listen to him!" said Jonas. "He only speaks gibberish. None of us can understand a word he says. He thinks I'm afraid of him . . ."

"He is afraid," said Shungmanitu Hokshila, "because I am the only one of us who understands him."

"I'm not afraid of you . . . I'll eat you up, and all the rest of you . . . so fuck yourselves . . . fuck, fuck, fuck, fuck!"

The boy was all a-tremble now, he didn't seem fearless at all. He snarled at the wind. Teddy didn't know what to make of him, so he turned his back and relieved himself as best he could, though the boy circled around to face him and danced about, trying to get in the way of the stream.

Suddenly the boy stopped. Listened. Teddy heard nothing but the sighing wind. "Food," said the boy. Teddy couldn't tell which of the voices it was. "Come on." Johnny led Teddy away from the stream, moving with a shambling, uncomfortable gait, like a dog made to walk on its hind legs.

A mouse deer lay dead in the clearing. Castellanos was crouched over it. He looked up. Blood dripped from his jaws, and Teddy saw that he had hamstrung the creature with his teeth.

Johnny laughed, a trifle nervously. Teddy began to build a fire. "I ain't eatin' no raw meat," he said to Castellanos, who was ripping off a hunk of the shank and tossing it at Johnny.

"You must grow big and strong," Castellanos said.

Teddy said, "That's true . . . he ain't growed none in these five years." It was something he had never ceased to marvel at since they had rescued him. Teddy himself had gone from an urchin, living by his wits, slipping in and out of the shadows, to a gunman who had killed men, who had shot to death Lord knew how many wolves too. Seemed like every time he saw a man die it aged him some more. He knew he looked a lot older than his nineteen years. But the boy, he didn't look any different. Not at all.

Seeming to divine his bewilderment, Johnny said, "Time hasn't passed for me, Teddy Grumiaux. But since you won't take me for your shadow, maybe I'll have to become myself; and then maybe I'll have to get older. And die."

It was another thing to puzzle over.

8
Winter Eyes
crescent moon, waning

THE LITTER WAS A GOOD ONE. NATALIA PETROVNA NEVER CEASED TO marvel at how she had been able to give birth to such beautiful pups—and only one of them stillborn.

They were in the nursery now, playing. The nursery had been the church once; now the pews had been knocked down, the altar covered with a tarp, and the nave was littered with toys. The four toddlers played rough; she loved to watch them. There was Sasha with the blond curls, who already had a howl like a full-grown pack leader; there was Katyusha, red-haired like her mother, slitty-eyed, slinking behind a stone pilaster; there were Kolya and Petrushka, stalking each other, softly growling, waiting to see who would be the first to pounce.

She clapped her hands. "Home now, children . . . dinner soon."

Sasha said, "Do we eat like people today or like wolves?"

"People."

A chorus of disappointment, then the four gathered solemnly in a line, tallest to shortest, in front of her. How quickly they had learnt their place in the hierarchy of the Lykanthropenverein! She glowed with pride. "But don't fret, children. If you finish everything on the plate, perhaps there'll be a little treat . . . something left over from the last full moon. . . ."

"Knucklebones!" Katyusha licked her lips. "Sucking the marrow!"

"Wanna bite balls off," said Petrushka, the runt, with gratifying relish.

"Children, children!" Natasha said, laughing. They had not even transformed completely for the first time yet . . . such an ability usually came a little later . . . but Sasha, in particular, could hardly contain his lupine nature within his human skin, and during the full moon he would become covered with a fine, blond down that Natasha loved to caress. Perhaps, when he was a little older, she would mate with him; that would go some way toward nurturing the purity of the strain.

"Milk, milk," cried Kolya and Petrushka, and leapt into her arms. Kolya's chubby fingers began to unclasp her stays and unlace her waist to uncover the breasts, still ripe, for she still fed them wolf milk now and then, believing that nothing else would keep them as strong. Petrushka sucked intensely, closing his eyes; Kolya tickled and bit, leaving tiny red marks from his developing canines.

"Mother, Mother," said Katyusha, "my turn, my turn!" For only during the full moon could all her brood suckle at the same time. Instead of feeding, she sprang up and locked her legs about her mother's neck; Sasha grasped her by the hand, and they prepared to return to the von Bächl-Wölfing house. A feeling of profound contentment swept over Natasha. I am a mother, she said. The wolves will grow strong. This town, this desolate place at the end of my people's Winterreise, will thrive after all.

Not, she reflected as they made their way towards the front entrance, without sacrifice. There were those who had not felt that Natasha was the true queen bitch; some of these she had defeated in single combat. She had had to cripple the Baroness von Dittersdorf, who had mated with everyone in sight, man or beast, a privilege that propriety, and the law, allowed only to the queen, whose duty was to the litter. Now the Baroness languished in an attic, and her lovers had all abandoned her, some even going off in search of the quasi-mythical firstborn son of the Count.

There was nothing mythical about Winter Eyes. None of Hartmut's flights of mystical nonsense. I am woman and wolf, and there is no contradiction, she thought. This world is real: my children, the moonlit blood feasts on the reservation and in the settlements, the midnight raids on mineshafts . . . a world of blood and flesh and death . . . a good world for my children to grow up in and to understand their true nature.

The five of them reached the doorway and began to walk out through the churchyard to make their customary obeisance to the spirit of Hartmut. Two young men, seeing her, hunched down as they scurried past; she flared her nostrils at them, casually confirming her dominance.

They stood before the grave of Hartmut von Bächl-Wölfing. The cemetery was, in a sense, a travesty, littered as it was with the symbols of the humans' superstitions: wooden crosses, here and there a saint or angel carved in stone. But it was necessary to maintain the illusion of humanity; Winter Eyes was not as wholly self-sufficient as Dr. Szymanowski had originally envisioned. There were industries not yet supported. Though there was a Chinese laundry, a blacksmith, and a general store, all operated by people recruited to the lycanthropic persuasion, there were no cartwrights and no seamstresses, and such skills had to be supplied by nearby towns. But Winter Eyes was flourishing.

"Yes," Natasha whispered as she knelt by the gravestone of her erstwhile lover, "we flourish . . . we grow . . . it is almost frightening, n'est-ce pas? but we flourish. Do not be angry that I concealed the contents of your will. I did it that your vision might be fulfilled. Oh, Hartmut, you lost your way, you did not stand true. You were swayed by that strange affection you have for lower beings. You were a hero with a fatal flaw—compassion."

She kissed the stone. The morning's roses were still fresh, but their fragrance could not utterly dispel the putrescence that seeped up through the rich humus. The children played, chasing each other around the markers. She did not stop them. It was not good to foster too much gloom here. The dying sunlight lengthened the shadows.

A man stood behind her. "Valentin Nikolaievich," she said. "You smell of bad tidings."

"Quickly, Natasha, gather the children. There is an urgent meeting of the elders."

"What?"

"Another one stricken with the new disease. We've asked that doctor in from Lead."

Dr. Josiah Swanson looked up from his patient as Natasha entered the town hall. The other citizens, who had been clustered around him, parted. When Natasha saw what had happened, she commanded the children to go and play in the vestibule. "Don't come inside," she told them. "Terrible things in here—terrible."

On no account must the litter be jeopardized. She trembled a little as they obediently slipped out. The sick man lay on a litter, having been brought in from Deadwood by cart. It was Joshua Levy. He had gone to Deadwood in order to transact some business at Wells Fargo. There was a delay of some kind, and the full moon had caught him unawares.

He lay now, his face covered with sores, his arms and legs blistered. His face was drenched in sweat, and his beard was soggy with drool and vomit.

"Sarcoptic mange," said Dr. Swanson. "The new disease the wolfers been using to try to wipe out the wolves that prey on the farm animals. I didn't know that you people were susceptible to it. I don't recollect any cure for it, and I reckon he ain't long for this world, ma'am."

"He may not die," Natasha said. "Diseases are not the same with us; we age, we grow weak, but not by the laws that rule the natural world. We are not of nature."

Baroness von Dittersdorf, in her wheelchair, attended by one of her latest beaux, said, "But he may be in agony for a long time." And shot Natasha a poisoned glance, to which Natasha responded with an impatient wave of the hand.

Natasha said, "Perhaps it would be better if we . . ." She did not need to utter what they were all thinking. When a member of the pack grows weak, the others may voluntarily elect to kill him themselves; the law was an ancient one, but had not been invoked as long as any of them could remember.

Except in the case of the late Countess von Bächl-Wölfing, the one whose statue still stood in the park outside the town house in Vienna, the very first Madonna of the Wolves. . . .

The Baroness thrashed about in the wheelchair while her attendant tried to restrain her. "*Luder!*" she shrieked. "*Hur! Warst nie das echte Weib des Grafen . . .*" She continued to screech ineffectively in German while Natasha turned her attention to the others.

"I do not have the authority; this must come from all of you." It would be an evening of deliberation, with all of them speaking their pieces, some arguing for clemency, others for ruthlessness, still others urging some nonexistent middle way. Meanwhile, Levy would continue to lie there, his body eaten alive by the disease. He could not even speak; his eyes were glazed over, and now and then a strangulated whimper escaped his throat. Seeing his agony would cause the other wolves to reflect on their mortality, and she knew that most of them preferred to see themselves as invincible.

They would not want to share the town with a continual, living memento mori. Levy would waste away. The mange would eat his skin raw, would blind him, would make him smell like putrid meat. She had no doubt what the town council's decision would be.

By dawn they will have torn him in pieces, she thought. Aloud, she said, "I must go and see to the litter," and stalked unceremoniously from the hall. She felt a sudden dread, as though the disease had already reached out with its claws to maul her children across the empty air.

They were not in the vestibule. Panicking, she went out into the street. The sun had set. Buildings in twilight; the streets deserted. "Katyusha . . . Sasha . . ." she said softly. "Valentin. . . ."

Then, abruptly, she heard children's laughter. They were chasing each other on the boardwalk across the street. Seeing her, they ran to her. Their laughter was shrill in the moist wind. Their smell reached her before they did, and brought a thin smile to her lips.

A shout from within the town hall. It was the death sentence. She had not thought it would come so soon.

9
Lead
new moon

SPERANZA HAD NOT USED COCA POWDER FOR SOME DAYS, NOT SINCE her hoard had been stolen from her in Bitter Creek. The nightmares worsened; the cocaine had numbed her mind to them before, but now there was nothing to deaden her to the horrors that visited her whenever she but closed her eyes. Time and time again she told herself: I must go home to San Francisco. What use is my presence here? I am thwarted at every turn; even if I were to find the boy, perhaps he no longer knows me, perhaps I will do him more harm than good.

Although she told herself these things, she knew she had to go on. To find Johnny was to end the nightmares.

In Cheyenne she purchased a bottle of laudanum before she boarded the stage for Deadwood and Lead. It proved to be a most unpleasant journey, for the coach was a rickety old thing, and so crowded with passengers that they had to resort to the offensive practice of dovetailing their legs; and the only warmth came from a hot brick wrapped in a blanket, shoved beneath their feet, changed only when they stopped to switch horses.

Speranza was not displeased to find herself once more in a real town of sorts, in a place that did not lurch and bounce and rattle and get bogged down in mud. It was raining in Lead, but at least she had the shelter of the awning above the boardwalk. She made her way to Dr. Swanson's office. Although her last visit there had been distressing, she thought that perhaps there might be letters from Herr Freud; having left so abruptly before, she had never had a chance to tell the doctor where such letters might be forwarded.

It was only drizzling, but the moisture was rank with the smell of rotting leaves. Many buildings were just shells now. A drunk,

nursing his bottle, leaned against a saloon door. An Indian, in
blanket and war bonnet, stood passing out political handbills
about the Chinese question. Was that not Dr. Swanson's place,
there, in the square where she had witnessed that terrible hanging?
But the windows were smashed, the gallows gone, the door to the
office swinging open and shut in the wind.

Slowly the rain grew heavier.

She let herself in. There was a sign that read "Dr. Josiah
Swanson, General Practitioner" and beneath that a smaller notice
that announced a cut rate on "tonsorial refurbishments." A
Chinaman and a Negro sat playing cards at a table, sharing a
hookah. The smell of opium pervaded the air, mixed with the
smell of wet earth and dead leaves.

"Is Dr. Swanson here?" she said.

The two did not answer for a long time. Then the Chinaman
peered at her without curiosity and said, "He go Winter
Eyes . . . no business here . . . town dying . . . no mo'
gold this here town."

"Winter Eyes?" Speranza said.

"Bad place. Many wolf," said the Chinaman.

Speranza turned away. There was nothing to be gained from this
place. She walked back out onto the boardwalk. Somewhere in the
distance came a burst of gunfire. Riderless, a horse raced down
the middle of the street, spraying her with mud.

She made her way back to the stage depot. She had no escort;
she thought of her husband and of little William, and wondered
whether the child thought ill of her for deserting him for so long.

Where could she go? To Winter Eyes, where the wolves would
surely kill her? To Fort Cassandra, whose commander was in
league with the Lykanthropenverein? Or abandon hope and return
to San Francisco?

But then the nightmares would never cease.

No, there was no real choice. She had to obey, not logic, not
common sense, but the prompting of her heart, which told her that
the boy lived, that he was crying out to her, that she must go to his
side whatever the cost.

The rain was driving hard now. She stepped inside the depot,
where her luggage was still piled, and asked the porter when it
would be possible for her to travel out of town.

"Next stage won't be for another three days, Mrs. Dupré, what with this here inclement weather, and the way business is doing poorly now."

"Would it be possible for you to see that my luggage is delivered to . . ." She paused, realizing she was making this up as she went along, realizing that she was still skirting the decision she knew had to be made. "To Deadwood. Yes."

"Will you be travellin' there, then, ma'am?"

"Eventually. There is a letter of credit on deposit for me at the local Wells Fargo which should take care of any eventuality; I should be most grateful were you to see to it that my belongings are kept for me at . . . the Diamond Spur," she said, naming the first hostel that came to mind. "Here," she said, pulling a twenty-dollar piece from her purse, "let me furnish you with some small recompense."

"Shouldn't be carryin' all that gold around," he said.

"No one will follow me where I am going," she said. "Perhaps you could tell me where I can purchase a horse?"

The porter gaped at her. "You aimin' to travel alone, Mrs. Dupré?"

"I surely am," she said.

"At least go down to Fort Cassandra, ma'am, and ask the major for an escort. . . ."

"That, sir, is the last thing I would want. And please, while you're at it," she continued, pulling from her purse the gold-tooled leather Bible she had been carrying since she left San Francisco, "perhaps you would care for this, too; you may have greater need of it than I."

It was a crutch, she told herself. I have hidden behind it long enough.

A flood of memories: the fat, plumed woman in Victoria Station, berating her for her scandalous appetites; the Russian woman with the flaming hair, her cheek marred by the deadly kiss of silver; the Count as he caressed the nape of her neck and softly touched her lips with his, inflaming her with the animal perfume he exuded; the boy with the angel's face, begging her to pervert a children's fairy tale; the boy pissing his anger against the train tracks, the boy weeping unconsolably as the blood of a fresh kill dribbled from the side of his mouth. . . .

"I was wrong to run away before," she said, not to the porter but for herself. "But Claggart is dead now. Perhaps the child can still be saved. Perhaps I can still redeem myself."

She pressed the Bible into the porter's hands, ignoring his uncomprehending expression. Quickly she pulled what she needed from her luggage and packed it in a single valise, then walked away in the rain toward the tumbledown livery at the end of the street.

I must ride into the forest, she thought. I must listen to the still small voice that cries out to me in the language of night.

I must ride into the forest of my nightmares.

10
The Black Hills
three-quarter moon, waxing

THERE IS A FOREST THAT COVERS THE WHOLE WORLD. HERE AND there, men beat back clearings, build cities, let in the sunlight, and have what they call civilization. But the forest, which knows not the nature of time, waits. Encroaches. Swallows up. No one knows if the forest has consciousness. Perhaps it knows only the need to devour, engulf. We can push the darkness from us, but we cannot wipe it out.

This was the lesson Speranza taught herself as she set off into the forest. She must forget that she was warned to stick to the path. She must put aside her fear of the dark. The forest was the womb of her nightmare, the trees bleeding with the putrescent moisture of autumn, the earth linking her to the dark like a placenta.

"I want Little Red Riding Hood . . . but make Little Red Riding Hood a boy . . ." That was what Johnny had asked her on the first train journey, so long ago, the winter journey in the snow. Why had such an innocent request sounded so obscene to her? Now she knew why. She knew why because she had entered the lair of the beast, she had smelled the beast's breath on her lips, she had loved the beast.

Gone were the stays and corsets. She wore a pair of cheap, creased, store-boughten Levi's; an oversized jacket; a shapeless old slough hat; all these things purchased in the general store in Lead. She did not even ride sidesaddle. Little Red Riding Hood had become a boy.

She had left the path somewhere on the road to Deadwood. She had forged uphill, always uphill, knowing that she was pushing farther into the territory of the dream. If the dream is real enough, she thought, I will find it. So she followed blind instinct, paying no attention to her surroundings. There were bleak crags, stark escarpments, twisted trees, angry waterfalls, vast vistas of evergreens from precarious ledges. She only half saw them. The dream was strong and it would lead her to him, as it had before. She rode uphill. Already, here and there, there was a little snow.

"Look," said Teddy Grumiaux, as they reached the creek beside the village of the Shungmanitu. Johnny crawled to the edge and lapped up water from the stream. It was sunset. Smoke tendriled from the vents of many tipis. There were more tents than before; somehow, despite the war with the *washichun* wolves, the tribe had grown more numerous.

"What do we do now?" Castellanos said. "It is true that I and the boy are wolves by nature, but I do not think they would necessarily welcome me."

"Got to do something first," Teddy said.

He led them downstream a ways. They forded. Tall rocks loomed. The ground sloped up steeply; they could see the village below them and smell the lodge smoke as it wafted. In a moment they reached the burial grounds, where the platforms were set up so the dead could lie exposed to Takushkanshkan, the sky, and Wakinyan, the sacred winged creatures that could prey on their flesh and absorb them back into the fabric of the universe.

Johnny sniffed the wind and said, "There are people I know here. Oh, Teddy, I don't want to—"

"Quiet. Got to find my ma." Skeletons lay on scaffolds decorated with shields and painted buffalo skulls and lances hung with scalps. Teddy shuddered. Victor Castellanos walked behind him, a bit of a swagger in his gait, whistling softly; Teddy knew he was trying to hide his unease. And Johnny was running from scaffold to scaffold, breathing in the perfume of decay, now and then crying out a name in the language of the Lakota. He's remembering, Teddy thought.

Suddenly he heard Johnny howl. He had found the resting place of Ishnazuyai. He cried "*Até, até,*" in the voice of the Indian boy. Teddy could see no trace of Jonas Kay in him, not in the way he moved, not in the way he sang a sacred song his Indian father had taught him. The wind whistled and he could hardly hear what the boy was singing, but Johnny seemed comforted.

Then Teddy turned and saw Little Elk Woman. He could still recognize her even though she was worn down almost to the bone; she was covered in a buffalo robe he knew well; he used to sleep on it when he was a child. She had no eyes, but there were still a few pieces of paper-thin skin wrapped around her cheeks, and a few hanks of hair, fluttering in the evening breeze. Standing there next to her dead body, Teddy felt the warmth of the presence of her spirit. "Never did cry for you, Ma," he said. "I was too busy fixin' to avenge you and all the others." As Catellanos watched him curiously he stripped off his shirt and untied the bowie knife from his boot, and made some deep gashes across his chest, calling out the name of the Great Mystery: "Wakantanka, Wakantanka."

Johnny sat at his feet, looking hungrily at the gushing blood. Teddy wept.

Only a smear of sun remained above the mountainous horizon. The boy stood up suddenly, cocked his ears; Teddy heard the crackle of moccasins on dead twigs. Then came voices; an old man singing a song in remembrance of a dead man. Teddy put out his hand, cautioning the others to silence. A slow procession was winding uphill. A dead man on a litter borne by two warriors, a *wichasha wakan* banging the slow drum of mourning, women with their piercing ritual grief-cries. Teddy hadn't heard such a thing since the time they laid Zeke to rest in the other village, before the Shungmanitu had fled the plains to seek refuge in the high remote places. It brought back memories and more memories, and he didn't feel rightly white at all anymore.

He went down to where the tribesmen were raising up the dead man onto a platform. He kept Johnny and Victor close to him. The medicine man showed no surprise when Teddy said, "I am the son of Little Elk Woman." He wore a wolfskin, and his face was painted like a skull.

The dead man's body was covered with suppurating sores. The face was eaten away; one eye dangled from its socket by a mere thread of tissue. Though he had been arrayed in a beautiful war shirt adorned with fine beadwork and with human hair, Teddy couldn't look away from the face. It looked like it had been turned inside out.

"I seen a lot of dead folks," Teddy said to Castellanos, "but I ain't never seen one that looked like it's been et alive."

"It is a new disease," said the *wichasha wakan*, "for which we have no cure. The white man give it to wolves, and sometimes to us. The wolves are dying out."

"But your village is thriving!"

"Humans, fleeing the reservations, swell our ranks. Some who surrendered with Sitting Bull became dissatisfied; those who did not stay in Canada came to us."

A woman, holding up the bleeding stumps where she had struck off fingers in her grief, hurled herself against the foot of the scaffold, weeping. Teddy carved another gash on his left arm to show his sorrow for the man's death.

"Give me the knife," said Castellanos. "I do not understand these Indians, but in my time with the Comancheros I learned to understand pain." And, taking the bowie knife from Teddy, he bared his chest and slit it in two places, and the medicine man nodded in approval as he began once more to pound his drum.

Johnny stepped forward. The *wichasha wakan* noticed him for the first time. In astonishment he missed a drumbeat. The women looked up from their wailing.

"*Wanaghi!*" someone whispered.

Teddy said, "This is no spirit. I've brought the boy back to you."

"You know me, don't you?" Johnny said in Lakota. "I've come back. I've come to lead you to the place of the moon dance. As I promised once, a long time ago, in the moon when the choke cherries ripen. I have returned. If the white wolves and the red wolves dance together, we can still renew the world and bring back the days of joy."

The shaman looked at him in disbelief. A warrior whispered in his ear, and he said, "There have been many evil spirits."

"I am no ghost," said Johnny quietly.

"There are some here who say that when you left on your spirit journey, you turned into a bird and flew so high that you were lost to us forever."

"I have come to lead the people to the place of the moon dance . . . as Ishnazuyai foresaw . . . according to my dream. I have been asleep for many years, and my body has seen many dark things, but my vision has brought me back to you. And we will dance the moon dance, for the great cycle has come around again, a great cycle of cycles."

"Poor child . . . it is too late . . . the people are too angry . . . all they want is to kill, even if it means that they too are annihilated."

Quietly, the boy repeated—and Teddy marvelled at the authority in him—"I have returned as my vision foretold, and I will lead all the wolf-peoples to the place of the moon dance, and those who have hurt us will be driven back across the great waters."

"The cage is shattered!" Johnny could hear the voice of Jake—fainter, distorted somehow until it was almost a mirror of his own voice. "We're free!"

But he could hear Jonas's taunting laughter. Even though the forest was awash with sunlight. The bars of the cage lay scattered; they were withering even as Johnny stood, marvelling at the light that streamed in with the leafy wind. There stood the Indian boy in a shaft of radiance, his hair windswept, looking upward at the sky. Perhaps he could see the sun; if he could, he was the only one in the forest who had ever done so.

The bars of the cage, the planks of the tree fort . . . rotting away, giving off the sweet scent of autumn.

The Indian boy turned to him. Spoke in the language of the Indians. But for the first time it seemed to him that he could make out the words: "There is still an enemy we must face."

Johnny went to stand beside the Indian boy. His gaze followed the boy's outstretched arm, but for him there was no sun. Only, perhaps, an eagle, swooping at his eyes, talons wide, screeching. . . .

The Indian boy said, "You see the edge of the vision. Soon you will see it all."

Jake's voice: "We're comin' together . . . we're joinin'

up . . . into one complete Johnny with all the memories and all the wisdom and all the—"

"Pain!" came the voice of Jonas. He was almost certain it was Jonas, Jonas who growled like an animal even when the moon was not full . . . yet the voice had a strange new quality, one that could almost be mistaken for compassion. Jonas, the dark one, even Jonas was beginning to be drawn into the circle of healing.

That was what chilled Johnny most. He did not want to accept the idea that, to become whole, he would have to stand face-to-face with this darkness and say to it, "I am yours and you are mine and we belong together."

All night, the people of the village sang of the return of the son of Ishnazuyai, returned to them out of the place of death.

11
Winter Eyes
three days before full moon

THE BROOD WAS RESTLESS. AND NATASHA TOO BROODED, FOR THE night was full of bad dreams. They were weighting her stomach with stones . . . she was sinking into the river of blood . . . blood streaming into her nostrils, flooding her lungs, her womb exploding as dead wolf pups clawed their way out, mindlessly chewing the flesh. . . .

She woke with the four children clamoring at her breasts, an hour before dawn. The scent of a stranger wafted in through the battened shutters of the von Bächl-Wölfing house.

She rose from bed and unlatched one shutter. Brilliant moonlight streamed in over the four-poster bed. The gauze drapes fluttered in the wind, cold, smelling of damp wormy earth. She drew on her dressing gown and stood gazing out onto the street.

The stranger stood at the graveyard gate. An old woman who smelled like a man. She recognized her now.

In their sleep the children squalled, groped for teats that were not there. Only Petrushka, the runt, lay absolutely still; his eyes alone darted back and forth, and Natasha wondered whether his dreams had been as troubled as her own.

She went to meet the woman.

The wind howled ceaselessly, and all through the town the shutters rattled like the bones of a desiccated corpse. The moon would soon be full; already Natasha could see with the eyes of night, and the skin beneath the fur patch on her cheek itched and ached and burned.

Gingerly she crossed the street, her bare feet sinking into moist earth. There was the church; the woman stood waiting, her face crisscrossed by the shadow of the railings of the cemetery gate.

"Juanita!" said Natasha angrily. "You were never to come here . . . you were to watch those two and never allow them to set foot in the Dakota Territory. . . ."

"And they never have," said the woman, pulling her shawl tighter about her face. "Did they ever consider going beyond Fort Laramie? A hundred times! And a hundred times I pluck death out of the tarot deck and I tell them: 'Turn back, turn back.' "

"I sent you gold and more gold, to make sure that Cordwainer Claggart and the child never came to this place . . . to make sure that the child would be treated with the utmost bestial cruelty . . . to make sure he would lose all human qualities, sit mired in his own excrement . . . the gold was not enough? Do you come to demand more?"

"No. I come to tell you Mr. Claggart is dead."

Natasha howled.

Overhead, clouds, billowing, darkened the moon's face. The grave markers' shadows yawned across the street to the muddy boardwalk and the dilapidated general store. "The child," she cried, seizing Juanita by the shoulders, "you must tell me he is dead . . . poisoned by the silver that imprisoned him. . . ."

"Liberated. Healed."

Lights came on in the upper-story windows. She howled and howled again, and the wind echoed her howling.

"A gunman came from the west . . . killed Claggart . . . stole the child . . . I think a man of your people was with him . . . I heard the name Castellanos."

She reeled. Suddenly Vishnevsky was there, a lamp in one

hand, to catch her before she swooned. She cried out in Russian:
"The children, Valentin Nikolaievich . . . the children . . ."
She felt weak. This must be the meaning of the terrible dreams
that had kept her tossing and turning these past days! Yes . . .
the dream of the prison that was a womb that was a prison whose
walls dripped blood that throbbed with the pangs of still-
birth. . . .

"Where did they go?" she said.

"Northeast . . . toward the Black Hills," said Juanita. "I read
it in the cards. And in Bitter Creek I met a woman who demanded
to know about the child. . . ."

Vishnevsky steadied her. She breathed deeply. Some other
residents of the town peered down from their windows; in the
distance, from the house, she could hear Katyusha call out:
"Mother, Mother."

"You must ride to Fort Cassandra, my cousin," Natasha said.
"You must tell Major Sanderson to come immediately . . . or
there will be no more future for us."

12
The Black Hills
two days before full moon

. . . THEN THEY WEIGHTED DOWN THE WOLF'S BELLY WITH STONES,
*and sewed him up, and threw him into the stream; and, as he
could not swim, he drowned horribly. . . .*

Speranza could not breathe. The womb was bursting . . .
blood seeping in . . . blood in her nostrils, blood pouring into
her lungs, blood. . . .

She awoke. In the forest. Awoke to darkness. The fire was
dead. The wind whined in the treetops. She could feel the blood
quicken. A keen odor: men moving through underbrush. The
rustling of dead leaves. The hunters are coming . . . the hunters

are coming . . . she thought of the dream . . . blood dripping from the womb walls, leaves bleeding from the dying trees. . . .

The horse whinnied.

A hand over her mouth and—

Laughter! Skull eyes stared back at her! She flailed, her hand struck the face, paint smudged, greasy on her fingers, provoked more laughter, masculine, ugly—

She tried to scream. The hand smelled of mud and horse dung. She was suffocating. Other hands pulled her up, she saw the glint of a bone-handled knife and—

Tore herself away as the scream tore from her throat—

More laughter.

"*Hokshila kin*—" said one of them.

She stood there. They were not touching her, but she could tell from the sound of their breathing that she was surrounded.

A flash of feathers . . . something hard struck her forehead and was retracted . . . a coup stick. A shriek of victory and delight. She reeled. The pain was making her dizzy. Blood flooded her left eye.

"*Onzé wichawahu kte lo!*" A soft voice, leering.

Another hand now, grasping her by the scruff, yanking at her jacket . . . she struggled, but other hands pinned her down . . . she felt callused fingers exploring the inside of her flannel shirt . . . oh God, they are planning to violate me, even thinking that I am a man, she thought . . . the stranger's nails raked flesh, skidded onto one of her breasts . . . she screamed again, screaming and wept . . . she felt cloth tear now, her breast felt the moist wind and the strangers' breath and. . . .

"*Winyan ye lo!*" a voice said, half in disgust.

A momentary pause. She managed to free herself. Her captors were close, almost touching her. The reprieve would be brief. They would rape her, kill her. The forest had engulfed her. There was no escape.

"*Winyan hecha* . . . " It was the same voice . . . she saw that the warrior was quite young, and that there was a certain bewilderment in his features, behind the mask of the death's head.

She shook the mud from her clothes. Three, four, five men perhaps. Eyes in the dark . . . faces painted to look like skulls. "Yes," she said, "I am a woman, and alone."

"*Wichakte po!*" a stern voice cried out. She knew from their tone that they were discussing her death. There was the knife again, teasing at her throat. She held her breath. A scream . . . a cough . . . and the knife would slit the skin. . . .

She closed her eyes. Somewhere, an owl hooted. She could hear the leaves stir in the autumn wind.

Then came a small voice, the voice of a child. The knife was withdrawn. She knew that voice. She felt heat . . . beneath closed lids she could sense flickering torchlight. The child's voice went on. It spoke in the language of the Indians, in measured tones that bespoke an ancient wisdom, yet the voice was still recognizably that of the boy she had come to seek out.

Slowly she opened her eyes.

He was standing at the far edge of the clearing. He was no taller than when she had last seen him. When he lived amongst the Indians, he had grown fast; had his sojourn with Cordwaiter Claggart stunted him? Like an Indian, he wore only a breechclout; a single feather adorned his shorn and matted hair. There were welts across his arms, his chest, thin ridges tipped with gray fur; she knew he had been touched with a silver lash. He was thin, emaciated, sunken-eyed. Yet he held himself erect, and there was a pride in his features she had never seen before. On either side of him stood braves who carried firebrands. Beyond she could see other Indians.

One of the braves handed her her jacket. She wrapped herself in it. The boy walked up to her slowly. When she looked into his eyes she saw a person she had never met. He blinked three times; his face underwent a swift metamorphosis; then, very quietly, he said, "Speranza."

For a moment she could not answer. At last she said, "I've come back."

He said, "They are very angry. They want to wipe out every trace of the *washichun* . . . I am sorry they tried to . . ."

He reached out his arms to her. And suddenly all that had passed—the journeys from darkness into deeper darkness, the years of loveless desolation in San Francisco—all that seemed meaningless. She remembered the first time he had clung to her in grief and terror—the first time she had embraced him, knowing what he was, knowing what he could become.

Johnny said, "We're going to Winter Eyes. I want to try to

make them see the light. I came to the Shungmanitu when they were on the verge of waging a war so terrible that all of us would have died, all the wolves . . . do you understand? I told them I could make the white wolves see reason . . . because I'm still the white wolves' king . . . that's what my father told me."

"Johnny . . . I've come to . . . take you far, far away . . . you're still a child, Johnny, and you'll be torn apart . . . Johnny, you must not remain amongst these people . . . that's why I've come."

"No, Speranza." This was not the frightened child she had left behind. He partook of many of the qualities of his other person-alities. She knew from this that he had begun to heal himself, to become integrated. "You didn't come here to drag me away. You came because you knew this is my destiny. That there's a part you have to play in it. You came because you love me. You truly loved my father even when you most loathed him. And I know you love me. All of me. Even Jonas. You're the only one who loves Jonas too."

It was strange to hear such a speech from the lips of one who seemed so young. Yet she knew these things were true. And though she was still a captive of the savage forest, among men who had assaulted her and tried to violate her, she knew she was no longer lost. I have found the path, she told herself. There was a new serenity in Johnny, and as the two of them clung together she tried, despairing, to draw some of that peace unto herself.

"Strange," she said. "I thought I was coming here to protect you, to release you . . . now I find that it is you who are comforting me . . . I am the lost child and you the father."

Johnny smiled a sad little smile. "There are many who are at war inside me," he said, "but the war will soon be over. We're not going to Winter Eyes to wreak destruction. We are going there to heal."

There came another voice, changed yet familiar: "Miss Speranza . . . I thought you was gone from us forever."

More light in the clearing. There was a man who came to her, held out his hand in greeting. She knew him at once, though he seemed immeasurably older.

"I saw you on a wanted poster . . ." she said.

Teddy Grumiaux laughed. "A mistake. I shouldn't never have

kilt them men in Utah. But I didn't know they was men; they reeked of wolf sweat."

"You've been hunting them down?"

"I killed Claggart. So I reckon I can stop killing now. And listen to what the boy says. About bringing peace betwixt the wolves. Mayhap it can be done."

More light. More Indians bearing torches. Firelight danced in their faces, faces painted like faces of death; could these really be harbingers of peace?

"Not all of them is convinced, Miss Speranza. They was fixin' to go on the warpath afore me and Johnny reached them. They was angry, and many of them still is."

"They won't be angry forever, Speranza . . . I promise . . . because I've had a true vision."

Johnny Kindred took her hand in his and led her to an embankment. Across the stream was a place she remembered vividly. But there were no tipis, and burnt-out fires smoldered in the drizzle. Some old men and women sat, wrapped in blankets, each one staring straight ahead as if already dead.

"Where is the village?" she asked him.

Teddy Grumiaux said, "They took down the lodges. Loaded the buffalo skins onto horse-drawn travois. Them old folks is staying because they'd only slow the others down; they aims to die here, beside the sacred burial grounds."

"Why is the village moving?" Speranza said.

"They're fixin' to take the whole village down to Winter Eyes . . . to the place of the moon dance."

"Moon dance?"

"When the moon reaches the beginning of a Great Cycle of Years," said Johnny Kindred, "the werewolves of the plains assemble at a specially appointed place sacred to them, and dance a dance that renews the universe. I am their seer, and I will lead them to that place, and you too have a role to play, Speranza, because my dream has brought you to me."

"Oh, Johnny . . . I know nothing of this moon dance . . . I came here for one thing only . . . I thought I could atone for abandoning you to that monster, Mr. Claggart . . . I thought I could bring you home with me, to San Francisco perhaps. . . ."

"You have a part to play," he said softly. And his eyes were flecked with cold yellow light, as though it were Jonas who spoke; yet she knew Jonas could not address her with such civility.

"But I don't see what I can do . . . I don't even speak their language. . . ."

"You're going to be standing beside me when I face the ultimate darkness; we'll dance together, you and I. Madonna and child, wolf and human, man and woman."

Again she felt that faint obscenity she had felt when he had asked her, so long ago, to tell him the perverted story of Little Red Riding Hood. And again she felt, behind the calm he exuded, behind the gentleness of his demeanor and the softness of his utterance, a ravening, insuperable despair.

"You think me mad," he said.

"Yes."

"Yet you still come with me.

"The Lakota think me mad too, Speranza." He smiled. And clutched her hand harder; his fingernails drew a drop of blood from her palm, but she did not mind. "But they believe it's good to be mad . . . they believe madness is holy."

And Speranza thought: Why, perhaps it is so. Was not St. Theresa, flagellating herself into the orgasmic ecstasy of communion with God, the kind of creature Sigmund Freud might have called a madwoman? And those who conquered the world, Alexander, Tamburlaine . . . were they not driven by insanity? Yet thousands followed to their deaths.

"I don't care about these things," she said at last. "Perhaps it was your dream that called me to this place; perhaps you've fashioned some kind of destiny for me that I can't understand. But I came here, as you say, because I love you; there's an end of it, Johnny."

It was raining harder as they rode down from the hills. She rode beside Teddy Grumiaux and Castellanos, a man she remembered vaguely from Winter Eyes as one of the Baroness von Dittersdorf's acquisitions. She retained her masculine dress, for they could not afford to be slowed down by a woman riding sidesaddle.

The women and children and the horses laden with their belongings marched behind. They rode in the open, for they believed that the dream protected them, that they could not be seen.

At sunrise the rain lightened. The morning mist coiled up from rocky clefts and mingled with the horses' breath.

In the light, she saw that this was no band of disorganized savages. Though each walked or rode his own way, seemingly unmindful of the others, there was a kind of secret rhythm to the movement; somehow they always arrived at some predeterminate place, be it a knoll, a copse, an outcropping, that was as familiar a landmark to them as the Staatsoper or the Houses of Parliament.

Johnny always rode ahead, flanked by the most distinguished warriors among the Shungmanitu. They carried ceremonial lances decorated with eagle feathers and human scalps. Each time that Johnny spoke, the chiefs heard him with reverence, and solemnly relayed his words to the others.

"That one there's Running Bull," said Teddy, pointing, "and that there's Man Who Talks To Himself; and there's Iron Hand, who ain't a werewolf, but a brave which rode with Sitting Bull down from Canada way."

She saw a man with a war shirt, every inch of which was covered with human hair . . . blond hair. She shuddered.

"All them scalps is white men's," Teddy said. "He's wearin' the hair of Curt Mortiz, Injun agent—there was a human slug if I ever did see one!—who traded whiskey for virgin squaws, which he sold to houses of ill fame for a hundred dollars apiece."

"I knew this Moritz," Castellanos said grimly, "for when I rode with the Comancheros, he forced us to cut the price of the liquor we traded the Comanches, and damn near drove us out of business."

Such was the nature of their small talk as they reached the vicinity of Winter Eyes. It was amazing to her that they had passed unnoticed even through areas the cavalry should have been patrolling. Perhaps there was something to this talk of dream power. But even as she tried to believe that Johnny could somehow make the drive real, the dread mounted.

And when at last she saw the town in the distance, under the shadow of Weeping Wolf Rock, the dread became almost palpable. She knew—they had told her—that Hartmut von Bächl-Wölfing was dead. He too had been driven by a dream, driven to his death. It seemed to her that his spirit was in the very wind as it sighed through the tall grass . . . the wind that caressed her and reminded her of his touch . . . I loved him! she thought.

And remembered the Chinawoman swinging in the summer sun.

Johnny was speaking animatedly to the chiefs. "What's he saying?" she asked Teddy, and they rode closer to the front of the line.

"He says they won't never talk peace if the whole tribe goes chargin' into town . . . that he has to go in alone. And they're sayin' they ain't lettin' him go down into the den of wolves by hisself because he's too precious to them."

"I will go with him," Speranza said.

Surprised, Teddy rode ahead and relayed what she had said. There was some more discussion. Then Johnny said to her, "Yes; I knew you would go. That's good. Many of the people of Winter Eyes still think that you are the real queen, and that Natalia Petrovna is a usurper. And Teddy Grumiaux and Victor should come with us too. The four of us can convince the others, I think."

"Convince them that a night of dancing is going to change the world?" Speranza said. Again the dread, teasing the back of her neck, knotting her stomach.

"Convince them that we, the wolves, are a single people who can share the land in peace," Johnny said.

With such despair in his eyes. Yet there was joy in the faces of the Shungmanitu. Far behind, she could hear the children playing hide-and-seek in the man-high grass.

"Soon will come night," said Castellanos. "We will enter the town now. I do not think they will harm us. At sunup we will return."

"And if we do not?" Speranza said.

"Then," Teddy said, "they swoops down and wipes them from the face of the earth."

"As the humans are doing to the wolves with their sarcoptic manage," said Victor Castellanos.

As she caught up to the others, she saw that one of the Indians—the one who wore the white men's scalps on his shirt, the one who was not Shungmanitu but pure Lakota—was toying with a silver bullet that he had pulled from a medicine bag around his neck . . . the medicine bag was encrusted with trade beads and with silver dollars. She stared at all the silver, wondering whether Iron Hand knew its power.

And two Sharps rifles hung from his saddle.

The dread grew stronger. Her stomach tightened and she could hear the pounding of her heart, though the wind screamed ceaselessly.

13
Winter Eyes
one day before full moon

AGAIN NATASHA AWOKE SWEATING. THE CHILDREN WERE POUNDING her sides with clenched fists, though their eyes were shut tight. There was a commotion in the street outside.

She hurried to the window.

People in the streets. The smell of strangers . . . and the smell of one she knew well . . . one who had touched the Count von Bächl-Wölfing, who still bore a trace of his marked scent upon her person. . . .

The children! The children had to be protected at all costs! She shouted for Vishnevsky, who stumbled, sleepy-eyed, into the bedchamber. "Didn't you send for Sanderson?" she said. "Didn't you—"

"Yes, yes . . . he is on his way with a troop of cavalry . . ."

"They're coming to kill the children . . ."

Vishnevsky rushed to the window. She knew that he saw what she had seen: the woman Speranza, and by her side that idiot boy, the one Hartmut had doted on, pinned his hopes on, left his kingdom to. . . .

"Come . . . we'll take the children to the church." Vishnevsky lifted up Sasha and Kolya in his arms and slung them, still asleep, one over each shoulder. Natasha gathered up the other two, the girl and the runt, and, cradling them to her breasts, followed her cousin down the stairs toward the back entrance and an alleyway.

Katyusha stirred. "Blood," she whispered, "blood, blood, blood." The moon, not quite full, was enough to make the child's heart pump and the blood race; perhaps tomorrow she would change completely for the first time. Snoring, Petrushka began to suckle. There was blood mixed with the milk. Her nipple stiffened. But she did not feel that disquieting blend of maternalism and eroticism that she usually felt; she was too afraid for the children's safety.

"Quick," Natasha said. They walked along the path. They could hear voices: "Right and proper . . ." "The true blood will tell . . ." "There's something in what the boy says. . . ."

They reached the back of the church. There was Hartmut's grave, illumined by soft moonlight. They entered by a back door and went into the vestry, a tiny, stone-walled chamber with a single, high window. Vishnevsky lit the lamps. Natasha ransacked a cupboard, found some musty surplices, bundled them up for bedding. They laid the four children down.

"Guard them," she said.

"What will you do?" said Vishnevsky.

"There can only be one queen bitch," she said. "Listen to the voices in the streets! I have no choice."

She left him, heard him bolt and bar the door, stepped out through the broken choir stalls to the nave. The voices were louder. Some were against her, some supported her. With the full moon so near, her sense of hearing was almost that of the wolves; she could hear them talking in low voices far down the street, down to the corner where stood the von Bächl-Wölfing mansion.

It was time to make the challenge once and for all.

Victor Castellanos found Baroness von Dittersdorf lying alone in an upper room, stricken by the disease that had claimed so many of the wolves. A naked youth lay snoring next to her. It was Joaquin Guzman, who had been a stableboy when they last met, and was now almost a man . . . who lay oblivious to the tumult in the street beyond. But the Baroness awoke as soon as he slipped in through the open window.

"You haven't changed," she said. And it was true; the moon lit up his strong features against the ivory-framed mirror on the wall. He could not say the same of her. She was dying. "You come to me, a withered woman, crippled from a battle for dominance with the queen bitch . . . dying of the mange . . . perhaps you've come to laugh at me?"

"I come with a message of healing."

The Baroness laughed bitterly. Her laughter turned to coughing. With a pus-gorged arm she tried to raise herself into a sitting position.

Castellanos wanted to tell her of the moon dance . . . of the coming of peace. "They were going to swoop down and destroy the village," he said, "and they were stopped by one child and his vision . . ."

"What difference would it make to me?" said the Baroness. She vomited blood onto piss-stained silken sheets. "Your wolves' utopia comes too late, too late—"

There was so much more to tell her! But he was choking on the words. Perhaps it would be best to forget her. Although he had once held her in his arms while she had sapped from him his humanness . . . even as he remembered how they had coupled, thrusting with a frenzied yet feelingless passion, on this very bed, these very sheets, the Baroness's latest conquest, without opening his eyes, put his arms around her and tried to drag her back into his embrace. . . .

"How can you do this to him . . . knowing of the contagion in your flesh?"

"He is young. The young will fuck anything." She spoke with a pathetic bravado; he pitied her even as he loathed her. "And I am old. Do you think the old have no needs, no desires?" Her voice had become a croak.

In his sleep, Joaquin mumbled: "Come to bed. Come on. Don't keep me waiting. Come on. Come to bed."

"Is he . . . one of us yet?" said Victor.

"Why? Can you not decide whether to use bullets of lead . . . or of silver? I know you have come to kill us all, you and your Indian friends."

At last, Joaquin sat up, rubbing his eyes. "Who is it?" he said. And then, seeing Castellanos: "Intruder . . . I'll kill you!" and reached for a derringer beneath the pillow and, without even thinking, fired at Castellanos's head.

"Don't be silly, you sweet boy," said the Baroness, stroking his head with a peeling hand. "You should know better than to kill a werewolf that way."

Castellanos felt something moist drip down his forehead. Blood . . . and something else . . . a wad of brain tissue peppered with pieces of his cranium. He barely noticed the agony. Already his body was repairing itself . . . the flesh knitting together . . . "I don't want to fight you!" he said. But another bullet ripped through his cheek, and another, and another, until the derringer was empty. He tasted blood . . . felt the flesh undulating, the sinews tying themselves off—

"Stealing my woman . . . that's what you're after. I could kill you ten times over." And the young man lunged at him, clawing at his throat, while the Baroness cackled like a fairy-tale witch.

He put out his hands to ward of the blows . . . felt the wolf strength flow through him . . . as his fingers touched the young man's chest he felt the skin tear, felt the hand rive the slippery flesh, felt the blood gush, felt the rib cage crack and the fibrillating heart as it squished into his clenching fist. . . .

He stared. "I do not mean to—"

The moon is gathering strength. The dream of the boy has terrible power to kill as well as heal . . . we are all pawns of the boy's dream, even the boy himself. . . .

And he stared into Joaquin's lifeless eyes as he slumped back onto the bed with the blood spurting from his chest and spattering the oily floorboards and he fell against the ravaged body of his lover, who screeched with inhuman laughter: "You have come to heal . . . to heal . . . to heal . . . ha! ha! . . . you have come to heal. . . ."

"But I *have* come to—"

. . . the body slammed down on the Baroness's body . . . the dull crack of splintering bone . . . the cackling mutated into a high-pitched wail that matched the squalling of the wind without . . .

The Baroness lay with her neck twisted at an impossible angle, yet she still screamed . . . "The mange . . . has eaten away . . . my power to heal myself . . . is weak . . ."

He knelt beside her. "Do you think I wanted to be what I am now? Do you think I would have willingly drunk the water from a wolf's pawprint if I had known that it was not the fine Alsatian wine you claimed it was?"

She clutched at his hand. Gripped it hard, so hard that a vessel popped between two of her knuckles and released a rivulet of blood and pus. He tried to yank his hand away, but her hand came away in his . . . blood dripped from the stump . . . he could see the nerves and sinews sizzling, flailing about as they sought to rejoin their severed ends . . . a capillary, wormlike, wriggled as it vainly sought its mate.

"I cannot heal," said Baroness von Dittersdorf, "and yet I cannot die."

With the arm that was still whole she caressed his neck, his hair, his cheeks. Her flesh was rotting as it hung limp on her bones. He felt both revulsion and pity.

"If I kill you," he said, "they will not believe we came to make peace."

But in his gunbelt there was a pistol with silver bullets; Teddy had loaded it for him so he would not have to touch the poison metal.

"You came to kill, not heal . . . always you have known this."

"Yes . . . perhaps I have."

He drew his gun and aimed it through her open mouth . . . remembering how her soft lips had closed on his stiff manhood once, and roused him to a passion he had not thought possible, when his only knowledge of women had been when the Comacheros gang-raped some squaw they had captured before selling her to a bordello . . . shoved the gun hard against the palate, wincing as the shaft grew slick with pus . . . and remembering how his seed had spurted and spurted as he drained the goblet of Alsatian wine not knowing it contained the water of transformation and that he would change forever and he spurted and spurted and . . . squeezed the trigger and heard the charring as the silver tore up through the brain tissue and erupted from the crown and the tongue shot out and . . . remembering the tongue teasing the tender tip as he . . . the whole body shaking now shifting from wolf to woman to wolf . . .

He got up.

Wrapped the lovers in each other's arms. So Joaquin had not transformed yet. That was why he had died so easily. Just put my fist through his chest, Castellanos thought. Never meant to. . . .

. . . turned his back on them. Went to the window. Stood awhile, watching. Blood ran down his palms and stained the windowsill. There was Grumiaux, waving at him to come down.

No one knew that the embassy of peace had already claimed two lives.

. . . the moon was moving to her destined place . . . the Indian boy dreamed while the others spoke to the citizens of Winter Eyes . . . the great circles of the sun and moon were going to intersect with the pathways of the stars . . . at the appointed moment it would be given to him to tap the power that flowed from the very heart of the earth . . . Shungmanitu Hokshila did not speak, did not open his eyes, though the body he inhabited spoke in the jangling tongues of the white men, pleading and importuning; Shungmanitu was the eye of the whirlwind, the utter calm at the tempest's center, dreaming the tumult still.

Teddy Grumiaux shinnied up the drainpipe to the window ledge where Castellanos stood. He knew there was something wrong even before he saw that his friend's hands were dripping blood. . . .

Speranza stood in the shadow of the town hall. One of the Count's retainers knelt before her, whispering, *"Gräfin, Gräfin. . . ."*

"You're shakin' all over," Teddy said. He looked past Castellanos into the room. Saw the dead bodies. "Shit," he said, "they must've tried to attack you—"
   "Attack . . . I myself . . ."

In the vestry, a clock on the wall ticked and ticked and ticked and Vishnevsky waited for sunrise.

The boy scurried across the rooftops. His feet thumped along the shingles and he howled in the language of the wolves: "Come with me to a place of beginning . . . come dance the moon dance with me . . . come to the place where the moon devours and gives birth to itself and where the world is reborn in love . . ."
   In their houses, roused from slumber, one by one, the were-wolves heard the words. They were new words, for the wolves of Europe had been cut off from the wisdom of the Shungmanitu Wakan, and knew themselves only as evil . . . some scoffed; others saw in the words a glimmer of ancient truth . . .

The boy cried out in the language of night: "It is true that we are the darkness but the darkness is the womb of the light! It is true that we devour but life springs from death as the maggot springs from the putrefying flesh! Weight not your wombs with stones, do not drown in the river of blood, but come with me to the source of the river and dance in the moonlight where past and future are one!" He spoke not with words but with howls that were carried on the shrieking wind . . . not with words but with the sacred scent of his own piss as he made water into the rushing air that carried the marked words to all the corners of the universe. . . .

And the children of the Wichasha Shungmanitu, even the forgotten children of the land beyond the sunrise, even they, came out to be anointed by the fragrance of the moonchild. . . .

"You and your demon child!" Speranza looked up to see Natasha standing in the doorway of the church across the street, her red hair billowing behind her, her dressing gown streaming in the wind and exposing breasts heavy with milk.

"I haven't come to fight you, Natasha," Speranza said. Warily she looked up at the roof of the town hall, where Johnny was leaping, dancing, somersaulting, howling.

A crowd was gathering around them. Many of them were rallying behind Speranza. "Fight her! Show your dominance!" whispered one of them to her. She stood, backed against a hitching post, watching Natasha through a flurry of wind-stirred leaves.

"How can I fight? . . . I'm not one of you—" she said. But Natasha was bearing down on her with eyes of crimson fire, hands wrenched into claws, the dressing gown flailing in the wind.

She could bear it no longer. She began to run down the middle of the street, her boots sinking into the damp earth and manure—

She slipped! Slid in the mud, her hands raking up dirt and wet leaves, and screamed—

Teddy said: "She's in trouble—"

Castellanos said, "It's the queen bitch, Natalia Petrovna . . . she thinks Speranza has come to steal away her title . . . she thinks that they must fight until one mauls the other to death . . . it is the way of the wolves."

"Come on." Teddy tried to lead the shaken Castellanos from the room with the dead bodies . . .

"Don't you see? First we must conceal their deaths . . . or else they will blame the boy and his vision will never come true. . . ."

"This ain't no time to be thinkin' of a mad boy's visions, Castellanos! We got to save Speranza from that queen bitch of yours!"

To his dismay, Victor was emptying the liquid from a coal-oil lamp onto the bodies . . . searching in his pockets for a lucifer . . .

"You ain't fixin' to burn up them corpses . . ." Teddy said.

. . . and one corner of the bed sheet was charring now, one edge of the fabric of the Baroness's puke-stained night-gown . . .

"Come now. Do not look."

For a moment Teddy could not tear away his gaze from flesh that just seemed to melt off the blackening bones . . . Joaquin's hair went up in a smoky flash, making his nostrils smart from the stink . . . "Hurry! Perhaps you have never seen a burning man before . . . I tell you it is much worse when the man is still alive. . . ." He had a haunted look and Teddy could just plumb tell that he'd seen a living man go up in flames, mayhap set him on fire himself, for he'd heard stories about the Comancheros that'd turn any man's stomach.

Quickly they quit the room and ran downstairs. They could feel the heat from the upper room, feel the fire raging above them. "It was necessary," said Castellanos softly, as they stepped out into the street and saw—

"Teddy!" she cried, reaching out her hand to him, trying to claw herself upright out of the mush—

And Johnny heard small voices, tiny scent-signals, calling out to him from the church. . . .

He climbed down to the high window. Peered down below; where a man watched four toddlers, each one asleep on his own pallet of heaped-up cassocks and surplices.

Johnny signed with his scent: "Don't be afraid, little ones. You'll all be safe soon . . . in your new life." And, because their sleep was troubled, he tried to comfort them. Their guardian did nothing but sit in a heavy wooden chair and stare at a ticking clock. . . .

"Teddy, Teddy," she cried again, but Natasha was on her, her fingernails raking her cheeks as she growled, kicking her in the groin so that she flew against a corner post.

"Fight me!" Natasha screamed. "Or should I just cut you down like prey that you are?"

Speranza slumped down on the planking. Natasha sprang, stomped hard on her hands, pinned her down with her knees. She tried to twist free. Shoved at Natasha's face with her fists, felt the teeth bite down on her knuckles, shrieked out in pain . . .

"Fight me! Oh, if only the moon were full, so I could transform and tear you limb from limb!"

Speranza punched with all her might at the fur scar on Natasha's cheek. Sticky blood oozed onto her fist. The Russian woman gave a cry of pain and surprise. Speranza seized the moment and rolled off the boardwalk into the muddy street. Natasha lunged, tripped, slid in the slush, tried to shake free, and smashed her head against a horse trough.

"You come here, woman in men's clothes . . . you think you can take Hartmut's place as well as mine? Which of us is wolf in sheep's clothing?"

Speranza panted as she tried to get to her feet. The Russian woman's eyes were the color of angry moonlight. The wind blew the mud-matted hair against her face.

The cheek wound quivered like a furry worm, and pus dripped from it like milky tears. That is her weakness! Speranza thought. The place where the silver poisoned her, the wound still quick after all these years!

Steadying herself against the trough, Natasha was pulling herself up. She stood in a shaft of moonlight. Speranza could see her drinking its power, drawing what strength she could from it even though it was not quite full . . . she could not transform, but she was as close to a wolf as she could be without transforming. She foamed at the mouth, she growled, her hands clawed the air.

The street was full of spectators now, some yelling encouragement, others shouting obscenities. The sky was getting light; soon

would come dawn, and they had not made peace with the citizens
of Winter Eyes.

She could see Teddy standing in a doorway. He was trying to
reach her, but could not penetrate the press of people.

For a moment she stood, staring wild-eyed at the watchers.
Then Natasha leapt. She had no time to think. The queen bitch
was on top of her, a tangle of claws and teeth, spitting in her
face . . . Speranza closed her eyes, but the sputum burned . . .
she struck at the cheek wound again and again, till her fingers
rived the flesh and gouged out a swatch of bloody fur and Natasha
yanked aside her dressing gown and stood naked as the moon hung
low in the sky and she saw the steaming stream gush forth as
Natasha leant back, knees bent, to shower Speranza with piss and
Speranza closed her mouth but the pungent fluid ran down her
nostrils, burning, so that she could not breathe and had to open her
mouth only to have it drenched . . .

"I have marked her!" Natasha stood exultant, kicking Speranza
in the ribs, raising her arms in triumph as she continued to urinate.
"I have marked her, she is mine, I am still queen, she is mine to
do with as I will. . . ."

Teddy was pushing his way through the crowd now, his Merwin
and Hulburt upraised . . . faintly above the crowd's roar and
the wind's shrieking she could hear his voice: "I got silver
bullets, Miss Speranza . . . don't you be afraid now . . . I'm
comin'."

She watched as members of the crowd tried to wrest the gun
from him, watched him as he hurled the weapon from him with all
his might and—

"Catch, Miss Speranza!" Teddy cried.

—it landed in the mud by her hand! Her fingers closed on it. It
felt strange . . . cold . . . she pointed it at Natasha.

The look of triumph faded from her face.

"You have silver," she said. "Oh, you usurpers are all alike.
You cannot fight with honor . . . always you must find way to
gain unfair advantage. . . ."

Speranza saw fear in Natasha's eyes for the first time. She
remembered the first time she had seen her, erect, splendid, proud
of her unquestioned queenhood as she greeted the Europeans in
the spring moonlight. How can I kill her? she thought. She
hesitated. Her hand trembled as it clutched the pistol.

"Weakling," said Natasha. "If you will not kill me with silver I will kill you with lead!" And she held out her hand imperiously as several guns were tossed at her from different directions. She caught one of them.

The crowd was silent.

"Or perhaps," Natasha said, and Speranza could see that the fear had been replaced by a gleeful irony, "it is simply that you wish to do me honor by killing me properly, in duel to death, as is my due?"

Still Speranza hesitated.

"In a few minutes it will be dawn . . . shall we say then? Ten paces, twenty? I shall say ten . . . since it is you who challenge, I shall call terms."

From somewhere upwind there came smoke, twisting around the awning supports, threading through the throng. Somewhere in the town, a building was on fire . . . but no one spoke.

Twilight seeped in through the clerestory window, nudged Vishnevsky awake. The children! Quickly he ascertained that they were safe . . . they were still asleep. Something moved in the high window . . . a shadow darted across the shadowed room. He stood on a chair to look at the alley beyond. Nothing. A cabochon of ruby light at the edge of the world. An unearthly, terrifying silence . . . for had he not drifted to sleep with the sounds of a crowd outside? He saw no one. He had an urge to run outside to see what had silenced them all . . . but he had to remain with the children . . . their safety was the most important thing in Winter Eyes.

Why in the name of God were they so silent?

A tendril of smoke wafted into the vestry. Little Petrushka coughed, but did not wake.

They crowded on the boardwalk, but the street was empty. They did not speak. Except Teddy, who had pushed through to the front of the crowd, who whispered to Speranza: "Don't worry about nothing, Miss Speranza . . . for she's goin' to get the sunrise in her eyes."

The two women, back-to-back, began to pace. Speranza steeled herself, though her blood was racing, though she knew that were

she wearing the corsets and tight garters of a woman she would
doubtless have already fainted quite away.

Perhaps this was why I've come, she told herself after three
paces. Perhaps I've got to kill her so that Johnny can return to
Winter Eyes and take his rightful inheritance and force all the
werewolves to follow his vision. . . .

It did not ring true.

Four paces.

Where's Johnny? she thought. I have to find him, comfort
him. . . .

Five.

She was walking straight into the rising sun now, but she knew
that the moment she turned, it would be Natasha who would be
forced to gaze at it . . .

Six. Seven.

This is ludicrous! How could I have got myself into this? I've
never even killed so much as a . . . a . . . well, I have seen
how they have gunfights on those Wild West shows, I remember
the time that William and I went to watch one at the Palace Theater
and the bullet ricocheted and knocked a piece off the chandelier
and—

Eight.

She stumbled a little; mud spattered her face, her arms; the wind
whipped up the leaves so that they tickled her cheeks, her neck;
she thought of all the times she had seen death when she lived in
Winter Eyes, seen the wolves ripping up the dead, pulling out their
intestines like balls of yarn, frolicking in the shredded bellies of
children still gasping for one last breath of fetid air. . . .

Nine.

It occurred to her that she was going to die. But she no longer
cared. She had seen the eyes of the huntress and she had made a
tacit gift of her own life. . . .

Ten!

And she whirled round, fumbling for the pistol . . . there was
Johnny in front of the spectators, staring at the sky with a look of
despair . . . and she saw Natasha with her fell eyes crimson as
the sunrise behind her, and she heard as though from a great
distance the pistol's report and the crowd roar, heard the bullet
sing in the wind and—

Suddenly the life seemed to drain from Natasha's eyes and—

A scream of shock and bloodlust went up from the crowd. In the distance came the pattering of hooves. Natasha did not scream; only a strange whine escaped her throat . . . for lodged in it was the shaft of a silver-tipped arrow!

Already her neck had begun to char. Speranza breathed in the fragrance of burning flesh . . . Natasha was groping her way toward the church, but already the streets were full of whooping Indians, and bloodcurdling shouts of *"Huka hey!"* rang in the air . . . her eyes were smarting from the smoke of the burning building, which billowed down the street, peppered with dust and mud flecks from horses' hooves . . . Speranza could barely see . . . she ran to where Johnny stood, slipping and sliding in the bloody slush . . . quickly she threw her arms around him . . .

"I didn't mean it to be this way!" he said, very softly.

There was Teddy now, motioning them to run toward the horse trough. Clasping the boy to her bosom, she ducked a flaming arrow and dived behind the trough. Teddy was there, and Castellanos. "You'd best start shootin' that there gun o' yours, Miss Speranza," Teddy said. He was alternately firing and ducking.

"Who are we fighting?" Speranza said.

"We said we'd be back by sunup, didn't we?" Teddy said. The street was stained with the dawnlight and with blood. She saw an Indian leap from his horse and yank one of the townsmen by the hair. He brandished a scalping knife . . . a knife with the dull glint of tarnishing silver . . . methodically scalped his screaming victim as though he were peeling a large orange . . . tossed the victim aside . . . he landed in the horse trough. Speranza was drenched with water and blood, and the man gasped for air, flailed, thrashed as the foul water poured into him and drowned him. . . .

"Why are they so brutal? How can they be so savage?" Speranza said.

"If you'd seen the way the soldiers raped their women and spitted their babies on their bayonets and burned their tipis to the ground, you wouldn't be asking me why they is so angry," Teddy said.

Someone lunged toward her. Blindly she fired.

A man tottered, fell facedown in the mud.

"Don't kill the Injuns, woman!" Teddy whispered harshly. "Just whose goddamned side are you on?"

"I don't know!" Speranza said, shooting blindly, as the recoil sent her slamming against the boardwalk's edge.

And Johnny said: "Speranza, I'm frightened," and buried his face in her bosom . . . and she remembered the first time she had held him so, how she had felt a strange sexual unease, a kind of obscenity in the touch of the innocent child . . . now, though he did not seem much older, though he still spoke as a child, she felt firm, animal musculature beneath his clothes . . . he looked at her with the eyes of a man and the eyes of a beast and she knew that he felt lust. . . .

Shattering glass . . . fire lapping at the swinging doors of a saloon . . . smoke coiling like a nervous cat . . . Natasha felt the poison of the silver eating away at her. Her vocal cords had been severed . . . only a feverish whimpering escaped her throat as she crawled toward the church over the scalped corpses of her people . . .

My children, Natasha thought, my children. . . .

. . . fire ran down the boardwalk in all the colors of autumn . . .

. . . a woman on fire charged through the streets . . . a man with no hands waved the stumps from which the blood welled up . . .

. . . dragging herself through the mud, she reached the portals of the church, she could see Hartmut's tombstone, its shadow long and fringed with dawnlight . . .

. . . *the children* . . .

"To the place of the moon dance!" Johnny cried. And twisted free from Speranza's arms, heedless of the blood and fire.

"Johnny, you must keep yourself hidden!" she shouted, trying to hold on to his sleeve. It tore in her hand, and she watched him leap over the trough of dead bodies into the middle of the street.

The head of an old man—she knew it was Andrew Raitt, a watchmaker—lay in the mud at the boy's feet. The morning sunlight, smoke-dappled, illumined his face; wordlessly, in time to a sourceless music, he began to move slowly in a circle, his eyes closed.

Terror gripped Speranza, and she could not remain concealed. She ran to him, tripping, sending the head flying down the street, she clasped the boy's knees, crying out, "Johnny, you must not let yourself be seen, you must not let them kill you . . ."

And for a moment she was inside her own dream and the ruddy sky was the wall of the womb that wept blood and the street was the birth canal and she was being thrust forth from the belly of the wolf. . . .

Johnny pointed at the sky. An eagle flew overhead, away from the sun, toward Weeping Wolf Rock.

"We will dance the moon dance," Johnny whispered. "We will drive them from the land . . . I give myself to redeem the tainted earth. . . ."

"Are you mad? Are you possessed?" she said, believing, a little, what Cornelius Quaid had intimated to her in Victoria Station so many years ago.

He opened his mouth. A high, ululating song poured from his lips . . . penetrating the shrilling of the wind and the screams of dying men and the war cries and the crash of burnt lumber. He opened his arms wide as though embracing the tempest, which gusted about him and crowned him with a whirlwind of smoke and dead leaves.

Many dropped their arms and looked at one another, filled with dread and self-loathing.

The boy sang. As though out of nowhere there came an answering drumbeat . . . and Speranza saw that one of the Indians had taken a rusty toy drum from a dead boy's body, and was pounding solemnly on it with his coup stick.

Teddy was beside her now, saying, "It's a new song for a new moon dance, Miss Speranza. He wants them to turn their backs on all they done. It's very sacred, big medicine."

The massacre had ended as abruptly as it had begun. The boy began to move slowly down the street, out of town. Wondering, Speranza followed. There was a single silver bullet left in the gun Teddy had given her.

Wounded men raised themselves up by their elbows and joined in the chorus. An old man drenched in blood wept and carved great gashes in his side with his knife as he joined the procession.

Here and there among the Indians were denizens of the town . . . she recognized some of them . . . Damaris Crites, who had wandered into Winter Eyes a lost waif and ended up as one of the most vicious of the wolves . . . Antoine Dozois, once a Canadian wolfer, now a wolf hunting men, his face eaten away from the sarcoptic mange . . . the white werewolves were swept up in the rhythm of Johnny's song . . . the eagle soared overhead . . . they were all at the edge of Johnny's dream.

Was that flute music above the roar of the wind? Was it her imagination, or was the radiance that suffused Johnny's features more than the glow of the rising sun?

Those who could hear the music followed. His face bore the light of Takushkanshkan. She was so terribly afraid for him. But his destiny must be played out to its end. . . .

Moving. Leaving the burning city. To the place of the moon dance.

She managed to push open the door of the vestry. She saw her cousin Valentin lying on the ground, his throat slit, in a pool of coagulating blood.

Katyusha had been nailed to the wall with silver nails. She was already dead. Sasha had been cut into three pieces. His head peered down at her from a bookshelf, a piece of windpipe trailing across the spine of a leather-bound Bible. Kolya had been scalped, and hung from a coathook over the door by a thread of his own intestine, a silver-tipped arrow rammed up his anus. His eyes were open in an expression of consummate terror. The carpet was matted with excrement where the children's sphincters had been loosened by fear.

"Ma . . . Ma . . ." It was Petrushka. He lay on the pile of surplices. He was soaked in blood, as though he had been dipped in red paint. His tiny arms had been cut off and hung around his neck. He was trying to crawl to her, but he was too weak. A fly buzzed about the stump of his left arm.

With a final surge of strength she seized the shaft in both hands and pulled the arrow from her throat. Blood soaked her dressing gown and drenched her lungs . . . I must not die! she thought. I must live . . . to bear a new litter . . . to bring the pack back to life . . . she wanted to scream out her rage, but only a piping whine issued from her ruptured throat.

Natasha wept.

* * *

It began to rain. Water cascaded on headless, limbless bodies strewn in the muddy streets. Torrents of rain on the husks of houses, dousing the flames and making huge smoke-clouds that engulfed the town. Rain that drained the blood from gutted faces. Rain that turned the mixed blood and earth, that turned the streets into an oozing river of red-dyed slush . . . in this rain, the Eleventh Cavalry entered the town of Winter Eyes, with Major James Sanderson at its head.

In this rain, the soldiers dismounted, gaped at the destruction. In this driving rain, Sanderson made his way to the church, where he found Natasha kneeling in front of the altar, where she had placed the eviscerated remains of her four children.

She smelled his presence before she saw him. Then she heard his footsteps.

Not turning around, she tried to say: "Why do you come now, now when my children are dead?" No sound came from her ravaged throat.

Major Sanderson approached. Removed his hat to reveal the patch of purple scar tissue that had once been his scalp, as though to show her that he too had suffered at the hands of the Sioux. "Natasha," he said.

She tried to answer him. The pain was unendurable. She turned to look at him. Blood streamed down her neck; she did not know how much she had lost; she wondered if her complexion had grown more pale. No human could have stood such loss of blood, such agony . . . but she was more than human. She was a supernatural creature, and a mother, and the guardian of the fate of the entire pack. She could not die yet. Even though the silver was racing through her veins, tainting her flesh, eating her alive. Had she not plucked out the arrow when she did, she did not doubt she would have been consumed long since.

"You want me to avenge these deaths?" said the major, surveying the carnage analytically. "You want me to wipe every last one of these savages from the land?"

She nodded.

"There was a thing you promised me once," said Major Sanderson, staring fixedly at her while he methodically unbuttoned his jacket. "You said I should rule this city by your side. You said you would whelp my pups, you bitch! And now you come begging to me for vengeance."

The jacket slid to the floor. She watched him, feeling no emotion save the emptiness of bereavement. She did not try to speak—as he unhooked his trousers, undid his fly, pulled out a rampant, gnarled erection. She could smell his lust, but it did not move her. He strode toward her, hunkering above her so that the penis teased at her parched lips, at the bloody neck wound.

She listened to the rain on the rooftop of the church.

Listened to the soldiers outside as they uncovered more corpses, as they questioned the survivors, as they catalogued the atrocities.

He pulled her up, forced her down upon the altar on top of the corpses of her children. She tried to protest, but the poison had invaded her muscles and made her veins seem like lead. She thought, My children, I am doing this to make more children. . . .

"I can't wait any longer, Natasha. You're going to give me everything you promised. A strong woman like you . . . you could bear children . . . better children than that Count of yours could give you. I'll go and I'll wreak all the vengeance you could ever want, Natasha, but first I'm going to have what I want."

He fucked her until she died.

Then, slowly and with infinite care, he put his clothes back on and walked outside into the rain to give the order to pursue the Indians.

14
Weeping Wolf Rock
full moon

SPERANZA NEVER LOOKED BACK AT THE BURNING TOWN, THOUGH SHE could smell the damp smoke. They reached the plain where the women and children were waiting. The music went with them and she could barely feel the rain. Always the eagle circled, and it seemed that Johnny, though his eyes were still closed, followed the eagle, stepping in perfect time, never needing to see the path.

They danced in the driving rain.

Johnny's eyes shone. The rain turned into sleet. The sky was gray, gray the tall grass, ash-gray the dancers' faces; they danced against the wind, each step as painful as giving birth.

They danced.

Riding beside Teddy Grumiaux, among the true humans who flanked the procession, Speranza saw no sun above them, only a cold and sourceless light behind the steel-colored clouds.

A blue radiance danced about Johnny's head and shoulders. He had not opened his eyes once since they left Winter Eyes. Often it seemed that the dancers' feet did not touch the ground, and even the horses floated on a cushion of mist. It seemed to her that the land was rushing past at a speed impossible even for a locomotive, and that time itself was streaming by, that the seasons themselves changed in the blink of an eye, autumn into winter into spring into brilliant summer . . . and she thought: We're wholly within his vision now. He has bridged the real and the dream.

The light swirled about the boy's head. It seemed to her that he was growing in stature, making up for the years he had been trapped in the body of a little boy . . . now he seemed on the brink of adolescence . . . now it was summer and the grass rustled and his golden hair was flung back as the hot wind raced over the plain and now it was autumn and the wind stripped the leaves from the oaks and roared and the grass was matted with rain . . . still the boy danced, and the men danced joyfully, leaping like young wolves eager for the hunt, and the women joined in the choruses with howls of hunger and desire.

"Teddy!" Speranza said. "Have you ever seen such a stirring, beautiful sight?"

"I only sees the sleet, Miss Speranza, and the rain which never stops."

"But the vision . . . the dancing lights . . . the songs of the wolves. . . ."

"Ain't my vision," he said. "Reckon I'll be goin' home soon."

"Home?"

"Knowed a girl in Lead named Nita. I wonder if she still remembers me."

It was beginning to snow. The wind was biting cold, and

Speranza shivered and did not guide the horse, trusting that he would follow the boy's dream.

"After this is over," Teddy said, "I aims to go looking for her. She don't deserve to end up a withered old whore. She's a good girl." There was a twinge of defiance in his tone. But Speranza did not condemn him; how could she? The time was long past when she believed that a woman, once fallen, was irredeemable. I too am a fallen woman, she thought. What a quaint idea it seemed now, with the millennium fast approaching, knowing what she now knew—we are all fallen, she thought, and all in need of redemption.

Still there was no sun. The dancers moved through mist and snow. There were no edges to the land; the mist shifted and the sea of snow-capped grass billowed and the wind sang. But she could make out Weeping Wolf Rock, a twisted gray thing that bestrode the ever-changing snowscape and seemed almost living.

Teddy went on, "I done kilt too many men . . . and wolves. I reckon it's time for me to get out of that line of work. I'm aweary of what I been, Miss Speranza, and I can't go on no more."

He was so young to think such thoughts.

"Mayhap I can find me a home amongst the Injuns. You think they might call me one of their own? The white men was always callin' me a breed and a bastard, and I allow as it's true that I weren't born on the preacher-blessed side of the blanket; but I got to say that the Injuns never called me them things. . . ."

He was lost in his own dreams; no wonder he could not touch the boy's grand vision. When the events of this night are over, she thought, he will pick up the pieces of his life. He has a home, he has a purpose.

But what of me? she thought. For better or worse, I have become a mere shadow of Johnny Kindred, the one who comforts him, who holds his hand when he faces the dark. But if he is victorious, if he is healed, what then for me?

A domestic life in San Francisco? Or a return to Aix-en-Provence, to face the family she had blithely left behind, with whom she had exchanged not so much as one letter during the years she had spent in America? Who else could she turn to? Sigmund Freud?

With a start, she realized she had not partaken of the coca powder for many weeks now . . . and that she had not even noticed. At the moment she had decided to leave the path, to go into the forest alone, she no longer needed any escapes from reality.

There was Weeping Wolf Rock now, riving the mist . . . the procession shuddered to a stop. The music ceased. One lone drum continued to beat in time with the pulse of the universe. She could not tell whether it was day or night, or what the season was, for the wind that pelted them with sharp-edged snow also carried the fragrances of spring. There was darkness, but that darkness was pregnant with daylight. The Indians and those who had left Winter Eyes gathered around Johnny.

"What cosmic splendor! What a serendipitous karmic juncture in our existences, isn't it, Countess!" She looked down to see a figure dimly remembered: the Indian astrologer Shri Chandraputra. "It is impossible for me to express the profundity of this moment; it is truly the birth of a new age." He stalked about, a bejewelled turban on his head, a Negro attendant at his side carrying a platter with some writing utensils. He was making notes in a journal. "The astral conjunctions," he said, "are such that today's full moon coincides with a great circle of Venus and a grand peregrination of the outer planets. . . ." She marvelled that he could still think about such things. He danced awkwardly alongside the others.

Then Johnny turned to her, summoned her with a glance at once imperious and vulnerable. Teddy dismounted and helped Speranza off her horse, and led her to where he stood, at the center of a circle.

Johnny and the chiefs of the Shungmanitu conversed in measured, lilting tones. A pipe was passed from hand to hand, and as each one handed it on he uttered the word "*Na*"; and the recipient responded: "*Ku*." The smoke from the pipe was the source of the mist. Its sweet scent blended with the smell of fresh grass thrusting from the ground, of decaying autumn leaves, of the hot wind of the plains of the summer, of the snow-laden storms of winter . . . all these things seemed to drift aloft from the bowl of the sacred pipe. And still the lone drum pounded. Until her very heartbeat seemed at one with it. She stood before Johnny and knew he had reached his journey's end.

The earth rumbled.

"It's the Eleventh Cavalry," Teddy said softly. "Don't know how far away."

One of the Indians crouched down, put his ear to the ground. He said, "Many horses."

"It's Sanderson," Teddy said. "He's fixin' to rub us all out."

"If my dream holds," said Johnny, "they will not touch us."

"You're goin' to die, Johnny-boy," said Teddy, "less we can keep them soldiers off our backs."

"Protect us," said Johnny, in a voice of quiet and profound authority.

The rumbling came closer now. She did not know if she or the ground was shaking. She was terribly afraid.

"Me and Iron Hand's men, we might be able to hold them off for a few hours," Teddy said, "but if you chooses to do your moon dance here, right in the shadow of Weeping Wolf Rock, there ain't but so much a few men can do against a troop of cavalry."

"But Teddy, we will not dance here," Johnny said. "I have seen the place of the moon dance in a vision. Tonight, there will be a darkness such as has never been seen, and when the clouds part, the light of the full moon will fall only on one place."

He pointed.

The crowd turned, following the curve of his arm. Gazed upward. Saw the ledge, precarious, inaccessible, a tongue of rock that stretched over the plain from atop the abutment.

A drumbeat.

Another.

Speranza said, "Oh, Johnny, surely now you can see that the dream can only lead you so far! There's not a soul among you who can climb that rock, reach that ledge . . . yet you expect them all to follow you . . . women and children even . . . you might as well ask them to follow you off the edge of a cliff . . . Johnny, you must see reason!"

Calmly, Johnny said: "Teddy will guard the base of Weeping Wolf Rock. And you will come with me, Speranza; you will be with me at the end. To this end I was born, to this end my father had me brought to this new world; to this end Ishnazuyai raised me. I shall renew the world."

And the drums beat faster, and the shamans blew upon shrill flutes, and the women began to chant and stamp their feet. "You are lost, Johnny Kindred . . ." she said, and with a passionate desire to protect him threw her arms about him, clasping him to her bosom, no longer mindful of those dark emotions his closeness aroused within her breast; she kissed him on the cheeks again and again, as she had done with poor Michael Bridgewater when he had lain alone and afraid of death and his servants and his family feared to come near; she held him suffocatingly close. There was no warmth in him, no substance; it was as though she had embraced a ghost, a shadow, the chill air.

"Believe me," Johnny said. "You must believe me. I have become the fabric of my own dark dreaming."

He turned to face the rock that could not be climbed.

Lifted up his arms, and began to murmur in Lakota. It seemed to Speranza that he was addressing the sky itself, or perhaps the eagle that wheeled above them.

Then he turned to the others and told them to follow. They gathered around him. He stripped himself naked to the wind. The others began to do the same. Speranza marvelled that they seemed not to feel the cold. He was still frail, still scarred in a dozen places by Claggart's lash. But she saw the strength in him too.

He took a deep breath.

Those trees . . . had they been there before? She blinked. More trees . . . lodgepole pines pushing up from the grama grass . . . the sky crisscrossed with spiderweb treetops, darkening . . . why, she thought, this is the forest of my nightmares . . . he's pulling the dream taut around us like a blanket, like a hangman's noose. The trees were thrusting up now, the ground quaking, great fissures opening up in the earth and spewing up conifers whose trunks raced up toward the roof of the world . . . the boy danced.

And she saw that the river of blood flowed from the summit of Weeping Wolf Rock, and the blood fell on the children of the wolves, and the very rain was blood, and they danced in the pouring blood, drinking it, drenching themselves in it, laughing, weeping for joy. It was the river of her dream, the very source of the river. The blood touched her and she smelled it and it was the smell of a bitch in heat and a woman who loves deeply and a mother giving birth.

Lightning lanced the treetops! The sky was burning! And still they danced. Sulphur fumes curled up from clefts in the earth. They danced. And Weeping Wolf Rock itself danced, the stone groaning as it shifted shape, and she saw that the very rock was living, that it breathed, that it danced to the rhythm of Johnny's song. And Johnny led his followers to the foot of the rock, and as he walked uphill the rock knelt down to support him, it bent, it buckled, transforming to fit the dancers' footsteps. The women and children moved solemnly along the edge of the rock, never faltering, never slipping. The forest sprang up, ever thickening, ever darkening.

Johnny said, holding Speranza's hand fast, "The world is a dream, Speranza."

She followed him. She stepped into thin air and the rock darted to catch her before she could fall. A chasm yawned and she leaped, not looking down at the void, and a whirlwind gathered her up and bore her to the far side, and she continued to climb as new trees blanketed the mountain . . . and still the drums kept pace with the racing blood and the pounding heart. The sky was on fire and the fire sprang from Johnny's outstretched hands. Up, up the mountain yawned. The mountain bucked and flung them up, up from ledge to ledge. Stones flew as they sprang. The earth itself was dancing.

And Johnny clasped her hand again and said, "Stay close to me, Speranza. Cling to the dream."

And the forest closed up around them and the fire in the sky was so thick with the fumes of hell that the burning sky was black as night. . . .

He couldn't believe his eyes. "Victor!" Teddy shouted, but his friend seemed not to hear him. As the rain lashed them the wolves seemed to grow faint . . . Teddy tried to touch Castellanos, but he was slippery . . . not quite real . . . slippery as the rain.

Teddy thought: It's Johnny's dream . . . the wolves is caught up in it, and pulling the real world along with them. . . .

The Indians had a special gift for dreaming. When they dreamed they could change the world. Teddy was only half Indian but he could feel the world shift. There were trees where no trees stood before. Weeping Wolf Rock seemed taller, the ledge harder to reach. Crags were tumbling into place, vantage points from which to defend the moon dance. Teddy and Iron Hand roosted behind a great big rock that seemed to have sprung up from nowhere. The Eleventh Cavalry couldn't be far away. He could hear the hoofbeats clearly. He crouched down. The rain was letting up a bit. You couldn't tell what time of day it was.

Teddy looked up at Weeping Wolf Rock.

They were up there. Speranza and all the members of the Shungmanitu, and some of the people from Winter Eyes. And Johnny. He could barely see them. They were up on that ledge. He thought: They couldn't of clomb up there by theirselfs. It was a dream.

The dream! When he thought about it, when he thought about Speranza and Johnny up there dancing on the rock, he could almost see the dark forest that had sprung up around them and the shifting pathway they had taken.

Iron Hand said, "The world will not hold this shape for very long. If the boy's dream is interrupted, it will melt away."

Teddy said, "What about the cavalry? Will they see the dream world, or their world?"

"I do not know." Iron Hand loaded his Sharps rifle and handed Teddy a second one. "Their captain, the one called Sanderson . . . the hate is so powerful in him that he may be able to burst through into the dream circle. Hate so strong can cast a man loose from the cosmos and into the spirit world."

"I'm skeered of that too," Teddy said. For Sanderson shared Claggart's nature. Mayhap they weren't supernatural creatures like the werewolves, but they too were monsters in their own right.

No time to think about dreams. He could see them now. Across the plain. Riding in from the west. A long wavery line that slithered along the horizon like a snake. Couldn't make out the individuals yet. The rain had lightened to a drizzle. He could hear the thump of horses' hooves on mud. He could feel the ground shaking. He didn't know how long they could last against Sanderson's men. There were only thirty, forty in Iron Hand's party. But they had the high ground and, long as they stood at the fringes of Johnny's dream, they could treat the dream boulders as the ramparts of a fort. But if the dream began slipping. . . .

Before he knew it they were halfway across the plain. They moved deliberately. Crow scouts in the van, and behind them the buglers and standard-bearers, and behind them . . . Teddy could not tell how many men. He guessed about a couple of hundred. And Sanderson at their head. One of the scouts was pointing up at Weeping Wolf Rock. Teddy wondered if they could see into Johnny's vison.

Suddenly he heard a distant bugle call . . . the charge! . . . and now the hoofbeats quickened and he could see the wall of cavalry racing toward them, and he sucked in his breath and waited, meaning to make every shot count. . . .

They were coming! Swarming through the spectral forest! Tiny lightning jags from drawn sabers, the screech of the bugle above the shaking of the earth, the stench of smoke . . . too soon they were within range. Gunfire . . . dull flashes in the gray . . . the rain clearing to reveal the faces of Crow scouts, white and red and yellow and black . . .

Arrows whistling through the air! Teddy fired and fired again, fired till the smoke made his eyes water . . . he blew a scout's face clear off, but the horse kept charging and he could see the brains dripping where the nose used to be and . . . a bullet squealed, grazed his cheek, he could hardly feel the pain . . .

"Iron Hand—" But the chief was no longer beside him.

He saw Iron Hand step forward as if the white men weren't even there, and tether one leg to a tree stump . . . he knew Iron Hand had pledged to die, killing as many soldiers as he could, because he was ashamed of what they had done in Winter Eyes. Teddy was alone behind his rock. Others were scattered on ledges overhead. Arrows rained down. One of them got it in the chest. He was twisting and turning and slumping forward on his horse. Teddy saw a man trampled by horses. He saw a severed arm go flying through the air. And the earth itself fought back with projectiles of burning stone flung from above.

Nightmare and reality intersected in a hundred places. Sometimes it rained fire and blood. Sometimes came torrents of real rain, dragging down the arrows, making the horses slide and smash their heads and limbs against boulders. Dead men lay by dozens in the mud. Still they came. Teddy fired and reloaded and fired and reloaded.

Still they came.

Dismounted now, they fought the Indians hand-to-hand, saber and bayonet against club tomahawk. Shrieking the war cry of "*Huka hey!*" Iron Hand's men leapt down from the treetops. Teddy was low on rifle ammunition. But he still had a gun—he'd thrown the prized Merwin and Hulburt with the silver bullets to Speranza, but he still had a single-action Colt.

He looked below. He saw that Iron Hand was surrounded. He was spinning around in circles, coup stick outstretched, smiting the soldiers as they tried to get closer. They were lunging, trying to jab him with their bayonets. He laughed at them, singing his scorn for them and his disdain of death. To kill was irrelevant. He must have counted fifty coups already. He would die with honor.

Mayhap its about time I died, Teddy thought. He wondered whether Nita was still waiting for him in that house of ill fame in Lead. He'd heard tell that she'd had a child, as red-skinned as her own savage paw, they said.

He tossed the rifle aside. He drew his Colt and leaped into Iron Hand's circle. Fanning the hammer, he took out six of the soldiers, enough to give them breathing space. He turned to Iron Hand as he reloaded. "Let me cut you loose, brother," he said.

"No!" He was spinning around so rapidly that the rawhide rope was reeling him in toward the tree stump, but he didn't seem to care. More soldiers were coming, stepping over the bodies of their slain companions. "Don't seek to free me," Iron Hand told him. "It's a good day to die. But free yourself." And he resumed his song, flailing at the soldiers.

Teddy looked down below. He could see Major Sanderson, erect, on horseback, driving his steed purposefully uphill— driving even when there was no purchase for his horse's hooves, driving even on thin air. He thought: It's true what Iron Hand says . . . his hate is giving him some dream power of his own.

Wildly Iron Hand swung. Teddy heard the snap of human bones above the war cries. Once more Teddy spun around and fanned the hammer of his Colt. Soldiers fell. He thrust his way through them. Others ran Iron Hand through with their bayonets, laughing. Sticky blood sprayed Teddy's face. The bayonets came out with a sound of ripping flesh. One of the soldiers had impaled the liver and was waving it like a guidon. Iron Hand's face showed only derision as he fell facedown into slick mud. Teddy looked the soldier in the eye. What he saw didn't even seem human . . . the eyes were fire-red like the eyes of a werewolf, the lips contorted in insensate rage . . . we is all turning into beasts, he thought, inside us we is all beasts no matter what we tells ourselfs we is all animals burning up with anger . . . the soldier's lips grinned to

reveal drooling fangs, the bloody liver dripped over his forehead
as the soldier waved it. . . .

Teddy blew away those lips and when the smoke cleared he
could see the jawbone come unhinged as the face splintered and
the skull cracked open like a soft-boiled egg . . . Teddy ran,
reloading, mounted the first horse he could see, rolled the dead
Indian off into the muck, rode toward Sanderson . . .

. . . full tilt, as Sanderson's horse struggled to climb the sky
itself . . . Sanderson smiling a little, untouched by the carnage
around him . . . calmly reading a leather-bound book in the
light of the fiery sky.

He looked up as Teddy charged him. "Why, what is the matter,
young man?" he said. "Don't you know that death is inevitable . . . but you are only a poor half-witted breed, trapped
between the Scylla and Charybdis of past and future . . . you
cannot know that I am not your mortal enemy, but a force of
history?"

"I kilt Claggart. I can sure as hell kill you, Sanderson, flesh and
blood." He fired. The bullet seemed to shatter against an invisible
shield.

"You didn't kill Claggart . . . Claggart cannot die . . . he
is within me. Don't have to be a werewolf to know the beast
within . . . Ah, you should have seen the beast-woman when I
made love to her until she became a corpse . . . you would
understand then . . . no monster is supernatural . . . all that is
monstrous is inside us. Man, poor fellow, is a fallen creature." He
referred to the leather-bound book. With astonishment, Teddy
realized that it was a Bible.

Memories raced: Claggart sneering sneering as he pumped him
full of lead sneering sneering blood on the autumn grass and—

"He's dead . . . he can't touch me no more." But Teddy
knew there was truth in Sanderson's words.

"Sometimes, my friend, it takes two to dream . . . hero and
villain . . . light and shadow." A high wind sprang up and blew
away the major's hat, and underneath he could see the mass of
bruises that used to be his scalp. But it seemed like his whole face
was peeling away. Sometimes he could see the skull beneath, the
worms crawling through the eye sockets. Maybe this ain't
Sanderson at all, he thought, maybe it's a kind of monster that the
body done dreamed up. Maybe I can't fight him. The wind blew

stronger. Plastered their faces with dead leaves and severed human hands. The trees and the sky were weeping blood and he could see the rocks buckling . . .

"I don't care how strong your hate is. You ain't reachin' them, not less you kills me first."

"Then I will kill you," said the dream-Sanderson, his dark horse rearing up, breathing frost and fire. And spurred his horse. And drew his saber and—

Teddy sprang up! The saber missed him by a hair's breadth as he jumped onto the neck of Sanderson's horse and—

—looked into the eyes of darkness and—

The earth heaved and bucked! Trees snapped and new ones sprouted up! Branches battered each other! Teddy saw his Indian horse get swallowed up in a fiery chasm . . .

—he pushed Sanderson's chest, slammed him down against the saddle as the horse raced uphill and the fluid rock ran to meet its footfall—

"Do not fight me . . . the white man has a destiny that will work itself out in the land . . . there's no place for people like you . . . it's fate, pure fate . . ." They were at each other's throats as the wind wrapped itself around them . . . Teddy hurt all over, but he couldn't let go . . . the major's fingers around his throat were bone-hard as he gasped for air. . . .

Through the fog, through the cacophony of death, the bugle call for the cavalry charge resounded. . . .

"There will be no moon dance," the major said. His face had melted away and there was only the death's head with the glowering eyes.

Teddy squirmed out of the major's grip, he brought his gun smashing down again and again against the grinning skull. The major laughed.

"Only a dream-thing can kill another dream-thing," the major said. And it seemed that he no longer even noticed the youth as he battered him with the butt of his Colt . . . even the flesh of the horse had melted away . . . the bones clattered and bit into him as the skeletal horse strode up the empty air . . . and behind, the hordes of death, skeletons in cavalry uniforms, and the charge still sounding, relentless. . . .

"You ain't even real . . ." Teddy said.

"No," said the major, mocking the young man's voice, "I reckon I ain't."

They were rolling the cannon uphill. As the major surveyed his troops, the ground flattened to form a ramp. The buglers blew madly. Guidons fluttered. The cannon wheels squealed, metal and wood against rock.

Fuckin' Jesus! thought Teddy. They're going to die up there. They're all of them going to die. Ain't nothing any man can do about it now.

"Time for you to get out of my dream." The major sat bolt upright and shook the young man loose just as if he were nothing more than a fly buzzing at his face. Teddy felt himself fall, felt the pebbles smashing into his face, felt the sharp gravel digging into his flesh as he rolled downhill . . .

He was fading out of the major's vision.

Out of Johnny's dream.

The moon was beginning to emerge from behind the clouds. He slammed hard against a clump of rock. His hands were raw and bleeding and one of his eyes was swollen shut.

He looked around him, trying to sit up. There were dead men all around him. Soldiers stuck with arrows, like dead porcupines. Indians with their bellies slit open and their guts crawling with rodents. The head of a young officer propped up against the stump of a tree, his mouth stuffed with earth and dead leaves. Twisted faces with jellied eyes. Men with their limbs ripped off, men charred, men crumpled, crushed, incinerated. No living men at all. Not one.

Fumes of sulphur and burning meat.

Where was Sanderson? Where were all his men? Teddy looked up at the ledge, impossible for man to reach except on the wings of the young werewolf's vision. He could see the figures of the dancers, impossibly small. He could not hear the music of their dancing through the blasting wind.

Suddenly he thought he could make out the horses and cannon of the Eleventh Cavalry, closing in on the dancers. I'm dreamin', he thought, as he staggered through the fog. Flies buzzed around Iron Hand, propped against a boulder with a dozen bayonet points bursting from his chest.

But in the forest of Johnny Kindred's mind, in the clearing at the center of that forest, at the eye of the tempest that raged about Weeping Wolf Rock, there was absolute calm.

The persons in the forest stood at the edge of the circle. The Indian boy called them one by one. Already Johnny had partaken of the Indian boy's wisdom, and could speak the language of the Lakota as well as his own. Already he had absorbed the humility of James Karney and the worldliness of Jake Killingsworth. One by one they fused as the Indian boy played the flute of love.

A few remained, among them Jonas Kay. Though Johnny had become much older as the other personalities became one with his, Jonas was still a child, still sullen. But he did not rage, though they could all feel the full moon tugging at them from behind the thick clouds that blanketed the sky.

Jonas Kay lay curled at the edge of the magic circle. He was sucking his thumb.

"Jonas," said Johnny, "it's time for you to come home now."

"I'm still . . . afraid." Where had his fear sprung from? One of the others, Johnny thought. Though he doesn't want to join us yet, part of him already has.

Johnny reached across the ring of pale blue flame. The fire did not sear him. He touched Jonas on the cheek. "We are each other," he said. "You can't be afraid now."

"You're going to kill me. But when the moon comes . . . then we'll really see. You've never seen me as I really am. When the moon comes, then you'll see. You won't want me. You'll drive me out . . . and you'll never be whole."

This was what Speranza saw: the sky electrified, colors dancing like the fabled aurora borealis; the wind whirling about them; the boy unmoving at the tempest's center. The dancers moving slowly to a sobbing threnody of flute and drum, moving yet still. Naked they danced, the women in an outside circle, the men within, the children imitating their elders.

And here and there were people from Winter Eyes too. Shri Chandraputra had doffed all his clothes but for his turban, and moved his withered limbs with a surprising elfin grace. There was Victor Castellanos, who had travelled with Teddy, leaping up and down, his dark hair flying in the wind, flinging about his buffalo robe cape as though it were a matador's.

There was still no moon.

He called her; she stepped into the circle. He opened his eyes. They shone with lunar radiance. He smiled and took her by the

hand. He marked her with his urine; it did not have the rank
animal odor she was used to, but smelled of the sweet autumn
earth.

He said, "We are going on a journey together, you and I. Be
with me."

"I'll go with you," she said, very softly. "I belong by your
side."

He gripped her hand more tightly. The dancers faded. The circle
was the bowl of the sacred pipe, the womb, the crucible of
creation. The world whirled madly, the world was the wind, the
wind was the fire that breathed life into the world. She saw all the
past, experienced it all at once . . . little Michael Bridgewater
scowling as they closed the coffin lid on him, the Bible and the
pressed rose in his folded hands and . . . Cornelius Quaid
handing her the purse of gold sovereigns, trying to conceal his
distaste and . . . the train rushing through the woods and . . .
tell me a story please Speranza tell me a story . . .

. . . then she saw herself . . . tall, stern-faced, looking
down from above . . . a child's eye view . . . "Is that really
me?" she thought wonderingly . . . the dark clothes, the prim
demeanor, the Bible tucked under her arm . . . the rocking of
the train.

. . . waiting for the hunters . . .

She heard the boy's voice: "We have to go and fetch Jonas
now."

And now it was an unfamiliar past that reeled by. The Indian
boy, toy bow in hand, crouching in the forest. Ishnazuyai
laughing . . . now a darker past, Claggart's silver cage, the
suffocating velvet that kept away the moonlight . . . the faces of
the women Claggart loved to kill . . . she thought, Oh, Johnny,
how can you have endured so much? . . . and the boy led her
on, down darker corridors of memory . . . the wolfling biting
down on the haunches of a drunk old man, warmed by the spurting
blood, driven to frenzy by the taste of liquor, and . . . the doors
of the Viennese town house flung open to the snowy night as the
wolves swarmed into the unlit alley and . . . Claggart's laughter
and . . . mocking laughter and . . . one time, shackled to a
board, cruciform in the moonlight, and the knife-thrower splintering the wood with silver blades that almost touched his flesh so
he could feel the glimmering poison as his skin prickled and his

hair stood on end and he struggled to control his terror so that the hair wouldn't touch the knives knowing the flesh would sear and sizzle at the silvery touch and . . . he led her by the hand deeper down into the memories and she saw corridors of the Viennese town house opening into other corridors and corridors on the train that rattled through the snow and corridors that were the banks of rivers that wept blood and corridors deeper and deeper into the womb of creation and . . .

"Where are you taking me?" she whispered.

"We can't fuse completely without Jonas," said Johnny, his voice becoming more and more childlike and . . .

. . . flung open the doorway of the Viennese town house and the sky raining blood on the statue of the Madonna of the Wolves and . . .

Another corridor. A stench of human ordure. A shackled man sitting in his own excrement; beard plastered to the face; drooling. A child without a mind, the eyes darting back and forth, back and forth with the regularity of a pendulum. A woman rocking a cucumber wrapped in swaddling clothes, singing a lullaby. Johnny led Speranza by the hand. An old man, naked, covered with syphilitic sores, muttering about a lost kingdom, methodically chewing, one by one, the petals of a geranium. All had shorn hair. The close-cropped heads of madmen and denizens of debtor's prisons, who had sold their hair to the wigmakers. A two-year-old child sucking laudanum from a bottle with a broken spout. Somewhere in the distance, the sound of flogging . . . a woman screaming . . . a woman being raped against a bust of Queen Victoria that stared severely over a pediment of green marble. . . .

In answer to her unspoken question, Johnny said, "The madhouse. I was brought to live here soon after it happened. . . ."

"What happened?" Speranza said.

. . . the madhouse disintegrated . . . now they stood at a crossroads . . . the wind was howling . . . howling . . . gray decaying buildings, piss-stained walls with crumbling bricks . . . Whitechapel.

Suddenly the boy clung to her in terror, though that terror was also a little bit like lust . . . and he whimpered, "Speranza . . . Speranza . . . Mother."

Angry men were digging at the crossroads. Dragging a woman

across the cobblestones. The woman wore rags. The woman's eyes were wide with terror. Her hair was long, blond, greasy . . . the resemblance to Johnny was unmistakable . . . "Bury her alive!" someone was shouting. "Bloody well deserves it . . ."

" . . . executed for having carnal knowledge of wolves . . ." another voice, solemn, sacerdotal . . . she did not know whether the voice came from Johnny's memory or her own memory of the Chinawoman in Lead . . .

Speranza saw a little boy running, shouting after her: "Mother! Mother! Mother!" and the woman looked up at him with listless eyes, already knowing she was about to die.

Ugly faces. Contorted. Angry. "They've got to be buried at a crossroads . . ."

The woman, prostrate, looked up at the child . . . and Speranza saw her with the child's eyes . . . she saw herself.

A man in black, on horseback, watched from the shadow of a charnel house.

The woman turned to the man in black. Pleading. The man in black said nothing, did nothing. The horse's breath hung heavy in the frosty air. It was morning. Blood streamed from the woman's nose and from cuts on her cheeks and arms. A man in a frock coat was flailing at her with a walking stick.

"Mother, Mother—" said the boy whose hand gripped Speranza's . . . a small boy, no more than three years old . . . a boy named Jonas Kay.

They dug her grave. They beat her with sticks and clubs. They raped her as they buried her alive. Jonas could feel her pain. He could smell her death. He tried to twist away from the men that held him, tried to run toward her. The men were crowding around the grave, watching the woman thrashing. Dirt and coagulated blood flew. Anger flowed in Jonas's veins. Anger gave him terrible strength. He wrested his arms free and ran to the woman's side but she was already dead, her neck snapped . . . a man was still thrusting at her lifeless body, his trousers down around his ankles, his fat buttocks quivering.

And Jonas turned to the man in black and screamed, "No no no no no I'll not run in your pack I'll not I'll not I'm me I'm me me alone alone alone!" but the man merely looked down from his horse with an inconstruable expression and Speranza saw his eyes and knew him for the man who had loved her and the beast who had possessed her and he stared back at her across the gulf of time and seemed to plead for her compassion, and at last he looked away and spurred his horse on and the hoofbeats clattered down the cobbled street . . . rage exploded in Jonas rage too huge to be contained by one person and he was foaming at the mouth and snarling and growling at the men who circled the dead woman's grave and she lay half buried in the dirt of the crossroads with her lips still red and a smear of blood on her left cheek and . . . furiously he bounded up to the man with his trousers down and bit off his penis and spat it out and the man howled and could not stanch the blood and Jonas was surrounded and he yelled for the man in black at the top of his lungs but the others crowded around him and cut off the light and smothered him with their chimney-sweep sweaty smell and they closed in on him and . . . closed in on him and . . . closed in on . . . closed . . . closed . . .

And then came Johnny, Johnny who could feel the pain, Johnny who knew how to weep . . .

. . . and Speranza embraced Johnny and comforted him and said, "It was a long time ago . . ."

"But do you know who the man in black was?"

"Yes," said Speranza. "But . . . he didn't mean it . . . he had his own grief, his own inner torment . . . I have heard him say that he loves you."

"I hate him! I hate my father!"

"You must heal now . . ." She embraced him and she knew that she embraced Jonas as well as Johnny . . . that she could no longer tell where the light ended and the dark began . . .

The moon began to emerge from behind the clouds.

The vision was slowly dissipating. Still the wind circled them. Still the Indians danced. Until Johnny said: "I see the man in black—"

"No, Johnny," Speranza said softly. "He is gone now. We killed him. We faced him together. He has gone away."

Then she heard the rattle of American snare drums and squeal of fifes and the blare of bugles and she saw the cavalrymen come at them and—

Moonlight! The first rays struck the women of the outer circle and one by one they transformed . . .

A swath of light swept the place where the children danced . . .

Trees snapped! Rocks blew apart! A dull thud and a flash of gunpowder and . . .

Soldiers. How had they climbed the face of Weeping Wolf Rock? Soldiers with their guns loaded with silver. Cannon. Some of the dancers broke ranks, leaped upon the soldiers even as they metamorphosed, ripping at faces, gnawing at hands.

Johnny still danced. The eagle was directly overhead.

They were falling on all fours . . . one by one . . . snouts pushing out, claws oozing out of fingertips, hair bursting out of their bodies and . . .

"The man in black," said Johnny. "My father . . . he is here."

And she looked up and saw a man in black on horseback with his saber drawn bearing down on them with his cape flying in the wind, but it was not the Count von Bächl-Wölfing at all, and she cried, "It's not your father . . . it's that monster, Major Sanderson, the man who wants to kill you all. . . ."

Cannon spewed silver fumes . . . silver particles fluttered in the moonlight like snowflakes . . . a child screamed as he breathed in glittering death . . . a woman scratched at the sores with her wolf paw, scratched until the wounds were raw . . . slowly, inexorably, Johnny was changing shape.

"Trying to hold on . . . long enough to . . ."

He danced.

The silver vapors gathered, swirled, dared not enter the inner circle. Heartened, some of the dancers resumed. Others were already dead. A group of them, completely changed, mobbed a soldier and were gorging themselves on steaming innards. But some still danced. An explosion . . . a wolf's head crowned with a jewelled turban flew through the air . . . "Chandraputra!" Speranza whispered. And Castellanos cut in half, his skull fractured by a silver tomahawk, the left half of his head still human, the other . . .

Screams of dying men.

"They are massacring us!" Speranza screamed.

"That is nothing new," the boy whispered. "Who is the true beast, Speranza—I, who can become a beast in outward form, or man, whose animal nature must always remain concealed, who is incapable of releasing the primal rage with which we all come into the world . . . the rage and pain of birth itself?"

A drum sounded in a dissonant counterpoint to the drums of the soldier. Major Sanderson rode toward them against a whirling nebula of silver dust, moving with agonizing slowness because he was fighting the boy's dream power.

"Do you love me, Speranza?"

The boy danced. A soft gold down was sprouting over his features. His eyes were narrowing. This wolf was neither the Indian boy nor Jonas Kay, but a composite of the two . . . a wolf infused with pity as well as terror.

"Yes, Johnny," Speranza said softly.

"Hold . . . me . . ."

They danced.

"Do you still have . . . the gun?"

"Yes. With one silver bullet left." She touched the barrel. It was clammy.

They danced.

"You must use it now . . . because you love me . . . kill me! I die that my death should propel the world toward the time of the next moon dance . . . I, the first sacrifice of the moon dance to have sprung both from the world of the beast-man and from the man-beast. . . ."

"You are mad, Johnny!" Speranza said, clasping the boy to her bosom, not caring that her tears flowed freely and were one with the blood and tears that rained down from the moonlit sky . . . "Johnny, you must not think of death . . . your dream was of life, not death . . . I did not come all this way to see you perish, but to make you whole again. . . ."

"Only death can heal me, Speranza."

Could she have heard aright? The boy's voice was harsh, distorted through the animal voice box; surely this could not be part of the dream. She stepped away . . . Hurt, perhaps imagining that she was abandoning him, he began to whimper like a child calling for its mother's breast, and . . .

. . . all at once she knew she had reached the most dreaded place within her nightmare, she knew that this death was the purpose for which she had been led to this place . . . weeping, she pointed the gun at the boy's head and . . .

(. . . the womb is the cage is the forest is the world . . .)

"We will be born together," said the boy.

(. . . and they weighed down the wolf's womb with stones . . .)

How can birth be so painful? she thought, as a terrible agony racked her body and . . .

The eagle was swooping down toward them.

Johnny saw her hesitate. Desperate, he said: "Don't you understand? You are the one who loves me, the one who can kill me . . . you have faced the shadow at my side . . . the first rays of the dancing moon are falling on us and if I die the dance will be fulfilled and then we will be at peace and the white wolves will be swept away and . . . having conquered the darkness within, I die that the people may live . . . to that end I was cast out of the place of madness, to that evil I was brought to this desolate place . . ."

(. . . and within the clearing, seizing the fearful Jonas by the hand, he made ready to pull him into the circle . . .)

Could she even understand him? She held the pistol, pointed it at him, and made as though to squeeze the trigger, and the wolfling roared his exultation, he howled out the song of death and renewal that was the same song with which the world had begun and . . .

Gunfire and . . .

Speranza toppled into his arms that were rapidly tightening, shortening into forefeet.

Dead.

He looked up snarling and saw Major Sanderson on his horse pawing the rock at the edge of the precipice with the horse's breath fuming in the moonlight and Major Sanderson putting down his rifle with a slow smile and . . .

Speranza lay on the ground. She is beautiful, the wolfling thought. And remembered his mother, being raped to death at a crossroads in Whitechapel, while his father did nothing. . . .

"Mother," the wolfling cried, but all that issued from his canine throat was inchoate rage as he . . .

Coiled up all his anger until he could bear the pain no more and leapt up over the horse's haunches and knocked Major Sanderson off his horse and fastened his jaws around his throat and . . .

Felt his teeth slice through windpipe and crush bone as they fell together, he and Sanderson, locked in an embrace of death, they fell from the towering rock, the dream shattered as the autumn wind streamed about them and he gripped the major's rib cage his paws sinking easily into flesh and they fell and fell as he snapped the major's neck between his jaws and . . .

Teddy heard the thud. He limped to find what Weeping Wolf Rock had spawned.

An eagle flew into the face of the moon.

The wind scattered the smoke, and the prairie grass swayed like an angry sea. Something had landed; there was a place where the grass was flattened and a shapeless lump lay motionless . . . human maybe.

It was Major Sanderson. What was left of him. He would not have recognized him at all but for the top of his head, the scars from the scalping. "Ain't pretty," he said softly to himself.

"No, it's not," said a voice. A long silvery shadow fell across the corpse.

It was a naked boy.

"Is you Johnny?" Teddy said. "Or one of the others?"

"I don't know," said Johnny Kindred, and wept bitterly.

"Did you just fall off that ledge?"

Johnny nodded.

"You ought to be dead."

"I can't die. My vision told me that only one who truly loved me could kill me . . . and she is dead."

"I'll get you something to cover you up . . . keep out the cold." He went to fetch a jacket from one of the dead. "Come on, Johnny-boy."

"The Indians . . ." the boy said. "My vision . . . betrayed . . . I betrayed them."

"Forget, Johnny. All of them is dead, all the soldiers, all the children of the Wichasha Shungmanitu . . . every last one of them gone to dust. You and me still got a heap of living to do yet."

"Where will you take me?"

"First we're goin' to head on up to Lead, where there's a woman waiting for me, I think. Then I don't know where we'll go. Mayhap we'll be settlin' on the reservation, for there ain't much left for me to love amongst white folks. Come on, help me saddle up one of them hosses."

A low rumble. Weeping Wolf Rock was shaking.

"Don't look back," Teddy said. "I reckon it's just the world sweepin' away the last pieces of your broken dream."

They rode away.

The earth swallowed up the dead.

Winter came, and the snow scoured the dried blood from the rock, and wrapped itself around the plains like a winding sheet.

EPILOGUE

Weeping Wolf Rock

1
1963: Winter Eyes
full moon

IT WAS THEN THAT DR. STERLING LA LOGE SPRUNG HIS THEORY OF "confrontation therapy" on me.

It was the day that J.K. told me the whole story of the abortive moon dance, the day I finally understood the role Preston and I were to play in the reenactment of the drama. I believed it all now. When he described the moon dance to me, I could see it as clearly as if I had been Speranza Martinique . . . Hope Martin . . . Hope Dupré . . . my great-grandmother herself.

La Loge took me aside in the corridor. J.K. was in his room, tranquillized to the gills. The psychiatrist led me by the sleeve to his office, sat me down, and explained his grand strategy—nothing short of a reenactment of Speranza's death.

"These lunar cycles are mysterious things," he said, watching me smoke the last of my second pack of the day. "I'm not an astronomer, and I don't really understand how they reckon the day that a moon dance is due, but it's something to do with various planets having to be in the right places . . . and the upshot of it is, sometimes it's frequent, but sometimes decades pass before it is the right time . . . but the knowledge of the right time is somehow instinctual with J.K."

"I know." Of course I knew. I had felt the stirrings of it myself. I knew that even I, far removed though I was from the generation of Scott Harper, could perhaps be impelled to metamorphose. I dreamed of it nightly.

"J.K. came very close to effecting a fusion of his disparate personalities that night in 1885," said La Loge, referring to his notes. "But Speranza's death robbed him of that moment. The Grumiauxes looked after him for a while, but during the Depression life became hard; Theodore Grumiaux had long since died, killed, I believe, in a train wreck; the Jonas personality became dominant. The Jonas personality looked up to Cordwainer Claggart as a father figure, and naturally, he attempted to follow in Claggart's footsteps, hence the strange psychosexual murders in Laramie . . . it was at that point that it was discovered that J.K. was in fact the heir to a small fortune . . . everything that remained in this town had been deeded to him in the Count von Bächl-Wölfing's will, discovered when the family ordered him exhumed and returned to the Wallachian mausoleum, which was discovered to be valid. The Szymanowski Institute (which, in name at least, J.K. owns) moved to protect him and. . . ."

I stopped listening. We were going over familiar ground now. "Something else has occurred to me, Dr. La Loge," I said. "What if Speranza hadn't been killed? True, J.K.'s personality fusion would have been achieved . . . but wouldn't Speranza have killed J.K.? Wasn't that the whole point of the exercise?"

"Well, perhaps . . . but once fusion has been achieved, I don't think it is necessary then to kill the patient! A sane man will not pay attention to the bizarre hallucinations from which he suffered during his madness . . . the delusions of grandeur, the odd notion that he had become some kind of werewolf messiah . . . these are aspects of his story that a rational man can do without, don't you agree?"

"Rational! We're talking about a werewolf, for God's sake . . . a supernatural creature. . . ."

"Nothing in the universe is supernatural," said Dr. La Loge, with that blithe confidence you will most often hear from the lips of a mad scientist in a bad horror movie.

Preston came to see me that night. He had a gift-wrapped box. He stood at the door to my room; I didn't know if he was expecting to come in or not.

"Happy moon dance," he said wryly.

"Do you want me to open it?" I said.

"Wait till I'm gone," he said. "Maybe you can use it as a dildo . . . seeing as I ain't capable of servicing you anymore."

A touch of the old Preston.

"Preston?" I said.

"What?"

"There's something I've always wanted to know."

"Not the length of my dick, I trust. Why don't you just open the package?"

Tomorrow would be the full moon, and we would do whatever it was Dr. La Loge expected of us. I sat down on the bed and opened the box. The wrapping paper was pretty tacky . . . it showed a smiling Jackie Kennedy in repeating patterns of full face and profile, with silhouettes of the White House. I had to laugh.

The box contained a Merwin and Hulburt pistol. There was a note with it, which read:

One bullet left.
It's been in my family for generations.
One silver bullet.

"You've always been a werewolf, haven't you?" I said. "I always assumed that that night, in the ghost town, when Johnny escaped and attacked you . . . that was when he converted you. But you've always had it in you . . . which means that Teddy Grumiaux must have. . . ."

He looked away. I did not know what to believe. But Teddy had looked after Scott, and then he had become Johnny's guardian until he died. Was it possible that he had somehow been induced to drink the dew from one of their footprints? Was it possible that Johnny had infected the child that Nita bore to Teddy?

Perhaps that was what explained Preston's alienation . . . and his animal magnetism. But he would not answer me, and I will never know for certain.

I put the gun in my purse.

Full moon. We got to the ledge by helicopter. Dr. La Loge said we could climb if we wanted to, but there was no point in not using modern technology, since it was available. Preston was there too.

J.K. stood in the middle of a circle that had already been drawn in advance in white chalk on the rock. He was naked . . . a shrunken, sunken man. They'd attached electrodes all over him, and they were linked to a battery of machines with weird flashing lights and oscillating patterns and levers . . . a Frankenstein movie kind of setup.

"If you really think that is going to work—" I said to La Loge, almost embarrassed.

The clouds broke. The moon came, and with it an eerie music that seemed to have been plucked out of the air.

Preston began to change first. He stepped out of his clothes. I could see Dr. La Loge gaping. I could smell the pheromones of arousal in Preston. I could smell them with my secret senses, the wolf-senses I had always known I had but had never been able to identify before. . . .

Slowly, the wires hampering his movements at first, J.K. began to dance.

It didn't matter that he was all withered. It didn't matter that the wires were dangling from his head, his arms, even his groin. It didn't matter that Dr. La Loge was gawking and taking notes like there was no tomorrow. J.K. was dancing, and he was beautiful. The wind rose, wuthering, toying with our hair. He danced and the music was in the wind and his face glowed with a cold blue light and he began to change . . .

Preston danced too, leaping, howling, rushing, whirling . . .

I heard the call of the moon. The moonlight touched the hairs on my arms and made them stand on end . . . the moonlight seeped into my pores and stirred up dormant yearnings . . . and I heard a small voice inside me cry, *Let me out I want to be born let me out let me out*, and my feet began to move in the rhythm of the moon dance, almost of their own accord, and . . .

"Speranza," said Johnny Kindred. The voice of a small boy. It called to me across the abyss of time.

And I answered, "I am Speranza. Speranza is in me."

Dr. La Loge looked approvingly at me and gestured as if to say, "That's the right sort of thing, say things like that, keep up the illusion for him." But I wasn't speaking for the shrinks and the scientists. I was speaking from the heart. And what I said next wasn't what La Loge wanted to hear at all.

"I am Speranza," I said, "but I'm more than her. I have her genes in me, but I also have the genes of the beast. I know what you've been through . . . even more than Speranza . . . I understand."

J.K. danced, flinging his arms from side to side, and the autumn wind whistled and whined and threw leaves in our faces. He danced, ripping away the electrodes, leaping now, jumping up high as though he were young again . . .

And I touched his dream and I stood beside him when he faced

the shadow and I held his hand when he said to the shadow: "Your
name is my name. We are one."

And Johnny Kindred and the myriad persons within him
became one soul.

I loved him.

Because of that love, I killed him, and in the morning I drove
away to California.

2
1988: Weeping Wolf Rock
full moon

NOW I AM A MIDDLE-AGED WOMAN. THIS IS NOT THE BOOK I SET OUT
to write. But now that it has been written, I realize that it is the
only book I could have written.

Another J.K. died that day in November. Everyone in America
remembers where he was that day. But I only remember thinking
about Johnny and wondering what the connection was. Sometimes
I wonder whether the death of a madman in South Dakota could
have anything to do with the death of a president. It seems almost
silly, but I can't help thinking about it sometimes.

I have a Volvo now. I have the chair of anthropology at an
obscure midwestern college. I have written other books, but they
are lies, shadows.

Lately I have felt an odd familiar stirring in my blood. I believe
that it is time for the moon dance again. That is why I have come
back to Weeping Wolf Rock. I am alone this time. There is no
helicopter to take me to the summit of the rock. Perhaps the rock
will bend itself for me, as it once did to a boy who could dream
the world into new shapes. I've been dreaming a lot too. It is only
in dreams that we can conceive of, battle, perhaps even conquer
an absolute evil.

Were the Shungmanitu the utterly beneficent totemic creatures—and the people of Winter Eyes the consummate evil—that the vision portended? I know the truth is a gray thing, like the clouds that obscure the full moon.

What was Johnny Kindred's moon dance designed to achieve? During his narration I often heard conflicting messages about the purpose of his grand vision. Did he really intend to send all the white werewolves back into the sea, to return the Great Plains to the Shungmanitu Indians? Was it something like the Ghost Dance, a few years later, which was supposed to rid the Indians of the white men and bring back the buffalo, but which ended in the massacre at Wounded Knee? What did Johnny mean by healing? Was it only himself that was to be healed, or did he want to heal the entire universe . . . and was this not some megalomaniac delusion?

I'm turning off the road, driving across grass that comes all the way up to the windows of my car. I can hear the shrill wind even with my windows rolled tight shut and the car CD blasting out the overture of a Wagner opera. There's no moon yet, but the sun is setting, bloated and bloody, against the outline of distant hills, and there are dark roiling clouds overhead.

I am thankful that it is not winter . . . that the moon dance falls in high summer this time.

Was Johnny's dance successful? Did his sacrifice bring about what his vision prophesied? Was the world changed?

Kennedy died. We lost the war. Does that count as driving the white men into the sea? Certainly we didn't do to the Vietnamese what we did to the Indians.

It only half fits the prophecy.

Why did I kill Johnny?

Was it merely that I was so caught up in his fantasy that I lost sight of all reality? I often wondered why La Loge didn't have me arrested; on the other hand, he couldn't have produced a body . . . not a human body anyway.

In movies, the werewolf always turns back into human shape after the silver bullet gets him. From experience, I know that it's sometimes one shape, sometimes the other, sometimes a chimeric conflation of the two.

Why did I kill Johnny?

Because I loved him—there's always that.

But also because it was part of the dance, and the dance was not complete without it, and because the rhythm of the dance impelled me, possessed me . . . because I heard the music.

Somehow I am not surprised to see a beat-up Dodge truck pull up to the base of Weeping Wolf Rock. I haven't seen Preston since he helped load my suitcases into the trunk of the Impala, twenty-five years ago. I guess he has felt it too. I won't be dancing the moon dance alone. Two to tango, I suppose. Perhaps one of us is meant to kill the other. I'm not afraid of that.

The woman in me is afraid, true. But not the beast. The beast knows that life and death is a game. The beast knows that when predator and prey gaze into each other's eyes and see each other's destiny, what follows, the chase, the leap, the frenzied gorging on warm flesh . . . is a dance. The same dance that the cosmos dances. The dance is the father who kills and the mother who gives birth. The gazelle dances into the jaws of the lion. I have danced with many men. A sock hop can lead to a dinner date. The moon dances in me. It is a dance of absolute and relentless grace.

Only a human would see horror in such a dance.

The moon will touch me. I will relinquish being human for a while. I will be a beast. I will forget speech. I will forget thinking. I will dance.

Eat my shit! Smell my piss! I am the queen!

—Phoenix, Alexandria, Deadwood, Los Angeles
1985–1988

S. P. SOMTOW

was born in Bangkok in 1952, a grandnephew of the late Queen Indrasakdisachi of Siam and son of the celebrated international jurist Sompong Sucharitkul, Vice-President of the International Academy of Human Rights and a judge on the World Bank court of arbitration. He grew up in various European countries and was educated at Eton and Cambridge, where he received his M.A. in English and Music. His first career was as a composer, and his work has been performed, broadcast and televised on four continents. He was Artistic Director of the Asian Composers EXPO 78 and Thai representative to the International Music Council of UNESCO.

In the late 1970s he took up writing speculative fiction, and won the 1981 John W. Campbell Award for best new writer as well as the Locus Award for his first novel, *Starship & Haiku*. He has also won the Daedalus Award for his historical novel *The Shattered Horse*, and his young adult novel *Forgetting Places* was selected as an "outstanding book of the year" by senior high school students participating in the national Books for Young Adults Program. His short fiction has twice been nominated for the Hugo Award, the science fiction equivalent of the Oscar, as well the Bram Stoker Award for horror; and one of his short stories won the 1983 Edmond Hamilton Award for "sense of wonder in science fiction."

1984 saw the publication of his first horror novel, *Vampire Junction*, which is now widely believed by critics to be of seminal importance in the modern "splatterpunk" movement. *Moon Dance*, his second horror novel, appears in the year that also sees the release of the horror film *The Laughing Dead* by Skouras International—a film that represents his debut as a director, and for which he also wrote the screenplay and the score.

He now resides in Los Angeles and works alternately on books, music, film, and reviews for the *Washington Post*.